CW00889031

Amy J. Smylie

# Out of Ashes

Book One of the Grenamoya Island Saga

To Auntie Thelma,

With all my love. I hope you like the book!

- Amy
x
x

GB

Cover Design, Text and Illustrations copyright © 2006
by Amy J. Smylie

First edition published in Great Britain in 2006
by BookForce UK

The right of Amy J. Smylie to be identified as the Author
of the Work has been asserted by her in accordance with
the Copyright, Designs and Patent Act 1988

A Galaxy Breakers Book

All rights reserved. No part of this publication may be
reproduced, stored in a retrieval system, or transmitted, in any form
or by any means without the prior written permission of the Author

All characters in this publication are fictitious and any resemblance
to real persons, living or dead, is purely coincidental

ISBN 123456789

BookForce UK's policy is to papers that are natural,
renewable and recyclable products and made from wood grown in
sustainable forests where ever possible

BookForce UK Ltd.
50 Albemarle Street
London W1S 4BD
www.bookforce.co.uk

The first person from the world of Grenamoya, Ramsey, walked into my life when I was about eight years old. He was a friend for me on the school playground, sitting with me and talking with me when I was able to escape from my throng of classmates. He even predated the island itself, as I remember telling my grandfather about him before the idea of a novel series had ever sprung to mind.

Since that time, and after the death of my grandfather, Grenamoya Island has grown, little by little, gaining new kingdoms, species and characters, evolving into the vast world that it is today. Some creatures and characters are born out of dreams, or little ideas that spring to mind; places I have visited, people I have met, feelings that I have harboured about the world around me. Writing their individual personalities as well as capturing them in artwork makes me feel very close to them, and in that way they are as real to me as the people around me.

Part of me wishes I could give a deeply profound reason for writing these stories – that I am trying to change the world, or convey some deep-rooted political opinion – but in all honesty I write for the enjoyment of it, and my desire to jot down the adventures and perils faced by the characters I love so dearly.

There is such a great multitude of legends about Grenamoya Island, a lifetime would not be enough to write them all. Of these recorded tales, this is the first. Ramsey the goblin carries the fate of Merlockiara, and the future of all Grenamoya, in his hands.

*For nine-thousand years, Emperor Pain ruled over Grenamoya Island.*
*Two-thousand years ago, the northern armies toppled him from his reign.*
*Five-hundred years ago, he tried to reclaim the island, but was defeated.*
*This time, he does not intend to fail.*

For Andrew –

thank you for loving me, supporting me, and appreciating Grenamoya Island as much as I do. You have brought me through so many hard times, and given me a million wonderful ones in return. Love you, forever more. xxx

and

For Grampa –

with gratitude for how you encouraged me to draw and make up stories. You left my life too soon. Though you were gone before Grenamoya was born, I hope you are proud of me. God bless. xxx

# Out of Ashes

## Book One of the Grenamoya Island Saga

# Chapters

| | |
|---|---|
| One – The Meeting | 1 |
| Two – Prince Morgan Goes Missing | 19 |
| Three – A Way Out | 61 |
| Four – Another Meeting | 93 |
| Five – Ramsey And The Troll | 129 |
| Six – A Break In The Wilderness | 153 |
| Seven – Enlightenment | 179 |
| Eight – Blood And Venom | 207 |
| Nine – Past Shadows | 239 |
| Ten – The Mountain Crossing | 271 |
| Eleven – Ramsey's Demon | 299 |
| Twelve – Where Loyalties Lie | 325 |
| Thirteen – Stronger Than Ever | 351 |
| Fourteen – The Eve Of Creation | 377 |
| Fifteen – Number Seventeen | 401 |
| Sixteen – Dying Dreams | 429 |
| Seventeen – Ramsey, Theron And The Dragons | 457 |
| Eighteen – The Climb | 485 |
| Nineteen – Dragon Flight | 505 |
| Epilogue | 529 |

# Chapter One

# The Meeting

In a land out of our reach, far across the ocean in a place unknown and uncharted, life was changing. The Earth breathed, struggling against the mists that threatened to choke it. Rolling green hills, deep valleys and crooked, crumbling mountains darkened as grey clouds engulfed the expanse of glittering night sky, the moon becoming little more than a dim glowing memory behind them. The wind blew, sharp and cruel like ice, and it seemed that the towering silver mountains, their foundations rooted deep into the Earth, might surrender and cower against it. It wasn't raining, but still the scattering silhouettes of night animals darted across the landscape in hurried fear, dread that something great and terrible was going to happen. There was a race for cover, a rush of cries, then all fell silent, and was still.

This was Grenamoya, a vast island untouched by modern Man, still retaining all the natural beauty it possessed when it was first forged out of the Earth. Untainted by car fumes, fossil fuels and factories – as it was always intended to be, but now growing dark, drawing in on itself, deepening. Grenamoya was inhabited by creatures found all around our discovered world, those oppressed by Man's interference and development. Dragons, goblins, elves and trolls, in vast numbers spread all across the land, dwarfed the human population. Man has a limited understanding of the world in which He lives, and though the darkness spread to the human communities across the island, they remained blissfully unaware of what evil was brewing in the mountains.

Grenamoya was a divided island, like a distorted, stretched-out, jagged circle, with rings and zones that set divisions and kingdom boundaries. The inner circle of the island contained mountains, which sloped up abruptly from the surrounding land, rendering it inaccessible to most. Only winged creatures made frequent visits to this sector, deemed 'sacred' by believers of the island due to its association with dragons. The five Great Dragons of Grenamoya were believed to bring the seasons every year.

In recent months, however, the elements had become unsettled, irregular, and it was this that gave the island leaders cause for concern. Without pattern, the Great Dragons were not controlling the seasons, and as all sacred matters were above and beyond the inhabitants of the island, they were helpless, and it frightened them. All they could hope for was that things would return to normal, but as the darkness spread across the whole of Grenamoya, the central hallowed mountain totally engulfed in shadow, they began to fall into despair, waiting and hoping for change.

Scaless Mountain, the most sacred peak in all Grenamoya, named after the divine Grenamoyan goddess of creation, appeared ragged and torn amongst the swirling mist of black clouds that hung low above its peak. The dark fog seemed to be bearing down against it. The rock itself appeared pale and wearied; the dull marble Temple of the Dragons, immense and immaculately designed, looked too cumbersome now to be supported by the mountain. It had been built many millennia ago, and had withstood years of thunderstorms, wind and rain.

Delicately sculpted dragons two-hundred feet tall in the columns and walls, each single scale painstakingly detailed like a precious jewel, stood strong against the darkness, as they had for centuries before. The rest of the world might tire, but they would never yield to the clouds closing in around them. They could not speak, but they resisted, and their stone hearts were steadfast as the day they were carved.

*They're weakening...*

*I can feel it in my bones...*

In a room in the highest tower of the temple, itself as vast and wide as a lake, he watched over the island through an arched window. He saw it all from there – the mountains, the land beyond, with darkening forests, hills and houses. He saw the people inside, he felt their coldness and fear; he knew that they feared him, whether or not they themselves knew it. It was the power he enjoyed, the fact that he was bringing about so much anxiety and doubt, and that he was the one who would determine the outcome of it all. There was nothing he wanted more in all the world. For centuries he had waited for this moment, and now he revelled in it. He turned from the window, a long, curved, sharp-toothed grin on his hairy, brown face, and started back towards the staircase.

*They are here...*

His voice rumbled like an alligator's chuckle inside his own head.

*Remember last time? Do you remember what happened? Of course you do. She ruined it. She ruined everything, she ripped you up, sliced your heart in two and crushed you. She destroyed you, she did it before, and she'll do it again. It kills you, you know it does. I know it does...*

*Not this time...*

He strode down the wide, winding stairs, claws tapping against the smooth marble, his smile quickly fading. His dark eyes narrowed, his face as severe as one who saw everything wrong with

the world and did nothing to put it to right. He had watched over the world since the beginning, and nothing about it had ever pleased him. His heart was hardened to the goodness, he was blind to the love and devotion, for none of it had ever been his. He had never known anything of the sweetness of life – his existence had seen nothing but hurt, contempt and rejection. He knew what he was, and that was Pain.

*If only you'd done as I asked. If only you had come to me when I called you. That's all I'm worth then, is it? You shoved my face in the dirt once too many times.*

He reached the bottom of the staircase and walked to the end of the corridor. The huge building contained passages and rooms wide enough to support his bulky frame many times over, yet he felt as though the walls were steadily closing in around him. He knew the kinds of enchantments placed upon the temple, and so thought it wise to keep up his guard, despite the fact that it was surely just his tortured mind playing with him once more.

*Don't start again…just keep strong, it will all be over momentarily. You'll be rid of this burden soon…*

*They are here…they are all here. They feel so…mortal…*

In the towering entrance chamber of the Dragon Temple, five anxious creatures waited side by side. Being summoned to such a hallowed place so secretively by a cloaked messenger would have anyone's blood surging, especially when given precious little other information, and all five of them were seething with expectancy. They stood in a row, fur bristling, tongues flicking, twitching in anticipation. They were tense, and hardly spoke, but the clear outcast of the five was receiving some unpleasant glances from the others. He was a large, brown reptile, the height of a man, and he walked strongly on two legs. He had a large snout, a long, pointed tail for balance, and on the innermost toe of each foot was a sharp, curved talon.

Nervously, he tugged on a chain around his neck, from which hung several glinting yellow stones. The gentle scraping noise they made as they rubbed together echoed faintly around the entire hall; to his either side, the other waiting creatures twitched with irritation.   Even the wailing winds outside seemed to be drowned out by the constant grinding noise of the five small stones.

Finally driven to the brink of madness, the large, tiger-like creature to his right lashed out and toppled him to the cold, marble floor, necklace and all, and stood over him, his massive body weight and strength combining to pin the reptile to the ground.  He snarled in a voice as deep as a volcano, whiskers bristling and jaws inches from his victim's face. "Stop it!  Stop it – will you just be quiet?  I've had it with you, Valdemar!"

Valdemar let out a terrified, wavering laugh and showed two rows of sharp teeth, meaningless while he had no courage to use them in self-defence. "I, er, um, ha ha, well-"

"Shut up!  Shut yourself up, you worthless little lizard!" He reached forward with one huge paw and pressed it against Valdemar's long, sinewy throat, successfully keeping him silent. "I have had just about enough of you and your stupid jewellery.  Now, you are going to be quiet, you are going to stay quiet until you are far, far away from here, understand?  You just leave those annoying little beads alone until you get home, hmm?"

The tiger was leaning gradually closer to Valdemar's scaly face, whipping his silver, pronged tail through the air threateningly. Valdemar blinked fearfully, staring up into a pair of eyes just as yellow and ten times more deadly.

"Understand?" spat the tiger, raising his free paw in preparation to strike Valdemar across the face; but before the blow landed, a seemingly distant wisp of a voice placated the tiger, and Valdemar craned his neck to find its owner.

"Surely you have more pressing things to do right now, Zoomana, than smack that intolerable little weed around the room?" Valdemar was relieved to feel the tiger's weight shifting off his body, and he instantly got back to his feet, brushing himself down with spindly, clawed fingers. "He is hardly worth your time."

This was Kaena, part snake, part dragon, part scorpion. Grenamoya contained clans of 'cobra dragons' in its darker regions, particularly the southernmost kingdoms of Utipona and Xavierania, and she was quite obviously one of them.  From the neck upwards,

6

she was, indeed, a cobra with a broad, dark hood, and her body was that of a dragon, sleek and scaly, entirely blue, with a crest of deep red hair along her back that slithered like a congregation of tiny serpents. Her thick, segmented tail stood out from the rest of her body – it was that of a large scorpion, sickly yellow, menacing and incredibly flexible, tipped with a bulbous, black stinger. At present, that most sinister part of her body was curved placidly over her back, shielded by her azure wings. There was nothing of beauty about her, but more of mystique, as she seemed to be speaking on a different level from that on which she existed. Whenever she opened her mouth, a black, forked tongue slipped out from between her lips.

"Valdemar, so much as touch those ridiculous stones again and I'll shove them down your throat."

"Yes, m'lady."

There was something in her hollow voice that commanded obedience, and Valdemar hurriedly moved out of Zoomana's way, trying to shield himself behind one of Kaena's folded, blue wings. On her other side, Kaena's brother emitted a hiss of laughter that sounded like a kettle letting off steam. His grotesque body was a mass of green and purple stripes, and, compared with his smaller sister, he looked positively toxic. For a moment, both cobras locked gazes with the two tigers, Zoomana and his winged, sour-faced mate, and swapped silent nods of acknowledgement.

Valdemar felt thoroughly left out, but was wise to the fact that cobra dragons were known relatives of the deadly basilisk reptiles of the south, and was therefore quite relieved to avoid eye contact with them. Any creature that could kill him with one look was not worth his time when he had an entire kingdom in his charge, and he was determined to return to Krakrakara alive.

Zoomana, still somewhat subdued from his brief encounter with Kaena, continued to eye both cobras warily, the fur all over his body bristling uneasily. He, unlike Valdemar, didn't rule anywhere on the island, nor was he the leader of his species. All he had was his expanse of territory, like all male cats, in the eastern edge of the island. His mate, a winged female known as Visciouss, was his constant companion, and the only other big cat in his bare, rocky domain.

Apart from Valdemar, all the creatures in this assorted gathering had very little to their names; nothing in the way of wealth, land, power or followers. In their lack of these things, what they shared was a deep hunger to possess them; this, it seemed, was the reason they had been chosen for the unknown task ahead of them. As they stood in the towering marble hall, analysing one another and muttering, a sudden, cold breeze swept into the room, and they fell entirely silent.

*Ah, there they are…*

*Yes, let them stare…let them stare 'til their souls are sucked out of them…it makes no difference to me…*

*Nothing makes a difference…*

Five pairs of eyes were suddenly drawn towards the large figure that had appeared at the entrance to the north corridor. The silhouette was faint and deep blue in the misty light of the storm brewing outside, but it was clearly huge, as tall as the cobras and broader. As it advanced, its vile form gradually taking shape, its body rattled. It was a strange sound, like hundreds of swords clashing together at once, and though they may have felt the urge to flee, none of them moved an inch. Maybe deep in their minds they knew what approached them. At the same time, they were excited and terrified.

*Yes, stare, get a good look at me…it feels so good to be feared again…*

*Now you know, there's no way to escape it. I'm a living, breathing creature, as much as you are…*

The whole mountain shook with his every step. He grinned, scanning over the five nervous faces as he stepped into a pool of shivering moonlight before them. They all looked up at him in quiet reverence, and he looked back at them with a sort of amused contempt. His sneer revealed a mouth full of sharp teeth, and he clawed at the ground impatiently – still they made no sound.

He was a massive creature, tall and wide with a crest atop his head and a body covered in enormous, black quills. The spines

8

started at the top of his neck, and spread over the whole of his back, all the way along to the tip of his club-like tail, and as he shook his body again, they rattled and clattered like knives. His cumbersome body was covered in brown hair, and his face resembled that of a malformed rat or a dog, with cruel, narrow eyes. There was no mistaking who he was – even as Valdemar averted his gaze to peer around the chamber, that same gruesome face stared out at him from the sculpted walls.

Amongst the lithe, glorious forms of dragons upon the walls and pillars, this ugly, unwieldy creature stood out like an imperfection, some horrible mistake of creation. He was a misshapen monster, fallen from the grace that the Great Dragons possessed, doomed to be forever hated and feared by all on Grenamoya. It was he who first brought evil to Utipona in the south, and fought against everything Lady Scaless stood for.

In the beginning, Grenamoya had been a barren world under his charge, where he exacted his bitter vengeance against Lady Scaless and the Great Dragons. Feeling rejected by his divine family, the already fragile Pain had been corrupted by hatred, and claimed the island for his own. He remained in power for over nine-thousand years of Grenamoya's history, and almost every race on the island had lived in fear of him. Acting under the prophecies of the elves' ancient religious tome, the peoples of each kingdom finally fought back, sacrificing themselves in great numbers to restore freedom for future generations. Brutally wounded, but not defeated, Pain remained in seclusion in Utipona, plotting, for so long that his name was almost forgotten.

Over five-hundred years ago, he had risen great armies in the south in an attempt to reclaim the island, but the alliance between the northern kingdoms had been too strong, and he failed. It had been foreseen by scripture readers of the alliance that he would rise again with unstoppable force unless he was destroyed, but as it was said that Pain remained only as a state of mind, created out of those that served his bidding, they mistakenly believed that it would never happen. Because of this wide-spread creed, the five creatures standing before him were in disbelief, but they knew in an instant who he was. Valdemar flinched. Pain took in a breath, and opened his mouth at last to speak. Silence fell.

"Before I show you all why you have been summoned here, I have to know this -" He didn't even bother to address them by name; he just looked down upon them, as though analysing each of them in turn, and continued in a voice both solemn and powerful. "Do you know me? In your feeble souls, in the darkest reaches of your minds, do you know me?"

His words hung in the air before them like icicles, echoing around the hall, until the wailing storm outside swept them away into nothingness. Of course they knew him. They knew him as well as the very island they stood upon, and the terror that the mere mention of his name struck into every mortal heart on Grenamoya. His presence was enough to freeze the icy, raging gusts that swept in through the bare windows.

"Kamror," He turned sharply to Kaena's brother, quills clashing together as he did so. "You know me, don't you?"

Kamror didn't move for a moment, then slowly bent his supple, serpentine neck, bowing his green snout to the marble floor. He lowered his scaled eyelids in a gesture of reverence, though his expression was poisonous. "Yes, my lord. I know you." Unlike his sister, Kamror's voice was low and sinuous like a boiling cess-pit. Following her brother's lead, Kaena imitated the motion, and, one by one, so did the others. Pain nodded and gestured towards the western corridor, causing the five pairs of eyes to turn accordingly.

"You may come this way, but do not touch anything."

He turned as though to lead them through the sculpted arch to the west corridor, but before any of them had taken a step, he whipped back around to face them, his eyes wild and threatening.

"Nothing that takes place here tonight is to be spoken of outside these stone walls. If you dare to back out, or betray my trust, I will take you down, and not even Scaless herself will be able to reach you. You swear yourselves to me, and you will have all you ever wanted, but you must obey me and do as I command you. Do you understand? You may not go back on this, you must honour this promise to me – that you will obey my orders and give yourselves to me and me alone. You are all vital to me, and I will not let go of any of you easily, but if you so much as put one toe – or claw – out of line, you will suffer my consequences. Is that clear?"

He looked at each of them in turn once more. He was starting to tire of their silence.

"Is that clear, I said! Am I staring at five statues?"

They flinched a little, but didn't speak in time.

"*Answer me!*"

"Permission to speak, sir-" started Valdemar tentatively. He had barely got the words out when he was interrupted by a howl of laughter from Pain, whose eyes were wild again.

"I do not believe this! Valdemar, my friend, you have the rule of an entire kingdom, yet you are so feeble and *stupid*. I would gather, then, that it is true that your advisors rule your kingdom for you, while you just sit in your fancy castle and play with rocks all day." Valdemar's long face fell as the others shared a chuckle at his expense. "Come now, you have a chance to do something fantastic in your time as king – isn't that what you always wanted, Valdemar? The will of a true king, the charisma to take some form of control over your people? You aren't much of a king at all, lizard."

Leaving an embarrassed Valdemar for the time being, he turned to the two tigers and advanced towards them with clattering steps.

"Zoomana, ruler of Fire Mountain – and your lady friend." Zoomana's mate still had the facial expression of a hairy, irritable toad, but Pain seemed charmed with her all the same. "You do me a great honour by coming here tonight. Certainly you have pressing matters to attend to in your kingdom."

Zoomana didn't rule anything apart from that which he claimed as his, but this term of address was very pleasing to him, and he bowed once more to the huge, spiny demon before him. "Nothing could honour *me* more than to serve you this night, my lord." His gleaming, silver tail was coiled submissively under his body, and he looked to be nothing more than a kitten next to the

11

towering monstrosity that was Pain. "We will both serve you to the utmost of our ability."

"Good, good." Kamror and Kaena were shooting identical glances at Pain from several metres away, and Pain picked up on them even before he had turned to look. "And my cobra friends," he began, ignoring the fragile form of Valdemar shivering in front of them. "I knew your father. He was a good and loyal companion, and it would please him greatly if I were to give you the means of power he never had. I never repaid him for his lifetime of service to me, but now, through you, I shall."

He made a brief glance at Valdemar, then turned from him, and set off towards the western corridor at an unhurried, determined pace.

"Come, all of you, and see what I have for you."

Row upon row of dragon-decorated columns lined the ever-darkening passage, which gradually seemed to be sloping upwards, as the air felt thinner in the gloom. Occasionally, a flash of lightning would illuminate the tunnel, making the frozen stone dragons flicker to life and dance across the ceiling. Pain strode noisily several paces ahead of the others, who were huddled together for safety. There would be no easy escape from the cramped passage.

That thought was running through Valdemar's small mind at an alarming rate as his eyes darted all around him, and he cursed himself for getting into such a potentially dangerous situation. Pain was bound to have an explosive temper, and he was already picking on the reptile. The others were much bigger than he was, which left Valdemar feeling at a loose end, like a worthless object to be made an example for the others. He was disposable. He whimpered and hurried along until he was walking two feet behind the hulking forms of Zoomana and his mate, and kept a firm eye out for any sudden movements.

Pain's walking pace decreased when they reached a wider part of the corridor, and finally entered a tall room, entirely structured out of marble like the others, but in the centre of which sat a small, round table, partially covered with a cloth. The demon said nothing, but approached the table, and indicated for the others to follow him. They all gathered around the elegantly polished, deep brown table, and watched as Pain took hold of a corner of the cloth. He looked at them, and tensed his claws around the fabric.

"What I have upon this table must not be revealed to anyone beyond this room, under any circumstances. I hope I have no further reason to elaborate on what your fate will be if it does." They shook their heads, each one still with a firm eye on the table. "Very well then. I know that I can depend on you all to serve me well, and to keep this magic hidden from the world, until I have gained enough power to use it. Then it all will be yours, to spend as you see fit. I promise you, it will come in time, but for now…"

Something about Pain had changed since he had entered this room, as he now appeared pale and weary, and had lost the timeless quality that prevented him from looking wizened. His body seemed to be too heavy for him to carry when he stood near the table, like some force was pulling on him, making him old. He glanced back at the table, and his large, hairy paw, with tired eyes. "…for now, keep it secret, and keep it contained."

With a flourish, he whipped the dark cloth away and lifted himself onto his thick back legs; he stood over the table, and lowered his head pensively, watching the others intently for any sign that they might change their minds.

They all leaned close to the table at once, and gaped at the four glowing, coloured crystals upon it with wide eyes. Each one seemed to radiate a cool warmth, and streaks and sparkles of glittering colour fluttered around inside like hundreds of tiny fairies. One was yellow, one green, one blue, and one red. Occasionally, the vague outline of an eye or a wing swam past the surface, and the colour inside the crystal erupted and burned more strongly.

Valdemar cocked his head in wonderment, and an inward desire to snatch all four. This had to be some kind of test, as Valdemar of the Sun Jewels was renowned for his obsession with shiny objects. Pain wasn't looking at him, though. Either way, these were the strangest crystal balls he had ever seen. They were only given a few moments to look upon the stones before Pain drew their attention once more with his sharp voice.

13

"There is one for each of you, to have, and to protect, for as long as I require you to. Their value is immeasurable." He bent forward and leered over the table towards them. "Keep quiet, and do not let them fall into the wrong hands."

Kamror, his cobra snout mere inches away from the blue crystal, scoffed and spat indignantly. "These rocks may be as big as human heads, but they are still rocks, and my sister knows all the magic stones on this island. She would know of these if they were at all magical."

Zoomana growled at Kamror's comment. "They're seeing stones, snake. There are images inside them – look." Pain was smiling silently, as though something had deeply satisfied him, and Zoomana's confidence mounted. "Definitely, seeing stones they are."

Pain looked at both of them and his smile broadened into a familiar, toothy grin. "They are not seeing stones, nor are they magic rocks, or anything of that sort." This sparked some curiosity in the others at once; Pain's voice deepened. "They are dragons. Inside each of these stones is one of the Great Dragons, captured by myself many months ago. They are caged inside the crystals, and all their power with them. They are mine, and now I give them to you."

The hush that had fallen over the other five creatures was incredible, but expected. The three pairs of reptilian eyes bulged with amazement, and Zoomana turned to his mate with an almost insulted expression. She raised her top lip in something of a reply, and her whole face scrunched up like a striped, orange lettuce. Pain suddenly burst out laughing.

"You weren't expecting something so wondrous to be placed in your care, were you? Exactly. Nobody on this island would ever suspect the four of you to be in charge of such magic, so who better to entrust it to? Most certainly, Valdemar, you can't even take care of yourself, let alone one of the most powerful entities of all time."

Valdemar still hadn't adjusted to having quips made at his expense, and shifted uncomfortably on his toes. Visciouss, though not officially involved in the ritual, felt a great deal of self-importance being there, and tossed her foul head.

"Therefore, let me give you some words of encouragement…" Pain held one palm over the yellow stone, and then hovered his large paw over each crystal in turn before snapping his gaze back upon the five of them. "…You have no alternative."

One by one, Kamror, Zoomana, Kaena and Valdemar stepped forward, and one by one, the demon Pain distributed the four imprisoned Great Dragons. With a final, sharp warning, he dismissed them, and was at last left alone with his thoughts. Outside, the bitterly cold winds howled over the temple, and the mountain silently screamed in agony. Inside, Pain was also screaming.

His whole body felt old and worn, as if he hadn't slept in years. True enough, he was incredibly old, and in all his centuries of existence, his dreams had been filled with too much horror and hatred to allow for decent sleep. It had begun to catch up with him at last. His head felt heavy as he lumbered back up the staircase to the tallest tower to watch over the island once more; a few moments' peace were most definitely needed. A few hours of deep meditation would help to suppress the adrenaline rushing through his cold body.

The view from the highest window hadn't changed in the least. Grenamoya was still a vast, jigsaw landscape, stretching hundreds of miles into the misty distance to merge with the oily night sky. Pain inhaled deeply, and took in the scent of wet stone; his dark pupils narrowed as the grey, glowing moon slipped out from behind a storm cloud, blurred and drizzled by the ever-falling rain. There were no stars now. The air was damp and murky, and his coarse, mud-coloured hair did little to keep out the chill.

It was done. The four dragons were gone, they had changed hands and were no longer his concern. They couldn't drain him any more. He knew that Kamror, Kaena, Zoomana and Valdemar would keep them guarded. They weren't his responsibility, after all…

But still they drained him. They plagued him, they made his quills stand on end. How could he have been so foolhardy, so reckless in his desire to unload them? What if something went wrong? Something would, he just knew it. They were all easily corrupted, but Valdemar, in particular, was stupid, and might give the presence of the magic away. It was bound to happen. He had come so close to victory in his first attempt, why should he have another chance?

It was fate...most definitely, it was inevitable. It had been written in the island scriptures. Pain could never be defeated, and he would rise to power again, bringing destruction upon the whole of Grenamoya. He had to be strong. Though he felt completely drained, this was his last chance for revenge, and he was going to take it.

*Look at that rain...so cold and cruel....the land is dark and lonely...*

*That's how you see me...it's how I feel. I don't know what to feel any more...I'm tired...*

*I'm so tired...*

He sighed heavily, his breath misting the air in front of his muzzle, and slowly panned his vision across the room, unblinking.

*Can you hear me? Oh, I know you can...you've got no choice but to listen now, have you? Have you?*

*You see what I do for you? What lengths I go to, just to make you listen?*

A broad grin returned to his face, hiding an eternity's worth of hurt pride and rejection. He was being drained again, and he began to laugh, feeling so exhausted that he could do nothing else but mock himself. His laughter finally ebbed away into a low, crocodile snigger, and he clenched his teeth together, rattling his quills in a threat to the silence.

Before him, sitting beautifully upon an ornate stone table, was another crystal – glowing brilliant white and surrounded by a haze of glittering, silver light, reducing everything else in the room, including Pain, to a lifeless, grey shadow. It surged and swelled with the agony of a caged life, and the torture shot through Pain's whole body, nearly crippling him, yet making him feel more elated than he had ever felt before.

*You have no idea how much you've destroyed my soul. I need you, I need you so much, but you kill me, each and every day you kill me! You knew it would come to this, you knew I would stop at nothing to hurt you, and make you feel how I feel...but I can't...*

*You'll never know the torment I endure for you, you'll never understand me. Nobody else in the whole world will ever understand me. And now...my destiny is to destroy you...to kill you, slowly...and softly...and eradicate this whole damned island with you...*

# Chapter Two

# Prince Morgan Goes Missing

Many hundreds of miles away, the light of dawn was gradually slinking towards the peaceful, green kingdom of Merlockiara. The elongated shadows of tall trees crept over the grass as the sun began to rise over Merlock, the capital town surrounded by a towering, immensely ugly, grey wall. The town was well-known for its bustling activity, expensive housing and twice-weekly markets, and was so large and densely populated that, beyond its protective stone wall, Merlockiara was mostly deserted.

The land was uneven and hilly in parts, which made it useless for farming, and the vast forests that covered most of the kingdom meant that few ever ventured far from the capital. The eyesore that was Merlock may have been a safe and comfortable place to live, but it was crowded, noisy, and had earned its inhabitants a reclusive reputation. The goblins of Merlockiara, however, didn't appear to care.

Goblins were never renowned for exquisite taste, as clearly illustrated by the ugly stone wall that surrounded both the town and the goblin castle beyond it. It was never really understood why, but goblins had always held a grudge against outsiders. Like most species on Grenamoya, goblins were very diverse in appearance. They could have long noses, large ears, pointed chins, tall or short stature, meanly thin or grossly fat – but, through all the variations, the goblins of Merlockiara had a collective distaste for those not their kind.

Merlockiara was ruled at that time by a dim-witted goblin known as Viktor, and though, as royalty, it was his duty to take charge of his people, he did a very poor job of it, and had little connection with the rulers of other kingdoms. He had one son; a bright, talented young goblin called Morgan. The presence of the prince gave some hope to the rest of the island, as he longed to see outside the town walls, and it was hoped that he would rebuild Merlockiara's frayed links with the rest of Grenamoya once he was king. The goblins may have done their utmost to remove themselves from the rest of the island, but they were strong, resourceful allies to have during troubled times, and the other kingdoms were reluctant to abandon them completely.

Not far from Merlock town, in a lone oak upon a grassy hill, was the small, poorly constructed wooden tree-house that was home to a goblin named Ramsey. For almost six years, the feeble shack had been his only home, and it had seen the goblin through his lonely adolescence. He had no parents, no siblings, and didn't know anyone in the town, which meant that he never had to bother to get up in the morning if he felt like sleeping in, and he had no obligations to do anything whatsoever all day. He had settled into this existence, and was at his least miserable when he was by himself.

Ramsey could barely wake himself up that morning. It was the first market day of the week, and he had to get himself down to Merlock before huge crowds gathered in the town square. As he lifted his head, his vision obscured by a mess of spiky, black hair, he found that the air was too cold for his liking, and tucked his legs up to his body. He tried to wrap his blanket fully around himself, but he had long out-grown it, and his toes poked out at the bottom.

Though he felt tired, he sat up on the bed, his blanket still around his shoulders, and got to his feet. The wooden planks creaked under the weight of his scrawny body as he felt around for his only clean shirt. Ramsey, though young, was quite tall for a goblin, and looked disproportionate with his thin body and large head. Ramsey had a long nose, pointed ears and fairly large, youthful eyes. His hair was unkempt and coarse like steel wool, and he forever looked malnourished and uncared-for. His skin, however, was unblemished, with the leathery feel of all goblin skin, vibrant orange in colour.

The only clothes he owned did little to compliment his complexion – stained, baggy, worn garments in tan and brown tones. Even his cleanest shirt beside the bed was dirty in parts, and had been nibbled by various creatures over the years. He put it on all the same, fastening the remaining buttons and attempting to cover some of the holes with his arms. Right on cue, his stomach grumbled loudly, and he began to make his steady way down from the tree-house.

Merlock was always ugly to behold, but to Ramsey, it looked worse in the mornings. Whenever he went to town, there would be goblins rushing frantically around the square, animals being ushered this way and that, and the dark, imposing shadow of the great wall would always engulf the town until noon. It was a town with nearly twenty hours of darkness per day, and Ramsey, living in the sun away from Merlock, found it terribly stupid. He had lived there as a child, but was kicked out of the town after his father's death because he couldn't support himself. He always resented Merlock, the whole kingdom, as well as the monarch who had thrown him out of his home. The law, along with treacherous surrounding forests and mountains, prevented him from finding refuge too far from the town wall, but in his mind, he was as far removed from Merlock as he could possibly be.

The drawbridge that led into the town had been lowered, as it was every morning, and Ramsey walked across it, taking a brief downwards glance at the wide, slimy moat surrounding the wall. He couldn't afford to miss a market day, as they were the only way he would get open access to food during the week. Not that he had any money to speak of. Already, the many colourful market stalls had been set up in the town square.

Small, hairy dogs were scrabbling and yapping around the central fountain, but otherwise, the square was abandoned. Ramsey almost stopped in his tracks as he beheld the unusual sight – instead of the overwhelming chatter of crowds and market sellers, the high-pitched barking of six dogs echoed aimlessly across the cobbled streets. Lining the square, houses had their windows and doors closed, curtains pulled across; they too appeared abandoned, silent and still.

Unnerved but not terribly deterred, Ramsey quietly made his way around the market stalls, looking them over and picking at the items on view. He took a few bites from what turned out to be a cooking apple, then sliced a chunk of butter from a large pat on the butcher's stall and ate it. Still hungry, but unable to carry much with him, he took a string of smoked sausages from the same stall and slung it around his neck. This immediately caught the attention of the six resident dogs, which scampered over to him, much to his annoyance, and started tugging on his trouser legs. He kicked two of them away and tried to carry on as normal, but was bitten on the ankle by one of the larger mutts.

"Ow! Hey, get off, will you? Get off my damn leg!" he exclaimed, but nobody came to his aid, and the large terrier wouldn't listen. "What are you doing out here anyway? Go and find some food from someone who cares, leave me alone!"

The dog bit down harder on Ramsey's bony ankle, and he angrily tossed them a sausage and tried to pull away. The food instantly diverted the attention of all six, which began to fight amongst themselves, and Ramsey hurried towards the goblin castle just north of the town, where he hoped he might find some signs of life other than mangy animals.

The extravagant finery of the goblin castle was perhaps the one exception from the goblins' distinct lack of taste. It was an old building, with tall, pointed towers, large windows and a decorative courtyard; King Viktor and his son lived there in total luxury, apparently paying little heed to the overcrowded, ugly town of Merlock below.

As soon as Ramsey set foot beyond the town, it was obvious as to where most of the market-goers had vanished to – littering the castle gardens and gathered beneath the king's main balcony were maybe seven-hundred goblins, shouting about something that Ramsey couldn't make out. Standing out on the balcony, where King Viktor always made his self-centred 'royal announcements', was a pair of castle guards, bound up tight in leather and body armour. Ramsey's keen eyesight could make out the scene, but he was still in the dark as to what had happened there.

The sound was incredible; goblins of all shapes and colours, young and old, were wailing and moaning to one another. Some were in hysterics, others remained solemn, but it was the most social interaction that Ramsey had seen amongst goblins in a very long time.

"I never thought I'd live to see the day!" exclaimed a rather fat goblin to his left, who he instantly recognised as the butcher. "It's terrible, really, but I can't say it wasn't deserved."

Ramsey was grinning inwardly that the string of sausages around his neck was completely unnoticed, but found himself absorbed into what was being said. Another goblin, a female with a lined, sagely face, made a reply. "But that poor little boy. He never harmed anybody, he was always so sweet, everybody said so. If it was up to me, I would have gotten rid of his father long ago."

Though not terribly friendly with the locals, Ramsey held a goblin's instinctive curiosity, and broke into their conversation. "What's wrong? Why has everyone left the market? There are dogs out in the square, taking their pick of anything they want."

The female turned to look at him worriedly, and the butcher remained oblivious to the sausages. "Oh dear, it's awful. We were just getting started with our shopping, when all of a sudden one of those palace guards came down to the square and announced that Prince Morgan is missing." Ramsey raised a thin eyebrow; the butcher tutted to himself and rubbed his broad, greasy forehead. "He's been kidnapped; apparently King Viktor has gone hysterical and they can't make sense of him. It's a terrible thing, really, to lose your child like that…"

Ramsey couldn't have cared less about the king's trauma. "Where has he gone, then? Who took him?"

"The castle woke up this morning to find half of the courtyard and one of the towers on fire," she continued, matter-of-factly. "And the prince was gone. We've been told that it was most likely a dragon that kidnapped him, but we're not to fall into a state of panic."

"As if we would," interjected the large goblin. "Especially after being told that there's a ruddy big dragon on the loose, burning up our kingdom."

Ramsey pursed his lips and looked over towards the castle, beyond the throng of panicking townsfolk. It struck him as odd that a dragon might have taken the prince – after all, a large, winged reptile would have little to gain from kidnapping a scrawny twelve-year-old. Not only that, but Merlockiara had never suffered from dragon-related abductions, and to suddenly have one out of the blue was, needless to say, puzzling. Ramsey was a smart goblin, and could work things out when he wanted to. Obviously it was too late to save the prince now, but their useless king was suffering for once, and Ramsey felt like gloating.

"Of course, now Viktor'll probably tighten our kingdom security and all that," grumbled the butcher. "I heard Gregg saying just five minutes ago, they've told him he can't leave town to take his crafts cart to Kinmerina next month. Everyone's gonna be paranoid!"

"Scaless save us!" exclaimed the female opposite him. "This is absolutely dreadful!" Ramsey was still squinting in the direction of the king's balcony, and at last saw some movement. The two guards moved aside to let another goblin, more colourfully dressed with a sombre expression, step to the front. The female to his side noticed the movement also. "Oh, look!" she said, exasperated. "Maybe they have more news about the prince. I do hope it's good news, bless him."

24

Ramsey was tempted to point out that Prince Morgan was probably being digested in the stomach of a huge, slimy lizard at that moment, but decided that a sarcastic 'ho hum' was sufficient.

All the goblins fell instantly silent upon noticing him, and the loud, frantic squabbling faded into a lull before dying altogether. Somewhere beyond the castle, a bird was singing. Ramsey hated birds, and was almost distracted from the present situation by thoughts of sparrow pie.

"Goblins of Merlock," began the herald in a sonorous voice, unrolling the paper in his hand, "I regret to inform you that Morgan, our dearly beloved prince, has been taken from us. King Viktor is devastated, and is being seen to by our best doctor. Sadly, he may be unable to take charge of his kingdom for a few days, so until then, I shall keep you all up to date with the latest news from the castle."

He had obviously rehearsed this speech several times already, as his voice was stilted and devoid of emotion.

"In the meantime, nobody is to leave Merlock for any reason, merely as a safety precaution. The town drawbridge is soon to be raised, and shall remain so until further notice. Also, a curfew shall be introduced as of this evening – there is to be no activity in the town streets after ten o' clock. We regret the inconvenience, but these measures are for your own good."

Ramsey cursed and grumbled quietly.

"For any of you that may have heard about the fires earlier today, rest assured that we now have everything under control. Furthermore, we have not found pieces of Prince Morgan's dismembered body all around his bedroom, as some individuals seem to have been told."

Too bad, thought Ramsey; that would have made things more interesting.

"There is no cause for panic, so please do not do so."

The piece of paper was rolled back up, the herald nodded, and then he retreated from the balcony. Once more, the crowd swelled into an uproar. "Ah dammit!" huffed the butcher, louder than ever. "It's all useless, you'd think they'd tell us more than that!"

Ramsey edged away from the cooking-fat smell of the larger goblin, trying to work out what he should do next. If he wasn't allowed to leave Merlock, he wouldn't be able to get home – maybe if he acted quickly, he could get out of the town without being noticed. Discreetly, he turned from the group and sneaked away, back to Merlock town itself.

Absolutely nothing had changed in the town square; the quiet market stalls were still unmanned, and the streets were empty apart from the few small dogs that remained around the fountain. From the way they were yapping and sniffling in a cluster, it seemed like they had found something to interest them, as Ramsey was totally ignored.

He hurried past them and through the town square, hoping to make it back to his tree-house before Merlock was closed up. Annoyingly, as he approached the drawbridge, he noticed a burly, stern-faced guard holding an off-putting weapon, and he knew that any attempts to get back home would be useless. The guard watched him draw to a disappointed halt, and called out to him.

"Hey you, nobody's to leave town without official urgency. The drawbridge will be pulled up soon, and you don't want to get stuck out there with a dragon about."

Ramsey sauntered nonchalantly towards the other goblin, keeping a safe distance and trying to look uninterested. "Well, that's a pity. I really need to travel to Hanya to-"

"I don't think so," interrupted the guard, raising his short spear. "You just get back into town where you belong, there's nothing for you here."

Ramsey glanced briefly at the bakery, inn and pottery shop to his either side and huffed. "What if I came out here to buy some pots?"

"You'd have done it by now. Get back there before I *throw* you back."

Ramsey was thin with stringy muscles, and knew that the thick-set, plum-faced guard could make short work of him; still looking uninterested, he turned on his heel and strutted back towards the town square, brushing past yet another guard who was making his way to the drawbridge. Curious, he slowed his pace to listen in on their brief, rumbling conversation.

"They've been told about the curfew – we can close up the town immediately. Had any bother?"

"Not at all, sir, none whatsoever. It gets you a little on edge, though, knowing that thing is out there somewhere. I'll be pretty glad once we've secured everything." Ramsey picked up on the sound of movement, and then a grinding, creaking noise as the Merlock drawbridge was slowly winched up. "But what if the thing flies in over the wall? That's the only way it could've reached the prince's bedroom window, it could get in just as easily again."

"I don't want to think about it. I'm looking forward to getting back indoors myself."

Ramsey was starting to get fed up with all this talk of dragons. There was always something about the subject that made everyone become frightened and mystified. Of course, a dragon was something to fear by anyone's standards, but Ramsey did not believe any of that 'Great Dragons bringing the seasons' nonsense. He had never seen a dragon bigger than his own head, and suddenly there was a huge one invading Merlockiara and stealing princes. Whatever spirituality and magic these dragons represented, Ramsey considered himself too smart to follow suit; he just wanted to get home and go to bed, to get away from the citizens of Merlock and their reverent aura.

As he approached the square once more, he couldn't escape the feeling of entrapment created by the towering wall surrounding the town; the cobbled streets in shades of sunny grey, dull in the shadow of that wretched wall, looked sickly and pale. Ramsey had no love for this place – not even memories of his father could brighten him, because all his recollections were of detachment and loneliness. A father who maintained his distance, and was so ashamed of his son that he kept him indoors for almost twelve years, away from the townspeople who might have hated him.

There was nobody in the town square yet. Ramsey picked up some more food from the butcher's stall and took some time to regard his past home on the opposite street – a cramped, tall house like all the others, bricks painted dull lemon and white, dismally reflecting his less than sunny mood. He was starting to remember why he never stayed in the town for too long; now he had a whole day and night, and possibly countless more, to endure there. He would need to avoid the other goblins as much as possible, of course, just in case he was recognised by anyone.

He knew that this was going to be completely awful, and he dwelled miserably on his predicament, wanting nothing more than to be back in his tree-house with his bed, blanket and other comforts. Merlock was too enclosed and full of memories for him to cope with how he was feeling, and he quickly stole away before anyone returned to the square.

***

By nightfall, there was a bitterly cold chill in the air, and Ramsey's poorly-clothed form felt the full force of it. The market stalls had been cleared away several hours before, and he had at least managed to pilfer some more food before then. The rumbling of his sore stomach echoed up and down the back streets, as he crouched beside a rubbish bin, trying to keep out the cold. His body felt brittle and vulnerable. He took a bite out of a slab of cheese, one of his remaining bits of food, and dropped the rest into the empty bin.

"What was I thinking?" he asked aloud, as though trying to keep himself company. "I don't even like cheese."

Heaving a sigh, he leaned against the brick wall behind him and shivered. Normally, the back streets of the town would be crawling with other goblins at night, but all of them had a home to go to, and they were afraid that the dragon that took Prince Morgan might return. Ramsey was stuck by himself in the dark, and felt dreadfully unsafe.

A sudden, swift movement overhead made Ramsey yelp and duck behind the bin, and he cowered there until he saw that it was only a flock of night birds in the sky. His heart raced in his chest, and he gasped quietly for breath. The fuss everyone was making about the dragon must have made him more nervous than he realised, and he felt embarrassed, though there was nobody around to see him. Still, he stayed behind the bin for protection, and piled up some old boxes to either side of him. He had only been sitting there for twelve minutes, and already he was cold, hungry, frightened and miserable. He didn't want to think about the possibility of spending hours, days, weeks, *months* waiting out in alleyways every night, jumping at the slightest sound of movement. At least for the moment, he was alone.

As each second passed, Ramsey found something new to despise about the town. Merlock had vermin that stalked the streets after dark, and he was none too fond of rats. The cobbled ground was hard and cold against his feet, and felt even worse against his scrawny pelvis. The cold wind whistled over the rooftops, and the steady creaking of the tall, thatched houses rang in his sharp ears. His breath misted the air in front of him, making him gasp and shiver.

He was so bitterly cold that he felt he might die there; alone, huddled between a wall and a rubbish bin for warmth. It would be a sorry end to a sorry existence, he mused. Still, better to freeze to death in an alley than to beg others for a place to stay. He would never degrade himself to that level, not for all the food and thick winter coats in the world.

Though it took him a while to realise it, Ramsey finally decided that it was a bad idea to stay out in the cold all night. Picking himself up off the ground, he made his way back out to the town square, silently, hugging himself.

As he passed several houses and an inn, shrouded in a blanket of blue darkness, a sense of uneasiness overcame him. Merlock was never this quiet, not even in the dead of night. There was always someone a little too loud for their own good at the ironically named 'Dragon Sword' inn, then a fight would break out and wake up the whole town, including Ramsey, far away in his tree-house.

Far, far away... How he longed to be back home right then. He couldn't feel safe in Merlock. His wide eyes scanned the bleak scene, making out every intricate detail in the dark. The houses were all the same, row upon row surrounding the square, piled close together in darkness, hiding the equally deserted back streets from view.

As he crossed the square, Ramsey could make out the shape of the goblin castle to the north. Without the hordes of townsfolk, the building looked old, pointless and fragile against the town wall and night sky. It was truly huge, and looked steadfast, yet it had only taken one dragon to pillage it, and perhaps destroy the goblin monarchy forever. One of the towers had clearly been badly burned; it seemed as though half of the east wing had just dissolved into nowhere. There were no lights in the castle, apart from one of the very lowest rooms, in which several guards were no doubt waiting for the beast to return.

Ramsey hurried quietly across the square, making sure to watch his feet on the cobbles. He could feel his heart racing again. It was so quiet, he could barely keep his mind straight. He headed past the square and continued stealthily towards the town drawbridge, a little way down a wide street. He was in luck to find that the one guard on duty was clearly asleep – standing with his head bent forward on his chest, leaning against his spear.

Though tempted to go and push him over, Ramsey crept forward, shadows gliding over his body, and stood right next to the guard. His arm was just slender enough to reach behind the large goblin to the drawbridge mechanism. He gripped one of the wheel handles firmly and pulled with all his might; nothing happened. He cursed and tried again, but his arm gave way, and he quickly withdrew it.

"For goodness sake...!"

He pulled up his short sleeves and reached behind the guard with both arms, clenching his teeth and trying desperately to turn the wheel. He could barely see where he was putting his hands, and felt around tentatively to get a firmer grip on the handles. He could feel his hands shivering, completely numb with cold. He didn't know how a town with a huge outer wall could be so cold and gusty, but he knew that he was far too exposed, and was going to collapse from hypothermia unless he found shelter.

He pulled on the wheel one last time, and felt it give way, but as he moved to withdraw his arms, he caught himself on something, and pain shot through his frozen left hand. He screamed loudly and tried to free himself, pulling his bloodied hand from the mechanism and reeling with agony.

The guard woke up, lost his balance and fell over, almost crushing Ramsey's limbs further, but the smaller goblin leapt aside, clutching his hand, and darted into the shadows. Adrenaline surged through him and tears welled up in his eyes, but he stifled himself. His whole body was shaking, and he almost cried as the guard stood up off the ground and looked at the blood on the cobbles at his feet. The goblin held up his spear and shouted to the darkness.

"Who's there? Show yourself!"

He wasn't looking in Ramsey's direction, but the pain searing through his left hand was overwhelming, and he was scared he might make a noise. His breath stung in his lungs as he inhaled the cold night air. Blood stained his shirt and trousers as he crouched in the gloom. The guard shouted again, and Ramsey's heart leapt to his throat. Desperately, he shuffled sideways in the shadows, feeling behind with his good hand for an escape route. His fingers clasped a doorknob, and he stopped still, rigid with fear.

"You're out there somewhere – show yourself!" The guard turned as Ramsey clicked the doorknob. "You know the law – get back to town! If you're hurt, it's your own fault!"

Ramsey didn't know where the door behind him led to, but it was his only way out. The guard hadn't seen his face; he would be safe by morning, if he lived that long. His hand was numb again with pain, and he quickly ducked into the doorway, slamming it behind him and pulling the bolt across. Outside, the guard yelled for a few moments more, but made no attempts to break in. At last, his words faded.

Ramsey was stuck in an unidentifiable black room, and his hand was swollen and bloody. He didn't care where he was – all he knew was that he was indoors, it was warmer than it was outside, and he had somewhere safe to sleep. With a final sob of pain and exhaustion, he fell to his knees on the wooden floor, and collapsed into unconsciousness.

\*\*\*

*Burn it...burn it...*
*We burn you because we love you...*
*Burn him, burn him 'til he bleeds!-*

Ramsey woke up suddenly in the middle of a nightmare, beads of cold sweat upon his forehead, and found himself lying face-down on the floor of the pottery shop. On shelves all around him were piled various bowls, vases and clay lamps. A pale beam of rainbow-tinted sunlight illuminated the dusty air through a bright stained glass window.

Ramsey was panting hard, and it took him several moments to focus his vision through the dull red glare in front of his eyes. He rolled over onto his back, still breathing hoarsely, and looked hazily at his left hand, resting on the floorboards in a patch of smeared blood. There was nobody else in the shop, but he could hear a gentle hum of voices outside, and tried to motivate himself to get up.

He often had nightmares when he felt unwell. All the hype about dragons and burning castles must have sparked something in his brain to make him dream about fire. He had lost a lot of blood. He felt terribly faint, and, looking at his blistered hand, remembered that he must have caught it in the drawbridge mechanism in the dark. His palm and fingers had been scraped raw, and the side of his wrist had been severely ripped. On closer inspection, he found that two of his fingernails had been torn out, and were bleeding quite considerably. He groaned loudly and tried to curl himself up, but his body was too stiff.

32

"Damn it...I wish I hadn't done that..." There was a loud thump on the door, and he jerked his head up. "Argh, what now...?"

He managed to sit up, nursing his left hand gently with the other, and crawled towards the door on his knees. Using a shelf to pull himself to his feet, he leant against the door-frame and pulled the bolt across. The door swung open, flooding the room with light; Ramsey was greeted by the sight of a crowd gathered in a circle in front of the shop.

He groaned, but was too drained to react further, and just slumped himself in the doorway. He could smell burning. Someone in the crowd noticed him and shouted, and several more followed suit, and soon he was surrounded by a group of frantic goblins, fussing over him and dragging him this way and that. His vision was becoming hazy again, and he felt himself collapse onto someone.

"Oh, can't you people leave me alone?" he mumbled.

Ramsey was too weak to realise that he had staggered out onto a scene of carnage, and didn't notice that he was stained with his own blood from head to toe. The crowd absorbed his feeble ramblings as they carried him towards the castle in an uproar. The burning smell became more potent as they crossed the square, where many houses were smouldering. All Ramsey could see was the sky and the looming grey wall all around. He wanted to sleep, he wanted to die, absolutely anything to shut out the noise. He closed his eyes, but the smell of ashes just brought images of fire back to his broken mind. He felt giddy as the sound of cheering and shouting gave way to that familiar voice...

*Burn it, burn it, feel it burn...burn, burn, burn...*

\*\*\*

When Ramsey next opened his tired eyes, he found himself surrounded by an eerily bright whiteness. His body felt stiff, yet loose and droopy. His waking thoughts were that he must have died, but the pain he still felt in his left hand suggested otherwise.

He had been dreaming again. All he could smell now was the clean aroma of potted plants, and perhaps a hint of tea leaves. He moaned loudly with discomfort and tried to turn himself over, but his chest felt like a lead weight. Gradually, the bright orange hue of his skin came into focus, and he stared wistfully at his own arm. He heaved a sigh. He wasn't dead.

"Euch…" He opened his mouth and tasted something awful. Stretching himself out, he tried to feel where he was. He guessed he was in some sort of bed. Everything started turning grey. "Where am…I…?"

He made out a window on the far side of a large, stone room, through which he could see the sky. He swallowed some air and slowly lifted himself onto his pointed elbows. His head felt too heavy for his neck, so he supported it with a pillow. The bed he was lying in was completely white, with a deep brown wooden frame, and on a table next to it were a bowl of fruit and a glass of water. He blinked again. It was most definitely real food. With somewhat less enthusiasm, he discovered that his clothes were missing, and all he had on was a pair of red shorts.

"Oh Scaless…what's happened to me?" In a sudden panic, he pulled the blanket off himself and moved to stand up, but he remembered the state of his hand just in time before supporting his weight with it. He scrambled around the bed, unsuccessfully looking for his clothes, and glanced towards the window. He could see the vast, cloudy blueness that was Merlockiara's endless sky – it felt like so long since he had seen it. "Where in the world am I?"

In order for him to see the sky clearly, he knew that he had to be either very high up, or somewhere outside the town wall. Curiosity overcame his need for adequate clothing, and he approached the window cautiously. His bare feet were as cold as ever, but strangely, the room was quite warm. He was glad of it. He gazed out upon the view, placing his elbows on the broad windowsill, and beheld the entirety of Merlock town far below.

The breeze rustled his wiry hair. The air was cold, and the rows of thatched houses looked pale and miserable. Miniature goblin figures pottered around the streets in small clusters. Beyond the foul town, the hazy green landscape of Merlockiara stretched as far as Ramsey's acute eyes could see, dappled with trees and dark, distant patches of woodland. He realised that he had to be in a tower of King Viktor's castle.

He was so absorbed in looking longingly out of the window that he didn't notice another goblin enter the chamber. Clad in a loose robe of purple and green, the royal herald stepped into the room with a look of expectancy on his long face. He began to say something, but silenced himself upon noticing Ramsey's trance-like state, and just stood motionless in the doorway. Ramsey's figure was a lean mass of bones from behind, with angular shoulders and a very defined spine that protruded through his orange skin in bumps. He looked horribly malnourished, which was clearly worrying to the other goblin, who at last decided to speak up before Ramsey turned around.

"Ah, you're up." Ramsey was so attentive to the landscape that he barely acknowledged the other goblin, and just nodded slightly in reply. "You really had quite a near-miss out there. How are you feeling after your ordeal?"

There was a pause; gradually, Ramsey turned from the window, and looked questioningly at the herald. Nobody else had been around when he had his accident, and the sentry didn't see his face, so wouldn't have been able to identify him. He couldn't think what had happened. All he remembered was hurting his hand when he tried to lower the town drawbridge and finding refuge in the empty pottery shop. There was a crowd outside, there was a lot of noise...and he started dreaming again, as though he was trapped inside a burning building. Everything had smelt like fire. Ramsey tried to find an answer that wasn't too suspicious. "My ordeal?"

"Poor boy," said the other, wringing his hands. "I suppose you've been too traumatised by what happened. But if possible, we need some information from you as to the dragon's appearance, method of attack, and direction."

Ramsey growled with irritation. "What are you talking about? I haven't seen any dragons around here, and it's pretty likely nobody else has either. I don't know where all this nonsense has come from – someone took Prince Morgan and set fire to the castle, but nobody here has any actual proof that it was a dragon!"

The shorter goblin stepped forward and held up an accusing index finger. "For your information, young man, somebody lost his life that night before you were found, and clearly you escaped the attack while he wasn't so lucky. We need your help if we are going to protect the rest of Merlock from attack."

"I don't know what you're talking about, I didn't see any dragons last night."

The herald still looked disagreeable, crossing his arms firmly. "You were found three days ago, boy, you've been in this room since then. We thought you might find it hard to recall what happened that night, since you also managed to bump your head rather badly, but you're our only witness. Please, you *have* to remember." Ramsey frowned when the other goblin took the liberty of holding him by the shoulders. "All we found of that guard was a dagger and part of his arm, you were lucky to survive. We need you to help us locate the dragon so we have a hope of rescuing Prince Morgan."

Ramsey suddenly realised what was going on. The crowd that took him must have told the castle where he was found, and from his injuries they assumed that he had escaped from a dragon attack. It was certainly interesting, and something of a relief, as now they wouldn't arrest him for attempting to get out of town.

The problem, however, was that he didn't have any information to give. They could throw him in prison if they discovered he tried to tamper with the drawbridge. Taking a deep breath, he put on his most thoughtful expression and pretended to wrack his brain.

"Now that I think about it," he began, pensively, "I can remember...voices, and a lot of fire, and shouting-"

"Yes, yes!" exclaimed the other, gleefully. "The fires in the middle of town, you can remember! We were so worried you wouldn't regain consciousness – I'll get the doctor here at once. Don't go anywhere, young sir, I'll be right back." With that, the herald turned and hurried out of the room, holding his robes up off the stone floor. The sound of his brisk footsteps faded along the corridor. Ramsey took a deep breath and looked around the room again.

"What a moron," he muttered to himself, sitting down on the edge of the bed. He lifted one of his feet onto his lap and inspected it for a moment, then glanced sombrely at his left hand. He felt grotesque and deformed whenever he looked at his scarred fingers, yet he could do little to stop himself checking them. They didn't look quite as bad, now that they had been washed and cleaned up a little. Still, he felt angry with himself for being so stupid. "That's the last time you do anything like *that*, isn't it? Bloody idiot."

For now, Ramsey knew he was safe enough. King Viktor and his advisors wouldn't do anything bad to him if they were counting on him for information about the dragon. If he could hold out the charade for a while, maybe he could get away with it and go home.

The goblin castle was a little different from what he had imagined it to be; it smelled better than he expected, it was clean, and he was being offered fruit and medical attention, which was not typical of the goblins' stingy nature. Then again, they were only treating him well because they thought he could help them. He wouldn't want to, even if he could.

He sighed loudly and flopped back onto the blanket with his arms and legs spread out. The ceiling was exactly the same as the walls and floor – dull and boring. A tapestry covered one of the walls, woven in gold, purple and green, but it too was quite grey. Most definitely, King Viktor didn't have the best taste in all Grenamoya, but at least his minions were treating Ramsey with respect.

Reaching over for a bunch of grapes, he closed his eyes and relaxed in the silence. Hopefully, the herald wouldn't be back for a while, and he would have time to gather his thoughts. Maybe he had been traumatised by his accident. He wanted to find some explanation for his garbled dreams over the last few days.

Ramsey often had nightmares when there was something wrong with him – maybe it was all caused by that disgusting piece of cheese he picked up in the market. He hadn't felt so disconcerted in years. His dreams were often about being burned, beaten, trapped inside a fire, and always there would be that voice wailing in his ear. Sometimes he would wake up terrified, and frantically trying to get away from that imaginary pain. The only person he had ever really known was his father, and he wouldn't put it past that cruel goblin to leave him in a smouldering building to die. Just thinking about it made Ramsey shiver.

What frightened him was that he couldn't remember what might have happened to him to make him feel so scared, hated, unable to trust others. It was always fire, burning his skin, searing away at his fragile body, and no matter how much he ran, it would always catch him again. He felt constricted, chained up, choked. He felt his limbs tense, and quickly tried to think of something else. He was safe, he was being well looked after, and soon he might find his way home. More than anything else, though, he had power that he had never possessed, power over goblins who had shunned him in the past, and he intended to abuse it to the full.

*** 

After a change of clothes and two adequate meals, Ramsey began to feel more settled. Though angry that his worn, blood-coated shirt and trousers had been thrown away, he was more than happy to receive several new sets in return. He thoroughly refused to be touched by anyone in the castle to begin with, however, and stole away to his chamber once they had ceased pestering him about dragons.

Every time he went to the window of his room, goblins in the square below would hurry towards the castle for a better view of his distant, orange form – it was certainly a change from what he was used to. Sometimes they would gather outside his window, waiting to cheer at their first glimpse of the amazing 'dragon survivor'. To any decent soul, this undeserved adoration would have evoked feelings of guilt, but Ramsey felt they deserved to look foolish for once, and enjoyed his royal treatment.

He allowed the castle doctor to wash and dress his sore hand, but otherwise didn't let himself get too close to the other goblins. So far, he only had to recall vague, fake memories of the night in question, and they would rush to him with extravagant meals and fresh pillows. Despite his comfortable situation, he decided to mull over some possible stories to tell once King Viktor's subjects became more probing.

On the third day or so, after Ramsey had finished his breakfast of toast and cereal, the royal herald returned to the former's room to retrieve the dishes and deliver some news. "I have just spoken with the doctor, young sir; he says your hand is healing nicely."

Ramsey, who was lying on his blanket, swung both legs over the side of the bed and sat up. "Yeah," he said, looking at the hand in question., "it doesn't hurt as much any more. I can feel my fingers properly again, and the doctor said my nails will grow back."

The herald nodded. "Yes, that is wonderful news. Now that you're on the mend..." The tone of his voice changed, becoming more urgent, causing Ramsey some discomfort. "...Now that you're on the mend, I wonder if you could recall some details of the creature to me. Just you and me, sir, no pressure...please, can you tell me about the dragon?"

Ramsey knew this time would come, but strangely wasn't prepared for it at all, and he froze for a moment, thoughts racing through his head as to what he should say.

"Um...I...I can remember a..." His words trailed off into nowhere, and he swallowed hard. He didn't know what a dragon was supposed to look like. "I..."

"Please, we need any information we can get."

"Give me a second," he grumbled, holding his head. "I *did* get a concussion, you know. I remember...uh...oh, it's gone. I'm sorry, I'll try again tomorrow."

The herald sighed loudly and wrung his hands together. "Very well, then. I had an idea that might help to boost your memory, but I don't know if it would be too upsetting for you."

"What is it?" he asked, a little apprehensive.

"Oh, nothing invasive, don't worry," said the herald with a slight smile. "We have discovered a few clues in Prince Morgan's room as to the type of dragon we are dealing with. It has been left quite untouched after what happened, so maybe if we discussed our findings with you, it would help to jog your memory of the beast."

Ramsey was not going to pass up an opportunity like that, even if it meant going into a repulsive child's bedroom, and nodded without hesitation. "Sure, I don't mind having a look, especially if it might help to rescue our beloved prince." He grinned inwardly – he was as smooth as the butter on his toast.

"Splendid, wonderful, oh thank you!" Ramsey pulled away from what threatened to be a full-on embrace, but the herald didn't take offence, suddenly overflowing with joy. "We may yet save Prince Morgan after all! I'm sure King Viktor would thank you too, if he was at all coherent right now."

"For goodness sake, what's wrong with him?" Ramsey snapped, more forceful than he intended to be. "Has he gone nuts or something?"

The other goblin's lined face became sombre once more, deep blue, accentuated by his green and purple robes. "Well, no…but he has been terribly upset over the loss of his son. It will just take him a while to get his head together, that's all. Nothing irreversible." He noticed Ramsey's unconvinced frown, and faltered. "Well, maybe he has become a little strange, but he will get better in time. You can count on it."

Ramsey still didn't believe this for a moment, but decided not to pursue a topic he didn't care about. "So, where is Morgan's room?"

"Ah, I'll take you there now, sir. If you are done with your breakfast, of course."

"Yeah."

"Good. I'll take the dishes now – the kitchen is along our way anyway."

Though he had seen some of the castle during his stay there, Ramsey couldn't help but be amazed at the sheer size of the interior. The kitchen was in fact not along the way to Prince Morgan's room, but was situated on the ground floor at the opposite end of the castle – needless to say, Ramsey saw at least half of the entire building during the excursion.

As he looked upwards, broad staircases criss-crossed high above his head, carpeted in purple and green velvet. The tapestries on the broadest walls were as gaudy as the rest of the décor, and ten-foot tall oil paintings of the pompous monarch himself dominated the remaining ones. As they passed, the herald made eager, informed comments on each one, and Ramsey mumbled meaningless agreements.

Each room was huge, and there seemed to be hundreds of them. The kitchen was as big as a house, and packed full of cooking utensils, pots, pans, stoves and piles of food. The cook, who was red in the face from chopping onions, seemed to materialise from behind some potatoes to take the dishes. At last, they made their way back up towards the prince's room.

"Now, don't feel the need to hurry yourself," said the other goblin, walking briskly several paces in front of an uninterested Ramsey. "We understand that you have been through a lot, and it may take you some time to fully recall what happened."

"Mmhmm…" Ramsey glanced at each tapestry and painting on the walls as he went past, and began to notice a theme emerging, besides that of King Viktor with his fat stomach strapped up in tight armour – the wall hangings in particular showed what looked to be dragons, with what must have represented goblin kings of the past, locked in battle. He wanted to ask the herald about the pictures, but thought he might receive a long-winded answer if he dared to show interest. He stayed quiet.

At last they came to a large wooden door on the left, into which was carved various images of trees and birds, as well as some sort of ancient writing. It was firmly closed, and the herald took a gold key from his robes to unlock it.

"This is Prince Morgan's room;" he said. "Our king had this door created from the tallest tree in Merlockiara when Morgan was just three months old. The writing around the frame is an old inscription that members of the royal family traditionally have carved into doors, tables and bed posts."

"Oh." Ramsey was casually regarding the nearest wall hanging, which featured a strange-looking dragon attacking a rather small goblin. The herald didn't notice him, and swung open the door, catching the other goblin's attention.

"Here we are. Feel free to have a look around, and if anything refreshes your memory, be sure to say. I'll be right here behind you."

He gestured for Ramsey to enter the room, which he did with some caution. He expected to find a lot of torn furniture and bloodied walls, but to his surprise, the room was tranquil, and just felt very empty. He took a deep breath.

Prince Morgan's room was at least twice the size of his own, but contained little extra furniture. The stone walls were the same dull shade, and the painting of Morgan and his father on the west wall was old and a bit smudged. Near to the four-poster bed, a desk and chair were overturned, and one corner of the colourful rug was rumpled. The single window, as tall as the one in Ramsey's room and far broader, gaped out into an emptiness of sky, and the edges were slightly crumbled, as though something a little too large had tried to force its way through. Near the window, several small drawings had been pasted to the wall, each one signed 'Morgan'; one of the pictures was slightly splashed with red. Ramsey inhaled heavily. The herald spoke up.

"I know it might be distressing," he sighed, "but if you can help us, Prince Morgan may still have a chance."

Ramsey remained quiet as he traversed the room, trying to pick out every last detail. He was starting to feel very uneasy. The state of the window in particular made him reconsider the likelihood of a large dragon being responsible for the carnage – it was one of the only creatures on the island that would be capable of reaching Morgan's room from the outside. The chamber was bitterly cold, deathly sad.

Ramsey walked over to the window, looked briefly out onto the small stone balcony, and turned towards some of the drawings nearby. One in particular, entitled 'Morgan-age 5', was obviously meant to portray the goblin castle. On top of the very simplified, angular building shape were two stick figures, one with a crown and the other without, in bright red and yellow crayon.

"I was with him when he drew that one," said the other goblin, approaching Ramsey by the window. "It's a picture of him with his father."

"I could've guessed that." Ramsey crossed his arms and moved towards the stained picture of what seemed to be a tree wearing a hat. The deep red colour was most definitely not paint, but it was the only splash of blood in the whole room.

As he took a closer look at the drawing, he noticed something else on the paper – something transparent and wet, shiny like saliva. Without thinking about it, he reached out and touched it with his finger-tips. It clung to his skin, and he immediately felt a sting in his hand. It burned. Ramsey frantically tried to wipe it off on his trouser leg, but it stuck firmly to his fingers, and he scraped his hand against the stone wall in desperation.

"What *is* this stuff?" he yelped.

"Any recollections yet, young sir?"

Ramsey almost screamed. "This is really painful, give me a second!" He rubbed his hand against the wall until the sticky fluid came off, but his skin still burned, and became red and irritated before his eyes. He growled to himself. Now he had two sore hands. The herald didn't offer any comfort, and just asked him again if anything was familiar. "Just tell me what that sticky stuff is. You said you had some ideas of your own."

"Well…" began the other, after a slight pause. "we have reason to believe that it was a particular kind of dragon that took Prince Morgan and attacked you. Namely a cobra dragon."

Ramsey turned to stare at him. "A *what* dragon?"

"A cobra dragon, young sir. They live mainly in the more southern kingdoms of Utipona and Yirsan, but we have reason to believe there is at least one colony in northern Oouealena. They inhabit mountainous regions, so we can determine where this creature is probably based. Within the last week, Merlock has suffered ten major fires in various parts of town, and nothing but a dragon would have the power to inflict so much damage."

Ramsey was beginning to find it hard to stay sceptical, but didn't allow any emotion to show on his face. The herald seemed to be distressing himself with his own words.

"The only problem is that cobra dragons aren't able to breathe fire, but there is no other explanation for the venom on that wall. We've had it analysed by two doctors and the local reptile keeper, and it is definitely potent cobra venom. Though we are possibly dealing with more than one dragon, I find it far more plausible that we are being plagued by some kind of advanced dragon that has many different attack methods. If two or three dragons were responsible, no doubt our town would have been completely burned to the ground by now, therefore I feel we are dealing with one incredibly dangerous beast, which we must locate and destroy soon if we are going to save our prince."

Ramsey hadn't spoken in a while, and found it difficult to relocate his voice. The information was overwhelming, and more than a little daunting. "...So, is it a snake or what?"

"Scaless, no, it's a dragon." The herald was gazing out onto Prince Morgan's balcony, as though waiting for the said creature to return. "It's a dragon that is part cobra, from the neck upwards, but it is a dragon and not a snake. Does this help you at all? Were you hit with venom during the attack?"

"No," he answered instantly. "I tried to run and the thing grabbed me by my arm, in its jaws, but I couldn't really see because it was so dark."

"Did it poison you with its fangs? No, I suppose it didn't, otherwise you would have died." The herald turned to face Ramsey again, a look of repressed desperation on his long face. "How big was it?"

"I don't know, I couldn't see it, could I?"

"Approximately."

"Okay, very big."

"What colour was it?"

Ramsey seethed. "I just said I was in the bloody dark!"

"Did it make a noise?"

"Um, yeah…it roared."

The other goblin raised an eyebrow in an unimpressed manner, but persisted patiently with his questioning. "And it was a cobra dragon?"

"It must have been." Ramsey managed to reclaim his cool, but couldn't help longing for his small, private tree-house right then, where nobody ever bothered to talk to him. He would have to play along until he could get back home, without suspicion. "It was really big, and it hissed quite a lot, and it had these really, really long teeth that dug into my arm."

He quickly shielded his injured hand in case the other goblin decided to inspect it, but he needn't have worried. The herald was evidently very excited again, and performed a little hop on the spot, his robes bouncing around his feet.

"Then my theory was correct! I must go and inform King Viktor at once – oh thank you, thank you so much, young sir. You really have been such a help to all of us in such an upsetting situation."

Ramsey huffed, averting his gaze to the window once more. "I haven't done anything apart from answer a few questions."

"But without you, we wouldn't have so many details about the creature. We've had virtually no reliable information so far, apart from what you have told us. This good news might be just what King Viktor needs to return to his senses. You may have saved our whole kingdom. Thank you so, so much."

He moved to hug Ramsey again, but thought better, and withdrew his arms back into his robes.

"I'll go and inform the king right away. Will you be all right here for a moment, until I return? I'm sure all our castle advisors will want to talk to you."

Ramsey was busy looking out at the view, and nodded half-heartedly. "Sure."

"Very well then. I'll be back sharply."

The herald hurried out of the room, pulling the door half-closed as he left. Ramsey hardly cared. He was by himself in a room than oozed vibes of death, looking out at a distant view that glowed with the warmth and freshness of a green summer day. The weather of Merlockiara never looked more inviting than when he couldn't get out to enjoy it. It unnerved him slightly that there were no birds in sight; though the sky was calm and beautiful, it looked barren and somewhat foreboding, as he found himself subconsciously watching for a dragon-shaped silhouette on the horizon.

Though he abhorred himself to do it, as he stood there in the abandoned bed-chamber, he found himself feeling somewhat sorry for Prince Morgan. Having to live pent-up in a mouldy castle with a moronic father who was full of himself was a life Ramsey wouldn't wish on anyone. Morgan was only a child, he had never known the anguishes of adolescence that Ramsey still dragged himself through, had never known what it was like to be truly free of his duties...

And now he was dead.

Ramsey knew it would happen, though it never should have – he was feeling guilty. Only a tiny bit, maybe, but he felt ashamed. It was hidden beneath his skin, unwilling to show itself, but it was there. He only wished that someone in his own life, anyone at all, cared for him the way the royal goblins cared for Prince Morgan. Thinking about that melted away his feelings of remorse, and made him angry again.

"Well, it's a sad, sad world in which you've got to be important to be cared about." He spoke aloud and leaned out of the window, addressing the balcony. "Yeah, it's an awful world sometimes, but too bad. Prince Morgan gets eaten by a dragon, King Viktor goes insane, no more goblin monarchy, everyone's happy. Well, apart from those two. Not that you can feel especially happy or sad once you're dead."

Sometimes, Merlockiara was beautiful. Often Ramsey resented every last bit of it, but beyond the town wall, in his little tree-house, he was free to be by himself, to look out for himself and nobody else. His body ached to be out there again, in the sun. Not that he liked the sun at all, but out in the fresh air, where it was warm, open, and the world stretched far beyond him at every angle, fading into the murky greenness that made Merlockiara so uniquely pleasing.

He was catered for in the castle, but the immense stone building was not his home, and he knew he couldn't stay there. He had come too far to admit that he had lied about the dragon attack; but otherwise, he feared, they might keep him in the castle forever, waiting on tenterhooks every day for a new drop of information on this imaginary snake dragon.

Ramsey had never faced such a dilemma in his life. He was too turbulent to be surrounded by other goblins twenty-four hours a day, and hoped he could find an adequate excuse to get himself freed from the town before the situation escalated further. The sound of fast-approaching footsteps along the corridor outside made him cringe.

He didn't feel as though he had been in the room very long, but the concept of time must have slipped past him, as the herald burst back into the room with a cluster of about ten other goblins in multi-coloured robes. They swarmed around him, frantic to get a good first look at him, though he distinctly remembered about half of them from sometime earlier in his stay. The herald was beaming with pride, as though boasting that it was he who first addressed Ramsey on the matter, and he raised his remarkable voice over the chatter of the excited group.

"Everyone, please meet our new informant, who has given us new hope in our quest to rescue Prince Morgan. You have been of such great service to us, Mister…" He paused for a moment and shook his head, laughing slightly. "I'm sorry, I never asked your name, did I, young sir? Please tell us who you are."

Ramsey almost couldn't recall his own name, but then again, the matter of thinking is made much harder when one is

47

faced with a buzzing throng of wide-eyed, loud-mouthed goblins. "My name is Ramsey."

"Ah, Ramsey – what an intelligent name."

He began to feel quite sick with need for his crummy tree-house. "Not really."

The herald clapped a hand onto Ramsey's pointed shoulder and started to lead him out of the room; the other goblins followed. "Nonsense, Ramsey. You have done for us what nobody else in Merlock has been able to do."

There was that annoying feeling in his stomach again. He wished everyone would stop praising him.

"We must go and announce the good news to our people – now all we need is a well-equipped search party, and Prince Morgan will be back home in no time."

Plus the automatic assumption that Morgan was still alive was *really* starting to bug him.

"Don't you worry though, sir. We will keep you and all the goblins of Merlock safe from that dreaded beast. We're posting more guards around the town on lookout duty, and we will get some new dragon-sized catapults and spears to protect our citizens in the event of further attacks. That should show the thing who is in charge, eh?"

The herald was clearly on some sort of high, as he was trying to integrate feeble jokes into the conversation. He was obviously confident that Prince Morgan would return alive and well.

"You are free to stay here at the castle if you would feel safer. Perhaps you could supervise our developments in the case, see if you can provide us with more information."

"I don't think I'll be able to do that," said Ramsey, keeping his voice as emotionless as possible. "I really can't remember any more. I wouldn't know what was real, and what could be a dream or something. That attack really affected me, I might never get over it."

The herald steered him around a corner and down a wide staircase, in the direction of Ramsey's room. The others still followed, in a contained state of awe. "That's dreadful to hear. You poor boy; so young, and to have something so horrible happen to you. You must tell us if there is anything we can do to help you get over your terrible experience."

"Well," he began, raising his tone a little, "what I would like is to go back home. My house is just outside town. Maybe then I could relax and get all this stuff out of my mind." The other goblin didn't respond right away, so Ramsey continued. "I don't live far from here, I could still keep in contact with you."

"I'm sorry, Ramsey, but it is Merlock's law – now that we are facing this dragon crisis, nobody is allowed to leave town, and if you were to leave we would be unable to let you back in." Ramsey frowned. He needed to find his way out soon or he would go crazy. "It is for your own safety, I'm afraid."

"And who made up that law?"

The herald tensed his grip on Ramsey's shoulder. "Well, I did, but I believe it was a decision for the best. That dragon could take every life in Merlock unless we protect ourselves somehow."

"But that hasn't stopped it setting fire to buildings all over town," Ramsey pointed out, glancing briefly sideways at a portrait of one of King Viktor's ancestors, wearing a dragon-skin cloak. "What's the harm in letting me go home?"

"I'm afraid that is quite simply out of the question."

The herald quickly dismissed their enthusiastic followers, telling them to organise a royal declaration, and took Ramsey back to his room in complete silence. The latter was none too pleased to be back in his boring, stone room, and automatically went over to the window to look at the view.

The herald stood in the doorway, idly brushing dirt off his robes and tutting to himself as he watched the other goblin at the window. He seemed to be waiting for something to be said, but Ramsey felt too frustrated to talk, and just leaned out over the windowsill, longing to be free of the wretched castle. His tree-house was only a brown speck on a grassy, green bump from the high window; all the same, he would sooner be back in that leaky, wooden hut than living in King Viktor's castle. The herald cleared his throat.

"Pardon me, sir," he began, "but I have noticed that you spend a lot of time looking out at the view. Even in Prince Morgan's room, you seemed to be drawn to the window."

Ramsey grumbled. "I just told you, I want to go home."

The other goblin was undeterred from his own theory. "I think you look out at the view because you are thinking deeply about something. Ever since we brought you here, you've been rapt in looking out of your window. I mentioned it casually to our doctor once he said you were recovering; he said that you might have developed some form of paranoia. Are you waiting for the dragon to come back? I assure you, sir, you're safe here."

Ramsey could have sworn quite bitterly at that moment, but stayed his tongue. If he lost his temper, he would stand even less of a chance of getting home. He would keep the royal goblins pleased, talk to them on their own terms, play along as far as he could, and he might at least get out of the castle, if not beyond the town wall.

"My every thought doesn't revolve around that damn dragon, you know. I was just thinking about…well, about Prince Morgan."

The herald swallowed.

"He must be so scared out there, all alone, without his father…" He gritted his teeth slightly and thought. "…In the clutches of an enormous, grotesque dragon, not knowing what is going to happen to him."

"Oh Scaless!" exclaimed the other, throwing up his arms. "We must get to him at once!"

Ramsey rolled his eyes. This guy wasn't even a challenge. "Because you know what dragons do to princes, don't you? They hold them for ransom, they love gold and jewels, but if they get too impatient, they *eat* the prince and steal the gold anyway. Sneaky creatures."

The other goblin gasped with nausea.

"And oh, the riddles they ask! You'd need someone really intellectual in your search party to challenge the dragon to a game of wits."

"But we have no intelligent warriors, and all the scholars in our town are feeble and weak…"

"Exactly. Maybe it would be better to evacuate Merlock and move everyone somewhere safe; then you could call in strong, clever soldiers from the other kingdoms or something. And they would need to be very discreet too, because dragons have excellent eyesight. A whole army wouldn't stand a chance, they'd just be torched the second they left town." Ramsey was gazing wistfully out at the view, hardly regarding his own words, but the herald thought he looked wise, and took his every word to heart, making frequent 'um' and 'ah' noises. "Only suggestions, of course."

"Clever sir," said the herald, his voice hopeful. "You should be on our royal council. You really have such good ideas, but I'm afraid no other kingdoms would be willing to aid us. King Viktor does not like to associate with-"

"Yeah, well, he's babbling nonsense right now, so maybe it would be safe to call in Ooealena or Hanyaliamaya for help." He craned his neck out of the window, watching the static movement of nervous goblins in the town square. They seemed to be miles away. Ramsey was starting to feel very distant and tired. He longed desperately to get back to his tree-house and be alone. If he became more deeply involved with activities in the castle, he was going to feel guilty again, and that was a sensation he would rather not feel. There was no real harm in giving hope to desperate goblins, after all, even if it was false hope.

And of course, it was amusing to see the royal herald so worked-up over the brain capacity of Merlock's citizens. He could still hear the other goblin behind him, muttering to himself in a worried squeak of a voice.

At what seemed to be the other end of the world, Ramsey observed the speck that was his home, swaying gently in the branches of that distant oak tree, as always. He never, ever dreamed that someday he would feel homesick for it. It was another part of his life; albeit a shabby, unstable, damp part. It was one of the few things on the planet that he could call his own, it had stuck with him through his life when nobody else would. There had to be some way for him to get back home…

"Will you do it?"

Ramsey blinked, halfway through reminiscing about his tree-house, and turned to the other goblin. "Sorry, what was that? I was miles away…"

The herald, if it was indeed possible, looked more nervous than ever. His whole body was twitching. "Will you go and rescue Prince Morgan?"

Ramsey blinked again, stared for a while, and finally reached the closest he had come to a laugh since his father passed away. One corner of his mouth raised slightly. "You've got to be kidding. What would I want to do that for?"

The other goblin had obviously expected a different reply, as his face fell completely, and he was overwhelmed with embarrassment. "Well, I thought you implied that maybe you wanted to…but…no, it doesn't matter…I just thought that you were suggesting yourself for the task. You're clearly intellectual, and you have come through so much, you've faced this dragon before…"

Ramsey pursed his lips and took another brief glance out of the window. Normally, he would have just laughed off the suggestion, and he wasn't sure why he couldn't find it in him to scoff or make a snide remark. Maybe he was just tired again. Wherever the dragon was, it was certain to be a very long way from Merlock. "That doesn't mean anything."

"But you have the brains, you have good ideas and you know what to expect from the dragon," argued the other. "And you're small, you would be able to evade the beast easily."

"I'm taller than you," huffed Ramsey, leaning one elbow on the windowsill.

"That may be, but you're very…well, *thin*, so you might go unnoticed by even the sharpest dragon eyes. And with the right equipment, a map, weapons, plenty of supplies, you could find your way to the dragon's lair, get Prince Morgan, and come back to

Merlockiara unnoticed. That way, you could avoid fighting the creature." There was a hint of longing in the herald's voice. Ramsey rested his sharp chin in his hand.

"That doesn't make any sense – you don't know where that dragon's lair is, and even if you did, I don't have the time or money to waste on a pointless journey like that."

"Oh, but we will pay your way, we'll make sure you have all the equipment needed. If you would only consider it, for a moment or two. I think you are just the goblin we are looking for."

Ramsey's lack of interest had no effect on the other goblin's desperation to rescue the missing prince. Though Ramsey wasn't being as irritable as usual, he still felt a little confused and angry in himself. It was fun to wind the herald up, but again he was in two minds about what he had done. He didn't want to commit himself to something knowing he had deceived a whole kingdom to do so. On the other hand, he hated Merlockiara, and he yearned to get out of the castle and back to his humble tree-house. If he could get beyond the town wall, he would be free to return home.

"So, would you send me off to find this dragon by myself?" His focus was by now entirely upon Merlockiara's green, hilly horizon.

"Well, from what you said previously, I would guess so. If you were by yourself, with enough money to buy food and supplies, your presence might be discreet enough to go unnoticed by the monster. You clearly have the brain power to outsmart this dragon." Ramsey gloated a little, still staring out of the window. "The whole of Merlockiara would be indebted to you, sir. You will be forever immortalised in our kingdom's history if you do this. I beg of you, young sir, I have come to know you over these last few days, you are brave, and you obviously care for our beloved Prince Morgan."

"You can read me like a book, can't you?"

The herald continued with a nod. "Merlock is falling apart right now, King Viktor is getting worse by the day, everyone in town is paranoid that the dragon will come back and destroy more homes. We have to do something quickly before this situation becomes worse, we cannot cause our citizens any more panic, and I for one am finding it difficult to cope with the fact that we may never see Morgan's chirpy little smile again."

Ramsey felt something painful in the pit of his stomach; the herald was starting to cry through his words.

"I raised him from when he was a baby, I've known him all his life, and it's killing me that I can't do anything to save him. But you, you are responsible, you are strong, you pulled your way through a horrifying dragon attack to help us, and I know our kingdom can rely on you. Please, I'll do anything, this kingdom means everything to me, the royal family can't be destroyed this way. Our king can't get a straight word out of his mouth, the heir to the throne is gone…"

At that point, the herald's voice dissolved into tearful sobs, and he buried his face in his embroidered sleeve. Ramsey could feel himself tensing. He hated Merlockiara so much, it made no sense for him to feel bad for what he had said. He took a deep breath, unable to look at the other goblin. "Yeah…Okay, I'll go." The herald kept sobbing; Ramsey raised his voice. "I said I'll do it."

"Oh Scaless…!" wailed the other, muffled by his sleeve. "Oh sweet Scaless, thank you…I know it is an awful lot to ask of you…"

"No, I'll do it. Just let me go alone, I'll do whatever I can to bring Morgan back."

"I will never be able to thank you enough, young sir…oh Scaless, bless you for sending us a hero…"

Ramsey felt angry again. "Stop giving thanks, really, it's all right. I want to keep this as low-key as possible, Okay? You don't want the whole kingdom getting agitated or anything." The herald nodded, acknowledging the logic in his statement. "Get me all the money I'll need, and at least one good map of the island. I want to set off as soon as possible, before I change my mind."

The herald leapt to attention at the possibility of such a thing. "Don't worry, sir, I'll get started on the arrangements straight away. Thank you so very, *very* much."

"I said you're welcome, now please, just go…I need to think…" Ramsey crouched down onto his knees on the floor, resting

54

his elbows on the windowsill and his chin on his arms. The herald, smiling broadly through eyes filled with tears, agreed that he deserved time to consider the task ahead of him, and left the room with a giddy spring in his step. Ramsey sighed gently, looking past his nose to the wide landscape ahead of him, and tapped his sharp fingernails on the cool stone. A wisp of a laugh escaped his thin lips. "That was too easy by far...what a gullible moron..."

Soon he would be home free – even better, they wouldn't be able to stop him leaving Merlock, leaving the kingdom if he wanted to. Since his youth, Ramsey had always felt the need to get far, far away from his childhood, even if that meant getting physically removed from Merlock; several hundred miles away would suit him just fine. If they thought he was going to rescue Prince Morgan, they wouldn't stop him leaving, and if he never returned, they would just assume he had died heroically on his quest.

He could live somewhere far away, in a forest or up a mountain, completely isolated with nobody to bother him; he would no doubt have enough wealth to live comfortably for the rest of his life. After the childhood he had suffered through, the discrimination he had endured, he felt he deserved to be remembered as a hero, dead or alive.

Whoever said that lying never solved anything was obviously never in Ramsey's position. He was going to be free, free and rich, free and rich and *heroic*; and he owed it all to an injured hand and the assumptions of some incredibly dim goblins. At least something had worked out well in his eighteen years of life – finally things were going the way he wanted. It was too good to be true. Right on cue, the royal herald interrupted Ramsey's train of thought with a loud, eager cry as he hurried back into the room.

"Wonderful news, sir...!" he exclaimed. "I have several of our advisors working on a journey plan for you right now, they're making some last decisions on the type of equipment and protection you will need. The public hasn't been informed yet of the developments, and I will make sure things stay that way, unless you have a change of heart."

"Right you are."

"And one more thing, sir…" he added, tentatively. "I have told King Viktor of your proposition, and he demands that you see him at once, so that he may thank you for your kindness and bravery."

Ramsey was certainly not in the mood to receive further extravagant 'thank you's, especially if accompanied by cries of 'hail Scaless!', but he didn't have much choice if he was going to be freed from the town. He stood up off the floor and brushed some dust off his trouser legs. "So he's making sense now, is he?"

The herald smiled. "Well, sir, there's some hope at least. I told him the good news, and he calmed a little, and asked to see you. It took him a while to get the first word out, but his speech was normal for the first time since his son was taken. It seems he may recover; the doctor is thrilled, we all are. It won't take long, but I'm sure it would mean a lot for him to meet the goblin who is going to save his son. It isn't far to the throne room." Ramsey crossed his arms. "I assure you, it really isn't far."

"I hope not. All these heroic decisions have made me tired. I need my bed." The herald agreed as though it was the most natural thing in the world, and gestured to the door. All Ramsey wanted was to stay in his room and enjoy thoughts of freedom. "I'd like to leave by tomorrow morning."

"Yes, sir," said the other, ushering Ramsey through the door with shuffling footsteps. "As soon as we have your supplies together, you can leave at any time. Everything will be as 'low-key' as possible, don't you worry."

Ramsey sighed aloud. He really wished he didn't have to go through this part of the plan – the last person he ever wanted to meet was the odious King Viktor. All he really knew about the king was that he was fat, lazy, enjoyed having flattering portraits of himself commissioned, and that he must have liked green and purple hues, as almost every decorative element in the castle was either one or both colours. The carpets, rugs, tapestries, even the robes of his advisors seemed to adhere to the theme. Maybe it was some sort of ancient 'royal goblin colour code'. Whatever it was, Ramsey decided there was no feasible excuse for décor that was so harsh on the eye, and guessed that Viktor was not a goblin of much sense or colour co-ordination.

Most of the dragons that featured in the castle's wall-hangings were green and purple now that he recalled it. That must have just been the way dragons were painted, in poisonous colours – but then, it was strange that the entire theme of the castle would be the same.

As they neared the corridor to King Viktor's throne room, the colour scheme became increasingly apparent. Once more, Ramsey wanted to inquire about the wall-hangings and ever-present dragon images, but declined. If there was anything important to be said, the herald would tell him. At least, he assumed so.

The other goblin was silent from the moment they left Ramsey's room until they arrived outside the door to King Viktor's throne room. It was closed, decorated in a similar fashion to that of Morgan's room, but much taller, and some parts were painted gold. Ramsey looked at the herald as the two of them stood in silence, grating his teeth quietly together, listening for any sign of activity. He could hear muffled voices on the other side of the door, but couldn't make out what was being said. Several long, slow minutes passed uneventfully before the door was opened from the inside, and a rather stocky goblin called both of them into the room.

Ramsey was so preoccupied with daydreams about his future that the herald had to practically pull him into the chamber. He was shocked at first by how dark the room was – opaque curtains covered all the open windows. The only light in the room was the glow of a large log fire at one end of the chamber, as well as several torches lining the walls. Not much could be seen in the dull orange glow of the flames, but Ramsey could hear low-pitched muttering somewhere to his left; as his eyes adjusted to the darkness, he beheld the outline of several other goblins, along with what must have been King Viktor's throne.

Indeed, there was somebody sitting on the carved, regal chair, and the herald began to steer him in that direction. He became tense again. Everything was moving ahead so rapidly, he couldn't afford to ruin his chances now.   A loud, chesty cough erupted from the darkness, and he jumped with surprise.

"Don't be scared, Ramsey," said the herald, keeping a firm, slightly uncomfortable grip on his arm. "Everything's fine. Greetings, Your Majesty…!" Ramsey looked all around as the other goblin addressed the throne. "This is the heroic young man I told you about.  He's going to rescue Morgan for us."

Ramsey stared intently as the outline of King Viktor solidified before his eyes. "…Hello."

There was another cough, and Ramsey saw the goblin before him quiver pathetically.  Viktor was a plump, sweaty figure, like a roast pig wearing a green shirt, purple trousers and a lopsided crown, strapped up in a thick leather belt.  He was clutching at his own face as if it perplexed him, his eyes were wide and pale, and he shivered in his seat as though plagued with a terrible fever.

Ramsey was thankful that the herald didn't attempt to move him closer; Viktor looked ready to lash out at any moment like a crazed man, but nobody in the room expressed alarm.  He must have been acting this way, if not worse, for many days beforehand. All of a sudden, he noticed Ramsey properly, and his ragged breath calmed slightly.

"Y…y-you will…rescue…my son?" He spoke as though every word was barbed wire in his throat.  A long pause followed, and he gasped loudly for breath to keep talking. "My son…my son, oh my son…"

The herald shook Ramsey lightly. "Yes, Your Highness, young Ramsey here has sworn to rescue Prince Morgan and bring him home safely.  He has been ever so selfless in his decision."

Ramsey stuck close to the other goblin at his side, unwilling to move any closer to the king.  He had never seen anything so strange.  King Viktor acted as though he could barely breathe, like he was horribly constricted.  His expression was manic, he was twitching randomly, and his breath was becoming shallower the more he spoke.  It looked like something on the borderline between extreme illness and madness.  He began to sob.

"My son…oh my son…my only son…" He gasped again, sobbing against his hands. "My flesh and blood, my son…!"

"Calm down, Your Majesty…" urged one of the attendants nearby, as three of the goblins attempted to placate their king. Ramsey stepped backwards, feeling more than a little disturbed. Everything was happening at once, soon this would be over and he could go home – he never expected anything as alarming as the state King Viktor was in. It was clearly something far beyond hysteria at the loss of his child.

At last, Viktor began to calm, rubbing his face with his palms and tugging slightly on his short, spiny, black hair. His chest heaved. "My son…my son…" His crown slid sideways off his head, and one of his attendants attempted to replace it, but Viktor pushed him aside and leaned towards Ramsey, breathing heavily. "You must save my son, he must come home…"

"I will," said Ramsey, a waver in his voice. "I promise I will."

"He is only small, fair, brown eyes…he wears a leather bracelet on his…left wrist…he is so small, what if his bones are broken? What if he's hurt? Oh Scaless…!" Ramsey cringed as the attendants calmed Viktor once more. After a moment of gasping and shivering, the king continued. "You will…y-you…will know him when you see him…he has brown eyes, blond hair…h-his skin is…v-very, so very pale…and his right cheek has…has a scar across it…please, please, save my son…!"

King Viktor continued sobbing; the goblins around his throne tried to get him under control again, and the herald moved forward also to give assistance. Ramsey stood alone in the dim light, watching the sorry scene before him with a great deal of tension. It was frightening to see anyone in such a state, even if it was the goblin king. He was feeling pity for the ugly old thing – here he was, delirious, screaming for his son, looking like an idiot, clearly not caring who this supposed rescuer was. Ramsey got the feeling he could have been a convict, a troll or an apple pie and he still would have received the same reaction.

Viktor didn't know where he was, who he was or who anyone else was, but he knew he had lost his son, and needed to get him back. He was screaming in absolute hysterics as the other goblins swarmed all over him, trying to hold him down in his chair, but Ramsey stayed put, somehow unable to move himself away. He couldn't get out of this disturbing situation now, and well he knew it. Viktor was a father...he may have been a dim-witted, self-serving goblin, but he was the father of a missing child, and Ramsey began to fear once more that he might have taken on more than he could handle.

"M-my...son! My son, oh Scaless, Scaless...! My blood, please, *please* save my son...!"

# Chapter Three

# A Way Out

Ramsey couldn't sleep that night. Every time he lay down, he found himself thinking about King Viktor, and the peculiar behaviour he had seen earlier that day. There was certainly something strange about the goblins in the castle. He had the feeling that he wasn't being told everything he might need to know about the kingdom, in particular its past association with dragons. There had to be more to the situation than met Ramsey's eager eyes, and though he had no intention whatsoever of rescuing Prince Morgan, he couldn't help but wonder what information the herald and other royal goblins were keeping from him. It was in his nature to be inquisitive, whether he liked it or not.

As one could guess, in his absence of sleep, Ramsey spent hour after hour looking out at the night sky through his window. When he became a little too tired, he sat down on the very edge of his bed, making sure to keep his eyes fixed upon the view, but soon returned to his former post to see more clearly into the distance. Apart from the moonlight illuminating the clouds, there was very little light by which to see, as Merlock town below the castle was completely dark, its inhabitants locked up tight inside their cold houses.

The night air was freezing, and Ramsey appreciated the warmth of a thick outer shirt, though it made his arms itch horrendously. He estimated the time to be around one o' clock, maybe later. The darkness seemed to stretch decades into the future, foreboding and black like a blanket of death – his own way of thinking was starting to unnerve him. It had certainly been a peculiar week, and now he had images of King Viktor lodged in his troubled brain. It made him all the more thankful for his sanity.

No, the night sky wasn't deathly. It was dark blue, beautiful, and it didn't harass him whatsoever. Ramsey was glad for every quiet second he could muster since arriving at the castle. Almost all the skin on his body was prickling and turning into goose-bumps. His bed was warm, but he stayed at the window, if only to gaze into the distance and envision himself as a free goblin at last. The whole world was his, and he would never have to look back on the town again. The rooftops down in Merlock seemed to glow under the pale moonlight as the clouds gradually parted. At least in the middle of the night with hardly any light, the town wall didn't look so horribly ugly.

"If only I liked it here, I'd miss it," he pondered, scratching his chin. "But I don't, so I won't."

He scanned the landscape, sighing gently to himself. Hopefully it would only be a matter of hours before he was somewhere far out there. He stretched his arms out, pressing his palms against the windowsill, and turned to retreat from the window, but as he did so, he caught sight of a bright flash from somewhere amongst the clouds. He gripped the ledge and leaned out of the window, squinting to work out if he had seen something real in the sky. As he stared out into the night, he saw it again – a brilliant, fiery flash shot through the dark in a long stream of flaming red, then disappeared. He saw something blurry moving where the flames had emanated from; it was coming towards the castle, gliding and somersaulting through the air. The fire came again, this time much closer – Ramsey felt a surge of heat, and smelled burning. He could see nothing more.

For about two minutes, he stood frozen at the window, clenching his teeth to contain his fear. He turned to run out of the room, but the lower half of his body was too scared to move, and he fell sideways onto the cold floor, landing on his injured hand. "Argh! Ow, oh damn it, be quiet...!" He trembled, panting heavily, and dragged himself back up to the window ledge, eyes wide. There was nobody awake in the castle, maybe nobody else had seen the thing. A loud, high-pitched hissing cry rang through the night air, and Ramsey heard a hollow, hot sound. The burning smell grew stronger. Something was moving above the castle.

All of a sudden, it was in his view again, whirling majestically above the royal gardens, a dark object gradually taking form. Though it flew too fast for Ramsey to properly make out what it was, in his mind he knew it was the cobra dragon that the herald had spoken of. It was a strange shape, with huge wings, a long body, and what appeared to be some kind of flared hood around its neck. It shot more flames from its gaping jaws and set the foliage alight; then it swerved in Ramsey's direction.

He tried to yell, but his voice was lost to him. It moved at an incredible speed directly at him, but soared vertically to the top of the castle before it collided with the window. He saw its smooth underside and sharp, green tail disappear up beyond his window, almost blown back by the heat that radiated off its shiny body, and tried to lean out for a better view. It was gone again, somewhere far above him, as the sound of a raging fire reached his ears. Along the corridor outside his room, he heard someone shout, and suddenly the castle came to life.

"Scaless save us, the dragon's back!"

"Don't panic, don't panic! Someone sound the alarm!"

"Sweet Scaless, protect our town!" exclaimed a voice that Ramsey recognised as the herald's. "Get everyone to safety, try to bring that beast down!"

"It's going back to the town, sir, it's burning up the square!"

Ramsey whirled around when the herald shouted from directly behind him, and clutched his chest with shock. The herald was, oddly, wearing the same robes he wore every day, but they were wrinkled due to being slept in. In his arms he held a large, leather pack, and around his neck was what appeared to be a string of garlic cloves. Ramsey was too scared to be angry with him.

"Young sir, I don't mean to alarm you, but-"

"I know, there's a bloody big dragon out there...! It's massive!"

"Yes, and it's attacking Merlock town at this very moment. You must escape, no matter what, we have to get you out of here. Take this pack – in it there is everything you need for your journey. I was going to give it to you in the morning, but..." He paused, and Ramsey heard the long, low rumble of a distant horn being sounded. "...there may not *be* another morning for us. Take the pack, I'll show you the emergency path out of town. We haven't a moment to spare."

Holding Ramsey's wrist firmly, the herald pushed his way through the goblin-filled corridors, past all of Viktor's portraits, and led both of them down to the ground floor of the castle; he then took Ramsey through a locked door to an undecorated passageway, at the end of which was a large, mostly empty room with a metal grid in the middle of its floor. They moved so fast and stopped so abruptly that Ramsey almost lost his balance, gripping the straps of his leather pack firmly. The herald, clearly distressed to his utmost capacity, knelt hastily by the grid and set about prising it open. Ramsey didn't like the look of where this was going.

"Hey, what's that?"

"It is the secret way out of the castle grounds," said the other, lifting one end of the grid with a loud grunt. "It's your only safe escape route – just drop yourself in, quickly, and you can navigate your way out from there."

Ramsey stepped back, holding the bag. "Where does it lead?"

"Just outside Merlock's wall.  It is a little bit murky down there, but you shouldn't get wet any higher than your ankles, I would guess."

Ramsey's mind was suddenly filled with disgusting thoughts.  Maybe the dragon wasn't such an awful thing to deal with. "It's not a sewage pipe or anything, is it?"

"No, it's merely an outlet for rainwater when the moat gets flooded.  Just be thankful the heaviest rains came months ago, otherwise you might have to swim your way out." The herald pulled the circular grid completely away, and rolled it over to the nearest wall. Ramsey peered down into the hole – it was about four feet in diameter, more than enough for him to slip through, but he couldn't see the bottom, and was, needless to say, a little wary of jumping in. The other goblin looked expectantly at him.

"Well?  Oh, please don't tell me you are having second thoughts.  We're relying on you to rescue Prince Morgan, you have to get out safely."

Ramsey crossed his arms over the leather bag. "And I want to, but I'm not sure if I want to jump down there.  You could be sending me to my death or something."

"Why in Scaless' name would I do that?  I want to help you, sir, please hurry and escape before it's too late.  Once you're down there, it is only a short trek to the outside, you will be fine, I promise you." More shouts were heard from above them, through the endless thunder of frantic, heavy footsteps. The herald jerked with fear. "Please, you must get out – go now." Ramsey eyed the hole again. "Now…!"

Clutching his leather pack and thinking of nothing but his imminent freedom, Ramsey nodded to the herald and crouched by the opening, hanging his long legs over the side, and dropped himself into the tunnel below.  There was a splash as he landed in water halfway up his calves, and he exclaimed loudly with disgust; the herald didn't react. Reaching out to his side, he felt a slimy wall, and he leant against it to catch his breath, blinking in the darkness. Overhead, the herald wished him good luck and instantly replaced the grid – within a matter of seconds, he rushed off, no doubt to raise further panic upstairs.

Ramsey panted heavily, listening to the sounds that came from above him, and slumped completely against the wall with relief. Now he only had to find his way out of the tunnel and he would be free. He could practically smell the entirety of Merlockiara's countryside all at once, it called out to him in silent tones. Wanting to make a dash for it, but finding himself stuck in three inches of slimy mud, he trudged with heavy footsteps towards the pale shaft of light at the end of the passage, clutching firmly to his supplies. He felt more elated than he had ever felt in his life, despite the fact that he was cold and wet in a tunnel that was almost too low for his head. The sludge loosened around his feet as he broke into a stilted run towards the light of the overhead grid – all regard for what he had left behind was gone. Slinging the bag over his left shoulder, Ramsey reached up and pushed on the stiff grid from below. Beyond it, he could see Merlockiara's night sky once more, now lit in red from the glare of fire coming from the town's blazing buildings. He gripped the cold metal and pushed upwards, trying to make full use of both hands. A loud, chilling snarl and the smouldering of many houses drowned out the screams from behind the town wall.

"Come on now, you can do it – just think, you're free...!" The grid jolted a little; Ramsey clenched his teeth and used every ounce of strength in his svelte body to force it upwards. It gave way with a jolt. He slid it aside with his good hand, making room for him to climb out, and tossed his bag of supplies up.

Now came the hard part – he had to lift himself out as well. Under normal circumstances, it wouldn't have been a problem, but he didn't trust himself to support his full weight with a damaged hand. Still, he had to try, or else stay down in the damp tunnel for the rest of his life. The grid opening was only a little way above his head, and he could easily reach it with his arms outstretched. With a huff, he gripped either side of the rim and tried to lift himself by his fingertips. He tried again, tucking one leg up to his body, but still he was too scared to test the strength of his injured hand. A fresh wave of cries from within Merlock heightened his sense of urgency, and he jumped up as far as he could, lodging himself halfway out of the opening with his elbows. He gasped and spread his arms, keeping the majority of his torso out of the tunnel, and lifted one foot out as well, getting a firmer grip on the ledge outside. He hoisted his remaining leg out of the passage, replaced the grid and quickly retrieved his leather pack, keeping himself in the shadow of the town wall.

His heart was racing. He was standing on a narrow stone platform, just above the water level of the moat, about eight feet from the opposite bank. He would need to jump over the water to get back to his tree-house, but the Merlock goblins were too unimaginative to add jagged rocks or crocodiles to their moat, so he didn't let it worry him. The outside world was so free, so open that he could barely contain the urge to run around, but he had to stay still – he could see the dragon again, moving far overhead.

It soared over the wall, extending its wings majestically in flight. It was leaving Merlock at last. Moonlight shone over its slender, green body, and in its claws, Ramsey beheld the outline of a large goblin – most likely another unfortunate guard. His breath caught in his stomach, throat and lungs all at once. For a while, the creature circled the town threateningly, and at last it glided away in the direction from which it came. Ramsey was at the front of the town wall, facing south – the dragon was flying north. Though it took him some time to feel safe, he at last began to breathe normally again, and the rising tone of shouts within Merlock reached his ears. It sounded as though half of the town was on fire. His tree-house had thankfully been spared, and it was there that he needed to go first, if only to take an inventory of what the herald had given him.

\*\*\*

Ramsey didn't remember his small home feeling so empty – after all, it was hardly spacious. He was relieved that the dragon hadn't been intent on total destruction, otherwise he might not have had a home to return to. Everything was just as he had left it over a week ago, as messy and feeble-looking as ever. He felt miserable; his trouser legs, coated with tunnel slime and green-tinted water (after he somewhat misjudged his jump over the moat), were giving his feet a chill, and he didn't want to catch a cold on top of everything else.

He straightened the blanket on his hard, low bed and sat down, lifting the bag of supplies onto his lap. He then unfastened the top and emptied the contents alongside him on the bed. It didn't look as though anything had been broken.

As he sifted through his supplies, it became obvious why the large pack felt heavier than was possible – it was so tightly-packed inside that Ramsey feared he wouldn't be able to fit everything back in. He had a metal compass, a rolled-up map with the Merlockiara seal on it, several clean shirts and trousers bound up tight, a dagger with a leather sheath, a roll of bandages, a drink flask, several pieces of fruit, and a fairly large purse in pale leather, tied with string. He opened the purse excitedly, and several multicoloured 'scales', the decorative Grenamoyan currency, fell out onto the blanket. From the look of things, there had to be hundreds of them in his possession.

"I'm rich…!" he exclaimed, reaching into the purse to feel exactly *how* rich he was. "I could buy my own kingdom with all this money…!"

After several moments of revelling in his sudden abundance of wealth, he stashed all the coloured scales inside the purse once more and fastened it tight. It went back into the very bottom of the bag, just to be safe. Feeling that they were valuable enough, he also replaced the official map and jewelled dagger – they could be sold if he became a little too luxuriant in his new lifestyle. Finally, he decided that everything in the bag might be useful on his way, and he packed it up again completely, with more than a little difficulty. There was nothing of any real worth in his tree-house, so all he took from there was his hair comb; though it was missing a few teeth, it still served some purpose to de-tangle the bristly mass on top of his head. He felt ready to go. The last thing he needed was to hang around so long that the dragon had time to come back – now that he was certain the dragon *did* exist, he found no reason to stay and every reason to be on the move.

Slinging his pack over his shoulders, Ramsey climbed back down from the tree-house, glancing briefly at the smouldering, red-glowing, grey form of Merlock to the north of his humble shack. The dragon had flown that way. He decided to head eastwards, where he could see at least some form of tree cover within a quarter of a mile or so, downhill from where he stood. He would be safe once he was hidden.

Clinging to that thought, and also to the straps of his leather pack, he set off at a brisk pace, down the green, dewy slope of the hill. The grass was damp and springy under his feet, and the feeling was incredible. With all the money the herald had given him, he could buy a big estate to run around on, or a whole mountain. When one is suddenly confronted by more money than one has ever had in one's life, there is a natural lapse in judgement over how it should be spent. Ramsey didn't care as long as he was able to get away from Merlock and run around.

To his left, and painfully in clear view, the goblin town was still burning. The wall drowned out plenty of the noise, but Ramsey could still hear the screams of petrified goblins fleeing their houses, animals crying out with panic, and the surging sound of flames rising higher over the town. The inside of the wall glowed violently, giving it the appearance of an enormous, stone campfire. To Ramsey's keen vision, the goblin castle was the only area within the wall that hadn't been destroyed, although one of the tall eastern turrets was burning furiously. Great clouds of putrid smoke rose up from Merlock, spreading out like a suspended black quilt above it. Before him was a patch of typically green woodland, the kind that Merlockiara was best known for – cool and wet from rain the previous day. The grassy ground gave way to a maze of tall evergreens, a small wood perhaps, but enough to protect him for the time being. He had truly had a lucky escape.

He hurried himself down to the final drop of the hill, where the patchy woodland began, and took shelter between several large trees, keeping himself hidden. Merlock wasn't going to leave his mind any time soon, though he wished it would. Hundreds of lives had probably been lost in the fire. At least he was free, and he had survived the carnage. His body was shivering with a mixture of fear and cold.

"Damn it..." he gasped, leaning against one particularly large tree and opening his leather bag. "That stupid water...damn dragon, scaring the life out of everyone..."

From the bag, he pulled a pair of dry trousers, which he laid out on the ground next to him. His bare feet were completely frozen, but as it was a basic trend that only wealthy, high-status goblins wore shoes, he never did anything about it. Goblins tended to have long toenails, which made the act of putting shoes on very tiresome. He did have a certain amount of money on his person. Shoes would be affordable...but the last thing he wanted was to be associated with goblins like King Viktor in any way. He complained to the trees about his icy toes, but didn't do anything practical.

In all, it took Ramsey half an hour to complain about his feet and attempt to change his trousers. Another attribute that most Merlockiara goblins shared was a tendency towards being prudish, unlike the trolls in the south of the kingdom, which were largely physical in everyday life. Trolls were also something he despised. He looked around in case there was anyone else there, and though there clearly wasn't, he took some time to investigate the small copse he was in before he decided to take his dirty trousers off.

Pressing himself against a tree trunk, he quickly dropped his trousers and pushed them aside, frantic to be fully clothed again, despite the fact that he was wearing quite long shorts underneath; he grabbed his clean pair and pulled them on. He breathed a sigh of relief. Though his old trousers were wet, if he had the chance to wash and dry them, he could wear them again, so he hung them over a low branch out of his way.

He wished he had a blanket to wrap around his shoulders, as he was very chilly, but he had to settle for the shelter of the tall trees to take the edge off the freezing gusts. In comparison, Merlock town was still a raging mass of fire over the hill. Inside the wall, houses had been reduced to ash, and hundreds of goblins had been burned to death, lying in the streets. The castle stood over it all, a crumbling mass of stone and vile décor. Within the space of a few days, Merlockiara had lost everything – it had no heir to the throne, the king might never be fit to rule again, and now Merlock itself was being burned to the ground. Far off along the horizon, a grotesque cry rang through the air as the silhouette of a large, hooded reptile crossed the moon.

\*\*\*

Grassman was a small village, only three miles or so from the capital. Ramsey decided to go there the following morning, in order to get some proper food and to see how much he could buy with all the money in his purse. The early morning sun lit up the landscape, transforming it into a luscious, green ocean. Though the village was faintly marked on his large island map, he had heard enough about the area to know that it was a small settlement with very little tourism, and so it would be grateful for Ramsey's wealthy presence. Maybe he could find some information on vast properties for sale in other kingdoms. Even if he couldn't, this village was his first stop on the road to freedom, and he was going to make the most of his brief stay there.

The village was little more than a dirt road lined with small houses, surrounded with trees and the odd field. A wooden sign, reading 'Grassman Village – Population 54', told Ramsey that he was in the right place. Though it was very near and in clear sight of the burning capital, there was no evidence of panic, or anything at all out of the ordinary. Ramsey had vague memories of the village from his childhood, but couldn't really discern why, as all his other recollections were based on the idea that his father never took him anywhere. Maybe he had stashed Ramsey in the back of a cart or something, then taken him out for the day. Ramsey had no idea; maybe his mind was just wandering again. Whatever the reality was, he knew he was in Grassman Village now, and that at last he had an important title to brag about.

With a spring in his step, and vowing to never again look back at Merlock, he strode into the village square, a patch of ground where the rows of houses appeared to converge. There were a few stalls set up alongside the houses, selling fruit, vegetables and home-made ornaments, and several goblins were happily going about their business without a care in the world. Ramsey wasn't noticed. He cleared his throat and strode right up to the rickety fruit and vegetable stand, scratching his chin and trying to look important. Though the pleasant village seemed quaint and homely, Ramsey had never before felt so eager to be on the move, and knew he had little time in which to enjoy the local atmosphere. He would make a name for himself in this small community of laid-back (and selectively blind) goblins, then go on his way.

On seeing him approach, the two other potential customers moved away, and the seller perked up curiously. She was female, freckled, apparently a little older than Ramsey, and she had shoulder-length purple hair tied up in a plait with a red ribbon. She looked intrigued by him, and similarly, the other market sellers all turned in his general direction. In a village with such a small population, a new face would, of course, attract plenty of attention. Ramsey felt that he was interesting them, and smiled inwardly.

"How much would you charge me for..." He scanned the stall, and pointed at a basket of red apples. "one of those?"

She stared at him for a moment or two, then followed his long finger to the basket. "Oh...um, those are one brown scale each, five apples for one yellow scale." He returned his finger to his chin, and proceeded to scratch again, as though contemplating his purchase. The seller looked up at him, not hiding her obvious fascination with him. Though she wanted to wait for his decision, her curiosity got the better of her, and she blurted out, "Who are you?"

"Excuse me?" Ramsey crossed his arms and puffed out his chest as much as he could to accentuate his importance; the girl started to turn red all over with embarrassment. The remarks of disapproval from the other goblins in the market were subtle, but very audible. Ramsey figured they were directed at the girl and not him. He swept around majestically, still puffing himself out, and spoke in a manner that struck them all dumb. "I am a hero amongst goblins, I am the only hope for this kingdom – the fate of your beloved Prince Morgan rests in my hands!" They all gasped. "King Viktor himself has chosen me to rescue his precious son from the vicious claws of a cobra dragon. A suicidal mission at best, but Scaless help me, I will rescue Prince Morgan or die trying!"

"Big deal!" grumbled one of the crowd. "King Viktor is a bastard anyway, we don't want him ruling us!"

"Well...yeah, but once Prince Morgan is on the throne, we'll be much better off, so I need to rescue him and bring him back to rule us. Basically, I'm very important, and I need a place to stay here for a day or two, maybe, while I stock up on supplies for my journey."

The girl behind the fruit and vegetable stall squealed ecstatically, and the noise shot through Ramsey's brain. "Oh goodie! We've got a hero in our town again! Daddy, daddy, look, he came to our stall first!"

"Who in Grenamoya are you, anyway?" asked another goblin in the crowd. He was round like a barrel, the colour of an unripe tomato, and wore a white apron over his clothes. "Who are you really, Mister Hero-amongst-goblins?"

"Daddy, please, don't be rude...!" urged the excitable girl. Ramsey double-checked both of them, more than a little confused by the contrast in appearance between the two. He wanted to say something, but stayed his tongue before he could insult either of them, and concentrated once more on making himself look heroic.

"My name is Ramsey, I left Merlock last night to start on my journey north."

"Ohh, really?" asked the round goblin, pressing down his mucky apron with his fingers. "So, how's Merlock then?"

Ramsey couldn't believe his ears. He pointed fixedly back in the direction of the town, his expression almost wild. "It's on fire! he said, exasperated. "Look, it's one big ball of fire back there, a dragon attacked it last night! Didn't you notice?"

Gradually, and clearly in no kind of hurry, all the other goblins, fat and thin, young and old, followed his gesture and gazed at Merlock's wall, rising over the green hills only a few miles away. Though it wasn't burning as strongly any more, it was still on fire, and the smoke had turned a vast expanse of sky overhead a murky grey hue. The smell of it hung strong in the air. They looked silently at the ruined town, and the fat, green goblin raised a hand to his head.

"Well, I'll be! Look at that, Mister Hero is telling the truth!"

Ramsey clenched his teeth and dropped his arms. "Of course I am! Don't you ever bother to look at Merlock or something?"

"Well, not much point normally," he said, as the others gradually returned to their shopping. "Nothing ever happens over there. And it's a bloody awful place, too. We don't care for Merlock one bit. I don't, anyhow."

Ramsey nodded and hoisted his pack more firmly onto his shoulders. "Yeah...I don't either, really." It wasn't hard to believe that these goblins didn't care for the capital, but Ramsey had thought that he was alone in his distaste for the town. It wasn't just his problem, then. He didn't know if he should feel comforted or not.

"...Do you still want your apple, sir?" asked the girl behind the stall tentatively, as she could see that Ramsey was thinking about something. Her lilac, freckled face was full of wonder, but Ramsey didn't notice. He looked at the basket of apples again, and the fat goblin nudged him.

"Go on, buy something from my girl. I know a place just down the lane where you can stay for a few nights."

"Oh yeah?"

He tugged on his apron proudly. "Certainly do. I own the place."

Ramsey caved in, though he wasn't terribly endeared to the fat goblin or his daughter. "Okay. I'll have five apples, then."

He bent to the ground and put down his backpack, shuffling around inside to find his money purse. The girl eagerly took five apples from the basket, dropped one, picked it up again, and put them inside a brown paper bag on the side of the stall. Ramsey retrieved a yellow scale, making sure not to expose how much money he was carrying, and handed it over to her. She put it in a small tin near to the bag of apples; Ramsey noticed when he took his purchase that there was no other money in it. The round father patted her on the shoulder, and then gestured for Ramsey to follow him down the lane to the only guest house in the village.

\*\*\*

It took the space of five minutes or less for Ramsey to reach the Grassman lodge, guided by the other goblin, who kept stopping randomly along the way to talk to neighbours and point out the different small shops that might be of interest. Ramsey hovered along behind him as though in an aggravated sleep – not really listening, but looking around, trying to analyse everything in his own mind.

The dirty ground left a coating of dust on the soles of his feet, and the sky overhead whispered of something in the distance. It chilled his whole body, though the sun shone purple through a dark cloud in the east. He saw a feeble settlement all around him, and goblins who knew one another only because their village was so small. It made such a contrast to Merlock, where everyone was living on top of one another, and nobody even cared for those around them.

The guest house was located at the end of one row of houses, past a small armoury shop and saddlery; like the other houses, it was a wooden cottage with a curved door and small windows, decorated with a few flower-less window boxes. It wasn't the most upmarket place Ramsey had ever seen, but he didn't have the energy to complain. The squat owner ushered Ramsey inside rather bossily and took him through the tea room, a medley of lace doilies and round tables; on each one sat a vase containing a piece of holly or bramble (goblins never cared much for flowers). It was warm and dusty inside, but Ramsey didn't have long to dwell there, as he was quickly escorted out through another door to a staircase and the lodging rooms. Several tea-drinking goblins watched them pass through, then instantly returned to their gossip.

"Got nobody staying here right now," said the owner, gruffly. "You'll be the first in two weeks."

"Aha," said Ramsey, not really listening and trying to avoid bodily contact with the other.

"I mean it," he continued, as he led Ramsey across the upstairs landing. "Folks 'round here really need trade from a lad like you."

He chose a room, one with a view of the lane below, and took a key from one of his overflowing pockets. He turned the key in the door forcefully and pushed it open with one shoulder. Ramsey stood still apprehensively and peered past the other goblin into the sparingly decorated room.

"This'll be your room – leave your stuff inside, I'll give you the key. Then maybe I can show you around the village a little."

Ramsey shrugged, agreed half-heartedly, and walked past him into the room. It was just as dusty as downstairs, if not more so, and it smelled like old books and furniture. It had a rustic appearance, with wooden walls, dried flowers (mainly thistles) and a burgundy armchair in one corner of the room, which had obviously seen its share of occupiers. The windowpanes were misty, and the bed had been tidily made. The owner followed him inside as Ramsey set about an investigation of the room. He closed the door, and addressed Ramsey harshly.

"What do you think you're doing, eh? Coming to our village, talking about dragons and burning castles! Really, I've never seen the likes of it!"

Ramsey was caught off-guard by the other goblin's words and turned abruptly, his pack hanging off one shoulder. "I'd say it's amazing that your whole village was too blind to see that the kingdom capital is on fire just a few miles away." He pointed to the window. "I can see it from here!"

"Don't give me that! Everyone knows there are no dragons within bloody miles of Merlockiara."

Ramsey flung his backpack onto the bed. "I know what I saw, and it was a dragon! Clear as day, I saw it setting fire to the town! You must have at least *heard* it!"

"No, I did not!"

"It was screeching its head off, you must be either moronically ignorant or terribly deaf." The other goblin swore at him, but he stood his ground. "I saw a dragon, a dragon took Prince Morgan, and that's why I've been sent to rescue him!"

The owner frowned at him, sceptically. "I don't know…"

"What more proof do you need? It's all true."

The other kept frowning, rubbing his thick neck ponderously, and looked angrily at Ramsey. "We folks here don't like to associate very much with Merlock. That King Viktor's no good to this kingdom or Grenamoya."

"I've said that I understand where you're coming from, but Prince Morgan'll be a better king than his dad. I care for this kingdom as much as you do." Ramsey was lucky that his nose didn't grow any further. The other goblin seemed somewhat convinced, though, and just sighed to himself.

"Well, whatever you're doing, don't let it interfere too much with our lives, Okay? Buy supplies, stay here a few nights, that's fine, just don't go upsetting our little village with tales of dragons."

"No problem." Ramsey sat down on the edge of the bed, suddenly feeling the urge to do so, and looked around. The owner offered once more to help, seemingly back to a pleasant state of mind; Ramsey admitted to being fine, and the other goblin returned downstairs.

He stretched his body and lay flat on the bed with a sigh. Outside, the sun emerged again, streaking a pale ray of light across the room. Ramsey was content in himself once more, and got comfortable on the bed. He turned onto his side, resting against some fluffy cushions. He blinked, closed his eyes, and opened them slightly; then he closed his eyes again and drifted into sleep.

\*\*\*

Several warm, static hours passed. Ramsey blinked awake once more to the sound of a large *thump*. His mind was full of heat and darkness, and he sat up with slight giddiness, half of his hair over his eyes. His back and shoulders felt as though they were on fire – the scalding pain in the middle of his back felt like the remnants of a bad dream, but he didn't remember having a nightmare. He reached anxiously over his shoulder and into the neck of his shirt with one hand, feeling the top and middle of his back for any cuts or swollen bumps, but found nothing out of the ordinary, apart from the fact that his skin was remarkably warm. He saw that he had knocked his bag onto the floor in his sleep, and deduced that he had been woken up as it landed on the wooden floor. He hadn't realised how tired he was from the previous night. He also hadn't intended to sleep for so long.

Outside, the sun had risen past its mid-point, and had begun to set in the west once more. It was the late afternoon, and he was still really tired. Though at that moment he felt as if he could sleep forever, he forced himself to sit up, and held onto the bedside unit to get to his feet without falling over. He hadn't seen it before, but as he stood, he noticed a large, leather-bound book on the cabinet beside the bed. He inspected it briefly – on the front cover was written 'The Scaless Scriptures' in tall, gilded letters, and the border was decorated with dragons and snakes in the same style. He lifted it open at a page, glanced at the words briefly, then let it fall shut again.

"Oh, you've got to be kidding."

Ramsey may not have been the most religious individual on Grenamoya, but he was smart enough to know what the Scaless Scriptures were all about. He'd heard the messages in Merlock a thousand times during King Viktor's rambling public speeches. This book was the foundation of Grenamoya's most ancient belief system. In it was found the reasons why the island was created; what every man, woman and child should be doing with his or her life; and the best way to find guidance from Lady Scaless, the great snake who watched over the whole of Grenamoya – all the answers together in one handy, dusty book. The scriptures had definitely not been there when Ramsey went to sleep, or he would have shoved them in a drawer. He was never one who tolerated being preached to, and at that moment, he felt positively violated.

Feeling suddenly energetic with anger against religious propaganda, he practically hurled himself across the room and out of the door. For once, he didn't care about the state of his hair or clothes; he did, however, return to the room seconds later to retrieve his purse from his leather pack by the bed. Then off he went again, marching downstairs at top speed towards the tea room. He didn't bother to lock the door behind him.

The plump, cabbage-coloured owner and his beanstalk of a daughter were sitting at a table in the tea room, talking rather edgily about the goblin who had arrived in their village that very morning. All the other patrons had gone home, presumably to continue their gossip in private; the owner sat with a yellowed newspaper (yesterday's) in his hands, and the other clutched a cup of lemon tea in her long fingers, mumbling hushed words about their latest customer. Dust settled on the windowsills in the deep, glowing light of the evening. Then Ramsey burst in through the door, his face a picture of outrage, and the quiet was lost.

"What do you think you're doing, putting that book in my room?" he asked bitterly, his teeth clenched. The fat goblin lowered his paper, raised an eyebrow, and inquired quite calmly as to what book Ramsey was referring. Ramsey tensed up. "You know fully well what I mean – that book of scriptures or what-have-you, it wasn't there when I went to sleep, then when I woke up, it was sitting on my bedroom cabinet." The other goblin just looked at him. "It's damn creepy!"

"Oh, right you are. I put a copy of the scriptures in every room in my establishment, guests find it comforting I s'pose." He stuck his large nose back in the newspaper. "Sorry if I disturbed you or anything."

"If I wanted a book of...snake-related *clap-trap*, I would have asked for it," grumbled Ramsey, if only to have the last word in the argument. Neither of the two responded. "Well, anyway..."

79

The owner didn't look up. "Sorry if I inconvenienced you, lad. Just a habit, I guess." Ramsey agreed pointlessly. "So, have a good rest, did you?"

"Yeah, but I didn't realise how tired I was until I lay down. I had a very late night, running from a you-know-what."

"I'm not phobic of the word 'dragon', boy, no need to be so secretive."

Ramsey huffed and leant against the back of a small chair. "Okay. So, when are you going to show me around this place so I can buy some supplies for my epic quest?"

"I'm not too busy right now, if you're ready. Everyone 'round here knows about you coming to Grassman, so they'll be eager to see you if you're in the mood to spend some cash." He folded his newspaper and put it aside, then pushed his chair back from the table heavily. His daughter watched anxiously, still holding her cup of tea, and made a fleeting glance towards Ramsey before diverting her gaze to her drink. Ramsey somewhat noticed her behaviour, and deduced that it was a feminine thing to do. Whatever it was, it made her oblivious to the fact that her tea was cold. "Come on then, young Ramsey Hero-amongst-goblins," barked the owner, taking a coat from a stand near the front door.

"All right, just tell me where I can get what I need."

"Certainly will, lad." He turned to his daughter as Ramsey made his way towards the open door. "Keep an eye on things here, Okay, sweet pea?" She nodded and set about clearing the table of cups and saucers. Her father smiled and closed the front door behind them, guiding Ramsey back down the lane towards the village square.

Grassman Village was basked in the orange glow of an impending sunset, and, Ramsey realised, looked far more comely than it had in the pale morning light. The long shadows of its small houses criss-crossed over the square like smeared tiger stripes; the market stalls were gone, and there was nobody else outside, as far as Ramsey could see. The lodge owner, for some reason, emerged as an incessant talker once they reached the village square, and set about telling Ramsey where he should go for good bargains and

80

quality gear. Ramsey didn't see the point of such deliberation, as the village was so small that it had only one armoury, one blacksmith, one tanner, one grocer, one of everything.

"The handy thing about living here is that lots of shops provide more than one kind of service," began the owner in a typically long-winded fashion. "Our armoury – known the guy since we were kids, he used to steal my marbles – stocks weaponry, navigational equipment, lots of useful information, as well as body armour of course. There's not much space here for businesses to spread out, see."

"Uh huh." Ramsey was eyeing a piece of gruesome-looking equipment in the foggy window of the blacksmith's shack. The other carried on, taking hold of Ramsey by the shoulder to keep his attention. Ramsey couldn't understand the apparent attraction that his shoulder held for irritating, know-it-all goblins.

"The blacksmith next-door has his shop joined onto the armoury, since they're in pretty similar interests. Might as well join forces to help business, I say. Well, I think you'd better have a look in the armoury here, and in the grocer's of course, for food and the like."

Ramsey perked up at the word 'food', and realised that it had been quite a while since he had eaten. He agreed eagerly. "Oh, sure, whatever you think is best."

The other goblin nodded and advanced towards the armoury, with its dark door and nearly opaque windows. A cold wind rustled through Ramsey's entire body at once, and he jumped uneasily; he was starting to notice a collective habit of not washing the windows in this village. "You know something," said the lodge owner suddenly, causing Ramsey to jump again, "you're a very strange lad…one minute you're shouting your head off, next you're all accommodating…you got a problem or something?"

Ramsey put his hands on his hips and stopped in the street. "I beg your pardon? What are you talking about?"

"I mean, you've got some very serious mood swings going on there." He didn't stop walking, and, quite in contrast, shoved the armoury door open with the force of his shoulder and carried on inside with a jovial cry of, "Hello Mick!"

Ramsey stood outside for a moment or two, aggravated. How dare that fat, ugly goblin accuse him of having a problem? There was no problem. Ramsey knew exactly where he was at, and what he was doing. He didn't have a personality problem. Well, maybe a slight one…there had to be something wrong with him. Nobody ever wanted to be around him for too long, and he was fine with that. Maybe there was some sort of personality defect in him. Some sort of…'social disadvantage'…'social *maladjustment*', that was it.

That was something he did remember of his father; he told him that he was maladjusted. But he couldn't remember why. That was one of his first big words, maladjustment. It was an ugly word; he knew inside that he was an ugly person. He had to be. That was why the world viewed him so strangely.

His mind had almost completely wandered from the subject of Prince Morgan and the dragon. It shot back into his brain with alarming ferocity, and his whole body froze up again. Maybe he had really done an awful thing by misleading the goblins of Merlock the way he did. Again, that was a maybe, not a certainty. If the world didn't want him, he didn't want the world, and once he was living in total secluded luxury, thoughts of them wouldn't plague him any more. There he was once again, trying to make sense of something that made no sense at all…no wonder the world despised him. He was a truly despicable person.

"Hey, what're you doing standing out in the cold? Get in here, Ramsey, Mick's got some great gear to show you!"

Full of self-hatred yet again, Ramsey took a deep breath and followed the lodge owner into the armoury; his conscience sunk into his empty stomach and concealed itself there.

\*\*\*

It was a great relief for Ramsey's chilled body to get back to the Grassman lodge after sunset. It was incredibly cold outside, and all the houses in the village had locked up their doors long beforehand. They returned to find the tea room of the lodge empty, and the tables neat and tidy once more. The larger goblin held the front door open, as Ramsey trudged inside, loaded with more equipment than he intended to buy and several paper bags of groceries. The owner did very little to help, and just laughed as Ramsey struggled inside and dumped his purchases on the nearest table. His orange skin was flushed pink from the effort and the cold evening air, and he gratefully slumped into a chair with a huff.

"Thank Scaless for the indoors, eh?" grunted the owner, taking his grubby apron off at last and hanging it up on the stand along with his coat. "If you're cold, how about I get you something warm to eat?"

Ramsey wheezed and coughed, his throat full of freezing air. "Actually, I think I'll just get to bed."

"Nonsense, let me fetch you some chocolate cake and a mug of coffee – always does the trick. I'm gonna get some myself. You stay put for a minute."

"They make cakes with chocolate?"

The other goblin laughed heartily again. "'Course they do. In Grassman we do it all the time, this place is famous for my chocolate cake and hot chocolate drink."

"You can *drink* chocolate?"

"Yup. You wait right here, I'll bring you some cake to try, and some of my special chocolate-seasoned coffee."

Ramsey almost melted at the thought of chocolate and cake mixed together. In Merlock's market, he had tried many different cakes, and occasionally a small piece of chocolate; he was so hungry at that moment that he could have eaten anything that would fit onto a plate, but the fact that he was going to try something so exciting made him all the more ravenous. Coffee was new to him. Previously, he had been able to get his hands on milk and fruit juice in the market, and of course, he had water in an abundant supply. Warm drinks were indeed a luxury. He would worry about getting to bed later.

Feeling optimistic about the chocolate cake and coffee, he sifted through some of his purchases on the table surface, which had landed in a disorganised mess due to his urgent need to drop them all at once. Mick, the goblin at the armoury, had successfully frightened him into buying unnecessary items. He was a tall, wide, steel-faced individual with messy, dark tendrils of hair that fell over his face. His hands, feet and chest were huge, and Ramsey was so terrified that he just answered a shaky 'yes' whenever Mick asked him a question. As a result, he now owned another dagger, a sword, a small wooden shield, a chain-mail shirt and several different kinds of compass.

The grocer, a small, elderly goblin, had been more helpful, and Ramsey bought some basic supplies like bread, cheese (which, yet again, he forgot he disliked), butter and plain crackers. Realising the need for one, he also bought a new leather bag from the grocer, one larger than his other bag, to carry all his extra supplies.

He looked up; the lodge owner was returning with a tray laden with mugs, sugar cubes, coffee pots and two large slices of the most delicious cake Ramsey had ever seen. It was dark, deeply rich in colour, and appeared moist to the touch, with a thick layer of icing on top and chocolate cream in the middle. He could smell it from across the room, and had to control himself as the other goblin put one slice of cake down in front of him on a plate.

"There you go," he said, arranging the rest of the crockery on the table also. "That's the best chocolate cake you'll get for miles once you leave Grassman. It's mainly wilderness from here on out, of course." Ramsey picked up a spoon and dug it into the slice of cake. "Where exactly are you headed, then? Far north, I'd say, if you want to find one of them dragons." Ramsey, his mouth full of cake, shrugged and continued eating. "Merlockiara's mostly forest up north, then you find the mountains in Oouealena and Ranmalona. You've got a map, right?"

"Mmhmm."

"Good, otherwise I'd not measure your chances. Oouealena's your best bet for dragons. Nothing much in Ranmalona but manearins and lizard men."

84

Ramsey wolfed down the last of his cake, wiped his mouth, and put his elbows on the table. "You travel much?"

"Nah, I've never been one for travelling. I read more about the rest of the island than I ever actually see of it." He poured two mugs of sweet-smelling black coffee, gave one to Ramsey, and indicated the cream. "Help yourself to cream and sugar."

Ramsey looked at his hot drink for a moment. "Why doesn't your daughter look like you?" he asked, as though it was a perfectly normal question to ask over coffee. The other goblin grinned.

"She's my adopted daughter. Had her since she was two years old, I have. That's why I pointed out Grassman house to you this morning on our way here. Most young goblins in this village are adopted."

"I don't remember a Grassman house."

"Well you weren't listening, then, were you?" pointed out the owner good-naturedly. Ramsey dropped some lumpy sugar cubes into his coffee, still leaning on one elbow. "Our village didn't have much to its name when it was first founded. About...well, must be thirty years ago, one goblin from our village, Shaun Grassman, made it his duty to free goblin children from slavery camps all across this island. He adopted a kid, you see, from what it later turned out was a labour camp, not an orphanage at all. So off he went, and he busted open about ten different child labour camps, and released countless numbers of children from slavery. They'd been taken from orphanages as very young children, then just forced to work from as young as two or three years old. Dunno how they were able to get any kind of labour out of such little kids, though.

"After Shaun died, we named the village after him and kept his house in immaculate condition for tourists. It's just a shame nobody bothers to come here and learn about him any more. The last place he freed was...must be...a little more than ten years ago, I think. Then a few months later, he died."

Ramsey stared intently at the other goblin throughout the story, idly stirring the eight sugar lumps in his coffee. Something came over the lodge owner when he spoke about Shaun Grassman; as though he felt sorrowful that Grassman's heritage was no longer of interest to outsiders. Well, it was a tiny little village, and Ramsey could see why nobody would bother with it. They didn't even mention their local hero on the sign outside the village. It had been quite wordy, but he had finally discovered why nobody looked like their children in Grassman Village. Now he had nothing left to do except taste his coffee.

"You sure you don't want any cream in that coffee? It's very strong."

Ramsey nodded confidently, though he had never tasted coffee before in his life. It was still hot, but not hot enough to hurt his mouth, so he tilted back his head and swallowed it all at once. The other goblin stared at him in disbelief as he finished the last drops of coffee and returned the mug to the table. He watched Ramsey for a long time, waiting for him to react in some way; eventually, Ramsey took a deep breath, picked up a sugar lump from the bowl and ate it. The owner raised an eyebrow warily.

"Are you alright?"

"Yeah, I'm fine. Get me some of that coffee stuff for my journey, will you? And some of this sugar. I didn't know it came in lumps like this." He popped another cube in his mouth and munched eagerly on it before taking another.

"If you eat any more of those you'll never get to sleep." Ramsey didn't listen, and brought the bowl of sugar lumps closer to his side of the table. The other goblin sighed and stood up. "I'll get you some coffee beans and sugar, then. Just don't blame me when you can't sleep for the next hundred years." He picked up his kitchen tray, as well as everything on the table apart from the sugar bowl, and started towards the rear door. Ramsey looked up.

"And get that damn book out of my room, will you?"

"Right you are…" He shuffled out of the room with heavy, lumbering steps, and closed the kitchen door firmly behind him. Ramsey was alone with his bowl of sugar lumps and new supplies; looking both ways, he discreetly retrieved his new leather bag and emptied the bowl into one of the front pockets. There was another bowl of sugar lumps on the table behind him, which he also took.

Full of energy from his sugar and coffee, he began arranging his new equipment inside the bag; his second dagger, his sword, his wooden shield (which didn't look as if it would do much good against a dragon's fire), his chain-mail shirt and small navigational objects, which looked rather complicated to use. His groceries went in on top, so they weren't squashed. It didn't occur to him at that moment that he would have to fit his old supplies in on top of his bread and crackers. Regardless, his coffee and sugar would be a priority.

He could hear was the other goblin moving around in the kitchen. Of course, he also had to give the lodge owner some kind of payment for taking him in, showing him around, giving him sugar and coffee...he didn't terribly want to, but he felt that he should all the same. Then he had the problem of not knowing how much would be appropriate to give. By the time the other goblin returned with two bags of coffee and sugar, Ramsey had decided once again to completely ignore the situation with the dragon and find somewhere more glamorous to stay, so that he could throw all his heavy, needless supplies down a well.

"I've got your stuff here. Do you want it now, or should I give it to you in the morning?"

"I'll take it now," he said, holding out his spare hand, one of his shoulder straps in the other. "I might leave very early tomorrow, I don't want to forget them."

He handed Ramsey the two bags and huffed. "You can't leave tomorrow, lad, you only just got here."

"I know, but I've seen enough here to know that your village is a...pleasant, interesting place." He reached behind his shoulders and put both paper bags in the top of his pack securely, so they wouldn't fall out. "The sooner I go, the sooner I can rescue Prince Morgan and slay the dragon."

"Oh, you're gonna *slay* it, are you?" he laughed, much to Ramsey's annoyance. "Well, be sure to stick your mighty sword right up through its brain – that's the way real heroes always do it."

Ramsey wasn't moved. "Oh yeah? How would you know?"

"I've read it in books. Dragon killing's not for me. Just do it right."

"I will." He hopped on the spot for a moment, once more testing the weight of his bag, and found that it was no lighter than before. "All this equipment is heavy. I think I'll get upstairs and try to rearrange my things so I don't do my back in." The other goblin sat down again and watched him pace impatiently between the tables. "Is that book still in my room?"

"I haven't had a spare moment to go up there, boy."

Ramsey growled. "Oh well, it doesn't matter. I just want to get up to bed."

"I can still take it out of your room if you want."

"Never mind. I'll just put it under the bed if it starts to bug me. Just don't put anything else in my room while I'm asleep this time." He motioned for the other to stay seated, and navigated his way past the tables to the back door. Neither one said anything more; Ramsey just left the tea room quickly and quietly, with a new sense of adventure, leaving the owner alone with his thoughts.

The corridor and staircase were surprisingly dark, as Ramsey hadn't noticed the time slip by; he picked up a lighted candlestick from the counter nearby and navigated his way slowly up the stairs. The floorboards creaked under his increased weight, but he paid the sound no heed, as there were no other guests in the lodge. Not that he was overly considerate of other people's feelings – he just didn't like being heard by strangers.

Once at the top of the stairs, he made a right turn and shuffled along the corridor towards his room; the door was still wide open, and was letting a draught in. He grumbled to himself and strode into his room, closing the door firmly behind him. His candle almost blew out as he did so. Taking great care, he placed the fading candle on his bedside cabinet, on top of the Scaless Scriptures, and sat down on the bed. He lifted his other bag onto his lap and started removing the contents, placing them alongside him on the blanket. Then, he figured, he would be able to assess how best to fit all his possessions into one bag.

It didn't really occur to him at that moment, but he had just been involved in perhaps the longest conversation of his life with another goblin. He was never happy when talking to others, he hated being touched or interrogated – which was why his stay in King Viktor's castle had been so excruciating, with the royal herald chasing him around persistently like a terrier. He wondered what was happening back in Merlock at that moment; though he was hardly on the other side of Grenamoya, Merlock felt like a distant memory, as his father was. Downstairs, the lodge owner's daughter searched for the candlestick she had left outside the kitchen, and tripped over her dressing-gown.

***

Ramsey didn't sleep a wink that night. For seven hours, until the first light of dawn, he lay awake on his bed, idly rearranging the contents of his travelling bag over and over again. Though there was enough room in the bag for all of his belongings, he didn't want to carry around a load of weapons that he knew would be of no use to him; at the same time, he couldn't let Grassman Village suspect that he wasn't going to rescue Prince Morgan. The bag was heavy, but he would eat his food items and lighten the load in no time. He felt a great surge in his metabolic rate, probably due to all the coffee and sugar in his system, and kept nibbling randomly at the bread and fruit as he repeatedly removed and replaced them in the bag.

At some point during the night, he had taken the liberty of hiding the Scaless Scriptures in a drawer of the bedside cabinet. His candle hadn't lasted long, and after its flame faded, Ramsey had carried on his activities by the blue light of the moon through the open window. He longed to be on the move again. If what the lodge owner told him was true, and Merlockiara was mostly deserted in a north-easterly direction, he wouldn't have to deal with any more awkward encounters with miscellaneous village folk. It would suit him just fine if he never had to see another living creature again. Nature would be his companion – the wide open, passive landscape of Grenamoya was all he needed, and as always, himself as his own travelling partner.

As soon as there was enough light for him to see clearly down the corridor, Ramsey made his way stealthily downstairs, complete with his backpack. He could hear snoring from a room nearby, and so moved as quietly as he could down to the lower landing, then walked through into the tea room. He glanced around briefly for any full bowls of sugar cubes, saw none, and made his way over to the table he and the owner had sat at the previous evening. Reaching into his pocket, he retrieved his money purse, untied the strings, and deliberated over how much he should leave, taking into account the fact that he had stayed at the lodge and taken liberties with the owner's hospitality.

The other goblin had never asked for any money, so he was tempted to abandon the idea; with a stiff hand, he reached into his purse and pulled out a handful of coloured scales – mostly yellow and red, with some varying shades of green. Of the colours, red was worth the most, then green, then yellow; Ramsey had never paid anyone for anything before in his life, not least because he never had any money. He took a guess as to the right amount, and left three red, five green and ten yellow scales in the empty, blue sugar bowl.

Already his right shoulder was starting to feel strained. With a very deep breath and a slight wince of pain, he pulled tightly on the straps of his backpack, lifting it securely onto his shoulders. He pulled the door bolt aside, opened the heavy door, and gazed out into the pale, dappled lane outside; the opposite row of squat houses were bathed in a pale, cloudy luminescence that made them look like decorated teacakes. He had delayed his big adventure long enough already.

As he closed the door behind him and stepped outside into the cool air, something passed over him like a shadow; he was going out into the immense, wide world, at last he would truly be free of Merlockiara's inhabitants. If there was nobody to bother him, there was nobody to stand in the way of his dream. All he needed was his map, his money, and an empty space, a secluded spot, to call his own. That was all he wanted, he was soon to have all that he ever desired. He had conned another whole community into believing his tales of nobility and self-sacrifice. Lying had made him a hero and given the whole of Merlock an empty hope to put their faith in.

He was thinking along those dangerous lines again. He felt so confident about the life ahead of him, and yet somewhere inside him was a nagging voice. He didn't know exactly what it was saying, but he knew it was there, and it had been driving him crazy all night. His head was hurting, and his back was still sore. The middle of his back was itching like one large insect bite, but hotter. Maybe his conscience lived in there and was trying to force its way into the open. At that thought, he clutched his bag more firmly against his back, and set off once again, down the dusty lane and into the wide open, tree-scattered expanse of Merlockiara.

# Chapter Four

# Another Meeting

Grenamoya seemed no more than a vast, blank canvas before the solitary orange goblin named Ramsey. Merlockiara was the kingdom that the rest of the island referred to as a 'patchwork quilt', and as he widened his scope to encapsulate more of the world around him, Ramsey finally understood why. It was a collage of green and earthy brown tones in the form of fields and forests, sometimes dotted with distant yellow flowers or white, fluffy sheep. Ramsey had never been fond of farm animals, or indeed any animals, but he passed many cows and sheep grazing in damp fields as he advanced further from Merlockiara and Grassman Village. Soon enough, he had reached the open, grassy plain of the kingdom, which it seemed nobody had bothered to colonise due to the irregularity of slopes and hills there.

Ramsey was notably more content to be by himself while on the move; by day he walked at a steady pace, not terribly caring about his destination, heading eastwards; and by night he set up temporary camp under any nearby shelter, be it a tree or a small patch of forest, and slept in several extra layers of clothing from his backpack. Though he was understandably irritated about it, the combination of falling into the castle moat and never wearing shoes had taken its toll on him, and he succumbed to a severe head-cold. To distract from the intense pain in his sinuses, he tried to concentrate on his left hand for a while; though healing, it still caused him slight discomfort when he moved his fingers, and so he clenched his hand repeatedly into a fist while walking to have another point of focus.

Merlockiara, like the rest of the island, was still trapped rigidly in the season of late spring. Brief showers of rain plagued Ramsey along his travels, seeming to emerge only when he was wearing a clean set of clothes or suffering acutely with his cold. He didn't care what everyone said about the Great Dragons failing to bring the seasons – as far as he was concerned, there was at least one Great Dragon out there that held a rainy vendetta against him.

Frequently, just to make sure that he wasn't heading into hostile territory, he checked the large island map that the herald had given to him on that terrifying night, seemingly weeks ago. As far as he could tell from his various compasses and navigational gadgets, he was gradually heading east towards the southern tip of Oouealena, the dragon and griffin kingdom. There were some attractive mountain ranges and wilderness areas in Oouealena, he decided, so he had no objections to going there. For days he continued east, glancing at his map and carrying a very heavy bag, finding nothing but even wider expanses of land, dotted with bushes and the occasional wild animal. Once or twice he came across some dirt paths, but they had clearly not been used for many years, and were severely overgrown with nettles.

At long last, Ramsey found himself enjoying a distinct change of scenery – the irregular, overgrown countryside gave way to an immense, dark forest that seemed to stretch for miles in a north-easterly direction. Deciding that it would do him no harm to do so, he continued onwards, into the depths of the wood. He was quite relieved to have constant overhead protection, as it was always lurking in the back of his mind that the cobra dragon could return to the kingdom at any time. Walking by himself across a bare stretch of meadow would certainly put him at risk of attack.

Curiously, the trees in this particular forest were unlike any Ramsey had encountered before, especially when compared with the comfortable oak tree that had been his home for so long. The trunks were straight, occasionally a bit crooked, but always thin and unstable in appearance, as though the slightest push might uproot them. The bark was almost blue in the dim light filtering through the canopy of what appeared to be pine needles above him, but otherwise the trees were bare. Though he had lived in a tree for most of his life, Ramsey was fairly sure that he wouldn't be able to scale one of the narrow, branch-less trees without some kind of grappling hook.

Frustrated and tired, after two full days or wandering uncomfortably through the hazy forest, Ramsey sat himself down heavily on a rotting tree stump and wrenched the island map from his backpack. His feet were aching, and there were far too many pine needles between his toes for his liking. They stuck to the soft skin between each toe, and made him itch dramatically. His cold had barely improved, he was sporting a runny nose and brown, bloodshot eyes that gave him the appearance of someone horrendously ill – needless to say, he looked like a mess. He spread open the map, ignoring the chilling, distant sounds of wild animals in the wood, and placed a finger on his approximate location within Merlockiara.

"According to this map," he mulled, out loud, "...there is no forest here." Briefly he paused, checking once more that there was no record of a forest anywhere nearby the location of his finger. He glanced around, eyeing the tree trunks and needle-infested woodland floor, and lowered the map. "Oh fiddlesticks..."

\*\*\*

A fair distance away, at the eastern-most edge of the lizard men- and frona-inhabited kingdom of Leal, a meeting was about to take place. Not a sinister sort of meeting, but a constructive one.

The UFC, more lengthily known as 'The Union of Fantastical Creatures', was due to gather together for the sole purpose of discussing the changing state of the island. Normally, a meeting was held every six months or so, but this latest one had been called as an emergency.

The UFC headquarters was little more than an ancient stone shrine that had been abandoned five-hundred years ago. The walls were subtly decorated with carved images of Lady Scaless and the Great Dragons – Amelia, Elkodina, Zared, Trahern and Leoma – to remind the UFC members of their just cause. The vegetation in this part of the island was lush, leading towards a vast area of sparse grassland and desert; shrubs with bright flowers crept in through the wide windows, entwining themselves around the embellished stone pillars. After only two months of neglect, the temple was almost overgrown, and as they arrived, members of the alliance began taming the foliage.

Standing at the broad stone table which took up most of the floor space in the temple was a tall, elegant creature resembling a dog that had decided to walk on its hind legs. He was a manearie, a bipedal canine, with luxuriant black, white and terracotta fur all over his strong body. On a leather collar around his neck he wore the Merlockiara kingdom symbol.

His name was Collinad, the unofficial leader of the union. He was trustworthy, strong-hearted and had a natural charisma that encouraged the others to follow him. Alongside Collinad at the table was Lothar, the king of the lizard people – taller than his friend, with blue scales, a long snout, and wearing a brightly-coloured uniform of Ranmalona regalia. Both were studying a tattered map that Collinad held open on the table with both paws. Without a prompt, Lothar crossed his arms and huffed noisily, causing the collie to look up.

"What is it?"

Lothar shook his head. "Trust that cat to be late as always," he growled, his voice rough. "Maybe he won't get here at all this time."

Collinad glared at the reptile down his muzzle, but it was a good-natured glare, and he was soon smiling. "My friend, it isn't fair to judge our comrade simply because it takes him longer to get here."

"Hah! See here, Collinad, it takes me far longer to get here from Ranmalona, because I have to divert all the way over here." Reaching out with a long index finger, Lothar indicated the path of his voyage from his home kingdom on the map. "See?"

"Don't wrinkle my map, Lothar."

"I'll wrinkle it if I wish."

Collinad smiled more broadly, as was his custom, and glanced over his shoulder to where another UFC member, an elf, was hacking at the overgrown shrubs with his sword. "How are you managing, Elwin? I'm dreadfully sorry to be of so little help."

"Not a problem, I'm doing fine here." He took another swing at a particularly large branch, and it fell at his feet. "Terak will help me once he gets here."

"*If* he gets here," said Lothar, leaning on the table. "Where *is* everyone?"

Collinad let go of the map, which instantly rolled itself up with a snap. "They will get here, I sent out messages of urgency to all of them." He held up one of his paws and started counting on his claws. "You and I are here, Elwin is seeing to the plant life...we need Terak, Karri," Lothar grumbled. "Nyx, Viktor...um..."

"Nyx won't get here. We haven't seen her for months, Collinad, I think she's become a recluse, like all unicorns."

The collie sighed. "It doesn't hurt to have hope. Oh, *Valdemar*, how could I forget Valdemar?"

"Oh, we'd certainly miss his wonderful presence if he didn't turn up." Lothar's voice was rank with sarcasm, and he shook his head again. "Apart from maybe Terak, we don't know for certain that anyone else will come. I say we get this meeting over with now, between the three of us. After all, it's you and Elwin who say you have something important to tell. Is it something about the dragons?" Elwin stopped swinging his sword; Collinad crossed his hairy arms. "It is, isn't it? Well then, for the love of Scaless, tell me!"

"No, my friend, we must wait – this is an official meeting, and it will be held as such."

Elwin put his sword away and approached the others, a consistently calm expression on his serene face. He was a typically fair elf, with silver-blond hair down past his shoulders and a healthy, golden shine to his skin. Though the atmosphere was formal, he held an air of youthful vigour and joviality – along with Terak and Lothar, he was one of Collinad's oldest friends. He put a hand on Lothar's shoulder to placate him. "There's nothing to be said immediately that cannot wait five minutes for the others to arrive. Be calm, don't get impatient – we need to rely on one another to get through all this."

Lothar hissed grumpily. "All what?"

Elwin laughed. "I'm not telling you."

"Well fine, I'll just wait here while the tension slowly builds up in my body until you feel the need to disclose your information."

"That's an excellent idea, Lothar, just don't let it damage you too greatly." He patted the reptile on the back and glanced at the doorway, as the sound of approaching footsteps reached them. There was a brief commotion outside, and then another humanoid figure entered the temple, brushing dust off his knees. Too pale to be human, the new arrival had the complexion of ice, dark hair, eyes and lips that were parted slightly by two small, protruding fangs. He was clad entirely in grey and black, and his thick, black hair was laced absurdly with pink and blue ribbons. Elwin abandoned the seething Lothar and extended his arms to the pale figure. "Terak, you made it."

"Barely," grumbled the vampire, clearly exhausted from his journey. "You wouldn't believe what a basilisk did to me just coming out of Xavierania. It killed off one of my best horses, I had to walk for miles before I could get another; and then it rained for *days*, until I was about half a mile from here. I've never been so irritated in all my life."

Collinad looked up. "Your hair looks nice, though."

"Did Synor do it for you?" asked Elwin, knowing the answer already. Terak nodded and rolled his eyes.

"You know it. I swear to Scaless, I brought home a few ribbons from town to lace a shirt he made, then he put them on me instead. That is probably the stupidest thing I've done since I let him have that pet he wanted."

Elwin put an arm around Terak and led him over to the table so that he could sit down. "So he's keeping well, then? That's great news. And yourself?"

"I'm all right, considering. Just been curious as to what your news is."

Lothar piped up. "He won't say until the others get here."

Terak sat himself down on the edge of the table, and the others did the same, all around the square, stone structure. "I saw Karri pulling up just at the top of the lane. Who else are we missing?"

Collinad sighed and looked at the others with a noble, yet slightly saddened expression. His brown eyes were suddenly full of worry, and it disconcerted the others greatly. Lord Collinad never felt despair.

Well...we may not have any others to wait for. Nyx probably won't be here, and Viktor and Valdemar were never the most devoted individuals...which would mean that we've lost the goblins, unicorns, land dragons, cave dragons, trolls, griffins, fronas and manearins all in the space of three years." He shrugged. "Which is rather disheartening, I'm sure you'll agree. I suppose I can speak for maneries and manearins, and Karri can represent fronas as well as froneks, but that isn't sufficient. We need the support of every species possible."

"I'm here!" shouted a voice from just outside, causing everyone to leap off the table. A five-and-a-half foot, bipedal, brown and white cat ran in through the doorway, picking grass and leaves off his fur. With a gasp, he came to a halt in front of the others and bent forward to catch his breath. "I'm here! Has Lothar arrived ye-" He noticed two long legs and a scaly, blue tail right in front of him and jolted upright. "Oh, there you are." He brushed some more dirt off himself and crossed his arms, looking up at Lothar's superior expression. "You been here long?"

"Oh yes," replied the lizard, "several hours, in fact. You're late."

"I am not. I got here no earlier and no later than I intended."

"Then you intended to be late."

Collinad held up his arm and intervened between the two. "Let's have some order here, please – Karri, did you see anyone else on your travels? Is anybody else on their way?"

Karri blinked a pair of bright yellow eyes thoughtfully and put a paw to his chin. "I don't think so, Collinad. I'm afraid I haven't really seen anything at all during my journey. The weather's been awful, though."

Terak looked at Elwin. "See, I was correct. You elves always take the good weather with you."

"Now I don't think that's true," said the accused with a smile, "but if it is, I'll try to transfer my best ray of sunshine onto you."

It felt good for all five of them to be together once more. Elwin and Terak, both immortal (as elves and vampires were fortunate enough to be), had been members of the UFC ever since it was founded, over two-thousand years before. Collinad, at the relatively young age of two-hundred, was not the oldest of the group, but very much took charge of them. Lothar, though older, had joined the UFC later than Collinad, and thus the collie had superiority over the strong and sometimes violent lizard.

Karri was the youngest and the last to join, and Lothar had an immense dislike for him, the reasons for which were never discussed. Their rivalry had prompted some tension between the reptiles and felines of the island, though not as strongly as the full-blown feuds between canines and felines on the island before Karri's father and Collinad had resolved the differences between the species many years ago. Grenamoya was still an island of rivalries, but now something far more deadly threatened to pull it apart. Though Collinad wanted nothing more than to relax with his friends, he had his duty to fulfil. He raised his voice.

"I think we had better start now," he said, turning to Elwin, "Viktor and Valdemar won't show up. Elwin, would you please retrieve your findings?"

"Of course." Knowing that this realisation was hard for the manearie to cope with, Elwin decided to get everything over with as soon as possible. He picked up a heavy, wooden box from underneath the table, and lifted it up onto the surface. Collinad wasn't looking at it, but was instead gazing out of one of the windows, waiting for somebody, anybody else to arrive. The elf quietly opened the chest and pulled a big book from inside, as well as some loose leaves of paper and a map similar to Collinad's tattered one. He addressed the company. "To begin with, I would like to thank you all for coming."

"Get to the bloody point!" yelled Lothar, grabbing the elf by the front of his shirt, "For Scaless' sake, tell us what's happening!"

Elwin put a hand on Lothar's shoulder, gently holding onto him, and the lizard submitted without a further word. Collinad glared and Karri whispered something unpleasant, but Lothar was as docile as a mouse, and looked plaintively at the others before Elwin spoke again. "Getting to the point, then, I would have to say that we are in great peril. I took the liberty of re-reading some of these old scripture books, and I believe that we may currently be facing the second uprising of..." He glanced briefly at the others to check if they were going to silence him, but they just looked intent, so he carried on. "Pain."

"Finally," said Lothar, still a little tuned out. "Now we can get on with our lives."

"Actually, it means that none of us will be able to get on with our lives until the threat is ended," continued Elwin, opening the book at one of its many book-marked pages. The words on the page were unintelligible to the others, but Elwin placed a finger on the text and began to read. "If I may – '...Until the tides turn and the elements become unrestrained, and the sky grows cold and the innocent die of discourse of the mind, then he shall come again, and bring his terrors with him'."

Elwin spoke solemnly in a voice that whispered summertime, and sought the next page. Lothar, Karri and Terak looked at one another, mumbling, as Collinad stood his ground with a determined glint in his eye.

"'Grenamoya will no longer be a free land if Pain cannot be thwarted – find four warriors of a comrade lost to avenge the island and bring Pain to his end. History repeats itself, as it is warrant to do; one among you is not a friend. Where loyalties lie, there must you question, and beware of taking an ally for something he is not.'"

"Damn it, Elwin, that makes no sense," said Terak, peering at the pages and trying to decipher the words. Behind him, Karri and Lothar were eyeing one another sceptically.

"There's more, don't worry." He searched for another page and continued, "'No single life has ended, but thousands will be lost – be wary of the one who hides behind the disguise of others.'" He turned to Collinad. "And we know who that will be." The collie sighed heavily and slowly nodded. "We know what the danger is; Pain will try to take the island, and he still has that *disgusting* malformation of a companion with him." Elwin couldn't hide the contempt in his voice, and the others made comments of agreement.

"I knew he survived. Damnable monster." Collinad covered his face with a paw and made an aggravated, distressed noise. His voice was strained. "We'll never rid this island of his intolerable, evil existence, all we can do is try to stop Pain where he stands."

"But where *does* he stand?" Karri moved closer to Elwin, pushing his way past Lothar, and stood at the elf's side. His young, furry face was inquisitive, ready for a challenge, and like Lothar, he hardly seemed fazed by the news. Though he had never before dealt with such a crisis in the UFC, he was energetic and eager to prove himself. Lothar hissed at him. "Do you know where he is?"

"Where else would he bloody well be? He's in Utipona, sending his cronies out to do his dirty work." Lothar's rancid voice didn't move the cat, who merely poked out his tongue. "Stop that! I'll have you know this is a serious situation, you gutter-crawling alley cat!"

"Gentlemen, please!" urged Elwin, pushing between them once more, "Yes, Lothar, granted, this may be a matter of most dire importance, but the last thing we need is for you to lose your temper. Settle down, we need to consider these implications from the Scaless Scriptures as a group."

The cat and the lizard continued to size one another up, but they refrained from insulting each other or starting a fight, so Elwin was satisfied that they were under control. Collinad looked even more distressed than before, and was nervously running his claws through his long fur. Elwin adopted a more formal tone, and closed the book in front of him.

"As you know, the prophecies contained within this most ancient copy of the Scaless Scriptures are nothing short of inevitable. This elvish copy has been in my monarchy ever since our island was born, and it has given us great guidance in the UFC through many trials. As much as we do not wish to face it, Pain has indeed risen again, and is forming his hateful empire in the south once more."

"Which explains all the activity along Utipona's borders," said Lothar, sounding intelligent. "So what exactly are we meant to do about it?"

"If I could give you a short, convenient answer to that question, Lothar, I wouldn't need to consult all of you about it. Collinad and I have come to the decision that the answer lies in 'four warriors of a comrade lost', whom we need to find and bring before the UFC, then send them away to combat Pain's forces, I presume."

"You're just grasping at straws here," Lothar growled. "I bet you don't have a clue what you're doing – the line itself makes no damn sense."

"History will repeat itself, Lothar – don't you see? This will be a re-enactment of Pain's uprising five hundred years ago. He gathered four allies, one in the north, one in the south, one in the east and one in the west. That was the distinctive element of his attack. They were in the four corners of the island, and he-"

"And he was right in the centre, in the Sacred Mountains, I know," huffed the lizard. "But that was all the way back then, he's not going to resort to such a needlessly complicated plan of attack this time."

"His plan is even more complicated this time, Lothar. Five hundred years ago, he imprisoned the five Great Dragons inside their own temple – when the goodness of their magic bestowed upon Pain's allies was released, they broke free, and we brought Pain's armies to the ground all in one day. He lost total power. Now, on the other hand, there is no evidence of the Great Dragons' presence anywhere on the island. They've completely vanished, and we need to determine why."

Terak, who hadn't spoken for a while, decided to make himself heard. "So you believe that he will have four allies in the four corners of the island, as he did before? And they need to be defeated one by one, as before, in order to weaken Pain for when we attack him in Utipona? Well then, when, and who? These warriors of a lost comrade...we don't have any lost comrades, do we?"

"We hardly have any left..." sighed Collinad woefully, gazing out of a window once more, "Elwin and I were considering the possibility that Rayven's four children might be those warriors, but they are only young, and are not yet old enough to be trained."

"That troll was one of the closest companions I've ever had, he did wonders for our alliance," said Terak. "His children are sure to be as strong and skilled as he was."

"But they are still young."

Elwin looked across the congregation thoughtfully. "There is time. There is nobody else that the scriptures could be referring to. We must wait for them to be of age, and then we can approach them and decide what best to do. Pain's forces will not threaten the island on a vast scale for several years yet; if my thesis is correct, he will bide his time once more until he can unleash a full-scale attack. However, we must remain vigilant, in case he plans diversionary tactics as he did last time, when those awful ten-foot mountain trolls attacked most of our northern kingdoms."

Terak was the only other member of the group who had been alive during Pain's previous uprising, and so spoke to back up Elwin's claims. "The damn things came out of nowhere and started pillaging everything in sight. They made up a great deal of his armies, along with goblins, dragons, those contemptible kamrin creatures..."

"Speaking of goblins," began Collinad, his voice elevated, "it looks as though our friend Viktor's carriage is coming to a halt at the top of the lane! Oh wonderful, we have another comrade to add to our group – we must greet him at once!"

The manearie was overjoyed, and discarded their discussion in an instant at the approach of their Merlockiaran ally. Elwin, somewhat alarmed, looked at the others for a moment before following him; Terak, Karri and Lothar trailed behind. Collinad hurried out of the temple, with the others in pursuit, and ran up to the top of the lane where the carriage had halted. Outside, the hot sun bore down on their bodies through the tree cover. The air was thick with bird song, and the temperate afternoon air beat against their cheeks.

King Viktor's carriage was at a stand-still at the top of the bright lane, glimmering in the sun. Like all of Viktor's royal accessories, the carriage was an eyesore to say the least, decked with extravagant gold décor and bright flags. The driver at the front of the carriage steadied the grey-dappled royal horses, and looked down at the approaching creatures hesitantly. He appeared to be heavily stressed. Collinad felt a twinge of anxiety as he beheld the driver's expression, and waited for the goblin king to step out of his carriage.

Around them, tall trees rose up out of the ground like immense soldiers, casting cool shadows over the scene, the wind whistling through their leaves. The horses stamped at the ground. Lothar did the same, tense and impatient, which caused Karri to toss his feline head and make a random complaint about reptiles. Terak, eternally full of conflict, felt the urge to shout to the driver, but retained his gentle, vampiric cool. His ebony hair rustled in the breeze like liquid feathers.

"What is wrong?" called out Elwin, addressing the only goblin they could see. "Is King Viktor with you?"

105

"Sure is," replied the other, "but he's not feeling very well at the moment. He will be with you shortly."

Collinad turned to Elwin, rubbing his white paws together nervously. "Wonderful. Maybe even more of our comrades will start to appear now that Viktor has arrived. In fact, I'm sure of it, we're bound to have a bigger group than just the six of us for such an important meeting."

Elwin sighed and rubbed his chin, taking in the whole image of King Viktor's carriage and horses. His elven intuition told him that something was awry, but he couldn't quite place where the uncertainty lay. "This is very strange...I wonder what's wrong with him?"

They stood stationary for many minutes more out in the sun, which warmed their blood most agreeably. Lothar in particular flared his red nostrils and soaked up the heat – there are few things more enjoyable to a reptile than a good bask in the sun, and the lizard men of Grenamoya were no exception. The enjoyment was, however, tainted by anxiety as they waited for the goblin king to emerge. In what state or manner he might do so they had no idea, but they were tense, and waited for the remainder of the time in silence, breathing gently. In one of the tall trees nearby, a large raven with deep purple eyes watched the scene with interest, barely blinking, hissing softly through its beak.

Finally, some movement emanated from the carriage. One of the doors swung open; the group expected to see the king of Merlockiara step out to join them, but were instead encountered by Viktor's royal herald. He was wearing his usual clothing, as though he had no other garments to choose from, and wore a weary, nervous expression on his long face. He stepped down from the carriage and addressed the company, apologising once more on behalf of the king, who wasn't feeling 'at all well'. Collinad sighed.

"Phil, for goodness sake, what's wrong? Is everything all right? We didn't think you would make it in time for the meeting."

The herald took one look at Collinad, and was suddenly overtaken by grief. He sobbed aloud and almost stumbled to the ground at the manearie's feet. "Terrible, terrible news, Lord

106

Collinad! A dragon has stolen Prince Morgan from us, our town is now little more than a burned-out shell, and His Highness has been struck by a terrible illness! I've never seen the likes of it, he acts as though something terrible plagues his every waking moment – please help me, my lord, I have tried everything to keep our kingdom from falling apart!" He clutched Collinad by the ruff of long fur around his neck and wailed pleadingly, jerking the dog forward. "Please, please my lord…! I have tried everything!"

"Oh sweet Scaless above…" Collinad turned to Elwin, who appeared equally perplexed and distressed. He patted the herald on the back with a paw, trying to be comforting, but found that it made the goblin cry more than ever. He tried to speak clearly and with an air of authority in an effort to calm him. "Phil, listen carefully. What dragon took Prince Morgan?"

"An awful dragon, my lord," he sniffed, "a cobra dragon, the biggest our kingdom has seen in years! It took Prince Morgan, then came back and torched Merlock. Almost every goblin in the town was burned to death…! I'm sorry we are late…"

Collinad would have smiled had the situation not been quite so upsetting. Ever since Prince Morgan came into the royal family, the herald had been his most dedicated teacher and babysitter; whenever Viktor brought this attendant with him to previous meetings, the herald would carry on and on about the prince throughout, unless he was politely subdued. With no children of his own, Collinad found the notion of caring for a child difficult to sympathise with, but he had his own emotions and could see that the goblin was devastated. Elwin touched Collinad's shoulder, and whispered discreetly in his ear.

"This may be the work of Pain, Collinad – to distract our attention. We must find a way to track this dragon, it could lead us to the source of our problem."

Collinad nodded, and spoke to the trembling herald once again. "Do you have any more information on this dragon, Phil? Please, if you can give us some more details…"

"We already have a goblin on the case," he sniffed, wiping his nose with a long sleeve, "a fellow by the name of Ramsey…he saw the dragon himself, and bravely volunteered to find it and rescue Prince Morgan. He's one in a million, that boy. But so far, we haven't heard any more news of him. I just pray he is alive and well."

"Ah yes, brave indeed," agreed the collie, looking briefly at Elwin, who was moving towards the carriage to peer through a window. "Phil, I don't mean to cause you undue alarm, but as you well know, recently the island has become unsettled, and the seasons unchanging. Therefore, we can assume that-"

"Don't say it!" snapped the herald, pushing away, "He's coming again, isn't he? He's getting ready to destroy Grenamoya all over again. My lord, it scares me horrendously to even think about it, especially with His Majesty in such a poor state!"

"I understand, really I do, but what I mean to say is that this kidnapping may be a diversionary tactic from Pain, before he begins to mass his forces once more – there was no purpose to the kidnapping, other than to disrupt your lives." The herald's mouth fell open, and he became angry once again. "Remember, back during his first uprising, a very prominent cobra dragon was one of Pain's chief acolytes."

The herald couldn't speak to defend his kingdom. When Pain first rose to near-dominance of the island, his so-called 'first ally' was a dragon known as Merlock, who had previously ruled over Merlockiara, which was in the beginning a kingdom of cobra dragons. The problem the dragons faced in the flat, forested kingdom was the lack of decent mountain ranges to inhabit, and so goblin invaders stole the rule of the kingdom early on in Grenamoya's recorded history. After this, the goblins built a capital for themselves, and a royal family descended from the original dragon-slayers of Merlockiara's early days. As in the case of most of Grenamoya's kingdoms, the capital settlement had originally been named after the true founder of the kingdom – Merlock, the island's very first cobra dragon.

After they had been hunted almost to extinction, rumours spread that the dragons were planning to pillage the land and take back what was rightfully theirs; the presence of a cobra dragon now, many hundreds of years after the species was driven out of the kingdom, therefore horrified the goblins far more than the presence of any other monster. Merlock, the first cobra dragon, was so filled with hate after their merciless eviction that he joined Pain's forces during the first uprising, at the promise that Merlockiara would be reinstated to its rightful owners. Of course, it was this scorned cobra dragon who fathered the monstrous Kamror and Kaena, before his demise at the hands of elven soldiers five-hundred years ago.

"I...but...it isn't fair...Prince Morgan never did a thing to hurt anyone!"

"I know, my friend, but I'm afraid we have to face reality...Pain has, in all probability, sent one of Merlock's descendants to abduct Morgan to exact revenge upon your kingdom, and to divert our attention from other developments in Utipona and the Sacred Mountains." Elwin approached the group once more, a look of urgency on his face, and Collinad took it as a prompt for another pressing question. "What is the matter with Viktor?" he asked the herald, "Is he just unwell with a fever or something of that sort? How long has he been ill?"

The herald sniffled loudly and sobbed against his sleeve. "He's gone mad, my lord, just mad...! He acts crazed and wild, as though he cannot see or hear, he has strange turns that make him scream and gasp for air...none of our best physicians have been able to help him..." His voice was full of distress, and tears streaked down his face relentlessly; every passing second seemed to upset him further. "I'm sure he will be unable to contribute to your meeting, my lords, but I felt it my duty to escort him here, as you went to the trouble of sending that message to our ruined town..."

Terak, tall and pale like a column of marble, stepped forward and stood by Collinad. He placed a cold hand on the herald's shoulder, and the collie pulled away. "You've done a good thing by bringing Viktor to us. What state is he in?"

"Maybe all six of us will be able to carry him inside," said Karri perkily, moving forward also. "Collinad and Elwin will be able to talk to him." The herald sniffed. "Won't you?" Karri looked at the manearie and the elf in turn, expectantly, but neither one responded. Collinad braced himself, and Elwin moved towards the carriage again.

"Come on," he said, shielding his earthy eyes from the sun, "we can't just leave Viktor out here all day. Phil, come over here and help me." Collinad approached also, while preparing himself for something terrible to meet his gaze. Karri and Lothar stood at a distance, and Terak guided the sobbing goblin back towards the carriage, with one pale hand still on his shoulder.

"I must warn you," said the herald, anxiously, as Elwin climbed up into the carriage heroically, "His Highness really is not himself, don't hold his behaviour against him. I've tried so hard to get through to him."

Elwin, though rather trim, could summon a great amount of physical strength during strenuous situations. After disappearing into the royal carriage, with an alert Collinad waiting below, it only took him a minute or two to get the goblin king to his wobbly feet and attempt to lower him out. Collinad was amazed by the lack of noise that came from the carriage, as he had expected Viktor to be kicking and screaming hysterically from what the herald told them, and readied himself to aid the king during his shaky descent.

Viktor looked horrific, though not much more so than when Ramsey had encountered him in the castle. He had deteriorated somewhat; it appeared that he had been pulling his own hair out, as large patches of his meaty scalp were bare, and his co-ordination was incredibly poor. It took the combined strength of Elwin and Collinad to get his rotund form down the steps, and then Karri and Lothar assisted also to guide Viktor down the lane to the temple. Behind, Terak and the herald followed slowly and hesitantly, due to Viktor's constant stumbling and swaying on his feet. He was babbling and muttering quietly to himself, his whole body red and sweaty in the heat, and he looked as though he was suffering with a phenomenal fever.

"Once we get inside," puffed Collinad, quickly wearied by the goblin's great weight, "we can rest him on the table."

"Good idea," replied Elwin, "then maybe we can deal with this strange sickness and find out what's going on in his mind."

Viktor shifted sideways in mid-step, forcing his entire weight onto Elwin and Karri's side – the herald squealed with fright and ran forward to help, but Viktor righted himself and leaned forward instead, driving his escorts in the same direction. They hurried onward to prevent him tumbling over; much to their surprise as they took him into the temple, he shouted at them and tried to push them off. "Get away from me! Get off, let go, I don't need any damn support!"

"Your Highness!" exclaimed the herald, darting up to him, "You're speaking again!"

Viktor's pale eyes glared all around madly, and he cast his gaze onto the herald with contempt, lunging at him. "Who in Grenamoya are you? Get away from me!" The lunge toppled his carriers, and Karri, the smallest, was flung away into a bush. The cat swore and kicked around angrily, fully submerged in the foliage apart from his legs, and the others took a much firmer grip on the goblin, dragging him forcefully inside as he tried to escape again. "Get back, get away! You're all with that bloody dragon, trying to steal my son from me! My own flesh and blood, flesh and blood! Get off me!"

"Viktor, be still!" shouted Elwin, grasping him around the neck, "Morgan isn't-"

"Get back!" He kicked out with a stubby, purple satin-covered leg and caught Lothar in the ribs. They wrestled him onto the table on his back, kicking and screaming, and the herald ran around frantically, wanting more than anything to see the king return to his former coherent self. His articulate speech didn't last very long. By the time Karri had run back in through the doorway, Viktor was delirious again. "Blood, flesh and blood...my only son...!" He curled up on the table surface, shuddering and sobbing, his face covered by his oily palms. The herald, terribly upset, stepped aside for the other members of the UFC to deal with the king.

"How peculiar..." mused Collinad, still panting, "Elwin, have you ever seen such strange behaviour?" Viktor writhed on the table, then curled back up into a foetal position and lay still, mumbling and crying against his knees.

"I can safely say that, in all my years on this island, I have only ever seen sickness as severe as this on two occasions," said the elf analytically, finally taking his strong hands away from Viktor's greasy throat. "This is far from good, my friend; there is no known cure…" He locked eyes with the manearie, and both took a deep, remorseful sigh. Viktor's tears ran down onto the stone table, darkening the thin layer of dust in black stains. Elwin leaned over the goblin's dishevelled form, his long hair hanging down in blond cascades to either side of his face, and confirmed his beliefs about Viktor's illness.

The delirium had been referred to five-hundred years ago as 'Utipona madness', or by creatures of lower intelligence as 'the evil fever'; of the two cases Elwin had encountered back then, a troll and a goblin from the UFC, both had died within a month of contracting the madness. It was rumoured to be one of Pain's 'silent killers', an illness that affected seemingly random island inhabitants, and often killed as suddenly as it appeared. Thousands of creatures on Grenamoya had been infected by the illness during Pain's uprising, and as far as Elwin knew, all had ultimately perished. It was not really known why or how it appeared, or why only certain members of society caught it. The king of the goblins was most certainly not a random target – deep inside, Elwin feared that other members of the organisation might be affected by the disease, but he refrained from saying so, though Collinad intuitively guessed what the elf was dreading. Elwin and Terak presumed themselves safe from infection due to their immortality, but this was no relief when they knew that Collinad, Karri and Lothar were vulnerable. Elwin often felt guilty for being immortal, while his friends lived far shorter lives and were most definitely mortal. He had seen many of his close friends come and go over the years, and did not want to lose any of them prematurely to one of Pain's more sinister attacks.

As they stood over the goblin king, recalling the illness from Pain's first uprising, Valdemar, the UFC representative for 'ground-dwelling dragons', shuffled in through the doorway, his usual chain of yellow stones around his thin neck. Nobody noticed him. He took a deep, raspy breath, his eyes darting all around the chamber; he clasped one of the jewels firmly in his right hand and approached the group with a shiver. He stood still for long enough to grasp that they were discussing a kind of sickness. And then, the name 'Pain' reached his ears.

"You can't prove I did anything!" he shrieked, causing the others to leap around with shock, "Don't speak of me as a traitor!"

"For Scaless' sake, Valdemar...!" gasped Elwin, panting hard for breath, "What do you think you're doing? Our comrade Viktor is sick, we need calm to assess how to help him – conduct yourself in a more orderly fashion, for the love of Scaless...!" Viktor was twitching again, moaning about his son and his possible injuries, and Karri and Terak subdued him once more. Lothar took one look at Valdemar and flew into a rage, in stark contrast to Elwin's comparatively gentle reaction.

"Ah, so you decided to show up after all! Brilliant – Valdemar, you useless idiot, have some sense and stop shouting!"

"I'm not shouting, you're shouting!" responded the other reptile, snarling contemptuously at Lothar, "I have done nothing for you to address me in such a way!"

"You damn stupid beast – get out of here before you make things worse."

Collinad turned around to face Valdemar and Lothar, desperate to calm them before they upset Viktor any further. Lothar, who had moved to draw his sword, stepped back and shot warning glances at the other reptile, who bared his fangs and clacked his large talons against the smooth floor threateningly. "That's enough, Lothar. Valdemar, we thought you wouldn't come. How have you been? Is Krakrakara prospering?"

Valdemar growled and looked at Collinad with a simpering smile. "You could say that."

"...Very well."

Suspicious, Lothar stood his ground as Collinad returned to the table. Viktor's flailing had stopped, and he was merely whimpering once again with his hands over his face. The herald stood over his master with the others, helpless to aid his king, and looking to Elwin and Collinad for comfort. Karri's attention had been diverted by Lothar's shouting, and he watched the two reptiles from the corner of his eye, expecting something dramatic to happen at any moment.

As Valdemar turned to the table, Lothar continued to eye him suspiciously. Nothing physical about him had changed – indeed, he had been wearing that same necklace for over one-hundred years. Something in his behaviour was alarming; normally Valdemar was a servile individual with no point of view to put across, but the ability to agree with others to the extent that he seemed useful. If Lothar had confronted him so aggressively in an earlier UFC meeting, he would have expected the weedy reptile to burst crying or run back home. He had shouted back. Something was definitely altered about the ruler of Krakrakara. Lothar cleared his throat and spoke loudly.

"We've just been discussing the second uprising of Pain in the Sacred Mountains."

Valdemar bared his teeth again. "Have you really? Well, that summarises what I missed then, doesn't it?"

"Lothar, for goodness' sake, hush…!" urged Collinad, "Leave Valdemar alone, it's not his fault he was late."

Viktor squirmed on the table and shouted again for his son; though they held him down and tried to speak in clear, calm words, he became worse, and caught Elwin in the face with his fist. The elf reeled back, and the others dove onto him – he kicked and screamed wildly as Karri and Lothar grabbed hold of one arm each, and Collinad gripped his round torso.

"Viktor, listen to me – it's Collinad, I'm speaking directly to you, Viktor. Can you hear me? Viktor!" The goblin kicked again, and produced a chilling scream of desperation that shot through all of them like a bullet.

"No, my son, he's taken my son!"

"Viktor, steady yourself!"

"Someone hold that leg, he keeps getting me in the armpit!"

"Can you hear me, Viktor? Stop it, you're only making this more difficult!"

"Scaless, someone hold that bloody leg of his!"

"I've only got one pair of paws, Lothar!"

"Useless cat!"

"Shut up both of you! Viktor, can you see me? It's Collinad, Viktor, please stop this!"

Valdemar's breath caught in his throat as he watched the jumble of bodies before him. It was terrifying. Something was taking him over again, and his breath came in short, ragged bursts, causing him to lurch forward uncontrollably. He caught his balance before falling, and found himself shouting with terror; he had to get out of the building. "You can never prove I did it! Get back, all of you!"

Pulling away from the fray, Elwin turned towards him. "What are you talking about, Valdemar?" He approached the brown dinosaur tentatively, and held out a hand towards him. "Are you quite all right?" Naturally fearful that Valdemar might have contracted the same madness as Viktor, Elwin was the only one who went to him. Valdemar shook and shivered in a manner similar to the goblin king, but he was still on his feet, and he pointed an accusing finger at Elwin, clutching his precious necklace with the other.

"Get back! Get away, you cannot prove I did it!"

"Did what?"

"Back off, or I'll kill you!"

Elwin moved away, knowing better than to defy the wishes of a potentially dangerous creature such as Valdemar. All of the others were still struggling with King Viktor, who by now had gone completely wild again and was scrambling around on the table, pulling away from his restraints and hitting out violently with terrified cries. Valdemar shouted at Elwin once more, and he moved further back; Terak noticed the reptile's behaviour from amongst the gathering, and readied himself to run to Elwin's aid.

"Valdemar, I mean you no harm – what is the matter? Let me help you, my friend-"

"*Friend*?" spat Valdemar viciously, taking a step backwards toward the door, "You are no friend of mine, elf! Keep away! Valdemar's only friend is Valdemar, me and myself and I – Valdemar! You want my sparklies!"

Elwin raised an eyebrow, still keeping a fair distance from the ranting dinosaur. "Your sparklies?"

"You want them, don't you? All of my lovely jewels and crystals, and the big, yellow sparkly I love above all! That's all you've ever wanted me for, I know you think I'm useless! Lothar has told me so!"

"Lothar says a lot of things, Valdemar – come here, calm down. You're not yourself, I can help you."

"Don't tell me I'm sick!" he snarled, "I'm not sick! I've merely come to my senses, I have to protect myself and my riches, as of now, anyone entering Krakrakara without my approval will be killed and feasted on by my fellow dragons! Stay back, or I shall kill and feast upon *you*!"

"He's gone nuts!" exclaimed Karri, who had been watching the exchange between the two, despite holding onto a persistently struggling Viktor, "He's wilder than Viktor, we should jump on him instead!"

"Stay back!" yelled Valdemar again, shakily stepping backwards to the arched temple doorway, still clutching his beloved jewellery, "I'll kill you all!"

"I'd like to see you try, dragon!" challenged Terak, drawing a dagger from his belt, "You know your place, get back in line!"

"I'll kill you all! You've only ever wanted me for my jewels and diamonds! Stay back, you'll never have them!"

"See?" said Karri, "Bloody nuts!"

"Shut up and hold onto this goblin, stupid moggie!"

"Go and talk to him then, Lothar, you're both lizards, aren't you?"

"I said hold onto him!"

Viktor gasped hoarsely for breath, then lost all energy, and slumped down onto the table surface, face-down, with Karri, Lothar and Collinad pinning him down with their combined body weight.

The manearie instantly abandoned the goblin king to confront Valdemar, who was shrieking accusations at Elwin and Terak with his wild, yellow eyes gaping. Collinad was exhausted, but he couldn't abandon his cause, and knew he had to restore peace in the UFC no matter what the cost.

"Valdemar, cease this at once! What in Grenamoya has gotten into you?"

"Keep away, Collinad! All of you! Just stay away from me and my kingdom!" Like a cornered rat, Valdemar saw that he was truly outnumbered and turned on his tail, tearing out of the chamber like a creature possessed. Collinad shouted, and Elwin moved to follow him.

"No, Elwin, don't you go – Lothar, you're his fellow reptile, follow Valdemar as far as you can and try to talk some sense into him. We have enough problems to deal with right here."

"Right." Lothar unsheathed the sword at his belt and strode briskly after the dinosaur, into the hot glare of sun and up the slope of the path, out of sight. Collinad watched him go, despairingly, inwardly praying that he would return in one piece. Even Karri expressed nervousness with his pointed ears pinned back against his neck. Half of him wanted to follow Lothar and help, but the remainder of him gloated in the fact that reptiles were clearly more insane than felines. Collinad sighed with dismay and leant against the stone table with one paw over his eyes. Elwin sat down with him. Nearby, the royal herald was frantically poking at Viktor with a finger to see if he was still breathing. Indeed he was, but at last he was quiet and still, with only an occasional mumble or twitch.

"All wrong…" said Collinad woefully, drawing his paw down one side of his face, "it's all gone wrong…Elwin, I don't know what happened to make everything go badly. We're in such a state so early on…we cannot submit to Pain's influence, in whatever form it may take. Surely we can help our comrade Viktor somehow…"

Elwin shook his head, stray tendrils of his hair framing his cheeks. "I'm afraid not, Collinad. There's nothing we can do to save him." The herald heard his words and cried pitifully, feeling the king's wrist for a pulse. "I'm so sorry, Phil…for five-hundred years, we have been unable to determine the cause or remedy for Utipona madness. I am so, so sorry...all you can do is make sure he rests, and doesn't do anything to inadvertently hurt himself."

"B-but...maybe this time we can find a way...oh Scaless, no...don't let this happen to my king..." He sobbed and fell to his knees beside the table, his elbows on the surface and his face in his hands. Elwin felt a chill all through his body. Alongside him, Collinad subdued some tears that threatened to fall. The elf put a hand on his shoulder.

"Collinad, it will be all right. We will adhere to the prophecies, our island will be safe. Pain will never rise to great enough power to cause irreversible damage to Grenamoya." Collinad smiled slightly, but the smile didn't last. His sleek, canine complexion was tussled and exhausted.

"I feel so helpless, my friend...Viktor's illness is incurable, Merlock has been burned down by a dragon, and his son has been kidnapped, it just feels so *unfair*. So much has happened to that single kingdom, and we can do nothing to aid him..." He sniffed and looked directly into Elwin's strong, tender face. "We've known Viktor for years, Elwin...we cannot let this happen to him..."

The elf nodded, sharing Collinad's pain but unable to offer any condolence. The collie leant against him sadly and breathed heavily. All that Elwin could do was pat him on the shoulder; he could offer no answer that would solve all their problems. Earlier than any of them had predicted, Pain was making his first move, whether in the Sacred Mountains, Utipona, or both. Indeed, with the apparent absence of the Great Dragons throughout recent months, it seemed that he had taken over the temple on Scaless Mountain, as well as initiating development along the borders of Utipona – the adjacent kingdoms, Gratokinya and Xavierania (Terak's homeland), had reported increased conflict along their southern borders, and thus it stood to reason that Pain's armies were accumulating once more in the wasteland of Grenamoya's southernmost kingdom.

When Lothar finally returned to the temple, he was in a weary state. His clothes were torn in places, and his expedition to retrieve Valdemar had obviously been fruitless, though he still held his sword resolutely in one hand. After his reappearance, he and Karri made no form of communication whatsoever, and kept at a respectful distance from each other.

Terak, who was still trying to comfort the herald, managed to convince the devastated goblin that it would be in Viktor's best interest to return to Merlockiara. With Viktor in a calmer state of mind, Terak and the royal herald were able to escort the goblin king out of the temple and back to his carriage with little trouble. Terak may have been a cold-blooded vampire, but his heart was full of compassion for those around him, and he used every ounce of muscle within his body to get the king back inside his royal carriage. Once laid out on some grass-coloured cushions, Viktor seemed to drift into a trance, and the agonised expression left his face, enabling him to sleep without a care, for the moment at least. The herald thanked Terak profusely, though with tears in his eyes, and at last the Merlockiaran royal carriage set off on its way back home.

\*\*\*

Ramsey, meanwhile, was more hopelessly lost than ever before. Having wondered for a time whether or not the forest around him was a figment of his imagination, he gave up on that theory after being plagued by a group of grey squirrels. Deeper in the forest, his visibility range was reduced to a metre or so in places; a thick, low-lying black fog crept through the trees at night, and there was little he could do to protect himself from potential woodland predators, so he stayed awake. As much as it worsened his state of health, he was at last rendered too terrified to close his eyes at night, and he kept a wide-awake vigil from the second he spotted the mists gathering until they dispersed in the morning light. Very few rays from the warm sun could reach the forest floor, but Ramsey's acute vision made daytime travelling more easy than it might have been for a human in his situation. All the same, he was beginning to wish that he had stayed home.

Though the rigid tree trunks were quite widely spaced deeper in the forest, the tangle of spindly branches and sharp, needle-like leaves overhead made the woodland darker than ever. Ramsey had tried only once to climb one of the trees during a moment of extreme panic the night before, but found that the tree bark was not as bare as it appeared, and was in fact covered with tiny, needle-sharp spines that cut into his skin the minute he grasped it. These trees were too aggressive for his liking; what he would have given for the sight of his comfy, gnarled, easy-to-climb oak tree...

As soon as the squirrels encountered him and found that he was fun to play with, they never went away. Ramsey kicked and shooed them with all his might, but for some reason he held a kind of attraction to them, and they refused to leave him for a moment. They leapt onto him, scratching him and sniffing him without mercy, and were always trying to crawl into his sleeves, trouser legs and, most of all, his bag of supplies. Grenamoyan squirrels are incredibly similar to our own, but are if anything more mischievous, and Ramsey had the displeasure of experiencing it first hand. He felt a brief moment of triumph when he managed to squash a particularly fat squirrel under his foot as it ventured towards his trousers, but it turned out to be stunned rather than dead, and quickly scuttled away again.

"I hate this place!" Ramsey collapsed onto a small rock formation in the middle of the forest after several days of wandering blindly through it, and covered his face with his hands, "Why do you guys have to follow me all the time?" Two squirrels, who had been following him mischievously all evening, merely stared vacantly at him and twitched their noses. "For goodness' sake, you think you're so cute, don't you? Well fine, take my food -" He reached into his bag, grabbed some bread rolls and crackers and flung them towards the two infidels. "Take all of it! And get out of my damn face, for a millisecond, please!"

Apparently satisfied, the squirrels gathered the food in their mouths and forepaws and scampered away into the deep blue mist.

Ramsey gasped, almost choking on his own breath, and slumped backwards onto the hard rock. His chest was heaving.

"I can't keep going on like this..." he muttered, "I'm much too tired...you've got to stop talking to yourself, Ramsey, you're going to go mad in the end...they all do..." He huffed, and grinned to himself. "Well, in any case, you're not going to end up like that lunatic Viktor, are you?"

Night was falling again. Ramsey decided not to journey further east until the next morning, when he would feel more confident to be on the move, and chose the pile of rocks as a temporary base of shelter until then. He moved around to the other side of the formation, which he believed to be the more sheltered side, and opened up his bag of supplies again to retrieve his blanket and extra clothing. Above him, owls and other birds of the night were rustling the needle canopy, and all around the swaying trees creaked and groaned in the gentle breeze that sifted through the wood.

He pulled his long-sleeved, itchy shirt over his head, and huddled against the cold, damp rock with his woollen blanket wrapped tightly around his fragile form. He was resting against a slight indent in the rock, and so felt more protected than usual, and hoped that he might be able to sleep that night, at least for an hour or two. In the dark woodland, surrounded by the deepest shades of midnight blue and black, and skeletal, towering trees, Ramsey's bright eyes darted all around for the slightest indication of movement, the tiniest threat, anything that might be lurking in the gloom. His breath rattled noisily in the dead silence of the forest; another owl hooted, something small stirred in the undergrowth, then all was mute once more.

Ramsey was starting to feel a sense of fulfilment at last. He was alone. He was completely and utterly alone. He loved being alone, he loved the silence of a world in which nobody else ever spoke a word; his life felt strangely as though it was his own at last, and nobody else's. He could do what he wanted; fair enough, if he wanted to die, he could die. He was determined to survive and escape from this non-existent wood; finally, he would find a piece of the island to call his own, somewhere remote and magical where nobody would ever bother him. Hidden in the shadow of the rocks, Ramsey began to feel less intimidated. He was certainly cold, and it frightened him somewhat that he could barely see, but he was truly free to do as he wanted without anyone knowing about it.

*You're all alone…*

*You're all alone and nobody loves you…*

*You're all alone and nobody loves you, nobody cares, nobody loves you, nobody cares, nobody loves you, nobody cares…*

Ramsey jolted upright suddenly with a gasp. He blinked, and looked around for a moment to make sure that he was still where he thought he was. The forest was still there, the familiar dark mist still enveloped him. Damn it, he thought. He had been on the verge of sleep at last, and something had woken him up. He hated being half-asleep, when he could hear his dreams, but still had his eyes open and could see the waking world…the dreams he had when he was only half-asleep confused him perhaps even more than those he had when he was deeply asleep. They narrowed the line between fantasy and reality. Nobody could have been talking to him, there was no sign of anyone around for miles, with the exception of the odd squirrel or two. And squirrels couldn't talk.

He huffed. "Must be getting a fever again…" he grumbled. "Damn cold, why can't it just hide out in my backside for a while or something rather than stick in my head all the time…no wonder I'm going crazy."

The dark mist was gradually closing in, and already Ramsey couldn't see further than two metres beyond his person. It had been that way since he first wandered into the wood; but with the mist that night came a smell, a rank, sweaty, earthy smell like moss, or a badger. Or perhaps a badger covered with moss. Something stale and animalistic, yet with the scent of soil and roots. Ramsey, with such a prominent nose, was very sensitive to changes in smell, despite his head cold. It was something abhorrent that made him screw up his face with disgust, and he muffled his nose and mouth in his woolly blanket irritably. He wanted it to fade away, but it never did; it was as though the night mist was seeping directly out from a rotting mire.

"For Scaless' sake..." he snarled under his breath, "something really massive must have died out there or something..."

Ramsey had never smelled anything like it in all his life, and he knew he never wanted to again. It was nauseating. Already weakened by lack of sleep, Ramsey felt his head starting to spin, and become increasingly heavy on his neck. With a moan of exhaustion, he closed his eyes and fell sideways against the rock, sliding out of the protected dip and onto the prickly ground, practically bent double with his blanket scrunched up on his lap. He felt himself snort tiredly, then his aching eyes closed fully, completing the darkness around him. Even then, the smell seeped through his airways like a disease, and it remained acute through his dreams.

*Nobody loves you, nobody cares, nobody loves you, nobody cares...nobody ca-a-aares...*

That stupid sing-song voice. Ramsey didn't know who was singing to him, but he couldn't recall any similar songs from his lifetime, and tried to dismiss the voice. Still it carried on, in lilting tones:

*Nobody loves you, nobody cares, you're stupid and you're ugly, nobody loves you...*

*If you love us, you'll let us love you...this is how we love you...we show the world that we love you...*

*But nobody loves you, you're thick and you're ugly, nobody loves you...*

Ramsey clenched his teeth and turned awkwardly in his sleep.

*You know we'd never hurt you unless it was necessary...*

*Burn him, let it all rip off! Rip him until he can't see for the pain...!*

He jolted and clutched at the needle-covered ground in a delirium of fear, not knowing where he truly was or what he was doing. He couldn't wake up. "G...g...get off...get off me, no...!" He screamed, his frantic voice echoing all through the forest and

123

rendering all other living creatures silent in awe. "No, no, help me...! Daddy!"

With a desperate cry he was awake, and clutching at his body in a cold sweat. He could have sworn that he was somewhere else, but he didn't know where. The voices were unfamiliar, he couldn't place them in his mind, there was no specific memorable incident that he could link to those voices...that confusing, singing voice, and the other one that changed from gentle to ferocious within a matter of seconds. His head was throbbing in agony, and he couldn't remember why he had fallen asleep in the first place. He looked around, focusing on the world around him as clearly as possible, and took a deep breath. He was safe and alone.

But almost as quickly as he had awoken from his nightmare, he found that he was neither safe nor alone any more. Gazing through the night mist, at the top of a shallow slope just above his hiding place, a massive, blurred figure was illuminated by a pale purple light; the shape of a bear or some kind of enormous tiger, and it was moving closer. The smell reached Ramsey's senses again, and his breath caught harshly in his throat. He couldn't feel his body any more. Rigid with terror, he felt behind him for some kind of weapon, anything that he could use to protect himself, and found nothing. A few feet away, his backpack had tipped its contents onto the forest floor.

He shuddered and stared helplessly up the slope to where the figure stood; suddenly, another joined it, and then a third, and the first let out a monstrous, roaring cry. They bolted towards him, a thunder of massive limbs and snarling fangs, and without thinking, Ramsey ran for his life.

His legs ran independently of his mind, which was barely functioning as he tore between the trees and through the dark, unable to see the way ahead but knowing that anything was better than standing still. They were faster than he was, and soon he could feel them getting closer, their galloping strides making the ground beneath his feet shudder.

The birds and squirrels overhead were rushing around and calling with distress. Ramsey just ran, he ran as fast as his goblin legs could carry him, even though his brain was weak from exhaustion, his legs were unwilling to give up. He caught a fleeting glance of one of the creatures to his left, gaining on him and moving ahead, in an attempt to ambush him – at least ten feet tall, it was like a huge, muscular lion weaving through the trees, which barely seemed to hinder it despite the creature's size. He felt the two others behind him, moving close, and suddenly they were upon him.

One of them dove past him and held its ground in front of him, and Ramsey finally saw exactly what he had been running from – truly huge, the creature was a mass of grey and brown hair with sharp claws, a lion's tail and a grotesque, snarling face. From its jaws dripped a massive glob of saliva, and its large, pointed ears were ripped. The other two were just the same as the first, if a little smaller, like monstrous lions with large noses, fangs, and dark manes of hair along their necks, past their shoulders. Ramsey couldn't scream. The largest one lunged at him with a mouthful of sharp teeth, and the others flanked him from either side.

"Looks like we caught a traveller, eh?" His voice was deep and husky, like someone who had swallowed something particularly sharp, "'Fraid we can't let you go any further, goblin." Ramsey screamed at last when the biggest monster lunged at him once more, and he turned to run, but the creature tripped him over with one swipe of his large paw. "You're not going anywhere!"

The mist in his lungs, Ramsey whipped around and spat forcefully in the creature's face. He didn't know how he thought to do so, but the creature reeled backwards in shock, giving him enough time to scramble away and flee once more, this time in the opposite direction. Uselessly, the other two creatures stood by their leader rather than chase after Ramsey and drag him back. The largest one bit each of the others forcefully on the neck and pushed past them, calling out to Ramsey, "You can't run forever!"

Ramsey's felt as though his feet would never stop running. He darted back through the wood the way he had come, weaving through the narrow trees, occasionally stumbling, but never looking back. He was ahead of them, but they were angry, and he was almost out of options. Even if he was able to grab his weapons, he knew he couldn't stand and fight all three. He had been even more terrified by the fact that the monsters could speak, and that there was anyone else in this forest apart from the usual flora and fauna.

They were gaining again, their heavy bodies were making the ground tremble. He ran, screaming, clutching a stitch in his ribs with both hands, frantic, desperate for some way to escape, or a hidden cave where he could hide, anything – they were surrounding him, he could feel them close, they were snarling and hurling insults at him. He was more terrified than he thought he could ever be.

The cold air beat harshly against his cheeks, and he felt himself slowing down. No, he couldn't give up so easily...he just *couldn't*...but his legs were so exhausted that they were practically failing beneath him

Seeing purely by chance an area of forest where the trees were more densely-packed, Ramsey gritted his teeth and lurched painfully in that direction. Somehow, he forced his way to the trees and was able to get through before the forest creatures could reach him. Everything felt distorted, he could hear them cursing behind him; though he knew he couldn't be safe just yet, his body could do no more and he slowed dismally to a stand-still.

He was gasping for breath, his throat raw from the cold night air, and the stitch in his abdomen throbbing like mad. He looked around feebly for a rock or tree-stump by which to rest, and instead beheld through his hazy, adrenaline-blurred vision something far more unwelcome. Another monster, like the ones that had been chasing him seconds before. He was so terrified that he could barely cry.

"Oh Scaless, no, don't do this to me..." he wheezed, his voice far weaker than he would have liked. "No, don't come any closer...! Stay back...!"

The creature loomed over him, and he turned to run, but was met with the sound of the other monsters roaring through the trees. He cried out in despair and pain ripped through his leg, intense and overwhelming, causing him to fall forward to the forest floor. He screamed and tried to kick out, but his attempts were futile, and he felt himself being forcefully dragged through the brush by his spindly right leg, which was bleeding onto his trousers.

"No, Scaless, no, don't...get off me, please! I'll do anything...!"

He knocked his head against something hard and cold, and once again his world descended into darkness and colourless memories.

# Chapter Five

# Ramsey And The Troll

Ramsey's brain kick-started itself abruptly sometime during the following day. His mind switched on at last, and though he could not open his eyes, he could feel his body slowly coming back to life. He knew that something had happened the night before, but like so many crucial events from his past, he could barely recall the details. He remembered an awful smell, something massive chasing him through a mist; he tried to remember more, but his head began to throb with exhaustion, and he stopped instantly. He had survived such a terrifying encounter with three monsters – he could survive the next few minutes at least.

His senses began to sharpen, but his eyes were still painful, itchy and watery, as though he had slept in contact lenses. Maybe he didn't want to see where he was at that moment. His nose detected a stale, muddy smell, and he reached out with one hand to feel the ground. He was lying face down on what felt like damp, bare earth. His leg was sore and splayed out unnaturally to his side, but otherwise he was relatively unscathed. With a wince, he tried to open his eyes, and found that his vision was cloudy and vague. That suited him just fine. The last thing he wanted was to open his eyes and find another one of those monsters lurking alongside him.

"I have..." He coughed and cleared his throat, forcing out a hoarse, feeble voice. "I have to...stop passing out like that..." He coughed again, trying to regain some strength in his vocal chords, but they felt tired and rusty like the rest of his body. "I have to stop passing out and...and getting myself injured all the time..."

His head was ringing with loud, unheard noises, and he rested his face flat against the lumpy ground. He couldn't feel a draught, and he was warmer than before, so he assumed that he was in a sheltered area within the forest. The deep, musty smell in the air most definitely attested that he was still in the never-ending woodland. Loose soil stuck to his damp, orange skin as he lay; his instinct told him to curl up into a foetal position, as he always did when feeling afraid, but his body wouldn't obey. Semi-conscious or not, Ramsey was glad to have escaped from his attackers.

"I mustn't let myself faint all the time like that," he asserted, his voice stronger, "or else the world'll think I'm some kind of wimp."

With a strong blink, his vision cleared, and he beheld the outline of what appeared to be his backpack lying on the dark ground a few feet away. He swallowed and looked upwards; above him was a tangle of pale roots and branches lacing the deep brown earth. No wonder the smell of soil was so intense – he was actually underground.

Not very deeply, however, since he could see a wide opening in the corner of his eye, framed with plants and thick tree roots, that led up to the open forest. A mist was gently seeping in through the entrance and dampening the earth inside. Ramsey found the strength in his body to sit up, and he anxiously reached for his bag of supplies, keeping both eyes firmly on the opening. If another one of those creatures had indeed dragged him to this underground den, then it was certain to return shortly to make sure he wouldn't escape before supper.

"You going somewhere?" enquired a gentle, deep voice to his right.

Ramsey spun around jerkily and staggered backwards with fright, clutching the earth wall behind him, his chest heaving. Hidden in the shadows nearby was another one of the creatures that had attacked him the night before. He could see its vague shape in the near darkness, but he was as close as he ever wanted to be, and he continued edging away. The creature, sitting like an enormous dog in one corner of the den, lifted its large, round head and clacked its teeth together.

"I can tell you that the last place you want to go is out there. The others will get you if you go out there."

Ramsey's heart was racing frantically in his chest, pounding against his ribcage like a jackhammer. He knew that the other monsters would probably catch him if he went into the open again, but this creature before him was just the same, and would eat him for sure if he stayed where he was. Desperate, he fumbled for his weapons in his backpack, crouching nervously to feel around amongst his supplies. The creature just stared plaintively at him from the dark with its round, almost cat-like head and deep eyes, flicking its tail with interest. It could speak. That aspect freaked Ramsey out even more, and he was certainly not going to listen to a word it said.

"I'm telling you," it said again, the dim light reflecting off its yellowed teeth, "you do not want to go back out there."

"Well I don't want to stay *here* either," snapped Ramsey, desperately rummaging for something to defend himself with. "Why did you bring me here, and why didn't you just eat me when you had the chance? I'll fight you to the last, I can tell you that…!"

"And I can tell you," said the creature again, "that if you go out there, you'll be eaten, and it won't be any fault of mine. I'm not going to eat you, I don't need to. I ate something last month – I'm good to go for another year now." Ramsey stared at the creature, not the slightest bit comforted, and it smiled a wide grin that was full of sharp teeth. "My name's Theron. What's yours?"

Ramsey felt himself becoming angry as well as terrified, and he grasped the handle of his jewelled dagger within the backpack. "Jonathan Witherbottom. What difference in Grenamoya does my name make? Just get away from me, don't make any sudden moves!" Theron looked at him for a moment, then stood on his four muscular legs and slowly advanced towards Ramsey, who was still clutching the dagger but couldn't think to use it. He just stared up at Theron, a creature standing at least eight feet tall and resembling a tower of pure strength; completely terrified and humbled, he dropped the weapon and turned to flee.

"Hey, come back!" Ramsey almost made it to the mouth of the den when Theron's large, clawed paw deftly tripped him, and he was pulled back into the earthy darkness by the back of his shirt, shouting and screaming. Theron dug his claws into Ramsey's skin and the goblin fell silent. "Stop it...! You don't want those other guys to come running here, do you? They'll wrestle you out into the open no problem if they find out I brought you here. Be quiet."

Ramsey swallowed, on his back on the bare ground, gazing up at Theron in order to capture his entire form at once. He was somewhat softer in appearance than the other creatures, with greyed purple hair all over his body and what looked like a pair of furry brown trousers covering his lower body and hind legs (with the exception of his tail, on the tip of which sat a tuft of long brown hair). Ramsey had never seen a creature like Theron before, not even in books, and was therefore too wary to trust him. The creature's face was more rounded than those of his far less accommodating associates, and a large nose took up the centre, pale pink like the colour of salmon. His eyes were brown, like Ramsey's own, but far larger in comparison, and in Ramsey's mind, much too threatening. Theron's bulk was deceptive, as he could clearly move very fast when he wanted to.

"What was the big idea of attacking me like that?" he shouted all of a sudden, causing Theron to reel backwards, "Look what you did you me! Why did you have to go and ravage my bloody leg? Answer me that!" He pointed at his still sore, swollen leg.

133

"I had to get you out of the other trolls' way, of course," replied Theron simply. "If I had left you on your own for a minute longer, you might have been dead."

"Yeah, well, you didn't have to mutilate me in the process. I have enough bad luck and plenty of accidents without your help, thank you." He kicked out at the troll, missing him, but causing him to back off a little further. With a deep breath, he tried to stand, but the pain in his leg was suddenly overwhelming, and he slumped backwards against the earthy wall gracelessly. Theron watched him, pulling back into a sitting position, benignly letting Ramsey explore his surroundings. The goblin felt the wall for a moment, a little soil crumbling beneath his fingers, and then looked at the other creature again with a hint of annoyance. "You're a *troll*?"

Theron smiled and nodded like a well-meaning spaniel. "Uh huh."

With a questioning look, Ramsey turned his body fully in Theron's direction and crossed his arms. "...You don't look like a troll."

Theron continued smiling, apparently not concerned that Ramsey might be a possible threat. Ramsey was increasingly irritated by the moment. "Well, I am a troll, but maybe not what you think one would look like. We forest trolls are a separate...uh...a separate type of troll from what you are probably used to."

"Oh great." Ramsey began to feel that Theron was too mellow to be feared, but was still uncomfortable, and bent to the ground to retrieve his dagger; Theron didn't react. "So you're a different genus of troll or something, right?"

"Yeah, that's it, that's the word I meant. Yes, I'm a different kind of troll than the usual sort. There aren't many of us left because men have taken over our forests."

"Mmhmm," pondered Ramsey, sliding the dagger into his belt.

"Trolls and fronas are sort of related in some way, and we are one of the mixed species. There are loads of different trolls like us on this island. I'm not the first troll you've ever seen, am I?"

"Well it's hardly a monumental occasion, is it?"

134

Theron fell silent, then cocked his head confusedly at Ramsey. It was going to be hard learning the ways of this goblin. "What do you mean?" he asked, genuinely unsure. Ramsey just waved a hand to dismiss his comment and returned to his backpack. "Oh, after I picked you up, I went back out and found your bag, and I brought it here, in case it went missing before you woke up."

"Yeah," Ramsey opened the top of his backpack and briefly checked inside – everything seemed to be in order. "Thanks a lot."

"You're welcome." Theron huffed and watched as Ramsey continued to investigate his supplies. The goblin pulled out various items and inspected them, including a small purse with hundreds of shiny things inside, and then returned them to the bag with a satisfied smile. In spite of one full inspection, Ramsey proceeded to repeat the investigation, rooting through the contents of his bag, seemingly to make sure that nothing had moved since he last checked. Theron began to feel that Ramsey was doing so to avoid speaking to him. "You still think I'm going to eat you?"

"You'd better not," replied Ramsey in a threatening tone, not averting his eyes from the bag. "For all you know I could be poisonous."

"I'm sure you aren't, I've had goblin before and it tasted just fine." Ramsey stopped dead in his tracks like a rabbit caught in the headlights; Theron laughed heartily. "You are listening to me, then?"

"Have I got a bloody *choice*?" snapped Ramsey, angrier than ever, "You just leave me alone, I need to get moving as quickly as possible." Grabbing hold of his island map once more, he stuffed it into the top of his backpack and tried to stand, holding onto the dirt wall for balance. Theron watched him with interest. "Just get out of my way and let me leave, for crying out loud!"

The bulky, purple forest troll sat down more firmly in front of the only exit and looked at Ramsey with defiance, as though fully understanding a certain concept at long last. Ramsey glared up at Theron and shouted for him to move back, but the larger creature held his ground. "You're a very angry person, aren't you?" he said at last, in a surprisingly gentle tone. Ramsey stamped his foot, and in the process almost dislodged his wounded knee from its socket.

"Well I guess I am, but that's only because you're sitting in front of me like a useless lump!"

"I can't let you go back out there, it'll only make me feel guilty if you get eaten," said the troll matter-of-factly, turning to glance out of the den entrance, into the hazy blue forest. "They're still out there, you know, they never give up."

"Since you want to protect me for whatever reason," said Ramsey assertively, trying to hold his temper, "why don't you just tell those others that you've eaten me already and that there's no need for them to wait around?"

Theron laughed loudly, still facing the open woodland. From behind, if it was indeed possible, he looked even bigger. The thick, brown hair covering his legs and rear end was matted slightly from lying down on the bare earth for so long, and his slender, purple tail swished from side to side slowly as he spoke. "I can't talk to those guys, they're much too dangerous. Why do you think I live underground to keep away from them? They hate me."

"Well that's something I can agree with them on, but only because you're in my way at the minute." He stayed silent for a moment, expecting Theron to move or at least reply, but he did neither. "Move your fat arse out of my *face!*"

Theron slapped Ramsey across the face with his long tail and remained vigilant at the root-infested opening. His fur smelled of dirt and decaying wood, and Ramsey wiped his nose furiously with his sleeve to remove all traces of the odour from his skin. Becoming increasingly frustrated, Ramsey lifted his heavy backpack onto one shoulder and tried to force his way past, but Theron was a hairy mass of solid muscle and bone, and Ramsey couldn't move around him.

"You can't keep me here forever!"

"I'm not going to," echoed the troll's mellow voice from outside. "Once I know it's safe, I can let you go. There's no point in sending you out to your death, is there?" Ramsey fussed and complained from behind him, but didn't attempt to escape again, and Theron contentedly lay his head down on his large paws and kept watch in silence, surveying the woodland around him.

Underground, trapped behind Theron's immense body, Ramsey was feeling many emotions at once – mostly related to anger, but there was plenty of confusion mixed within him at that moment. The night before, he had been running terrified from three creatures that looked just like Theron, thinking that he was going to be ripped to shreds and eaten mercilessly. Now he was stuck with Theron, some random empty-headed troll, and was feeling far more aggravated than afraid. Normally he wouldn't have felt so confident, but Theron was in the way of his freedom, and that was something that Ramsey would fight to the death over. He hadn't come this far from Merlock just to be confined in a smelly troll lair.

Impatiently, he slumped back against the wall of the chamber, causing more of it to fall away, and hopped slightly on the spot, calling out to Theron in irritable tones. "You just tell me when I can continue my quest, Okay? I don't want to be stuck in here forever with only you for company."

"I will, don't worry," he replied, then after a further moment of consideration, added, "You're on a quest?"

Ramsey smiled inwardly. Of course, this was the response he had hoped for. His heroism tactic had worked on the goblins of Merlock and Grassman Village, so logically it should work on a dim-witted forest troll. Though Theron did not turn around, and remained on guard at the opening, he certainly sounded curious. Ramsey had really underestimated the power of false impressions. "Oh, I most definitely am," he said, trying to sound casual. "Just the usual stuff, you know. Vanquishing a dragon, rescuing an innocent prince, that sort of thing." Theron's body shifted with a gasp. "I was chosen by the goblin king himself to rescue his son, and I hope that you will allow me to continue on my journey."

"Of course...!" came Theron's somewhat muffled voice, "That's so amazing, I had no idea that goblins had a prince."

"Well, not any more we don't."

"Heh, that's true." The troll's body shook slightly with laughter, and Ramsey backed away a little further, just in case

137

Theron moved backwards and squashed him. "You're very witty. What is your name? Oh please tell me, it isn't really Joshua Something-bottom, is it?

"Nah, not really." Ramsey kept one eye firmly on the troll, just in case an opportunity arose for him to make a break for safety, but Theron made it quite clear that he was not going to move. Ramsey cursed inside his head a few times, but managed to maintain a mask of composure. Though he stayed silent for a moment, hoping that Theron would turn around to check on him, he quickly abandoned any further attempts to distract him. "My name's Ramsey, and I've come here all the way from Merlock on my dangerous quest. I need to continue east and then north to the Ash Mountains of Oouealena."

"...Merlock?"

Ramsey stood still as Theron shifted his bulky body and turned around to face him; the troll's face was full of wonder, and apparently he wasn't worried about the possibility of the other trolls appearing and attacking his rear end. "Yes, *Merlock*. You know? The goblin settlement, capital of this kingdom?"

Lines marked Theron's hairy forehead for a moment as he pondered this answer, and finally unable to confirm or dismiss this fact, he just nodded and smiled. "Oh yes, I remember now."

"Good, then you realise that my mission is of real importance. I want to get on my way as soon as possible, so don't keep me down here for the rest of my life." Ramsey cringed; he had sounded like the Merlock royal herald for a moment or two. At least the language was emotive, but whether or not Theron could understand some of the long words, he couldn't tell. The troll just nodded and reacted once in a while with non-committal, throaty sounds. "I'm doing all this for the sake of an innocent child."

"Ooh," said Theron, shuffling a bit closer to him. "Have you been on a mission like this before?"

"No, but I'm clearly qualified if the goblin king himself chose me."

"So why're you going to the Ash Mountains?"

"Because that's where cobra dragons live," said Ramsey with confidence, knowing that he could lie to Theron as much as he wanted without the troll being able to question him. "A cobra dragon kidnapped the prince, you see. I know they come from the south as well, but in the north section of the island where we are, it makes sense that this particular dragon came from the Ash Mountains."

Theron continued to agree with everything Ramsey said, and Ramsey kept describing in great detail how he was on a mission of 'great significance' and was going to rescue the 'beloved Prince Morgan' from certain death in the vicious cobra dragon's clutches. The more he spoke, and the more Theron responded, the more Ramsey despised him. Though he couldn't logically argue that he had been happy on his own in the middle of the forest, he still wanted to get this troll creature out of the way as quickly as possible.

To begin with, there was the smell to deal with. Until Ramsey found himself in such confined space with a troll, he hadn't appreciated their awful odour. At least the odour of this particular sort of troll; if indeed, as Theron said, there were many different kinds. It was an intense, rank smell like rotting organic matter, wood and meat. Secondly, the company was terrible. The three trolls in the forest outside had tried to eat him, and Theron had the intelligence of a baked potato. On the plus side, he wasn't obliged to have any in-depth conversations, as had been enforced on him by the herald and the Grassman lodge owner.

For whatever reason, though it seemed that the coast was clear, Theron was reluctant to let him leave. Instead, he asked Ramsey question after question, all related in some way to Prince Morgan's rescue, for what seemed like a decade to the frustrated goblin. He began to feel quite sick of all the simple questions after a while, and it was most definitely a feeling of illness separate from that of his head-cold. His sinuses were pulsing with all the dust in Theron's underground lair. Nonetheless, he tried to stay sweet for his cumbersome host; after all, he didn't want to end up as dinner for a relatively pleasant troll.

"So, what's Prince Morgan like?" asked Theron, for about the third time, "Is he nice?"

"I told you," growled Ramsey (albeit composedly), "I have never met him before in my life."

"Then why would you want to go and rescue him?" Theron lay his heavy head down on his paws and gazed at Ramsey intently. "I mean, isn't it a bit of a waste of time?"

Ramsey looked back at the troll, trying to stare him out and make him avert his gaze, but Theron didn't move. He just kept watching Ramsey curiously, like an overgrown kitten, waiting for him to respond in some way. Ramsey had to think about his answer for a moment – now that he considered this, it did seem strange to set off on a quest to rescue someone he had never met, and in all honesty, didn't care for in the least. Oh well, it was a *fake* quest after all, and therefore not as strange as one might think. "Well...not really," he replied at last. "It's for a good cause if I can rescue the future king of Merlockiara."

"True." Theron tilted his head from side to side for a moment, as though thinking again. "You're a real hero then, aren't you?"

Ramsey clenched his teeth; these questions were slowly and surely driving him insane. "What else would I be?" he growled, "Look, there's no sign of those other trolls outside, why can't you let me go?"

"You can't go now. They can hunt you more easily in the daytime, they can see better. We must wait until night falls, then you can go."

"But no sunlight reaches down here during the day anyway, and they were chasing after me last night! Wouldn't it just be easier to let me go now? You don't have to do anything else for me ever again, just let me leave, please...!"

Theron shook his head and Ramsey cursed to himself again. "We usually hunt after dark, but it's harder for us to see when the mists come. And when the mists come, it is easier to smell the other trolls coming out to hunt. You're safer if you stay here for a while."

Ramsey was seething, but knew he couldn't do anything more to increase his chances of a premature escape; frustrated, he crossed his arms and sunk into himself, refusing to look at Theron. This troll was the most aggravating individual he had ever met in his life, and he could feel himself beginning to lose grip of his sanity, not to mention his temper. Theron would probably be too slow to react if he managed to grab one of his weapons and force his way out of the lair, Ramsey pondered.

Then again, he didn't want to put his already frail body at risk of being crushed by the troll's heavy bulk. If Theron didn't need to eat too often, Ramsey could easily guess where all his body fat was stored; the troll's stomach was large and round, but muscular like the rest of him, and Ramsey dreaded the thought of seeing a huge belly looming in his direction. No, he had to stay where he was and remain in one piece.

His thoughts about Theron's abdomen had made him suddenly hungry. Frustrated, and knowing that he had thrown plenty of his good supplies to the meddlesome squirrels the previous day, Ramsey delved once more into his bag with the aim of finding something edible. All he had left were his sugar cubes and bag of coffee from Grassman Village, but he was still thankful that they had been spared in the carnage. Ravenously, he grabbed a handful of white sugar cubes from one pocket of his bag and shoved them into his mouth, crunching them into liquid sweetness with his sharp teeth. Theron watched him, and though Ramsey knew this, he didn't offer the troll any of his precious supplies. Theron just sat still, gazing at him enchanted, his eyes following the goblin's every move. His purple hair twitched a little, as though troubled by a flea or two, and his tail thumped noisily from side to side against the ground.

"What're those?" he asked at last in his deep, harmless voice, "Are they food?"

"They're sugar cubes, they taste sweet, and I'll thank you not to stare at me while I'm eating," grumbled Ramsey, munching on another couple of sugar lumps. "What do you eat, anyway? Apart from goblins, I mean," he added with disgust; Theron smiled.

"Oh, I eat anything that comes along really. Mostly living things, but I like apples. We used to have some apple trees in this forest, but humans cut them down." Ramsey grimaced, thinking back to the bitter cooking apple he had stolen from a market stall in Merlock, right before he embarked on his journey. The familiar surroundings of Merlock and its marketplace, alleyways and rowdy 'Dragon Sword' tavern were beginning to fade from his memory. "Just as well we don't need to eat all the time, because there isn't much food around any more."

Ramsey was packing up his backpack once again, hoping that this action would prompt Theron to let him go. "Why not? What about all the stupid squirrels and everything? They were always in my face from the second I wandered into this forest."

"You don't want to eat them," said the troll instantly. "They aren't nice to taste, and they're full of bones and fur. They aren't good to eat."

"Good thing I'm bony and hairy, then," said Ramsey, "or you might have eaten me."

"Of course I wouldn't have eaten you." The troll laughed again; Ramsey really could not see what was constantly so funny. "I told you that I've eaten this year, so I don't need to again. And I saw you had all those things in your bag, so I knew you were important. I hope you rescue the prince, and become a hero. Maybe they could name a place after you."

"Hey, yeah..." Ramsey smiled, thoughts of road signs reading 'Ramsey Forest' and 'Hillock of Ramsey' racing through his goblin mind. Now that was something worth thinking about. Oh, how happy he would be once he was famous. He didn't know for sure – maybe he already was famous. After all, the goblins in Merlock were sure to have been told all about his departure, and to be saying special prayers to Scaless in hope of aiding him spiritually in his quest. Perhaps his commemorative statue was under construction at that very moment...

"...Are you Okay, Ramsey?"

Ramsey snapped back to reality, where sadly there were very few locations with his name in them as of yet. Theron's face was alarmingly close to his own, and he pushed the troll away sharply with an elbow before crossing his arms over his body again with a sigh. For a moment at least, he had escaped his current situation; now he was depressed once more, and itching to be on his own. "Yeah...I'm just fine."

Theron didn't catch the undertones of anger in Ramsey's brief response, and continued to smile in a pleasant manner while keeping his brown eyes directly focused on him. His tail twitched with curiosity every time Ramsey moved or made a sound, but despite occasional pleading glances from the goblin to endear him into moving, Theron refused to let him go free. The troll's response was always the same, relating in some way to his species' sense of smell or hunting patterns, and Ramsey became increasingly frustrated that he could not win the debate though his opponent was someone of comparatively little brain.

Finally, in an attempt to avoid Theron's insistent questioning for the rest of the day, Ramsey curled himself up against the wall, with his backpack for a pillow, and feigned sleep for a few hours. The second he closed his eyes, Theron became silent, and instead began to shuffle idly around the den; from the sounds that reached Ramsey's keen ears, he guessed that the troll was rearranging the primitive décor, as he could hear movement of soil and earth around him.

With his dark hair over his face, he sneakily glanced at the other creature once in a while, to determine if he could make a desperate sprint to the forest outside; as before, these ideas soon faded from his mind. Theron seemed too stupid to lie to him, and so Ramsey had no logical reason to fear him or try to run away. It was just the sheer size of Theron, the sharp teeth and claws, and the experience of the night before that kept sparking fear and panic within him.

This troll was unlike the others, though, Ramsey knew that very well. He wasn't unpredictable, nor malicious. He seemed genuinely interested to hear about Prince Morgan's kidnap, and Ramsey's quest to free him from a fire-breathing dragon – after all, it wasn't the sort of story one would hear every day, particularly if one lived in a deep forest.

When at last a sneezing fit betrayed the fact that he was awake, Ramsey opened his eyes completely and sat up, expecting the troll's questioning to begin again. Much to his surprise, he could see no trace of Theron anywhere within the lair. His smell still lingered in the gloom, but physically, he was nowhere to be seen. Ramsey jerked awake instantly and grabbed hold of his backpack, his breath quickening. He had a clear run to the woodland outside.

Hastily, he shoved his arms through the straps of his bag and readied himself to sprint into the open, but his injured leg gave way in mid-step. With a shout to nobody in particular, he crawled towards the opening on his hands and knees in desperation, dragging himself along the damp, dirty ground, lurching his limbs forward like a maniacal animal. He had to get out – if he couldn't escape now he might never see the sun again.

Suddenly he found himself in the shadow of a large creature, as Theron descended into the lair once more, his hair and mane ruffled and full of twigs. Ramsey cursed loudly and collapsed face-down onto the ground with frustration, but Theron, as usual, didn't recognise this reaction as one of anger towards him. He proudly dropped a limp squirrel in front of Ramsey's pointed nose and sat down alongside him patiently.

"...What do you want me to do with that?" asked Ramsey, blinking at the furry thing on the ground before him. Theron leaned down towards him, his breath rustling the fine hairs on the back of Ramsey's neck. "Eew, get away from me!"

Theron moved back to avoid a swipe from the goblin's spindly arm and stared blankly at him with dark eyes. "I just thought you might be hungry, that's all."

"Eew!" exclaimed Ramsey again, sitting upright instantly and shuffling away from the rodent. "I thought you said that you can't eat the squirrels here!"

"I said that they don't taste nice and you shouldn't eat them, but you can if you want to. I just wanted you to have something to eat, in case you were hungry."

Ramsey hugged himself irritably and glanced down at the squirrel, which gradually regained consciousness, stood up and scampered back into the forest. Theron watched it leave, then turned his attention back to Ramsey, who was sitting hunched-over and looking unwell. He noticed that the goblin's nose was starting to drip slightly, but didn't mention it. With a sigh, and feeling heavily guilty that he had offended his guest, Theron sat at the mouth of his lair once more and gazed out into the darkening woodland. It was already evening.

"There's something funny on the wind tonight," he said in his rumbling, earthy voice. "I can smell something different, it isn't a troll. It smells like burning."

"Oh *wonderful*." Ramsey picked up a clod of dirt and threw it at the troll, standing up rigidly with his bony fists clenched. "What are you talking about? That doesn't have anything to do with...*anything*. Just let me out of here, stop making up excuses for me to stay, or I'll force my way out!"

Theron stood up on his four muscular legs and clenched at the ground with his claws, his eyes focused on Ramsey, pleading and confused. "What are you talking about? I haven't made excuses."

"Okay, so I know you aren't going to eat me – then why keep me here, eh? Can't you see that all I want is to get away from you? I need to go and rescue Prince Morgan from imminent death, I can't afford to waste time around here with you!"

Pain flashed across Theron's wide eyes, and he moved a bit closer to the goblin, slowly, so as not to alarm him further. Though as a troll he was not very intelligent, he had lived in the same forest for over thirty years, and as a result had a keen grasp on how to survive in the wild. Frightened prey would run if he moved closer, and he figured that Ramsey would do the same. He was not prepared to let Ramsey risk his life out in dark woodland alone. He was on a quest to save an innocent child, after all. "What's wrong with me? Don't you like being with me?"

"No, I don't."

"But why? What have I done to make you hate me?"

Ramsey crossed his arms. "I wouldn't say that I hate you, exactly...actually, I probably do. At any rate, I hate the way you're keeping me here for no reason, other than to barrage me with questions about who I am, where I'm going and whatever! Maybe I don't want to talk about myself, did you ever think of that?" Theron winced. "No, I guess you didn't, because you're stupid!"

"I haven't done anything..." whined Theron, hanging his head, his large, triangular ears folding slightly with dismay, "I don't know why you feel so angry towards me, all I have done since I found you is try to help you...and I haven't lied to you, I promise."

"All this stuff about smells on the wind, and the way your species hunts, and those damn mists that bring the sound of death or whatever – I don't believe a word of it! If you want to eat me for the sake of it, then go ahead, just don't keep me in here for the rest of my life! All those questions, too, let me tell you, I don't appreciate being interrogated like that!" Ramsey bent to pick up another clod of soil from the ground, but Theron didn't seem to be listening any more. Strangely, he was craning his neck in all directions, and moving towards the lair opening, his lips tight and his expression focused. Ramsey glared at him, and hurled more dirt in his direction. "Hey! Are you listening to me?"

"Shush a minute..." Theron moved forward with deft, silent steps, sniffing the air with his large nose, and peered out into the forest above. Ramsey was so unnerved by the sudden change in behaviour that he decided to obey; quietly, he tried to listen for any unusual sounds, though all he could smell at that moment was Theron's dirty hair. He couldn't hear anything of special interest, and moved closer to the troll, listening keenly with both pointed ears. Theron's heavy breathing began to fill the lair, his sides were heaving greatly and he was making a low rumbling noise with every heave. Impatient, Ramsey poked him in the thigh with a sharp fingernail, and Theron moved quickly backwards, almost squashing the goblin in the process. "There's something here..."

"What are you talking about?" asked Ramsey in a forced whisper, copying the troll's urgent tone, "What can you hear? I can't hear a bloody thing!"

"Shush!" Theron moved again, causing Ramsey to leap aside with panic. "You can hear it, it's getting closer...I haven't heard such a sound in all my life..."

"What, a non-existent one?" He drew back his arm to give Theron a forceful blow on the leg, when suddenly a deep, echoing sound rang through the forest. He tensed. "Stop trying to scare me into staying here!"

"That wasn't me, Ramsey."

The noise was coming from a fair distance away, Ramsey could discern that, but it was strangely loud, and it felt like it was getting closer. Silence fell, then the cry came again – it started as a high shriek, then deepened into an eerie, echoing noise, like a fog-horn. It filled the air over and over again, getting closer, but still distant. The forest outside came to life, animals and birds appeared from nowhere and tore away through the trees, past the opening of Theron's lair. Theron gasped and moved into the open woodland, his rear end still blocking the entrance, and Ramsey dove forward, holding the straps of his backpack tightly.

"What's happening? What's wrong?"

Theron sniffed the air noisily and retreated back into the den, his face a picture of dread and his voice full of urgency. "This isn't good, Ramsey, I can smell fire. We have to get moving right away."

"Moving where?" A loud snarl came from directly above them, and Theron shuddered, grabbing hold of Ramsey's sleeve with his teeth and pulling him forward. "Get off me!"

"We have to go, Ramsey, something has set the trees on fire." Though he was obviously frightened, the troll didn't raise his voice; instead he persisted in pulling Ramsey forward by his sleeve until the goblin began to comply on his own two feet. "That's it, come out here and follow me." He turned quickly on his tail and headed outside, leaving Ramsey to follow on his own. "This has happened before, I've seen forest fires wipe out loads of trees in one go."

"It can't be anything serious, it's not as if we're in the middle of a hot, dry summer. It must be your imaginati-"

147

With a loud creak, the tangled branches overhead collapsed down onto them, scattering sharp needles all around and smouldering harshly. Heat billowed out in all directions, more burning twigs rained down upon them. Ramsey screamed and tumbled sideways against a spiny tree trunk, his face livid with fear, and Theron knew they had to act fast.

Shouting and crying out in panic, Ramsey slid down the tree trunk, tearing the back of his shirt to pieces, and curled up into a muttering ball as the smoke engulfed both of them. Theron called to him, but Ramsey couldn't hear; terror was overwhelming his senses, all he could see was pale light and flashes of grey before his eyes, and his ears became deaf to the world. His body jolted and squirmed in the litter of needles that coated the forest floor.

"Aargh! Get away from me!"

Theron couldn't see Ramsey through the thick smoke that was burning through the murky dampness of the wood. He shouted to him, but his voice was lost in the loud crackling of fire all around him. "Ramsey! Come to me, we have to get away!" More of the canopy gave way in a cascade of hot sparks, and Theron felt them singeing his body hair. Overhead, a streamlined green creature swept over the flames, shrieking as it flew, and another patch of trees nearby caught fire in a spectacular explosion of heat. The fire beat against Theron's heavy body, but he pressed himself forward through the red glare of the ruined trees, desperately seeking for Ramsey somewhere beneath the debris.

"Aaargh…" Ramsey turned over in the hot undergrowth, his eyes clouded over completely with fear, "it's so hot in here…" He pushed his body upward, summoning all the strength inside him, and leant up against the tree, scraping and bloodying his back severely but not realising it. His pale vision was turning yellow, then orange, and it glowed under his eyelids like the sun, becoming too harsh and painful for him to bear. He heard Theron's voice at last, but couldn't discern where it came from. He felt himself crying. "Oh Scaless no, don't let me die here…!" The trees around him were alight, blackening and crumbling into ash. "Don't leave me here…!"

*We only burn you because we love you…*

"Don't leave me here!"

*Where's your daddy now? Left you to burn until you die!*

"No, I won't die here!" Something heavy pressed against his face, and Ramsey screamed and kicked out. Theron grunted as the goblin's foot collided with his chin, but was far too relieved to be angry with him. With a swift motion, he grasped the front of Ramsey's shirt in his teeth and pulled him through the embers; breaking into a run, he hoisted the spindly goblin onto his shoulders and galloped away through the trees, in the opposite direction from which the creature's horrendous shrieks sounded.

Ramsey was being savagely pulled between semi-consciousness and his fiery memories, finally grasping hold of reality as he bumped up and down on Theron's back, clutching the troll's brown mane of coarse hair tightly. He screamed again and clung to Theron for dear life, pressing his sweaty face against the broad shoulders, ducking from the branches that streaked past as they tore through the trees. The ride was turbulent and fast, but seemed to go on forever, the flames rising higher and higher behind them. Ramsey could feel the fire surging until it seemed to pass through his body; his back was cut and bleeding, but the cold air numbed his bare skin to the pain. He heard the creature's eerie cry once again, and at last recognised it as the call of the cobra dragon that had terrorised Merlock. It was louder than ever, coming from directly behind them. There was an explosion of flames to their left, and Theron turned sharply as the blackened tree trunks crumbled and snapped.

"We're going to die..." moaned Ramsey against Theron's hairy back, pressing his cheek against the fur and closing his eyes tightly, "it's the dragon that I saw back in Merlock, I know it is...!"

"We won't die," panted Theron, swerving and breaking down some flimsy trees in his haste, diving down past a fallen log and through a small, rocky stream. "Just hold on tightly, don't let go. I know there's a break in the forest somewhere near..."

A branch cut Theron's cheek as he ran, and Ramsey pressed himself flat against the troll's body, gasping, feeling the panic start to take him over again. He heard a rush of air from somewhere far behind them, and the familiar hot sound that caused another patch of trees to ignite. Though the sound of the dragon receded, the flames continued to burn, and Theron found himself moving towards even greater danger. It was as though there was nothing else left in the world but the two of them, the dragon and the burning trees.

Ramsey was screaming inside his head, tensing up his whole body to protect against the sharp branches; he opened his eyes briefly and saw the sky. The sky, scattered with blue stars and a pale, cold moon, high above them through the thinning cover of the trees. Ramsey would have felt relieved but was too terrified to feel anything other than the freezing air.

Theron's endurance and determination didn't falter for a moment. His legs carried him almost independently of his mind, as instinct drove him onwards to find safety for himself and his bony passenger. He too saw the sky, and the break in the trees ahead told him that he was going in the right direction.

Overhead, the stars were blotted out by the slender, winged outline of the striped cobra dragon, which seemed strangely oblivious to the movement of the two creatures below. It soared past, faster than Theron could run, and expelled a torrent of fire from its gaping mouth, directly at the edge of the forest, trapping them within a circle of flame. It shrieked its horrific cry once more, then danced away through the sky like a dolphin in the sea. Theron gasped and watched the dragon's heedless and graceful disappearance, driving himself onwards to the wall of fire that encapsulated his beloved woodland home.

"We can do it, Ramsey, don't worry," he panted, his hair bristling and his muscles tense; but Ramsey didn't hear him. The goblin had been frightened into blind panic once again, gripping so tightly to Theron's thick hair that his nails dug into his own palms.

"Oh Scaless, no, don't leave me here...!" he squealed, banging his head against Theron's left shoulder blade. "Argh!"

"Just a moment now and we'll be safe, Ramsey, just hold on." The wall of flame was drawing near, completely blocking the troll's view of the other side – all he knew was that anything would be safer than the burning forest. He felt Ramsey's grip loosen slightly, the goblin continued to babble and beg him not to leave him alone to die. Theron couldn't get through to him, and turned his head quickly to lift Ramsey's dangling right leg back onto his shoulders. "Hold on, Ramsey, don't let go, we're almost there!"

"I can't, I can't...!"

"Hold on, Ramsey, for the love of Scaless!"

Theron pulled down his head, flattened his sharp ears and sprinted towards the fire, every last drop of energy within him driving him forward. Like a cumbersome, bear-like cheetah, he swept through the dying woodland on four heavy paws, streamlining his body by lowering himself towards the ground, both eyes set on the small gap in the flames before him.

He shouted for Ramsey to hold on tightly, and felt the goblin clutching at his fur with both hands. Confident that the goblin had a secure grip on his back, Theron clenched his teeth and dove through the flames, scattering ash and fiery sparks in his wake. Ramsey almost lost grip on the troll as the intense heat stung his tender skin, and his back began to throb again with deep-rooted, boiling pain. He kept his eyes shut, not wanting to see where they had ended up.

Theron, panting heavily, galloped onwards, away from the ruined woodland and out into the cool night air.

# Chapter Six

# A Break In The Wilderness

Beyond the crumbling inferno of the forest, the grassy hills were green and laced with evening dew. It was raining slightly, but not enough to quell the flames that Ramsey and Theron left behind. The moon hung lazily in the sky, watching them with its cold, blue gaze from amidst the dense scattering of stars that twinkled in the dark. The dragon was gone, the only sound that loomed over the land was that of the gently howling wind.

The woodland burned furiously, but it didn't look as though the fire would spread further. Something was dulling it as it ripped through the trees, and the smell of murky smoke rose up to the clouds. Downhill from the burning forest, two insignificant figures hobbled through the wet grass, exhausted and frightened, but safe for the time being.

"You didn't have to help me, you know." Ramsey walked with his arms across his chest, glancing at the troll who walked beside him. Theron's lumbering pace quickened slightly when Ramsey pulled ahead, but he kept his head down, staring wistfully at the ground beneath his big feet. Uncomfortable, Ramsey secured his bag over his injured back and slowed down to allow Theron to catch up. "I mean it, you really didn't have to do anything for me, let alone save my life…"

"Mmhmm…"

The goblin huffed, voicing his displeasure out loud so that Theron might feel guilty and respond. "Why aren't you talking to me now? Come on, what have I done? A few hours ago you wouldn't shut up."

"I don't feel like talking right now," sighed the troll, slowing down and finally coming to a stand-still halfway down the hill. "I've lived in that forest ever since I was born, and now it's gone…"

"So, why not find a new home? A place where no psychopathic trolls will attack you." Ramsey stopped also and turned to face Theron, who was sitting down on the grass like a massive dog with his purple tail wrapped around one leg. "There are loads of places to live on this island, you couldn't get much worse than that creepy place back there."

"But it was my *home*, that creepy place back there," said Theron in a touchy manner, advancing slightly. "I lived there all my life, and now it's been burned down. You don't have to understand if you don't want to, but I loved my home there."

"Hey, no need to get angry," replied Ramsey, holding his orange palms towards the troll in defence. "I just said that you didn't have to save my life back there, that's all."

"I don't get angry, Ramsey. It isn't healthy to be angry all the time, my mum used to say. And if you find someone who's angry, well, then you have to make their day so they *will* be happy."

"What are you talking about?"

"I just think that you're very angry, and I never did anything to make you mad." Theron walked up to Ramsey at his slow and steady pace, and the goblin ambled alongside him, unhurriedly. "You threw stuff at me, and you called me names even though I didn't say anything bad to you."

"Like I said, you didn't have to save my life."

Theron nodded his heavy head and looked down at Ramsey with a smile. "I wanted to, though. And I think that if it came down to it, you'd have done the same for me, because you're a hero."

Ramsey didn't need to wrack his brain to discern what he would have done, had the situation been reversed. On the surface, he was heroic and righteous, and a good hero would always help an innocent person in need. However, beneath all that, he was self-centred and uncaring.

"That's right, of course I would have. Dunno how I would have managed to carry you out of the fire, though." Theron didn't catch on to anything sarcastic in Ramsey's speech, as always, and smiled wider than ever. "So, I guess this is where we go our separate ways."

"What do you mean?" The two stepped over a patch of rocky earth and continued down the hill, where the ground levelled out into a flat, grassy plain. Their feet disturbed a clump of yellow flowers, causing dusty, pink pollen to billow up around them. "I thought you said you were going to save the prince from a dragon."

"I am."

"Well then, I should come with you. I want to help you on your quest."

Ramsey's whole body drew to a halt at once. "What?" he exclaimed, louder than he had intended. "No, no, you just stay here. You need to find a new home, after all."

"I won't find a home if I just stand here, Ramsey. This is a hill, and it's all bare." Ramsey surveyed their surroundings, confirmed this fact, and rested his eyes on Theron once more. "Oh let me come with you, Ramsey, I can protect you on your journey. I want to help."

Ramsey coughed, wafting some of the stray pollen away from his face and trying to look serious at the same time. The other finally stopped moving. "Come on, troll, this quest is too dangerous for me to bring you along. I don't need to have you around me, messing things up. The only reason I set out on this journey by myself is-"

He inhaled and swallowed some pollen, coughing furiously for a moment or two. He knew the reason he had volunteered himself for the mission, he knew it very well, but he couldn't reveal it to Theron. Though the troll was a little dim, he was still big, and Ramsey had already boasted of his royal mission far too much to let it drop from the conversation. He punched himself in the chest harshly to clear his throat while Theron watched him, intrigued and waiting for him to speak once more.

"...Is so that I can be discreet and unseen. If I brought you along with me, therefore, it would defeat the whole purpose of being on a solitary mission."

Taken aback slightly, Theron nodded and returned his gaze to the ground. "I guess you're right."

"Yes, I am. Look, I appreciate you saving my life, I really do, but I can't jeopardise the future prince of Merlockiara just so that you can come with me and have a good time."

"But I don't want a good time," persisted Theron, a hint of pleading in his deep voice, "I want to help you on your journey, I can protect you from danger and everything. Besides, you aren't being very crafty if that big dragon was able to follow you all the way here." Ramsey opened his mouth, but no sound came out. "You said it was the same dragon, it followed you here so it must have seen you...so then you're the one to blame for my home being burned down...!"

"I am not!" Ramsey crossed his arms obstinately and turned on his bony heel. "That dragon couldn't have followed me, I saw it flying north after it attacked Merlock, it didn't notice me at all, I know it didn't. Otherwise, it would have chased me down and torched me, too."

"What was it doing in my forest, then? Ramsey, there was no reason for it to burn my home, none at all," he added with a sigh, leaning back on his hind legs and crossing his large arms, facing away from the skinny goblin. Ramsey huffed and took several steps in the opposite direction. "I hope you didn't lead it here on purpose."

Ramsey's teeth ground together and his shoulder blades clenched up with anger. Hot fluid was searing inside his head. "What the-? Oh for pity's sake- Why in bloody Grenamoya would I-" He lunged forward with enough ferocity in his eyes to startle Theron, but otherwise was nothing more than an aggravated, orange stick-figure. His blood was boiling; all he wanted was for Theron to get out of his face, but the troll was being awfully stubborn about parting ways. "...ah, never mind! You just cannot grasp anything that makes sense, can you? Either way, I'm carrying on by myself, and don't you dare try to follow me, all right?"

Theron kept his eyes fixed on Ramsey, unblinking and pensive, and, when Ramsey showed no sign of backing down, made a massive shrug and clawed at the ground, crossing his arms once again. "Okay, Ramsey, whatever you want." The goblin nodded with triumph and instantly began to march onwards, striding extravagantly with his long limbs, his backpack tightly secured on his shoulders. Theron watched, unmoving, as Ramsey continued forward without so much as a backwards glance at the troll who had saved his life. The evening air was cool and gentle, though the smell of burning pine-wood still festered around them. Theron made a whinging noise at the back of his throat and got to his feet as the goblin faded from view in the dark. "Oh Ramsey, please let me come with you...! I want to help!"

"Not interested!" called Ramsey over his shoulder, one spindly arm raised in the air. Theron shouted to him again, but the goblin just waved his hand without turning back. "You're better off back here!"

Theron's body hair bristled indignantly in the cold; he bounded after Ramsey at top speed, his heavy footsteps thundering over the grass, and the goblin turned just in time to find Theron's purple face right in front of his own. "I am coming, Ramsey, I want to come with you and save the prince."

"Whoa, what's gotten into you all of a sudden? No need to be so angry, troll. I didn't lead the dragon to your forest, I had no reason to, despite how much you're annoying me right now."

"Okay, I believe you. I still want to come with you, though." Theron was heaving slightly for breath, but his expression was still placid and soft. Ramsey clearly wasn't afraid of him, which was a positive thing, but Theron hoped that the goblin would soon feel more kindly towards him. Ramsey had a consistently pointed face and a sharp expression that betrayed no signs of tenderness whatsoever. His black hair was tousled and his orange cheeks were dusted grey from the fire. Theron smiled at him. "You're a real hero, and I want to help you. After all, you are risking your life to save a little boy."

"Well, not really…"

"Of course you are. You could have died in that fire. I think you're great."

Ramsey put one hand to his chin, smiling to himself and brushing his two damaged fingers idly against his throat. "Yeah, you're right." With excitement, he felt the beginnings of two new fingernails scraping his neck. "Yeah, you are. But it's for a good cause. I've got a long way to go yet, but I can take the distance as long as I remember that I'm doing it for a little lost prince. Such responsibility, bestowed upon my humble shoulders…"

"Ooh, oh Ramsey, let me come with you, let me help! Then when you save the prince, you can tell everyone that I helped you, and maybe they can find me a new home." Ramsey didn't see much sense within Theron's starry-eyed logic, but decided to play along with the troll for a while. After all, the protection might be useful, and either way he couldn't confess to his rescue mission being a cruel farce. Then again, was the protection worth the torturously boring company? "Ramsey, please, let me come with you. I can keep you safe from danger, because if you're going north, you'll need me."

"And why is that, pray tell?"

The two travellers continued across the grassy plain, a vast area of lush, green life, shadowed in all directions by a thick border of trees. Though Theron's forest burned ever-strongly behind them, it was the only area of woodland that was on fire. All around, the dark trees were tall and strong, like a protective barrier that Ramsey

158

hoped would offer some shelter from the cobra dragon. The beast didn't return, much to his relief. He looked around, and realised that they were walking through a massive clearing in the centre of an even more immense forest.

"Anyway, I thought you said you lived in that forest all your life."

"I did, but I do know some things about other parts of this island. My mum used to tell me stories about different trolls that live in the mountains."

"Oh, let me guess:" interrupted Ramsey, "*mountain* trolls."

"Uh huh, mountain trolls. But not the sort that live in the...uh...what are they-? The Sacred Mountains, I mean. They aren't like the ones at the Sacred Mountains," Ramsey groaned, sensing a long-winded, pointless explanation. "The ones like humans. They're more like...well...they're not like big humans, they're more like..."

"You?"

"Yes, they're like me, but not as big, and not as nice."

Ramsey rolled his eyes, already regretting his decision to let Theron tag along. This was too tedious a conversation for him to deal with so late in the day. "So basically, these mountain trolls are like smaller versions of those buggers that were chasing me through your forest last night?"

"Yeah."

"Brilliant."

"But my mum said that there are loads of mountain trolls in the mountains, more than twenty, sometimes hundreds..."

Ramsey picked up his pace, causing Theron to fall behind slightly. It was getting late, and he knew they would have to find somewhere safe to rest before it became too dark to travel. Instinct told him to head towards the cover of the forest, but he couldn't be sure of what else might be lurking in the trees.

Though he now had the added protection of Theron acting like a hairy, purple tank, they would be in serious peril if they ran into any more forest trolls, which would no doubt be even bigger and stronger than Ramsey's companion. To rest in the open air might put them at risk of exposure, and make them vulnerable to attack. Behind him, Theron was still talking about stories his mother used to tell him as a child. Ramsey had no memories of his own mother, so Theron's recollections quickly made him irritable.

"We've got to find somewhere to stop for the night," he said, interrupting Theron's train of thought. "Should we go under cover or should we stay out here? Will there be more trolls in the forest here?"

"There shouldn't be." Theron lumbered up to him like a bear and walked at his side, his stomach swaying from side to side as he strode. "The forest ahead is a different forest from the one we just came from. It looks like one big forest, but really it's different over there. We'll be safe, either way."

"Are you sure? I don't trust this place one bit, and the last thing I need is to get eaten before I even leave the kingdom."

Theron nodded. "Mmhmm. I think we'll be fine. See up ahead, over there?" Ramsey squinted in the direction the troll indicated, and beheld the fuzzy outline of some broad-leafed trees near the eastern edge of the clearing. Still sick with longing for his tree-house and oak tree, Ramsey felt himself instantly drawn towards the vague shapes. "We can go over to those trees, they look like they will make a good shelter."

"I couldn't agree more – let's go." Ramsey would have dragged Theron behind him had the troll not been so heavy. The weight of his backpack was putting great strain on his shoulders, so he had no strength to run, but he refused to let exhaustion get the better of him. Despite his excitement, he was forced to trudge slowly onwards at Theron's lumbering pace. "It'll be good to get out of this damn rain."

Theron nodded in agreement, shaking rainwater from his back and mane. His pink nose was glistening with moisture, slightly bumpy with a few small hairs on the tip. Ramsey's hair still stuck out stubbornly in all directions, the light rain deflecting off the wiry strands. Through his tough skin, he felt the cold biting him with a vengeance. The warmth of the blazing woodland was now far behind them, glowing brightly, sending dark clouds of smoke into the night sky.

By the time Ramsey and Theron reached the small patch of trees, the rain had died down, and they were traversing a downward slope once more. They neared the oak-like trees, which appeared almost half grown, and found that the foliage bordered the edge of a large lake that had formed in the dip of the slope. The corners of the lake were lined with reeds and duckweed, and small insects darted across the water's surface.

Ramsey hurried past Theron towards the largest tree and set down his bulging backpack with a sigh of relief. Theron sidled over to another tree and sat down heavily on his backside, by which time Ramsey had opened his bag and was unloading some equipment onto the grass. His clothes were only slightly damp, but he was more concerned with the damage inflicted upon them from their escapade in the forest. He reached one hand over his shoulder and touched his back through his torn shirt, and felt the gashed, swollen skin beneath his fingers. He needed to find some clean clothes.

Plaintively, Theron looked up at the dark blue sky littered with stars, taking a deep breath. A cloud had drifted over the moon, dulling the pale glow that seeped through the grey scattering of smoke in the air. The breeze had dispersed the signs of fire, and it seemed that the rain had largely extinguished the blaze. Only the very middle of the forest, where the dragon had first struck, still flickered with the remnants of huge flames.

Theron lay down on the cool grass and looked towards the slope from which they had travelled, where his life-long home stood still, black and silent as though in mourning. He didn't think that the other trolls would have survived the terrible business, but didn't allow them to play on his mind.

He was on a mission now, a quest to save a kidnapped prince. All his life he had lived in that forest with only tales of the outside world; now, the great, wide land beyond his woodland home was unable to daunt him. Ramsey bustled noisily through his travelling bag all through Theron's reverie, and finally spoke.

"Hey, I'm gonna get changed, I want to clean myself up a bit, all right?"

"Uh huh."

Ramsey huffed and poked Theron in the backside, causing the troll to turn. "I'm going to bathe in this lake for a moment or two, Okay? So don't turn around or try anything indecent."

"But you poked me, Ramsey."

"I mean, don't turn around once I *tell* you not to turn around," explained the goblin gruffly, a bundle of fresh clothes under his arm. Theron looked at him, one eyebrow slightly raised in confusion; Ramsey pointed a finger at him. "Turn around!"

"Okay, Okay…"

Theron obliged tiredly, and returned his attention to the ebbing forest fires once again. With a final check to make sure that the troll wasn't peeking, Ramsey clambered down the narrow bank with his clean clothes to hand, and placed them neatly on the grass. He felt disgusting and grimy, with cuts and dirt all over his body, not to mention ash and twigs in his hair, and was very relieved to take his dirty clothes off. His shirt was the most painful part; as he lifted it over his head, the patches of congealed blood on his back snagged in the material, and he had to peel the garment off at an agonisingly slow speed, which left him both sore and cold.

"Are you Okay, Ramsey?" asked Theron, in response to the various wincing noises coming from his companion. Ramsey almost leapt off the ground.

"Don't turn around!"

"I wasn't going to…"

Shivering from the cold, Ramsey pulled his shirt off completely and tossed it aside, further dishevelling his hair in the process. Afraid that Theron might yet turn around and embarrass him, he removed his trousers as quickly as possible, along with his underwear, tossed them aside and stepped into the cold water. Though he was frozen the second he placed his leg in the water, he was desperate to be covered, and waded further into the cold lake, which was far deeper than he had first thought. He moved onwards until the water level reached his lower chest, and then began to swim around a little, though he had never been a confident swimmer. Theron had kept his promise, and was staring quietly into the night. Ramsey kept a firm eye on him as he paddled about in the water, rubbing his skin with his palms to remove grime and unpleasant smells.

"You just keep looking over there, troll! I'm watching you!"

Theron made a noise, but didn't turn. Ramsey had expected him to slip up and turn around almost instantly, but the troll was strangely focused. He was glad of it, though, as he didn't want to end up travelling miles with someone who had seen him naked. It made him wonder how much the goblins at King Viktor's castle had witnesses when they changed his clothes...

"Eew..." he mumbled to himself, paddling around in a circle with small strokes, lowering his chin to the water. With a deep breath, he held his nose and ducked beneath the water completely, emerging seconds later with his soaking hair draped over his shoulders in wiry tendrils. He wiped his eyes, wishing that he had something to dry his face with, but at least he was cleaner than before.

The lake bed was very muddy, and as he walked, his toes stirred up dirt that clouded the water brown. Moving over to one of the banks, where the water was clearer, he stood in amongst the reeds with the water up to just below his navel, breathing deeply. He was frozen all through his body, but felt invigorated and energised despite his physical exhaustion.

He looked down at himself, his narrow chest, small stomach and stringy muscles, and ran two fingers across the uneven appendix scar that fissured beneath the right-hand curve of his stomach. His wet hair stuck to his shoulders, and drips of water fell from the tip of his long nose.

Something about himself captivated him at that moment; his body was frail and weak, he was sore, cold and injured, and yet he had survived several near-death experiences on his dishonest quest so far. Maybe he was worth something, maybe he was meant to survive, to do something important. But then again, it was probably just good luck.

Still stroking the indent of flesh in his stomach, Ramsey barely noticed that he had disturbed a frog from the reeds. It leapt from the bank, croaking, and splashed into the water, swimming out of sight. Theron, alerted by the noise, turned and got to his feet. All he could see was Ramsey standing peacefully near the bank, with his back to the troll; the water's surface was barely disturbed.

He was about to call out to Ramsey when he noticed the awful injuries that criss-crossed the goblin's back. Many fine, vertical cuts were set into his skin from sliding against a tree trunk back in the forest, and his arms and sides had various other wounds; but in the middle of Ramsey's back, below his shoulders, was the strangest looking cut Theron had ever seen. From a distance, it looked almost like a perfect circle of raised, red skin.

Theron couldn't guess at how Ramsey had acquired such an injury, but as he moved to speak, Ramsey noticed him, and spoke first.

"Hey! I said don't turn around!"

"Sorry, Ramsey, I heard a-"

Ramsey fell sideways into the water spectacularly in his surprise, and surfaced in a panic moments later covered in mud. Shouting and yelling at the top of his voice, regardless of what other threats might be lurking nearby, Ramsey quickly splashed himself with more water to remove the dirt and marched up towards the bank. "Stop looking!"

Theron gasped and turned in a hurry, keeping his eyes fixed on the nearest tree while Ramsey emerged from the lake and began to dry himself with his old clothes.

"What are you, a pervert or something?" he shrieked, almost stumbling over with one foot caught in his trouser leg. "I told you specifically not to look! Do you know how that makes me feel?"

"Embarrassed?"

"Yes, embarrassed, exactly!" Hastily getting into his clothes, Ramsey grabbed the dirty ones, shoved them back into his bag and sat down in a huff with his arms crossed and his knees drawn up to his chin.

164

Theron averted his gaze again. He was starting to feel as though he couldn't do anything right. Ramsey scratched his arm and twisted his torso around to face further away from Theron. His heart was racing from the shock, his skin was flushed pink with cold, and he felt so overwhelmingly angry that he would have stormed off into the night, had he known a safe place to go.

The slight breeze froze his damp skin and made him shiver profoundly, but he found himself unable to move. Theron didn't speak. Ramsey didn't want him to speak; he wanted him to apologise, to beg forgiveness and feel sick with guilt. Ramsey's body, though by no means perfect, was the only one he had, and he felt horrifically violated at the mere thought of someone else staring at it.

"...You can look now, if you want. I'm not naked any more, but all the same, you can look at me if you bloody well want."

The troll sighed and faced him at last, confusion in his brown eyes. "I didn't mean to upset you, but you made it so difficult to tell whether or not I could look, and...I'm so sorry...I thought you might have fallen over or something, and I promised to keep you safe..."

Ramsey shrugged and leaned back against the tree, hugging his knees with one arm, the other resting across his lap. "Don't worry about it, it doesn't matter...just do what I say in future, eh? It'll make life easier."

"Okay, Ramsey...I'm really sorry."

"Forget about it. I only needed a brief wash anyway, I'm clean enough."

These words seemed to comfort Theron, who lay his head down happily upon his arms and looked up at the sky, his eyes picking out the twinkling patterns of the stars. His tail, wrapped around his body protectively, twitched every now and again, as though an invisible butterfly was trying to settle upon it.

Ramsey, on the other hand, felt far more vulnerable at that moment. Not only was he much smaller than Theron, as well as skinnier and weaker; he felt confused and thoughtful, though he didn't know what exactly he was trying to think of.

Knowing that Theron was distracted, he reached tentatively underneath his cream, embroidered shirt and touched the scar on his stomach again. He had never owned a mirror, and it felt like so long since he had noticed that line just below his abdomen. So long since he had noticed it, or even remembered that he had it...

Like all goblins, Ramsey was of a prudish nature, and so thought nothing of the fact that he hated to be seen in anything less than full clothing. Now that he had found this scar again, however, he wondered if his fear lay in viewing himself as unattractive. It was an awful thing to look at – uneven, long and deeply-cut, slicing the right side of his body in two rather messily. Sometimes it seemed small, but at that moment, it couldn't have looked bigger or more disfiguring to Ramsey.

Now that it had been rediscovered, the scar wouldn't go away. Ramsey felt so angry with himself at that moment; always, he thought, why was he always trying to open up old wounds? He couldn't very well just ignore them, but all the same, thinking over his past injuries all the time was not a very healthy thing to do. He kept confusing himself and becoming angry with nobody in particular, so the only person he could take his anger out on was him. Which was why he kept hurting himself inside.

With a sigh, he realised that he couldn't remember how or when he acquired the scar on his stomach. He was educated enough to know that it was an appendix scar, but he must have obtained it when he was too young to recall any memories.

It was with a certain degree of surprise that Ramsey realised that his eyelids were closing by themselves, heavy and weary like the rest of his body. He was too cold and nervous to doze off, he had too much to think about, but the temptation of a good night's sleep crept up on him like a serene, ethereal snake, lulling him gradually into the land of slumber. He was uncomfortable. Barely able to stay awake, he lay down on his side on the soft, cool grass and tucked his legs up to his body.

Quite suddenly, Theron's tail slapped against his face, and he jolted back upright. The coarse hair felt unfamiliar against his cheek. He grumbled silently, unable to find the strength within him to wake the troll from his apparent slumber, and curled up again on the grass, shivering slightly. He didn't remember that he had another clean, warm, long-sleeved shirt inside his backpack.

Theron wasn't asleep yet. He was breathing deeply and quietly, taking in the world around him with a sense of wonder. He had always been a great nature lover, but never before had he been out in the open, experiencing the various sensations of the world from all angles. Grenamoya suddenly seemed far bigger than he could have ever imagined. In wonder, he watched the silver stars overhead as they glittered silently, undisturbed and unaltered since the beginning of time.

But people can change, he thought, nobody has to stay the same forever – neither did he. He had left his home and was on the move for the first time in his life, with a goblin he had only just met. But he trusted in Ramsey; he knew that his own judgement had never been too reliable, but Ramsey, he knew, was a genuine individual, who just acted a little rough to disguise a tender, heroic heart. Theron's mother had always taught him to believe the best in everyone. Unfortunately for Theron, he was dealing with a goblin who had little better side to show.

Finally overtaken by fatigue, Theron too closed his eyes and fell asleep, a menagerie of dreams dancing in his head. He slept uneasily, so tired from their fiery encounter that his brain could barely focus on its own dream sequences. The sky was peaceful and barren, save for the fading stars that sprinkled across the darkness until morning. The cobra dragon was nowhere to be seen, and little of its presence remained on the landscape, apart from the western region of the great forest, Theron's home, which lay completely blackened and disintegrated under the first light of dawn.

\*\*\*

With much relief, as they journeyed eastwards into the great forest, Ramsey found that the trees in this part of the woodland were far more endearing, some reminiscent of his home tree near Merlock. They entered an area of forest that was far less dark and gloomy than Theron's home, and accommodated a wider variety of wild creatures. Though Ramsey wasn't fussy on the animals, he was glad that the trees were different, with no spiny bark or harsh needles for leaves. The broadleaf trees were very tall in this part of the kingdom, ascending many metres over Ramsey's head in places, and the ground was grassy and soft with the odd trace of green leaf litter. In a far better mood than before, Ramsey continually advanced past Theron to scout ahead, or scaled a random tree to get a good vantage-point over the canopy. Theron was humble, and just followed behind the goblin at his steady pace, his eyes and ears open to detect any danger.

The troll wasn't actively being a burden upon him, but Ramsey felt apprehensive all the same; after all, he wasn't travelling across two whole kingdoms with the honest intent of rescuing Prince Morgan. With Theron constantly by his side, Ramsey couldn't divert his mission – at least, he couldn't do so in any obvious way.

But then he had another problem, because try as he might, he couldn't navigate the island by himself. He blamed the useless map the royal herald had given to him, but in reality he knew that it was down to his own terrible sense of direction. He had never travelled anywhere before in his life, it was understandable that he couldn't work out distance or determine his route via a compass.

Theron seemed to have a general 'feel' for their location on the island, as well as what lay ahead, and kept bringing up various stories his mother had told him as a young troll. Ramsey didn't really listen, but tried to keep his travelling companion in good spirits; he needed the protection and navigational advice, at the end of the day. Theron said that he could tell by the stars which direction they were journeying in, but since they were travelling through thick woodland and could barely see the night sky through the leaf cover, Ramsey inwardly questioned the validity of this claim.

Theron also seemed to have forgotten about the incident at the lake just days before, something that Ramsey would never disregard, and nor would he forgive Theron for disobeying him.

Ramsey despised not being in control, but his greatest anger lay in the fact that another person had seen his scarred, skinny body against his will. As long as he could remember, he had a near obsessive fear of being naked in front of another person, but he always attributed this to his species; goblins were always prudish, every goblin he had ever met adhered to this general rule.

It was a somewhat strange thing, whenever he thought about it, and it must have had its roots somewhere far back in goblin history. Maybe one of King Viktor's great-great-great-grandfathers had been caught in the middle of a bath once. Ramsey liked being clean, but he vowed to measure the risks in future, and make sure that Theron was many metres away behind a tree before taking his next bath.

Trudging alongside him pleasantly, Theron was clearly laid-back about wandering around with no clothing. True enough, he wasn't humanoid and looked more like a large, lilac dog than a goblin, so maybe he didn't need anything more than the hairy brown 'trousers' that covered his lower body.

The troll was certainly a strange-looking creature to Ramsey, who had heard about and seen pictures of many different kinds of trolls, but hadn't been prepared for a real one. Still, it was better to travel with a gentle, four-legged troll than one of its unpleasant, two-legged counterparts. Theron's thick body hair guarded against the cold far more effectively than Ramsey's many layers of clothing during the coldest nights, and much to his own disgust, Ramsey found himself leaning against Theron every now and again to take advantage of his body heat.

He was completely deficient in the way of supplies after several days on the move; even his coffee and sugar cubes had been totally devoured out of desperation. Theron helped by catching a couple of pheasants in the forest, but after failing to start a fire to cook them over, Ramsey ate them raw and gave himself a dreadful stomach upset that lasted for two days. Theron readily carried the ailing goblin on his back, but still Ramsey remained unappreciative and awkward, complaining that he felt he was going to die and that it was Theron's fault for catching contaminated birds.

Several bouts of sickness and three days of fruit-picking later, they reached the eastern-most edge of the forest, where the tall trees thinned out into bushes, saplings and patches of flowers. Most importantly, however, they emerged into the warm open air at brim of a shallow valley, in the midst of which lay a town. Ramsey could have jumped for joy, and wasted no time in leaping onto Theron's shoulders and steering him down the short ridge towards the settlement. Theron didn't protest, glad to be of service to the fearless adventurer, and followed the orders at his steady, determined pace.

All around them, the land was green and fresh, with more colour than could be found in Merlockiara – flowers and bright shrubs added flecks of pigment to the landscape, and to the north, Ramsey could see rolling hills and farming fields. Further north and to the east lay the misty silhouettes of sleepy grey mountains, distant and serene, framed by soft clouds and basked in the invigorating glow of the sun. The rays beat against Ramsey's vibrant orange skin, and fluttered in his dark hair, refreshing him immensely. Theron looked up at the bright, yellow circle in the sky, and a slight breeze ruffled the ridge of brown hair along his neck.

Ramsey rode into BlackField Town on Theron's back like an orange-skinned knight on a very strange steed, regarding the sign on his way down. It was a far bigger settlement than Grassman Village, but not as big as the capital; it was a happy medium, with bustling activity and goblins passing to and fro between houses and talking to neighbours. Even as they entered the town, attracting their fair share of attention, a troop of goblins on horseback, who looked like soldiers of some sort, rode away in the opposite direction, a banner flapping over their heads.

Theron was fascinated by the activity around him, having never been in a town before, and investigated signs and windows as he walked past without diverting from Ramsey's instructions. The smells and sounds were overwhelming; fresh bread, horses, hot iron and young children all reached Theron's senses, and he wanted to pursue every one of them to discover more about this place.

Ramsey was having none of it, and instead kept jerking the troll harshly by his hair whenever he strayed off-course. He enjoyed being at such an elevated position, and looked down at the other goblins as he rode past with a superior expression on his face.

"This place is much bigger than Grassman," said Ramsey in Theron's ear as they traversed the main street, past a group of young children playing with a leather ball. "I'll be able to stock up on food again, there should be a place to stay, too..."

"Ramsey, I don't know if the people here like me very much, they keep staring at me."

"Of course they're staring at you, you're a huge troll walking through an entirely goblin community." Two small, hairy dogs crossed the street in front of Theron's big paws, reminding Ramsey feverishly of the goblin capital and its canine vermin. Theron stepped over them carefully, not allowing his claws to pass near them, and continued straight ahead, ignoring the goblins around him.

"Stand aside," said Ramsey, addressing the crowd, "hero of Merlock coming through!" Theron grunted with surprise as Ramsey's sharp heels dug into his ribcage, and picked up his pace slightly. "That's it, troll, onward!" With a certain degree of nervousness, Theron hurried along at a brisk canter, Ramsey bouncing proudly between his shoulder blades with a firm grip on his mane.

"You don't need to tug on me there, Ramsey, just tell me when you want me to go fast."

"Go fast then, troll, I need to find somewhere to dismount. Where do you suppose the town square will be? Even Grassman Village had a square, and it was just grass and dirt. This place is bound to have a big square, like Merlock."

"I don't know, Ramsey."

The buildings in BlackField Town were tall and dark, and so they suited the name perfectly. The town was even bigger than Ramsey had first estimated, though still not as big or ugly as Merlock, and the many routes leading away between the buildings around them looked just as busy as the main street. This settlement didn't seem to have a market place, but the many varied shops that lined the avenue compensated for the loss of a Wednesday market. Ramsey also noticed one or two taverns and a small doctor's office. He was so enraptured by his surroundings that he had to order Theron to slow down so that he could get a better look.

"I guess this place looks Okay, Ramsey," said the troll, keeping his eyes on the distracted locals that were gradually abandoning their tasks to watch the strange pair. "I feel a little silly right now, though..."

"Nonsense, you're just a troll. For a troll, you look perfectly normal. Besides, they're all looking at me, not you, so don't worry...hey, look there – I think that's the square, there's a fountain. We had a fountain back in Merlock, but I never remember it working. It's probably been burned down by now, though."

Wanting to avoid any physical assault, Theron briskly followed Ramsey's indication and wandered towards the town square, which he guessed was located more in the north-west corner of the town than in the proper centre. He didn't know why this seemed strange, but from what Ramsey had told him about Merlock, he expected all town squares to be in the centre of their respective towns.

The buildings around the square were taller than the others, and cast long shadows across the grey paving stones. In the middle of the square was a small ornamental fountain, surrounded by several planted apple trees that emerged from the pavement like proud soldiers; they bore green, unripe apples and leaves that swayed gently in the wind. A few wooden benches were arranged around the square in such a way that each one offered a pleasing view of the fountain or the badly dilapidated white statue of what appeared to be a goblin located towards the southern corner of the square, which had obviously seen better days. Some goblins were distributed around the fountain, tossing some spare change into the water, and didn't notice Ramsey and Theron approach from the main street.

Ramsey was amazed at the size of the town, especially as he had expected nothing but wilderness from Grassman Village onwards. There had to be hundreds of goblins living in BlackField. Good, he thought, more people to get housing information from. Thoughts of buying his own secluded property had become increasingly appealing ever since the pheasant-poisoning incident, and he felt that this town was far enough from Merlock for him to be able to settle down happily. At least he could put his mind to rest and stop thinking about Prince Morgan. Great, now he had remembered the name again...Morgan, the kidnapped prince, the final hope for the goblins of Merlockiara.

"Yeah...well, too bloody bad..."

"Pardon, Ramsey?"

Ramsey blinked and shook his head, realising that he had spoken aloud. "Oh, nothing, just thinking...come on, we need to get a better look around, don't we? Let me down, it's too high up here."

Like a relaxed cat, Theron lowered himself onto his belly, his paws underneath his body, allowing Ramsey to safely slide down from his back. The goblin scratched himself briefly, stretched, and gestured for Theron to get up again.

"Come on, we're going to investigate for a while. Stay close, I don't want you getting lost." Theron got to his feet slowly, his brown eyes fixed in Ramsey's direction, but looking beyond him. His face was curious; Ramsey glared at him, then turned around. "What in blazes are you looking at?"

"Look, Ramsey, it's a temple," responded Theron simply from behind him, as the goblin's eyes beheld the form of a tall, stone structure at the end of a short, wide street that led away from the square. "My mum used to tell me about temples, where everyone goes to pray to Lady Scaless, and thank her for all she gives us..."

"Well, how about that?" mused Ramsey half-heartedly. "Come on, Theron, we need to have a proper look around and find somewhere for me to stay. We don't need to go to a temple- hey, get back here!"

Against his orders, Theron was ambling away towards the route that led to the temple. Ramsey knew he couldn't forcibly turn the troll around, and just followed him with a scowl on his face. He hated being small and weedy.

The front of the temple was decked with white pillars and carvings, and the whole structure was illuminated by the sun's rays that streaked through the wispy clouds overhead. There was a small group of goblins in formal wear outside the entrance, but overall there was relatively little activity in this vicinity of the town.

For some reason, Merlock had never featured its own place of worship; something that Ramsey was quite glad of, since he disliked having the beliefs of others thrust upon him. Theron trotted along the street and up the short series of steps that led to the elevated plateau on which the temple was situated, his expression one of mute wonder, and Ramsey trudged behind with his hands in his pockets, glancing at the nearby citizens with distaste. Of course, he disguised his revulsion for these temple-goers with a charming grin, and followed the eager troll with as much composure as he could muster.

Stopping briefly to sniff the long flower-beds that framed the entrance to the building, Theron didn't think twice about heading onwards into the temple, his tail swishing behind him. Ramsey prayed that the troll wouldn't embarrass himself, and hurried after him, passing a goblin with a very holier-than-thou expression, who merely smiled and said that they accepted worshippers of all shapes and sizes at 'The BlackField Church of Scaless'. He found that Theron hadn't progressed much further than the entrance portal, and marched up to him, panting slightly. The troll was gazing up at the vast, painted ceiling with marvel, his face glowing.

"Okay, you can have a look here, but I really need to find a place to stay, all right? So make it brief."

Though it was by no means as large as Merlock, BlackField Town certainly had a lot to offer – not that Ramsey had interest in the temple, but BlackField was a buzzing community of goblins very different from those that one would find back in the kingdom capital. There were no gaudy colours, everything was a pleasing mixture of monochrome shades; there was no town wall that shut off all daylight, nor an imposing castle nearby.

Ramsey's first impression of these goblins was that they were more community-orientated than the Merlock goblins, less stressful, quite peaceful. Nobody had bothered to confront them as they walked through the streets, despite the numerous strange looks they received. He was proud to have made an impact upon them, and hopefully soon he would be staying somewhere comfortable and warm for the first night in ages, eating real food with a roof over his head. He didn't consider what Theron would do in the meantime, assuming that the troll would be content to stay outside.

With a heavy breath, Ramsey moved over to one of the nearby mahogany pews and sat down, too exhausted to remain standing with his heavy backpack. He placed the bag onto the bare stone floor at his feet and leaned back against the wood, keeping his eyes on Theron at all times, to make sure he was behaving. The troll was quietly looking around, his massive bulk appearing out of place in a setting of serene elegance.

There was no carpeting on the floor, and twenty pairs of dark, wooden pews faced the rear wall of the tall room, into which was carved a graphic, two-dimensional representation of Lady Scaless – an almighty snake with feathery 'quills' that framed her cheeks and traversed the entirety of her spine. She was depicted majestically, intertwined between clouds, stars and the moon, and like the rest of the temple, apart from the ceiling, was a combination of white and pale grey hues, etched into milky rock.

The high ceiling of the temple had been painted in a mixture of dark and lurid colours, the bright outlines of blood and fire standing out against the black background. Ramsey rotated his neck to change his perspective as he looked upwards, and decided that the painting showed Lady Scaless in shades of dark green and yellow, surrounded by flecks of red and orange flame, with some kind of battle scene in the far corner, showing an army on horseback wielding spears and Scaless' official banners. Ramsey didn't believe in tales of a massive snake creating Grenamoya Island, but all the same felt that it was a reasonable painting.

Theron, meanwhile, had reached the back of the room, where the stone alter and carving of Lady Scaless were situated. He passed near to a pair of middle-aged goblin women who were sitting in silent prayer, causing them to look up, but did not notice them. He was too enraptured by the beauty and serenity all around him.

There were so many things that Theron had never before seen, and he had Ramsey to thank for taking him beyond the closed-in monotony of his woodland home. Sculptures, paintings and buildings were all foreign to him, but if Ramsey said they were safe, then he didn't mind experiencing them. In fact, it was very exciting – he felt as though his life was starting again, anew and enriched with the culture of the outside world.

He approached the Scaless carving, recognised it as the almighty snake, and lowered himself clumsily to his elbows with his head on the floor, in a four-legged 'bow'. This motion attracted Ramsey's attention, and the second he beheld Theron leaning down with his bottom in the air, he could barely suppress his laughter.

"Troll, what in Grenamoya are you doing?" he called out, leaning forward with his elbows on the back of the pew in front, "Get up, you can come back here later! See if we can find a place to stay, all right?"

Theron was unmoved by his words, and stood from his submissive position of his own accord several moments later, his head still lowered towards the carving, and turned around slowly with a sombre expression. Ramsey saw this and eagerly stood, grabbing hold of his backpack again.

"That's it, come on. No sense hanging around here doing nothing when there's a boy's life at stake, is there?"

With a fleeting glance, he noticed that he had attracted the attention of the other worshippers, and smiled to himself as he waited for Theron to reach the entrance where he was standing. Theron arrived at his side soon enough, albeit somewhat dejectedly, and followed him back into the open air where the sun's glow rippled across their bodies once more.

There was little else in BlackField Town that was of interest to Theron, who decided that it would be least painful to follow Ramsey's plan and stay near to him. For some reason, though

Ramsey decided to journey back through the town on foot, he refrained from trusting Theron to carry his supplies. On the ground, he figured, he would be easier to see, and the townsfolk could get an even better look at him before he found a place to stay overnight.

By now, it was mid-afternoon, and the streets were at their most active; here and there, goblins hurried, or casually strode, in all directions past the duo. Each and every individual made at least a slight inclination to watch them go by. Ramsey loved having the open, blue sky overhead instead of the looming silhouette of a stone wall, and was in the habit of breathing deeply to inhale as much fresh air as possible before he ended up in another claustrophobic environment.

Theron held his tongue and didn't complain when Ramsey selected the Bull's Head tavern for his custom and left the troll outside with no apology. It was an average building in a street of matching houses, near to the southern edge of the town, with a faded sign and a black front door with a knocker that resembled, appropriately, a bull's head.

"This looks like a good enough place to cater for a hero like myself, don't you think, troll?"

"I guess so, Ramsey. What do you want me to do?"

Already halfway through the front door, Ramsey turned around with one hand grasping the door-frame, the other on a handle of his backpack. Unfortunately, his expression was casual and uncaring. "Well, it's good weather and everything, isn't it? Why don't you just stay out here?"

Theron blinked slowly and glanced to his either side. "Here, in the street?"

"I dunno, but I'm sure they won't let a troll like yourself inside. You're too big, to begin with. Try losing a little weight." Theron sighed loudly and nodded, realising this predicament.

"Okay, Ramsey, I'll stay out here. I hope you don't mind if I go back to look at the temple again."

Of course, he could have predicted this request. He smiled falsely and turned back to the doorway. "Knock yourself out," he said, as he slipped out of sight into the musty dimness of the tavern. "Just don't get lost."

Theron stood outside for a while, half expecting Ramsey to re-emerge, then ambled away down the street to the edge of the town where grass and trees framed the last of the paving stones. On their way into town, he had noticed that some of the windows of these houses faced rural Grenamoya at the other side, and he decided that he might be able to see Ramsey through a window to let him know where he was. The goblin didn't come to any one of the tavern's windows, and so eventually Theron lay down on the grass, his head on his paws, and rested his tired body under the shade of a tree.

# Chapter Seven

# Enlightenment

The very second that Ramsey stepped over the threshold of the Bull's Head and closed the door behind him, he found himself presented with a very different world from that of BlackField Town's composed, cultured exterior. The air was thick with sweat and tobacco, and the murky windows allowed scant amounts of daylight to pass through. The hallway was lit by candles along both walls, and consequently was illuminated with a dusty, yellow glow. There was noise coming from every doorway, and goblins passed back and forth between rooms, carrying assorted cargo and plates of food.

Ramsey felt perplexed to begin with, but nonetheless decided that the Bull's Head tavern would be his safest bet for a place to stay. 'Safest' being the operative word. As he strode down the short corridor, glancing through doorways to locate the reception desk, he could have sworn that he heard what sounded like several glass bottles being shattered at once somewhere to his left.

The low ceiling brushed against his wiry hair, so he bent slightly forward to compensate for the lack of space. The carpet was brown, he noticed, and was somewhat sticky to the touch; with what exactly, Ramsey didn't want to think about. He took a deep breath that was heavy with dust and smoke, almost choked, and abruptly found himself face-to-face (so to speak) with a straggly, blue-skinned goblin wearing a thick jumper and a sour expression. Ramsey stopped in his tracks and looked with some deliberation at the short figure, who glared back with an aggressive, almost manic look in his eyes.

"All right, whaddaya want?" snapped the short figure, waving a fan of crumpled menus up at him. "You want ta' stay here? Fine, that's just fine, but get out of my hallway, I've got other people to worry about besides yourself!"

"I-"

"Get outta my hallway, for Scaless' sake, boy!" The menus wafted through the air again, and Ramsey felt his composure starting to slip away. "Yes, yes, we've got rooms, get yourself to the desk over there, but for pity's sake, get outta the way!"

"Okay, calm down, I don't-"

"Get back there!" he shrieked again, his thinning, dark hair glued to his forehead with sweat. "I won't stand for it, get out of my bloody hallway! I've got other people to see to!" Sounds of shattering china and drunken laughter burst forth from a nearby room, and the short goblin seemed to grow madder still before Ramsey's confused eyes. "Argh, see what you made me miss? Get outta my way and over to that desk before I kick ya out!"

With a flinging arm gesture in the direction of an open passageway at the very end of the corridor, the blue goblin marched away through a half-closed door, clutching his menus to his chest. Ramsey watched him disappear into the other room with a hint of apprehension, and shuffled quietly over to the other doorway, holding tightly to his backpack for fear of pick-pockets.

He felt as though his heavy breathing could be heard all through the tavern; his eyes were starting to water, having never before been accustomed to concentrated smoke in a close

180

environment. Through his slightly blurred vision he made his way to the doorway and found himself in a somewhat different room. It still smelled unfavourable, but was brighter than the hallway and had a different carpet – less sticky, Ramsey noted.

At the back of the room, flanked by two large vases of dried flowers and bird feathers, was what appeared to be the reception desk, but otherwise the room was quite bare apart from some paintings and gilded maps that adorned the dark cream wallpaper. The windows were small and rectangular, but somehow provided enough light for the contents of the room to be clearly seen without need for candles. It was only when Ramsey had finished evaluating the room that he noticed the young girl sitting behind the desk with a pen in her hand, and he quickly approached her, though a little wary of how she might address him.

"Hello, um…I'd like a room…please." The girl, pale-skinned with blonde hair tied up in a pony-tail, looked up at him casually with the tip of her pen in her mouth and reached into one of the desk drawers quietly. She fiddled around inside the drawer for several minutes before Ramsey felt the need to speak again, this time more assertively. "I'd like a room, if it's not too much *trouble* for you…"

"Fifteen's free," she mumbled, handing him a brass key with her pen still between her teeth. "Lunch ended two hours ago, dinner's at seven, just go into the restaurant anytime if you want sandwiches. Thankyou for choosing our tavern for your dining and/or drinking pleasure, the customer is always right, BlackField is the town of new beginnings…"

Ramsey took the key possessively and raised one eyebrow, slightly concerned. "…Um…"

With a huff she placed the pen onto the surface in front of her and crossed her arms, a wry expression on her face. "They pay me to say that," she said with a grumble, as though resenting every single aspect of her life at once. "Just 'cause a place got burned down once doesn't make it a town of new beginnings, and just because we say the customer is always right doesn't mean we won't kick you out if you complain."

"Ah...well...thanks, anyway..." said Ramsey, backing away with one eye fixed upon the door. "I'll be on my way now..."

"Out of the door and to your right," she gestured with a flip of her hand. "You can get into the dining room and have some food, or go straight through and up the stairs to find your room."

"Thanks. And, uh...how much does this place charge per night?"

She grinned. "Never mind that. Just wait 'til you're ready to leave, then the boss'll give you a right old shock. Believe me, you don't want to question his reasoning."

Ramsey winced slightly as the sound of high-pitched yelling reached his ears. "Is he the short guy?"

"Yep."

"...Right. I'll just make my way to the...um...I'll be off, now."

With an understandable feeling of peculiarity, he hurried out of the room and down the short, musty corridor, then through another doorway on his right into what was clearly the dining room. Several rectangular, wooden tables sat alongside one another in neat rows from wall to wall, covered with faded tablecloths and each with its own set of salt and pepper pots. At the far end of the room was a vast bookcase, filled with books that dripped with loose, yellowed pages; and located insignificantly alongside it was a worn, brown loveseat with hundreds of faded designs stitched into the fabric.

Ramsey swallowed in the warmth of the well-lit, pale room, his shoulders suddenly aching once more beneath the weight of his backpack. The faint scent of spoiled milk stung inside his nostrils. It was only as he turned his head to wipe his nose that he noticed the other person in the room – only one, another fairly short goblin wearing a heavy coat and nursing a large tankard of something. Ramsey couldn't help but wonder if the individual was feeling uncomfortable in the heat of the room.

To his left, propped up against the wall, was a rack of newspapers (simply entitled 'The Merlockiara Bulletin'), above which was positioned a hand-painted sign that read: 'Free

182

Newspaper – Residents Only'. Well, he had the key to one of the tavern's rooms, and thus he was a 'resident', so he decided to take a newspaper if only to have something other than his island map to read. He noticed that it was up-to-date, with a recent date printed in the top corner, and a headline that read 'Merlock Plagued By Dragon – Burned To The Ground'. Not very imaginative, but still, it might be worthwhile to read.

Disregarding his need for food for the time being, Ramsey sat down at the nearest table, tucked his backpack safely between his feet, and spread the newspaper out on the tablecloth with eager hands and eyes. He scanned the page hurriedly, searching for any trace of his own name in the print, but he was not mentioned. At least, he wasn't mentioned in the headline.

As he could have guessed, the journalist described the 'recent' attacks on the town, the fact that a very sophisticated dragon was the obvious culprit, and that King Viktor had become unwell following the disappearance of his son. And then, at the very end of the headline story, Ramsey came across a couple of peculiar paragraphs. The reporter, working for a somewhat sensational (and not completely factual) newspaper, had a few strange remarks to end her story:

'...citizens have always questioned the rationality of Viktor's mind. After all, we're talking about the same king who never married, then adopted a common boy as his son without giving an explanation for his lack of interest in a wife. Is it just me, or could he have been hiding something from us for all these years? At least now that Morgan is gone, royal officials say, there will be no peasant blood contaminating the goblin throne. As our king has no living descendants, we are left with the problem of who will become king. Who knows, maybe we'll end up with an admirable monarch at last.'

Ramsey pursed his lips, one index finger pressed against the page in front of him. It was astounding that journalists could get away with such slander against the king. It was even more astounding that Prince Morgan was, in fact, not a prince at all. And it had been stated as though it was a well-known fact – Ramsey knew that the Merlockiaran royal family had their share of scandals surrounding them, but this was one rumour he had never heard before.

And it was more than just a rumour, it had to be. Regardless of the fact that The Merlockiara Bulletin was an unreliable source for factual information, Ramsey knew that this was the basic truth.

It made sense: Morgan was slender, handsome and much adored, whereas Viktor was fat, ugly and resented by the general public. Why hadn't he seen it before? It seemed so obvious now…Morgan may even have been adopted from one of the enslavement orphanages that the innkeeper in Grassman Village had spoken of. So it made perfect sense – an adopted prince in a castle near to a village comprised entirely of adoptive families. Well, maybe not every child in Grassman was adopted, but for the purpose of Ramsey's inner-workings, he disregarded those families that had made their own offspring.

"Hey, you!" Ramsey looked up from his newspaper to find himself at eye level with the same short goblin who had shouted at him in the hallway. In the absence of menus, he was shaking an empty fist through the air, and his grey eyes were frantic and wide as though he had just caught someone kissing his wife. "You took one of the newspapers, did ya?"

Ramsey could feel another senseless argument looming. "Yes. It says over there that it's free."

"Not if you pick it up and take it over to a table and sit down like you own the bloody tavern, it isn't!" he shrieked, pointing at the spread-out copy of The Merlockiara Bulletin. "One green scale for the paper, boy, and what are you waiting around for? Food you want, is it? Right, I'll get back into that kitchen and slave away so that tardy folk like yourself can have something to fill their bellies, shall I?"

Ramsey stared blankly at him with both elbows on the table, gritting his teeth silently. The owner smelled unfavourably of smoke and bile. "Don't you have a cook?"

The other goblin's eyes narrowed bitterly. "It's his day off."

"Ah...well, if I can't get any food here, then I'll-"

"Sit back down!" he growled, as Ramsey threatened to stand. "I'll see what I can get for you. Just sit there and don't think about running off without paying, all right? And you still need to pay me for the paper."

Ramsey sighed and complained within his own mind, but reluctantly paid the owner for use of his newspaper. The other goblin quickly took his leave, grumbling out loud, and Ramsey couldn't have felt more relieved to see the back of him. Goblins in BlackField Town had some sort of compulsion when it came to interrupting him in the middle of a sentence.

With a deep breath he returned to his casual reading, turning the flimsy page and setting his eyes upon some new headings. 'Mother seeks compensation for Son's schoolhouse injury', 'Dragons also kidnapped my Child, says Lakeside Town goblin', 'Pedigree Battle – annual Merlockiara sheepdog trials held'. Finally, at the bottom of page five, Ramsey found what he had been looking for – 'Merlock's hero visits Grassman Village'. Ramsey's heart leapt to his throat as he lowered his face to the page for a better view of the small print. His name was written in a newspaper. It was only a short article, but he was riveted from start to finish.

"...Merlock has issued a brave goblin to rescue Prince Morgan..." he mumbled to himself, under his breath so that the other goblin in the room would not hear him. "Grassman Village...local innkeeper claims that the boy, Ramsey, stayed at his lodge overnight..."

A grin played on Ramsey's thin lips as he read the innkeeper's statement about him. As one could guess, it was highly praising, and named him as 'one of the most generous goblins ever to stay in Grassman'. That comment must have been referring to the money he left before departing the lodge; perhaps it had been a little much. No matter, though. He still had plenty of currency left over to pay for food, clothing, free newspapers...

From the remainder of the article, Ramsey discerned that the royal goblins had disclosed very little information about him to the public, which he was very thankful for. True enough, he liked being noticed and revered when he was in the right mood, but all the same he didn't want the whole of Grenamoya knowing his name or what he looked like. If he was easily recognisable, he would not be able to enact his plan of starting anew elsewhere on the island.

Of course, he had other problems that threatened his luxurious, isolated future – namely a big, purple, hairy problem called Theron. The troll may have been irritating, boring company, but he was very kind-hearted and clearly believed the best in Ramsey. It was this fact that made Ramsey feel resentful towards himself once more. It was unhealthy for him to keep turning back and forth within his mind. He knew what he really wanted at the end of the day, and that was freedom, a place of belonging, somewhere of his own where nobody else could hinder him. He would have to discard Theron at some point, in order to achieve what he had always wanted; but the troll's trusting, compliant nature made it harder for Ramsey to find justification for his intent of abandoning him.

He idly flipped through the pages of the newspaper, glancing at headlines but paying little attention to their actual content. In the corner of his eye, he noticed that the other goblin, seated hunched-over at a nearby table, was looking at him. Ramsey didn't know how long the other person had been watching him, but he quickly returned his gaze to the page in front of him, not wanting to attract any attention. The last thing he needed was the focus of an aggressive, intoxicated goblin.

Though he kept his eyes fixed upon the writing beneath his nose, he could feel the other goblin's gaze upon him still. The *clunk* sound of glass being placed upon a wooden surface reached his ears, and he heard the other goblin take in a deep, ragged breath from amidst the heavily-furred collar of his thick coat. Still refusing to look up, Ramsey heard the low rumble of the other's voice at last – it was set at a slow pace, and weighted by drink.

"You're that guy what rode into town on that big, purple thing with horns, aren't ya?"

Ramsey felt obliged to lift his head, though there was still a considerable knot in his chest. He had learned in Merlock that it was never wise to be exposed to drunken goblins; for the time being at least, this one seemed harmless. Ramsey nodded and confirmed this fact, not rising from his seat.

"Weird looking thing, if ever I saw one...huge, purple thing with horns and hair and claws...you'd best keep away from creatures like that, ya know..." The other goblin waved one green hand through the air and slammed it against the table, though the better part of his face was hidden within the hood of his big coat. "I've seen 'em before - great, big trolls that'd swipe your head off as soon as look at ya! But we don't get many around these parts any more..."

Ramsey didn't know what to say, and just grinned silently.

"But you know where ya *will* find them, lad..." he continued, pressing one hand to his chin. "You will find them in the mountains, but they never come down no more...they're too scared to come down the mountain, so you should stay away from there...you're new around here, boy, I can see that...don't go doing anything...stupid or nothing..."

"Okay...I won't." Ramsey would have made another sarcastic comment about mountain trolls, had the situation been more comfortable. The other goblin lay completely slumped across the table surface, his face flat against the wood and the frona fur hood of his coat bristling out in all directions like an aggravated weasel.

In Grenamoya, where the humanity of the fur trade was being debated at the time, you would have to be a very rich person to own an article of genuine big cat fur. Ramsey might have found this interesting if he had been in a good position to steal it, but he really had no taste for fur taken from wild animals – as long as he kept his own skin well intact, that was all he needed. Maybe he could tame a few fronas once he was living in isolated luxury. After all, large animals like fronas, maneries and certain kinds of dragon were becoming increasingly popular as pets for rich people. Failing that, he could play with Theron's mind for a while and tame him instead.

On second thought, Theron was too smelly for Ramsey to want to be indoors with him for more than five minutes. Nor would he want to wear the troll's skin around his neck. Even now that they were many miles away from the so-called 'great forest', Theron still carried the incessant odour of pine-needles, soil and decaying things. Although, thought Ramsey, he would be less irritating company if he was turned into a fur coat.

With a snort and a grunt, the other goblin raised his weary head once more, and looked at Ramsey with a distant, vague gaze, pointing clumsily at him as though trying to summon the power of speech by directing his finger at someone. He remained fixed in this position for a moment or two, deliberating his words; Ramsey just kept still, not wanting to make any sudden movements.

"You know something, boy?" he mumbled, his ageing vision cloudy and dull. "You come wandering around here when there's dragons on the loose…let me tell you something, you need to respect dragons, kid. Dragons made the island you're standing on, so they deserve some damn respect, all right?" He couldn't get up, but shifted in his chair as though it was his intent. "You know something? You're not from around here, are you? Well then, I bet you don't know that this town has been burned down by dragons before. Twice, in fact! What is the world coming to, eh? Mark my words, if there's a dragon about, it's going to burn this place down…"

Ramsey couldn't believe his ears – BlackField was steadily becoming a stranger and stranger community. Every time he encountered someone, he found a new reason to appreciate his own company. At least he was still sane.

A slender waitress skulked past him with a tray of empty glasses, and he took the opportunity to attract her attention and ask for a strong coffee. She instantly responded, with many pleasantries, and Ramsey recognised her as the same girl that he had spoken to at the reception desk – pretty, pale and blonde, now with a creased apron over the front of her dress. Standing near the doorway, also weighed-down with crockery, were two other female goblins, apparently her work colleagues and friends, who shared a giggle with her as she returned to them with her order.

Ramsey paid them no heed, oblivious as he was to the customs of females. He knew he needed something powerfully strong to help him keep his wits, and it had been so long since he had tasted coffee. His latest taste of caffeine had been in the form of dried-out coffee beans from his backpack; all in all, not overly thrilling.

The goblin with the empty tankard had apparently fallen asleep in his seat with his head on the table, and Ramsey knew better than to disturb him. One distinctive aspect of the relationship between goblins and alcohol, far removed from that of humans or trolls for instance, was the way in which goblins had a very low threshold for toxins in the body. With slow-working livers, goblins were less able to deal with high levels of alcohol in the bloodstream; as such, an intoxicated goblin could remain so for days, feel seriously hung-over for longer, and even die from the slightest overdose. Goblin drinkers in Grenamoya were very hard goblins indeed.

Ramsey was more than happy with his black coffee. It arrived quickly, carried loftily upon the silver tray of the blonde waitress who had taken a shine to him. Still, there was no mention of any sandwiches. She lowered the tray, which also held a few dirty mugs and pieces of cutlery, and placed the striped cup on the tablecloth in front of him, along with a bowl of brown sugar-cubes and a jug of cream. He thanked her casually, and set about adding cream and sweeteners to his coffee.

She smiled, but did not move away. She watched him, leaning against the back of his chair with one pale elbow, the broad tray balanced neatly upon her other palm. Ramsey scooped five sugar-cubes into his coffee, stirred it, and lifted the mug to his lips; but before he had even tasted it, he noticed the waitress standing alongside him, her velvet green dress glimmering ever so slightly in the warm light and her long, blonde hair tied up in a tight ponytail with a ribbon of matching green colour.

She smiled lengthily at him, not taking her eyes away from his face as he slowly moved the coffee mug away from his mouth. He blinked. She blinked. For a split-second, Ramsey felt a surge of annoyance, and wanted her to know.

"Stop staring at me like that...!" he growled, mug in hand. "What's wrong with you? Why does everyone in this town seem to have a problem with me?" She wasn't moved by his words, and just smiled more widely at him. "...Why are you staring at me?"

"Why else would I be staring at you?" she replied, laying one pale hand upon his nearest shoulder. "You're really cute. As if you didn't know..." Ramsey hated being touched in any way, and tried to pull away from her, but her grip was strangely tight for a girl, and he couldn't move.

Putting his coffee down on the table (there was no point in spilling it, after all), he yelled at her to let go of him. Contrary to his pleas, she entwined her fingers in his thick, black fringe instead. He struggled, but she clung, and he squawked with embarrassment. She was on the verge of pulling his hair out, and he stood up from his chair in an effort to make her let go. Still she hung on, despite the fact that he was taller than her; she just laid her tray upon a nearby surface and kept a vigilant hold on his hair.

"Ow! I mean it, really, you're hurting me!"

"But you're the first decent man I've seen in this town for so long," she insisted, pinching his cheek with her other hand.

Ramsey snarled and grabbed her wrists, forcing her to let go of him, though he lost several hairs in the fray. He clutched her arms forcefully, staring directly into her face, teeth bared. "What do you think you're doing? You carry on like that for long enough and I'll be bald!"

"But you're so lovely."

She grinned at him, and the other waitresses were smiling in the doorway. Ramsey couldn't have cared less about them at that moment. All of a sudden, without prompt, the blonde girl lunged forward and kissed him on the mouth, and he was so startled that he fell right backwards. He collided with the edge of the table, and suddenly he was on his back upon the tablecloth with the girl

190

slumped over him, having been dragged down with him when he fell. He was about to yell at her and kick her away; but then he saw something he prayed he would never see again.

The girl was a replica of Prince Morgan. Morgan, blond hair, brown eyes, pale skin and soft features; Ramsey had seen the same face littered across portraits all through King Viktor's castle. It struck him like lightning, and with a scream he pushed her away into another table, livid and horrified as though he had seen a ghost. She tumbled against the table, barely catching her balance, and glared at him, her chest heaving and her long hair tousled.

"What in Grenamoya are you playing at?" she exclaimed, straightening her clothes while gasping for breath. "It was only a kiss!"

He was going mad. He had to be going mad. There was no other explanation for it. He couldn't possibly have seen Prince Morgan's face on another goblin's body. Weeks of travelling with insufficient food, water and shelter must have sent him into a spiral of madness. His first kiss from a girl should have been a pleasant experience, but instead he was seeing images of King Viktor's son. He felt utterly foolish, beads of sweat trickling down his face slowly like transparent treacle. He could barely speak.

"I...I'm sorry, I didn't mean to..."

He didn't know why he was apologising. As a rule, Ramsey never apologised to anyone willingly. He felt embarrassed beyond belief, not least because the other two girls, as well as a group of newly-arriving tavern occupants, were staring at him with mixed expressions of shock and amusement. He didn't know where to turn. He could still feel her hands upon him, but this feeling quickly turned into the cold, leaden weight of guilt. He wasn't thinking about Prince Morgan; something in his brain had just tweaked unfavourably for some reason, and left him scared and confused.

From the crowd of stunned onlookers suddenly loomed the short figure of the tavern owner; still as threatening as ever despite his small stature, covered with grey fleece and thinning black hair, a hefty bunch of keys in his hand. He looked maniacal, and swiftly turned his attention to Ramsey's love-interest, who was firmly on her feet, tidying her wrinkled attire. He shouted at her to get on with her job, flung similar threats at all the others, ordered that the passed-out goblin at table seven should be forcibly removed, and mercifully left Ramsey unscathed.

Ramsey couldn't stop his heart from racing. He felt morbidly embarrassed, like he wanted the floor to open up and swallow him as a frog would devour a slug – quickly and with minimal mess. The blonde girl shot him a glance equally embarrassed and aggravated before exiting the room the way she had come, complete with tray. Seeing no reason to abandon a perfectly good cup of coffee, he hurriedly drank it, returned the mug to the table and stashed the remaining lumps of sugar in his pockets.

It was still daylight, mid-afternoon at the latest. He could afford to get away from the tavern for a while. He had barely been there for half an hour, and already he had humiliated himself beyond belief. He needed to get out, into the open air. He could clear his head. He would never have to envision Morgan's mild-mannered, adopted features again.

He hurried out of the room at a brisk pace, though not quickly enough to attract further attention; after a very brief encounter with an angular waiter, to whom he entrusted his backpack to be taken up to his room, he made his way to the black-painted door at the end of the burgundy-carpeted hallway and desperately made his escape into the gently warm climate of BlackField Town.

In comparison with the dull corridors of the tavern, the outside world was overly bright and glaring, so Ramsey shielded his eyes from the sun with one arm until his vision adjusted to the light once again. The heavy door closed behind him with a deep *thump*, and he breathed a sigh of relief, his thin arm still raised in front of his face. His narrow chest was tight and riddled with a tense, hot sensation that he could only describe as an incredible feeling of relief.

Outside the Bull's Head, the town was dark but gentle, entirely chrome shades like an ornate black and white photograph; here and there, bunches of flowers and bright window-boxes

192

splashed colour amidst the grey shades. Back in Merlock, even in Grassman Village, the goblins expressed a specific distaste for flower arrangements, but in BlackField, these bright, living decorations littered the scenery as though they too staked ownership upon the town.

This was certainly a curious settlement of goblins; externally, the town was serene and beautiful, with its own temple and rows of picturesque housing, but inside the tavern, Ramsey found an entirely different class of goblin altogether. Sure enough, goblins in a tavern were likely to be eccentric, but the exterior of the town was far more deceptive than that of Merlock. The Dragon Sword was a rowdy tavern indeed, but Merlock itself was also a disreputable, ugly place. Still, Ramsey couldn't escape the fact that neither Grassman Village nor BlackField Town had any sort of surrounding wall – if only the goblins of Merlock would consider the possibilities achievable by removing the damn thing.

Much to Ramsey's surprise, Theron was nowhere to be seen. He hadn't been inside for very long, and already the troll had taken the initiative to wander off by himself. Having said that, Ramsey could take a reasonably good guess at where he might have gone, and so took a left turn and proceeded back towards the town centre, from where he would navigate his way to the Scaless temple.

\*\*\*

The wind had picked up. Murky clouds danced and dispersed high above the Scaless temple, and parted every now and again to let a brief glimmer of sunlight shine through. It was amazing how quickly the weather deteriorated. Ramsey could have sworn that in the time it took him to walk from the Bull's Head to the temple, the sky suddenly darkened and a complete change in climate occurred overhead. The faint prickle of rain threatened a few rooftops, but it looked as though the worst rain was yet to come.

Ramsey wanted to get indoors before he got soaked and contracted another head-cold, and so hurried along the street with his arms wrapped around himself for warmth, trudging across the damp paving stones and ignoring the muttering comments of those around him as he passed. If there was one meteorological phenomenon that he disliked as much as rain, it was blustery weather.

He leaned into the wind, which was gradually picking up, and one by one the passers-by began to file back into their comfortable houses. It was only mid-afternoon, and yet suddenly the sky was dark and grey. Late spring was an awkward season to be suspended in – not enough sun, too much rain and unpredictable hail and snow on occasion. He was glad that the weather hadn't become any worse. At least, it hadn't done so yet.

The temple of Scaless stood steadfastly in the cold, its slightly crumbled pillars standing up to the harsh gusts with ease. It was tall, white and magnificent like an ivory sculpture against the bleak monochrome textures of BlackField Town, and called out to Ramsey like a beacon through the chilling gales that beat down upon his fragile body. He squinted his eyes against the cold, hugging himself tightly, and made a beeline for the massive specimen of dragon architecture.

The streets were almost deserted now. He shielded himself against the wind and hurried onwards, up the wide steps and past the long flower boxes to the grand, arched entrance. He sneezed into his palms, ignoring the concerned comments from a waiting cleric, and bustled into the temple, leaving the cruel elements behind him for the time being.

He breathed heavily with relief and shook some dampness from his hair before surveying his surroundings; there were additional goblins lining the mahogany pews in silent prayer, and rain gently tip-tapped upon the stained-glass windows, but Theron was nowhere to be seen.

Ramsey ran a hand through his hair, slicking it back temporarily, and slowly traversed the majestic, serene building with his other palm lodged within a pocket. His skin was prickling with goose-pimples, and his eyes felt raw and reddened from the cold air. He couldn't return outside to face the turbulent elements yet. Theron could take care of himself, and Ramsey had no real concern after all. He clenched his teeth as he felt a harsh knot develop in his stomach.

"Oh Ramsey, what in Grenamoya did you do that for?" he hissed under his breath, his thoughts returning to his foolish actions back in the tavern. "There's no doubt about it, you're going mental if you see that kid everywhere you turn..."

He put one hand to his face and clutched angrily at his orange flesh. He felt like such an idiot. Okay, so she had looked somewhat like Prince Morgan, but that was only because she was blonde and had creamy skin. It was Viktor who should have been seeing his son's face on other people, not Ramsey. But she *did* look very much like Prince Morgan...only taller, with breasts and wearing a dress.

"That was the stupidest thing you have ever done in your life, you know..." he growled, his breath tight in his throat. "You've really messed things up now."

Still angry, Ramsey marched towards a nearby sculpture of one of the Great Dragons and sat down upon its base, not caring if it attracted further embarrassing attention. He put his head in his hands, with both pointed elbows resting on his knees, and closed his eyes to think. He had a better chance of hearing his inner voice in this place of peace and solace. He needed to find an explanation for what he had seen. Alas, nothing from within his mind spoke to him, and he hunched himself up in silence, his sharp chin pressing into his chest.

Quietly, and with no hint of invading Ramsey's personal space, a lofty goblin who was clearly a priest of the temple approached him, and stood at a respective distance with his hands clasped behind his back. Ramsey only saw the other goblin's bare feet, and refused to look up. He felt so confused that he could barely make sense of the world around him. Without moving any closer, the robe-wearing minister addressed Ramsey in a soft, baritone lilt, and inquired what was wrong.

"I say, my boy, are you quite all right? You look most distressed all by yourself."

Ramsey didn't reply; he generally made a point of not conversing with religious types.

"I see you have sought the strength of almighty Trahern in your moment of upset," said the other in a conversational manner, though he still did not approach. "Do not worry, my boy. May the enlightenment of the divine Lady Scaless shine down upon you and remedy your problems."

With these words, the cleric made a small hand gesture and closed his eyes in reverence to the statue that loomed over Ramsey. Ramsey looked up at the huge, sculpted dragon above him, seated behind him on the same engraved pedestal. It looked like a run-of-the-mill dragon to his cynical eyes, but it clearly inspired great awe in those who had faith in Lady Scaless.

Ramsey didn't know very much about the complexities of the island's faith, but gathered that the Great Dragons were supposedly the offspring of Lady Scaless and existed to remind the native inhabitants to keep their faith. The other goblin made another hand gesture, and looked upon Ramsey with a welcoming smile.

"Inspiring, isn't it?" he said, motioning towards the statue. "Our carvings of Lady Scaless and the Great Dragons were the only artefacts salvaged when this temple was originally burned down. We lost all our windows, tapestries, and half of the building was destroyed, but nothing could hinder our great lady or her offspring." Ramsey blinked, absorbing the information with a dry gaze. "It just goes to show you that nothing can overcome one's faith," concluded the other, pressing a hand proudly to his chest. "Divinity stands strong in the face of adversity, no matter how devastating."

"Could've fooled me…"

The priest was mildly surprised by Ramsey's response, but clearly was experienced in dealing with individuals who had no faith left within them. He still did not approach, but waited patiently for Ramsey to stand of his own accord. "Everybody goes through times of sadness in their life, son, but that does not necessarily mean that there is nobody in the world who is on your side. And Lady Scaless' love for us will remain, even when we exist no longer."

"Look, why don't you go and preach to someone who gives a damn?" snapped Ramsey, hopping to his feet. "I don't want to listen to this now, I've got too much to think about!"

"Calm down, there is no reason to be angry. I understand that maybe you are not comfortable with discussing how you feel." Ramsey crossed his arms and began to protest. "No, don't worry, it's perfectly understandable. There is nothing wrong with standing out from the crowd and feeling like you cannot belong, but we all belong to Lady Scaless, and at the end of it all, she will always love us and protect us from harm."

"I'd like to know what theory you're basing that on."

The priest looked at him harmlessly; though Ramsey felt angry, he couldn't just march away for once in his life. "There isn't necessarily a theory to the ways of Lady Scaless," he began, after deliberating the answer for a moment. "Theory is for doctors and scientists, but I am a simple man, and I know that Lady Scaless loves all her living creatures because I have faith. Dear boy, I saw you outside – you looked as though everyone in the world hated you. And that is no way to live, I can tell you."

"I hate the world because it seems to have some kind of problem with me!" he exclaimed, ignoring the other Scaless worshippers as they stirred from their silent praying. "Is it so wrong to want to live your own life? I just want to be me, I don't need anybody else, but the rest of the world keeps interfering with me. I want to be left alone, and by that I mean that I don't need anyone preaching the lessons of a gigantic snake to me, either. How can I be a child of Scaless, anyway? How can any of us be? She's a snake, we're all goblins – even the most basic elements of your theory are nonsensical!"

"For Scaless' sake, boy," He made another hand gesture and looked up at the statue of Trahern, the dragon of summer, "not every aspect of our faith is literal. We may have our own parents, and we may not be snakes, but we are still the fruit of the island that Lady Scaless forged out of the earth when the world was new.

Everyone on Grenamoya is a product of Lady Scaless' creation, and we must respect that."

Ramsey seemed unmoved, and he glanced awkwardly at his feet.

"Having said that," added the priest, feeling it would be tactful to do so, "you don't have to believe in Lady Scaless. She loves all of us, from the most holy to the most heretical. After all, my boy, do not forget that her own son turned against her and ruled our island for thousands of years, and even then she loved him and was willing to forgive him. One can only hope that such forgiveness and love will not be wasted upon others."

By now, the other goblins in the temple had stirred from their silent reverie and were craning their necks to listen to Ramsey and the cleric. The topic of their discussion had immediately attracted the attention of everyone else, the words resonating around the walls of the building. Ramsey, a bedraggled-looking young goblin with his stick-like arms wrapped around himself, stood transfixed in front of the robed, ageing priest as one might regard someone who could explain the deepest secrets of the universe. He could still find no rationality within claims of an enormous snake crafting the whole of Grenamoya without the use of limbs, but was beginning to lose his will to argue as the holy goblin elaborated upon the ancestry of the island.

"Okay, so Lady Scaless had a son who ruled our island?" The other goblin nodded wisely. "...I thought her sons were the Great Dragons."

"Zared and Trahern are her two sons who normally bring winter and summer to our island, yes, but she had a third son who...well, he just went 'bad', I suppose." Ramsey knew to expect a long and tedious story when the other goblin took the liberty of sitting down upon a table littered with prayer books; he too sat down, returning to his former post beneath the shadow of the dragon. "Everybody loves to hear a tale, my boy. Surely you won't object if I take the liberty of passing on some of my wisdom?"

Ramsey leaned back against the stony form of Trahern and shrugged. "Go ahead if you like."

"Well then, how shall I begin? You seem to be a bright young lad, I am surprised that you haven't heard more about our island's humble beginnings."

"I don't like to read about stuff that goes against what I believe. I've heard enough about Lady Scaless from far too many people, and the basic information is different each time."

The priest would not be deterred. "Well, surely you will listen to a harmless extract from our native folklore? When Lady Scaless created the island, or so they say, she made a beautiful place for her to rest, amidst the sacred mountains. When she came to rest, and looked upon our humble island with its new beginnings of life, she decided that she would create offspring of her own. Thus, she made a nest at the peak of Scaless Mountain, and incarnated six eggs, which would contain the divine creatures of our island. She decided that they would control the seasons and the elements, and watch over the island that she had crafted. She left the six eggs in safety at the top of the mountain, and departed to form Grenamoya's Great Lakes and the deep forests."

Ramsey drummed his fingers against the stone pedestal upon which he sat. Everyone else in the temple was listening to the cleric's story, somehow uplifted by his words; a strange, nostalgic bliss was plastered across their faces. The other goblin cleared his throat.

"However, while she was away, one of the eggs rolled towards the edge of the nest. The moment it was separated from the others, the very nature that Lady Scaless had created for her island seized it – thorns and brambles entwined around it, clutching it in place as all kinds of crawly creatures infested it. The egg was corrupted, it became blackened and evil."

"Ah...it was an evil egg."

"Lady Scaless returned days later," continued the cleric, regardless, "and discovered that one of her eggs was missing. She found her sixth egg and freed it, and placed it back amongst the others. It wasn't long before she heard the egg shells cracking, and she watched as her five beautiful offspring entered the world – four to bring the seasons, and her pure daughter, Leoma, to govern them.

When the sixth egg hatched, what emerged was a deformed, impure creature. Lady Scaless still loved her third son, but the other dragons never accepted him because he was ugly, and not a dragon at all. He and Leoma were meant to take charge of life and death on Grenamoya, but...well, he took things into his own hands and took charge of the island. And he ruled over us for thousands of years before anything could be done."

"That's because Lady Scaless promised him the island in return for his ugliness!" shouted a middle-aged female goblin wearing a grey and yellow bonnet, who had been listening intently all through the tale.

"Well I heard that Pain loved Leoma and she rejected him," said a teenage boy in the row behind, who was sitting between his parents in the pew. "But why would he have fancied his own sister?"

"Brendan!" hissed his mother, tapping him on the head. "Where did you come up with such a foul idea?"

"Dad said that he heard-"

"I've heard enough!"

Both the boy and his father received a scolding from the animated, portly woman, and the family was soon on their noisy way out of the temple, protesting amongst themselves. Ramsey watched them leave, a slight smirk threatening his expression. What a load of weirdoes. Everybody in the temple had been glued to the story, which no doubt was one that they had heard countless times in the past. Now that Ramsey thought about it, he had heard about Pain before, and recalled reading about how he used to rule over the island. But then again, that could have been another graphic metaphor for the fact that the island used to be a less pleasant place to live...

"And so you see," concluded the priest, his eyes bright, "that is why dragons never hatch more than five eggs. If a mother dragon has six eggs, one will be crushed before it can hatch. Dragons are superstitious, and they don't want another Pain to be born into the world. It's all quite fascinating really. I dabble in dragon behaviour in my spare time, I find it so incredibly intriguing

201

how aspects of the legend are recreated in the behaviour of our modern dragons."

"So, have you ever actually seen one of the Great Dragons?"

With a laugh, the other goblin nodded and crossed his arms, his face mirthfully crinkled with laughter lines. He seemed younger, though nothing of his age was hidden. "Oh yes. I remember once when I was a little boy, working on my father's land in late August. I saw Amelia – beautiful, fiery red and orange and brown, like she had autumn leaves sprouting from her scales. She was the most amazing creature I've ever seen. She swept over the farm, and the air just changed, just like that."

He snapped his fingers and nodded again, thinking back to that magical moment. Ramsey felt a twinge in his stomach. He could remember nothing from his childhood that warranted such a fond expression.

"And the second she was out of sight, it was autumn all around us. The leaves began to change to yellow and brown and orange, like the colours of her body. Autumn became my favourite season from the moment I saw Amelia. She made me realise how incredible our island actually is. They are definitely Lady Scaless' messengers, my boy. They certainly remind me that Lady Scaless watches over us."

Ramsey pursed his lips, moving to stand once more as the sound of raindrops pattered against the stained glass windows. He had been in the temple longer than he intended. "So, what do you think about the fact that we're stuck in late spring for some reason? I keep hearing all this stuff about the Great Dragons going missing."

"I know, son, it is very worrying, but everything will be all right. May Scaless have mercy upon all of us." He looked at Ramsey, his brow lined with the pang of worry, and instead of moving to touch him, he merely closed his eyes and made the S-shaped mark of Scaless in front of him, which Ramsey was thankful for. Finally, an interfering goblin who didn't demand physical contact with him. "You should get home before the weather becomes worse. I hope that I have given you some assurance for the future, and reminded you that a power greater than Pain watches over us. I'll be praying for you, son, and I hope you are able to work through whatever problems are distressing you this evening."

Ramsey muttered a terse 'thank you', and walked past the other goblin in an unhurried manner. Before, he would have felt the urge to escape from the temple as quickly as possible, but something within him was calmer than before. He could honestly no longer recall why he had been so upset. But he was still in a temple, and he felt strange to be there.

It was cold, and Ramsey knew it would be even colder, and far wetter, outside. If only he had thought to buy more clothes; he logged this idea in his memory, and decided to purchase some kind of heavy coat before he left BlackField Town.

As he turned towards the arched doorway, the relatively small, painted sculpture of the Great Dragons above caught his eye – below it was written 'Goblins of BlackField Town – Gone but never Forgotten. May Scaless and her Dragons shield You.' To either side of the statue, in very small writing, was a list of at least two-hundred names, but Ramsey could not read them.

Though not as immense as the other works of architecture in the building, this six-foot tall piece was intricately carved and heavily detailed. The eyes of each dragon were positioned as such that they seemed to follow Ramsey as he moved. He swallowed, stepping discreetly from side-to-side under their collective, frigid gaze. It was as though they were accusing him of something. Maybe they disapproved of him entering the temple when he had no faith in Lady Scaless. No, that was silly, they were just five dragons carved from stone and painted with ordinary paints.

Ramsey was not the type to let religious disapproval worry him, and though the silent dragons stared judgementally at him still, he found composure within himself to take a deep breath and walk past.

***

The staccato rhythm of rain beat heavily against the windows of the Bull's Head that evening. Ramsey sighed and shivered, sitting hunched-over at the edge of his small bed in the dimly-lit room, his backpack and meagre possessions scattered over the only table, near to the misty window. He had picked up another 'free' newspaper on his return, so as to have something to read in bed, but so far hadn't found any more interesting headlines. The ceiling was low, and slanted in one direction so that he could barely stand in the far corners.

He was exhausted and desperate to get a good night's sleep in a safe bed, but he couldn't relax. Every inch of clothing upon his body was damp from the rain, and his skin felt chilled and clammy beneath it. His fingers and toes were numb with cold. The bed he sat upon offered little warmth, and Ramsey knew he wouldn't be able to sleep. He breathed, his chest and stomach rising and falling with a subtle shiver.

Reaching for the clean set of clothes that he had draped over the headboard, he grudgingly got to his feet and began to remove his damp garments. He didn't trust his feeble immune system to defend him against further head-colds.

Quietly easing the unlocked door open, the blonde-haired goblin waitress entered his room unnoticed, as he had opted to face a bare wall while getting changed. The rain, too, had flustered her complexion, and her torso was wrapped up in a thick velvet coat with angora lining. She smiled.

"Hello there again," she greeted, perkily.

He whipped around, his damp shirt in his hands, and hurriedly tried to cover his bare chest with it again. "Hey! What are you doing in here? Didn't you think to knock or something?"

"I just came to apologise for my behaviour this afternoon." Though her intent seemed honourable, Ramsey was not swayed. He pointed to the door and shouted for her to get out. She didn't move. "I want you to know that I wasn't just playing with you earlier. Okay, so my friends gave me the idea, but I really think you're cute, you know."

"Oh really?" he grumbled through clenched teeth, gesturing to the door. "Look, just get out, I don't need apologies. You don't need to apologise anyway, it was me who acted stupid, so let's just forget about it."

She kept smiling and moved towards him, an intent glint in her brown eyes. "Oh good, because I just got off work, and I'm in the mood for some fun. How about you and me go out somewhere?"

Ramsey pointed fixedly at the door, the knot in his chest restricting his breath. "Whatever you're going on about, I don't care, so get out."

"At least let me take a look at your back." With an intrigued expression on her face, she reached out to him. He recoiled from her hand like an insulted snake. "You've got a really sore-looking spot on your back. I can get you some ointment for that."

"I said get *out!*" He took hold of her wrist, and escorted her brusquely over to the door. "Just get out, leave me alone and don't you dare come barging in here again! I need privacy, and if you're just going to come in here and make a joke out of me, you can forget it!"

He forced her out of the door and slammed it behind her, making sure to turn the key in the lock. Gasping, he slumped forward against the door and breathed against the wood. He closed his eyes, unclenched his teeth and huffed to himself. The adrenaline rushing through his veins had heated his body to uncomfortable levels, and the pit of his stomach was churning with anger. He felt so embarrassed; his face was hot and flushed. He heard her footsteps fading away down the stairs.

When he was certain that she was gone, he returned to his bed and changed his clothing as quickly as possible, hanging his older ones over the side of the nearby table to dry out. He fastened his leather belt tightly around his trousers, and began to pace feverishly up and down the room. He felt like a complete and utter idiot. His romantic prospects for the future certainly did not look promising.

With his hands on his hips, he went to the window and stared out through the misty panes at the rain-soaked scenery beyond, distorted by raindrops that dribbled in long streaks down the smooth glass. It didn't look as though the outside world would ever be dry again. The evening had loomed darker than usual, and the grass, trees and fences outside his window were drenched in deep blue, like a watercolour painting. The sky was foggy and nearly black, the only exception being the vast, slate-coloured clouds that gushed their freezing load relentlessly from above.

Scantily sheltered beneath the leafy bows of a tall tree was the equally dismal form of Theron. He lay with his head between his paws, resting on bare mud, and his tail wrapped around his body as a feeble form of protection. He looked completely soaked from head to toe, but didn't appear too upset about it.

Ramsey sighed. Like it or not, he knew what his conscience told him to do. He withdrew from the window and retrieved his dagger from the table; sliding it into his belt (just to be sure), tucking 'The Merlockiara Bulletin' under his arm and pulling his itchy, woollen, long-sleeved shirt over his head, he ambled over to the door, unlocked it, opened it, and made his way downstairs.

# Chapter Eight

# Blood And Venom

Theron blinked back the cold water that ran into his eyes and shook his head, shaking raindrops in all directions. He snorted, and more rain dripped from his nose, so he wiped it with one of his big paws. His body hair was heavy with moisture, and would only become heavier if he stayed outside with no shelter. As Ramsey had said, there was no tavern in BlackField Town big enough for him to lodge in. The rain wasn't too bad. It was only water, and Theron had fought off far worse things than water in his lifetime.

He glanced around at the water-logged fields and glistening houses through the grey-streaked landscape, and wondered where Ramsey was. Of course, he was certain to be inside the tavern, warm and comfortable in his bed. Theron could have tried to stay at the temple, but didn't want to desecrate the house of Scaless by walking in while dripping rainwater. No, he was content outside; his body fat was keeping him comfortable and moderately warm.

As Ramsey's frail, irritable figure came into view, Theron got to his feet and clawed at the ground like an excited dog on the return of its master. Water ran down his purple hair in rivulets, forming puddles at his feet. Ramsey trudged bitterly through the wet, marshy grass, bundled up in heavy, brown wool, and sat himself down in the mud alongside Theron, his knees firmly tucked up against his body. Theron lay back down next to him, his face a sopping-wet picture of joy, and nudged Ramsey's arm with his pink nose.

"Hello Ramsey," he smiled. "Why have you come all this way through the rain? You didn't need to visit me, but thank you."

Ramsey looked less than enchanted by the smell of wet troll, and pressed himself against the smooth bark of the tree, trying to shut out the cold. "You're welcome, just don't touch me."

"Oh, sorry, Ramsey." Theron moved backwards, putting the majority of his rear end in the path of heavy rain, and continued to look intently at him. Ramsey's soaked hair was plastered to his face and neck, with a few random bristles sticking out behind his pointed ears. He looked wholly different with wet hair, although the orange skin and long nose stayed the same. "It's very wet, isn't it?"

"Yeah, well, rain normally is, I'm afraid." He snorted some water from his nose and grumbled, sinking into the itchy wool of his outer shirt. It was too big for him, so he withdrew his arms from the sleeves and wrapped them around his chest once more, still within the relatively warm confines of the thick material. His elbows poked through the sides of the garment in two angular bumps. "Bloody cold."

Theron pricked his ears and glanced upwards at the mottled, unfriendly clouds that hung far above them in the sky, as though waiting for the rain to stop there and then; it showed no signs of relenting, and if anything got a little worse. "Yes, it is cold. At least when I was back in my forest, the rain wasn't so bad. This one tree isn't doing much to stop the rain, is it?"

He sneezed. "Nope."

"I wonder what Prince...uh..."

"*Morgan.*"

"I wonder what Prince Morgan is doing right now..." pondered Theron, still gazing up at the ever-thickening veil of grey clouds. "I guess he's waiting for you to come and rescue him. That will be so wonderful, won't it, Ramsey? Just imagine being all alone with a dragon, and then someone comes to rescue you without you even knowing. I've been thinking," he continued, much to Ramsey's dismay, "that you're doing so much to help the prince, I'm really proud to be coming with you. I've never been on an adventure before. Where are we going next?"

It took Ramsey a moment or two to realise that Theron had addressed him. He cleared his throat. "We're still going east, I think. And...um..." He thought for a moment, trying to recall the bearings on his map of the island. He would have to check once he returned to his room, whenever that would be. Miserable as their situation was, he was rooted to the soggy ground. "And I think we're going north next. I'm really not sure."

"Oh Ramsey, I can't wait to rescue the prince. I want to see what he looks like."

"He's nothing special, like I said; just blond hair, brown eyes, pale skin, a scar on his cheek and a spring in his step, what-have-you..." His words trailed off as he dug his face into the neck of his shirt, and buried his mouth and nose into the sheltered warmth within. He narrowed his eyes against the cold and dampness. "I don't suppose there are a lot of female trolls on this island, are there?"

Theron looked at him with a wrinkled, hairy brow, and shrugged his big shoulders. He was still coated in several inches of mud along his forearms, lower legs and stomach. "Of course we have girl trolls, Ramsey, or we wouldn't have any baby trolls." He stated this as though it was the most obvious response in the world; Ramsey supposed that it was, and conjured up a rather amusing mental image of Theron wearing lipstick and a dress. "My mum was a girl, Ramsey."

"'Course..."

"But since you haven't seen many trolls apart from me, I guess you won't have seen a girl one. They look a lot like us, you know, but they're smaller and they don't have horns like me."

Here he gestured to the two small horns behind his ears; Ramsey slunk further into his woolly shirt, ignoring the rain that still beat down upon them like a bitter, foreboding reminder of what they might face when they reached the nearest mountains. He shivered. Theron shook himself again, sending raindrops flying in all directions and disturbing mud that splattered onto Ramsey's trousers.

"And you know that girls are different from us in lots of other ways, too, but I don't need to go into that."

Ramsey laughed. He was soaked, frozen and muddy, but from the inner-regions of his clothing, he let out a shudder of laughter, though the shudder may have been due to the cold. "Yeah, don't worry, I know." Theron was greatly encouraged by the goblin's laughter, and joined in mirthfully with his own deep, rumbling chuckle, only slightly hindered by the tickling of water in his nose. "*Women…*"

"What about them?" Theron sniffed.

"Some of them are damn near impossible, I can tell you that. You just can't work them out for some reason. I had this run-in with a girl in the tavern, see, and…oh well, stupid girl." It suddenly occurred to Ramsey that he had started to tell Theron about his strange encounter with the waitress, and he felt the urge to change the subject. The troll probably wouldn't understand, anyway.

Theron bobbed his head, as though expecting more to the story, and finally said, "My mum was never impossible."

"She was your mum, though, wasn't she? I'm not saying that mothers are awkward, I'm saying that girls your own age are awkward. The sort that would want to get close to you romantically or whatever."

He blinked at Theron with his head almost completely submerged within his shirt, and realised that he was talking to a purple troll of limited intelligence. He didn't need to discuss the intimacies of the opposite gender with such a creature, and dropped the subject again. Theron clearly hadn't grasped what he was talking about, and wasn't disappointed when the goblin said no more on the matter.

"Scaless, how long is this rain going to keep falling?" he muttered. "We're going to get soaked to the bone out here."

"You can go back inside if you want," said Theron, earnestly. "I won't mind."

"Nah, it's all right...I can't be bothered to go back in. I don't want to bump into that crazy girl again." The rain lashed down upon them with increased ferocity, tussling the boughs of their tree as though it was made out of rubber. "Argh! Damn it!"

Theron shuffled closer to him, so that Ramsey was sheltered between him and the tree trunk, and lay his head down on his paws. He breathed a sigh that sent a cloud of water vapour into the air, which dispersed quickly amidst the rain. His brown and purple hair glistened with accumulated rainwater, and his large nose shone like polished leather. Ramsey shifted, feeling the damp newspaper wrinkling against his side. "Ramsey? If you don't think that Lady Scaless exists, why do you keep saying her name?"

"I don't," he responded, his keen eyes tracing the contours and points of the distant, mountainous landscape.

"Yes you do. You just said 'Scaless' a moment ago."

"Did I? Oh...well, you know, just as a phrase. It's a figure of speech all over this island to say 'sweet Scaless' and things like that. It doesn't mean anything, though. You just pick these things up once you've been in the world long enough." Theron didn't move. "I keep forgetting that you haven't seen the rest of this island before."

"I'm glad I met you, Ramsey." Theron turned his head and smiled merrily at his companion, though raindrops still ran down his cheeks, forehead and nose, causing him to shiver and pin back his ears against his neck. "You're a really nice person, and I think the rest of the island is lovely. It's so green and bright, and the sky...it's wonderful to see the sky. Well, it's not very nice right now, but otherwise I think this place is really pretty. And everyone is so friendly, too. I went for a walk through the town again earlier, and everybody was really nice to me. I told everyone that you and me were on a quest to rescue a prince from a dragon."

"What? Didn't I tell you we need to be discreet if we're going to get to Oouealena alive? For goodness' sake, Theron, why don't you just tell the dragon where we are?"

He held his head. Theron apologised, but Ramsey didn't seem to care. Theron's blabbing, he thought, must have been the reason why that girl in the tavern had found him so suddenly interesting and gone to the trouble of entering his room. She must have realised that he really was someone worthwhile after all, and decided to try her luck again. He sighed and pressed himself bodily against the tree, wanting to shut out all his senses at once and find some way to get to sleep. He still couldn't face returning to the tavern. Theron asked him if he was all right, and he replied that yes, he was. Just tired.

"And I'm not a nice person, troll. I'm not a nice person at all, so be thankful I let you come along with me. I pray you'll turn out to be more of a help than a hindrance."

Theron couldn't understand him. Try as he might, he couldn't analyse his companion, but felt stupid whenever he had to ask Ramsey to explain himself. He moved his paws, which sank further into the marshy ground, determination in his face.

Ramsey was, by now, no more than a brown, woolly jumper with limp arms, two stick-like legs coming out of the bottom and a mess of black hair sprouting from the neck, and apart from his occasional shivering, it was impossible to tell if he was alive or not. Theron looked at him with concern. He didn't know what approach to take with his companion; though it seemed that they had been bonding for a moment or two, that closeness had vanished, and now Ramsey was as distant as ever.

"Just because you don't think you're a good person doesn't mean I can't say you are," said Theron at length. "If you can use Lady Scaless' name as an empty phrase, I can tell you that you're a good person. Everyone is a good person inside."

Ramsey scoffed. "You sound like that priest in the temple. He went on about how Lady Scaless even loves the son that turned against her, or whatever. You're absolutely full of it, troll, and that's fine with me. Just don't try to impose your views on me, limited

212

though they are. I've survived by myself in this kingdom for over six years, and clearly my way of life works, or I'd be dead by now."

Theron shrugged and turned his attention to the sky once more. "Say what you like, Ramsey, that doesn't make it true. If Lady Scaless doesn't exist, how can we exist? And how can the island be real?"

"And how exactly did a ruddy big snake carve this island out of the earth with no hands, pray tell?"

He emerged from his shirt, sprouting bony hands and a pointed face with a familiar wry expression once more. Theron ignored him, his eyes fixed on the clouds, which were gradually beginning to disperse. A few luminescent stars glinted silently in the tiny gaps of clear sky.

"I've heard enough about that snake and her children to last a lifetime, I really have. I don't know why I stood there and let that mindless priest go on and on and *on* about our ancestry when I went looking for you. I guess I was bored, I must have been out of my mind to listen to a word he said."

"You don't have to make a big thing of it, Ramsey, I was just asking…"

He huffed and crossed his arms over his body, trying to ignore the rain, though it had moistened his clothes and made his toes prune. The soles of his feet were slick with mud and grime. "Right, well, don't you forget that I'm managing fine, regardless of whether a big ol' snake made the very island that I stand upon. I suppose I should be grateful to call her my 'mother', because she's the only one I'm ever going to have."

He swallowed. The rain was still stinging in his eyes. There was a brief, though imposing, rumble of thunder in the distance, but otherwise it seemed that the weather was improving. The dark, turbulent sky overhead was gradually clearing, and twinkling stars were revealed one by one beyond the conflicting clouds.

He felt suddenly unwell, and rested his head against the tree bark, looking up at the huge bustle of branches above, which had been torn asunder by the storm so that some now hung treacherously at odd angles, threatening to fall upon them at the slightest disturbance. This made him feel slightly worse.

"…Do you hate me, Ramsey?"

He smiled, though it was something of a grimace as a result of his stomach ache. "Nah…no, of course I don't. Just forget it, troll. You can believe whatever you want, but, like you said, that doesn't make it true. Think anything you like, but don't keep talking about all this nonsense with me, Okay? Don't want me getting upset with you and sending you back home, do you?"

At this, Theron shook his head and promised to agree with any guidelines that Ramsey put forward.

"Great. All I ask is that there be no more of this 'great snake' talk, and that from now on, I decide when we should let others know about our quest. We don't want anyone sending the dragon on our tails, now do we?"

"You don't have a tail, Ramsey."

"I mean *your* tail, then," he retorted with a sigh. "At least it looks like the weather might be good for tomorrow. Damn it, I should have brought the map out with me so I could work out where we're heading…no worries, I'll have a look in the morning. Since it's getting better out here, I might as well stay. Eh, troll? Could you use my thrilling company?" Theron didn't reply. Ramsey resented the pain in his neck as he lowered his gaze with a *crack*. "Oh great, you haven't fallen asleep, have you?"

Theron's head was lifted well above the ground, so that wasn't the answer. Ramsey growled, feeling more than irritated about having to move from his comfortable position, and finding himself unable to move further, stretched out his leg and tapped Theron in the side with his foot.

"Stop playing around!"

Theron lifted himself onto his forelegs, staring out into the distance for a moment longer; then suddenly he stood up and looked at Ramsey, his hairy stomach tangled with mud and grass. "Sorry, I thought I saw something again…"

Unnerved, Ramsey got to his feet also, and shook the rain from his heavy shirt and trouser legs. He looked in all directions with a single, fleeting glance, then fixed his eyes on Theron. "I wish you'd say so! Don't keep leaving me in the dark as to what you're doing, Okay? What did you see? That dragon again? Well, we're miles from your home, and there's no reason why that dragon should be here as opposed to any other corner of the island."

There was a high-pitched, shrieking cry somewhere in the distance, in the direction of the rolling thunder, and Ramsey froze on the spot. Theron leapt to attention, his four feet placed firmly on the mushy ground, scanning the horizon furiously for any sign of movement. The cry had been very distant, and could have come from miles away. There was nothing to be seen, no silhouette, no burst of flame, nothing.

Ramsey couldn't speak, and tentatively backed up to the tree trunk, against which he pressed his body as though praying the bark would ingest him immediately. That sound struck terror in the depths of his body, no matter how distant. Theron panted, his breath fogging up the air in front of his face.

"Ramsey, I think we're Okay. It's very far away in that direction." He pointed with one of his paws towards the nearest mountains, which lay in an easterly direction. "Don't panic..."

Ramsey could feel his heart-beat in his throat, pulsing and constricting his every gasp. He looked wildly in every direction, in case Theron hadn't noticed something important on the landscape, but there was nothing visible, though they could see for miles all around. His chest was so tight that it crushed his lungs. It couldn't happen to him, not again.

"Don't move..." whispered Theron in the near darkness, his bulky form silhouetted against the moonlight, shiny with rainwater. "Stay still, just in case..." He stood before Ramsey, solid and muscular like a shire horse, unmoving, his face directed towards the distant mountains. His sides heaved like a huge barrel being filled to its breaking point. Ramsey could only focus on him; everything had merged into a murky blur. Something inside him said that he would soon have to run for his life.

The island seemed peaceful all around them. There were no birds in the sky, and there was little movement on the ground. The

215

trees swayed gently in the dying breeze, though it was still cold. The crisp form of BlackField Town was barren and icy – everyone was already indoors, tucked-up in bed. The paving stones shone like silver under the light of the moon. The lazy dips of distant hills, and the jagged, lonely mountains beyond, were still and unmoving, as though in a comfortable sleep. Beyond Merlock, the world was beautiful.

Theron swallowed, squinting into the distance. There was something else in the sky. At first it looked like a cloud, but it was approaching too fast to be anything other than a living creature. It moved silently in flight, though it cried out again, and disappeared amidst the remaining clouds above BlackField. Theron was scared, but knew he had to act quickly, and he turned to Ramsey.

"Ramsey, stay here, don't move. I'm going to go and have a better look." Ramsey had pressed himself completely against the tree, clutching the bark with his fingernails, a bizarre look of phenomenal terror upon his pointed face. Theron tried to get his attention, but Ramsey didn't respond to him. He had to raise his voice; he shouted at Ramsey and smacked him on the face, causing the goblin to regain his senses, but also sparking off the attack upon BlackField Town.

Like a seal into the ocean, the dragon dove from the cloud cover and soared above the rooftops. It jerked in its flight, as though looking for something, then turned on its tail and flew in the opposite direction, back over the houses, to begin its assault. With a shriek from the dragon, half-a-dozen houses were ablaze in an instant, and it wasted no time before diving down into the main street, setting the town alight as it did so.

Theron tore away across the marshy field, gushing water and mud in his wake, and up into the street, where tongues of fire already lashed the buildings. He looked around, blood rushing through his body; the dragon was above him, a sleek, green monster with a flared hood of bone along its neck, and fire burst from its jaws in all directions.

Theron couldn't understand it; as with his forest, the dragon seemed intent on torching the area without a plausible reason. It was a mindless, fire-breathing machine. Theron would have tried to fight it, but it soared ever higher into the air, only to swoop back down to earth again, its monstrous head shooting fire like a flame-thrower.

From somewhere to his right, in one of the burning houses, he heard a child screaming. Smoke already poured from the coloured windows like black vomit. With a surge of determination, he barged down the wide front door, which fell easily from its hinges, and forced his way into the burning kitchen. The smell of ash filled his nostrils and stung his eyes. It was impossible to see, but, driven onward by the child's screams, he navigated through the kitchen into a bedroom, where he found a terrified young boy screaming for his parents.

Theron gritted his teeth, feeling sick from the smell, but unwilling to let instinct override his desire to save a life. Already the walls were blackened with smoke, and more than half of the bedroom was on fire, including a tall dresser that was collapsing shelf-by-shelf onto the rough carpet. He picked up the child firmly but gently with his jaws, and though the boy began to scream more than ever, he ran from the kitchen and into the open, fire-ridden street.

Two goblins, obviously the boy's parents, ran to Theron and took the child from him. They thanked him, grimy tears running down their cheeks, but Theron could not wait around, and quickly ran to the opposite house to free a trapped woman who was trying hysterically to break through her living room window. With the sound of hissing laughter, the cobra dragon passed overhead, fire gushing in its wake.

Staggering forward, as though he had suddenly lost his sense of balance, Ramsey made his unsteady way towards the town, his arms out in front of him so that he resembled some kind of orange-skinned, drunken zombie. He didn't know where Theron was, he couldn't see him, and so ambled down the main street, as though blind to the fires that blazed to his either side.

The world around him was frozen, unmoving, though terrified goblins fled past him, parting around him, some almost leaping over him in their panic. Ramsey barely registered them. He was terrified; of all the things, natural and supernatural, on the island, nothing could inspire such primal dread within him as fire.

The sky above BlackField Town was ablaze with streaks of red and orange and black, and the dragon rose high over the flames, its green, serpentine form glistening amidst the smog like a curved arrow. Its vast wings spread across the sky until it seemed to embrace eternity, soaring with silent, horrific grace through the darkness. Its harsh voice struck the air like lightning; beneath it, slate roofs were crumbling in jagged pieces onto the street, showering down upon goblins who could see nothing but the dragon high above. Several were struck down by falling slabs.

Before Ramsey could think to flee, Theron's blackened form burst forth through a flimsy wall, which fell around him, dusting him with clouds of grey dust. He set two small children down on the paving stones, both of which were coughing and smeared with ash; then he darted away down the street, away from Ramsey, and further into the fire.

"Hey! Come back here!" Ramsey yelled, still swaying with the giddiness of fear and confusion. "Come back!"

He didn't know what he was doing there. He should have just stayed by the tree outside town, where it was safer, where he wasn't standing in the middle of a fire. He couldn't turn and run. His brain was overridden with a dense fear that rooted his bare, muddy feet to the spot in the centre of the street, and deafened him to the words of those around him. They shouted at him to move, to save himself and get out of the open and away from the blaze, but he couldn't move.

The dragon danced through the air, whirling through the flames as though in jubilation, caressing the thick smoke with its sinewy, pale wings. Ramsey couldn't fathom a creature more contemptible. He wanted to help, but Theron was gone, and he was too small to do anything by himself. He was too frightened to barge into a burning house. He could do nothing but stand and look in fixated awe at the creature that had destroyed Merlock and Theron's forest homeland, and now was ruining more innocent lives.

Then, as quick as a blink, its eyes were upon him. Ramsey almost swallowed his own throat. The two yellow eyes were fixed upon him, distant though they were, they were aimed directly at his scrawny, soaked body. He trembled, realising for the first time that he was truly alone. Everyone else had long since abandoned the smouldering town, which still crumbled and fell to pieces around him, the flames burning higher with every falling beam and piece of slate. The heat was intense, and he was blinded by the glare.

The dragon's shadow swooped over him, and it fell to the ground, landing several metres in front of him on its four feet like a cat that had been dropped from a windowsill. Its watery, yellow eyes struck him dumb as it reared up on its hind legs, letting out a deafening cry and flaring its striped hood in a challenge. Ramsey was no match for such a creature, and he knew so; he couldn't run.

He felt his jaw drop open, and heat rushed into his lungs. The dragon was huge, towering more than nine feet over him with all four feet on the ground. As it rose its forequarters into the air, coiling its neck and hissing at him, it seemed to stare down upon him from miles above. Its sleek, green and purple body burned yellow in the fierce glow of the fire to either side of them, and Ramsey felt himself fall over.

He was on his back, crawling away feebly from a gigantic, serpentine monster that was certain to end his life within seconds. He could only look up at its slender, gleaming body and colossal bat-like wings, shining against the landscape of fire behind it. It shrieked and, seeing that Ramsey was clearly not able to fight back, made its attack.

Ramsey expected the dragon to burn him to death there and then, but instead the creature recoiled its neck, and with the speed of a falcon shot its head forward, catching Ramsey by the shoulder with its eight-inch fangs. Ramsey screamed more loudly than he thought possible, and flailed helplessly in the cobra-dragon's fearsome grasp. It shook him, and dragged him off the ground; it began to hurl him from side-to-side through the air, its hold tightening on the nape of his neck, and Ramsey felt his body going numb.

The heat of alarmed blood surged in his muscles, and he knew that he was being poisoned. He began to lose consciousness, he could literally feel his brain being tossed around inside his throbbing skull and taste the metallic sweetness of blood in his mouth. The dragon never ceased the relentless torture of its puny victim, shaking Ramsey to-and-fro like a limp and lifeless rag doll.

He struck the ground harshly and felt the cold, smooth paving stones against his skin. He couldn't move, he was certain that he was dead. The terror of the experience alone would have been enough to kill a man. Ramsey opened his eyes; his head felt swollen and bruised, and his vision was cloudy, but he made out enough of the scene to realise that Theron had returned. He saw the troll's bulky form shrouded in the yellow light of flames, dancing back and forth in front of him. He was snarling and slashing at something that hovered just out of Ramsey's sight. It gave a cry. It was the dragon.

Theron leapt at it, catching the creature by its lithe neck and pulling it to the ground, and then he beat down upon it with all the instinctive aggression in his body. The cobra creature hissed at him, and spat a torrent of venom that landed mere inches from Ramsey's injured shoulder. Theron was making strange noises that Ramsey had never heard before; he sounded like a dog or a lion, and roared at the dragon, pinning it to the ground by one of its wings.

The dragon shrieked, constantly aiming futile attacks at Theron. It finally caught him on the cheek with one of its talons, and the moment the troll reeled backwards, it got to its feet and tore away from his grasp. Its right wing was ripped in the process, but in spite of that it instantly fled and took flight, flapping away from BlackField Town with a cry of injured pride.

Ramsey could not feel his body, only his head – the area above his left temple was throbbing painfully, and he felt as though his one eye was completely swollen shut. That was the last straw. He now knew that he officially had the worst luck in the whole of Grenamoya. The dragon had chosen BlackField Town as a target, then honed in on Ramsey himself, and now he was injured again. Could he not spend one day in his life without getting hurt?

He shuddered, still cold and wet, despite the heat of the fire that still burned. He could feel blood trickling down the inside of his shirt. This was it. He wasn't dead now, but he soon would be. With an agonised gasp, he closed his heavy eyelids and prepared himself for death. It shouldn't happen...not like this...

Though Ramsey felt the world slowing to a stand-still, Theron reached his side in a split second, blood trailing through the fur of his right cheek. He had a deep gash running beneath his eye, but apparently was not aware of it, as he instantly began trying to revive his companion. Ramsey didn't get up. As far as he was concerned, it would be safer to stay still and wait to die. Theron wouldn't give in.

"Ramsey? Ramsey, speak to me! Get up, please, get up!" He pressed his nose against Ramsey's damp face and nudged him once, then a second time, more forcefully. "Ramsey!"

The goblin murmured slightly, but didn't move. He didn't even open his eyes. Theron looked around desperately for anyone who could help, but there was nobody left in the town; all had either fled the area or been burned to death in their homes.

The air was still murky with smoke, but the wind had picked up, and was dispersing the odour across the nearby fields. A slight, stinging rain tickled Theron's nose. He sniffed, and looked down at Ramsey as though he was the only thing that mattered in Theron's whole world. He nudged him again, then lay down beside him on the wet paving stones and rested his head next to Ramsey's pained face. The goblin, though chilled, was still alive, and had a visible, fast pulse.

Theron needed to try something, anything possible to save him. Mouth-to-mouth resuscitation would have been impossible due to their size difference, but Theron still knew how to bleed a wound to remove poison. Ramsey's thick outer shirt was already stained dark with blood, so Theron could only guess at the size of the injury.

Suddenly motivated by desperate hope, Theron held Ramsey's torso with a paw and used his teeth to lift the thick, woollen shirt over the goblin's head. He set it aside, and readied to inspect the wound, exposed by the open neck of Ramsey's purple inner shirt.

To his surprise, Ramsey had taken very little damage in the attack – it seemed that the majority of the cobra dragon's grasp had been on the heavy material of Ramsey's outer clothing. Ramsey had sustained a raw cut to his left shoulder, and it still bled dramatically onto his chest and clothing. With any luck, the dragon had not injected much venom into the skin, and Theron quickly set about deepening the wound with one of his teeth, causing it to bleed more than ever. Ramsey winced and tried to turn over, but Theron held him steady.

"It's Okay, Ramsey, you're going to be all right. Don't move, I will look after you…" He bit into Ramsey's shoulder again, and the goblin squealed. "Sorry, but I'd rather you be in pain than be dead."

"I'm going to die, troll, leave me alone…"

"You are not going to die, I'm going to help you."

Theron pinched Ramsey's shoulder between two of his claws, and more blood, slightly darker than the rest, oozed out. Ramsey writhed and complained, but Theron persisted in holding him down, and did not yield until he was satisfied that Ramsey's heavy bleeding had surpassed the amount of venom in his system. He had never known a goblin to bleed so much, and he had certainly seen goblins bleed in his lifetime.

He lay beside Ramsey in the abandoned street, surrounded by the burning remnants of houses, until at last the rain returned and gradually doused most of the flames. There was nobody else to be seen for miles. Theron guessed that they had all run for safety when the dragon attacked Ramsey, but where they had gone, he could not understand. The fields were bare as far as he could see, and no living creatures, apart from himself and Ramsey, remained in the town.

Next to him, curled up on the smooth, stone slabs, Ramsey stirred slightly in haunted sleep, occasionally muttering to himself in mumbled tones. Theron watched him, and draped the woolly, brown shirt over his small body, to shield the goblin from the worst cold. With a sigh, he crossed his arms and lay his head down upon them thoughtfully, blinking quietly into sleep. He knew that they would be safe for the time being, as the burnt-out shells of BlackField's houses served as a protective barrier around them.

The dragon was long gone, and it was too late, or indeed too early, for them to journey on. They would wait until it was light, and they could travel more safely. Near to Ramsey's sleeping form, caked with ash and soot so that it was barely recognisable, the painted, wooden sign for the 'Bull's Head tavern' lay insignificantly amongst the rubble.

***

At the first sallow light of dawn, the two travellers abandoned BlackField Town, which remained black and brittle, like the broken skeleton of a great dinosaur protruding from the ground. Ravens had already perched there, and pecked away sombrely at whatever remains they could salvage in the coating of ash that choked the streets.

The entire expanse of the town had been levelled and destroyed in a single night, apart from one particular building, the Scaless temple, which, though it was missing a wall, was the only structure left standing. It hadn't been burned, but the cobra dragon had clearly been intent on breaking it down by force. Some of the larger stained-glass windows had been shattered.

Ramsey was still weak, but extraordinarily lucky to have survived overnight. The dragon's deadly fangs had pierced right through his shoulder, and injected their poison into the material of his shirt. There was seemingly no trace of poison in his body, but he was still fatigued from blood loss, and though he could barely sit up, he made no secret of the fact that he resented Theron's blood-letting actions from the previous night.

Theron accepted Ramsey's anger without complaint, as was his manner, and continued onward beneath the first glow of morning, heading in the direction of the mountains with Ramsey's listless figure sprawled on his back. The lanky arms and legs swayed gently with Theron's every step, and once more wrapped up in his outer layer of brown, blood-stained wool, Ramsey began to realise how miraculous it was to be alive. Anyone else on the whole island would have been killed by such an assault, but he was still there, traversing the kingdom on the back of a big, purple troll. If he had stayed in the tavern much longer, he could have been burned to death as he slept.

There was something altogether strange about his persistent bad luck but inability to die. If he was dead, he wouldn't have to deal with the dilemma of escaping Theron's attention as soon as possible. For the time being, he was too exhausted to move of his own accord, and closed his eyes as he bobbed up and down on the troll's back.

Ahead of them, the sky was paling gradually, and night succumbed to the warm breath of the new dawn. The stars faded into nothingness, falling away behind the murky, ragged shadow of the mountains. These stretched up to the clouds like clutching, haggard fingers, flanked by mist that shrouded the more distant peaks from view. Theron turned his head and gazed northwards; there were mountains in the north, too, but they were even more distant than they had seemed from BlackField Town, and were merely irregular, grey points that flecked the landscape beyond the rolling hills and forest.

He snorted and pressed onwards. Without a map, they had no way of navigating the island apart from Theron's own instinct, and so he continued in a north-easterly persuasion, towards the mountains. They looked threatening, and Theron knew the dangers of travelling across mountain ranges in the area, but he distinctly recalled Ramsey recommending that they travel this way, and so, confident that he would be better able to challenge the dragon at high altitude, he trotted onwards.

Ramsey slept for the majority of the journey, weakly gripping Theron's mane with his head nestled between the troll's shoulder blades. His skull was throbbing so dramatically that he could hear the swelling and pulsing in his ears, and his whole body felt utterly shaken and dislocated. He hadn't broken anything, but all the same he couldn't have felt much worse. He hadn't had enough sleep to satisfy his exhaustion, and flopped around like a fish whenever Theron made any harsh movements.

The troll was well aware of his sore passenger, and moved as smoothly as possible to avoid keeping him awake. He rose to the top of a broad, green hill, and cantered down the shallow slope with an excited spring in his step. They were both free, they were alive, and they had almost left the kingdom altogether.

Daffodils bowed in his wake, though he took great care not to tread on them, and the grass beneath his paws released mild sprinklings of dew that moistened his toes. The air was cold and revitalising in his vast lungs, and every paw-print brought them closer to the next stage of their journey.

At the edge of a shallow, grassy ledge, in clear view of the mountains and the morning sky beyond, Theron finally stopped to rest. He had not slept well that night due to watching over Ramsey until dawn, and had been unable to gather much sleep in recent days, even before the dragon reappeared and struck new fear into their hearts.

It took a great deal of energy to manipulate his heavy body, and so he wearily laid himself down on the grass, near to some scattered clumps of white flowers, to rest his muscles and close his eyes, if only for a moment. Ramsey was somewhat perkier by this time, and had regained the use of his legs and arms, not to mention his mouth. Theron was so overwhelmed by sudden fatigue that he didn't even care what Ramsey had to say, and he had only laid his head down for half a minute before he drifted into sleep.

Ramsey could do nothing to stir him. With a sigh, and a stretch to test out the function of his limbs, he leaned against Theron's large ribs, looking out over the green landscape. In the direction of the mountains, which were seemingly many miles away, the greenness gradually merged into brown, and then from brown into grey, where the peaks stuck out from the earth like daggers. They were tall, indeed they pierced the sky, and were decorated sparsely with clouds, but Ramsey knew that more fearsome mountains awaited them in the north. Which was why he didn't intend going there.

Something in his memory echoed a lost fact about these nearest mountains, and he remembered that they had planned to cross them and continue northwards from there, but the more that he thought about it, he realised that these mountains offered him the perfect location to live in isolated comfort. He could live at the top of a mountain where nobody else could reach him.

Then, with utter dismay, another fact came to mind – he had no money. All of his money had been left in his room at the tavern...all he had to his name were the clothes on his back, his jewelled dagger and a soggy, smeared copy of 'The Merlockiara Bulletin'. He felt sick to his stomach, his whole body convulsed with desperate frustration. Why hadn't he thought to take the money with him?

He shuddered and dug his fingers into his scalp, scolding himself for being so foolish, but though the bile rose in his throat, he couldn't vomit. He had nothing in his stomach. He smacked himself on the forehead and gritted his teeth, as tears streaked down his face, dark with grime. He collapsed onto the grass and cried with appalled devastation, his hands over his eyes, and he stayed this way for several moments before he managed to stop shaking.

Nothing could ever compensate for the loss of so much money; without it, he couldn't be independent in the way he dreamed of. The front page of his moist newspaper was smeared beyond recognition, and he was certain that a stubby, ornamental dagger would do very little good against a nine-foot-tall cobra dragon. Even his clothes were unsatisfactory. If he had known that all his other clothes would be burned, he wouldn't have decided to salvage a bright purple shirt and green trousers with an itchy, brown jumper. He felt like one of Viktor's nonsensical escorts when he looked down at the colours he was wearing.

Theron was asleep, and snoring gently with every rise of his rib-cage. Ramsey sighed and pulled his newspaper from beneath his shirt, flattening it out on the ground in an effort to discern some of the words. He turned the pages, and found that some were more water-logged than others, and that a few were still readable on close inspection. He placed his nine-inch dagger on the newspaper in front of him and looked down at it, as though trying to work out their location on an invisible island map. He spun the dagger around like the point of a compass, and rested his chin in his hand.

"I'm not well..." he mumbled. Theron snorted and opened his eyes. He looked plaintively at Ramsey, still with the vagueness of sleep in his face. "There's something wrong with me. Every time I get hurt or get scared, I can hear people talking to me who aren't really there. I can feel...people touching me, and hurting me, and I can never tell who they are, except my dad..." Theron mumbled, and Ramsey took this as an indication that the troll could hear his words, though his eyes had closed again. "I started telling you about that girl in the tavern...when she was near me, I could see Prince Morgan's face on her body, and I panicked. I felt like a complete idiot..."

"Mmhmm..."

Ramsey looked at the troll, whose ears seemed awake though his eyes remained closed. "I thought I was going to die back there, I'm sure I would have been dead if you hadn't come to help me. But really, I'm not well, I'm sick, and I'm getting sicker. My body can't take much more of this adventure. I didn't believe it before, but that dragon must have followed me from Merlock...one look at me in the town and he singled me out from all the others...I'm sorry, but I can't keep this up, not even for a prince." Theron stirred slightly, and nodded against the grass. "Before all of this happened, I was fine, I never had hallucinations or anything. Now I know that I'm going crazy, and more than anything, it *frightens* me."

"Mmmph..."

"I heard them again last night, after I hit my head...I heard them, and then I know I heard my dad. I can remember him just enough to know his voice, troll, but I don't know what he said." Ramsey held his head and took a deep breath, as though a painful weight was being lifted from his soul. Theron listened, but he did not register the words. Ramsey could feel his eyes stinging again. "I

227

need to know what's going on in my head, and to do that, I have to be alone," he explained, his gaze constantly upon his companion. "Away from you and this quest, I might recover my health, and that is what I really need."

Retrieving his weapon and newspaper, Ramsey stood shakily, still somewhat stiff, and panned the whole of the landscape with his bright, tawny eyes. Birds were gathering on the horizon beyond the mountains, speckling the amber sky with a flurry of buzzing outlines that danced in unison this way and that. He looked at Theron, who was blissfully ignorant in his sleep, swallowed to clear his dry throat, and ambled away down the side of the shallow cliff, possessions in hand.

The sky was brightening, but Theron did not stir. Still with a slight limp in his gait, Ramsey navigated around the broad ledge, dropped a little way to the ground below, and strode on towards the mountains alone.

***

At the peak of Scaless mountain, from the broadest window overlooking most of the island, Pain still watched, unflinching, his expression rarely changing. The island definitely had a different aura to it now. There was movement of some sort to the north – his kingdom of Utipona in the south remained as frigid and threatening as ever. Pain loved the island as much as he hated it, and the mere thought that it would soon all be his once more sent shivers through his body. Cold, like slivers of frost.

The sky was darkening, as the clouds gathered over the sunset in the west, and he watched in quiet meditation. His body was beginning to relax again, though he knew it would not be for long. It never was. Something always interrupted his thoughts. The current interruption made itself present in the shadows behind him, and something of a smile crossed his face.

"What is it now? What news have you?" Pain turned his daunting, four-legged form in the direction of the nearby life-force,

228

and clacked his claws against the marble. "Has there been any word on this movement I feel in the north?"

From the shadows stepped a humanoid creature, his skin a mangled texture of muscle and tissue, like a human being that had been turned inside-out. His form was that of a man, over six-feet tall, and in a constant slouch. He was unclothed, and somewhat reptilian in his grim, fleshy face. Small spikes protruded from his body in various places, and beneath the skin covering his large skull glowed the murky, yellow hue of a pulsing, turbulent brain.

Pain looked down upon him expectantly, somewhat patronisingly, but though he treated the creature harshly, he relied on him as much as the island relied on the Great Dragons. This man-thing was Pain's window to the intimacies of the outside world, his informer and confidant, his ever-reliable source of information. The creature wrung two large, long-fingered hands together, and looked up at Pain with a pair of alarmingly brilliant purple eyes.

"Sir, I believe now would not be the best time to initiate my plan of infiltrating the collie's inner-circle. They are still too strong, and on constant guard. I shall wait for an opportunity to act, but until then, I cannot advance with that angle of attack." As he spoke, fine dribbles of bloody saliva fell from his lips. Pain whipped back towards the window, as though searching for a distant signal.

"Very well, Ulyssis, whatever you feel is best…but what of this activity in the north? Tell me this instant."

Ulyssis crossed his sinewy arms and flared his nostrils. "Kamror the Nefarious has bade his son kidnap the heir to the Merlockiaran throne. The whole kingdom has closed itself up, and a rescue party has been sent north to retrieve the prince. I believe this serves as a sufficient distraction for us to make further progress in Utipona."

He spoke matter-of-factly, though with a slight dribble – but inside he seethed anxiously. He wanted Pain to make his take-over as soon as possible, so he could see some action at last, but the porcupine would have none of it. Pain nodded, and snapped harshly.

"Then get yourself back to Utipona and inform me of our development. Get messages to Kamror, Kaena, Valdemar and Zoomana to keep guard of themselves. We shall make our move soon enough."

Ulyssis the man-creature nodded and bowed low, then approached the wide window-ledge alongside Pain, gazing out into the night. He gripped the surface, took a deep breath, and hunched himself over with a grunt. Pain gave the impression that he wasn't looking, but he watched his informant in the corner of his eye, curiously. The other creature's abilities never ceased to impress him.

As Ulyssis stood, gripping the marble, his whole fleshy body began to writhe and pulse with energy. He started to pant, his long tongue lolled from his mouth, and he gasped in agony as his body began to change form. He arched his spiny back, his flesh-coloured body began to turn green, two of his sharp ribs broke away and formed bat wings behind his arms, as his already reptilian face elongated into that of a dragon. He howled and snarled as he transformed, and part of the windowsill broke away beneath his claws, but at last there was an elegant green dragon standing alongside Pain, with only a hint of agony, and eternally stunning eyes.

As though nothing had happened, Ulyssis climbed up onto the ledge and swept downwards over the mountain peaks in a perfect mimic of a dragon's flight. He flew silently away into the night sky, ducking and diving amidst the clouds – at last he vanished. Only a slight, swirling distortion of the clouds remained to show that he had passed by at all.

Pain exhaled and bowed his head, staring out at the rain as it fell down and down through the sky, over the mountains below, until it disappeared completely from view amidst the fading mists. Even a cursed being like Ulyssis could have the freedom of a dragon in flight. Pain knew he would never feel that for himself.

How he envied that wretched shape-shifter and his freedom. Pain would normally do away with anyone who displeased him, but Ulyssis was invaluable to him, and he knew it would be a very, very

230

long time before another human decided to sacrifice themselves to an eternity in his service. He often did not keep Ulyssis in his presence for long periods of time, because company other than his own tended to make him angry, but still, the 'non-human' had his uses. Hopefully those errands would keep him busy for several days at least. Pain knew he should try to get some rest.

Something in the back of his mind jolted to life suddenly. He froze in mid-step, and craned his neck upwards. It was as though a new section of his brain had been switched on. He pricked up his ears; he could hear nothing, but he could feel it.

*There's someone here...*

He returned to earth quickly, and, with silent, creeping motions, he hurried out of the room in the direction of the disturbance. He could sense a solitary presence in the temple other than his own; he could feel it, sense it and smell it, almost taste it, but he did not know what it was. He was alone. Ulyssis was already gone. He knew he would have to investigate himself.

With fevered caution in every step, Pain deftly descended the curving staircase, ignoring the flickering streaks of rain outside, which had dampened the steps through the tall, uncovered windows. He moved so quietly, so stealthily that it was hard to believe a creature so large could creep in such a way. There was at an element of dark enchantment in his motions, as he remained entirely undetected, and utterly dangerous.

As he neared the bottom stair, he saw the creature whose presence he had sensed upstairs – a slender male elf, decked from head to toe in green and brown, was dismounting from a large, agitated grey griffin, which stamped its claws on the marble floor as its handler made futile attempts to soothe it. Neither elf nor griffin noticed Pain, who remained stationary in the archway like a living nightmare, his eyes dark and gleaming dully like unhealed scars. The crest atop his head bristled in the breeze that invaded the arched windows. He retreated as the elf moved away from his feathered, storm-like steed.

"You stay here, all right?" the elf asserted once more as he turned. "Don't worry, I won't let anything happen to you. I will return shortly, I promise."

Pain shuddered, peering through the passage at this sleek intruder, his whole body out of view. As the elf advanced, Pain moved further away, back up the stairs, making sure to keep out of sight for the time being. He didn't seem to be armed, but Pain knew that elves were all too often surprising, and didn't trust his judgement. It made no sense sending a single, unarmed elf to the temple, when surely the island leaders already suspected that he was there.

Of course they would know he was there. Pain may have hated them, but he knew they were not stupid.

The elf continued his vague inspection of the main chamber in a rather wistful manner; he did not approach the corridor, he didn't even seem to know what he was looking for. He tidied his autumn brown hair with one hand, bending to inspect a piece of broken marble on the floor.

Pain gasped, trying to hold his breath in. He could see the elf clearly, but something inside him was strangely frightened. He wasn't scared, he knew that he could handle anything Grenamoya had to throw at him. He didn't know why his heart was pounding in his thick chest. The elf was still crouched on the floor, examining the loose chips of rock as though he had come with the intent of refining the architecture.

*Ulyssis, get back here now. We have an intruder. Don't question me, just come back here instantly.*

Pain swallowed; he felt Ulyssis' mind churning within his own brain for a split-second, and scowled.

*Don't ask questions, just get back here, damn you…*

The elf looked up suddenly, as though he had heard something. Pain slinked back silently, his breath cold in his throat. The elf stared questioningly at the carved doorway for a moment or two, noticed that it led to a staircase, but didn't see anything suspicious. He just knelt back to the ground to examine the fairly large chunk of marble that had come loose from the ceiling. It wasn't a good sign, as the Great Dragons always kept the temple in perfect condition.

It is just as Lord Elwin told us, he thought; something destructive has manifested itself here.

He ran his deft fingers over the marble, and, to his great disgust, found that it was splashed with blood. Instantly, he dropped it to the floor and wiped his hands on his tunic, backing away as though the blood had bitten him. His hair fell in messy curtains around his face.

"Scaless above..." he gasped, his voice as frail as the rain that pattered against the temple walls. He stood like a pale child, wrapped up strangely in suede and satin, as he craned his neck towards the ceiling; his body jolted, and he wanted to run, but he could not move, or even make a sound.

Above him, strewn randomly across the marble ceiling, were what looked like bloody egg sacs, blistering and shining putridly with clotted, red fluid. They took up all the corners of the ceiling, some in the middle, and more stuck to the indents where the walls joined the roof. There were about ten in total, and the largest, situated right over his head in the centre of the ceiling, was glistening, bulbous and dripping pale globs of blood. Many dangling tendrils of what looked like bloody glue hung precariously over his head.

Too appalled to remember where he was, the elf stumbled backwards, his eyes locked upon the huge growths on the ceiling. They seemed to be alive, but it was impossible to tell. The griffin, its attention also drawn to the bloody, tumour-like infestations, began to screech and rear up wildly, threatening to tear off through the sky with no heed to its rider.

"No, Dancer, stay!" he commanded, though his voice was still weak and ailing. "Do not panic, I say! Hold yourself calm!" His words did little to placate the griffin; it continued to writhe and yawn agitatedly, but something overcame it in an instant and rendered it silent, as though its voice box had been plucked from its throat. The elf held up his hands towards it. "Be still...!"

The griffin didn't look at him. Instead, it gazed fixedly at something beyond him, its beady golden eyes gawking like an owl's. Pain hissed quietly, lurking at the bottom of the staircase, invisible like a murky shadow; the elf still didn't see him. Pain's brain seared angrily. Ulyssis should have returned by now. Transfixed, the elf squinted towards Pain, apparently blind to his presence, and began to creep forward, reaching into his tunic. The griffin made a sound like a beaten dog, and backed away through the temple entrance with its wings folded submissively at its sides.

"...H-hello?" he called out, now brandishing a pair of attractive knives that he had concealed about his person. "If there's somebody there...show yourself...!"

His voice was even more strained now, barely strong enough to penetrate the air in the chamber. Pain snarled, his brown eyes fixed upon the elf – though standing mere feet away from him, he knew that the elf could not see him. He kept silent, lurking just beyond the doorway with his tail coiled around his body. His quills clattered together like curved, black swords.

"Who is it?" squealed the elf, jumping at the sound. He approached the archway, leered through it for a moment before turning away, and went hurriedly to the adjacent window. He obviously knew that Pain was there, though he could not see him. He had a job to do, he needed to find evidence of Pain's presence in the temple, and he certainly had, but he was too terrified to fight.

He jerked away from the window and called out to the griffin that he expected to see waiting for him at the main entrance; to his horror, he found that the eagle-lion hybrid had vanished into the swirling rain. His mouth fell open, his knives clutched tightly in each hand.

"Dancer!" he called, but he was answered by silence, apart from the constant crackling of rain against the temple walls. He cried again and moved to run to the entrance, but before he could move any further, a huge, black club of knife-like spines struck him from the side, and his body was smashed into the wall; great, blood-laced quills stuck through his flesh, pinning him to the cold marble.

His head hung limp and rested on the shaft of one ebony quill, which dug brutally through his slender throat.

Pain finally breathed. His raspy breath echoed through the chamber as he wrenched his tail free from the wall, leaving many quills still embedded in the blood-soaked stone. They would grow again. He backed away, admiring his work, watching as the fresh blood ran down to the damp floor and transformed the marble into a mottled, crimson watercolour painting. His paws washed the blood and water and swirled them into strange shapes on the ground. He looked at the blood, his hairy face pensive and unfazed. In a second, this neutral expression had changed to one of deep anger.

"I told you to come back instantly!" he barked, not taking his eyes off the gory new addition to their wall. "What does 'instantly' mean to you, Ulyssis? I was waiting for you to return, but I don't need you now. I took care of our visitor myself."

Ulyssis, once again in his semi-human form, soaking wet all over, approached his master and heeded the bloody display of the elf with sword-length spines slicing through his body like knitting needles through a fleshy pin-cushion. His pus-coloured brain throbbed and swelled from within, as though his thoughts were determinable from outside. "You most certainly did, sir. What was his business here?"

"I suppose he was one of Elwin's scouts. That elf is just the sort to send others to do his dirty work, to determine if I've taken up my base here. Well, there's one scout, at least, who won't be returning home with an answer anytime soon."

His mouth curled up into a sharp-toothed sneer, and he cackled like a crocodile; though it was not an absurd, maniacal sound, but a cruel, calculated snicker of laughter that unnerved Ulyssis still, after more than eight-hundred years in his service. Ulyssis trembled slightly with the cold, and sank into himself like a limp rag, still looking at the mangled elf's corpse. It seemed to twitch before his eyes. Pain noticed Ulyssis' silence, and glanced down at the man creature from his great height.

"That is something you can do for me...go to Hanyaliamaya and pay a certain King of the Elves a little visit. It has been rather a long time since the two of you got together, hasn't it?" Pain said this with an amused sneer, but Ulyssis looked up at him with a mixed expression of anger and tiredness. His purple eyes gleamed, reflecting the blood that cascaded down the wall.

"What would you have me do?" he asked at last, staring directly into Pain's dark eyes. Pain could read Ulyssis' feelings in his eyes just as well as he could read his thoughts in his mind.

Psychologically linked, Ulyssis' life-force and power tied to Pain's own, they shared more than the temple in which they lived. Pain could speak into Ulyssis' mind as he could to any living creature; but his link with Ulyssis was far stronger, the mutual wounds more deeply cut.

Pain had been near powerless when Ulyssis was a young boy growing up in Kinmerina, one of the island's north-eastern kingdoms. The fresh, angry soul had been Pain's vehicle for re-establishing his power, which he transferred onto Ulyssis, giving him immortality in exchange for his undivided lifetime servitude. Ulyssis had gained power beyond his wildest dreams; he could change his form into any living thing he desired, he could summon powerful magic out of thin air, he could sense how his enemies were going to move before they did so.

As part of their bargain, although Ulyssis was immortal, he was not actually alive. He was not immortal like Elwin, who was very much alive and would live forever unless killed; he was a by-product of the black magic Pain originally used to create his armies of vampires when he ruled over the island. Ulyssis was 'undead', like Terak, the vampire lord of Xavierania. Unlike Terak, he was part of Pain's psychosis.

Whatever Pain felt, Ulyssis would feel it too; if Pain was injured, Ulyssis would bleed twice as fast. Their power was tied to one another, and ultimately, if Pain died, Ulyssis' life, too, would end. They both lived in suffering for sins they had committed. Ulyssis had been vain as a human, and was determined never to age and die; what he didn't realise was that he would have to spend the rest of his immortal life as the ugly, flesh-seeking creature that he was.

"That elf is not the threat to me," mused Pain in his deep, swamp-like voice. "I can feel it…he is not the threat to me, but he knows something that can break both of us. I want you to make your way to his castle and tear apart anything you can find relating to the scripture prophecies."

Ulyssis gave a sharp nod.

"He has that ancient copy of the scriptures, he's bound to keep it locked somewhere in his castle, where he can consult it frequently. Find it and destroy it. Don't worry about Elwin – the most he can do to me is send his feeble minions after me. I think I can handle that, without your help."

Ulyssis nodded again, in the direction of the ravaged, bloody wall.

"I can sense that he knows something that could endanger us – go quickly, and get back here as soon as you can."

"Immediately, sir. I shall be back straight away."

Pain laughed, his eyes wide with amusement, and Ulyssis looked both ways to see what was so funny. The porcupine sniffed and grinned at him. "You should have seen the way this poor wretch reacted when he saw those tumours of yours on the ceiling. He was so terrified that he did not even notice his own death approaching. It just goes to show what can happen when you stupidly let your guard down."

"It certainly does, master."

Pain stood up onto his four, hairy legs and approached the nearest window, which the elven spy had turned to mere moments before his death. The rain was lashing across the sky in thick, silver sheets and beating down upon the Dragon Temple with such ferocity that the raindrops bounced right off the marble. Torrents of freezing water gushed down off the roof; up in the mountains, the weather was far colder and harsher.

The floor was slippery and damp beneath Pain's clawed toes. The rain was brash enough to harass him, to dampen his fur; it had been so long since sunlight had graced his hard, canine-like face.  Storms brewed in his wake, the sky darkened and became turbulent like his mind.  He had grown used to it over the years.  Behind him, he heard Ulyssis draw a pained, rattling breath.

"You may have that elf if you wish – I have no use for it," said Pain, understanding what Ulyssis had wanted to ask.  The non-human thanked him profoundly, and set about his grizzly business, tearing clothes and skin from the dead elf.

Pain occasionally stayed to watch, but it suddenly occurred to him that he had not yet found time to meditate and calm his mind.  Without excusing himself, he departed back up the staircase with the intent of returning to his chamber at the top of the temple, where Leoma, encased within her crystalline prison, waited for him at the end of every long, tortuous day.  She did not have much choice, after all.

Pain's body was heavy with tension.  He suffered with headaches almost constantly, but this time he felt different.  He could cope with danger himself, he had survived thousands of years long before Ulyssis came into his service.  He was not as strong as he had once been, all those years ago when the island had been completely in his charge.

Only after he had been toppled from power had he realised how truly weak he was without the island and armies of followers – he had nothing to his name any more, apart from the white orb that glimmered and shone relentlessly up in the tower.  Ulyssis possessed half of his power.  It was no wonder Pain sometimes felt so drained.  He was at his strongest when Ulyssis was with him, when their minds and powers worked together.

He had once been so powerful, he had clutched the entire island in his claws, and for all his toils, he now stood alone in one passage of the Dragon Temple, cold and damp, a changed and weak individual.  Angry, he struck the nearest wall with a heavy blow from his quill-coated tail, causing the mountain to shake, and trudged exasperatedly to his room.

# Chapter Nine

# Past Shadows

"Ramsey! Ramsey!"

Theron dragged himself to his feet the moment he woke to find Ramsey missing. He darted in circles, calling out to him, his fur damp and smelling of daisies. It was morning already, the sun had risen over the mountains. He didn't know what to do with himself.

He sniffed frantically at the ground where Ramsey had been sitting what felt like mere moments ago. Ramsey had a particular smell to Theron, like cold sweat; the excursion in the tavern had left a tinge of smoke in the goblin's otherwise familiar scent. Theron knew that Ramsey had sat there next to him, but he was not a bloodhound, and could not have tracked the goblin had his life depended on it.

Ramsey's somewhat sour smell didn't lead anywhere that the troll could follow, though he scratched desperately at the ground for a moment or two. Maybe the dragon had taken him, lifted him clear off the ground and returned to the mountains to eat him. Theron whined and moaned like a grieving dog, running back and forth over the plateau for any signs of his goblin companion. He trampled the flowers beneath his heavy paws and stirred up mud from the soggy ground. Ramsey was nowhere to be seen.

"Ramsey!" he cried out again, over the cool landscape that spread undeterred towards the grey mountains in the east. "Ramsey! Please, Ramsey, if you can hear me...!"

His deep voice echoed fruitlessly over the land, causing the hills to ring resonantly, but offering no condolence to his anxious soul. He whimpered and jumped off the grassy ledge onto the mildly sloping ground below, craning his neck outwards to the mountains. He couldn't bear the thought of Ramsey being held captive by a dragon.

He felt passionate enough about rescuing the goblin prince from the dragon, a child he didn't even know. Ramsey was someone the troll would be willing to fight tooth and claw for. They had battled their way through the great forest, survived two horrific fires and endured countless days of wandering unguided across the kingdom, with want for food and water. Ramsey had almost died the previous night. Theron was not going to give up on him; he would find him, though he did not know which way to run.

Terrible thoughts racing through his simple mind, Theron turned in a circle, as though trying to hone in on the correct direction; finally unable to determine which way Ramsey had gone, he spun around and galloped back towards the skeletal remains of BlackField Town.

***

Ramsey hadn't moved far away in the short span of time in which Theron had been asleep. He guessed that he was at least three-quarters of a mile away from the troll, and felt confident enough to stop for a rest. He was hungry, and a small fruit tree next to a jumbled collection of large rocks offered him an opportunity to fill his stomach.

Skilled at climbing trees, he easily scaled the branches and sat down in the crook of a large bough, no more than six feet off the

240

ground, and helped himself to the dark, mango-like fruit. The breeze fanned his hair into his face as he ate, making it sticky with juice, but Ramsey was so relieved to find food that he hardly cared. He chewed pensively on the soft flesh of the fruit, gazing into the distance with his eyelids half-closed.

It would be a very long walk to the mountains; longer than he had expected, at least. The sun, hovering like a spherical, golden bird to the east, cast long, bent shadows over the land. Ramsey's tree was darkened in one such shadow, of perhaps the tallest mountain. It was not the closest, but it was dull and mean looking, lightly capped with snow that Ramsey could barely see through the clouds.

The air smelled of precipitation; no doubt, he thought, it would soon be raining again. Grenamoya saw plenty of rain all year round, particularly in the northern kingdoms. He had become used to the miserable weather long ago, and was at least thankful that goblins have thick skin. He took another bite from his dark green fruit, juice spilling from his mouth and down his neck. He was damned if he let anything get in the way of his hunger. Without a full belly, the mountains would be crueller still upon his stick-like form.

He picked three more fruits from the tree and crammed them into his trouser pockets for later. If only the pockets were more spacious, he would be able to take sufficient food with him. He had survived in poverty for most of his life, he could make the fruit last longer than most men could. As though for reassurance, he tucked into another dark-skinned fruit, and decided to keep his place for a while longer. He was safe, raised off the ground, and he could see for miles. No dragon would be able to sneak up on him now.

Damn that wretched creature...Ramsey's bite wound still stung as though a blistering poker had been dug into his flesh. At this thought, he pressed one hand to the area through the neck of his shirt, and squeezed it to stem the pain. Blood came off on his hand, he could feel it tickling his fingertips.

He closed his eyes tightly, casting his half-eaten fruit aside, and grumbled aloud. Goblins were meant to have a high threshold for pain...Ramsey didn't know what this threshold was supposedly compared with. Trolls? Trolls hardly felt anything, they just kept on fighting as long as they could stand. Ramsey had plainly seen this trait in Theron the previous night. Humans? Ramsey huffed, the hairs on the back of his neck bristling. Humans were weak creatures that screamed a lot.

In comparison with a human, maybe he was quite resilient, but at that moment he wanted to curl up into a ball, to scream and cry and be the only person left in the world; to be able to unleash his feelings upon everything, the air, the mountains, the very tree he was sitting in.

He was in so much pain that he could barely look up from his wound. It was ugly, it marred his skin like a living parasite. It hurt so much that he could feel nothing else but the pain sensors swelling and buzzing inside his head. He couldn't begin to think about how he felt inside. He was angry; he was relieved to be alive, but he was angry to be so.

He should have died. Anyone in his situation, staring into the soulless eyes of that striped, serpentine face and withstanding a deadly bite, would have perished. Ramsey should have felt elated. He had another chance, he was alive, and he could still salvage his freedom from this whole escapade, even if he had no money. But he didn't even feel happy. He felt anguished, from his burning mind to the pit of his stomach. He had eaten, but his soul was empty, and he felt as though he could scream with the confusion of it all.

He had been dreaming the previous night; a heated, feverish sort of dreaming that had left him feeling sick and breathless when he awoke. Every time he thought about his dreams, the way he was subconsciously thinking about Prince Morgan despite his apparent disdain for him, he became a little more certain that he was indeed going mad.

Before he had left home, he had not been a frequent dreamer. Guilt never plagued him, whether he was stealing an apple from the grocer's stall in the market place or kicking a couple of mangy

242

animals around the square. It was an unfamiliar feeling to him, and he didn't know how to deal with it.

He had hoped that the further he travelled from the capital, the less his mind would dwell upon Prince Morgan. He had been hopelessly wrong. The boy was plaguing his thoughts, now more than ever. He had seen Morgan's face on another goblin's shoulders – if that was not a sign of madness, nothing was. He suddenly felt much worse, and placed his sinewy hands on his stomach, as though to stop himself from throwing up.

Morgan was nothing special. Ramsey gritted his teeth, reminding himself that it was highly likely that the prince was already dead. It shouldn't matter any more. Morgan was just a young boy; he wasn't royalty, at least by blood. He wasn't anyone important, but Ramsey could not shift his milky, blond face from his thoughts.

"He's just a kid," he mused to himself as a breeze shook the branches of his tree, sending a few leaves spiralling towards the ground. In all his years of loneliness, talking to himself had become as commonplace as talking to another goblin at his side. Though for the sake of his sanity he aimed to stem this habit, he could find no other way to effectively voice his thoughts to himself. "He's about the same age I was...when I...when..."

He growled and clenched his eyes tightly shut, trying to focus himself. He had been thrown onto the streets when he was twelve years old, he had been shunned and forced out of his home, but he couldn't remember why. His father had just...not come back. He couldn't remember where from.

"Damn it, Ramsey, you delirious git..."

Every now and again, a voice returned to his ears, as though echoing inside a particularly large cauldron – 'We only hurt you because we love you...let us show you how much we love you...'

Whenever Ramsey came close to recognising the voice, to recalling the face that owned it, he would snap awake and the sounds would be gone. It was a melodic, fairly high-pitched voice, though it had the slight edge of gravel about it. It was a male voice.

Sometimes it lilted back to him when he was only half-asleep. He felt compelled to run and escape from it, as though the very words burned him, licked at him with a ferocity that he could vaguely remember, but could not grasp. He had not heard this sing-song voice prior to the cobra dragon's first attack on Merlock; at least, not in his dreams.

He had tried to place the voice ever since he first recalled it, and knew he would get no further by moping in the branches of a tree. Still, it stung at his consciousness. He wanted to know if it was his father's, he had always expected it to be.

His few remaining memories of his father involved being smuggled into cupboards and locked inside, being told that he was not allowed to go outside and play with the other children in the square. The last he remembered of his father was fire, screaming, and a door being slammed and locked. Ramsey couldn't get out through that door. He was too small to reach the handle.

The fire…it felt as though the fire had occurred long before the locked door, or maybe just afterwards. He couldn't remember.

These few memories had only reached him over the last couple of weeks, while stuck with Theron for company. His mindless presence must have sparked something hidden within Ramsey's mind, he thought. Either way, they were the few memories he had, and they pained him more than they answered his questions.

The night before, amidst the usual consternation and vagueness that his recent dreams always carried, Ramsey had seen an altogether different scene while he slept. He had looked upon a figure, tall, skinny and orange, which he had finally identified as himself, running through a corridor, which opened into a room, which became a whole house. The house opened wider, it seemed massive, and as it grew, it filled with smoke.

He had watched the scene from high above, as though having an out-of-body experience – a phenomenon that Ramsey thoroughly dismissed, though many Scaless scholars from all over the island claimed to have been lifted from their bodies in the coils of an almighty snake at some point in their lives. He knew enough about dream interpretation to know that a house indicated his life, but this knowledge was useless to him. Unless he viewed his existence as being exceptionally smoky and house-like, he could not decipher any deeper message.

The slender middle finger of his right hand sunk into the fleshy cleft of his appendix scar beneath his shirt. He sighed. He was feeling very confused. It had to be the fact that he had been thrown out of Merlock at a similar age that made him feel pity for Prince Morgan.

Before his stay in BlackField Town, Ramsey had viewed Morgan as a member of the royal family, the same monarchy that had forced him out of his home when his father went missing. Now that he knew Morgan was in fact not related in any way to King Viktor, his sympathy had increased ten-fold; though he still had the desire to be by himself and start a new life in the wilderness.

"But I don't have any money..." he reminded himself out loud. "And this wilderness isn't exactly the *friendly* sort of wilderness."

If only he had a mug of steaming coffee in his hands, something to warm his soul and comfort his mind. Tragically, to Ramsey at least, the sugar lumps in his trouser pockets had been crushed to smithereens when he was thrown to the ground the previous night, and he had nothing too pleasant to munch on. The fruit was nice, but it didn't exhilarate him the way that caffeine and sugar did.

There was no real reason behind his fondness for strong coffee, apart maybe from the fact that it sent a riveting rush of excitement through his whole body whenever he drank some. It was something he knew he was certain to miss if he had to return to his old way of life, scrounging around at the Merlock market. Coffee, tea; all warm drinks and sweet, sticky substances seemed to be privileges available only to the rich and powerful, so Ramsey associated them with his own feelings of power and advancement. Advancements towards his dreams of freedom, not towards mental health. He felt as though he was drastically receding in that particular field.

"Damn..." He choked slightly on this single word, and shuddered, pressing his knuckles to his eyes, which were tight-shut and stinging again. "Damn it...damn it, what's wrong with me?" His pointed knuckles pressed deeply against his eyelids, sending flashes of red and indigo across his vision. "Get a hold of yourself, idiot...you didn't come all this way from Merlock just to break down and give it all up..." He gritted his teeth. A sharp intake of breath paralysed his throat for a moment, and he gasped on his words. "Get a hold of yourself...this doesn't mean anything. Curse it all, what's wrong with me?"

*You're ugly, that's what's wrong with you.*

Ramsey clenched his eyes shut tighter, hot fluid rushing in his ears. "I don't care about that any more."

*You're stupid, you're ugly, and you'll never amount to anything more than a screaming little baby. Just look at you, crying like a girl. Don't think you can escape by running from me!* threatened the voice, for Ramsey had moved to climb out of the tree, *You carry me everywhere with you. I am in your skin.*

Ramsey couldn't remove his hands, afraid to open his eyes and find himself alone again. He was not going crazy, he couldn't be hearing voices other than his own inside his head. The voice was different this time. It was more focused, he heard it as clearly as though it were the wind chattering in his ears. It surrounded him. He wasn't even asleep, and he could feel the presence of another person around him.

"Who are you?" he asked, aloud, his voice thin. "If you're going to follow me everywhere, at least tell me who you are." He heard the other voice mumbling almost inaudibly for a moment or two, as though it was deliberating how to answer. It was so familiar. He swallowed. "Are you my father?"

*Your father? My goodness, you are confused aren't you? You barely knew your father, you know as well as I do that you couldn't possibly carry him around inside you. You feel the pain that your father caused you every day.*

"Who are you then?" Ramsey could feel himself shuddering again, as though an icy wind had clutched him by the neck. "Please, I can't go on like this. I'm suffering because of you."

He couldn't hear his own words any more; he didn't know if he even spoke them. He could feel the voice in his head fading away, then drawing near, only to pull away once more. It was a memory, a memory of something horrific, amazing, or somehow significant. The voice wasn't singing to him any more. It was deeper, more composed, and far more sinister. It spoke to him steadily, like someone standing at his side.

*You are, without a doubt, and always will be, the most despicable, worthless child I have ever laid my eyes on.*

Ramsey's narrow chest rose and fell slowly, his fingers tightly curled together against his eyes. He released the pressure slightly as his knuckles began to feel uncomfortable, his hands shaking ever so slightly. "This is mad. I'm talking to someone inside my own head..."

*Your parents never wanted you, insolent boy!*
*Or they wouldn't have left you here with us, now would they?*
*Yes, that's it...you know you can trust me...*

Ramsey could feel the slick friction of skin against corneas as he anxiously rubbed his eyes with his palms. "Why are you speaking to me? Can you hear me?" The voice didn't reply; all he could hear once more was various taunts being thrown at him, insults, endearing pleas for him to trust the owner of this disembodied voice. His throat tightened up. "You're not real...this has never happened before, I'm going crazy...!" He tore his hands away from his face, but his eyes remained closed so tightly that they were painful in their sockets, as though fire burned behind them. "No, I will not give in to this..." he growled through gritted teeth. "Drive me stark raving mad if you will, but I'm not just going to sit here like a fool and let you terrorise me!"

*Rip it off! Tear him to pieces!*
*Let's see that skin...*

Ramsey jarred and instinctively reached around to his back, pressing the fabric firmly onto his body to protect himself. One

247

hand clutched his stomach, and covered his appendix scar with clasping fingers, as though it was suddenly open and bleeding. He could feel pain all around him, but could not understand why.

*It's no use screaming, you wretched urchin!*

*Nobody will come back for you...*

"Whoever you are, I hate you!" cried Ramsey, writhing and jerking around in the boughs of the tree, trying to escape from the voices that seemed to be getting louder than ever. He bumped his cheek against a branch, but didn't notice. "Get away from me! I never want to hear you again – you're not real!"

*You'll be joining all the dead little boys if you don't stop screaming!*

Ramsey coughed, and tried to talk, but the voice wasn't responding to him any more. Its pitch rose, and it became so ragged that it was barely intelligible. It was louder, but strained, like a screeching radio station fading into static.

*Stop screaming! Daddy will never come back!*

*He's dead...*

"No...!"

The voice shrieked, barely audible over another sound that screamed and buzzed louder still. *We'll never leave you, you know. We'll stay with you forever.*

"You're not real!"

*THUD.*

Ramsey was knocked unconscious, but only for a moment or two, as the world came into focus once more. He had fallen out of the tree in a rather awkward manner; his arms were spread out at his sides, and he could see his legs in the air, his feet and bony knees dangling above his head. He was bent double, upside-down, his back against the tree trunk and his head tilted wearily to one side on the damp, grassy ground.

He blinked slowly, and with much discomfort; over him, the fruit tree stood like a sentinel, giving him adequate shelter against the gusts that blew across the hilly terrain. He lifted his head, his chin making contact with his left knee, but had to lower it again. He felt as though his skull was full of metal. At least that would explain the ringing in his ears.

He gasped hoarsely, and suddenly felt a moist, burning sensation on his cheeks, searing his tired eyes. He was crying. Ramsey had never been one to cry, not even during those first few weeks without his father, not knowing where his parents had gone or if they were even alive.

He hadn't noticed himself start to cry; all he knew was that he was staring up at the pale sky, with uncomfortable pressure on his innards, and that hot tears were rolling across his cheeks and down his temples, for he was still upside-down. He clenched his teeth, feeling the hot flush of anguish grace his cheeks, and he sobbed aloud, more salt water ebbing from the corners of his eyes, making shiny trails across his orange skin.

He inhaled the phlegm in his nostrils, much to his distaste, and reached feebly towards his face, to wipe his bloodshot eyes, reddened with anger and terror felt in the same moment. The mild, temperate wind swept past him, chilling the wet paths etched by tears on his pointed face.

The feeling of heat combined with the faint sting of cold was enough to awaken Ramsey to the real world once more, and he didn't hear the voices again. He kept crying, unable to stop, feeling like a fool though there was nobody to watch him.

There was a slight rumble somewhere amidst the airbrushed grey of the clouds above him, though he could not judge where it came from. The sky was endless, a single, slate shade, and it was all he could focus on through the sobbing that shook his whole body, convulsing his stomach and chest with a different kind of pain. Ramsey had felt real agony moments before, the realisation that there was something seriously wrong with his mind, and barely cared that he had lost all control of his angst-ridden body.

He was so distracted that he didn't notice Theron running to him, leaning over him, casting a broad shadow him, and bending down to sniff and nudge his face. It took several moments of provocation from the concerned troll to restore Ramsey's full consciousness, and he looked up at Theron, his cheeks red and soaked, and could do nothing but cry. It was a sound that distressed Theron phenomenally, and he desperately tried to calm him, and encourage him to say what had upset him.

Ramsey could not reply, the sobs catching painfully in his throat due to his uncomfortable, upside-down position, in which his chest was severely compressed by his own knees. The troll hurriedly turned Ramsey onto his side and helped the goblin support himself against the tree. His expression was one overcome with concern, flecked with traces of fear for Ramsey's health and safety. Theron was furious at himself for falling asleep when Ramsey had needed to talk to him, for almost losing him in the wide-open emptiness of Merlockiara, and he tried to talk to Ramsey in a thoroughly exasperated manner.

Ramsey brushed Theron away the moment he could muster enough composure to stand, resolutely claiming that he was perfectly well. Theron shot him a strangely perceptive look, which made Ramsey feel quite embarrassed. Slick streaks of drying tears painted his face like the trails of tiny slugs, standing out starkly in the light of the morning.

Theron could see that Ramsey was upset about something, and he vaguely remembered the goblin mentioning voices in his head, and being fearful for his sanity. Theron knew that this was most likely what had troubled his companion so, and was trying to find a few comforting words when Ramsey spoke first, his voice brittle from crying so hard.

"Come on then, troll...let's get going before anything else happens to me."

"Are you sure?" asked Theron, looking down at Ramsey with a fretful expression. "You look terrible."

"Thanks."

"No, I didn't mean..." Theron fumbled for words, and sighed. Ramsey's brown eyes were puffy and red, but strangely deep at that moment, as though he had seen something that would change his life. "I am sorry, Ramsey. I never meant to sound unkind. But I do care about you, and I am worried for you." The goblin nodded stiffly. "If you ever want to talk about something, I am here for you, all right?" Ramsey didn't react. Theron looked quizzically at him, then added, "I am not as smart as you, Ramsey, and I might not understand what you talk about, but if you need me, I'm here."

The goblin was still for a moment, staring vaguely at the ground. Skinny and fragile, all knees and elbows, the very breeze seemed enough to shatter him at that moment. Theron saw something different shining within him, wholly unlike Ramsey's usual coarse, dismissive nature. He looked as though something inside him had broken in the brief time they had spent apart; something deep-rooted and essential to the person that was truly Ramsey. Theron did not appreciate the way that his companion constantly cast him aside, but there was something disconcerting about this docile, vulnerable manner. Theron could hardly bring himself to touch him, for fear of breaking him in two.

"Yeah...thanks."

Ramsey looked up at Theron for a moment, the itching of a sarcastic smile on his lips. He wanted to grin at himself for being such an emotional idiot; if Theron wouldn't ridicule him, he felt he should do so himself. Theron's brown eyes were filled with pity, and Ramsey found himself unable to feel angry.

"Thanks, troll...I appreciate it." Somewhere in the direction of the mountains, an animal cried, though it was certainly not a dragon. Theron looked up; Ramsey just hugged himself. "...What did you say your name was, again?"

Theron instantly cast his eyes upon Ramsey, and a smile spread across the whole of his hairy face, from ear to ear. Ramsey felt sheepish for being so inattentive, but the troll didn't look the least bit insulted.

"My name is Theron," he said, in his deep, good-natured voice that was so unlike the cries that plagued Ramsey's mind. Ramsey was relieved to have escaped from the words that had haunted him for so long. Theron was smiling as though his birthday had come early. Ramsey could not frown in return.

The clouds gathered overhead, and dispersed in time, dancing wistfully across the sky like sea foam on the gentle ebb of an afternoon tide.  It didn't rain on them again; a fact that Ramsey was very grateful for, given his lack of clean, dry clothes to change into.  On a positive note, he found it quite a relief to be travelling with such a light load.  Without a heavy backpack, he felt as though a significant weight had been lifted from his heart at the same time.

Though he was still a goblin of a decidedly fickle temperament, and he was not entirely fond of the prospect of a mountain hike with Theron, he realised that he felt less unwell, and healthier without the unnecessary bulk of supplies.  His headache faded, and miraculously, the voices in his head, which had been infesting his dreams and waking thoughts as of late, barely troubled him.  It was as though his assertion that the voices were not real had indeed driven them from his mind, if not completely.  He felt strangely inspired, though still confused as to the origins of the voices he could hear.

'Stop screaming!  Daddy will never come back!'

The voice had mentioned his father.  Therefore, the person speaking had not been his father.

'Your parents never wanted you, insolent boy!

Or they wouldn't have left you here with us, now would they?'

They had left him somewhere.  He had been told that they were dead.  He was instructed to stop screaming…

With a sigh, Ramsey reached over his shoulder with one bony hand and felt the sore patch of skin in the centre of his back, beneath his shirt.  It consisted of bumps of raised skin that hurt whenever he touched them, as though something sharp had cut into his skin long before the incident in Theron's forest, making its mark on his flesh.  His appendix scar stung slightly.  His body felt vulnerable, as though it had been exposed to more acute feelings of pain.  Though, strangely, in general, he felt healthier than ever.

They journeyed onwards, on fairly civil speaking terms, until the ground became rocky, and sloped upwards in the lee of the majestic mountains.  Tall trees and scraggly clumps of lichen adorned large boulders as they drew near to the base of the huge, jagged turrets of rock, starting on a shallow slope that abruptly stretched upwards, high into the sky, ultimately disappearing far above them.

Ramsey was not very enthusiastic at first, but as they managed to scale the lower slope of the eastern-most mountain (and the first of the 'Troll Teeth' peaks), his spirits were raised, and he scampered ahead of Theron, through the sharp-leafed shrubs and patches of mountain flowers, as though there was no pain weighing upon his soul. Theron watched him in amusement, ducking between tree branches, and with a renewed feeling of optimism, cantered behind his companion, leaping over the randomly-strewn boulders, hoping the horror of their recent experiences had finally been left behind.

*** 

Hanyaliamaya, the elf kingdom on the eastern side of Grenamoya Island, was, in many ways, similar to Merlockiara. It was very green, mostly due to the presence of nature-loving elves that had inhabited and tended the kingdom over the years, with mountains in the north-east, deep woodland in the south-west, and one of the island's eleven 'great lakes' taking up the centre.

The capital, Hanya, was located to the west of the lake, and was home to hundreds of the mild-tempered, fair-skinned folk, as well as the ivy-decorated palace of the elven king, Elwin. Hanya was the perfect place to live if you enjoyed breath-taking sunrises, the scent of dew on the air and the feel of a cool, damp breeze against your skin. The elves loved all of these things, and though they were not fond of travel, the other races and species of the island were allowed free passage to and from the kingdom, for few things intrigued an elf like an interesting new face.

The sky was dark that night, and barely a cloud ventured across the endless, black plane, as though nervous about the lack of stars in space. There were a few stars, enough to catch the interest of those who watched from far below, but not nearly as many as the elves were used to. On perfect nights, the sky would seem enchanted, as though a solitary person in black had scaled a tall ladder and randomly scattered the contents of a bag of silver dust, thickly and brilliantly, all across the darkness.

All consuming and morosely black, there was nothing to illuminate the sky and remove the sinister air that Grenamoya nights so often held in recent times. The sky was an empty void, bereft of more than a few stars, or even moonlight. The waning crescent of the crater-ridden, pearl-white moon hung mutely in the sky, as though a clean bite had been taken out of it. It was nothing intriguing on that night, and remained suspended in silence, pale and sorrowful.

Elves had never really possessed much of a monarchy, for elves are immortal and will live forever unless killed; therefore, an elven king might still be on the throne when he had children, grand-children, great grand-children and more beneath him. This seemed wholly impractical, and so it became necessary for the reigning elf king to refrain from having children throughout his lifetime. Then, when and if the king happened to 'pass on' (as most elves preferred this phrasing), a successor would be chosen from amongst the late king's closest associates and advisors.

Most elves were strong believers in fate and the enactment of prophecies, which made this system of selection all the more plausible. Elwin had been on the throne of Hanyaliamaya for two-thousand years, since the previous king was killed in battle against Pain's forces during the first great battle, and everyone in the kingdom admired and respected him.

It was getting late, well past eleven o' clock in a world with no artificial lighting, and Elwin was on his way to his chamber at long last to get some sleep after an arduous conference with his advisors. They had begun discussing matters of the union, and ended with some long-winded plans for repairing and improving the Hanya Temple of Scaless – by the end of the debate, Elwin was understandably fed up, and was desperate to catch some sleep. He had been up since dawn, as many elves were in habit of doing, and though he had only been reading in his bedroom for several hours, the lack of rest had finally caught up with him.

What a relief it was to return to the main hall of the palace, with only a single staircase to scale to reach his chamber. His long hair, normally smooth and sparkling like the cascades of a blond waterfall, was dull and drab, framing his face as though it was exhausted also. He felt too dressed-up to be comfortable, and made his way around the gilded, decorated hall with its high, painted ceiling and pillars of white, pink and green marble.

A serene, curved portrait of Lady Scaless amidst wispy clouds graced the ceiling, lit up by two immense, golden chandeliers, the pastel hues flickering orange above the hundreds of small candles. Elwin had lived and ruled in the palace for many generations, and yet the great hall still captivated him.

He remembered being young and not so troubled, sitting for hours on end in the hall upon one of its polished marble benches, reading, writing, and listening to the voices of other elves echo meaninglessly around the walls. That had been a golden time for him. Now, at last, he was beginning to feel the strain that his long-term reign had inflicted on him, and for the first time in his life, he felt as though he was ageing.

Two broad, carpeted staircases followed opposite curves of the wall, and converged at a plateau that opened onto one of the palace's many corridors, which led to, among other areas, his living quarters, and the locked study where he kept his most crucial books and documents. He moved towards the curved staircase to the left, and as he passed, a lean, waxen-haired elf sentry addressed him with a traditional elven greeting; *"May Scaless heed your blessed rest."*

Elwin smiled and returned the greeting in their elvish language, though his head was heavy with exhaustion. The stairs, which were normally so much fun to hop up and down, were yet another trial beneath his weary legs, and he could barely muster the strength to climb them at all. Behind him, the elf guard watched the blond, heavily-clothed king trudge tiredly up to the top of the staircase and disappear to the left, down the corridor; then he returned to his uneventful duty, leaning his ornamental bow against the banister, and sat down on the bottom step with a yawn.

The corridor had never felt longer, wider, or darker. Elwin kept forgetting how late it really was, though his eyelids were persistently heavy. The glow of lighted candles lining the passage began to merge together with the dark doors and decorated walls into a dull, ebbing pulse of orange and brown, until he managed to jerk himself awake again. Just a bit further, then he could rest all he wanted. He swallowed, alert for the time being, and managed to smile at a troop of attendants as they walked past, taking the opportunity to lightly smack a distracted girl on the rump as he went by.

The candlelight was gradually fading as he neared the end of the corridor, from which a sharp right turn would take him directly to his room. His five layers of clothing kept out the cold, but also made him feel horrendously stuffy.

With a stifled yawn, and still ignoring the indignant stare of the molested girl, he unfastened the clasp of his heavy, brown cloak and shrugged it off his shoulders, hooking it under his right arm. He shook his head as though to remove the last traces of boredom from his gold-tinted skin, and readied himself to get inside, lock the door and slink into bed. As he vanished down the corridor, the other elves continued the way he had come, downstairs to the dining room.

Elwin was in the middle of unbuttoning his third shirt when he heard a peculiar, muffled crash from behind him. Being a creature of usually calm temperament, he didn't jump, but instead turned around slowly, still unbuttoning his shirt, and peered down the corridor in the murky, orange light. He couldn't see anyone there, and so, still fiddling with his clothes, he walked quietly along the corridor with soft steps, expecting the other elves to have made the noise. He couldn't hear anything else.

It suddenly dawned on him how black the corridor appeared so late at night – were it not for the brightly-lit main hall at the far end, the dark passage would have blackened forever onwards. The slightly sooty smell all around was intoxicating in his sleep-deprived state, and once more he yearned desperately for his bed.

His dextrous steps carried him tentatively down the corridor, and all the while he was loosening his heavy clothes, until all he wore on his torso was a single shirt made of thin, leaf-coloured cotton. With his spare clothing under his arm, he came to an instinctive stop in front of the door to his ornate study, where out of habit he would sit every evening and peruse his extensive collection of literature. Elves were fond of faces and of words, and were always avid readers.

He took a step back from the dark, carved door, flickering dull red in the fading light, and reached out for the golden handle, lightly pressing one pointed ear against the wood.

*Thump.*

Elwin's heart missed a beat, though his expression remained composed. He didn't call for help. Instead, he turned the door handle, still clasped firmly in his slender right hand, and pushed his way into the room without thinking. Vandals, he thought; he had faced more challenging opponents single-handed in his lifetime. He was king, and therefore appraised for his rational thinking and good decisions. It remained to be seen whether or not this move was a wise one.

The door creaked noisily as he stepped into the faintly-lit room. There were no candles, but vague, strained streaks of light penetrated the grand, arched window, the only one in the room; it had been shattered from the bottom right-hand corner, and flimsy shards of glass hung from the frayed, jagged opening, breaking off one by one with a soft tinkling noise.

Elwin's sharp eyes quickly adapted to the poor lighting, glancing apprehensively in all directions for the culprit, though he knew better than to shout. Surely the vandal had heard him open the door, and had fled.

His study was the only untidy room in the whole of the elf palace – papers were always strewn here and there over randomly placed desks, that had once been new and intricately painted, now remaining as shabby, dull shadows of their former appearance. There were three of these long desks in the study, and the walls were completely lined with tall, pine bookcases, practically spilling over with gilded, leather tomes and dusty stacks of parchment.

Cabinets with glass doors showed dusty rows of tightly-bound books, and on the shelves, amidst the numerous volumes, were various trinkets collected by the elven monarchy over the years; a wooden bowl of wax fruit, an empty, antique wine rack, and tiny glass sculptures of humming birds and swans, to name a few. Of all the rooms in the palace, in the whole of Hanya, Elwin loved this room best.

At last, he noticed some movement. The murky shadows around him sharpened, and he beheld a figure standing beneath the shattered window, moving silently, slinking like a bad dream next to the lectern that held Elwin's prize possession – the most ancient copy of the Scaless Scriptures in existence.

The creature had its back to him. The bumps of its bare, exposed spine were illuminated like stepping stones under the faint light, and the whole individual seemed to expel a light of its own, as it stood out starkly against the otherwise black and murky scene. It moved like a spider towards the book, and Elwin saw it open the cover, slowly, as one would handle loose leaves that were not joined together – deftly, as though the pages might break apart under his touch.

Elwin's breath shallowed as he tried to keep silent. His name was written in that front cover, along with the names of all the elven monarchs who had preceded him. He couldn't feel afraid, for the deep sickness of utter loathing swelling in his stomach had drowned out all other emotion. Though he could not think immediately of how to act, he knew that he had to do so quickly. The creature had not heard his rather clumsy advance through the door, and so, still standing with his fingers wrapped around the door handle, he shuffled sideways.

His blond tresses floated with every jerk of his head as he neared a large display of various war weapons that he kept propped up against the wall. He was barely twenty feet from his potential attacker. Reaching out with one resolute hand, he grabbed hold of the nearest weapon, a particularly heavy sword, and drew it near to his body, his breath becoming more ragged with every passing second.

He kept his earthy eyes fixed on the other creature, knowing better than to let down his guard. The intruder was, apparently, doing no harm – it appeared to be reading the dedication in the front cover of the book, as casually as if it were reading a magazine at the hairdresser's. It also seemed rather deaf, for as Elwin retrieved his weapon, a couple of other metal objects had clattered dully to the floor, unnoticed.

The long sword gleamed brilliantly in the feeble light, as though streaks of luminescent blood remained on the blade from a long-forgotten battle. Elwin swallowed, trying to wield the sword properly, though it was a troll warrior's sword and too heavy for him to carry. No matter – if he could swing it just *once*. He was certain that the whole palace should have heard him, with all the noise he was making at that moment. His hands tightened around the rough handle (he had to use both hands in order to lift it), and he strode boldly forward, lifting the blade as he did so, both of them glowing pale blue in the emerging moonlight.

As he exasperatedly raised the sword to strike a blow, the other creature whirled around, its clawed hand still resting upon the page in front of it. With a single flash of its purple eyes, Elwin lost the feeling in his arms, and the huge sword fell to the ground with a deep *thunk* that resonated through the room and along the corridor outside.

"Leave your weapon, Elwin. I am, after all, unarmed."

Elwin had expected this to happen, but the vain hope of striking a blow unnoticed had driven him beyond reasonable thought. He glanced fleetingly at his discarded weapon, which was smoking slightly, then fixed his eyes once more on his sinewy opponent. He was staring into a pair of eyes that he hadn't seen for five-hundred years.

"Ulyssis," he began, and his voice was strained, "what do you think you are doing in my study? Get your hands off that book."

There was menace in his words, though not in his gaze. Ulyssis cocked his head in his own unique manner, like a corpse that had been dead for too long, and long tendrils of saliva fell from his partially closed mouth. He removed his yellow-clawed hand from the page, and it hung benignly at his side. His deep, violet eyes were pulsing from within, glowing at the edges and bloodshot in the corners.

"It's been a long time," he hissed at last, his voice slowed slightly by the amount of viscous saliva in his mouth, which spilled gradually over his lips, dripping onto the floor. For once, Elwin had no concern for his carpet.

"Yes," he replied, "it has been a long time. You haven't changed at all." His eyes narrowed; these were not the words of a friendly acquaintance. Ulyssis turned his head slightly, glancing at the weary-looking elf from a different angle. Elwin returned the surveying look, taking in the entirety of Ulyssis' bony yet muscular form, and finally spat, "You repulse me! I cannot even look at you any more, Ulyssis!"

The other creature was taken aback by the fury in his voice, but stood his ground, pulling back his mouth into a fang-filled grimace. Elwin looked at him, unable to take his eyes off Ulyssis' gently moist, fleshy body and the yellow spines that protruded from his legs, back and hands. They regarded one another poisonously for a moment in the near-darkness. At last Elwin spoke; his tone had lowered.

"…Have you come here to kill me?"

"Of course I haven't!" snarled Ulyssis, indignantly. "Do you think I would be inept enough to stand here and gape at you if I had been sent here to kill you?"

Elwin kept his eyes on the semi-human creature – a man who had once been so beautiful – with an unflinching, measured glare. He had never felt so hateful, so pitying, so full of despair all in the same moment – except maybe when he had beheld this creature a long time ago, and found not companionship, but the cold, ebbing flourish of hate in those eyes. They had once been blue, the most brilliant blue eyes that Elwin had ever seen; now, they just looked toxic, as though poisoned from the inside. "Then what are you doing here? Surely you didn't come here just to visit me." His fists, subtly clenched, were dormant by his sides, and bitterness tinged his voice.

"I am not here to kill you, Elwin," he insisted, more drool gently dripping from his chin. His eyes were dark, and his expression was guarded. Elwin trusted Ulyssis not to attack. "I cannot tell you what I came here to do, and quite frankly, I wish you hadn't happened upon me in this room. I stand by what I said before, Elwin, and I have never, ever wanted to face you again in this way." He inhaled deeply, and the ridges of his rib cage swelled outwards, his flesh stretching like elastic over them. "This isn't easy for me."

"Ha! Don't make me believe that you're going soft, Ulyssis. I know you'd probably relish the chance to get your claws into me, and rip me to pieces. You've got a chance, Ulyssis – attack me if you will, but I will fight you with every last bit of strength in my body before I let you threaten my kingdom in any manner."

"Elwin, I'm not here to kill you. I've got my task to do, and I'm not leaving this room until it is done."

"And I'm not going anywhere until I get some damned answers!" shot Elwin, taking a bold step forward, though he had no weapon. Ulyssis lowered his gaze slightly to meet the elf's slender height. It was amazing how unfazed he was by Elwin's threats, though he had good reason not to fear him. Ulyssis was not a creature who was easy to kill; eight-hundred years of near-death encounters and gruelling physical pain were enough to prove it so.

They regarded one another, mere feet apart; close enough to reach out and touch the other. Neither one moved. The crackle of rain against the arched window fractured the silence. Elwin broke their intense eye contact to look out at the falling rain, scattered drops littering the sill through the broken glass, and his body heaved in a sigh.

"It never goes for very long without raining any more," he said, returning his eyes to Ulyssis'; the part-human creature blinked slowly, the edges of his mouth glistening. "I knew I would see you again, Ulyssis, though I never wanted to."

The scripture book seemed to have been forgotten amidst their relatively calm discussion. Ulyssis smirked, though interpreted through his thin lips it looked more threatening than he meant it to be. "And why would you prefer not to see me again, pray tell? Am I not your favourite person in the whole of Grenamoya?"

"Not any more, you aren't," responded the elf, his arms wrapped around his slender, green-clad torso. "You bring back far too many painful memories of yourself, Ulyssis, for me to want to be in your company."

"You make it sound as though I am a bad person."

"That's just it, Ulyssis!" snapped Elwin, though he wished he had not reacted so strongly, for the smile was instantly struck from Ulyssis' gaunt face. "A person! A person, you were once a *real* person, a soul, a human being – now look at you!" Ulyssis hissed. "When I look at you, all I can see is how horrid, how ugly you've become…but it is more painful whenever I see that flash of your true self in your eyes."

"You don't know what you're talking about."

"I'm an elf, Ulyssis, I happen to have very good perception," he huffed. They were still close, dangerously so, but the creature did not attack. "I can see it in your eyes, still, after all this time. That tiny smudge of yourself, in the way you still look at me. I saw it back when we last said goodbye, and I can see it now." Ulyssis was shooting daggers at him, his amethyst irises glowing like purple flames. "Well, not any longer, but a second ago, when you looked at me that way…"

"You're wasting your breath."

Elwin frowned and bowed his head, his expression severe. "Yes, I am. I am wasting my precious time on you, when I already know that I can do nothing to save you now. You're corrupted, Ulyssis. You're corrupted, you're evil, and you are positively foul to behold. That is what hurts me so much, you know." Ulyssis opened his mouth. "You may not think I have feelings, but I do, and I used to have wonderful feelings about you when you were younger. I was proud of you, Ulyssis, honoured to be in your company."

"Give it up, Elwin..." Ulyssis had averted his eyes, and returned his focus to the scripture book, but the elf king would not be swayed. He had waited so long to say the words that so avidly poured from his mouth and from his heart – rampant mountain trolls could not have torn him away.

"You know something? I remember when I first saw you, and you gave me that fascinated look. I couldn't get over how perfect you were, Ulyssis, you were a bright and handsome young man. I used to envy you because of it, for Scaless' sake!"

"Don't spit that name at me."

"You have no idea how much I wanted to tell you how incredible you were, how much I admired you for all that you went through! All the time we spent together, we bonded, Ulyssis, and for what? Absolutely nothing! You're a traitor and an idiot, Ulyssis, look at what has happened to you! What has become of your good looks? All you ever loved about yourself is gone!"

"Shut up!"

"And don't you dare try to tell me *that* doesn't make you the stupidest human being on Grenamoya!" He finished, lost for breath, and had to take a few gulps of air before he could summon his weary voice again. "Which is saying a lot, considering all the disastrous decisions that humans have made since then, Ulyssis."

Ulyssis was glowering at him with the sharpest, most injured and insulted look that Elwin had ever seen. His fleshy body heaved with suppressed anger that he was unwilling to unleash, though the pain surging through his head was urging him to do the contrary. Pain...

Pain could probably sense that he was hurting, that he was more aggravated than usual. He didn't want his master to know that he had been on casual talking terms with the enemy, and began to fear exactly how much Pain could determine via their psychological bond.

Ulyssis looked at Elwin; the elf was unerringly perfect, with a soft, yet defined face, lit up with the natural glow of healthy skin.

His blond hair was slightly flustered from the ordeal, but even under pressuring circumstances, he remained composed and unaffected. Ulyssis took in the image before him, and it sparked more anger within him; the anger of loss, of helplessness, of jealousy and damaged pride.

"Don't touch me!" he shrieked, as Elwin reached out tentatively towards him. "I don't need your sympathy!"

Elwin's hand shot away, and he stepped back, his expression now one of deep concern. Ulyssis was disgusting to behold, and foolish in the decisions he had made; but at the end of the day, he was still partially human beneath the gruesome veil of bony flesh. Pity had overwhelmed him for a moment, but now he was afraid. "Ulyssis?"

"You're right, I've made a royal mess of my life, I don't need you to tell me that!"

"I am sorry, but that is how I feel."

Ulyssis swore and lashed out at him, missing the elf's face by an inch, though he did not advance. The ghostly light of the rainy landscape lit up his features; his cheeks, snout and eyelids glowed faintly blue, the colour that his agonised eyes had once been, hundreds of years ago when he was still human.

"Back off!" he snarled, streaks of saliva dangling from his jaws. "I was a fool to let you distract me this way, Elwin! Get out of my sight, I will do my bidding and then I'll be gone, and I'll be out of your life forever!"

"What are you going to do?" asked Elwin, in as firm a voice as he could muster, still backing away, until his face was in shadows. Ulyssis glared after him, his mouth wide open and gaping fiendishly, as he was a skilled shape-shifter and could elongate his body at will. He snapped his abnormally long fangs in Elwin's direction once, spattering the carpet with saliva, then turned back to the scripture book. Elwin shuddered. "Don't harm that book, Ulyssis!" he shouted, but Ulyssis was deaf to him. "Please, no! It is all I have left of King Galewyn and his kindness to me!"

Ulyssis looked fleetingly in his directly, then glanced down at the book once again, sitting eloquently upon its carved lectern, the pages startlingly bright in the moonlight. His eyes narrowed, and he clenched up his body, his fists scrunched into tight balls, his spiny knuckles pale. For a moment, he tilted his head to the ceiling, his mouth open and his long tongue lolling from between his lips like someone who was overwhelmed with nausea.

Then he made a deep, choking sound, brought his chin back down, clutched the lectern, and vomited a mingled mess of blood and bile onto the front of the book, retching painfully, the thick fluid sloshing all over the cover and stand, onto his hands.

Elwin cried out, but Ulyssis didn't heed him, his eyes tightly closed as he emptied what appeared to be the contents of his entire body onto the ruined book. His stomach tightened and seemed to invert on itself, leaving Ulyssis with an altogether hollow appearance as he staggered backwards and held his head with his blood-soaked hands.

"Gah!" Elwin gasped and reached quickly for a decorative silver arrow displayed upon the closest bookcase, still mostly hidden in shadow. He drew the gleaming shaft to his body, concealed within his sleeve. "You came all the way from Utipona to destroy a book? You're mad!"

Ulyssis looked incredibly ill now; his body was shuddering and pale, his hands still clutching at his protruding brain with no small measure of giddiness. He was able manipulate anything about his physical form – he could cut out his whole digestive system and grow a new one, he could slice his heart in two and reform it to beat once more in the blinking of an eye. He would recover; but not quickly enough, for Elwin was upon him the moment he turned.

Livid, the elf knocked him off his feet, striking him across the face with something sharp that Ulyssis could not see. The semi-human choked again, involuntarily lacing Elwin's fringe with the remnants of vomit. "I cannot believe you did that! You abhorrent monster! I could murder you right now!"

"Get off me!" snapped Ulyssis, though his voice lacked decent threat due to his combined shock and exhaustion. He kicked up at Elwin, striking him a painful blow in the crook of his right thigh, and quickly overpowered the elf, who was very light for his size.

He pushed away from Elwin, panting raggedly, his mouth tinged with his own bodily fluid, and watched as Elwin also stood, and put a respectable, though still dangerous, distance between them. Ulyssis gasped, his voice raw with the sting of acid in his throat, and the pain of unavoidable emotion that he had been afraid to face for over five-hundred years.

"I don't want to fight you, Elwin," he shuddered, his throat tightening with a swallow. Elwin's eyes burned brilliantly in the dim light, unable to believe the other creature's words.

"You've got a peculiar way of showing it!" he replied with a mocking laugh. "You came all the way here to obliterate a *book*, Ulyssis!" He held the silver arrow, the only weapon available to him, and deftly disguised it behind his back.

What he beheld in the intense, violet eyes at that moment was striking; Ulyssis' gaze was heated yet weary, focused yet vague, resolute yet somehow softening. He was breathing deeply, and before Elwin's eyes, his sinewy body was gradually 'filling out' once again, like a flat tire being pumped with air, so that his muscle-covered skin became taut over his bony form, like a perfectly fitting layer of thin rubber all over his body. His entire form gleamed with perspiration, and traces of blood-tainted vomit still adorned his mouth, chest and stomach. He didn't look proud of himself; he looked pensive.

Elwin regarded the rather reptilian face – the eyes without eyelashes, the eyebrows replaced by two rows of yellow spines, the small nostrils flaring slightly with every fevered breath. All he could see before him was a monster, and a boy that he had once known, who was now an unrecognisable, depraved excuse for a man.

"I don't know what I thought I could see in you," began Elwin, Ulyssis' tired gaze still upon him, "but whatever it was, it is most certainly gone."

Ulyssis twitched as though readying to move, but Elwin moved first; once more, he leapt upon his unprepared opponent and pushed him backwards against a bookcase with glass-panelled cabinets. There was a loud crash as they collided with the heavy piece of furniture, as one of the panels shattered under contact with Ulyssis' shoulder, causing him to swear blatantly, knocking Elwin aside with one sweep of his hand.

Elwin fell against the cabinet again, and with a firm grip on the wood, he clutched the silver arrow firmly in his left palm and stabbed it deep into the back of Ulyssis' bulging, pus-coloured brain, as the creature fumbled to remove glass from his skin. Ulyssis screamed the most gut-wrenching scream that Elwin had ever heard, and he stumbled onto the floor by his side in his horror at what he had done. He had done it to an evil being, but a being that still played an important part in his life, and his heart.

Ulyssis shrieked and bawled, lashing out, trying to reach the slender, silver shard that was embedded seven inches deep in his skull. No blood fell from the wound, but Ulyssis was certainly in pain as he clutched at the arrow, unable to get a grasp on it due to it being almost entirely submerged in his brain. Elwin knew that this injury wouldn't kill the creature. Hundreds of years spent trying to find Ulyssis' weakness had been unsuccessful, but he had immobilised him enough to make a quick escape.

Yet, he couldn't force himself to leave. Ulyssis tore insanely up and down between the desks and bookshelves, scattering books and leaves of paper in his wake. Elwin took a breath and grabbed the side of the cabinet to support his shaking body. "You have achieved nothing by destroying that one book, Ulyssis!" he shouted, his tone exasperated and triumphant. "Get back to Utipona and tell Pain not to send any more of his minions to do his dirty work!"

Ulyssis screamed once more, a cry that gurgled deep inside his throat; then quelled himself completely, and, summoning what must have been a great deal of determination, turned around to look at Elwin, his pupils narrow, like the eyes of a cat. Disregarded books and withered sheets of parchment were scattered at his feet, some of them glistening with bloody bile.

"Pain isn't in Utipona!" he spat, his mouth moist. "We're stationed in the Scared Mountains already, both of us. He has few others to do his 'dirty work' thus far, but believe me, he will resume control of those who are rightfully his, and soon he will reign over this miserable island once again, for all eternity!"

Elwin's eyebrows drew together as he stood, leaning against the bookcase for support. Ulyssis was at the opposite end of the room, and worse for wear, but he still looked defiant and dangerous. Elwin didn't want to imagine how painful it was to have an arrow sticking into his brain, but could hardly find it with himself to praise Ulyssis for his bravery. The air was rank with the stench of vomit. "Those who are rightfully his?"

"You know what I mean, genius!"

Elwin thought for a moment. It was morbidly obvious. "*Terak*."

Ulyssis rolled his eyes, though in the dim light it was difficult for Elwin to make out these more obscure movements. "Clearly! Pain is already taking hold of his children, and it will not be long before all of them, and I mean *all* of them, are under his complete control, and killing at his will!"

The vampires and similar creatures of Grenamoya differed from the other races on the island, in that they had actually been created by Pain himself, when the island was new and Pain ruled over all. The vampires, under the same black enchantment that Ulyssis was subjected to, had been blood-hungry creatures, as one might expect, that feasted upon the flesh of Pain's enemies when instructed to do so, and whenever the urge to kill overcame them at night.

Pain had been so fond of these creatures that he had even given them two kingdoms solely to occupy – Utipona, now famed as Pain's base of attack, and Xavierania, to the north of Utipona, where Terak and the other 'reformed' vampires now lived and worked in relative peace.

Though they had progressed far over thousands of years, they were still bound to Pain, no matter how remotely so, by the bond of their ancestor's blood. Ulyssis was directly linked to Pain's heart and mind in a way that far surpassed any other pact forged upon Grenamoya, but nonetheless, if Pain wished to resume control of his 'children', then a mere thought could alert them all to his dark bidding. Elwin hadn't considered these implications before, and the realisation of Ulyssis' truthful words struck him like a crushing blow.

"...Damn it, Ulyssis!"

He drew himself up to his maximum height and found himself storming towards the other creature, who, as could be predicted, was standing perfectly still without a hint of weakness. Ulyssis was panting like a dog, his tongue hanging several inches from his lips, curled and pointed, tipped with saliva, as always.

"To think I was beginning to feel sorry for you...!" Elwin held his hands up to his face, staring at them briefly before flicking his gaze back to the monster before him. Ulyssis was sneering; that empty, smug look made Elwin feel positively sick. He knew that nothing he could do at that moment would affect Ulyssis, physically or mentally, and felt despair start to envelop his heart. "Get out of my house..."

"What?" drooled Ulyssis, for Elwin had spoken faintly.

"I said get out!" The elf grabbed Ulyssis by the shoulders and pushed him backwards forcefully, but felt it would be futile to strike him. This creature knew a deeper pain than that which was physical. He pushed Ulyssis again, digging his nails into the smooth skin, feeling it break slightly beneath his touch. "Get out!"

"I said I won't fight you, Elwin," growled Ulyssis, looking down at him with lofty, purple eyes. "But I have done what I came here to do, and now I must leave you."

As quick as a flash, but with no such spectacle, Ulyssis was gone, and Elwin was left clutching at thin air, his hands coiled around invisible flesh. Shocked, Elwin quickly withdrew his hands, but found himself entirely alone. Ulyssis had dissipated, without so much as a sound, or a puff of smoke. Elwin stared at the nothingness that surrounded him in his desolate, ransacked study, and his heart sank.

He had seen that person again, looked into those eyes, felt that familiar feeling of sadness whenever thoughts of Ulyssis dawned in his mind, normally last thing at night when the darkness brought such miserable memories out of hiding. There had been no laughter in those eyes, and not even the hint of a warm smile. Elwin felt foolish; for a moment, the briefest of moments, he had hoped that there was still a shred of goodness in Ulyssis' hollow heart, but he had met with bitter disappointment in return.

There was nothing to be done to save a soul that was already lost. He had to concentrate on saving the lives of those who still had a chance for salvation, the innocent beings who were under threat from an evil force that gained momentum with every passing day.

Thoughts of Ulyssis and Pain dashed across his mind; and he dwelled uncomfortably on the mention of Terak, one of his dearest comrades, before striding resolutely to one of the uneven tables and taking a fresh piece of leaf-printed parchment from one of its drawers.

'To my dearest friend, Collinad,' he wrote, his penmanship unfaltering and curvy, 'please come to Hanya at once for an urgent council. I will send letters to the others, do not worry about contacting them yourself. I am afraid we have some rather unfortunate affairs to consider...'

# Chapter Ten

# The Mountain Crossing

Despite Ramsey and Theron's initially high spirits, the Troll Teeth Mountains were not a place where optimism could easily thrive. The weather turned harsh, the sky grew dark like steel above them, and soon the trees and plants died out, leaving their path up the mountain barren and dreary. The wind howled and cried all around then, whirring in their ears, and every now and again the weather became worse, and sheets of icy rain, sometimes even hail, would batter them from all sides.

As they climbed the great peak, following a jagged mountain road that seemed to curve gradually northwards around the mountainside, they were always sheltered from one side; far too often, however, they found themselves walking against the restless gusts, with the wind and rain in their faces.

Ramsey had thankfully heeded the words of one brief article from 'The Merlockiara Bulletin', that detailed the convergence of manearins in the valley just beneath the shadow of the Troll Teeth Mountains. This was more than enough reason for them to skirt the edges of the low-lying land. Even now as he gazed giddily down to the landscape they had left behind, he could see the fleeting movements of the wolf-like manearins, working as a pack and chasing some poor creature up and down the hills. He and the troll were hundreds of feet up the mountain, and so all he could make out of the chase was a collection of dark dots chasing after a somewhat smaller smudge, which tore back and forth over the ground, trying to avoid its pursuers.

Ramsey felt sick at the mere thought of how high up he was, and could not bear to look back down the mountain for prolonged periods. He and Theron had travelled onwards and upwards without stopping for the best part of two days; Theron, blissful in his good-tempered resilience, had barely said a word unless Ramsey bade him speak.

Ramsey, on the other hand, was feeling awfully miserable and grumpy in the cold weather, with his hair constantly being blown in front of his eyes. He would be glad if he never had to set eye upon another mountain ever again, and for a while even contemplated how much worse the situation could have been, had they travelled across the flat, green land instead. The haunting cries of twenty manearins in the valley was enough to snap him out of this contemplation, and he continued behind Theron bitterly, sucking his arms into his clothes for warmth.

Once or twice they encountered blockades on the road, and had to find an alternative route. Large boulders the size of Theron obscured their path on the evening of their first day of hiking, but with no small measure of gratitude to the troll's stocky build, they had managed to break their way through and continue onwards.

Every now and again Ramsey found himself glancing over the edge of the trail, at the fading, bumpy land of Merlockiara, laid out far below them like an uneven blanket, if only to watch for familiar points on the landscape. Miles away, he could see the ashen remains of BlackField Town like a tiny pencil mark upon the land, and just beyond that, the Great Forest sprouted and spread out as far as his eyes could see, dotted with a hundred shades of green and brown.

Theron occasionally turned to see what the goblin was looking at, but seemed rather unconcerned about the view they had left behind, beautiful though it was. Every minute or so, he would sniff the air, searching for any trace of unfamiliar smells in their midst. There was nothing interesting to be smelled that evening – just the usual scent of rocks, clouds and dust that was always associated with mountains.

The sky began to darken and grow faintly pink at Grenamoya's usual sunset hour. The cirrus clouds stretched into the distance like wispy fingers reaching out to caress the dying sun, which sank low over the Great Forest to the west. Ramsey trained his vision as far as possible, but the sea of trees expanded further than his eyes could fathom. Perhaps he was searching for the gloomy, grey speck that was Merlock on the horizon, still shadowed by the wall that enclosed it on all sides.

He sighed, shivering slightly with the deepening cold that seemed to affect Theron very little. The troll shook himself briefly, but otherwise did not react to the steadily mounting chill in the air. His face was neutral; which, for Theron, meant a calm expression with the faint traces of a smile.

Ramsey had hoped that they would stop for a rest during the evening, due to insufficient rest the night before, but he realised that, even if he had possessed a comfortable blanket and a pillow, the sounds of manearins in the valley and the rumblings of unknown creatures from above them would have kept him awake. He was a light sleeper at the best of times, and figured that he wouldn't have the slightest chance of a rest with so many unwelcome distractions.

The road narrowed slightly, meaning that he and Theron could not walk side by side for a brief way. As the path widened once more, and became broader than before, he walked around the troll and resumed his previous post, striding alongside, towards the outermost edge of the path. It was important to Ramsey that he could see around, and though he was at times precariously close to a lethal fall, he was more content being able to see the breathtaking landscape below once his vertigo began to subside. Something

273

moving caught his eye once again, and he realised that there were large creatures wandering in the valley.

Stopping briefly for a better look, though Theron kept walking, he moved closer to the edge and peered down to the distant valley. The manearins emerged at dusk and dawn to hunt, but the creatures moving below were different; they were larger, and from what Ramsey could tell, they all had dark fur, ranging from black to petrol to burgundy. They were certainly four-legged creatures, and they approached the manearins with a loping gait, dwarfing the wolf-like creatures in comparison. They shattered the pack, sending faintly outlined manearins darting in all directions, and the cry they gave was completely feline, like the roars and snarls of a dozen lions.

Ramsey was too far away to feel afraid, but all the same wished that he could get a closer look at the commotion. Visibly, some of the manearins had been killed and lay motionless and vague on the ground, with the other creatures dancing and cavorting around them in a circle, some of them turning to pick off the remaining manearins one by one, chasing them over the hills. Ramsey was so eager to see more of the battle that he leaned dangerously far over the edge.

"Ramsey!" called Theron, his voice urgent and suddenly near. "Be careful, don't lean too far over!"

The goblin pulled upright once more, brushed himself down, and without a word followed Theron as though nothing had interrupted their journey. He could still hear the yowling and calling of the animals in the valley, but compelled himself not to look, in case he was unable to hold himself back from falling forward the second time.

They journeyed on for hours, long after the reddened light of the sunset had faded over the trees, and night crept towards them from the east, clutching the island in its black, icy grip. Theron commented about the lack of stars, claiming that it was a warning of bleak times ahead, but Ramsey found this notion too morbid for his liking, and complained that he was cold and tired.

Adhering to the goblin's wishes, for he could see that Ramsey was genuinely miserable, Theron suggested that they look for a place to rest for the night, and that they could travel onwards when the morning came. Ramsey hadn't noticed the moment when Theron had assumed control over their quest, and didn't enjoy the fact that the troll was making decisions; he made a mental note to resume his dominant position in the morning.

It did not take them long to find a place to rest. A hanging boulder, which looked fairly stable, served as shelter for both of them overnight. It was an unexpected lip of protection along an otherwise vulnerable path, and Ramsey didn't know how it had been formed, but all the same was thankful that it had been. Theron laid himself down on the cold ground against the wall of rock that was the mountain face, and Ramsey joined him, sitting not too far away, but not very near to the troll, either. He was currently wearing all the clothing he owned, and so did not have to fuss about getting changed before he settled down to sleep.

The wind howled around them, tempered slightly by the presence of the mountain. The sky was empty and black, like the inside of Ramsey's eyelids whenever he closed them. He had tried to think more clearly ever since he and Theron had reached the base of the mountain, but had been too exhausted and flustered by the weather to do so. Sitting against a wall of solid rock, with Theron drifting to sleep beside him, he tucked his knees up to his body and attempted to recall something, anything at all from his past, so that he could begin to remember.

The voices were gone. Or rather, the one voice that followed him, echoed by many others. At times it had been as though ten or more speakers were clamouring inside his head at once, thus rendering all of them unintelligible. But now, he could hear none of them. Not one. Not since he had fallen out of the tree two mornings ago. He had told them that they were not real, and they had faded into nothing. For a split-second, he wondered whether he had not heard the voices because of the awful weather, and the wind screaming in his ears, but he knew in an instant that this was not true.

He was free. For the first time since his accident in Merlock, he was free.

Seeing that Theron was asleep, for he was still quite possessive when it came to food, he took one of the dark-skinned fruits from his pocket and eagerly sunk his sharp teeth into it, though he would have been thankful for something warmer in its place. The subtly bitter taste filled his entire mouth with a single bite, and he slumped contentedly against the hard rock behind him, finding some enjoyment in the moment. Theron had clearly been more exhausted that he let on, because he was already sound asleep and gently snoring over the whistling gusts that encircled them.

Ramsey took another bite, staring thoughtfully out at the swirling fray of wind and rain. It looked as though a storm would be upon them soon, and no doubt there would be little shelter further up the mountain. Theron made small noise; a slight snort seized Ramsey's attention, and he looked quietly at the troll, thinking back over all the trials they had faced together.

He was still unsure of how he felt about Theron – after all, it was Theron who had found him after he fell out of the tree, Theron who had gone to the trouble of looking for him, and offered him a listening ear. Theron had saved his life mere hours after they had first met, he had defended him from a dragon far bigger than himself.

And even now, Theron was sticking at his side. Leading the way, in fact; pursuing a quest that Ramsey had falsely promised to, a mission that he had never intended to act upon.

He finished his fruit, idly tossing its bitter core over the side of the rocky ledge in front of him, where it fell hundreds of feet to the ground below without a sound. Theron breathed heavily, his pink nostrils flaring gently, and Ramsey glanced at him again, wondering what exactly he should do. Something in his heart felt sullen whenever he looked at Theron nowadays. Here was the only person who had ever cared about him, and Ramsey had enough of a shred of goodness in his soul to know that it would be unforgivable to abandon him.

The troll was company, even if he was not the most riveting sort, and Ramsey had finally begun to comprehend why he had felt so wretched and miserable before he set off on his journey. This quest to rescue Prince Morgan from a dragon had won him recognition – finally, he was not known only as the homeless boy who stole food from market stalls in Merlock. He was a hero, something he had yearned to be when he was a child. Even the praise of faceless goblins had encouraged him to think he was truly somebody, and now the boundless devotion of a single, even-tempered troll had made him realise how deeply he had once pined for companionship.

Ramsey was good company for himself, sure enough, but the sheer relief of talking to another living creature instead of the unknown voices in his head was incredible.

Part of him wanted to tell Theron the truth, how he had agreed to rescue Prince Morgan with no real promise to do so, but another part of him told him that this would be unwise. The troll had complete faith in him, and told him that he was a hero, a good person. Ramsey would not give this up for the world, knowing that if he lost Theron's friendship, he might never have another's. Theron was his last hope for companionship. He was determined to cling to that, whatever the cost.

Even if it meant going to the Ash Mountains and slaying a cobra dragon to rescue some kid who wasn't a real prince, he pondered.

There was no doubt in his mind. Something about him had changed during that morning, two days ago. He had battled his demons, and, as far as he could tell, he had won at last. He was shivering with cold, and wet from head to toe, but a new surge of energy was building within him; the healthy sort of energy that made him feel as though he could face the whole world at once. He resolved to talk to Theron in the morning; he would tell the troll how much he appreciated his company. That shouldn't be too hard, he thought, even though he had little experience when it came to thanking anyone.

Tucking himself into the folds of his itchy shirt, and curling himself into a ball, he closed his eyes and tried to sleep, sheltered from the furious gusts by the wall of rock and Theron's bulky, hairy body.

*\*\*\**

The next day dawned bleaker than ever. From the moment he awoke, Ramsey could feel the extremities of his body stinging with a frozen numbness that refused to fade, even as they continued on their upward trek. Theron had actually opened his eyes to find that his fur was brittle with frost, and as they trudged onwards, the ground beneath their feet crackled with a thin coating of ice.

Incredibly, just as Ramsey was beginning to feel that their situation could get no worse, the ominous storm that had been brewing overhead for more than a day finally broke, sweeping rain and hailstones over the mountain, and finally besieging them with a thick barrage of unrelenting snow. When he was younger, Ramsey had felt more fondly towards this sort of weather, despite living in a desolate tree-house. However, the snowstorm in the mountains, on top of the icy temperatures, howling winds and lack of food, made him exceptionally sick with frustration.

Theron ploughed ahead through the snow (which in places reached as high as Ramsey's scrawny thighs), allowing the goblin to follow with relative ease. Only twice did overhangs of hardened snow above them give way, submerging both of them in the freezing, powdery white flakes, and they stopped for a rest once, at about midday when the rising sun melted the majority of the fresh snow into grey slush. Their respite was brief, and soon they were forced to continue, for fear that the weather at the mountain's peak would worsen during the night. They aimed to reach the summit of the mountain before nightfall, and journey to the more sheltered side, from which they could descend once more to the low-lying ground, still skirting the territory of the resident manearins.

All conversation ground to a halt. For some reason unknown to Ramsey, Theron was acting strangely, and seemed to be in an apprehensive mood from the first light of morning. Ramsey couldn't work out what was bothering his companion, because every time he opened his mouth to ask, Theron would tell him to be quiet, albeit politely. Ramsey was unwilling to be governed by a troll of any description, but finally defeated by Theron's insistence, he fell quiet and slunk moodily behind him as they advanced through the thick snow. He could not remember why he had ever considered Theron a useful companion; now, the troll was just bothering him again.

Grumpy as he was, Ramsey hugged himself to keep warm against the storm, though his hair was flustered in all directions and his nose was cold and running. He was forced to press his body against the mountainside as they walked, to avoid being blown off the ledge; Theron, persistently strong and sturdy, ambled ahead of him, with a dusting of snowflakes all over his brown and purple hair.

The thick fur on his hind-quarters must be comfortable and warm, thought Ramsey bitterly, who was certain that his limbs would soon turn gangrenous with frostbite. Theron always seemed to have an easier time than Ramsey, no matter what the situation. Thoughts of a troll fur coat began to appeal to him once again.

Ramsey found it hard to believe that they were still moving in an upward direction, and had lost count of how many arduous hours they had spent climbing higher and higher up the mountainside, through the raw weather. The clean smell of fallen snow was fresh in the air, and the gloomy sky above them was windswept with grey clouds. A slight rumble of distant thunder told Ramsey that the storm was not going to subside anytime soon. Theron glanced up at the sky for a split-second, then picked up his pace, urging Ramsey to keep up; Ramsey, slouching against the wind, hurried along behind the troll, his expression hard and his toes numb.

At last, they reached a section of the path that was bereft of snow, for they were no longer in the direct path of the chilling gusts. The stone was still cold, and cracked slightly as they walked over it, but it was a broad, secure walkway, and far preferable to the path they had followed before.

They were so very high above ground level that they seemed to have passed above the clouds, as a dull, grey mist hung all around them. It was not as cold as the snow and hail had been, and it left a slight feeling of dampness on the skin, rendering their visibility very poor. Ramsey could not see far in front of him, and was reminded of the creeping fog that had surrounded him in the Great Forest; but something heartened him.

"We must be getting near the top," he said, "otherwise it wouldn't be so damn hard to see."

"Mmhmm…" responded Theron. Ramsey looked up at his companion, and found that the troll's face was caked with snow, like a pair of white sideburns and a beard framing his cheeks and chin, flaking off gradually as he spoke. "I don't think it could be much further, Ramsey. We must try to keep quiet."

"Still? Oh, for crying out loud…!" Theron shushed him, and Ramsey crossed his arms again, a miffed expression on his face. He had only tried to make pleasant conversation, after all.

It had, indeed, taken them an insanely long time to scale a drastically tall mountain, for the sake of avoiding a small group of wolf-sized predators. Theron could probably have faced them with no problems at all. For some reason, Ramsey felt compelled to go out of his way to keep them as safe as possible, even though the risk had been small.

Talking to the innkeeper in Grassman Village, reading that one article in 'The Merlockiara Bulletin' – something had been imprinted on his mind that warned him starkly not to risk travelling over the open land. Had he known that the weather would be so unpleasant, and that the Troll Teeth Mountains were as tall and inhospitable as they were, he would have thought again about his decision.

Like it or not, he had already made his choice on the matter, and it would be fruitless to attempt climbing back down the mountain. With the recent storm, Ramsey knew that conditions would get no more pleasant further down the peak. They had already come half-way, and journeys downhill were always swifter than those uphill – they could withstand the weather for another day or two.

He shivered, and closed his eyes against the cool water vapour suspended around them. If they had risked travelling over the flat land, they might have been the ones under attack from the creatures with dark fur that had attacked the manearins the previous day. They hadn't seemed as big as Theron, but there were several of them on the scene at once, and surely even a huge troll like Theron would have lost the battle against them all.

Though he had never been to school in his life, Ramsey was fond of information that he could acquire from anywhere and everywhere – but even in wildlife books that he had stolen from the Merlock market, he had never read a description of such creatures. He was just thankful that they hadn't scaled the mountain behind him and Theron; they had been high enough so as to be entirely unnoticed by the animals.

"Theron?" Theron grunted. "You know those animals I was looking at yesterday, when-"

"Keep your voice down, Ramsey."

"...*when I almost fell over the side of the path*?" hissed Ramsey in an exaggeratedly low and husky whisper.

The troll sniffed and shook his head, sending loose snowflakes fluttering to the ground. "Uh huh."

"Well...did you know what they were?" Theron shook his head again, answering Ramsey's question this time. "Hmm...well, they were really weird looking. They sounded like cats, so I guess they were fronas of some sort. Too big, though." Theron grunted again. "And they were peculiar colours, dark green and dark red and black..."

"Ramsey," said Theron, his voice a low growl, "for the last time, will you please keep quiet? I don't mean to be rude, but this mountain feels strange to me, and we can't let our guard down. I get the feeling that we have been followed for a while."

Ramsey blanched instantly, through his cheeks were flushed pink from the cold, and he quickened his steps to keep pace with the troll. "What? Followed? By what? Not the dragon?"

"No, Ramsey. I am not sure what it is, but it may still be following us, so we need to hurry up."

Theron promptly broke into a brisk trot to illustrate this point, and Ramsey had to start jogging in order to keep up. By now, they had reached a point where a natural arch of stone had formed over the path, making a narrow tunnel for them to pass through, which offered shelter for a moment or two. Theron did not linger, however, and continued under the arch and along the mountain path, which took a sharp right turn into a fissure that had formed in the mountainside.

Ramsey still could not see very far due to the low-lying clouds, but could make out that they were passing across a section of the path that was inverted with the inward curve of the mountain. Another pathway, hanging far above their heads, coiled away even higher above the mist, out of sight. He figured that somewhere along their current path, they should come across some way to reach the trail above, which, it seemed, would take them to the peak of the mountain, and over.

The wind blew in their faces. The sheer wall of the mountainside was all they had to steady themselves, faced with a black ravine immediately to their left, a fall from which, it could be certain, neither one of them would survive. Amidst the fog-like covering of clouds, a few gnarled, unhealthy looking trees twisted their way out of crevices in the rock, and brittle shrubs sat like hedgehogs on either side of the twisting mountain road.

The snow had all but stopped falling, and as they could no longer gaze upon the flakes cascading over the distant landscape, their only way to determine the fall of snow was by the number of snowflakes that landed directly upon them. Ramsey fussed immensely when some snow made its way into his eye, because he already had a generous amount of the white, powdery substance in his hair, which made his usual coal-black locks appear grey and ageing. Normally erect and unkempt, Ramsey's hair was damp and flustered by the storm, and thus it fell drably over his shoulders, plastered to his neck with frost.

Only now, as they neared the peak of the mountain, did Ramsey notice a bitter, rank smell on the air, like that of a severely infected wound or of meat that had been left in the kitchen for too long. It was the scent of something that was dead, some kind of rotten flesh. It suddenly overpowered his senses, and he scrunched up his face, pinching his nostrils shut with two fingers.

"Eugh!" he exclaimed, producing a startle from Theron, who walked a metre or so ahead of him through the mist. "What in the name of Scaless is that disgusting smell?"

"Ramsey, please," urged Theron, not stopping, "the less we say out loud, the better. This is a dangerous place, we should never have come here."

"What in Grenamoya is so frightfully worrying?" he snapped, his hands in his pockets. "You've been in a bad mood all day, and it would help if you'd at least say what the matter is!" The troll's rounded outline, obscured by the cloud cover, became fainter through the mist, indicating that Theron was moving more quickly. Ramsey now had to run to keep up with him, though Theron continued without faltering, as though he knew the mountain paths well. "Hey, wait a minute!"

"We should never have come here, Ramsey," repeated the troll, his voice somewhat strained. "It was foolish of us to come this way."

"Oh, so now it's my fault, is it? Well, I'm sorry, Theron, but for your information I was trying to keep us safe when I said we should cross the mountains! Did you see what happened to those manearins down there?" He gestured obscurely downwards, though Theron had his back towards him. "They were practically massacred by a load of off-colour frona things! That could have been us, if we'd gone that way!"

"Ramsey, keep up."

Ramsey was running as fast as his legs could carry him, but was quickly fatigued due to the lack of oxygen so high up in the air. He gasped for breath and leaned against the mountainside, instantly losing sight of his companion in the thickening fog. "Oh, so now you're just going to leave me? Fine! Carry on if you like, but I'm not going to tag along behind you without knowing what you're running away from!"

He waited in silence for a moment, his frozen breath catching in his throat; Theron did not come back through the cloud. Ramsey was suddenly aware that he could neither see nor hear anything apart from the bleak mist that surrounded him on all sides, clouding the path ahead as well as the way they had come. A sinking feeling found its way into his stomach, and an overwhelming sense of dread engulfed him. He was alone.

Frantically, he ran onwards in a blind panic, calling Theron's name, and abruptly bumped into something firm and hairy – he had collided with Theron's backside. He instantly steadied himself to find that the troll was looking over his shoulder at him; Ramsey glared, and fury erupted inside his head.

"Why did you just *wander off* like that, Theron? Some friend! I thought you'd been killed!"

"Of course not."

Ramsey grabbed at his own hair with impatience. "What do you mean, 'of course not'? I didn't know, did I? You won't tell me what we're running from!"

Theron did not turn around, partially because his bulk on the narrow path prevented him from doing so. "Ramsey, be quiet! We can't be too careful!"

"You've got a habit of doing that, you know! You go all obscure and weird, and say that bad stuff is going to happen, but you never bloody well tell me until it's too late!"

"Ramsey-"

"And to think I was starting to see you as a friend!"

Theron still did not turn, but his gaze was imploring. "I *am* your friend, Ramsey."

"Ha!" He stamped at the ground, disturbing a few broken fragments of rock with his bare feet. "If you're my friend, don't keep blaming me for bringing us up here!"

"I'm not blaming you!"

"You've been acting funny for ages, so at least tell me what's wrong! I do have a right to know when my own life is in danger!"

By now, the whole mountain seemed to echo their argument, up and down every crevice, each path, each cave. The creatures in those caves rattled and stirred with hollow intakes of breath, drawn to the sound of the two companions feuding. Theron moved ahead once more, losing his patience with Ramsey, who indignantly tried to keep pace with brisk, bony steps. The mist closed in around them like a gloomy veil.

"If you'd just give me a straight answer, troll!"

Theron growled, his claws scraping the path. "I have a name, you know."

"That's what has always annoyed me about you, troll – you make out like you know all the secrets of nature, all these cosmic signs, which are a load of-" (Here Ramsey said a word that Theron had not heard before, but he knew it was an insult.) "You pretend that you know all this stuff I don't, when you're as thick as a fence post! And this is *my* quest, not yours, so you should bloody well let me take control of it!"

"I know it's your quest, Ramsey!" Theron's voice was now little more than a beastly snarl, but Ramsey was not intimidated; he still walked a few feet behind the troll, fuming. "You let me come along on this journey with you! I didn't just invite myself along!"

"Like Pain you didn't!" snapped Ramsey, and the sentence seemed to strike an acute blow on Theron. Ramsey hadn't thought about what he was saying. Something within him sparked anew as the four, simple words left his lips. "You wanted to come so badly, and I only let you come because I felt so bad for you after your home was destroyed! I never even liked you, and now you're saying that you're my *friend*? Act more like a friend, then, Theron, and stop keeping stuff from me!"

"I've been trying to keep quiet in case we were in danger, you can't blame me for wanting to protect you! I've got half a mind to leave you here by yourself in the snow."

"You've got half a mind *full stop*."

Ramsey felt sick and empty, as though he might start to cry again out of sheer frustration. A powerful anger surged through his body, numbing him to everything else. Theron would not stop; he marched forward out of sight, but still called over his shoulder, "You're a very sad person, Ramsey, if you can't appreciate me trying to help you, and you never have!"

"Shut up!" screamed Ramsey to the mist. "Shut up, shut up!"

He clutched his scalp, his eyes red with the threat of tears. The last person he had spoken those words to was the one he could hear in his head, harassing him, telling him to feel pain, to bear it or be killed. He felt a pain far more excruciating than death somewhere in the back of his mind. He couldn't understand what had happened to him all those years ago. All he knew now was that, once again, he was alone.

He blinked, and then tore along the winding road behind Theron, the frantic fear of abandonment icy in his chest. Only a few metres along the path, Theron had stopped, and Ramsey ran to his side. Before he could speak, however, he noticed was Theron was looking at.

Sprawled out on the path, which was almost ten feet broad at this particular site, was the mangled, frost-bitten body of what at first appeared to be an immense bird. On closer inspection, they found it to be a griffin, which had probably been grand and intimidating in life. Now, bloodstained, snow-covered and stripped of most of its flesh, it was an altogether mournful sight.

Plucked feathers strewn across the plateau danced away from Theron's feet as he approached the carcass, taking great care not to disturb it out of respect. Ramsey, literally frozen to the spot, could find no more coarse words for the troll.

"What in Grenamoya could have done that?" he asked at last, his mouth dry. "That griffin is huge!"

Theron peered closely at the dead animal without touching it, then stood at his full height again, craning his neck to the sky. His large, triangular ears twitched slightly, listening for the lowest growl or the tiniest disturbance of rock. Ramsey could have screamed at him again, desperately wanting to be heard. "Hey...!" was all he whispered.

Theron had no time to respond. In an instant, his eyes were fixed upon the dark, murky silhouette of a wide cave that opened onto the path, for something was moving inside. Ramsey followed the troll's line of vision and beheld movement within the vague blackness. The sound of rumbling, unintelligible voices muttering a deep language, the scrape of claws against rock, the feel of a foul presence in the air.

First they saw one, then two, then five, then ten, all emerging from the cave through the murky cloud cover; creatures with different coloured fur, brown hair on their hind legs and black manes running along their necks. They whooped and muttered in unison like a clan of hyenas stalking a particularly vulnerable pair of gazelles. Acting on instinct, as terror had halted all independent thought, Ramsey shuffled closer to Theron, who stood his ground, his chest heaving steadily though he too must have been afraid.

The mountain trolls were all that Ramsey had imagined – in the same instant, they had all and nothing in common with Theron. They had the same appearance, but stretched over a far bonier structure. Their barrel-like chests sunk away into mean, malnourished stomachs; their limbs were lean and their faces were shaggy. They were shorter than Ramsey while standing on four legs, but not by far. Though Theron was big, the mountain dwellers were numerous, and were evidently more malicious than any manearin could ever be.

For a brief moment, they stood still amidst the fog, as though summarising the challenge that Theron might present. Then, as suddenly as they had appeared, the mountain trolls let out a uniform snarl, and sprang into action.

Ramsey could feel nothing below his neck, and was suddenly dragged to one side as the largest mountain troll leapt towards him, missing its prey by inches. All he could see for a moment was a swirling barrage of colours, and then it all fell into place; he was atop Theron's back, as they fled for their lives yet again.

Ramsey pressed himself desperately against the troll's body, gripping onto his mane, closing his eyes against the cold wind that lashed at his exposed skin. Theron did not falter for a moment, darting sideways, turning sharp corners, searching for a path of escape. Frightfully close behind them, the other trolls were clamouring noisily in their frenzied manner, as sure-footed as mountain goats as they sprinted over the crumbling rock.

The rocky path was heavily weathered beneath Theron's paws, and seemed to get narrower with every turn. Dead, brittle shrubs were crushed to fragments as he passed over, followed by a group of at least fifteen mountain trolls, all snarling and snapping at his heels like mindless animals. They were not deterred by the fact that Theron was their kin; if anything, they were more excited at the prospect of bringing down a large victim.

Ramsey got the feeling that he would not make much of a meal, and clung onto Theron for dear life, trying to keep his eyes focused on the way ahead through the diminishing clouds. Theron's footsteps thundered over the whole mountain, dully echoed by the collective noise of rabid predators behind them.

The fog cleared, and finally Ramsey saw the wide landscape once again, stretching away to their left as Theron ran. To their right, the rigid wall of rock offered no escape. Theron's body was heaving dramatically, no doubt due to the thinness of the air, and he slowed briefly, only to be spurred on once again by a sharp jab from Ramsey's ankles. Resolute to keep going, the forest troll galloped onwards, leaping over a fallen pile of mis-matched rocks and around another sharp turn in the indent of the mountain, the smaller trolls in hot pursuit.

"No! Stop, stop!"

Ramsey shrieked, and Theron came to a halt mere inches from the summit of a vast drop, formed where the road had been abruptly cut short. Theron gasped loudly, his claws teetering on the edge of the crevice; he took a step backwards and turned to face their attackers. A sea of malnourished, shaggy bodies had converged several feet away from the pair, and the troll at the front, its face tight and aggressive like that of a bulldog, took a bold step forward, its bristly mane of black hair wafting in the breeze of the ebbing storm. It was still snowing, and small flakes caught in the creature's dark blue body hair.

Theron drew himself up to his full height, his breath misting the air in front of him, and made a strange, barking noise at the mountain troll, which Ramsey could interpret as some kind of challenge. The smaller troll snapped back with a spitting retort, and suddenly Ramsey felt himself being pulled forward by his arms as Theron charged towards the mountain trolls and leapt over their heads.

Ramsey screamed and clenched his teeth, but found that they landed with a thud on solid ground, on a narrow shelf that led to another climbing mountain road, above the broken path they had previously followed. Just beneath and behind them, the other trolls stared confusedly for a moment, then awoke to the situation and followed Theron, scrambling up the ledge and tearing after them once more.

Ramsey gasped and held onto Theron so tightly that his knuckles turned white. The endless landscape of green and brown was now to his right, and seemed further away than ever. The wind whipped at his face. It was colder than before, and they were dangerously exposed. They must have been nearing the summit, he hoped. He prayed.

"It was not a good idea to come this way, Ramsey!" panted Theron, snow in his eyes as he ran. Ramsey lifted his head, astounded that Theron had raised the topic at that particular moment.

"Oh give it up, will you? It's not my fault, I didn't know this would happen!"

Theron's voice was hard and unsympathetic, sending a more devastating wave of terror over Ramsey's being. "I'm never going to listen to you again! You'll get us both killed!"

"Just shut up, will you? I feel bad enough without you being mad at me!" Theron let out a strangled cry, and Ramsey whipped around to find that one of the scraggly mountain trolls had latched onto one of Theron's hind legs. "Argh!"

Another troll leapt forward at its comrade's initiative, and clung to Theron's left side, digging its sharp teeth into the fur and flesh. Theron snarled and bashed himself against the solid mountainside with the force of rhinoceros, and the green-furred troll, crushed and instantly killed, let go of him and fell behind, slowing its accomplices. This only served to make them angrier, and they pushed the hairy body aside, fury now adding to their speed.

"Oh no..." moaned Ramsey, as he watched the dead troll slide to the ground unheeded. "Oh Scaless..." Suddenly, the other mountain troll that was still attached to Theron reached upward and grabbed Ramsey by the belt. Toppled off-balance, Ramsey yelled and almost fell to his death, but a sudden jolt from Theron jerked Ramsey back into a sitting position and dislodged the offending mountain troll. "Ow! Theron, you're bleeding!" he said, noticing the blood seeping through Theron's thick, brown leg hair. Theron shook his head and took a deep, loud breath.

"Don't bother me with that now, Ramsey!"

Ahead of them, there loomed a break in the road that looked just narrow enough for him to jump over. Ramsey had not noticed this at first, but the moment he did, he yelped and pressed himself against Theron's back, not caring that he and the troll were at loggerheads with one another. Theron, his eyes set upon the broad gap and the crumbling rock that bordered it, quickened his run, his claws scraping upon the stone.

As he ran, he kicked an opportunistic troll in the jaw by accident, thus saving himself from further grievous injury. The trolls yowled and screamed resoundingly behind them, but their cries faded somehow in the impending presence of the broken trail. Ramsey heard their snarls echo almost meaninglessly behind him; distant, like threats heard from underwater.

The sky above them shattered with thunder and lightning, and the clouds were suddenly lit, foggy behind the cascade of falling snow. The mountain trolls faltered, some cowering behind the others. Theron charged ahead, his mind numb to the rest of the world, and he sprang from the ground, leaping over the fissure of missing rock. Ramsey felt it all in an instant – the air streaking past his face, as though he was atop some mythical, flying creature, and then the harsh bump as they struck stone once more. He lost his grip, and was thrown several metres through the air, coming to a rough and awkward landing upon the icy path. He slumped onto his stomach, twisting his neck rather painfully, then lifted his head to see where he was.

Metres away, Theron was struggling to climb onto the jagged ledge, clutching at it with claws that scraped long gashes in the stone. Hanging halfway into the abyss, he was struggling to support the weight of himself and three vicious mountain trolls with only his arms. His eyes were wild and panic-ridden, and he barely saw his companion lying sprawled-out on the path before him.

Horrified, Ramsey scrambled to his feet and ran back to help, but he could do nothing. Theron, either due to waning strength or out of self-sacrifice, lost his grip on the edge, and quick as a flash he was gone. Ramsey felt a stifling grip on his throat; delirious with fear he ran back down the path too late, just in time to see Theron disappear through the fog, his trio of assailants screaming as they fell.

The mountain trolls on the other edge of the path wailed and snarled, and their gaze was instantly upon Ramsey, who froze. One troll leapt forward to bridge the gap, but missed the ledge and fell into the chasm with a rusty cry. Its comrades stared after it for a moment, then returned their attention to Ramsey; and then, much to Ramsey's relief, they just spat at him, turned, and set off in the opposite direction, back down the mountain towards their cave.

Ramsey swallowed the massive lump in his throat. The trolls knew the mountain far better than he, and almost certainly would find another way of reaching him. Turning around, and tripping slightly in the process, he bolted up the road, not knowing where he might end up. The wind swept his hair from his face as he ran.

He did not know how far he ran or how long it snowed upon him. The storm was rumbling overhead once more in a dark and grumpy manner, like the growling of the mountain trolls still so freshly etched in his mind. He stumbled blindly through the fluttering snow, and the sheets of hail that occasionally bore down upon him. Lightning streaked across the sky, but it was mostly distant, striking the peaks of the other Troll Teeth Mountains in a most alarming way. At that moment, Ramsey knew he couldn't have felt more miserable if he happened to be struck by lightning – who knows, he thought, maybe it would help me think straight.

All around him the mountain was white and silver, the grey stone glimmering with an icing of frost. Below, and as far as the eye could see, the green, misty land of Merlockiara was damp and serene beneath the gradually fading light. Oouealena, now also visible from his lofty vantage point, was equally green, but somehow seemed more static and weary than his home kingdom, scattered here and there with brown patches of sparse grassland. Frona hunting-ground.

Fronas sounded like a blessing in the aftermath of such a traumatic, troll-related experience. He held his head, his clothes stiff and grimy from the chase. Snow crunched morosely beneath his bare feet, and low-lying cloud began to close in once more, fading the white flashes of lightning above him.

Finally, feeling his way tentatively along the mountainside through the storm, he came across a relatively dry, goblin-sized crevice in the rock. It was tall enough for him to walk in with a slight slouch, and more than wide enough, so he quickly clambered inside to escape the hail.

Thankfully, the small cave did not have the slightest hint of troll smell, so he pushed his way past the lumpy, eroded walls and sat down at the very back of the cave, with enough room to stretch out his legs if he wanted to. All the same, he did not stretch himself out, because he was feeling so cold, wet and ill. He tucked his legs up to his body, shrouding them within his large, brown shirt, and put his head in his hands.

"What have I done? Oh Scaless..." The weak, withering quality of his own voice scared him at that moment. He was completely alone. He had once heard someone say that one day he would be all alone and it would be his fault. He swallowed and thought for a moment. That voice was not the same as the others. It was a completely different voice. He swallowed harder. "Oh no, please don't let me hear them again..."

*One day you'll end up all alone...*

There was no grim pleasure in this voice. It was filled with a kind of sorrowful acceptance.

*And you'll have nobody to blame but yourself.*

It was a different voice. So different.

*One day you'll be all alone, and you'll have nobody to blame but yourself.*

It was a female voice. It was a higher octave that the usual voices in his head. The number of thoughts racing through his mind meant that he could not decipher any one singularly. Maybe he deserved this. His eyes were so painful that they burned, combined with the sting of sorrow and self-hatred in his heart.

"That should have been me falling to my death out there...oh Scaless, just let me die here!"

Forks of lightning graced the sky, and the thunder was suddenly deafening, as though the sheer anger within him was being voiced by the heavens. He shrunk back inside the cave, his fingers tightly coiled against his cheeks, seeking to grab onto something and throttle it just to vent his grief. He closed his eyes tightly, and saw the swirling colours glowing beneath his eyelids. They began to form a picture as he sat in the dark, a very vague, watery picture, and then they vanished once more.

The voice kept repeating its haunting mantra inside his head, and he felt the glands in his throat swelling with emotion. He had thought, just possibly, for a very, *very* brief moment, that he had seen his mother. Her blurry, inexact mouth had moved with the contours of each word;

*One day you'll end up all alone, Ramsey, and you'll have nobody to blame but youself...*

'*Ramsey*'. She had said his name. The flitting remembrance of her partially formed face stung the edges of Ramsey's consciousness like a poisoned needle. He had seen those eyes, that skin, he had felt that silky hair before, entwined between his fingers, his other hand clutching a fraying, home-made stuffed animal.

He swore under his breath, realising that he had remembered something.  He saw a blank, glass-eyed face gazing emptily up at him, held securely in his arms; a face so expressionless and dead, but full of warmth.  The scent of raspberries where an old jam stain had never fully been washed from the brown, woollen face.  Wool, like the thick shirt he was wearing at that exact moment.

In an effort to conjure up further wispy memories, he pressed his face against his sleeve and breathed in the slightly damp scent of the wool.  It was not the same, but it awoke something forgotten within him.

*I will not keep him here!  This will be the death of him, the death of you.  Don't you see?  He will die if he stays here with me!  They will take him from me, you know I cannot stand up to anything the king might do, Ramsey.  If I lose my only child, Scaless help me, I may love you, but I swear I will kill you if they don't get to you first!*

The words were as clear as day, spoken firmly, sending boiling messages to and fro across his mind.  He couldn't open his eyes for fear that the voices would end; for once in his life, he yearned to listen.  His heart thumped erratically in his chest, seeming to resonate around the entire cave.  The female speaker's fearful, yet dejected voice faltered slightly, and he felt his concentration dying again.  He was so upset that could not prevent his thoughts from racing.

*Please…no, Ramsey, please, take him from me!*

Ramsey could see her now; she was a lemon-skinned goblin standing on the brink of nothingness, surrounded by nothing but a vast, empty void, and she was speaking not to him, but beyond him. He could see her makeup smearing down her cheeks.

*You cannot send your own son to his death in this way!  I am powerless!*

*We love you, Ramsey…we only press this against your skin to show you our love…*

His heart jolted and ricocheted around inside his ribcage. The familiar, sneering voice had returned, yet it was still faint and obscured by a screechy, humming undertone. Everything else that was dwelling on his mind suddenly fell away, leaving him on the brink of consciousness alone, standing between two contrasting voices that spoke at once. One of them clear, the other scratchy and waning. His stomach turned.

*I cannot send you out there to die, and I cannot sacrifice our son to them. Please, you must stay and help me. If you have any heart at all...*

*Hold him down, hold him down! Rip the skin, peel it off!*

*It's all right, my love, we will be fine, you and I...*

*Tear it off! Look at all that blood...*

*Don't pull on mummy's earrings, dear.*

*Slice him open! Quickly now, before he bleeds to death like the others...*

*...I saw what you did last night, Ulyssis.*

Ramsey gritted his teeth, his breath coming hard and fast. The two voices had suddenly subsided, and all he could hear now was the deep tone of a new one. It was cold, thunderous, and he instantly knew that it was detached from his memories. He opened his eyes, but the sound remained, and grew stronger.

*I suppose you derive some twisted satisfaction from sticking your claws down that elf's throat...*

Ramsey was wide-awake and fully conscious. He could hear this new person as though they were discussing something face to face, though the hail battered against the mountainside like a thousand woodpeckers all working together. Too entranced to be worried for his sanity, his listened, knotting his brow with curiosity.

*No, your worship, it is not what you think!* cried a second voice, not as deep, but somewhat coarse.

*I can see anything and everything you do, Ulyssis, as quickly and as clearly as I wish. You displease me, you treacherous cretin!*

The owner of the second voice was silent for a moment, then said in a simple manner, *I was attempting to kill him.*

*Then why did you not fulfil your intent? Answer me that, Ulyssis! You still have feelings for that repulsive elf, don't you?*

Ramsey could feel the pain in the second voice's response; *No! No, I have never felt anything towards Elwin apart from hatred, master, and that is the honest truth. I would never deceive you, for I know I never could, even if I wished to.*

This response seemed to please the first voice, for it spoke again in a calm, measured tone. *Very well then. Do not take any more initiatives, however, Ulyssis; I do not want that elf dead just yet. Return to me immediately, and no diversions.*

Ramsey's throat was so tight that he could barely breathe, even after his world had descended into silence once more, apart from the sound of the raging weather outside. He blinked, staring out at the hail through the mouth of his cave. Somehow, he got the feeling that he had just acted as an uncertified eavesdropper upon a very crucial conversation.

Everything fell into place once again, sweeping over Ramsey like a devastating, polar tide. Theron was gone. He was all by himself, stranded at the top of a snow-capped mountain, with probably an entire swarm of carnivorous trolls after his flesh. It was his fault that Theron was dead. The troll was right; if Ramsey had not led them up the mountain, they would have never run into such trouble.

But he had only wanted to protect them...

An encounter with the frona-like creatures in the valley, whatever they were, would maybe not have resulted in the death of his companion. He felt as though he had dragged Theron into that abyss himself. Theron had not quite been able to reach the other side because of the three other trolls clinging to him. If Ramsey hadn't shouted so much, maybe they would not have been chased.

With all these thoughts and more now weighing on his frail mind, Ramsey sunk against the sharp wall of the cave, covered his face with his hands and cried until sleep overcame him. Outside, the darkening sky veiled the mountain in an eerie blackness, casting shadows over the mountain trolls lurking upon the trails in search of griffin eggs, and the solitary, motionless body of a forest troll that had fallen through the mists.

# Chapter Eleven

# Ramsey's Demon

The first thing Ramsey noticed from the moment he awoke, besides the dull splatter of raindrops at the entrance to his cave, was a sharp, aching pain in his right calf. He grumbled to himself, suddenly awake as though every tired inch of his body had been called to attention at once. He had no hope of getting back to sleep, though from the faint, white glisten of clouds on the horizon, he realised it was very early morning. The sun had not yet risen over the mountains.

Infuriated, he realised that he also had a throbbing headache in his temples. He had been so bouncy, so healthy over the last couple of days that he had forgotten how truly awful he usually felt. He closed his eyes tight, but on finding that this increased the severity of his pain, opened them once more.

The cave walls were blurred for a moment, then they came into grey, murky focus, and his skull pulsed more acutely than ever. He briefly pulled up his right trouser leg to inspect his calf. The old scarring, where Theron had dragged him through the forest so long ago, had somehow reopened, and around the wound, his normally orange skin was the milky, pink hue of unhealed flesh. It was bleeding very slightly. All he could think was that one of the mountain trolls had grabbed him the previous evening without him noticing.

His heart and stomach were heavy and painful inside him. Without Theron for protection, he was too afraid to wander beyond the damp protection of his small cave. If he waited in hiding for too long, he was certain to die of hunger. For the first time in what felt like ages, he was at a complete loss about what to do next.

He hadn't come all this way just to die. He wouldn't abandon his quest now that he felt some genuine urge to rescue Morgan and reunite him with his father. Viktor may have been a hopeless king, as Ramsey so fondly reminded himself, but Morgan was worth fighting for.

Something deep inside himself spurred him on; he would navigate his way down the mountain, across Oouealena and the Ash Mountains to rescue the prince, or he would die trying.

He just hoped his journey would not come to such a grim conclusion.

Ramsey reached out to his sides and pressed his flat, orange palms against the narrow walls of the cave. He uncurled his legs, and stretched them out in front of him. He gazed down at his long, lanky limbs for a moment or two, still gaudily clad in a purple shirt, brown over-shirt and green trousers; his feet, poking out of his trouser legs miles away, were dark and grimy from his journey. It had been so long since he had enjoyed a decent rest, or been able to wash himself. He sighed, remembering his memorable lakeside escapade with Theron weeks before.

When he saw past his own sheer embarrassment at being seen naked by another living being, it was actually an amusing thought. He must had looked crazy, wading through the lake and falling into the water like a lunatic, covered in mud and screaming. This contemplation brought a slight smile to Ramsey's pointed face, now lined by the trauma of recent days.

He had most certainly aged since he started out on his travels; not only did he feel entirely different, but he looked it. He was skinnier, his face was dirtier and his hair more unruly, black spikes streaking to and fro like the wayward strokes of an artist's paintbrush. His clothes were intact, and brighter than he was used to, with more buttons remaining than he had even known in his life.

But more than anything, his face had changed. As sharp as his wit, very distinct with a pointed chin, long nose and bright, brown eyes; now his eyes were dull, the colour of dead leaves, and masked with sadness. His face was harder, and yet something about him had softened, possibly due to his current grief, maybe founded upon something more permanent. His cheeks were dusted with dirt, and flushed from the cold. He knew he must try to regain his composure and continue on his travels if he was to have any hope of surviving.

There was no hint of troll smell in the air, so he tentatively crawled from the cramped confines of his cave, stepped shakily onto the mountain path, and stretched his arms above his head, allowing the raindrops to run down his skin and gather in his thick hair. The cool droplets were refreshing, and distracted him from the emotions he felt inside; an array of feelings so diverse that he could not begin to unravel them. He wanted to hide and never be seen again, he wanted to cry, he wanted to scream, he wanted to rescue Prince Morgan and take the poor boy home, so the prince would no longer be in the same situation as Ramsey; cold and stranded at the top of a mountain, with nobody to protect him.

Ramsey could feel that Morgan was alive. He knew it as surely as he had heard that strange, deep voice in his head the night before. Whoever 'Ulyssis' might be, Ramsey did not want to hear anything else about him if he had some kind of elf fetish.

He would not let the mountain conquer him; he would continue on his way, he would survive, he would rescue Prince Morgan, and somehow the two of them would find their way home. Theron was gone, but Ramsey would not let the troll be shaken from his mind so easily. Somebody had held faith in him, even though their friendship lasted only a brief time. Ramsey was determined to fight.

The morning sky was clear, offering Ramsey an acute view of the world below, and the rain clouds above. There were but a few clouds in the gleaming azure sky, and it did not seem that the downpour would continue throughout the morning. Regardless of how wet he became, Ramsey knew that procrastination would only make his situation worse, and perhaps give the mountain trolls time to sneak up on him; so without further regard to the crucial conversation he had heard the night before, he rolled up his sleeves and marched onwards, up the mountainside on the narrow, winding road.

Unfortunately (or perhaps not so) for Ramsey, he had barely been walking for five minutes when an abrupt scratching sound from behind him made him stop dead on the path. His first thought, of course, was that the mountain trolls had found him. To some extent, he was correct, for it was a mountain troll that turned the bend further back along the trail – it was, however, a rather small, podgy one that came toward him.

Ramsey turned, still apprehensive, as he knew that the other trolls would not be far behind the infant. The small troll did not notice him at first, seemingly scampering along the road looking for somewhere to conceal itself, in what must have been a playful manner. To Ramsey, it was just hairy, ugly and unappealing, despite its small stature. About the size of a beagle, with a small, tufted fringe of black hair on its head and purple fur, similar to Theron's, on its body, the small troll ambled closer and closer to Ramsey, until it was barely a metre from him. When at last it noticed him, it gave him an incredulous, fascinated glance, then began to growl in a feeble gesture of aggression.

Despite the possible danger, Ramsey could not help but feel the urge to kick the little troll around on the road – it reminded him far too much of the mongrels that infested the town square back in Merlock. He raised a thin eyebrow, temporarily forgetting his other troubles, and watched as the hideous infant began to maul his trouser leg with its blunt teeth. It clung to the green cotton for a while, then, upon noticing that Ramsey was not bleeding to death, decided to attack him verbally instead.

Ramsey stared at the troll with a smirk on his face, but as he readied himself to kick the hairy child over the edge, a fully-grown adult emerged from around the bend, causing him to seize up with panic. It was a female mountain troll; barely distinguishable from the male variety, but with no dark hair framing its cheeks, and a ragged garment around its upper body to conceal its chest. Ramsey was surprised to see such a wild creature wearing any kind of clothing, but was somewhat relieved.

The very second the female saw him, her face contorted into a hateful grimace, and she stopped in her tracks, her purple fur bristling irritably. No doubt seeing Ramsey so close to the baby troll had alerted the female that the goblin might attack. Ramsey realised this just in time, and for lack of a better plan and with no other way to save his skin, he hurriedly snatched the small troll by the scruff of its neck and held it aloft as it struggled and squirmed like an angry cat.

It swiped a handful of small claws at him, but he easily avoided its reach and held it towards the edge of the path, beads of sweat breaking out on his forehead. He had not spoken a word, but the mother troll instantly saw his meaning, and though she bared a mouthful of uneven fangs towards him, she did not advance.

Ramsey swallowed and shook the small troll slightly, causing it to snort and try to maul him once more. Its attempts were futile, as its four legs were dangling high over the mountain ledge, from which it would fall until it hit the ground hundreds of metres below. It glanced briefly downwards, fell silent, and hung harmlessly in Ramsey's surprisingly strong grip.

"I'll drop him!" warned Ramsey urgently as the mother troll took a step forward. "I swear, I'll let him fall!"

What am I doing? he asked himself, I'm talking to a wild animal…

Strangely, the female troll stepped backwards in a manner that suggested she had understood his words. Her teeth were still bared menacingly, and she growled fiercely under her breath, but at long last, and much to Ramsey's surprise, she sat down on her haunches and said in a rough, savage voice, "What do you want?"

Ramsey couldn't have made his eyes go any wider if he tried. He kept a tight grip on the wriggling form of the infant, and decided to reply in as steady and bold a tone as possible. "Y-you can…talk?" He could have slapped himself – he had sounded more inarticulate than fearless.

"Give me back my child!" she snapped, in much the same manner as the other mountain trolls had snarled while chasing him and Theron. "If you let him drop, I shall kill you!"

Ramsey had no doubt about that. He also couldn't risk the female returning to the other trolls and alerting them to where he was. He desperately tried to think what he should do. Right on cue, he felt a stabbing pain in his right leg, and stumbled very slightly, causing the mother troll to leap to her feet.

"Um…I promise to let him go if you fetch me something to heal wounds with!" The troll returned to her sitting position, cocked her head at him, then slowly nodded. "And some food, too. But nothing poisonous, or I'll drop him anyway. And I'll do the same if you come back here with any of your friends following you!" The female growled again; apparently, this had been her original plan. "Hurry up about it, too."

"As you wish…" She grumbled and raised her upper lip in a snarl, but still complied with Ramsey's demands. She turned on her tail and trotted back the way she had come, around the bend in the mountain path, from which point onwards Ramsey could see her no longer.

After standing still in complete silence for a moment, he returned his attention to the young troll, who was flailing around again, his grip still firmly on the scruff of its furry neck. He looked at the baby, which looked back with large, brown eyes staring out of an unsightly face. He put his free hand on his hip and spoke with a stern tone, assuming that the baby could understand him nearly as well as its mother. "Listen – you pee on my trousers, kid, and I'll drop you anyway." It glared reproachfully at him, then surrendered to his firm hold, and dangled quietly.

It took approximately twenty minutes for the mother troll to return. Ramsey noticed her approaching along the crumbling road, a few objects in her mouth that Ramsey could not identify at a distance.

Now that he was not fleeing for his life, Ramsey was able to have a proper look at the mountain troll's appearance more closely. This particular female was very similar to the males, and her face was not unlike Theron's, except that it was less rounded and her fur was more rugged and irregular. Mountain trolls, Ramsey concluded, had a moth-eaten, feral appearance that could be attributed to the harshness of life in such an environment. No wonder they had been so eager to attack and kill Theron for food.

The troll drew near, and sat down at a safe distance from Ramsey, placing the items on the stone path in front of her. Ramsey, waiting for an explanation, withdrew the child from the edge of the path and held it to his chest, allowing the mother to feel more secure. The female, her purple fur glistening with rain, spoke in a voice that sounded strained and passive.

"This plant will heal wounds," she said, gesturing to a long, green stem with many broad leaves and small red flowers that rested at her feet. She spoke the name of the plant, but the title was unfamiliar to Ramsey, and he hesitated. The other item she had brought, a large piece of what looked like tough, grey hide, didn't look too appealing either. "And that is food."

"What is it?" asked Ramsey, sceptically. "It looks like it's been dead too long."

The troll snarled at him. "Picky, picky, picky!" Ramsey stared at the mother and threatened to hold her baby over the cliff again, which made the female regain her former composure and guarded tone. "We do not get much food up here. That is hippogriff, very tough, long lasting."

Ramsey felt so unwell with the prospect of eating the skin of a half-eagle, half-horse creature that he disregarded the female troll's attempts to coerce him into letting her baby go. His head was hurting again, and he dwelled miserably on his predicament until the distant, echoing roar of an animal down in the valley snapped him back to the present. The female troll made a gruff noise at the prospect of Ramsey dropping her child from fright, then snapped at him with an equally gruff voice.

"Don't be so jumpy! They are just the rhôniae down on the hills, they can't reach you. They never come up the mountains." With another lingering gaze towards the baby troll, she added, "Now, return my child to me, as you promised!"

"Rhôniae? I thought they were fronas," said Ramsey, carefully kneeling and setting the small troll on the ground, while keeping a firm eye on its mother. She barked angrily at Ramsey when he refused to let go of the baby, but she did not move closer.

"They *are* fronas. They are big fronas, though, and very dangerous. I have seen them kill manearins and goblins in the valley. They have not been seen in this kingdom for many years."

"Are they evil or something?"

"Give me my child!"

Ramsey restrained the infant, which was trying desperately to escape from his grasp. It began chewing on his arm through his brown shirt, but this action went unnoticed by the goblin, who was still searching for answers. "I want to know. You must tell me everything that you can about those animals. I came over these mountains to avoid manearins, and then I saw those huge things running up and down the hills."

"My *child*."

"How can I trust you? You'll just run the second I let your baby go. And I don't even know if this plant has healing properties, or if that hippogriff meat is poisoned!"

She growled, becoming bolder with the prolonged separation from her baby. "I would not have carried them in my mouth if either one was poisonous, would I?" she snarled, her voice breaking with frustration. "Let my child go free, and I will tell you all that I can, though I know little, and I doubt it will help you much, because my pack will hunt you down eventually, even though I haven't brought them with me!"

Ramsey hesitated for a moment, weighing his decision carefully, and then let go of the struggling baby troll. It gratefully scampered free of his grip and ran to its mother, nestling itself between her forelegs and shooting Ramsey a look of pure hostility. On the face of such a small troll, it was laughable and by no means threatening.

The female troll took no time to reacquaint herself with her child just then; instead, with her eyes fixed sternly upon Ramsey to prove that she now held the upper hand, she delivered her promised response quickly and with no betrayal of emotion.

"The rhôniae are not ordinary fronas. They are very large fronas, with dark fur, and I have been told that they come from Utipona. I have heard that they use tentacles on their faces to grasp and kill their victims. More than that, I can't tell, and I do not know why they have returned now, but the mountains are safe."

Ramsey stood still, unable to find the urge to move as he absorbed the information. The female troll gave him one final, pensive look, and then turned and retreated down the mountain road, her infant tottering along by her side. He found that he was breathing heavily; he watched the two mountain trolls until they vanished from view entirely, and bent to retrieve the two items from the path.

The dark leaves on the plant stem were shiny with a dusting of raindrops, and the delicate, red flower petals stood out starkly like wild eyes gleaming in complete darkness. He briefly sniffed the piece of hippogriff hide, found that it did not smell as gruesome as he had expected, and sat down in the middle of the path, rain falling around him, to tend to his leg.

Not certain how to apply the plant, he rolled up his trouser leg, plucked a large leaf from the green stem, and rubbed it firmly against the bleeding gash in his right calf. It stung instantly, like bullets of fire rushing to his skin, and he winced with pain, but the sensation quickly dulled, and he found that the plant had numbed the wound quite effectively. He kept the leaf firmly pressed against his calf for a further two minutes, applying even pressure all along the wound, and then removed it and cast it aside on the road. There was no visible improvement in the injury, but he could no longer feel pain in his leg, and was satisfied that the plant had done its task well.

He put the remainder of the plant, with its several broad, shiny leaves, into one of his pockets, and hungrily tucked into the tough, leathery hide that the troll had given him. It was very difficult to chew, very dense, and he knew that it would keep him going for quite some time yet; he hadn't forgotten that he still had a fresh fruit in his other pocket, and though it might be already overripe, it was better than nothing.

The rain pattered softly against the road as Ramsey journeyed onwards. He was still cold, and his clothes were heavy with water, soaked completely through. He felt awful, but found that he did not really worry about himself that day. He had spent a lifetime holding concern for nobody but himself, and now it was as though he was devoid of the single part of himself that he had cared about. There was nothing worthwhile within him.

The only person he felt sorry for was, in complete honesty, Prince Morgan. It was a feeling that he never dreamed he would experience, but now it was genuine, and rooted so deep inside him that he could not shake it, regardless of how much he wished to dwell on his own sorrowful situation. Theron was gone, so there was no point worrying for him – the forest troll now dwelled with the ethereal snake, somewhere high up in the clouds, pondered Ramsey. If indeed there was any truth in the whole 'afterlife' theory, Theron was one person who certainly deserved an eternity of peace and happiness.

"And with a brand new, indestructible forest to live in."

He did not register the fact that he had spoken this final thought out loud. He missed Theron, he had pined for him from the moment the troll had disappeared from sight through the fog. He needed somebody to talk to. Even if Theron had persisted in telling him to be quiet, Ramsey would at least have someone to whisper his troubles to. He felt utterly confused, totally lost. He did not know how in the name of Grenamoya he was going to make his way to the Ash Mountains with such bad luck and so few provisions; and, not that Theron could have given him any answers, he wanted to ask somebody to explain the voices he had heard the previous night.

"I'm completely mental…"

He sighed, as though mourning for a distant relative. This was a fact he now had to accept; he had been hearing unidentified voices for a long time, he had heard and seen a goblin whom he recognised as his own mother, and to finish the bizarre list of disembodied voices, he had heard a sharp, clear conversation between two male creatures that had drowned out his fragmented memories.

It was as if the two voices, more than all the others he had ever heard, were genuine; they had not felt like memories. They felt as though they were being spoken in the present, directly into his mind via some sort of psychic channel, though he could not explain why he had heard the conversation as it had not included him in any way.

He had never heard of anyone called Elwin, and certainly 'Ulyssis' sounded so foreign to his ears that it had not seemed like a real name. It was like a word from some kind of ancient, vampiric language, and Ramsey was most certainly glad that he had not overheard any more of the discussion. The less he had to hear about claws in elves' mouths, the better.

Ramsey had been so dramatically deep in thought that he did not notice when the mountain path began to curl downwards; the instant that he found himself descending the peak, he was filled with so much excitement that he felt he could have sprinted all the way down in less than an hour. Unfortunately, he was not in a fit mental or physical state to do so, and followed the trail, gradually tilting downwards, his pace set at a brisk walk.

He had somewhat suspected that there would be a solid barrage of mountain trolls waiting to ambush him on the other side of the mountain, but he was in luck, for he met with no such threat. The sky was clear, and though he was still being rained upon ever so slightly, the sheer relief gushing through his veins muted the impact of the cold, hard weather.

He was now gazing out over Oouealena, a beautiful, new landscape that was even more wonderful now that he was closer to it. The land was flatter than Merlockiara, with twisted, but very alive, oak trees sprouting proudly from the ground, standing thirty feet or more above the green grass. Ramsey could see a narrow, winding stream that cut through the land, flowing down from one of the other Troll Teeth Mountains, and culminating in a large, misshapen lake that reflected the blue sky like a sheet of dappled glass.

He could see no manearins, or any other threatening wildlife from his high vantage point; a flock of white birds flew overhead, towards the lake, and he saw them land noisily in the luscious branches of a tree, where they settled and called out to the distant clouds.

A chill was ever crisp against his bright skin, but the sun fell upon his face, illuminating his forehead, his long nose and grubby cheeks in a warm, yellow glow. He looked up at the sun, which had risen high through the sky since he had begun walking early that morning, and he knew he was smiling. It was a smile of relief, of sorrow for what he had lost, but tinged with gratitude to the powers that be, whatever they were, for seeing him through. The last warmth he had felt upon his face had been the hot sting of spilling tears; he would have cried again, with gladness, but could not find the strength within him to do so.

He kicked aside sparse, fading patches of snow from the path with his feet, not caring how cold it was to the touch, or the way the iciness bit at his already painful toes. His leg had improved since that same morning. He was thankful to have met with the female troll and her ugly baby, and even more thankful that she had kept her promise not to kill him. No doubt she would have informed the rest of her pack about where he was the moment she returned, and he knew better than to linger on the mountainside and enjoy the scenery.

The downhill journey was far swifter than the trek up the mountain; facing the sun's rays, there was very little snow to obstruct his way, and the rain clouds had passed overhead, taking the remainder of the unpleasant weather with them. Without Theron nagging him to hurry up and shut up, Ramsey was able to take his time despite his enthusiasm; he stopped several times an hour to rest his muscles, which ached every now and again from the arduous uphill journey, and to have another bite or two of the hippogriff hide that he carried with him.

He figured that his taste buds had been left numb from the cold, because the meat was not repulsive to him – it smelled pretty awful, but once it was in his mouth, he barely noticed what he was eating. Normally a very picky eater (as the female troll had very rightly pointed out), Ramsey was unaccustomed to eating something so strange, apart from under dire circumstances.

He heard no more voices that day, and put the previous night's experience down to the bitter impact of losing Theron to the mountain trolls. The problem of hearing voices was certainly magnified whenever he was feeling upset or angry, but now he felt elated again, as he had on that first day after falling out of the fruit tree. He had fought his illness, and though it had returned, it now seemed to have faded. It was as though the two unknown speakers had somehow banished the old voices from his mind. Stopping once again by the side of the road, next to the remnants of a stripped and dead tree, Ramsey rested his weary legs and took a deep breath, looking out over the land, which now seemed close enough for him to reach out and grasp.

Evening was already looming on the horizon. Ramsey estimated that he was maybe one third of the way down the mountain; the path was steeper than it had been on the way up the mountainside, but it appeared more direct than the snaking road they had followed over previous days. It might take him another day or so to reach the base of the mountain, but certainly no longer. Ramsey had never expected the mountain to be so dramatically tall as to take them a number of days to scale it. As he looked to the south, he beheld the largest and most unpleasant of the Troll Teeth Mountains, and was overwhelmed with relief that he and Theron had not attempted to climb that one instead.

311

Not wanting fatigue to overpower him before he found some cover, Ramsey resolutely began to investigate his immediate area for any sort of cave, small crevice, or a sheltering boulder. He sighed, seeing nothing nearby, and was forced to make his way further down the broad, sloping path, skidding slightly on a pile of loose rock fragments that had converged in the middle of the road.

He was aware that there could be danger lurking around, and moved as silently as possible, without need for Theron at his side constantly reminding him to be quiet. He smiled a thin smile, realising that he was already starting to forget the troll's strong smell, the colour of his fur, the sound of his deep, gentle voice.

He knew that he felt upset at the loss of his companion – what was it he had said to himself two nights ago, about telling Theron how much he was appreciated? How he did not want to lose the troll's friendship? These thoughts were almost forgotten amidst Ramsey's burning desire to rescue Prince Morgan and make something of himself. He knew Morgan was alive. He just *knew*.

The grunting sound of what he recognised to be troll voices halted his tentative steps. He could hear more than one troll making noise further down the road, but in the gathering dark, Ramsey found it hard to determine where exactly the sound came from. Ducking behind a large pile of rough stones, Ramsey peered down the road, squinting his eyes in an effort to focus his sight upon the currently invisible trolls. These voices certainly did not belong to infants.

After a moment or two of waiting with baited breath, Ramsey saw a pair of bristly silhouettes forming where the road turned away from his line of vision. Two trolls, which from a distance appeared to be fully grown, were approaching along the path, climbing the steep mountain road and talking in growling tones, looking at one another's faces. As they drew nearer, Ramsey could determine that they were having an argument of some kind, but they spoke in voices so low and rumbling that Ramsey could not understand their speech. He lowered his breathing, trying to remain as still and silent as possible, even when the trolls were very close to his protective pile of rocks.

Ramsey's fingernails scraped noiselessly against the hard stone as the two trolls came dangerously close to his hiding place. He was ready to breathe a sigh of relief, when suddenly both of them stopped still on the path, glaring at one another; then they began a growling argument right alongside the pile of stones, and did not advance beyond Ramsey's concealed, skinny form. He cursed to himself, begging that the trolls would pass by without noticing him.

"You are foolish, Rafan!" snapped one troll, the larger of the two, which had slate blue fur covering its skinny body. "I told you this was a stupid idea! You will get us killed!"

Ramsey swallowed; this mountain troll was speaking Theron's words, but in a far more aggressive tone. The smaller of the two, which appeared to be the equivalent of a mountain troll teenager, looked away from the larger troll, its grey-green fur bristling with anger. "I was only trying to get food for the family. Do not blame me for trying to keep us alive."

"You will get us killed, brother! You try to attack the rhôniae, and you will not emerge alive! Father will beat you for this."

Ramsey shrank back behind his rock pile, listening intently and glancing nervously at the trolls from between two large stones. He hoped to discover more about the rhôniae creatures that the mother troll had spoken of, but he had no such luck, for it seemed that these two male trolls knew just as little about them as she had done.

They bickered for a while longer, still not walking past Ramsey's hiding place; he learned little from their conversation, but discovered that the larger troll was named 'Rikmir'. He began to think that trolls had a preference for names beginning with 'R', as he had heard of several more examples in his lifetime. The mountain trolls had a rather sinister, snarling way of pronouncing their 'R's, which gave words like 'rhôniae' a more unnerving connotation.

He began to tire of the troll brothers once he realised that they would not present him with useful information, but he could do very little to get rid of them. Apart from maybe showing himself and telling them to shove off, which would probably result in him being killed and eaten. So he was forced to stay where he was, listening to their tedious conversation about how they each hated the other and how mother and father were going to hurt them both.

Eventually, he became so fed up that he lay down on his side with his chin in his palm and his legs tucked up to his body, wanting to catch some rest that evening regardless of how many trolls were arguing. He could still hear them ranting and growling as his eyelids gently closed, and he dwelled for a moment on Theron, Prince Morgan, and finally on his mother.

It had definitely been his mother that he had seen in his partial dream the night before. Actually, he thought, it had been more of a vision than a dream. The briefest glance at her face, at her skin, her hair and her makeup. She had spoken to him, telling him that she loved him, but then she had spoken of her only son...Ramsey could not make sense of what he had seen. It might have been a memory, or some kind of symbolic dream, like that of himself running through a burning house.

Her words did not make sense in reality, for he had been her son, and nobody else. He knew that he had been an only child, that his mother had been with him for a while, then she was gone.

All he had left after his mother vanished from his life was his father, and a world of torment. For so many years he had owned no memories whatsoever of his mother, and now that he had seen her, felt her presence, he was strangely comforted, though it had been just a dream. Every time he fell asleep, and every time he dreamed, something inside him awoke; the knowledge that Prince Morgan was alive, that he was well, and that Ramsey needed to rescue him.

How do you know he's alive? Ramsey asked himself, making sure not to speak aloud.

He had no concrete answer to this question. All he could say in response was that he just did. He knew for certain that Morgan was alive. It made him wonder if the voices in his head could indeed convey factual messages to him. The message that Morgan was alive, and that some person called Ulyssis had an unhealthy elf fixation, and was working for a master of some kind. That much, he knew, was real.

With a heavy sigh, and unable to work out any answers inside his head, he stretched and got to his feet, gazing once more across the lulling pink and golden hues of the sunset. Grenamoya was a beautiful place through Ramsey's eyes, having lived a controlled existence since his childhood. It dawned on him that he truly had all the time in the world to discover this unique, untamed land, to find himself, perhaps to rescue a prince along the way.

The island was incredible, and as his eyes scanned the horizon, completely absorbed in the exquisite colours and lay of the land, he barely noticed the two shaggy-faced mountain trolls gawking at him until it was too late.

The larger troll leapt at him, knocking Ramsey onto his back, and instantly aimed for the goblin's scrawny neck with his sharp fangs. Ramsey cried out and kicked the troll hard in the stomach, grabbing the hairy creature by the neck and trying to force his gruesome jaws away from him.

Rafan stood by, watching, snapping and yowling with excitement without attempting to help his brother. Ramsey did not know what coherent thought possessed him, but he knew that he had to defend himself; his right hand found his leather belt and grasped onto his dagger. The stench of the troll's murky fur was overpowering, and he lunged towards Ramsey's face, his clawed paws scrabbling to pin Ramsey to the ground.

There was a flurry of noise, snarls and screams of pain, and Ramsey struck the troll in the ribs with his sharp dagger, which sliced deep into the furry flesh.

The troll made an incredibly grotesque sound of agony as he slumped on top of his victim, weakened by the pain in his side, but as Ramsey fought to pull away from the weight of Rikmir's heavy body, the troll latched onto him with his teeth and ripped the brown, woollen shirt clean in two.

"Get away from me!" yelled Ramsey in desperation, pulling his weapon from the gaping wound in Rikmir's chest. "Or I'll use this dagger to slice you both!"

The large troll did not cease, and instead continued to rip at Ramsey's torso, reducing the brown shirt to shreds, and tearing several buttons from the second, purple shirt beneath. Ramsey pulled away with a scream, desperate to maintain his fully-clothed state despite his situation, but as the troll dove to sink his teeth into the goblin's exposed collar, something made him stop.

Rikmir was panting hard, his blue fur darkened with sweat, and much to Ramsey's amazement, he began to back away cautiously, while keeping a firm eye on the goblin's exposed, orange skin. The blood gushing from the stab wound in his own chest barely seemed to faze him.

Rafan snarled and grumbled, rushing up to his brother with an agitated expression. "Why did you stop? He is food!"

The larger troll took a deep breath, his face set. "He bears the bite of the cobra dragon."

Ramsey shuddered, leaning up on his elbows on the cold mountain path, his face and neck etched with blood and cuts. The missing buttons from his shirt had revealed his unhealed left shoulder, where the bite wound from the dragon's poisonous fangs still burned through his flesh; a black laceration that had almost resulted in his death. Now, it seemed, this very injury might save his life.

Rafan looked incredulously at his brother, itching to eat Ramsey on the spot, but unable to do so without his brother's consent. Rikmir had a solemn expression on his rough face, tinted faintly with evident fear. Maybe he was wondering how much damage Ramsey could do to them both, if he had already survived a fatal attack from the dreaded cobra dragon. The dragon did not care who or what it killed, and had taken several members of the mountain trolls' group in the past.

As though it pained him to do so, Rikmir hung his head and admitted defeat, with a single wound to show for his efforts. Ramsey clenched his fingers around the handle of his dagger when the large, blue troll moved closer, but lowered his weapon as the trolls moved past him, up the mountain path, with no further hints of aggression. Rafan, clearly distraught at the prospect of missing out on a meal, scolded his brother animatedly until long after the trolls had disappeared from view. Their bickering resumed, and echoed once more along the road like a pair of chattering wolverines. They were gone, and thankfully for Ramsey, did not return.

Ramsey stood in the middle of the road once again, shaken but not gravely harmed. The troll's sharp teeth and claws had left graze marks on his skin, and his ribs felt bruised from the attack, but he was otherwise unscathed, save for the loss of a very useful brown shirt.

Tattered shreds of mud-coloured wool were strewn across the path, and the one sleeve that remained intact upon his right forearm slid miserably over his thin wrist and onto the ground. His smudged copy of 'The Merlockiara Bulletin' had fallen free of his shirt during the encounter, and he bent quietly to retrieve it, holding his purple shirt closed with his free hand. Even though there was nobody watching him, he wanted to keep his dignity, and at least cover up the unsightly wound at the nape of his neck.

He could hardly make sense of what had happened, for it had ended so quickly. His painful neck wound had turned out to be quite a convenience, though he did not think it would have the same effect on any other predators on Grenamoya. He had been insanely lucky. His breath was short and laboured in his lungs, and though he stood once more, willing himself to continue on his trek, he instantly sank to his knees with his arms wrapped around his body, unable to face any more walking.

His face stung at the brush of the breeze against his newly-formed cuts, and he could feel his body sagging with every intake of breath. Closing his eyes, he lay on his side and curled up in the middle of the mountain road, unable to even move from the spot where he had been attacked. A mixture of sleep and unconsciousness consumed him quickly, and the gathering dark swept over the sky like a black, silken curtain.

The night was kind to Ramsey's prone form. The tempestuous wind sang over him, ruffling his ripped clothing and chilling his tender skin, but he was mercifully spared the discomfort, lost as he was in a world of voices that excluded the rest of reality. The soft, contemplative tone of a low, animalistic voice cut across his mind as he dreamt, conjuring images of himself lost in smoke, flailing through the dark, only to emerge onto the mountain road and find that Theron had already fallen to his death. He ran to the precipice, calling out the troll's name, praying that he had somehow been spared, but the deep, bitter emptiness that ran all through his being told him that it was too late.

He felt the mountain getting broader, higher, until he was a meagre speck somewhere upon a twisting, narrow path leading to nowhere. He could no longer see his mother, or hear his manic tormentors, but the solitary, morose voice of someone in anguished meditation lingered in his head, quietening everything else within his head, and repeating a sorrowful, galling soliloquy over and over again:

*You drive me insane, you take the whole of my being and corrupt it with this tormenting, unreal emotion...I hate you more than you will ever know...*

*I hate you more than you will ever know...*

*I hate you...yet I cannot live without you near...*

Until morning, these bodiless words tortured him, filling him with a grief akin to that in the speaker's voice. He felt detached from these words, he knew that they did not apply to him in any shape or form, and yet they pained him with every uttered syllable. He could feel something grievous lurching in his chest, making him want to cry out, and this was what woke him.

The sky was azure and clear that morning, though Ramsey could not see the sun. He could make out a glow emanating from somewhere to the east, where, no doubt, he presumed that the sun was obscured by some distant, unseen mist that shrouded it from view. He took a deep breath. He was most certainly ill, for the voice remained vigilant in his waking hours; though it was dormant and subdued, he could feel its presence, even with no coherent words.

There was no doubt about it, he was completely insane, but that did not dampen his passion for battling his way down the mountain and northwards to Oouealena. Something about the presence in his mind gave him the clear message that Morgan was alive. He could not explain why, but he felt it instinctively in his heart.

His head was heavy as he descended along the narrow road, faltering occasionally over a crack or bump in the path. The demon inside his head, as Ramsey decided to call it, weighed heavily upon his body and his soul at once; the acute headache in his temples, combined with the confusion and discord caused by his recently unearthed memories, made him feel persistently tired and edgy.

Afraid to stop, for fear of being overtaken by a returning group of mountain trolls, Ramsey only allowed himself a single half-hour rest at midday to clear his head and eat some lunch, which by then had gone rather hard and strong-smelling. Repulsed by a mouthful of the rancid hippogriff meat (which, in all honesty, he had not been too fond of from the beginning), he resorted to eating the piece of fruit left in his pocket. Though slightly squashed from the impact of an adult mountain troll jumping onto him, it was still edible, and he quickly cleaned himself up before making his weary way down the final slope of the mountain.

Less than three hours from his lunch break, for he was moving at quite a brisk pace despite his headache, Ramsey found himself walking past scraggly clumps of grass and moss. All around him, with every step forward, the earth sprang to life out of what had been a barren, morose environment, and small flowers tickled his toes as he walked down the slackening slope. He heaved a sigh, realising that he was near the end of his memorable mountain trek. The slope was very shallow as he descended, and the land was soft beneath his exhausted feet.

He could see Oouealena before him, and now that he was nearly at ground level, he realised how thankful he was to be lower than the clouds once again. The world could not have been more beautiful than it was to Ramsey in that single, fleeting moment, as the nightmare of recent days blanked away to be replaced by an intense, exhilarating feeling of hope.

The bumpy, shrub-scattered slope was bathed in the healing glow of the sun, and dotted with sprouting trees. Their ash grey branches and small, glittering leaves stretched up towards the clear, blue sky, and Ramsey did the same, taking a moment to be still, allowing the vast, open wilderness of Grenamoya to witness him at the end of his ordeal. He was alive and he was free in this land, and the island beheld him, rejuvenating his weary body with its splendour and purity. A soft gust blew some of his hair into his eyes, and he lifted one hand half-heartedly to coax it away.

With his other hand still clutching his newspaper to his chest, and his precious dagger nestled snugly in his belt, he made his way down the final stretch of the mountain, which bore no resemblance to the cold, cruel environment that Ramsey had battled through in past days. Nothing could ever compare with that misery, that terror, and nothing could compensate him for what he had lost. Nothing could console him, and though it was hard for him to express sorrow for the loss of a companion, the remaining, frayed fringes of his sanity were enough to move him nearly to tears.

Ramsey was unable to find the strength to look for food, and as he was used to going without meals for lengthy periods of time, he did not let his hunger bother him. A fallen oak tree by the eastern bank of a large, shimmering lake offered him sufficient shelter from the cold. He had seen this very lake from high on the mountainside the previous day, and up close, it glimmered magically with the breeze, which tousled the water's surface and made it dance, like light flickering through glass.

He could hear nothing but the anger and confusion inside himself, he could see nothing but the broken water of the lake, which was painted dark blue with the onset of nightfall. Streaks of red and orange fluttered over the water like hundreds of bright snakes converging in the lake, lighting up the sullen, grassy banks that flanked it.

Ramsey tried to focus on the writing in his newspaper, which was by now very mucky and smudged, but his mind could not settle on the matter. His heart was thumping in his chest as though confined, as if it longed to leap out of his mouth. The painful lump in his throat was most certainly not his heart, however, though it refused to budge no matter how many times he swallowed hard or punched himself in the ribs.

With nobody but the lake and the fallen tree for company, Ramsey spoke to himself, trying in vain to find words that made sense. He could not explain what was happening to him. It was as though he was dying, as though some foreign creature in his head was sapping his energy, aiming to eat away at him until there was nothing left in his soul.

Prince Morgan gave him a focus – yes, he said to himself, the boy is alive, and I will rescue him. This was all he could concentrate on, for he knew that it was a snatch of reality in an otherwise vague and meaningless world. His whole world, his life, depended on the prince's survival, for he knew that something, no matter how trivial, would be resolved the moment he found his way to Morgan in the Ash Mountains.

"It's so far away..." he mumbled to himself, gazing wistfully northwards to see the distant peaks silhouetted against the orange, sunset sky. "I don't know if I can survive that long with this demon in my head..."

The realisation struck him anew with the sound of his own words; he slapped his hands to his face, clenching his fingers against his dirty, swollen cheeks, and wailed against his palms. He did not know what was happening to him – if he was dying, if he was simply unwell, or if he had imagined all the voices and pictures from the beginning. Maybe the sound of that patronising, lilting tone and the foggy hallucination of his mother were the products of a mind troubled by fever.

But he had felt so healthy, and his mind had been steady until Theron fell...

"Whoever you are..." he whispered through his palms, his voice muffled and wavering with tears. "Whoever you are, whatever you are, please, just leave me alone...I can't take much more of this..."

A brief, stabbing pain in the back of his head disrupted his speech, and he could no longer find the will to talk. It was over as quickly as it began, as sudden as a strike from an axe, but the agony lingered, as with any physical injury. He moaned angrily and covered his face more firmly with his hands, determined not to cry any more. He would not surrender to anyone, not even a person in his own head.

He was afraid; he admitted that to himself. He was scared, he was nervous to be alone, he was fearful for his own safety. It was as though the island had placed the entirety of its burdens upon his feeble shoulders. He could feel nothing but despair, overwhelmed by how truly bleak his situation was. He had survived the mountains, but he did not know how long he could keep himself alive with so many powerful, contrasting emotions inside him. Some of them seemed to stem from the creature that spoke into his mind, and Ramsey too had begun to feel angry, sorrowful and desperate whenever he heard that same, low voice.

"I can't cope…" he stuttered, his voice thin. "This is the sort of thing that people get locked up for…"

He felt a hot tear roll down his cheek, and forcefully brushed it away with his fingertips. There was nothing left for him in Merlockiara, he had known that from the start; now he was mere miles away from the borders of Oouealena, a kingdom that he had never been to before, and he knew that he should have felt excited. Even a matter of minutes beforehand, he had felt genuinely exhilarated to be so near the kingdom's edge, but something dragged him down, preventing him from feeling happy.

All he saw as he looked upon the looming landscape was a desolate world, and one that would probably claim his life. He had survived so many near-fatal encounters, and now he was throwing himself away in the faint, meagre hope that he might find his way to the mountains and rescue the prince. And Morgan was not even royalty. He was giving his life in order to save some anonymous 'peasant boy' from a dragon the size of a house.

Despite the leaden feeling of dread in his heart, Ramsey managed a small smile as this thought crossed his mind. "I guess Theron was right…maybe I am a nice person…" He blinked towards the mountains, pursing his lips. "Or maybe I'm just a suicidal idiot…"

As though there had been some incantation in those words, Ramsey suddenly turned to find that a certain hairy, purple forest troll had come to join him by the lake. His fur dirty and matted with blood in parts, Theron offered Ramsey a plaintive smile and hobbled unsteadily to him, a pronounced limp in his gait. Ramsey got to his feet instantly, unable to move closer for fear that this wonderful apparition might disappear if he did so.

Theron was battered and in pain, but he was real nonetheless; and finally unable to hold back any longer, Ramsey ran to him and grabbed the troll by his thick, hairy neck, hugging onto him for dear life like a child clinging to its beloved German Shepherd. Theron stumbled slightly with the force of Ramsey's tugging embrace, but he smiled, and lowered his head so that the goblin could keep a more comfortable hold on his neck.

Ramsey could find no words to speak, speechless as he had been two nights ago when he had seen this same troll, his only friend in his entire lifetime, plummeting hundreds of feet to his imminent doom. Ramsey did not care how Theron had survived, he did not care how the troll had found him; all he cared about was that Theron was with him, and he could not release his grip, no matter how much he wanted to. It was not in him to hug anyone, particularly not a smelly creature like Theron. Try as he might, that was all he could think of to do.

As soon as Theron could pull away from Ramsey's arms, he looked down at his goblin companion, and a look of concern spread across his furry face. "Ramsey…you look terrible."

Ramsey couldn't help but laugh, realising how bad he must have looked with his torn clothing and gashes on his face, neck and arms. "You don't look too great yourself."

The troll blinked at him, his round face tinted with fiery shades of orange in the dying sunset sky. His brown eyes were bright and earnest, without a hint of anger, though Ramsey was certain that the troll was still upset with him. He had made a mistake in crossing the mountain, but they had both survived, and nothing seemed to trouble him as much as before. Now that Theron was with him again, he stood a chance of reaching his goal.

"But that's not important," he said, an unguarded smile on his face. "You're back with me, and Scaless knows I've *missed* you."

They rested that night sheltered against the fallen tree, the moon like a milky, watchful eye above them, surrounded by stars that glittered in wispy bands all across the sky. Theron slept peacefully, as he always did, with Ramsey by his side. Unwilling to let go of his companion, Ramsey stayed awake all night, his spirit lifted simply because Theron was with him.

With the mountain far behind them, Ramsey could feel his heart beating with expectancy. He wanted to be on the move again as quickly as possible. When Theron had recovered and his pain had been relieved by the leaves of the healing plant, Ramsey would be able to tell the troll about the new voice he had heard. Maybe Theron had also heard it in the mountains, thought Ramsey hopefully. They would resolve all matters the next day, for at that moment, Theron slept without a care, knowing that no matter what troubles lay ahead, he could help Ramsey through them.

# Chapter Twelve

# Where Loyalties Lie

Just as Elwin the elf king had decreed, the next meeting of the Union of Fantastical Creatures took place in his home kingdom; and, more precisely, in his very own conference hall at Hanya Palace. Within a week and a half of Elwin dispatching his letter to the manearie lord via one of his swiftest messengers, almost all of the UFC members had arrived in Hanya, and were awaiting the news that Elwin seemed so unwilling to tell. He knew that, as king of the elves, he was obliged to relay all information to his comrades during their meeting, but he was hesitant to do so. This was partially due to his great shame at allowing one of their greatest foes to escape unscathed from his palace, and it was not his favourite pastime to pass along dismal news to his friends.

It was mid-afternoon, a typically green and sunny day in the kingdom of Hanyaliamaya, but the members of the UFC were unable to venture outside to enjoy the sun. In the conference hall – a tall, broad room with a marble ceiling and large, gold-framed portraits along the walls – Elwin waited despondently, along with

Collinad, Karri and Lothar, who had arrived, one by one, over previous days. An arched window set in one of the ornate walls, very similar to that in his beloved study, opened onto the rear of the palace, offering a generous, glimmering view of the gardens beyond, with their sculpted topiaries and trimmed hedges. The sunlight was strong, giving the glass a brilliant glow, and Karri could not turn away from the view, itching to be outside instead of cooped-up in the elf king's palace.

"It's a nice day," he commented, to nobody in particular; and as such, nobody answered him. Slightly deflated that nobody suggested he should go outside, the cat shrugged his furry shoulders and sat down upon the wide ledge to survey his companions.

A long, wooden table took up the centre of the room, and stretched almost the entire length of the hall. Boldly carved chairs were lined up at its edges; Collinad and Elwin both sat at the far end of the table, near to Karri at the window, facing one another and saying not a word. Their equally troubled gazes spoke volumes to each other, but this was nothing that Karri could pick up on, and he decided it would be best not to address them. Lothar had been gradually pacing his way around the hall from the moment they had entered, and was now almost at the other end of the long room, inspecting some carved, wooden ornaments upon an antique bookcase.

The elves' love of words was clearly expressed in all the important rooms of Elwin's palace, which seemed to team with bookcases and shelves of diverse literature. The walls of the conference hall were equally abundant with bookcases, similar to those in Elwin's study, for he loved taking up space with books and various trinkets. Lothar lifted a small, glass peacock on a crystal stand with a gold pen-holder, examined it briefly, then hurriedly replaced it on the shelf with a sharp noise.

The echoing sound of a creaking door handle reached them from the other end of the room, and Collinad and Elwin finally looked away from each other. A small elf, standing the same height as Karri (for elves were naturally tall, Elwin himself standing six feet

326

high), edged his way into the room with a mixture of excitement and nervousness on his freckled face.

"My king," he addressed, though Elwin was far away from him at the table, "Lord Terak has just arrived with his companion, and he wishes to enter. Shall I bring him to you?"

Elwin paused briefly, and looked down at his right hand that rested on the table surface, his fingers slightly coiled. All eyes in the room were trained upon him in an instant, and he felt them on his flesh, burning through him. He swallowed, then answered tersely, "Yes, if you will."

The elf bowed himself out of the room, not closing the door completely as he retreated to fetch the vampire lord. Elwin's skin was pallid, and his eyes were bright and dark. Collinad trusted Elwin with his life, but could see that his comrade was suffering with an internal dilemma, and feared for him in silence. When the small, sunny-haired elf returned, Terak the vampire lord was at his side. The elf smiled and gestured for Terak to approach the resident king, and Terak did so, as his escort hurried out of the room and closed the door.

"Elwin, my friend," began the pale lord, his long, black hair looking flustered as usual, "it is wonderful to see you. What news have you?"

The silence was deafening as Terak approached Collinad and Elwin at the far end of the table, his leather boots scuffling slightly on the marble floor. Lothar sprang to life the instant he saw the vampire advance, and he briskly paced his way towards the far wall, also. Karri jumped down off the sill, and moved behind Collinad's chair, just in time for the manearie to push away from the table and stub Karri's toes. His wince of pain went unnoticed, however, for Terak had drawn their attention to him in an instant.

Terak was quick to realise that something was awry among his comrades, and he voiced his concern. "What is wrong? Collinad, is it serious? Oh no, Viktor's dead..." Terak desperately wanted them to confirm that their problem did not lie with him, but he was offered no words of comfort, and before they could speak, he blurted out, "What in Grenamoya have I done? I assure you, I have done nothing for you to resent me."

Karri's eyes were as wide as can be, and indeed he seemed to be edging close to Lothar for protection. The lizard king paid no mind to Karri, and stood fixedly, his fist tight around the handle of the sword at his belt. Elwin looked at the vampire, but as Terak met his gaze, the elf turned away, a pained expression on his smooth face. Terak was beginning to feel highly unnerved, when Collinad spoke and eased the silence.

"As far as we can tell, you have done nothing," he said, but his tone was one of forced calm, and it made Terak feel worse. The collie stood from his chair, and Elwin did the same, his eyes fixed upon an apparently interesting spot on the floor. Collinad took a deep breath as though in anticipation of speaking some dreadful truth, but all that escaped his canine lips was, "You have blood on your mouth."

Terak raised an eyebrow, then quickly pressed an index finger to his lips; drawing it away from his face, indeed, the digit was stained with flesh blood. This was obviously why Karri was staring so fixedly at him, and Lothar had his weapon at the ready. With a laugh, which he uttered far too quickly, Terak looked imploringly at Collinad.

"Oh, think nothing of it, I must have just bitten my lip or something." The others did not seem swayed by his feeble explanation, and he felt his chest tighten uncomfortably. "What else did you think? Why else would I have blood on my mouth, pray tell?"

Lothar growled, showing his sharp teeth through his reptilian lips. "Why do vampires ever have blood on their mouths?" he questioned, though it was one that did not require an answer. Terak's face flooded with anger and fear.

"Ah, so that is what you have come to think of me! That I am some kind of blood-lusting maniac who wanders around killing people before I show up for meetings! Oh, charming, I assure you."

Collinad looked distraught. "No, Terak, we do not think such things of you, I promise. Please, gentlemen, do not bicker – it

328

is senseless in a world where there are far more important matters at hand."

"No-one's bickering!" huffed Lothar, who was then silenced with a startlingly aggressive glance from Collinad. He heaved a sigh and let his hold slip from his weapon.

Terak looked to Elwin, but the elf still would not glance at him. Fuelled by upset and frustration, he turned his attention back to Collinad and demanded, "What in Grenamoya has led you to act so strangely? The last time we met, we were comrades, not enemies! You are all beloved to me, particularly you, Elwin." Elwin blinked, but did not look up. "Please, no matter what has caused you all to behave so oddly, tell me of this news, so that I may remind you of my utter devotion to you. I would never do anything to endanger you, or anyone else on this island, by Scaless."

"At least wipe all the blood from your lips when you say that," uttered Lothar, his voice low and threatening.

Terak was used to Lothar's aggressive behaviour, but never from the receiving end. A pang of sadness shot through his body at the realisation that one of his oldest comrades now felt so apprehensive towards him, and he rubbed his mouth and chin to remove all traces of blood from his face. This seemed to make the others more confident, and they allowed him to approach and join them at the table.

Collinad and Elwin were both standing, so Terak did not sit, and leant against the back of a chair instead, his arms folded across his chest. The loose, white shirt he was wearing betrayed no extra traces of blood, though the open collar revealed a thin leather choker around the base of his neck that looked as though it dug sharply into his colourless skin.

Now that his companions seemed stable, Collinad cleared his throat, and spoke in the commanding tone that he always used to bring the UFC meetings to order. "Well, now that our vampire representative has arrived, it seems appropriate to uncover our new intelligence, don't you think, Elwin?" The collie looked sharply at Elwin, who had finally glanced up from the floor and had an earthy flame burning behind his eyes. "Considering that it is your intelligence, Elwin, will you please speak?"

Elwin nodded, though he seemed at great pains to find his voice. In silence, he looked at each of the others in turn, including Terak, then reached into a pocket of his brown coat, which he was wearing despite the warmth of the room. He withdrew what looked like a torn piece of thick leather with some gold lettering on it, and with a sudden rush of anger, slammed it down upon the table surface.

"This!" he exclaimed, the others reeling away from him in shock. "*This*! This is all that remains of the Scaless Scriptures, my most ancient, most sacred copy that has been in this monarchy for generations!" His voice echoed around the hall like a thunder clap, and he slammed his fist onto the table, his cheeks red with outrage. "Nothing remains of it. Nothing at all, except this piece of the cover! You all know how much I treasured that book, and just as importantly, how big a part it played in our lives upon this fragile island!"

Lothar swore under his breath, Karri jumped, and Collinad hurried forward to place his hands upon Elwin's shoulders; the elf was shaking with rage, and his eyes were glossy with tears that could not be shed. Terak went forward as well, but as he moved to touch Elwin, the elf shied away from his hand.

"Collinad, I know I have released more information to you than this, but…but still, it hurts me…" He steadied himself with the back of a chair, breathing loudly and with an air of hysteria. "You all remember Ulyssis, even those of you who had not yet been born when he came into the UFC. Terak, I realise that you are the only one, other than myself, who was alive when Ulyssis joined us – but to the rest of you, it does not matter that you never met him as a human."

Karri's ears were pinned back against his head in distress, and Lothar was stroking his sword again as though wanting to do battle with the said creature at that very moment.

"He returned to this palace, to do Pain's bidding and destroy the book of scriptures, and in the process, take revenge upon me, though I never did anything but try to support him. I was a friend to him..." Collinad patted him on the back, saying 'I know, I know', but this seemed to make Elwin more upset. "There are few things that I am so passionate about..." he explained, his voice wistful and sad at the same time. "But Ulyssis was my friend, and he knew exactly how to hurt me."

"Is he really as ugly as you've always said?" enquired Karri with no subtlety. "Is he uglier or what?"

"He is the most deplorable creature on the whole of Grenamoya Island," said Elwin, meaning every syllable of his words. "Pain may be evil and corrupted, but Ulyssis is a traitor. Pain clearly realised that we had access to the island prophecies in my copy of the Scaless Scriptures, and he sent Ulyssis to destroy them. Which leaves us with even more of a dilemma, for not only are the terms of the prophecies now lost to us, but in destroying the only tome in which they were written, Pain may indeed have destroyed our future."

Lothar growled. "Which means that...?"

"Which means that in destroying my book," Elwin clasped the remaining piece of the Scaless Scriptures' cover between his fingers and toyed with it angrily, "he may also have eradicated the prophecies. The parts that we read and remembered are most likely completely defunct now that my sacred copy has been destroyed."

Terak had a grim look upon his sharp face, his cheekbones glowing gently under the light of the window. He was relieved that the others were willing to talk in front of him, though they did not speak to him as readily as they once had. Seeing that Karri and Lothar were looking sceptical of Elwin's theory, he spoke, his voice as calm and guarded as the subtle undertow of the ocean. "Elwin, I presume that Ulyssis destroyed the book by vomiting upon it?"

Elwin nodded stiffly, a look of disgust flashing on his face. "Yes, he did."

"Which would have caused the book to disintegrate completely," he stated, his explanation directed at his feline and reptilian comrades. "Ulyssis is a creature of destruction, like Pain himself, and his bodily fluids..." He hesitated at his own wording, noticing a repulsed expression forming on Karri's face. "His bodily fluids are like acid upon anything truly hallowed and sacred, and so by vomiting upon the Scaless Scriptures, he was able to obliterate the book; and the nature of the poison in his body is so acute that it may have rendered the book's prophecies untrue."

"Prophecies, like those found within my copy of the scriptures, exist only as long as the book in which they are bound," said Elwin, continuing Terak's explanation with an air of irony. "Ingenious…totally ingenious. Pain thought out that plan, Collinad, it is far more destructive than one would believe upon first glance."

"These implications run deep…" mused Collinad, running a paw through his thick fur. "Pain may have sealed our fate by destroying that book. The path to our salvation was held in those pages…"

Elwin smiled a sorrowful smile and shrugged his shoulders, discarding the torn segment of book cover onto the floor at his feet. "It is just as well, then, that I did not probe too deeply into the prophecies. Now we are spared the fruitless longing for what might have been." He ran a hand through his hair, copying Collinad's gesture, and funnily enough, Karri and Terak did the same. Lothar, who had no hair, just folded and unfolded his arms. "Collinad, I remember enough to know that we need to seek for 'four warriors of a comrade lost' – did you have any success in contacting Celee Tergana?"

"As a matter of fact, I visited Mrs Tergana last week, to discuss what we deciphered from the scriptures," said Collinad, though his tone uncharacteristically lacked optimism. "I am afraid, however, that she did not welcome the idea of training her children as warriors for Lady Scaless. We must not forget that she is still mourning for Rayven – after all, it has been barely two years since his death, and she is understandably protective of them."

"As any parent would be," interjected Terak, the only present member of the UFC to have ever had children. Collinad graced him with a sad, sympathetic gaze, and Terak smiled without mirth.

Karri, who had barely matured since his teenage years, did not understand the concept of parenthood, and displayed his blatant lack of sympathy. "Didn't you tell her that she doesn't have a choice? They were mentioned in the prophecies, for crying out loud! Can't you force her to hand them over or something, for the good of the island?"

"I am afraid not, my friend. They are her children, not ours. In time, perhaps she will come to realise the importance of letting them fulfil their prophesised destiny, but at the moment, we should keep our distance and permit her to grieve without interference."

Elwin sighed, his expression troubled and turbulent, though his eyes remained as soft as ever. His skin was still unusually pale, as though something had upset him beyond mortal comprehension, though the faint tint of gold had returned to his cheeks. He was acting in a manner that did not suit him at all, his usual calm disposition darkened by frustration and sorrow. With another sigh, which drew the attention of the other union members like a secret signal, he turned to Terak, and gestured to the door behind him, which led outside to the back garden.

"Terak, I would very much appreciate it if we could talk alone for a while."

The vampire's gaze was unflinching, though he felt suitably anxious about what they would discuss once separated from the others. He nodded, and without a further word, Elwin went to the heavy, decorated door and opened it with a creak, allowing Terak to walk through in front of him. The elf looked briefly at Collinad, as though imploring him to keep Karri and Lothar occupied; then he too exited the room, pulling the door closed behind him and severing the ray of sunlight that had briefly entered through the doorway.

"Oh poo!" huffed Karri as soon as Elwin had left the room. "Terak gets to go outside and we don't? That's completely unfair – the guy doesn't even tan!"

Lothar rolled his eyes. "And you, my simple friend, have fur instead of skin, and cannot tan either."

"I didn't say I wanted a tan," grumbled the cat, pointedly looking away from Lothar, who was basking on the windowsill with his clawed hands in his pockets, "but it *would* be nice to have our meeting outside for a change. There's nobody around to eavesdrop on us!"

"We can never be too careful," said Collinad wisely, now sitting at the table with his paws on his lap. "Clearly, whatever Elwin wants to say in private is something that can be uttered outside, but I cannot think why. Elwin has been acting so disturbed lately, it is entirely unlike his character. I am worried for him."

"Yeah, but I mean...taking Terak outside, in front of us, to discuss something in private? Not very tactful, is it? It's like Pain sending that ex-human thing to vomit on the Scaless Scriptures and destroy them. Very spectacular way to ruin the prophecies, wasn't it? About as imaginative as calling a pet iguana 'Iggy'..."

Collinad turned to his feline comrade with a smirk upon his face. "Are you making allusions to the fact that I own a dragon called 'Dragon'?"

A look of shock and embarrassment crossed Karri's furry features, and he fumbled for words, trying to apologise, though Collinad smiled at him. He swallowed and grinned apologetically. "No! No, of course not!"

Lothar, who had watched the brief conversation from his snug position on the windowsill, crossed his arms and fixed his eyes on Karri from behind. "Well," he voiced, sounding detached and vaguely amused, "'Karri' is a girl's name."

Outside the palace, the green, flawless lawn and neatly trimmed hedges were shining like a field of emeralds in the warm sun. Elwin was a proud king who loved tending to nature, as all elves do, but he was particularly fond of neatness when it came to gardening, and enjoyed pruning the lush foliage all year round. Though most elves preferred the natural beauty of the trees and plants, Elwin was very dedicated to maintaining his immaculately straight hedges and ornamental topiaries, most of which were sculpted to resemble birds and animals. At the far end of the large, walled garden was a tall gazebo made out of white marble, which

Elwin would visit in summertime to relax with one of his many beloved books.

Terak had not visited Hanya for several years, and was caught up in admiring the garden when Elwin cleared his throat to catch his focus. The vampire turned starkly, betraying his heightened tension. The bright sun caught in his hair like silver light dancing upon coal.

"So...what is it you wanted to tell me?"

Elwin seemed at a loss for what to say. Looking at the vampire lord, gazing into those cool, velvet blue eyes, he saw the same person whom he had fought against back when Terak was working under Pain's command; the same person, also, who had joined with him to form the Union of Fantastical Creatures two-thousand years ago, and had stood faithfully at his side ever since. Terak meant a great deal to Elwin, and not merely because of his unfaltering loyalty. Try as he might, Ulyssis' foreboding words remained fixed in his head, echoing time and time again, making him feel paranoid and untrusting.

*He has few others to do his 'dirty work' thus far, but believe me, he will resume control of those who are rightfully his, and soon he will reign over this miserable island once again, for all eternity!*

He sighed heavily, not knowing how to voice his concerns, but try as he might, he could not let his suspicions go unmentioned. Terak's deep eyes were glistening with concern, reflecting the sun's rays that streaked across the pristine garden.

"Please, Elwin," he spoke, his tone imploring, "after all these years, I hope that you can find it within yourself to trust me under any circumstances."

Elwin shot back, his wispy, blond hair sparkling in the sun like spun gold; "It isn't as simple as that. When Ulyssis returned to me, he told me that Pain is going to regain control over 'those who are rightfully his', by which he meant *you*. Not to mention all the other dark creatures that inhabit our island."

Terak stared at him, with a mixture of disbelief and resignation on his colourless face. "As a matter of fact..."

336

"And it isn't that I would believe his word over yours," continued the elf, animatedly sweeping his arms as though trying to grasp a plausible train of thought. "But the encounter disconcerted me immensely. I do not know what to believe any more, my friend, but I hoped that a few comforting words from your lips might ease my torment..." He swallowed, and his gaze hardened upon Terak's perplexed face. "But instead you come here with blood on those lips, claiming to have bitten yourself by mistake. There can be no mistake, Terak, I know what I saw, and it was fresh blood falling from your mouth."

"I swear to Scaless, Elwin, that I have not attacked anyone – if indeed your mind has been baffled enough to make you think so! I have been in terrible pain as of late, and I must have just bitten my lip without noticing. Is your faith in me so shaken, Elwin, that you no longer believe what I say to you?"

Elwin kept his gaze steady upon Terak, but did not reply. Ink blue eyes pierced through earthy brown ones; finally, the latter, Elwin's, were drawn behind blond eyelashes as he looked aside.

"As a matter of fact, if you will hear me out," continued the vampire, "I have found that I can hear Pain speaking, late at night. For a few weeks now, I have heard him, and I have heard Ulyssis, in the back of my mind."

Elwin's head snapped back up at the mention of Ulyssis, though he remained quiet so that Terak could speak.

"And I heard a very interesting conversation a few nights ago, concerning Ulyssis and a botched attempt to choke you by stuffing his fingers down your throat. Does that recall any memories for you, Elwin?"

"Never you mind."

Terak crossed his arms. "I must say that it all sounded very questionable upon first hearing it, but then I realised that it was something serious, and I felt afraid for you. It is so satisfying to know that when you truly care about someone, this is how they treat you. As though they barely know you, let alone *care*! I have been suffering because of this bond to Emperor Pain, Elwin, and don't you forget it! I have seen and felt more hurt and sorrow than you will ever know."

The elf's eyes were burning again as he moved closer to Terak, his expression unreadable were it not for the threads of anger flitting across his soft features. "Oh, so you now speak of him once more as 'Emperor' Pain, do you? This is not the best way to plead your case, Terak, by addressing him in such a grovelling manner!"

"Oh Elwin, don't be so eager to damn me!"

"Damn you? It's somewhat too late for that, I would say, my friend." He spat out this last word as though it was poison on his tongue. Terak could feel anger and fear rising in his chest, for Elwin was acting like someone else entirely, and it struck an ashen terror deep inside him. "You were damned from the moment you went into Pain's service."

Terak could barely keep himself from exploding with rage, and he dug his sharp, dark fingernails into his own white palms. "I cannot help it that I was born into his servitude, Elwin! I hardly chose my path, it was chosen for me long before I came into being!"

"If Pain had not been overthrown you would not have abandoned him! And so, now that he is gaining strength once more, you have decided to return to him! Is that it, Terak? Have I struck the nail on the head?" Terak's blood was rushing through his veins, and Elwin could see the tension in his muscular neck. "I think I've struck the truth, you conniving, inconceivable-"

"Never!" roared Terak, his voiced ragged with despair. "Never, Elwin, *never* you speak of such a notion! That creature of destruction cost me everything I ever held dear, and you know it! Why do you torment me by bringing up the past? You are my friend, Elwin, I would give my life for you!"

Elwin felt a dense weight crashing into his stomach, and realised that he had pushed too far. Guilt welled up inside him, and he stepped back, unable to speak. The vampire's words were like lightning, his dark eyes sparkling with moisture and his fists clenched in front of him.

"Because of him, Elwin, I lost the only woman I ever loved, and the only daughter I'll ever have! They were my whole life,

338

Elwin, you have sat with me and comforted me as I have wept for them over these many years! The pain will never subside, Elwin, he took away everything that I..."

With a wavering gasp for air, Terak pressed his hands to his face and groaned deeply against them, his black hair catching the sun elegantly despite the anger that shook his body. He pulled his palms down his face, over his lips and the small, protruding fangs, and stared at Elwin through his fingers.

"He is Pain, Elwin...and that is all he gives, even to those loyal to him. And I know, because I have been there. Please, do not think so little of me...how could I return to him, knowing what I have lost because of him?"

Elwin pursed his golden lips, then held out his arms and approached his comrade in an apologetic gesture. Terak swallowed hard, allowing the elf to embrace him with warm, slender arms, and he found the strength in himself not to cry for his stolen family. Elwin hugged him firmly but gently, his head leaning against that of the vampire, who was an inch or two shorter than himself.

"I know, my friend...I am so very, very sorry for what I said, and what I implied...it has just been so very hard for me lately." Terak nodded. "But that is no excuse for my irrational behaviour. I apologise, my dearest friend...my oldest friend in Grenamoya."

"Why can't you let him go?"

Elwin blinked, still embracing his strong, pale comrade. "Why can't I let who go?"

Though he could not see his face, Elwin could sense the vampire's distasteful grimace in his words. "Ulyssis...Elwin, you cannot let him go, but for the sake of your own life, you must. He cannot be saved, my friend, he is not the boy you once knew."

Elwin knew the truth, but all the same, it made his heart wither inside his chest. He held more tightly onto Terak, his face pressed close to the long, dark hair. "I know that...but..." He closed his eyes. "Oh Scaless help me, I am a fool, but I cannot live knowing that he still exists in this world, and I can do not a thing to aid him. I saw it in his eyes, my friend, if only for a moment – that tiny fragment of his true self that remains. He was once so good, so loving, so…"

"It is hard to deal with, Elwin. I understand your pain. I am trapped inside a mould that Pain created to serve him thousands of years ago, for Scaless' sake, yet I feel barely one-tenth of the torture that Ulyssis must endure every single day." He patted Elwin on the back, disturbing the silvery-blond hair. "But I have heard them, Elwin, I have heard Pain and Ulyssis talking, and I can see them, and I can hear Pain calling me to him. Hear me now, Elwin, when I say that I will never return to him, and that I will stay strong against his influence."

The elf drew away from him at last, his golden complexion gleaming healthily in the sun once more. His cheeks were no longer pale, though his eyes were glossy and slightly reddened at the corners. Terak smiled at him, a picture of black hair, sharp teeth, wan skin and a dazzling, white shirt. He was the friend that Elwin had always known, and finally, Elwin felt that he could believe him.

"I am a man of few emotions, Elwin…" he said, his voice low and resentful, "…save one, I suppose. Whenever I feel strong emotion I hear him calling most acutely, so once more, I must accustom myself to shielding my feelings, for the greater good."

"Very well," said Elwin, smiling in the sunlight, "and if there is anything at all that I can do for you, you have only to ask, as always. I gather that you will be requiring some remedy to curb those outbursts of yours?"

Terak nodded. "Yes, I am afraid that they have returned, along with all this senseless anguish. I am sorry to have burdened your household with Synor's extravagant personality." He smirked, and the slight expression lit up his face. "He is probably harassing your staff as we speak. I am afraid that I have to bring him everywhere with me nowadays."

"Not a problem at all. For what I have put you through, my friend, I owe you and your companion far more than my hospitality."

The sun was brilliant upon the two of them as they returned to the heavy door of the conference hall, no longer at odds with one another. Elwin felt childish and embarrassed at his poor treatment of Terak, but the vampire rarely demanded apologies, and never held grudges against his closest allies. For this, Elwin was very grateful, for he most certainly did not want to cause a rift in the UFC, especially as there were so few remaining members.

They entered the conference hall to find Collinad and Lothar deep in conversation at the table. Karri, who was examining one of the bookshelves, whipped around at the creaking of the door; he dropped a small, glass fish onto the floor as he turned, causing it to shatter on the stone, and instantly broke into a stream of apologies.

"Oh Scaless, Elwin, I'm sorry, I didn't mean to, I didn't–"

Elwin held up a hand, his other resting amicably on Terak's forearm. "Do not worry, my friend. We all have bigger concerns to face at the moment. Collinad," He looked to the manearie lord. "Do not allow communication between yourself and Celee Tergana to fail. Do not pester her, or give her any cause to cut us out of her life. Once all her children are of age, we shall make our move, and it will be up to them to decide if they wish to be trained. They are Rayven's children – I am certain that they will embrace their destiny, as their father did."

"Rayven's destiny also led to his demise," crooned Lothar morbidly, moving away from Collinad. "May Scaless grant them better fortune than their father's."

Collinad heaved a sigh, his long, soft coat of fur shifting with his chest. "Do not worry. I know well enough to give a grieving widow enough space to raise her children as she wishes. But all the same, I will let her know that I, that *we*, will be there for her in times of need. I should remind myself of her children's names again...I know she has three sons and a daughter, and that her eldest son is called Rousoe – I recall Rayven telling me so – but other than that, my knowledge is limited. I will pay her another friendly visit when I return home." Elwin nodded, indicating that this would be a good plan. Collinad smiled, his dark leather collar and wet nose reflecting the light from the window. "I say, Terak, are you all right? You look ill."

The vampire forced a smile and nodded stiffly, as though attempting to mimic Elwin's brief gesture. His cheekbones were so prominent on his gaunt face that they seemed to break painfully through his skin, his deep eyes glowing beneath his eyelids. He raised one hand to his neck to loosen his already open shirt collar, and as he did so, his sleeve slid down his forearm, revealing a long, jagged twist of barbed wire entwined around his wrist. The coil was so tight that it was clearly piercing his skin, and as Collinad looked at him, blood seeped down the vampire's pallid arm in thin streaks.

"Yes...yes I am, I'm fine..." he asserted, when it became apparent that he was not. "I'm fine, don't worry."

Moments later, he collapsed to the hard floor with a strangled gasp, his limbs shaking and his hands tangled in his hair. Elwin visibly jolted into anticipated action and grabbed onto him as he fell, and they crumpled to the floor together, Elwin beneath him as he shuddered and groaned and twisted and shouted.

"Scaless!" exclaimed Elwin, along with an equally frantic expletive in his own language. "I knew this would happen, Terak, you imbecile!" Terak twisted on the floor, knocking his head against Elwin's stomach and prompting both Collinad and Lothar to back away with shock. Elwin grabbed the vampire's head harshly and shook him with the force of a mild earthquake. "Fight it, Terak, or so help me, if you betray us...!"

Terak stared at him with empty, wide eyes that burned and faded in the same instant, frosted like glass, and his mouth was drawn so tight that blood spilled down his chin. Elwin clutched the sides of Terak's face, nails digging into the frozen, pigment-deficient flesh, and Terak wailed with agony at his touch. The gruesome bracelet around his wrist dug into his skin, and soon blood was erupting from his grey veins and splashing the front of Elwin's clean coat.

"Terak! Speak to me!" He shook him again, but Terak did not respond, his stare distant and glazed like a dead animal. "Collinad, Lothar, help me!"

Karri ran up to them as they converged around the vampire, who was leaning more heavily with the weight of his torment. Still

342

he did not respond to Elwin's words. "What's wrong with him?" asked Karri frantically, ignoring the fact that he had stumbled over shards of broken glass in his rush. "What's happening? Why won't anybody tell me anything?"

"Karri, run outside and fetch Febril for me!"

Elwin, who was still supporting the majority of Terak's weight, could not rise from the floor, his hands and coat stained with blood. Collinad and Lothar knelt with him, watching Terak intently for movement, but the vampire was frigid, bleeding though he made no response to their words. Karri ran towards the door to the back garden.

"No, not that door, Karri – get Febril, he will be waiting outside!" Elwin made a fleeting arm gesture towards the door at the far end of the hall, to which Karri sprinted with his green cape trailing behind him. Elwin took a deep breath, fanning Terak's face with one hand. "You idiot, Terak, what have you done? You see this, Collinad? This is what happens when Pain reclaims the minds of his followers – I tell you, he's a traitor! He has returned to his master's service!"

"Oh Sweet Scaless save us," gasped Collinad, reaching out to feel for a pulse in Terak's bleeding wrist. His paw consequentially was stained red also, the blood lacing quickly through his white fur.

"He cannot help it, Collinad," scolded Elwin. "He is bound to Pain for his whole lifetime – of *course* he would return to him once he regained power!"

"My friend, there is no need to assume-"

"You know nothing of this, Collinad! Nothing!" The stark ferocity in his voice sent the collie backwards, blood still dripping from him. "You do not govern me!"

By now, Karri had returned with the small, freckled elf that escorted Terak into the hall. The elf was holding a damp, white cloth in the crook of one arm, and his fingers were tight around a tiny, glimmering glass bottle, which held a deep red liquid. Karri looked far more distraught than Elwin as the elf king retrieved the two items, and though Karri looked to Collinad and Lothar for answers, a sharp glance from the blue lizard made him turn away.

"Hold on, Terak, listen to me..." Elwin said repeatedly as he placed two fingers on his comrade's cold forehead. "Listen to me..."

"I want to know what's happening!" exclaimed Karri, his brown fur standing up on end. "Is he dying?"

Terak groaned, causing everyone to jump at once, and began to gasp for air, through which a few words were discernible. His dark eyes were wide and staring as though indescribable pain was surging through his body, and Collinad felt his blood run cold. "He's here...Elwin!"

"What is it?" urged Elwin, leaning down to him. His words held concern, but not for Terak's health.

Terak coughed, and blood swelled in his mouth. "I can hear him...I can feel him..." With every breath, his speech became clearer, though he still could not rise. Sprawled on the floor on his back, with his head and shoulders supported in Elwin's arms, Terak shivered and struggled to regain his composure. "He knows that Morgan is alive...I can feel him, Elwin, Morgan is still alive!"

"He is?" gasped Collinad, a smile sprouting on his canine face. "Oh Scaless, in all this confusion I almost forgot about poor Prince Morgan! What splendid news! I must deliver this message to Viktor as soon as I return to Merlockiara."

"Are you saying this to deceive us, Terak?" taunted Elwin, much to the shock of everyone else in the room, and even Lothar glared reproachfully at him.

"Elwin, it's one thing to be worried, but you'll kill him if you're not careful!" said Karri, jumping on the spot as Collinad tried in vain to master the situation. Terak's head jolted back and forth on his neck as Elwin did little short of throttling him. Defeated, Collinad stood back, subtle threads of anger bound tight in his chest.

Terak groaned, clenched his fangs, and fell limp. A split-second later, he rose, and began to struggle against Elwin's grip, attempting to stand. His bloody wrist had made its mark on the elf's beautiful coat, and the blood spilled everywhere as he moved. "Thank you...but you can let go of me now...I'm fine."

344

"Are you quite certain?" Elwin pressed the damp cloth against Terak's face and neck, dabbing him gently with the cool water while keeping him in place. "Scaless, I'm so sorry that I..." His hair was well and truly dishevelled, but his face softened and he seemed sad.

"Forget it," he replied, gruffly. "Right now, I just need to stand up and get hold of myself again. It's no big deal, Elwin, you can stop cradling me..."

Elwin reluctantly let go, and allowed Terak to find his feet. All the while, the elven attendant stood nearby, watching the exchange with interest, the sunlight gleaming off his sandy hair. Collinad, Lothar and Karri watched also; Lothar in the middle stood far taller than the others, dressed from head to toe in his usual colourful regalia, the sunbeams glinting off his elegant blue scales. Like a cat that had tripped by accident, Terak fumbled his way towards a chair with an air of broken dignity, and hoisted himself to his feet. He pressed his knuckles against his moist forehead, then accepted the bottle of red liquid that Elwin offered him.

"Thank you...again."

"You are welcome."

Terak lowered his eyelids and shot Elwin a jagged look, his fangs grazing his dark lower lip. "You do not want to know what I see when Pain speaks to me, all that I suffer through. You upset me, Elwin, and only when I feel such emotion do I feel him so strongly. I suggest that you make accusations more sparingly in future."

Taken aback, Elwin glanced at Collinad. Collinad's eyes were severe, but he could not turn to the vampire to speak. "I am sorry, my friend, I truly am. I have apologised to you."

"Yes, I know, and I am not one to dwell on petty grudges against my allies, but really, Elwin, think before you start pointing fingers in future, all right?" With one quick motion, Terak swallowed the contents of the small bottle and placed it upon the table with a terse *clink*. He shivered, tossed his hair, and furrowed his brows, recollecting horrific experiences from time gone by. "When he speaks to me, sometimes I can see him, sometimes I cannot, but sometimes I can see my family..." He ran one hand through his hair, looking at his comrades with an unreadable emotion. "I can see my wife and daughter...being murdered all over again...and it brings it all back to me, Elwin, it is torture..."

Elwin nodded sadly. "I am certain it is, my friend, and I am sorry that I can do nothing to help."

"As am I," said Collinad, standing at Elwin's side to show his support. Elwin turned to him appreciatively, and Collinad smiled, willing the elf to retain a prosperous mood in front of Terak.

"It is not your fault, so I do not wish to take my anger out on any one of you. Seriously though, Elwin, you cannot comprehend what I go through for the sake of remaining loyal to this cause. If I returned to Pain's service, it would be less than the torment I endure now. This horror has struck me anew as of late, which is why I have to bring Synor everywhere with me. But under no circumstances would I ever turn my back on you. It is an absurd proposition, when you consider all that I have sacrificed for you in the past."

Collinad smiled at Terak. "Never you worry, my friend. I could never turn my back on you. But this is a very peculiar phenomenon – are you sure you are not hurt?"

"I am hurt, but not incurably. It always passes. I could feel him, Collinad. Pain somehow knows that Prince Morgan is alive. Which means that one of his comrades must have apprehended Morgan in the first place." Terak pursed his lips and looked at the others, as though expecting them to question the truth in his story. "I know it sounds strange. Pain is weak, he has yet to regain his former power, and as far as I can tell, he has been unable to block his thoughts from reaching me. And I can feel what he feels..."

Karri's eyes were as wide as two yellow saucers. "Wow...that must feel really strange." Lothar grunted in the cat's direction.

"I suppose it would to someone who has never experienced it before." Terak still looked drained, and settled down on one of the decorated chairs with his hands on his knees. "But few people have ever been as close to Pain in their lifetime as I once was, and fewer who still live have ever seen the demon face-to-face. Elwin saw me through such awful times during Pain's first attempt to regain control of the island."

The sound of Elwin's attendant clearing his throat caused them all to turn. "Excuse me, Your Highness, but might this be an opportune moment for me to leave? Not to be eavesdropping on private conversations…"

Elwin nodded. "Yes, as you will." With a typically sunny elven smile, the attendant hurried out of the hall through the far door, taking the used cloth and empty bottle with him. As the heavy door swung shut, Elwin turned to the company, looking very misplaced with his thick, bloodstained coat in the warm room.

Terak's chest was heaving, his eyes were dappled with light, shining as bright as rain; they reflected pure disbelief, horror, anger, all masked behind a mounting shield of black. He was trying to compose himself, to control his emotions so that he would feel no further agony at Elwin's damning words. Elwin felt sick at himself, but could not ignore the strength of his own convictions. His body was unused to the feeling of guilt, and more so to the feeling of hatred. But he felt both.

Elwin could think of nothing to say, except (at Collinad's prompting), "It is fine weather. I say we take lunch on the garden patio."

"Brilliant!" shouted Karri, who had been yearning for the outside world all morning. "Great, then I can tell you all about that arranged marriage waiting for me when I get back home. I swear, if I put the story off any longer I'll already have a hundred children by the time I tell you."

Collinad laughed, joining Elwin as the elf coaxed Terak from his comfortable chair. "Ah yes, the marriage. Do tell, my friend, I promise that we will all listen this time."

"Marriage?" repeated Terak, who had not arrived in time to hear previous mention of the occasion. "Karri, you're getting married?" Intuitively, Lothar went to the chamber door to summon Elwin's staff members to assemble lunch. Karri's upcoming matrimony did not terribly captivate him.

Karri rolled his eyes and made a disenchanted facial expression to show his lack of enthusiasm. "Yeah, I've got to get married as soon as I return from this meeting, so I don't really want to go home. Something my mum and dad arranged from when I was younger, you know?"

"Well, as the only one of us to have ever been married, I suppose I am the best person to talk to on the matter. Although times have changed significantly since my own wedding day," said Terak, nostalgically, as he pulled away from Elwin to walk on his own. They opened the door and walked out onto the green grass, into the sun. His hair twirled as it was caught by the breeze, and Karri eagerly went to his side, assured that Terak no longer posed any sort of threat. "What is she like? Pretty?"

"That's the problem...I've never actually seen her."

"Ah..."

Karri perked up. "I know her name is Korin."

Terak laughed, a slight weakness in his voice the only thing betraying his inner dischord. He did not look back into the room, poignantly avoiding Elwin. The elf swallowed a hot lump in his throat. "Well, at least the pair of you will make for good alliteration."

"What?"

Collinad followed them, Elwin at his side, and Lothar striding quietly behind him. Once the group of three had fallen slightly behind, Lothar sighed, catching Elwin's attention.

"What has gotten into you, my friend?" mourned Collinad, his eyes weary. "This is not like you at all. I am worried for you."

"I want nothing more than to protect this island, Collinad, and I will not allow Pain to dispatch his spies to our meetings." Elwin looked to Terak, who was skulking away down the garden steps with Karri in tow. The fresh spattering of crimson on the vampire's crisp shirt caught his eye instantly, glowing dark red under the bright sun. "I will not hoard suspicions only to refrain from acting upon them."

"For one," said the manearie, his tone more assertive, "I feel that we are facing enough danger from outside our group, not to feel the need to raise conflict amongst our allies."

Karri made some kind of exclamation combined with a grand arm gesture as he and Terak descended the steps to the flat, immaculately cropped lawn, and the sun lit up Elwin's severe face like a scowling statue. His vaguely unusual elven features, his eyes placed ever-so-slightly too high on his face, were captivating even while grim.

"You did not know him when I did, as a boy, Collinad. When I first saw him in battle, as I stood by King Galewyn...there was so much hurt upon his face, yet his eyes were..." He looked at his boots, and drew to a halt. Lothar, striding behind them, stopped barely short of a collision. He was clearly lapping up this debate as though it fuelled his very soul. "...They were empty, Collinad, and icy, and dead. He is hearing Pain's words, Collinad, absorbing his commands. I *know* he is, and we must divide ourselves from him before he presents a real danger to any of us." Terak and Karri were well out of earshot in the middle of the lawn, talking face to face.

"Do not be hasty, Elwin. Just have some faith in him."

"You're too trusting, Collinad; that has always been a flaw in you."

By now, they were not even looking at one another, but were staring out over the garden, where the heir to the Kinmerina throne and the vampire lord of Xavierania were lost in discussion. Lothar craned his long neck over Elwin's blond head, listening.

Collinad's fur puffed out from his body. "Why can you not let Ulyssis go, Elwin? Dwelling on him is making you bitter."

The elf found no response. Collinad wrapped his hairy arms around himself, flattening the long, white fur of his chest and belly as he moved to join Karri and Terak on the lawn. As soon as the collie shifted, Lothar stepped forward to take his place and stood by Elwin. The elf's stance was tense like a taut bowstring, but once more he averted his eyes from the garden, ashamed, and caught Lothar in the corner of his eye.

"I don't much like the look of things, Elwin," growled the reptile, searing with aggression. "If even Collinad will ignore you, well, then at least I will stick by you." Elwin nodded his gratitude, with a grievous tint upon his face. He did not notice as a gaggle of elf girls emerged from the palace, laden with trays of food for lunch. "I dislike the look in his eyes, Elwin, you are right. And while we're at it," he continued, briefly acknowledging a plate of freshly-sliced bread as it was laid upon the table, "I'd have a security check on the other vampires of the island. Scaless knows there are enough of them to pose a real threat to peace on Grenamoya. There is nothing worse than regretting one's failure to act in retrospect."

Elwin blinked in the general direction of where Karri, Terak and Collinad were now laughing amongst their small group; Terak's grip on Collinad's furry, brown shoulder set a fire burning in his gut. The sun dipped lazily behind a cloud, dulling the painful glare of the grass and sky, casting gentle greyness over the embroidered, honey-coloured tablecloth on the lunch table.

# Chapter Thirteen

# Stronger Than Ever

"I just fell a long way, and I was alone. Then I set out to find you again, and I did, and here I am now."

That was all. That was all that Theron had answered, when Ramsey asked him the itching question; "How are you bloody well still alive?" There was no further answer, and Theron had immediately stood to greet the new morning, not willing to enlighten Ramsey with the full nature of his ordeal. Ramsey was frustrated, riddled with his typical goblin curiosity (some might say 'nosiness', literally so in Ramsey's case), but he was still content to have Theron back with him. To say he was content would be an understatement. He was absolutely elated, in a way that only a spindly, caffeine-loving goblin like himself could be.

The first morning after they were reunited passed by with a distinct lack of angst on Ramsey's part. Far too thrilled at having his companion back, Ramsey danced giddily around the lakeside, and had few qualms over venturing into the water for a bathe, though he decided to keep his trousers on. It was a sunny day, so he guessed that wet trousers would not remain so for very long. He sloshed around in the water, complaining that he was hungry in a suspiciously good-tempered manner.

Grinning, though still weak from his various injuries, Theron splashed into the water to do some noisy fishing, causing a tidal wave to sweep across the lake, toppling Ramsey temporarily under the surface. He scowled when he rose for a breath, but was placated by the sight of Theron plucking some fish from the water and tossing them onto the bank.

"Have you eaten anything at all?" Theron had asked, upon seeing Ramsey without his shirt. "You're going to fade away."

Though his stomach growled indignantly on a constant basis, Ramsey had joked about Theron's bulky figure, which led to some brief play-fighting – Theron batted Ramsey on the head with his claws, Ramsey tried to throttle him with his bare hands, and Theron had finally gained the upper hand, causing his goblin companion to tumble to the grass, his one, heavy paw pressing against Ramsey's belly. Thoroughly winded, Ramsey had feigned defeat, only to give Theron a swift, playful kick when he let his guard down.

The entire day slipped by in a dizzy haze; Ramsey overjoyed to see Theron alive, and Theron equally so at finding Ramsey in one piece. Birds frequented the skies over this part of the island, and without realising it, they slipped uneventfully into the neighbouring kingdom of Oouealena, and continued on their journey, skirting the Troll Teeth Mountains warily.

Ramsey told Theron all about his experience on the mountain – his encounter with the female troll and her baby, the dispute between the two male trolls, his unappetising sample of hippogriff meat, and most prominently, the voices he had heard so very clearly while surrounded by nothing but rain, snow and stone. Theron often walked by his side, frequently carried Ramsey on his back, but throughout the whole of Ramsey's animated story, the forest troll remained captivated.

Of course, thought Ramsey, neither one of us ever travelled much before this...shame he missed out on some of the best action.

"I should be dead by now," he sighed wearily one day, as they were bordering the slope of another bleak mountain beyond the kingdom border. "I've had all these stupid accidents, I've been attacked, almost burned to death – not to mention that I've narrowly escaped being eaten several times. Makes me wonder why in Grenamoya my bad luck is combined with good fortune nowadays…"

"I know you said not to say anything about this," began Theron, limping slightly a few paces behind, "but I think that you are still alive because someone is watching over you."

"You're right…" Ramsey paused, admiring a dark array of wild, bracken-like shrubs blossoming with white flowers. "I *did* say not to say anything about that."

Theron smiled, shrugging as he walked. A slight breeze caught his brown mane, tousling it. "You have made some stupid decisions, you know." Ramsey glowered at him, fondling one of the white flowers that he had plucked from the prickly bush. "You can't deny that. But you are still alive, and so am I. I am sure that the other forest trolls I knew were killed in that fire, weeks and weeks ago, but I survived. And I am here with you now, and as long as I have strength in my body, I'll follow you."

A brief moment passed between them, in which Ramsey just stared, lips parted, barely able to absorb Theron's words at once. Theron smiled, wincing slightly at the pressure of his weight upon his injured leg. He shifted on his toes, and still Ramsey did not speak.

"I had time to think about things before I found you."

Ramsey's thin eyebrows climbed his forehead, and he mirrored Theron's smile. "Yeah, it definitely shows." He crumpled the flower slightly between his fingers, the soft petals tracing the pale scars that remained on his hand. His black fingernails, now completely re-grown, if a little bent, split one of the petals in two; then he dropped it to the ground. A faint coating of pale pollen remained on his palm. "I can't believe I'm doing this."

"Doing what?" Theron bent to sniff the discarded blossom, and he groaned at the discomfort in his joints. Ramsey didn't speak for a moment, looking from the sky to the dark mountains, and then to Theron's open face, friendly, yet still feral. Theron's smile was soft, edged with concern. "Doing what, Ramsey?" he prompted once more.

With a tired smirk, Ramsey flung his arms around himself and trudged ahead, his dagger protruding from his belt, still stained with troll blood. Theron whimpered, but tried to keep up without displaying too much pain. "Just...I can't believe...when I was a kid, I would never have thought I'd end up doing this...going off to rescue a prince from a dragon, and genuinely wanting to do it. Nobody would have done this for me when I was twelve years old."

"I would have, if I had known you," said Theron with a suppressed gasp. By now, they had used all of the healing leaves, and Theron was in agony whenever he moved. Ramsey knew that the troll needed to see a doctor, but there were none to be found in the wilderness, miles and miles from civilisation. Ramsey knew a lot about some things, but was hopeless with medicine.

"You wouldn't have liked me when I was young," stated the goblin, treading over the somewhat pebbly earth as they bordered the mountain. "I've always hated everything about the world, I was never a nice person." Dry grass tickled his bare feet, sometimes managing to poke inside his trouser legs. Theron trampled it easily.

"You probably weren't much different from how you were when I met you. But I still liked you."

Ramsey laughed. "You do realise that I've come all the way from home, through loads of awful stuff, I met you, and now I've got to go miles and miles north, over mountains, only to reach some *more* mountains, and then I've got to kill a massive dragon, and somehow drag a twelve-year-old prince all the way back home to where I started from. And I've only got one clean set of clothes!"

Theron lowered his head and nudged Ramsey forcefully in the back, causing the goblin to flinch and fall forward. "I'm glad that you've got me, then. Or you would be lonely as well as tired and dirty and smelly."

"I do not smell! I only just had a bath, what, about four days ago?"

354

Theron grinned at Ramsey, who was attempting to stand on the loose earth, stepped over him and continued past him, still with a limp. Ramsey eventually scrambled to his dusty feet, brushed himself down, and ran behind with a shout, proclaiming that he smelled rather fragrant and not at all sweaty.

And thus it continued for days, even as they moved beyond the shadow of the mountain, and progressed to the free, flat landscape once more, heading northwards. Ramsey opened like an orange flower as the sun shone upon him, unhindered by the cover of trees or the darkness of mountains, and the more he spoke, the bouncier he became, until he was virtually hopping on the balls of his feet, even when the rain beat down upon them.

Theron, however, became worse as the days dragged on and turned into weeks. Days in which their progress was often slow, and became slower as Theron's limp became more severe. Some mornings, he could barely stand, could hardly walk. Ramsey tried in vain to ease Theron's discomfort, but cool water, leafy bandages and firm-fingered massages did little for the troll's pain. Visibly, his wounds no longer bled, but the damage beneath his greyish fur lingered.

One gloomy afternoon, when a slight dusting of snowflakes flittered down from the clouds above them, Theron once again drew to a halt, allowing the white crystals to settle on his fur. "I can't, Ramsey...I'm sorry...I can't walk..."

Ramsey ran back to him across the grass, which was crunchy and brittle with frost, and forcefully embraced Theron's head as the troll lay down wearily in the snow, trying to rouse him. Theron stayed still, closed his eyes and whined mournfully, clearly not wanting to give in – but the weight of his body combined with the weakness of his damaged back leg had defeated him.

"Come on, Theron, you can't just...oh, for Scaless' sake...!" Ramsey tugged on Theron's cheeks, his ears, even his nose, but the troll stayed motionless, his legs curled under him like a huge, weary cat. Ramsey grabbed one of Theron's big paws and pulled as hard as he could, but Theron just withdrew his leg under his stomach with a groan. "You can't just lie down there and die!"

"Don't worry about me, Ramsey, just go on…"

A hysterical, frightened laugh burst from Ramsey's chest. "What? Oh Theron, don't joke, I could never just leave you here! I…I could go ahead and find you a doctor!"

He glanced hurriedly towards the murky, grey silhouette of what appeared to be some kind of town or large village, no more than two miles from where they had halted. It was the first sign of civilisation since Ramsey had left BlackField Town – the fact that the cobra dragon had tracked him there and reduced the whole town to ashes did not fill him with much hope. They had walked too far and for too long, just for Theron to give up and lie down on the snow.

"If I run, it won't take long, but I don't know if that place would even have a doctor. I can hardly see anything of it from here." He squinted. "But maybe-"

"No, Ramsey, just give me a moment…I will be fine, honestly…"

Ramsey swallowed, bobbing tensely on the spot, not knowing what to do. "I can't leave you here, Theron, I spent far too long wandering over that mountain wishing you were with me!"

Unexpectedly, Theron swiped four sharp claws in Ramsey's direction, barely missing him, and it was not a playful gesture this time. "No, Ramsey, you can't stay here, you have to keep going! I just need to rest, but you mustn't wait with me, not when there's shelter up ahead."

"I am not going on without you."

Theron snarled at him, causing Ramsey to jump aside. "Go, Ramsey! I won't sit here and blame myself for keeping you out in the cold!"

"Are you mad? There's no way I'm going to just wander off and leave you alone when you're injured and can't move! What would you do to defend yourself?"

With an angry huff, Theron slumped back down on the frosted grass and heaved a sigh. "I'm big enough to cope with anything that might come along, Ramsey. There's been no danger for days."

Ramsey paced back and forth in front of him, the troll's tired breath warming his toes and melting the snowflakes. "All the more reason for some to show up at this very minute! No, you can't make me leave you, not here in the cold. I'll drag you along with my bare hands if I have to!"

Theron sighed again, mist rising in front of his nostrils. "You can't help me by yourself."

"Don't you think I know that? Give me a second to think, will you?" Ramsey grasped futilely at the breeze and twisted his thin fingers in his hair, pulling it. "I can't leave you like this, I need to be here to protect you. But at the same time I can't help you. So..." Theron grunted impatiently, batting Ramsey's feet with his paw. "Hey! You can't make me go! I know you'd do the same for me, Theron, you wouldn't leave me like this, and I certainly won't do that to you!"

Theron whined mournfully and covered his face with his claws, shaking his head. "But you can't stay here...!"

"And you know what, Theron?" continued Ramsey, regardless of the troll's objections, "I'm not going to abandon you, because you've shown me something that I've never had before. You've made me feel like I'm worthwhile, you've made me feel as though I can see this journey through to the end. And you're mad if you think that I would abandon you now, because you would stay by me until Utipona's volcanoes turned to ice if you had to – I know you would. And I know nobody else on this whole damn island would ever do that for me."

Theron shook his head, and Ramsey realised that the troll's whole body was shaking too, with deep, painful sobs. Ramsey instantly stopped pacing and knelt, hugging Theron's face with his bony arms.

"What's wrong? It's true, I know it's all true. You're the greatest friend I've ever had." Theron sniffed loudly, his injured leg bent under him as though it was devoid of all feeling. The unnatural angle of the troll's hairy limb made Ramsey hug tighter, with as great a depth of emotion as he could summon. "You're the *only* friend I've ever had."

357

"I'm sorry, Ramsey, I'm so sorry...I never meant to slow you down like this..." He snorted and closed his eyes tightly. "If I hadn't missed that jump and hurt myself...I'm so, so sorry..."

"Oh shut up," scolded Ramsey, who was now behind Theron, trying to push him from the back. "None of this was your fault – I'm the one who said we should go across the mountain, and now *you're* the one suffering for it. I'm an idiot, I admit that." He hurled himself at Theron's backside with a forceful shove, but the troll did not shift. "I'm not going anywhere without you, so I'll do everything I can to get you back on your feet."

"I'm so- oof!" he grunted as Ramsey tried to force him into movement. "Ramsey, no, I can't get up..."

"Yes you can, Theron, and I'll help you." He tried to push one last time; then, relenting, he stepped back. "Or maybe I should try to find some help that might actually do you some good..."

Theron nodded. "Please, Ramsey, just go ahead...I've been in more pain than this, and I was fine afterwards."

Ramsey stared up at the clouds miserably, his arms at his sides. "But it's really starting to snow...damn it, that's all we need!" He kicked angrily at the grass, scattering settled snowflakes in all directions, his toes stinging with cold. "I'm going to catch my death out here. I don't have enough layers on."

Theron growled, as though asserting his previous point. "For goodness sake, Ramsey, just go ahead. I'm all right here, I just need a short rest, then I'll be fine, and I'll come after you."

Ramsey was already gone. Theron lifted his head, which at that moment felt particularly heavy, and turned to see the orange-skinned goblin traipsing away through the snow. The grass was crusty with frost, and crunched beneath Ramsey's feet, the sound gradually fading as he walked further away from Theron, in the direction of the town-like blot in the distance. Too tired to keep his head aloft, Theron lay back down on the grass and allowed the feather-soft snowflakes to settle in his hair. His left hind leg was numb beneath him, pulsing gently with discomfort every time he moved.

He closed his eyes. He opened them again a moment later to find Ramsey's frost-bitten feet in front of his face, and his head jerked upwards to stare at him. "What are you doing?" he asked, his ears pressed flat against his neck to protect from the snow. "I thought you went to get help."

"No," said Ramsey simply, kneeling down so that he was level with the troll's worried face. "I saw a sign post, so I just nipped ahead to have a look. It said that the town up ahead is called 'Morfran Town', and that the capital Oouea is many, many miles to the east. So I think we need to try for Morfran, otherwise we'll be diverted a long way, and I'm not going to stand around and watch you get sicker. Morfran looks a big enough place to have at least one decent doctor or vet."

Theron nodded dimly; he did not know what a vet was, but felt it was a cruel-sounding word.

"So come on – and literally, I will drag you all the way there with my own two hands if you can't walk for yourself." Ramsey grabbed forcefully onto the sides of Theron's face, where brown fur sprouted beneath his ears, and pulled. "Come on, Theron, put some effort into it!"

The troll snarled and lashed out at Ramsey, pushing him aside. "No, Ramsey, I can't, I just can't! You have to go, please!"

"You can just say if you don't want my company any more!" exclaimed Ramsey, who had tripped onto the cold ground on his bottom, in the shadow of an ash-like tree as its branches waved sadly above them. The nearby trees were whitened and softly frosted with the traces of snow, a few of them bare, but most with thick plumes of tiny green leaves, which sparkled silver under the glow of the sun through snow-clouds. Theron looked towards one of the trees, and heaved a determined breath.

"Go on, Ramsey, I'll follow. If I can get myself over to that tree, maybe I can stand…"

"Whatever you want – just don't hit me again."

Ramsey stood by, not attempting to push or pull, as Theron slowly clawed his way across the grassy earth towards the tree. Still the troll insisted that Ramsey should hurry along to Morfran Town, but Ramsey stayed put like a stubborn rooster, his arms firmly folded across his chest. The few buttonholes bereft of buttons on his purple shirt were allowing a cold draught to flitter across his bare skin underneath. It was not a comfortable feeling.

To distract himself from Theron's growls as the troll attempted to get to his feet while supported by the relatively flimsy tree, Ramsey turned away with his hands in his pockets to survey the land; the path ahead, and the way they had already come. A cool breeze whipped over the grassy plain, tall trees bowing in its wake, and the mountains beyond looked so harmless from a distance.

Ramsey could identify it even now – the jagged peak of the mountain they had crossed many days ago, where he had lost Theron, and been attacked by so many different mountain trolls that he had lost count. Its head was completely under snow, and Ramsey was sincerely glad to be back on flat land.

Suddenly, in the very corner of his eye, he spied some dark, and moving, in the distance to the north. It was growing, moving quickly towards them, but he could hear nothing. His heart stopped.

Oh Scaless, no, don't let those be more mountain trolls…

I've had more than my fill of those things for one lifetime.

Were it not for Theron's loud grunting and the feeble creaking of the ash tree, Ramsey's world would have been silent, save for the frantic pulse buzzing in his ears. Ramsey could not hear the cries of animals, or any growls or snarls, apart from Theron's own. His throat closed up and he instinctively reached for the dagger at his belt, closing his fingers tightly around the jewelled handle. The shape approaching was definitely not a dragon.

"Theron."

Theron groaned, and unsuccessfully slumped onto the grass with one paw over his nose. "I'm sorry, I can't, I just can't get up…I'm so, so tired…"

"There's something coming this way. I can't tell what it is, though." He blinked hard and tried to focus his vision. Whatever it was, it was coming at them directly from Morfran Town. "Scaless, I

360

hope it's something friendly. If not, then I'm ready." Theron turned to gaze towards the town, his eyes slightly hazy with exhaustion, but for a moment he said nothing. He looked too dazed to register fear.

"No, Ramsey, you have to go..."

"Now why in blazes would I do that? And, I should say, if I *had* gone ahead to Morfran Town, and that thing is dangerous, then I would have been in worse trouble than I am now! So thank you for your advice, Theron, but I'm staying right on this spot!"

Like a sack of rocks, a dead weight suddenly struck him from above, and he was pinned to the ground by a massive, writhing mass of coarse, black fur and claws and teeth. A deafening roar sounded in his ears, and he could barely tell which way was up until the burden was suddenly struck away from him, and he saw Theron above him, struggling to stand, his mouth pulled back into a terrifying snarl.

Ramsey's hands shot to his ears, desperate to shut out the sound, and he turned, and saw in one fleeting moment, the muscular, hairy form of a partially scaly, lion-like animal, its fur completely black, and ghastly yellow tentacles sprouting from its face. Ramsey screamed and leapt to his feet, feeling Theron's fur beneath his fingers as he grasped for balance. Even as he stood, rigid with fear, he kept himself rooted to the ground between Theron and the hairy animal, dagger in hand.

The black creature bared a mouthful of knife-like fangs at them, and Theron tried to stand once again, only to collapse onto the grass with an angry grunt. He tried to pull himself up, but his leg gave way completely, and Ramsey was on his own. The animal was over ten feet long from head to tail, and its eyes glowed like coal. Ramsey edged around as the animal circled them, putting a permanent block between it and the frail form of Theron – and then the creature sprang, and Ramsey ran at it with all the fury in his heart.

His dagger slashed the creature's face almost in two, but it came at him again with a gruesome, gurgling cry, its fur standing sharply on end, the snake-like protrusions on its face writhing grotesquely, moist with some kind of dark fluid that splattered onto the grass. Its mouth gaped like some hellish gateway, and with another scream, Ramsey struck like a cobra, jamming his weapon into the creature's mouth as it roared. It tore away from him with a blood-curdling cry, ripping out the roof of its mouth as it did so, leapt at Ramsey again, and then crashed to the ground, dead.

Ramsey would have promptly fainted were it not for the adrenaline burning through his veins, and even as he turned to kick the dead creature out of his way, three more identical animals descended from the trees, and leapt at him, seeking his blood in return for their dead comrade.

Theron was down, so they ignored him, and all three set upon Ramsey at once, diving over one another and trying to avoid his dagger. Ramsey was not strong, but he was a goblin, and as such was nimble and exceedingly quick. He dodged them, his breath ragged in his chest, but not once did he leave Theron unguarded.

"Ramsey…" he moaned, as the goblin evaded a stealthy leap from one of the felines, "please, for the love of Scaless, get away from here…!" The animals ignored him, but Ramsey heard him through their cries.

"I almost lost you once!" he shouted, striking one of the animals across the neck and causing it to skid to the ground. "I'm not going to lose you again!"

And if we die here, thought Ramsey through the deafening shriek of terror in his ears, we die together.

Seeing no alternative, and abandoning Theron for the first time, Ramsey shot up a tree, still with his dagger in hand, to escape the slashing claws of his attackers. Of course, they could climb trees, but for some reason or another they did not pursue him, and instead circled beneath the tree, snapping their jaws towards him and roaring like shaggy-haired, scaly, black lions. The four tentacles on each of their faces – two above the eyes and two on the cheeks – constricted and danced like dying snakes.

One rammed its thick head against the tree trunk, almost causing Ramsey to drop, but he held on tight, desperately seeking for some way of escape. Apparently, he was not worth the creatures' effort to climb the tree, and instead they would wait until he fell.

Not thinking for himself, driven to insanity as the monsters moved to inspect Theron, Ramsey braced himself and leapt from the tree, landing on the back of one creature and holding on for dear life, gripping its muscular neck through its fur. The animal snarled indignantly and leapt around, jolting itself and trying to dislodge the nimble goblin, but Ramsey swung himself around and with one quick sweep, sliced the tentacles from its face, and it stumbled with pain, shaking him off at last. Ramsey landed hard on the cold ground and gaped at his surroundings, to find that the one animal still standing, the largest of the four, was charging at him like a bull, its sharp tail whipping through the air.

Ramsey jumped to his feet, not a metre away from Theron, ready to face the final battle whether he survived or not – but then, to his great surprise, a swift, feathered shaft came from nowhere and struck the beast right through its heart. Miserably, it fell, and came to a skidding halt in front of Ramsey on the snow-crusted grass, and its head lolled to one side, the tentacles swerving gently, then stilling altogether. Ramsey whipped around with understandable shock, to find that a line of pale, humanoid creatures on horseback, all armed with bows, were flanking the scene in a semi-circle. He dropped his dagger, swallowed hard, and could find no words to speak. Theron did not move.

"Hold, men!" cried one of the pale creatures, who wore an elaborate helmet and rode a particularly elegant, black steed. "There are some rhôniae that are not quite dead. See to them at once."

Ramsey stared, still beyond words, as two of the pale horsemen rode forward to the pair of twitching felines, and with subtle swiftness, put an arrow through each of their hairy skulls, finally quietening them. Ramsey stared even harder when the apparent leader of the throng approached him on horseback, and offered him a pale, slender hand.

"You are fortunate, young goblin. I saw you fighting those creatures on your own – I must say, it has come as quite a shock to find you still intact. I feared that we might not reach you in time, before the rhôniae attacked you."

"Yeah, well…thanks." Ramsey looked quickly to Theron, for some of the riders had approached him with dutiful curiosity. "That troll is with me, don't you dare hurt him!"

The lead horseman was still leaning down to him and offering one hand; his expression was fixedly sombre. "He looks in a bad way."

"Well, then, get him a doctor!" snapped Ramsey, not really meaning to be aggressive but being so all the same. "He's got an injured leg, which was entirely my fault, but anyway, he needs a doctor, or a vet, or something like that!"

The two rhôniae-killing riders returned to stand near their leader, and both looked down upon Ramsey with equally sombre eyes. He swallowed, and began to fumble on the grass for his dagger while keeping his eyes fixed on the fascinatingly pale creatures. "Yes, we shall see to it that he gets a doctor. Welcome, dear goblin. We shall escort you to Morfran Town, to protect you from any further attacks."

Ramsey finally accepted the proffered hand, and with a surprising amount of strength, the horseman lifted him up to sit behind him on the saddle. Ramsey had never been comfortable around horses, for they tended to bite him, but this colourless creature seemed to have his steed under tight control.

"I am sorry that we could not reach you sooner. Our sentry spotted you from a great distance, but once I feared that you might encounter some unpleasant creatures on your way, I decided it best to assemble my men."

"Mmm." Ramsey couldn't take his eyes from Theron, even as they turned and rode back towards Morfran Town. Not even the awkward bumping of his crotch against the hard saddle could distract him. He wanted to see Theron up and about, and smiling again – one of his altogether loveable smiles, which nowadays always made Ramsey smile in return.

"You see, there have been many rhôniae attacks in this kingdom in recent months, but we have been able to destroy most of them. Now barely a few remain, and regretfully, you ran into a group out of sheer misfortune."

"I'm used to it," he sighed, for Theron was now out of sight, obscured by the dark tide of horseback riders that followed them. "I'm not the luckiest goblin in the world. You just make sure that my friend is taken care of, all right? I'm useless without him."

"A funny thing," commented the chief rider, keeping a slack tension in the reins of his majestic horse. "to be travelling across Oouealena with a forest troll."

Ramsey's eyes were burning as the cold breeze whipped icy fingers against his cheeks. His hair was grey and fluffy with snow, even as the wind threatened to blow it away. He sheltered himself against the back of his rescuer, for they were now riding into the wind, and the horses stamped, their manes tousling to and fro. Snowflakes blew past almost horizontally as the breeze became more severe, and Ramsey closed his eyes tight, wishing for silence, some good food, and a warm bed. And, not least of all, Theron trotting once more by his side.

\*\*\*

When Ramsey was finally set down on the streets of Morfran, his rescuer shot him what could have been interpreted as a smile, were it not for the lack of mirth in his expression. Ramsey shivered, the cold gusts somehow penetrating through the tall buildings that surrounded him on all sides – Morfran Town square, he quickly noted, was more than massive.

"A safe and enjoyable stay to you, sir goblin. Pardon me, but what did you say your name was?"

Ramsey shuddered, very much intimidated by the huge, black horse glaring down at him. "I didn't tell you my name."

There was a brief pause, in which several of the other riders looked questioningly at one another, but the creature at the head of the team gave a proper smile, and the hint of a laugh. His horse stamped impatiently, making Ramsey jump. "A sharp mind you have, goblin. Enjoy your time here, and a very happy Eve of

Creation to you, as well." He steered his horse around sharply, and Ramsey hurriedly moved out of the way. "Worry not, for your companion will soon be returned to you. I shall see to it personally this instant, that he receives a good doctor."

"Thanks," replied Ramsey. "Always better than a bad one."

With a terse command in a language that Ramsey could not understand, the lead rider urged his steed into motion, and the elegant group galloped away in perfect formation, over one-hundred horseshoes clattering away over the cobbled square and down the wide street. Ramsey watched in silence as they disappeared as beautifully as they had arrived, and noted that several others stopped in the street to watch the riders go past; some waving, some cheering, and others just turning their heads. Ramsey took in a breath, turned to the sky, and felt his heart jump inside his ribs.

"This place is huge..."

It was a massive town, almost as big as Merlock, but open and beautiful, and overflowing with art. The carved statue of an elegant, humanoid creature in a long, flowing gown (though Ramsey could not tell if it was male or female) dominated the centre of the square. To all sides, Ramsey beheld ornate, painted houses, several theatres, half-a-dozen shops, and most prominently of all at the northern edge of the square; a beautiful, captivating temple carved entirely out of coloured marble, with a coiled, stone snake over the entrance doors, and a placard outside that read 'Come one, come all, to the Eve of Creation ceremony at the Morfran Church of Scaless, tonight at nine o' clock'. His heart was fluttering at the sheer scale and beauty of this place, that he could do nothing but turn in circles, staring up to trace the tall towers and the beautiful town clock with his eager eyes.

There was never anything like this in Merlock, he thought with glee.

"I'll never go home again."

The houses, the shops, the temple – everything was too beautiful to be imagined, as though the entire town had been plucked straight from a painting. The houses were decorated like

366

iced cakes, lacy trims of black on white bordering the sloped roofs. His face was alight with intrigue, and he knew that everyone else was most likely staring at him, but he didn't care one fraction. He felt as though the whole world had been created again, just for him, and nobody else – a whole new land to explore, and admire, and love.

It wasn't until he returned his gaze to ground level that he realised that everyone in the town looked rather strange. The square was busy, as any town square would be; but as the residents passed nearer to him, going about their daily business, he began to realise why they were all so pale. One goblin went past – nothing unusual about her, apart from the fact that she was talking to a creature that distinctly resembled a dead human.

A dead human, walking around the town square with a bag of shopping under its arm.

Ramsey shuddered at the sudden icy cold that swept over his skin. This was as bizarre as he could ever cope with.

"Hello, love," said the goblin girl good-naturedly, having noticed that he was looking at her. "New to Morfran, are you?"

Ramsey grinned anxiously; here he was again, inches away from a rather beautiful girl who just *maybe* was coming on to him, and all he could stare at was the gaunt, sallow face of her companion. He tried not to look, but it was hard to ignore. The dead-looking thing had a piece missing from its face. "Um...er...um...yes..."

The zombie-like creature spoke, almost shattering Ramsey's composure. "Oh dearie, don't worry about it. This place may look pretty big, but once you get to know the place – well, I tell you, the locals are great. The perfect place to pass the holiday season, I say."

The female goblin giggled happily in agreement. "So, have you got somewhere to stay? Visiting relatives, are you?"

"No...I just..." He could barely tell if the zombie was a man or a woman, and that unsettled him more than ever. "I just got here from...um..."

"Merlock?" she guessed, her odd companion fumbling slightly with the bags of shopping.

"Yes! Yes, that's it. Merlock. Lovely place." He thought for a moment, and realised that he was not unnerved enough to speak such a blatant lie. "Nah, actually it's an awful place, and I'm glad to be rid of it."

The girl smiled warmly. Apparently, she did not find her dead friend unusual in the least, and hooked her arm around that of her companion with a laugh. "Yes, I've heard nothing but negative things about that place. Stay here in Morfran Town, there's no better place in all of Grenamoya to spend the festive season. It was nice talking to you, sir."

"Um, yes...you too."

"Bye, dearie!" waved the girl's accomplice, who seemed to be female from the tone of her voice. "And happy Creation Eve to you!"

"Yes, you too." Ramsey was starting to feel physically sick by the time he became isolated once more in the crowd. All he could see around him, far from the majestic artistry of the architecture, was the dreary, wan faces of passers-by, some whiter than others, some male, some female, some in-between to Ramsey's eyes. And suddenly, all he could think of was getting out of the square.

Weaving his way through the crowd with some difficulty (for he was rather too nervous to risk touching any of the dead-looking locals), he escaped the enthusiastic throng without attracting too much attention. Clearly, everyone was too occupied with thoughts of Creation Eve celebrations to be concerned with the antics of a bony, orange newcomer; for which Ramsey was truly grateful. He also realised, with dismay, that if it was Creation Eve, he had missed the passing of his nineteenth birthday.

Separated from the dizzying hum of activity in the square, Ramsey ambled inconspicuously along one of the wide, cobbled streets that led away from the centre. He passed a line of small houses, a line of tall houses, a line of houses that were medium in height, all of which were white with elegant black roofs and beams; until at last, on his left, he found a rather unique-looking building. It, too, was black and white and very tall, but somehow it stood separately from the others – its steeply-sloping roof reached all the way down to the top of Ramsey's head, so that the whole building looked triangular from the front. The building's peak was lost somewhere high above him – most likely fifty feet or more from the ground.

Interested, Ramsey moved closer to inspect the wooden front doors (themselves rather slender and over ten feet high), and found that a decorated plaque was mounted on one of the wooden panels. It read; 'Andel's Tavern – Lodge, bar and restaurant. Mofran's most popular tavern!' and then, on a smaller sign beneath in curvy handwriting, were the words; 'Places available during Creation Festival. Come on in!'

Allured by his goblin curiosity, but wary of what sort of clientele he might discover inside, Ramsey hurriedly deliberated over what to do. A few steps led up to the doors, they were nothing imposing. The building looked pleasant enough from the outside. And he couldn't deny that he needed somewhere to stay, whether or not he had money. He would find some way to pay. His skin broke out in goosebumps at the very thought of the corpse-like people roaming the town square, so before any other dead creatures could approach him, Ramsey sucked in his stomach and took decisive action.

As he ambled up the stone steps and passed through the tall doorway, he was instantly struck by the strong smell of soap and cooking. He was standing in a narrow corridor with a floor of black stone; ahead of him was a half-open door labelled as the dining room, and to his immediate right, through a glass-panelled door, was a brightly-lit room with pine furniture and a stairway that disappeared from view, beneath which was a high reception desk, also labelled as such.

The strong, vaguely woody smell settled in his nostrils, and became quite pleasant. He pushed the door to his right, which swung open with the ring of a little bell, and stepped through, grateful to be out of the cold. As he entered, the individual behind the tall desk, visible only as a head of straight, purple hair, moved sideways, apparently standing from a chair, and finally peered over the top of the desk to greet him.

"Well, hi there, stranger! What can I do for you?"

Ramsey hesitated slightly upon noticing the deathly pale skin, dark lips and slightly protruding fangs that were present on the receptionist's grinning face. Ramsey was none too comfortable to be in the presence of someone who was obviously a vampire. He stood still; the receptionist cocked his head with interest, peering at the goblin with one arm resting on the desk.

"No need to be nervous, sunshine. I won't bite." He shot Ramsey a very sharp-looking smile, which made Ramsey feel more unsettled than ever. This was certainly a very odd town with even odder people living in it. The vampire, still not moving from behind his desk, leaned over and offered Ramsey a handshake. "Come on, I mean it! You can trust little old me. Want a room, do you?" Ramsey opened his mouth, but the vampire interrupted before he could answer. "What am I saying? Of course you want a room! Andel, I have to say some mornings – *Andel*, the reason people come here is always the same! They want a room, I say to myself, but *no*, I reply to myself – perhaps they just want to stay for dinner! But nonetheless, I think it's polite to ask whether somebody wants a room or not, don't you?"

Ramsey stared at him for a moment, unsure of whether the vampire was talking to him or not. Still uncertain, he took the vampire's cold hand in his own and shook it in as masculine a way as possible. "You're Andel?"

"Of course I'm Andel!" came the reply, though it was merry and by no means insulted. "I'm receptionist, owner, manager, what-have-you, all in one! And I'm a pretty good dancer, too, but I digress. I've owned this place for nearly fifty years, I'd wager. Ah, the good old days when I started out with hardly any scales to my name…"

He trailed off briefly, apparently lost in thought, then abruptly returned to the present and clasped Ramsey's hand tightly, still held in his own palm.

"So, you're new to Morfran Town, aren't you? I know you are, otherwise I'd know your face. I'm over a thousand years old and I still remember every face I've ever seen! Pretty amazing, don't you think?"

"Oh yes," replied Ramsey, genuinely impressed by such a talent but still wary, "absolutely amazing."

Andel smiled at him, two yellow streaks in his otherwise violet hair framing the edges of his face brightly. Ramsey's heart began to beat as normal, though he still readied himself to flee if need be. The vampire looked docile, and as though far too intrigued by the visitor to keep his distance, he walked around the side of the desk and came to stand in front of Ramsey. Ramsey realised that Andel was taller than he was, that he had indigo hair that came down almost to his shoulders, and that he was dressed entirely in grey and black.

"Um...how much do you charge per night?" he asked tentatively, humbled by the vampire's grand presence. "Because I don't have...very much money."

Andel pondered this for a moment, brushing some hair away from the left side of his face to reveal an ear riddled with metal piercings, and looked down at Ramsey through dark eyes, sharp with thought. "Hmm...well, you're new around here, so maybe I can stretch to..." He thought again for a moment; Ramsey braced himself. "Fifteen green scales per day?"

"Great," responded Ramsey too quickly, secretly wondering how he was going to get his hands on that sort of money before he left the town. "Can I pay when I leave?"

"Sure you can, mate. Honestly, I'd let you stay for free if only I didn't have all these bills to pay. It's like my mother used to say – a great...no, not that one...ah, she used to say – everybody loves getting something for free, and sometimes it's nice to give something for free. Honestly, I would, but...well, you know."

"Yeah, I know." Ramsey swallowed, and managed a smile, now fairly certain that Andel did not intend to kill him. As he thought about it, he realised that it was wholly unlike him to trust this kind of stranger. He had more faith in people these days.

Largely thanks to Theron, he mused. "Oh, and...I've got a fairly odd request."

Andel leaned on the desk, his elbow pressing against the pale wood. "Go ahead. I've dealt with loads of strange stuff while running this place."

"Well," began Ramsey, trying to find the best way to phrase his dilemma, "I've been travelling with a troll that I met back in the Great Forest, in Merlockiara, and...well, it would be really helpful if you could give him somewhere to stay, too. The problem is that he's very big."

"Hey, wow! You have a troll? That's amazing!" Andel's face became suddenly brighter than ever, and he positively beamed at Ramsey with eagerness in his eyes. "I used to have a troll! I kept him in my wardrobe when I was little. Mum eventually found out, but I kept him there for over a year without her knowing. I called him Archie."

Ramsey's face fell blank. This vampire was insane. "You...do know what trolls are, don't you? The sort of creature I'm talking about?"

"Sure I do. I'm guessing that you don't mean the big, ugly hairless ones that you get in the Sacred Mountains."

Ramsey smirked involuntarily, picturing Theron with all his fur shaved off. "You're right about that. I've been travelling with a forest troll. He's very big, I'd say around...seven feet at the shoulder?"

Andel smiled. "The way you were going on about it, I thought you were going to say he was much bigger. I used to have a mountain troll myself; the hairiest baby I've ever seen in my life. He was adorable, though...in an ugly sort of way."

Ramsey cringed, thinking back to his own unpleasant experience with mountain trolls. Andel noticed this, and laughed.

"Not a big fan of mountain trolls, then?"

"Let's just say we ran into a couple on our way here."

Andel laughed again. Ramsey was surprised to have encountered such a jovial vampire. At least he had discerned why everyone there was so unhealthy looking – most likely, all of them were vampires, or other varieties of 'undead' creatures. He had never really known if zombies were real until now, but on first glance, most of the residents of Morfran appeared to be regular vampires. It was very unusual to have a settlement like Morfran in the middle of Oouealena, when normally it was believed that all creatures of the undead variety lived in the south of the island. He was relieved to be off the streets, but was intent on helping Theron do the same once he was well.

"Certainly," said Andel at last, his elbow still on the desk top. "There's a stable out at the back of my building, and there's nothing else in there at the moment. I'm sure there will be plenty of room for your friend to stay."

"Oh, thank you," said Ramsey. "He's sick at the moment, and being seen by a doctor, I hope. But once I get him back, I'll need to get him out of the cold before he…um, catches a cold."

"You're worried about the creatures wandering around outside, aren't you?" said the vampire perceptibly, still with a smile. "Well, you needn't. Vampires, zombies, witches, warlocks (not that you see many of those nowadays) – we're all the same. We're like people, but with paler skin, if you think about it. Nobody here means any harm, buddy. Everyone I've even known in Morfran has been as friendly as you please. It's just a bit hectic at the moment, you know, because of the Eve of Creation and everything."

Andel seemed to slip into a dream for a moment, then a broad smile broke out on his face.

"I've got my banners and all my decorations ready for tonight. You've never been in my tavern for the Creation Festival before. Believe me, you're in for a treat. I hold great parties."

Ramsey smiled nervously. He did not want to be dragged into the festivities, not even by someone as friendly as Andel. There was something suspicious about such positive people. Andel began rummaging through his desk for the key to Ramsey's room, and as he did so, the tiniest little slip of a kitten hopped up onto the surface, and let out a wailing tone that made Andel bump his head under the counter with a resonance that rattled the room.

"Ack! Oh, Nemo, you little rascal!" he scolded, though his head was still lost beneath the desk. Ramsey leaned over for a look, and found himself smiling at the small cat. Its soft, black fur twitched slightly, and Ramsey couldn't help but thank Scaless that he had survived the attack from the rhôniae. The kitten, however, was far removed from the terror of those terrible creatures. It stared at him fondly with eyes as green as cut grass. "You like him?" asked Andel from the floor, on hearing Ramsey chuckle. "I only got him last week. Sharp as a button, he is."

Ramsey was so absorbed with stroking the kitten that he barely heeded the vampire's metaphor. It warmed lovingly to his hand, rubbing its face against the hard skin of his scarred palm, and he instinctively lifted it from the counter and held it in his arms.

"Great company," continued Andel, rising from the desk with a brass key hanging from the little finger of his right hand. "I called him 'Necromancer', but the name just felt so long after two days, I just call him Nemo. My dad used to have a horse called Necromancer. And a dog called 'Bobby', now that I recall..." He wandered off into his mind for a moment or two, then offered Ramsey the key with a quirky smile. "Here's the key to your room, by the way. Any luggage?"

"Nope. I just brought myself with me."

Andel pouted at Nemo, who just nestled more snugly against Ramsey's chest. "Treacherous cat. I swear, the first person to come along and give him a good cuddle...ah well. Yourself, you say? Yeah, it's always handy to take yourself with you. That way you can't lose yourself. At least that's what I always say. I think."

Unwilling, but desperate for a rest, Ramsey surrendered the squirming kitten and took the key from Andel, holding it securely in his palm. "Thank you."

"You're welcome, sunshine. And don't be afraid to nip outside later on for a bit of fresh air, hmm? Nobody will hurt you in Morfran Town. We all love each other to bits." Ramsey blinked, already halfway across the room in the direction of the staircase. Andel smiled and shrugged. "And you don't want to miss the

Morfran Church service this evening, either. I'll be heading down there at nine; I can come and get you."

Ramsey could not find the strength to object, and so just nodded as he ascended the stairs to his room. He noticed a pattern very quickly; a pattern of moving up, and up, and up, and *up*, until he felt as though he was walking above the clouds. He climbed many flights of stairs, advancing higher and higher up through the building, until he finally reached the topmost room – the door of which, he found, matched his key.

"It bloody well would be..." he mused to himself, for it was quite obvious that there was nobody else staying at the tavern. His legs creaked so painfully that he collapsed into the nearest armchair as soon as he pushed his way into the room. It sagged comfortably beneath his slight weight.

The whole room was white, with pale, wooden floorboards and clean, white bedsheets. With a contented sigh, he dragged himself, armchair and all, over to one of the small windows of his room; he leaned forward, drew the curtains, and lifted the glass to give himself a perfect, unobstructed view of the bustling square beyond. The cobbled town centre was teeming with people of all shapes and sizes and races, and they converged upon the temple, which stood glimmering in the serene, snowy sunlight. He put his elbows on the sill, rested his chin on his arms, and for the first time in many weeks, he felt content.

# Chapter Fourteen

# The Eve Of Creation

*"Scaless, Lady fair, your love for us all shines through this day! Sweet Scaless, you watch from above, beautiful reptile we love..."*

It was half-past six in the evening before Ramsey emerged from his comfortable, white room and ventured downstairs. To his surprise (though very little seemed normal in Morfran Town), he arrived in the reception area to find Andel the purple-haired vampire at the top of a tall ladder, with a thick garland of ivy around his neck, singing in an unfaltering tenor that echoed around the high ceiling. From the moment Ramsey noticed him wrestling with the garland, the goblin's pace slowed considerably as he descended the stairs. He was nervous of making a noise in case it made the vampire lose his footing, but the slight scuffle of his bare feet on the staircase was enough to make the pale figure turn.

"Oh, hiya," said Andel, half of his face shrouded in thick ivy. "How are you doing down there? How did you find your room?"

Ramsey drew to the base of the narrow ladder, hugging himself. "Up at the very top of about a hundred flights of stairs," he responded, noticing the black kitten playing with a discarded leaf next to the desk. Andel burst out laughing, hummed for a moment as though about to continue with his singing, then quick as a flash he slid down the ladder and landed with a slight bounce in front of Ramsey. The ivy leaves were still wrapped around his torso.

"You like your room, then?"

"Yes, I suppose, though it happens to be quite a long walk..." Andel smirked and went to Nemo; the kitten was by now badly tangled with a piece of gold twine. "Is there anyone else staying here at the moment?" asked Ramsey nonchalantly, prompting Andel to reveal why his room was such an inconvenient distance away.

"Nope."

Ramsey pursed his lips and scratched a mild itch at the back of his neck. The kitten was running in circles around the vampire's ankles. "So..." He was going to ask his intended question, then decided on a different one. "Why not?"

"Oh, nobody travels much over the festive season. It's been snowing more than ever since you went to your room. Looks like a big snowstorm. I'm surprised to find even one goblin out and about on the Eve of Creation without anywhere to stay. Everyone comes over after the service for my legendary Creation Eve party – that's become about as much of a tradition as the festival itself."

He paused for a moment, then sighed heavily, realising that he was now tangled with both Nemo and the gold twine.

"Basically," he continued, fiddling with the string, "everyone comes for the party, then goes home. It's always best to be with friends and family for the new year."

Ramsey nodded, though the vampire's attention was elsewhere.

"So, going out for some air, are we?"

"I suppose." Ramsey then noticed the rack of up-to-date newspapers sitting next to the reception desk, and remembering for the first time in ages, he lifted his untidy shirt and pulled his smudged copy of 'The Merlockiara Bulletin' from within. "Can I have one of those papers?"

Andel had already cut the twine away from the kitten's body, and he stared fixedly at Ramsey with wide-open blue eyes. He grinned. "Of course you can. What else are you keeping under your clothes, then?" Ramsey swallowed and placed his old newspaper on the desk, his cheeks flushed. The vampire just turned his attention back to the ivy around his neck. "Of course you can, sunshine. Feel free. You just enjoy your time out, Okay, and don't forget to be back before the service starts. I just have some final voice-tuning to do, and then I'm set."

Ramsey nodded, and decided to retrieve a newspaper once he returned, rather than walk around Morfran Town with another crumpled mass of paper under his shirt. The moment he left the room, he noted through the glass door, Andel picked up the small, black kitten and swayed gently with it in his arms, and of course he resumed singing. Ramsey didn't know any hymn words, for he had never been to a church service, but he didn't intend to learn; neither did he intend going to the service. He was going to rescue Prince Morgan, he had sworn himself to it – but changing his beliefs altogether was a step too far.

It is true what they say, thought Ramsey as he stepped out into the brisk evening air; experience inspires confidence.

He wasn't sure where he had heard those words before -- most likely in another dream-- but it was certainly true that brief snippets of conversation with a particularly friendly vampire had quelled his nervousness. Theron had made him a less cynical person, if only slightly.

As he walked by, the inhabitants of Morfran Town still swarming over the square greeted him – they smiled, called out greetings, raised their hats to him. Festivities are worthwhile, truly, if they make people act so courteously to one another. Ramsey was unaccustomed to feeling so excited. Theron was injured, and under the care of a doctor somewhere in the town, but Ramsey was not disheartened, not in the slightest bit worried. These people, these vampires, zombies and what-have-you – the more he saw of them, the more he realised with amusement that they were far more sociable than members of his own race back in Merlock.

Strangely enough, as he crossed the square, he once more passed the female goblin and her undead companion that he had met earlier in the day. The girl smiled enthusiastically and waved in a manner that suggested they had known one another for years. The sallow-skinned woman, now laden with more shopping bags, smiled jaggedly at him over one large, brightly-wrapped parcel, and then they both receded into the crowd. Something at the very brink of his consciousness sensed cold eyes upon him.

Fine flakes of snow fluttered through the air, and Ramsey could see the mountains that flanked the town, the southernmost range of the Ash Mountains, also dusted with snow. He would be thankful if he never had to look at another mountain again, after his awful experience while wandering without Theron in the Troll Teeth Mountains; funnily enough, now that he was so close to the rocky peaks that had been his destination for so many weeks, he felt detached. He was happy, he was smiling more than he had ever smiled before, and he couldn't feel intimidated right at that moment. He was too light on his feet, too careless, though he could not tell why.

A rather beautiful female vampire with long, white hair passed him with a cheery gesture, and he was drawn to the various carts strewn around the square, where people of different races were selling handmade wares and Morfran Town souvenirs. One stall in particular, set just outside the grand church, enticed Ramsey with bright ribbons and scarves, and not surprisingly, most of its featured items were religious in one way or another. Elegantly carved wooden snakes, of varying quality and price, sold out rapidly.

Ramsey was not a fan of religious advertising, but had to admit than some of the carvings were impressive. If nothing else, he would have bought one for Theron were it not for his complete lack of currency.

He wandered around the borders of the square twice in a row before selecting one of the side roads to investigate. Money had been far from his mind for a few blissful hours. It would work out somehow.

There were considerably fewer people beyond the bustling square, and Ramsey began to quite enjoy the feel of bumpy cobbles beneath his bare feet. This street comprised mostly small shops and a café or two, none of which he went into. He was so absorbed in admiring the beautiful buildings that he quite forgot how far he was walking, but on such a straight and direct road, he figured, he would have no problem getting back to the centre.

There it was again, ever so briefly – the tight, cold feeling of being watched. He looked over his shoulder, to either side, and squinted down the road in front of him. There was most definitely nobody there. He swallowed to regain his composure, then marched onwards, further beyond the centre to wherever the road might lead him.

He had wandered for so long, he estimated the time at around seven o' clock, maybe half-past. If he kept walking, by the time he returned to the square the church service would be over and done with, and that way, he could avoid explaining to his particularly cheerful innkeeper why he did not want to attend.

"Is it really so unusual," he murmured to himself aloud, "not to think in the mainstream? Even Theron thinks that the world was made by a big snake. I wonder where they get all this stuff…"

He heard something clatter behind him, like a rock skimming over the cobbles, and he peered over his shoulder again, through the now blinding sheets of snow that broke over the rooftops and across the road. He could barely see anything, but the sound came again, and he felt his stomach give an uncomfortable jolt. He kept walking, his eyes fixed directly ahead, and began to hum forcefully to himself to drown out the noise.

It came again, then again, loudly. Then a snort, and another clatter, and he found his feet carrying him forward at a suddenly frantic pace, leaving deep footprints in his wake. There was the sound of something metal, the hushed sound of somebody talking. Was it talking? Or hissing? Ramsey held his hands in front of his face to protect against the snow and ran blindly forward, the snow thickening as he ran until it reached mid-way up his calves, and still he hurried on, for the sound kept clanking behind him, and he heard no spoken words, only the remnants of what might be coarse voices.

He couldn't speak, and he couldn't think to hold his dagger and shout threats into the obscure whiteness of the road. He heard crunching in the snow behind him, matching his footsteps, gaining, and he caught himself from tripping as the snow became too thick around his legs.

In the moment it took him to think, he was grabbed from behind and dragged to the ground. A forceful, frozen hand was pressed to his mouth as he tried to scream, and solid muscle held him down in the snow, though he twisted and kicked and tried to escape. The grip tightened, and he heard some sharp words, unintelligible in his state of terror, but he knew that he was screaming and swearing and trying to work out where his dagger was.

The snow smothered him from all sides, he felt himself choking, his voice was lost in his throat as another hand closed around his neck. Through the murkiness of snow in his eyes, he stared up into the eyes of his attacker, brilliantly deep blue, and suddenly he felt himself go limp. He sagged in the snow, and despite knowing that he had to stand and fight as the tightly closed hands pulled away, his body would not function below the neck.

The fingernails were not the claws of a rhôniae, the eyes were not those of a dragon, and the hands, the sleek, deathly-cold fingers, drew the very life out of his body. He felt his head hanging limp on his neck, knew that he was being lifted from the ground, and he saw a face, unfocused and hazy, but recognisably the face of some human creature.

It wasn't Andel, though the hands felt like his. Ramsey had no voice for an instant, then the whole world seemed to crumble beneath him, and he felt himself crying and coughing hard for breath. He fell back into the snow, and the pain in his temples grew into sharp focus; then the face was near again, a male face, striking and concerned and masculine, as white as the snow all around them. Ramsey swallowed uncomfortably, and felt cold fingers stroking his cheek, though he barely noticed them through the numbness of his whole body.

"I'm not going to hurt you. Hold still."

He opened his mouth, only to find that his voice would not come. He wheezed feebly, angry with himself for such a lack of dignity. Somewhere beyond them, the clattering, stony sound came again, and his whole world became fuzzy and colourless.

"I won't hurt you. You'll be all right, you're just too cold." Fingers against his face again, touching his cheeks, chin and forehead; then he felt the same dead touch on the nape of his neck, where his bite scar still shone white in the evening light, and he winced, and the world drew itself back together.

"Don't touch that…" he gasped, and although his voice was barely audible through the howling winds, the hand was pulled away, and he felt himself being supported upright in the snow. "Nngh…" He coiled his neck uncomfortably. The scar was still tender.

"I am sorry…forgive me, but did you get that scar from a cobra dragon?"

Ruefully rubbing his shoulder, Ramsey looked up into the stormy eyes of a vampire with flowing black hair, strong cheekbones and a large, silver loop piercing in his right ear, which jangled in the heavy gusts. Ramsey blinked hard, and his focus moved beyond the face to the rest of the vampire's figure – like Andel, he was dressed entirely in black and grey with a heavy leather coat; unlike Andel, he was apparently quite muscular. The vampire offered Ramsey a hand once more, and this time Ramsey took it, and was hoisted unsteadily to his feet, frost sticking to his back and trousers.

"How do…how do you know about the dragon?" asked Ramsey, perplexed, the moment he regained full control of his voice. The vampire looked down upon him with a subtle smile, and mild sorrow lining his brows.

"I have heard about you and your quest, Ramsey. It is Ramsey, I presume?" Ramsey confirmed his name, anxious as to how this vampire came to know about him. "I could have guessed. I knew you from miles away and clear across the square. You look exactly like your father."

Ramsey was suddenly aware of how much he was shaking. He shivered pronouncedly in the extreme cold, and something new now struck his body, rendering him speechless and immobile. He was too frozen and too confused to talk. He was trying to find the words to ask the vampire's name, when a large, dark creature loomed through the swirling, white mists, and another vampire, this one far more similar to Andel, approached the scene on horseback. Ramsey was feeling terrible at the presence of so many horses in one day, and could only stare wordlessly up at the figure.

"I do wish you wouldn't go running off like that into the unknown," said the new vampire, a pout in his tone. Ramsey blinked, lifted one hand to his face, and discerned a slender, heavily dressed male vampire sitting side-saddle on the huge horse, foxglove-coloured hair blowing in the wind. "Let me know beforehand in future, Okay?"

"Don't worry," said the vampire with dark hair, who still hovered next to Ramsey like a marble statue in the snow. "I knew what I was doing."

"I can't drive this thing..." huffed the other, tugging on the green and silver reins in a particularly feeble manner. The horse came to a stamping stand-still alongside Ramsey, and the Andel-like vampire peered down at him with an expression that spoke a thousand words of intrigue and uncertainty. "Nice nose."

Ramsey instinctively covered his face with his palms, then realised that it was futile to hide his appearance, and that his long nose was prominent no matter who he was speaking to. He smiled slightly, but only *slightly* – no matter how much this smaller vampire resembled Andel, Ramsey would not tolerate insults.

"My name is Terak," spoke the other vampire over the noise of the snowstorm. Ramsey jumped on hearing his voice, having completely forgotten all company at the mention of his nose. "I do not know what you think you are doing, wandering out in the snow like this, but you will catch pneumonia if you are not careful. It is very fortunate that I found you." The other vampire cleared his throat angrily. "That *we* found you, I mean. I saw you coming into the town after that rhôniae attack. You weren't scratched or bitten, were you?"

"No," said Ramsey blandly, shivering in his shirt.

Terak smiled at this information, nodded, and then addressed his companion, who was bouncing irritably on the saddle. "This is the right goblin, Synor. Our search has not been in vain."

"Are you sure?" questioned the other, cocking his head with his bright hair blowing in front of his face.

Ramsey scowled. He was not too fond of Terak's accomplice. Therefore, he was surprised at the other vampire's reaction when Terak affirmed that Ramsey was indeed 'the right one'.

"Oh, great, we thought we'd never find you. Nice to meet you – my name's Synor. Get up here now, I'm fed up of being cold." He tilted his head towards Terak, smiling brightly. "You're brilliant, you are! His dad had a carrot nose as well then, did he?"

"*Carrot* nose?" spat Ramsey, feeling all too aggravated out in the freezing snow. "My nose does not look like a-"

"Come, come, now..." said Terak, his soothing voice calming both Ramsey and Synor in an instant. "The sooner we get out of the cold, the better. Synor, please stop jumping, you'll aggravate the horse. Ramsey, my young fellow, I'll help you climb up." Ramsey's lips and cheeks were completely numb, and he felt as though icicles should have been dangling from his body in various places. He could feel the sting of frost on his skin.

Completely unperturbed by the cold, Terak hoisted himself up onto the dark horse with muscular grace, and once more offered Ramsey a hand. Ramsey took it, and Terak whisked him up onto the saddle, to sit between himself and Synor; whom, Ramsey now noticed, was sitting with a cloth-covered bundle on his lap, which he cradled as though it was positively precious. Ramsey was too confused and cold to think any more of it, and did not even inquire about his father once Terak coaxed the horse into a gallop.

The world swept past him in a blur of grey and white. Suddenly exhausted and feeling rather helpless, Ramsey slouched forward to use the back of Terak's coat as a bumpy pillow. His head was hurting again, and he could not think straight; just like the time when he and Theron had been attacked outside the town. Something in the burning, red eyes of the reptilian frona creatures had sparked such primal fear and rage in him. Had there been a hundred of them, he would have fought to the death to defend Theron. How Ramsey missed him…

Vaguely, from seemingly miles away behind him, Ramsey heard the hushed tones of someone speaking to another person. It was Synor; Synor had a much perkier voice than Terak's. There was something about Terak that made Ramsey feel so weak. He didn't want an explanation. He just wanted Theron back, he wanted to know about his father, and he wanted to rescue Prince Morgan and go home. Anywhere that wasn't smothered in snow.

Even at a brisk gallop, it took the trio quite some time to arrive back in the town square, and as Terak moved to dismount, Ramsey could barely lift his head. Synor laughed behind him, and he felt, rather than saw, Synor drop to the ground from his position astride the saddle. Terak reached behind his back, gently supported Ramsey's shoulders, and helped the weak goblin to the ground. The square was considerably less noisy by now – most of the locals were already taking their seats in church.

"Where are we?" asked Ramsey dreamily, his head spinning. He heard the rapid scuffling of boots on cobbles, and guessed that the smaller vampire had run off.

Terak cleared his throat and brushed some snow from the breast of his jacket. "Don't worry, Master Ramsey, we are back in the town centre. Synor's younger brother owns a tavern here, so that is where we always stay. Just a few steps, now – watch your feet."

Ramsey swooned at the feel of Terak's solid arm around his narrow shoulders, and he swallowed a heavy lump in his throat. The vampire's grip was firm, but not unkind, and Ramsey realised that he was being far too trusting of others. Surely, trusting a vampire that had just tackled him in the street was not a good idea. He lifted his heavy eyelids, and read before him, mounted on a plaque, the words; 'Andel's Tavern – Lodge, bar and restaurant. Mofran's most popular tavern!'. He found it necessary to smirk.

Terak dragged him inside, supporting the entirety of Ramsey's slight weight with one arm, and a heavy, leather pack with the other. He nudged the glass-panelled door open, and they beheld a delightful, if somewhat strange, scene in the reception hall. Synor was waiting by the desk, lumpy bundle still in the crook of one arm and his coat already discarded on the coat-stand, calling out a certain familiar name.

The moment Andel appeared at the top of the creaky staircase, his face lit up and he scrambled down two at a time, pulling his brother into the tightest, most heart-felt embrace that Ramsey had ever seen. Indeed, he managed to sweep Synor right off his feet, and then, much to Ramsey's shock, gave his brother an enthusiastic kiss on the lips.

"Oh, oh, oh!" was all Andel could say for an instant, gripping Synor like a vice. "Oh, Synor, you're here! I didn't think I'd see you this Creation Eve!" Synor laughed joyously, an infectious sound that echoed off the walls, and he still held tightly to his concealed, lumpy bundle. "You look fabulous, as always. Terak here with you?"

"Yes, I'm here," said Terak with a smile and a wave, losing none of his composure. Ramsey was still leaning against the side of his body, looking bewildered and interested at once. Andel's blue eyes were shining with happiness, and he kissed Synor again, this time on the neck; where, Ramsey noticed, Synor already had an unusual scar.

"And I see you met my new friend, Ramsey," continued Andel, at a slightly lower pitch and with no less enthusiasm. "He just arrived today, so I gave him the best room in the house. Oh Synor, please say you'll stay! It would mean the world to me if you and Terak would stay for a while. Me and Ramsey don't mind, do we, Ram? Can I call you 'Ram', Ram?"

Ramsey felt so delirious with confusion and relief and sudden warmth that he could not stop himself from laughing. Terak set him down at a small table, where Ramsey continued to laugh until the colour returned to his orange cheeks. Andel was all smiles, ever so slightly taller than his brother, whose luminous magenta hair was complimented by traces of yellow, like Andel's. They were startlingly similar in appearance.

Ramsey wondered how similar he was to his father. If indeed Terak knew his father, Ramsey was keen to find out. The world felt less cold, and more open, as he watched the two siblings hug and kiss one another while Terak stood by like a gothic statue.

It's funny how it takes vampires, of all things, to prove that there is some genuine love and kindness in the world, he thought. That must be the definition of 'irony'.

He was lost in a dream world when a sharp, gleeful exclamation from Andel snapped him back to reality, and he realised that Synor had unwrapped his mysterious bundle on the floor. From the folds of heavy fabric came the squirming, knobbly form of a small, white goat with messy fur, small horns and large ears. And, as it turned to face Ramsey with an eager bleat, he realised that the left half of its face was missing, and made up of nothing but bare skull and an empty, skeletal eye-socket.

It was with amusement that he noticed how little this revelation unnerved him. It clip-clopped in a small circle, its hooves making hollow clacking noises on the stone floor, and Andel clasped his hands together in obvious mirth.

"Ooh, oh Synor, he's so cute!"

"Yeah, he's called Sweetness!" replied Synor proudly, fussing over the goat and patting its head. "Terak got him for me for my one-thousand and fifty-seventh birthday, at Xavi's market. I don't know what would have become of him if I hadn't asked Terak to buy him for me." The brothers shared a worrisome expression, as though imagining the poor, beloved half-dead goat being used for soup. "But never mind, because he's mine, and I love him, love him, *love* him!"

Terak did not smile, but cleared his throat loudly, also catching the attention of Ramsey, who was watching the pale siblings with intrigue.

"Don't worry, Terak, I love you too, for getting Sweetness for me!"

"No, I wasn't objecting to not being loved," asserted Terak, though the tiniest hint of a smile touched the corners of his mouth. "I just wanted to remind both of you about the church service tonight. Presumably you both still want to go?"

"Oh, yes!" said Andel, leaving Synor to play with the semi-skeletal goat. He pointed over his head to the tall ceiling, and both Terak and Ramsey looked to see the many streaming garlands that hung across the black beams. "I've got all my decorations done, and the dining room is ready for our big 'do'. So let me just grab something warmer to wear and I'm ready. Oh Synor, you must see my new kitten Nemo while you're here."

"Nemo?"

"Named after father's old horse."

"Oh yes, Necromancer, I remember."

"Wasn't he gorgeous?"

Synor snickered, and wrapped his pet goat up in the blanket as though fearful he might catch a cold. "I guess, by horse standards. Smelly, though." Sweetness bleated and stared at Ramsey with one glassy eye, bizarre yet adorable at the same time. It also had a few segments of its left side missing, exposing a smooth, white skeleton that glowed in the candlelight. "Ooh, I hope we'll get a good seat in church. I've practised my singing."

"Me too." Andel was shrugging his way into a heavy, woollen overcoat and searching for his keys at the same time. "Ram, you have to see the inside of our church on Creation Eve! I swear, every year it gets lovelier and lovelier. A bit like me, really." With no surprise, he found his keys sitting openly on the reception desk and clasped them firmly in his right palm. Synor was settling his unusual pet on the chair opposite Ramsey, turning its blanket into a makeshift basket for the goat to sleep in. "I can't believe we both got new pets, Synor! Isn't it great?"

389

"Yeah," beamed Synor. "Once you get your cat in here, we can race them!"

Most of this animated conversation was lost upon Ramsey. He stood from the table, scratching and stretching himself, and certainly feeling worse for wear. Yet he still found himself smiling, and feeling as though he was among friends. And with vampires, of all things. He could not ignore the fact that they all seemed rather fond of him. Terak observed Ramsey with interest, and upon noticing that the goblin had nothing warm to wear, removed his own coat and offered it to Ramsey.

"Here you go, lad," he said, his voice firm yet gentle. "It might be somewhat big for you, but I do not feel the cold. You smile, yet you seem sad." Ramsey's head jerked up at this simple comment, for he had been looking pointlessly at his feet. "Is there something bothering you?"

Ramsey tersely affirmed that he was quite all right, even as he was steered out of the tavern and back into the street by Andel and Synor, who continued to talk and laugh and sing random hymn lines over the wailing of the storm. Terak tramped through the snow alongside him, noting how his large coat dwarfed the shorter goblin and dragged along the ground behind him.

There were few people waiting outside the glistening temple by now, as the service was due to begin. The one large, hairy, snow-coated figure that caught Ramsey's eye was one that sent a flash of joy through his whole body, and he broke away from his escorts to greet Theron in the cold.

"Ramsey!" called the troll as soon as he saw the spindly, coat-engulfed goblin running towards him. He was waiting below the steps to the temple doors, and his injured hind leg, as well as one of his front ones, was bound up tightly in a stiff, white bandage. He looked absurd, but Ramsey dashed to him and hugged the troll with a ferocity that could have left bruises. "Oh Ramsey, it's so nice to see you! Where have you been?"

"Where have *you* been?" returned Ramsey, pressing his cheek firmly against the frosty fur of Theron's chest. Behind him, Andel, Synor and Terak halted in the street, and though they did not approach, they watched, and Synor took hold of Terak's arm. "Damn you, don't you ever, *ever* get sick again! I was worried to sickness myself, you great ninny. Oh, come here..."

Theron smiled like a labrador, not caring about the snow. "I'm surprised to see you here, Ramsey. Did you come for the service?"

"I'm only going because...well, because those vampires over there-" He pointed over his shoulder in the general direction of the three vampires, who were still standing patiently in the snow, the wind whipping their hair like spilled ink. "- want me to go, so I didn't want to disappoint them because they...well, they're nice. No point in being a spoil-sport, I guess."

Theron grinned delightedly, and Ramsey huffed. "Well, my doctor said that there was a service tonight, and that it was the last day of summer today and the first day of autumn tomorrow, and I was so excited, because me and my mum used to celebrate Creation Eve, but I've never been to a proper church service. I asked the doctor if I could go, and he said yes, and I think that if I wait right out here, I'll be able to hear the service and the songs."

Ramsey couldn't quip back in any way, shape or form; not while Theron was looking down at him with so much excitement and happiness in his warm eyes. He just hugged more tightly onto Theron, and lost himself momentarily in the comparative warmth of the troll's body hair.

"I'm so glad to see you, Ramsey. What you did, fighting those animals to defend me, it really touched me. You're a good friend."

Ramsey laughed and pulled away, wiping his face with the back of his hand. "Hey, you'd have done the same for me. Listen, Theron, I don't really want to go, but we're running late and I probably should. You stay here, all right? I found a place where you can stay for the night, near to where I am."

Terak walked up to Ramsey with his hands in his pockets and ice in his ebony hair. The brothers were not with him. "Sorry to interrupt," he began, not at all fazed by the unexplained presence of a seven-foot forest troll. "but the service is just about to begin. Ramsey, if we may...?"

Ramsey nodded, bade Theron farewell, and followed the tall vampire up the wide steps and into the temple, where there was no storm. The serenity of candlelit marble walls and ceilings and pews brimming with reverent worshippers created a peacefully humming atmosphere. Ramsey was struck dumb, having so many different things to marvel at in the same instant, and Terak ushered him over to one of the many pews that were teaming with believers of all ages and races.

Andel and Synor, already seated, had saved two places for them, and shuffled over to make room. The entire temple fell silent at that very moment; and then, from somewhere far off to the back of the church, beyond the stone altar, came the pure, lilting voices of choirboys singing in perfect harmony, and something inside Ramsey melted, leaving him humble.

He recognised the unaccompanied tune, and the words – Andel had been singing the same song earlier that day. Ramsey glanced quickly to either side to see what the vampires were doing, and if he should be getting ready to sing as well. Terak was seated to his right, Synor to his left, and Andel sat on the other side of his brother. All three were silent and still, except for the slight rustling of service leaflets that Synor was glancing at. In front of him, Ramsey traced his vision along a whole row of vampires, and in front of the vampires, an assortment of goblins, manearies and a few elves. Beyond them, to every side, the sea of bowed heads was varied and fascinating.

Ramsey could not stop turning and staring and absorbing the scene around him. Long, draped banners of purple, magenta, blue and gold decked the two rows of stone arches that ran the length of the temple; titles such as 'Mighty Serpent', 'Divine Lady' and 'Grenamoya Mother' were emblazoned upon them with elaborate patterns.

*"Sweet Scaless, you watch from above, beautiful reptile we love!"*

Ramsey now noticed a procession of goblins, vampires and corpse-like creatures walking down the central aisle towards the church altar, carrying lighted candles, but not singing. Suddenly the whole of the congregation burst into song for the next verse, and though Ramsey confusedly accepted a spare sheet from Synor, he did not know the tune, and remained mute, looking at Terak as everybody in the church stood to sing. Terak was not singing, and was instead standing silently with his hands clasped behind his back; to Ramsey's left, the vampire brothers were harmonising quite loudly.

*"And, when we fear, your love for us gives us your strength! O Lady, when you draw so near, elegant, divine and dear!"*

Paintings hung along the walls of the temple, alongside temporary wooden seating that had been added to the church for the duration of the festival. One painting in particular caught Ramsey's eye; very black, very big, about eight feet tall and five feet wide with a gold frame, featuring a rather murky image of Lady Scaless encircling three contorted humanoid forms. Over the swarm of heads, trying not to look conspicuous, Ramsey squinted at the painting and discerned the three forms to be a vampire with white hair, a green-skinned goblin, and a two-legged troll of some kind that resembled Theron closely in the face. All three were naked, but the picture was so dark that nothing offensive was on view.

*"Lady, in your great love, this Creation Eve you bless us with hope! Sweet Scaless, you watch us this day, in our hearts always to stay!"*

Ramsey groaned loudly, but was not heard over the loud singing. He couldn't believe how long the song was. Terak's mouth was tightly shut, and he was looking at the floor. Andel and Synor, on the other hand, were singing so animatedly that Ramsey was sure half of the congregation was staring.

He craned his neck upwards and blinked toward the high, curved ceiling. The temple was truly huge, bigger than the church in BlackField Town, and yet nothing about it was gaudy, nothing seemed excessive. It was quite invigorating, in fact, and Ramsey felt something inside himself become warm and cool at the same time, then fade, as though his heart had been cleansed.

Could it be that I am getting more laid back? he asked himself over the seventh verse of the same hymn.

Maybe he was just too tired to care.

*"Scaless, Lady fair, your love for us all shines through this day! Sweet Scaless, you watch from above, beautiful reptile we love...!"*

Great, thought Ramsey, now we're back to the first verse again...

However, the song ended there, and with a final, grand chord from the church organ, the entire congregation sat down once more with a rustle and a mumble. Someone coughed from the front pew, and to Ramsey's immediate right, Terak sighed and crossed his arms, his eyes trained on the front of the temple where a heavily robed vampire priest had stepped up to a golden, dragon-shaped lectern to speak. A hush descended over the crowd. Ramsey, comfortably warm in the folds of Terak's coat, managed to sit still at last.

"My children," he addressed, after clearing his throat once or twice in succession. "it is a glorious day in Morfran Town on this Creation Eve. For, as we see, Scaless herself is gracing our fair town with snow, which should suggest to all of us a chance of purification, cleansing of our sins – a chance for a fresh beginning in time for the new year."

On Grenamoya Island, as opposed to our twelve months of the year, the calendar was divided into the four seasons; autumn, winter, spring and summer, each of which traditionally heralded the appearance of one of the Great Dragons. Grenamoya's year lasted three-hundred and sixty days, for each season lasted for ninety days, and the new year began upon the first day of autumn. Despite the disappearance of the Great Dragons, the island inhabitants continued the seasonal tradition, though the whole of Grenamoya seemed fixed in a turbulent, springtime climate.

"I ask all of you now to join me in sending a prayer to Lady Scaless – a prayer for forgiveness for our sins of the year past, and for prosperity in the year to come."

And so the Eve of Creation service continued; and strangely, it was not as morbidly boring as Ramsey had expected it to be. There was a lot of singing, of course --that was to be expected-- but there was very little preaching involved. Once or twice, young choir members ascended to the pulpit to recite a reading from The Scaless Scriptures, but apart from a few brief reflections from the vampire cleric, who had a head of black, glossy hair that reached to the small of his back, nothing was actually said.

The words of the hymns created an atmosphere of reverent, exuberant worship, and though Ramsey could not manage to sing, the enthusiasm of the two brothers at his side warmed his heart and made him smile. This seemed to encourage Terak, who, Ramsey noted with vague anxiety, was keeping a firm eye on him.

An echoing chime from the town clock outside the temple alerted Ramsey, just as he was beginning to feel too tired to open his eyes. He blinked, glanced quickly to either side, and saw that his vampire escorts were still as vigilant as ever, particularly the two brothers. Andel, upon hearing the chime for ten o' clock, nudged his brother and leaned towards Ramsey with some green leaflets in his hand.

"Hey, don't be falling asleep before you get the chance to sample my famous Creation Eve cooking, Ram," he whispered, smiling broadly and offering him a leaflet. Ramsey, who was already holding several pamphlets of different colours, added the new sheet to his ever-accumulating pile. He looked at it with a small yawn. "We've got to join in the last prayer, then there's one more song," (Here Ramsey grumbled; Andel ignored him.) "and then we can head on home, and wait for everyone to arrive."

"Hush!" said Synor with a grin, poking Andel in the ribs. "It's starting...!"

Ramsey sighed and stared at his new paper as though he couldn't read a single word. His eyes just weren't working, and his eyelids were starting to close by themselves. He wasn't bored (which he realised with considerable surprise) – he was quite simply exhausted from his journey and the battle with four rhôniae fronas that same day. He just hoped Prince Morgan would be more than a *little* grateful when he finally managed to rescue him.

"And now, as I prepare to bid you all farewell in time for a brand new Grenamoya year, let us join together and recite the Prayer to Scaless. You will find it on the green leaflet."

The priest made the sign of Scaless in the air in front of him, touched his forehead, then his collar, and stepped up to the lectern. Ramsey realised by now that the lectern was supposed to resemble Leoma, the most powerful of the Great Dragons, who governed life on the island. He had gone to the trouble of asking Andel (whom he still liked better than the other two vampires) a few questions during the service, which the aforementioned innkeeper answered with good humour and the occasional perplexing anecdote.

Terak had not spoken a word since entering the church. One of the dark-haired vampire's few actions had been to write something on a small piece of paper he had been given during the central hymn, 'Scaless, In the Clouds we see your Coils' (one of the more unusual songs that Ramsey had heard – probably badly translated). As far as Ramsey could see, everyone had been given a small slip of paper during the service, including him, but not knowing what to do with it, he had just slid it into his pocket, unmarked.

Everyone rose to their feet, and Ramsey did the same, having shrugged Terak's heavy coat off his shoulders. He was a goblin, and as such was not as tall as he would like to be; the row of typically tall vampires on the pew in front blocked his view of the priest entirely. Not that he minded – it meant he could get away with not reciting the prayer. Religion still felt so foreign to him.

"Scaless, the mother of all life," prompted the robed cleric, and from the following line onwards, the entire congregation joined in, with perfect sync. Ramsey didn't realise he was mumbling the words until they were several lines on.

"You have bestowed your divinity upon us. Your children dwell upon the mountains, bringing life to the world. For us you have created the earth, and all evil quells in your wake. For you shall we strive each day, to be righteous, loving, and free of all sin."

"For sweet Scaless' sake," concluded the priest, his voice solemn, though Ramsey could not see his face. "let it be so."

*Ulyssis!*

It struck Ramsey's temples like a knife blow, and blackness overcame him for the split-second that it took to collapse back onto his seat. The entire gathering seemed to swell and gasp, and Ramsey saw one vampire in front of him stumble sideways and knock several others to the floor. To his right, a sudden movement caught Ramsey's eye, and he turned. Terak was clutching at his own face with white fingers, shuddering, covering his mouth, and to Ramsey's left, Synor cried out. In the confusion, Ramsey managed to see through the writhing congregation to the front of the temple, where the long-haired priest was draped across the elaborate lectern, his face shrouded by dark tresses.

*Ulyssis, I do not know what you're doing, but if you value your life, return immediately!*

*Curse you, you abomination, you must follow orders...!*

It's happening again. Oh Scaless, oh no, it's happening again... Ramsey felt as though his eyes were bleeding, and he pressed his palms to his cheeks to numb the pain. It did not work. That voice, that same, deep voice that he could hear so clearly, had been roused. He saw darkness, an orange-lit glow from the hundreds of candles and the bustling mass of panicking bodies all merged into one before his eyes, and he shrunk into a tight ball, hunched up on Terak's folded coat with his arms across his face.

Only then did he truly realise that most of the other creatures in the temple were reacting to the voice as well. They could hear it. He could hear nothing but the confused shouts and cries of hundreds of worshippers; vampires, undeads, goblins, elves, manearies, froneks and lizard people, clamouring and trying to lift fallen individuals from the floor, struggling to revive them.

This pain was more acute than he had ever felt, so much so that he could barely feel it at all – it overpowered him so greatly that he couldn't even hear himself scream. He felt hands on his face, freezing his flushed skin, and in a flash of vision he saw Terak, twisting and groaning and reaching across to Synor.

Ramsey shut his eyes tightly, but the burning struck through his skin and under his eyelids until he felt his fingernails cutting into his palms. Above him, Terak clutched Synor by the wrist, and Ramsey saw blood streaming down the taller vampire's arm. Suddenly they were both gone, and Ramsey fell onto his side, shapes moving above him, and the pale-faced figure of Andel leaning over him seared into focus.

"Aargh...!"

"Hold still!" urged Andel, shouting over the noise in the temple, one hand holding Ramsey's scrawny neck to the pew. "Calm down, Ram, you'll be all right, I'm here for you..."

*I do not appreciate such independent thought, damn you. Report to me at once, and I shall punish you then...*

*Return at once, or I shall not let you live.*

*And that is a promise.*

"It...it's going again..." Ramsey choked out his words, trying to push the vampire off, but Andel stayed firm, holding him down with both hands. "I can hear it, it's fading...oh no, oh please, no..."

The sound of everything else faded into the background, and he melted against something cool and soothing, though his orange skin was burning from the inside, feverish to the touch. Through half-closed eyes he saw the disarray of the row in front of them – eight vampires were stumbling over one another, and one of them pushed past the others with both hands clutching the sides of his head. This vampire forced his way down the aisle just as Terak and Synor had done, and disappeared amidst the panicked throng. He passed by, and Ramsey beheld a fleeting face that looked very much like Terak's. Overwhelmed, he leaned against the cold form that held him upright, and felt his fists clenching of their own accord.

"Shh, shh, it's all right, you'll be fine..." insisted Andel, holding tightly onto Ramsey's prone form. "It's over, don't worry..."

Ramsey could barely think straight. The corners of his eyes were stinging and every part of his body was boiling with fever. "You heard it?"

"Heard what?" asked Andel, stroking Ramsey's hair. At the front of the temple, two vampires and an elf were gently shaking the priest to revive him.

"The voice! You know damn well what I mean! That voice..."

Andel held more tightly onto him and swallowed. His coat smelled of peppermint. "Don't worry, you will be all right..."

"Where...where did your brother...?"

"They went outside, Ram, don't worry, they will be all right. I am sure they will return."

Ramsey couldn't believe his ears. It was almost as though it was commonplace for vampire priests to suffer unexplained blackouts in the middle of a service. Perhaps it was the norm for whole congregations to go crazy and hear voices without warning. He growled and pushed away from Andel, who surrendered his grip upon seeing the determined, frightened look in Ramsey's eyes.

"All right? How can anything like this ever be *all right*? No, I have to...I have to find out...you must hear the voices, you must have heard him speak!"

Andel stared at him with fretful, blue eyes as the uproar around them began to quell. The confused shouting and the scraping of chairs echoed all around the ceiling with a deafening resonance. "I am sorry, but I don't know what you mean. Speak to Terak if you must."

Ramsey was away, giddy with a massive headache but somehow able to run and push his way through the swelling tide of worshippers. He felt as though he could run forever, his feet quick on the cool stone floor. The moment he was beyond the thickest herd of people, he was free, and he turned right, hurrying to the wide doors which had been left ajar.

Someone must have heard that voice, he thought, and if I can guess right, that vampire Terak will have heard it.

It was worth a try.

He said he knew my father...how could he know something about me that even I don't know?

The door was heavy for his fragile, lethargic arms to pull, but he managed to force it open, and was immediately struck in the face by the heavenly sting of snow in the frosty air. His lungs ached at his first breath in the open. The snow had lain virtually undisturbed for an hour, and coated the streets, the square, the buildings and the town clock in a perfect, thick, fluffy blanket. It was utterly beautiful and completely bright white under the moon and stars that gleamed high above, and the sky was darker and more dreamlike than Ramsey could ever remember. His feet sank in the snow on the temple steps.

Snowflakes danced around him, blissfully cold against his cheeks and forehead. He could see the disturbance of tracks in the snow, leading away from the temple, but though he strained his eyes, he could see nobody near. Surely in the snow any figure of any description was certain to stand out. He blinked, and his head felt heavy again, so he crouched in the snow for fear of sudden dizziness. Theron was gone.

A sudden, loud flutter caught his ears, and he stared up into the night sky as a glossy raven as black as coal flapped away into the starry darkness over the rooftops. He could have broken down at that moment. No matter how close he arrived to getting any answers about his past, they were always snatched away from his fingertips.

"I just want to know who I am..." he moaned, his knuckles digging into his cheeks, dusted with crystals of snow.

With a sigh and a sob, he stared futilely at the snow at his feet, crushing it between his toes. Nobody would come after him. Nobody ever did. A soft, padding noise awakened him from his misery, and as he lifted his head, he beheld in front of him the black fur, burning eyes and yellow tentacles of a rhôniae. Ramsey stood, grabbed his dagger, and the creature sprang.

# Chapter Fifteen

# Number Seventeen

"No! By Scaless, you won't kill me!"

Ramsey dived and spun around in the snow. The hellish beast soared over his head and slammed into the temple doors, taking only a split-second to turn and strike again. Dagger against gaping jaws, Ramsey's feet skidded and swerved until the creature shook its mouth away from his blade and toppled him to the ground with a sharp swipe from its spiny tail.

It loomed above him, fur as black as tar and coated with melting snowflakes, tentacles reaching toward him like deathly, yellow fingers. In an instant he was on his feet, bruised, sweaty and frozen, and his voice rang around the square.

"You can't take me! I won't let you!"

Its roar was thunder and its eyes were twin fires. It was so large that it stood at eye-level with Ramsey. It drew back its leathery lips, glistening with spit, and lunged at him with a death bite to crush his skull. Ramsey cried and jolted forward with his dagger, lodging it deep between the cat's eyes, and it screamed.

Such force emanated from the creature that Ramsey stumbled to his knees in the snow, still forcing his elaborately jewelled weapon into the creature's face. It pulled away, blood falling from its muzzle, and its sickly tentacles danced in front of Ramsey's stricken gaze, ready to claim him.

But as Ramsey felt the agony of his headache overwhelm him, a figure loomed through the gleaming whiteness, one pale hand outstretched, and before his very eyes, the rhôniae stilled, fell back, and crumpled in a heap, its body surrounded by a swirling, pink glow.

He watched the rhôniae as it submitted to the bright light; he literally saw its face grow calm as it almost casually seemed to take a rest in the snow. He stared at it for an instant, and when it did not move, he scrambled to his feet and beheld the once murky figure, now clearly recognisable as Andel's brother, standing silently a few metres away. The vampire's slender hand was still outstretched, but nothing was glowing any more. As though a treacherous storm had at last subsided, Synor's body became still, his coat swirling gently around him. His eyes were alight and almost fearful.

Ramsey paid no heed to his dagger and ran to the magenta-haired vampire through the snow. "You saved my life...!" Synor raised his eyes to meet Ramsey's, neither smiling nor frowning. "I don't know what you did exactly, but you saved my life." The goblin was still panting. "Thank you."

"You're welcome," came the soft reply. His amber gaze shifted to the ragged body of the suddenly lifeless rhôniae, as though mildly surprised to see it there. From behind him loomed the loftier figure of Terak, who put his hand on Synor's shoulder. Presumably he had been watching the whole thing.

"Master Ramsey," he addressed with unnerving composure. "what are you doing in the snow without a coat?"

"I-" began Ramsey, before realising that he wasn't sure *where* to begin. He noticed that Synor was going to great pains to conceal his neck by tugging on the collar of his jacket. "I...I saw you two run outside, and everyone began screaming and the priest collapsed and-"

Terak smiled slightly and nodded, giving Ramsey cause to cease his explanation. "Ah yes. Typical goblin curiosity. Not to mention stealth and astounding speed. Very well accomplished."

"Thank you." Ramsey felt a pulsing, like an allergic reaction, from within his head. He didn't wholly trust the taller vampire. There was something about Terak that made him feel weak and compliant, as though he had no resistance. Maybe just a trick of the mind, pondered Ramsey as he allowed himself to be steered back to the temple doors.

As they crunched through the snow, Theron ran onto the scene, followed by half-a-dozen vampires on horseback. The troll's heavy limp meant that he slid uncomfortably in the snow, but when he drew to a halt and found Ramsey standing next to two vampires and a dead rhôniae, he almost lost his balance completely.

"Ramsey! How...how did you...what happened?"

The goblin laughed exasperatedly, pulling away from Terak's grip and striding back down the steps towards his friend. "Nothing you can't guess at, I'm sure. What in Grenamoya happened to you, though? Where did you go?"

By now, the exhausted and frightened worshippers were filing out of the Scaless Temple, supporting one another and talking in hushed tones, some of them in tears. The shock, more than anything, had drained them of the festive spirit. It seemed as though most of them were going straight home for the evening to take inventory of their families and be thankful for being alive. Very few of them looked at Theron, as they had seen him on their way into the church earlier that night.

"I was waiting outside, listening to the songs, and then I saw one of those big things that attacked us before." Here Theron motioned towards the dead animal with anger, but with no sign of disrespect. He kept his distance. "So I went to fetch someone who could help, like my doctor said. He told me that there might be some of these animals wandering in the streets tonight. I don't know why."

"Right, men," said the horseman at the front of the small group, the same vampire whom Ramsey had ridden with that very afternoon. "we cannot be too cautious. Follow me, and we shall search the town. Rhôniae do not hunt alone."

With those unsettling words, the troop fled away across the square and down one of the main streets, the sound of horseshoes muffled by the snow. Ramsey stared after them, half expecting to hear a gut-wrenching scream at any moment, but nothing happened. He was still breathing hard, and Theron smiled at him with concern, towering over the temple-goers that passed by.

The priest with long hair, who had apparently recovered in full, stood at the doorway in his grand robe, saying farewell to the worshippers and reminding them to attend the 'pool of remembrance'. Terak caught something in the priest's words and spoke hurriedly to Synor before disappearing amidst the crowd, back into the temple. Ramsey shivered and hugged himself, then turned to Synor. The smaller vampire looked distracted.

"Are you all right?" he asked, tentatively, for fear that things might start glowing again. "You don't look very happy."

"I'm fine. I will be as right as sleet, given a second or two. Where's my brother?"

Ramsey had a feeling that this final question was not directed at him, and instead turned his attention to Theron, who was spouting seasonal greetings to a group of passing elves. Of the congregation, the elves seemed to have been least affected by the voice. The fair-skinned folk were quite enchanted with Theron for some reason or another, and they gathered by the troll's feet like children at a particularly interesting zoo exhibit.

A familiar head of purple hair bobbed amongst the temple swarm, and Synor called out to his brother, having apparently shaken off his momentary strangeness. Andel waved and hurried towards the both of them, with Terak close behind.

"Would you believe it? Everybody's going home!" exclaimed Andel, utterly appalled. "Well, not everyone, but most of them...! Even my most regular customers...I don't know what in Grenamoya has made them lose their senses, but really, not

404

attending my famous Creation Eve celebrations!" He huffed and puffed until he had vented most of his anger, then without warning grabbed Ramsey by the shoulders and shook him. "For Scaless' sake, Ram! Where did you run off to? They said there were rhôniae wandering in the streets again, I thought you'd been killed!"

"Don't worry, I wasn't," replied Ramsey through the shaking, remaining rigid. At this affirmation, Andel stopped convulsing him and embraced him mightily instead.

"Thank Scaless! And Synor, where did *you* run off to? And Terak...!" He whirled around, checking that Terak was still there, and took hold of him as well. "You're all abandoning me!"

"No we aren't." Terak remained calm, despite the furious grip around his neck. Synor swallowed, and Ramsey was shocked to see a huge patch of blood staining the shortest vampire's shirt. Synor sensed Ramsey's eyes, and quickly concealed his throat within his collar. "I suggest that we return before any more rhôniae hone in on young Ramsey, here. He seems to be some kind of magnet for those monsters."

Ramsey quickly realised how much he despised indifferent people; he could not tell if Terak was being solemn or sarcastic. Nonetheless, he acted according to their wishes, and followed the three vampires back to the tavern, the snow still whistling through the air on invisible tongues of wind. Theron saw them leave, and hobbled behind Ramsey, slipping on the ice every now and again with a grunt.

\*\*\*

Despite the comparatively small number of locals that had decided to attend Andel's Creation Eve party, the sheer volume and atmosphere of buzzing excitement was more than overwhelming to an already exhausted Ramsey. He sat at a table in one corner of the dining room, picking curiously at a plate of seasoned rice delicacies that were rather like sushi, except they were flavoured with sweet and savoury foods instead of fish. Apparently it was traditional to eat such things on the Eve of Creation, and, knowing nothing to the contrary, Ramsey had complied with minimum fuss. Of the various classical dishes that Andel had had made for the occasion, Ramsey decided that the clumps of flavoured rice looked the least questionable.

Not many of the enthusiastic party-goers noticed him in his quiet corner. At the front of the room, standing upon a stage with a spare garland around his neck, Andel was shouting encouragement to his unusually scant group of guests and telling various tales of how his cooking exploits had gone awry over the years.

Twenty-nine creatures of varying species (Ramsey had been intrigued enough to count them) were assembled below the stage, mostly standing to eat, and one or two of them sitting at nearby tables within earshot of Andel's stories. Synor stood nearby with a rather large plate of rice in one hand, eating through spouts of laughter and occasionally berating his brother.

Ramsey stared blandly out from his corner, trailing his gaze around the white walls at the different portraits and busy paintings, hardly touching his food despite the vicious groaning of his stomach. Terak emerged from the chortling group, also with a large plate, and joined Ramsey at the table, uninvited. The goblin was so far removed from the action that Terak could not leave him to his solitude.

"Are you all right, Ramsey?" he inquired, sitting opposite the goblin at the table. He had apparently chosen to neglect the mild formality of 'Master' before Ramsey's name.

"I'm fine," sighed Ramsey, smiling vaguely towards his food, as though the very practice of eating had become foreign to him. Terak politely showed him how to eat the seasoned rice by impaling each cluster with a supposedly 'traditional' pointed stick. Ramsey picked at his food again, debating silently over whether to choose the chicken or the strawberry. "No...no, I'm not really fine. I haven't felt fine for quite a while now, and I haven't got the faintest clue why I'm trusting the lot of you."

"What do you mean, young one?"

Ramsey swallowed his words, for he had yet to place any food in his mouth. His body twitched and he hugged himself, still

406

holding the rice-eating stick between two fingers like a pencil. "I missed my birthday. It passed by a while ago, without me even noticing it."

The vampire seemed intrigued. "Really? Forgive me for asking, but how old are you?"

"I turned nineteen on the seventy-sixth day of summer."

Reaching reflexively for another piece of Creation Eve pancake from his plate, Terak nodded pensively and shot Ramsey a contemplative gaze that Ramsey did not altogether like. He should not have been revealing anything about himself to complete strangers. "You look older."

"Yeah, well, I'm not." From the far end of the room, Andel abruptly burst into song, dragging his brother onto the stage and catching Terak's attention completely. Ramsey glared at Terak with all the confusion and anger and frustration in his body, and maintained that same glare even as the vampire turned back to face him. Terak's expression did not change. "You knew my father."

"Yes, I did. He was a good man."

"He was *not*," snapped Ramsey, his shoulders rising. "He was a selfish, thoughtless bastard who left me to die in a fire. I have no love for him whatsoever."

He then turned his attention back to his plate and proceeded to pile several clumps of sweet and savoury rice into his mouth, chewing on them all at once and refusing to look at Terak. Terak breathed softly, unheard over Ramsey's loud munching. The goblin closed his eyes forcefully, and through his sloppy eating there emerged a pained sort of gulp, not the sort of gulp one makes when swallowing food.

"You have no understanding of the way your father was, Ramsey. He was a loyal friend and a devoted father to you." Ramsey shook his head. "I would not lie to you, my boy. How you can think such deplorable things about your own father defies all logic, I am afraid."

"What else am I supposed to think? I've been on my own since I was twelve. If he was any sort of devoted father, he would have been there for me."

"He *was* there for you. Can you not remember all that he went through, just to be in your life and save you from the...?" Ramsey was staring at him now, and the desperate, searching fire burning in his eyes made Terak stop in mid-sentence. The vampire clenched his teeth, and his protruding fangs lengthened ever so slightly. "You don't remember? Not at all?"

"Hey, you two are getting quite cosy!" exclaimed Andel exuberantly, having navigated his way to their table through the motley gathering. Ramsey felt as though someone had stabbed him in the head with a steel shard. Andel did not notice the goblin's discomfort, and quickly laid two small, heavy-bottomed glasses on the table, both of which were filled with something purple that smelled like fruit and medicine. "Here you go, Ram, get some of that down your neck. Can I call you 'Rammy', Ram?"

"If you like."

"Brilliant! Oh, I'm so glad to have made a new friend for the new year. Me and my best buddy Rammy, off to face the world and supply the needy with food and drink fit for a king!" His customers were not protesting his absence, their attention now focused on Synor, who was performing minor magic tricks with his slender legs dangling over the edge of the stage. "Terak, you miserable git, don't just stare like that!"

"I am not staring like anything," responded Terak, his black hair falling around his face as he moved his head. "You know I am trying to give up drinking."

Andel looked positively scandalised. "Oh, well! For your information, it's called *tradition*, and if you won't be a sport and join in with the festivities, well then, too bad!" Terak looked wryly at him, and Andel instantly broke into peals of laughter. "Aww, come on, Terak, you can give up tomorrow! Hey, Rammy!" Ramsey looked up, after focusing pointlessly on the scarred tabletop. "Drink that up, I only serve it once a year."

Terak drank his quickly, while Ramsey just picked up his glass and warily examined the contents. "What is it?"

"Andel's island-famous Creation Eve fruit cordial!" Ramsey grinned. Almost everything that Andel talked about was supposedly famous or otherwise traditional. "And if you don't drink it, you'll have bad luck for the new year. Drink it up, and I'll give you a kiss."

"I- what?"

Andel quickly amended himself. "Okay, drink it up, *or* I'll give you a kiss." Ramsey could have sworn that he heard Terak laugh, but he did not look. Unnerved by the prospect of further physical contact with vampires, Ramsey quickly drank the sickly-sweet cordial and set his glass back down on the table.

"That's better, sunshine. Not too long now until the new year!" He looked at the clock mounted on the wall, a rather brightly-painted wooden object with brass hands, and retrieved the empty glasses. "Only an hour to go! Won't you two come and join in the party? It must be boring over here."

"We are fine, thank you," responded Terak coolly, waving the other vampire away. One look at Ramsey told him that the goblin was regretting his actions of moments before. "It's exceedingly strong, Ramsey. Give yourself a minute or two, and the shock will fade."

"Who..." Ramsey winced at the sharp increase in his headache and laid his chin down on the table in front of him. "Who are you, anyway? How in Scaless' name do you know my name, and why do you keep saying that you knew my father?"

"Because I did know him," affirmed Terak, leaning one elbow on the table and gazing down at Ramsey with fond eyes. "And I know that you set off on a quest to rescue the kidnapped Prince Morgan from a cobra dragon. My name is Terak Richart; I am the First Lord of Xavierania, and I represent my own race in the Union of Fantastical Creatures. King Viktor is a member of the same organisation, and my comrades and I thereby learned of your noble journey. I had a feeling I would meet you here, my boy. Though I must say that at first I was rather concerned for your safety, especially as that cobra dragon seemed to be tailing you from the beginning."

"Uggh…" Ramsey could feel the strong-tasting cordial boiling in the pit of his stomach like severe indigestion. "But how did you know my father?" he repeated.

Terak pursed his dark lips. "I was introduced to your father by a late member of our union, who also lived in Merlockiara at the time. Your father was skilled in carpentry and cookery, and worked part-time in both. You were named after him, of course, which is how I recognised your name when it was first mentioned to me."

Too curious, and somehow very trusting, Ramsey leaned across the table to absorb the vampire's words. Andel and Synor had started to sing again, and were working the guests into an excited frenzy.

"Ramsey is a name that I have heard nowhere else amongst the goblin population," reflected Terak. He was smiling with sincerity and tenderness, and something genuine shone inside him, drawing Ramsey closer. "I am sorry that this is rather a lot to absorb in such a short time."

"I believe you."

Terak drew back in his chair and placed his hands on his knees. "I am afraid that I know little about your mother, but I do know that your father left you in her care when he had to flee from Merlock. For his own safety, you see…" Ramsey sniffed. Terak seemed to be dancing around his words. "Ramsey, your father was the offspring of royalty." He paused briefly to allow Ramsey to react, but the goblin stayed silent. Terak hurried on. "Your father was the child of King Kristofer, born of a young palace maid, before Kristofer went on to marry his rightful queen a few years afterwards…are you still with me?"

"Yes."

"Good…well, your father was a child born out of wedlock, so obviously his mother was ashamed, and never revealed anything of her affair with the king. So, your father grew up like any other boy in Merlock, eventually meeting your mother, of course. Then you were born – I swear, you are the exact mirror image of your father. It is quite astounding."

410

"Terak!" called Synor's sharp voice over the crowd. "Terak, get over here! I'm bored, and Andel's bullying me!" He then started giggling, discovered that he could not stop, and began wrestling with his brother, who was still attempting to sing. Terak aimed a smirk at Ramsey. The goblin's eyes were as glassy as sheets of ice, empty and sombre.

"Now that I look back on all this, I am very thankful that my friend and I went to the trouble of investigating the matter, otherwise I would not be able to relate this information to you now."

"Why did my father leave me?" asked Ramsey in a measured tone.

"I...well..." Terak searched long and hard for the most tactful and simplified explanation; Ramsey watched him plaintively, shivering slightly, sweat breaking out on his chest. "I know that there are certain people in Merlock who think along certain lines, and...not long after you were born, rumours began to circulate about Kristofer's secret son, and that this son now had a son of his own, and..."

He drummed his fingernails against the table with a hollow clacking sound; Ramsey waited patiently.

"Some bad people were sent after your father, to kill him and his family, for fear that the whole matter might escalate into a royal scandal. So your father left Merlock to protect you and your mother. However, your mother did not remain undetected, and you were seized from her and placed in an orphanage."

"I don't remember..." Ramsey held his head. "Oh, I don't know why I'm even listening to this..."

"They put you there because they thought you wouldn't realise your connection to the royal family, however distant," said Terak firmly, seeking to gain Ramsey's trust by asserting the truth. "You stayed at the orphanage for a few years, until your father returned to find both you and your mother missing. Then he visited the orphanage, and adopted you. I even remember the day he found you and brought you home, because he sent us a letter, saying that he had returned to Merlock and had his son in safe custody once again. And you lived with him for years, though he had to

411

work under a new identity and keep you hidden from the other goblins of Merlock, in case you were both discovered once more."

Ramsey was bent double in his seat, staring at his lap and rocking gently back and forth. Terak could hardly bear to speak, had he not known that it was in Ramsey's best interests to hear the truth. He cleared his throat. Nobody else was paying even remote attention to them.

"All the same, he was eventually apprehended when you were twelve…you were presumed dead, I suppose, for they made no effort to search for you. After I received the news of your father's disappearance, my companion and I gave up hope that you would be found alive. But for some reason or other, here you are."

Ramsey nodded, his eyes downcast. Memories as faint as breath had stirred within him. "I waited and waited…but he just…never came back. I waited for days by myself, in the dark, expecting him to come in through that door and…he never did…oh Scaless…he is dead, then?"

Terak looked down upon the figure before him, running one hand through his ebony mane. He knew that such revelations about one's parentage must be an unbearable strain upon the soul. "Yes, I am afraid so."

"And my mother?"

"Yes."

It all converged upon Ramsey in one tortuous instant, and he dissolved into sobs, his thin hands covering his face, bent double with his elbows on his knees. Terak steadied himself, though he wanted to offer comfort. By the stage, the thirty-or-so party-happy people were singing as one, some bawdy tavern song that Ramsey had never heard. They were sinking into madness, and Ramsey spiralled into anguish.

"Oh Scaless…oh Scaless, I'm alone…!"

"No you aren't." Terak's voice was firm. "You have a wonderful companion to travel with, to support and protect you. You have been fighting all across Merlockiara and Oouealena for the sake of saving a young boy in desperate need of help. You are a brave goblin, Ramsey, and you do your father proud."

412

"Why should I believe you?" cried Ramsey, his eyes red and sore. "Why am I bloody well listening? You could be lying to me, to hurt me...! My parents could still be out there somewhere..."

"They aren't."

"I don't want him to be dead..."

Terak straightened. "Not long ago you said that your father was a selfish, thoughtless bastard. Now you say that you don't want him to be dead. Do not be so quick to judge someone that you do not know, Ramsey. Not even your own parents."

"But that's just it...I never knew him...I should be able to remember, but I...I remember waiting for him, and I remember..." His voice grew strained; raucous laughter echoed around the walls. "I remember fire, and I remember...someone talking to me..." Something suddenly switched on inside his brain, and he looked at the vampire, his brown eyes bleary with tears. "That voice. I heard a voice in the temple, I have heard it for weeks. Everyone jumped and reacted when I heard that voice, but when I asked Andel, he said he didn't know what I was talking about. What's going on? What's *wrong* with me?"

"You could hear him?" asked Terak, nonplussed. Ramsey felt sick with frustration and embarrassment.

"You heard it, too...! Then please, just tell me what you heard...all my life I've thought that there were so many things wrong with me, and hearing this voice at night, on top of all my other problems, it just about finished me off! I would be dead now, or at least completely and utterly mental, were it not for Theron holding me together!"

"Have you told him so?"

"Yes, I have. He's my best friend. But he can't explain this to me...please...I always suspected that my father was dead, but still...you never quite give up hope, you know?" Terak regarded him with sadness. "Theron is all I've ever had, all this time. We need one another. But if you can help me, if you can put my mind at ease...it will make my life a little easier."

Terak gave Ramsey a full smile, and Ramsey returned it, though his eyes were red and moist from crying. Even as Terak

413

reached out to clasp Ramsey's slender hands in his own, the goblin was still dripping with tears.

He felt the world turn around him, hot and dizzying and purple, something soothed his body and made him hang limp, with only Terak's strong hands as an anchor. He stiffly turned his head to see Terak drawing close, and as the vampire held him, Ramsey grew weak, until the brush of something cold and sharp against his throat made him realise what was happening. Terak was trying to kill him.

With a start he attempted to kick and scream, but his body became weaker the more his brain fought for control. He sagged against the back of his chair, Terak's heavy presence bearing down upon him like a migraine. Then the vampire pulled back, and Ramsey felt his head jerk upwards with a snap.

"G-get away from me...!" The world fell back into place all too quickly, and knives stabbed at Ramsey's already miserable headache, making him sway on his chair and almost fall. Terak caught him, and Ramsey gaped fearfully at the dark mouth, for the vampire's fangs were longer than before, like a snake readying to strike; curved and pearly white. "Scaless, what are you doing?" he cried, his voice weak in his lungs. Terak's dark mouth was turned down at the edges with concern.

"Ramsey, look at me," he insisted, holding Ramsey's sharp chin and forcing him to look up despite his sudden lethargy. "This may be painful to hear, but..." He gritted his teeth and swallowed. "You have Utipona Madness, Ramsey. You have the beginnings of the same mental illness that has stricken King Viktor."

"What? No, I can't have!"

"You can hear Pain's voice, you practically fainted when I moved to touch you – you have the first stages of the madness, Ramsey. You believed me about everything else, so believe me now."

Ramsey sniffled, shaking his head despite Terak's solid grip. "I believe you, I believe you, but no...I can't have...I..." He blinked hard, gasping for breath. Still, the other creatures in the room disregarded the goblin and the vampire in the far corner. They were too occupied with their dancing. "P...Pain? That porcupine? What has he got to do with-"

"Pain causes Utipona Madness, my boy. It is his black influence that inflicts the disease upon the innocent. Those who are not already under that darkness. An impulse sent as a call to me would have devastating effects upon someone like you."

"I don't understand..."

Terak held tightly onto Ramsey's wrists, causing great discomfort and making Ramsey's world slow down. There was just something about his touch. "You heard him, Ramsey, and I heard him; but, chances are, nobody else in the whole temple heard him speak. We dark creatures instinctively react to Pain's presence. When Andel told you that he didn't hear a voice, he was telling the truth, for nobody else will have heard it. I am certain."

"But why me?" Ramsey tried meekly to pull back, but Terak held him firmly. The discomfort was beginning to disappear, much like the effect of the powerful fruit cordial. Ramsey's headache was still there, however slight.

"I heard Pain's voice because I was once his most trusted general, in charge of his armies in Utipona and my home kingdom, two thousand years ago. You heard his voice because you already have Utipona Madness, or at least some degree of it, which must have stemmed from somewhere. I could sense that in you from the moment I met you. No goblin should possess an aura so murky."

"Twenty minutes to go, everyone!" shouted Andel from the front of the room, keeping one eye on the clock. Synor was clapping enthusiastically to encourage his brother to continue his most recent story, and was in partial-conversation with a bipedal female troll, of the kind that resembled Theron in the face. They were quite tall creatures, rather stocky, and a group of them was making a great deal of noise around the refreshment table. Ramsey could barely hear Terak's voice over the uproar.

"This is too strange..." he breathed, determined to recall every last detail that the vampire had revealed to him. "So you're saying that Pain is...real?"

"Yes, I am."

The goblin scoffed, but it was an empty sound. "I find that hard to believe."

"Well believe it, young Ramsey, because Pain himself has been speaking directly into your vulnerable mind. You cannot possibly dispute his existence. I have seen him, I have served beneath him, and I have fought against him also. He is a literal creature, one of the oldest manifestations still existing on our island. He is as old as the Great Dragons, and they have existed as long as the seasons have fallen upon Grenamoya."

Terak allowed Ramsey to pull free from his grip, and watched the goblin with concern. Ramsey was twitching and frantically trying to distract himself by running his fingers through his rough hair. "I still don't know why I believe you, but...is this illness...fatal?"

"Yes, it is."

"Oh...!"

"*But,*" interjected Terak forcefully before Ramsey had the chance to grieve. "King Viktor has a very obvious disorder, that struck him quickly, and I fear will kill him just as suddenly. Whereas you, on the other hand, have endured this illness since your childhood. I do believe that you are the first person, throughout the whole of our island's history, to have survived this terminal illness."

"How do you know?" moaned Ramsey, sobbing harshly against his coarse palms.

"Ramsey, Ramsey, listen to me!" The goblin stopped convulsing. "This has plagued my mind since the very beginning, when you were first taken back to Merlock by your father. You had darkness inflicted upon you while you were in the orphanage. That orphanage was selected for you by the monsters that killed your mother, because you were a descendent of royalty. For several years, such establishments had been obtaining children to investigate the effects of Pain's darkness upon royals and more magical races. I know, because Synor and myself spied upon one such orphanage for a time, and we determined that it was being run

416

by a group of our own race that remained loyal to our former master."

"I'm not hearing this..." Ramsey's sharp fingers were lost in his hair.

"You were psychologically harmed by them, Ramsey, though you were thankfully in their clutches for a relatively short time. When your father took you away with him, he worked as hard as possible to offer you a normal childhood, though you could never be seen outside your home. You were scarred; and of course, literally as well as mentally. You wouldn't believe how devastated your father was when he realised how much damage you had sustained."

"It's just a little appendix scar," grumbled Ramsey, feeling hot all over and looking at his bony knees through his worn trousers. "Nobody ever has to see it."

Terak paused prominently, and returned his attention to the cold pancake on his plate. Ramsey was discouraged by the sudden lapse in information, and he assertively caught the vampire's gaze, mouth drawn tight with anger. "...I meant the brand mark on your back. I am sorry if I..." The look on Ramsey's face said it all. "...you've never noticed?"

"Noticed...what?" Ramsey reached under the back of his purple shirt to feel his spine, searching for something unusual, but despite being quite flexible, his hands found nothing. He prayed that there was indeed nothing there, and that Terak's story had been merely nonsense. He finally realised how much his ribs poked out, and one hand returned to rest upon his lumpy appendix scar. He could feel his eyes shimmering once more.

Terak did not look away from the flustered goblin, even as a very inquisitive black kitten started to scratch at his trouser leg. Ramsey, in his utterly confused state, still registered the display of tenderness as Terak lifted the kitten aside with his boot and laid it carefully on the floor near Ramsey's feet. It then noticed the goblin who had petted it earlier, and hopped up onto Ramsey's lap with a squeak. Too upset to think of much else, Ramsey abandoned his hated scar in favour of the small cat, running his fingers along its back to give himself a focus.

"I saw it myself, when you were a child," said the vampire at length, noticing the others' increasing fixation on the clock. Midnight was drawing near. "You have a brand mark in the middle of your back, below your shoulders. A circle, with the number seventeen in it. No doubt, it never faded."

Ramsey nodded to affirm that he had been listening. The kitten settled down and stretched languidly beneath the soothing scratch of Ramsey's sharp fingernails.

"That, I hope, will prove my story to be true. You were cruelly branded by people that considered you an experiment. Though few orphans from those establishments survived to be rescued, as far as I have heard, all have retained the identification scars inflicted upon them as children. Yours just happened to be a rather unpleasant and noticeable one."

Andel walked past, squeezing Ramsey's shoulder as he went and making the goblin jump. Nemo grumbled unappreciatively. "Three minutes to go!" beamed the purple-haired innkeeper, handing out more glasses of cordial to his guests. They were talking amongst themselves with unrivalled volume, and Terak beamed distantly for a moment, though his eyes remained on Ramsey, who looked up at him. The goblin's face was wet with tears, but he managed half a smile.

"Of course," continued Terak in a brighter tone. "Prince Morgan also bears that identification scar on his cheek. I was wondering all this time, if you realised that Morgan was adopted?"

Ramsey nodded. "Yes, I found out as much from a newspaper that I picked up...I didn't know that he was...he was in the same sort of orphanage as me?"

"Yes, he was. No doubt you have heard about the famous Shaun Grassman, a fellow goblin – Morgan was rescued from the final corrupt orphanage in Merlockiara, after Grassman closed it down himself."

"But if he's adopted, he isn't royalty, is he? So what was he doing there?"

Something in his question sparked an entirely positive reaction in the vampire, who grinned, showing a perfect set of white teeth that complimented his fangs quite brilliantly. Nemo stirred on Ramsey's lap, apparently alerted to the imminent arrival of the new year. "Morgan is a very fair young boy. Anyone who has ever met him in person can tell you so. He was taken to that orphanage because he very obviously has elven blood."

Ramsey's eyes went wide, and he choked out a laugh. "He's an *elf*?"

"No, he's a goblin. But to be perfectly honest, I have a strong conviction that he had an elven father." His smiled broadened. "And I have a stronger conviction that his elven father may, too, have been royalty. Something about him is far too fair for a goblin. Not to insult your race, of course."

"No, it's Okay," mused Ramsey, picking up the kitten as he moved to stand. "Most of us are ugly buggers."

"Now I didn't say-"

Ramsey laughed, properly this time, cradling the black kitten in his arms like a furry doll. "I know you didn't say so – I did. And I'm allowed to poke fun at my own species, if nothing else."

Terak chortled and stood alongside Ramsey, his strong arms crossed over his chest. On seeing the tall vampire stand up, Synor ushered his way through the crowd to Terak and latched onto his arm with excitement. Andel shouted over the throbbing noise of the crowd, still standing upon the stage, ringing a resonant, clanging brass bell that he seemed to have reserved for this singular occasion.

"Hey, everyone, I know you're all excited, but shut up!" Ramsey sniggered, his cheeks warm and runny, and felt something comforting coursing through his blood. As though in kindness, the kitten clambered its way up the front of his shirt, onto his shoulder, and began rasping the tears from Ramsey's cheeks with a rough, tiny tongue. "If you'll all be so good as to keep quiet for one millisecond, we should hear the chimes of the town clock heralding the new year! Don't stop enjoying yourselves, by any means, but it's tradition to listen for the bells!"

This mention of tradition was enough to silence the loudest of the trolls, the rowdiest of the zombies, and even the playful bleating of Synor's pet goat that was sneaking breadsticks from the refreshment table. Pure silence flooded the tall room, not the tiniest echo offended the high walls. Ramsey held tightly onto Nemo as the kitten curled up against his chest.

Then suddenly, as though booming from miles away, came the first, deep chime of Morfran's town clock, and as abruptly as they had quieted, everyone in the tavern erupted into joyous noise and exalted exclamations. Ramsey was hugged by everyone at least once, he was pushed this way and that, several anonymous women took the liberty of kissing him and ruffling his hair. It was so bizarre and frantic that he couldn't help but keep smiling. Perhaps mood swings were a symptom of this 'Utipona Madness' that he supposedly had. He felt whole. Nemo squirmed in his grip and wriggled free onto a nearby table, just as Ramsey was pulled into a suffocating embrace by Andel.

"Happy new year, Rammy! I hope things work out for you, wherever you're heading off to, Okay?"

"Yeah, you too." Much to Ramsey's frustration, Andel also took the liberty of playing with the goblin's hair, making it messier than ever. "It's been an odd visit, but I'm glad I came here. And again, thank you, for allowing my friend to stay in your stable. You've really gone out of your way to be helpful."

"Oh nonsense, Rammy. You're great company, you really are."

In a vaguely confusing gesture, Andel lowered his face to Ramsey's neck and gave him what felt like a tentative, toothy kiss, and then drew back without further explanation. Ramsey instantly touched the left side of his throat with his fingers, but felt no blood.

"I'll see you again in a minute, Rammy, I just need to see to Mrs Morris over there." He leaned close once more, and Ramsey flinched, but Andel did not touch him, and spoke in a whisper. "Some crazy old bat who lets her dog Harry piddle against my reception desk whenever she comes to stay. It might take a while."

Then he bustled away through the group towards a rather eccentric-looking goblin with blue hair and a furry coat.

Ramsey felt a hand on his shoulder and turned to see Terak smiling down at him. The vampire rolled his eyes. "The festive season can do strange things to people. Happy Creation Day, Ramsey. I know it is hardly the daytime, but midnight has passed. A prosperous new year to you."

"And to you, too," he responded mechanically, extending the gesture to Terak's magenta-haired companion, who was standing very close by. Synor still looked at Ramsey with measured caution, but two hours of eating and drinking and dancing with Andel had left him quite subdued, and his eyes held no fire. "You've definitely made me view things quite differently than before…"

Synor blinked. "What did you say to him, Terak?"

"Nothing that concerns you, my friend. Do not worry." Synor was clearly more tired than he was letting on, because he raised no further questions, and instead fumbled his way over to the nearest chair and sat down. Terak watched him for a moment, then turned to Ramsey and placed his hands on the smaller goblin's shoulders. "Vampire tradition. It is a gesture of utmost trust." Ramsey knew to brace himself for another touch from a vampire's fangs. Terak bent to Ramsey's height, but did not injure him. In fact, Ramsey didn't find it too strange the second time around. He supposed that for a vampire it would, indeed, be a very trusting display. "What?" inquired Terak when he felt Ramsey start.

"Nothing." Ramsey was smiling, astounded. "My species doesn't go in for the kissing angle, that's all."

"Do not worry. All vampires greet in this manner, so nobody will think badly of you." His inky eyes searched the room for a moment, then settled on Synor. Ramsey's line of vision followed.

"…Can I ask you something? Since you've told me so much this evening."

"Of course you may."

Ramsey tried his best to sound casual, and looked at Terak's collar, which was at his eye level. "Is that vampire with the pink hair...is he a relative or a friend or what? Because he's been acting more like a sulking wife, glaring daggers at me when you were talking to me."

"He is my apprentice," answered Terak, no guard in his tone. "He was placed in my care from a young age, because he was the son of one of Pain's most powerful sorceresses. Andel is his brother, of course, but Synor has inherited some aura powers from his mother that Pain might try to exploit if Synor was fighting on his side. I protect Synor and help him to curb his magic, and he lives with me, and travels with me."

Ramsey nodded distractedly, noticing as Andel joined his brother at the table and offered him the same trustful gesture. Synor looked far more drained than his younger brother, who pulled him into a hug. "I've never seen any goblins in Merlock hug one another like that...being in this town has made my own race look very dismal and frigid in comparison. But there is something else I want to know..."

"Yes?" Terak was not losing patience, and quite enjoyed answering the young goblin's insistent questions. Even the sudden attention of a female vampire with silver hair failed to distract either one of them.

"Synor saved my life from that rhôniae...and I was so thankful for that, but when I saw that he was bleeding, I suspected that you had attacked him, because I remember you running out of the church with him. So, did you attack him?"

The female vampire flounced off, directing her efforts at Andel instead. Terak did not notice her leave. His face was hard with what looked like regret. "I wondered exactly what made you act so strangely towards me." Ramsey felt embarrassed under those interrogating, dark eyes, but knew that no malice was aimed at him. "I took Synor out of the temple when I felt Pain's influence compelling me to kill at his command. Synor is my closest companion, he has been like a son to me, since I lost my daughter many years ago."

"I'm sorry," broke in Ramsey, his voice quiet. Terak bowed his head.

"To me, Synor is what my race refers to as a 'blood mate'. We share a bond so close that if ever I were to bite him, I would not kill him. He is the one person on this whole island who can survive an attack from me. Which is why I have to travel with him everywhere, nowadays. It is very shameful…" he added with a sigh.

"Does it hurt him?"

"No more than any other vampire bite would hurt a person. His company is the only thing that keeps me from posing a danger to other people."

Ramsey watched Synor for a moment with pity. "So, if you bit me, would I turn into a vampire?"

Terak laughed, showing his fangs and white teeth once more. "If I bit you, young Ramsey, you would have two puncture wounds in a crucial part of your throat that could not be healed, and you would bleed to death. Our bites are no longer the sort that convert others to our kind."

"Ah…"

Ramsey was thankful when the two of them returned to sitting down once more. The dull ache of tiredness had begun to wear away at his body. Synor looked to be only semi-conscious, and huddled against Terak's side the instant they sat down at the table. Terak winked amusedly at Ramsey and held tightly onto his companion, who promptly fell asleep and began to snore softly.

Andel, it seemed, existed without sleep, and was as bouncy as he had been that same afternoon. Upon seeing how tired his brother was, he offered to help him upstairs, but Terak declined the offer, choosing to remain still and allow the small vampire to sleep.

Ramsey was contemplating everything that Terak had told him. A brief search through one of his trouser pockets yielded the discovery of a single, small slip of unmarked paper, and he stared at it for a moment, trying to recollect its origin. Of course, it had been given to him at the church service. Terak instantly spotted it, and spoke to Ramsey in a hushed voice that was intended not to wake Synor.

"Did you not add your slip to the Pool of Remembrance? Oh Ramsey, I'm so sorry. After everything that happened, I forgot to offer to take your paper for you…"

"What is it?" asked Ramsey, examining both sides of the paper with interest. "I've never been to a church service before."

"You never…? Oh, of course…how thoughtless of me. I should have informed you. It's traditional in the Creation Eve service to write down the name of a deceased loved one on the paper, which you then drop into the pool of blessed water at the back of the temple. It's symbolic of…letting go of memories, I suppose. I wrote down the names of my late wife and daughter; Andel and Synor always write down a remembrance of their mother." Andel, who was still sitting at the table with them, nodded to confirm this statement. Ramsey swallowed.

"Before tonight, I didn't…I didn't really have anyone to remember." With a final, long look, he placed the slip back in his pocket and crossed his arms over his body. "I feel so strained and…like I've wasted my entire life on something that never existed."

"You have wasted nothing, Ramsey. You're risking your life to save a child who is completely unconnected to you." Synor made a mumbling noise in his sleep that sounded like an agreeing sound, but he was not awake in the least, so they did not disturb him. Sweetness, the partially decayed goat, was settling down next to Synor's crossed feet. "And though it may be strange to acknowledge, Ramsey, do remember that you have some remnants of a family left. King Viktor, after all, is your half-uncle."

Terak had explained it all clearly that same night, in black and white. Ramsey's father had been Viktor's half-brother. Of course that meant that Ramsey was Viktor's half-nephew. But somehow, that hadn't clicked in Ramsey's brain beforehand, and suddenly his head was heavy with sickness.

He was related to the ugliest, most unintelligent goblin in all of Merlockiara – he was the king's illegitimate nephew. He was more closely related to the king than Morgan was, for Scaless' sake. He wasn't sure what exactly it was that made him feel so deceived.

"Ramsey? Oh Ramsey, I am sorry...I am sorry that I brought all this upon you, out of the blue. Forgive me if I have upset you."

"No...no, honestly...I think I just need a little fresh air." Ramsey stood, forcing his chair backwards, and it shrieked against the stone floor. "Can you keep my seat for me?"

"Of course, Rammy, don't worry about a thing!" Andel promptly lifted his legs and rested his boots upon the chair, reclining comfortably while still seated on his own. "Goblins need fresh air. It's good for the soul, I say. Hurry back, though, Rammy, before we miss you too much."

"Okay." Ramsey caught a concerned glance from Terak before ambling out of the noise-ridden room, along the hallway and out into the cold, moonlit street.

***

Theron had been less than half asleep that whole night, and was eventually woken up by the deep chiming of the town clock. He could count fairly well, and had no trouble determining that he had heard twelve distinct bell chimes. There was nobody else with him in the musty stable, apart from a particularly impressive black horse tied up in one of the stalls, so he decided to continue his rest. The persistent throbbing of his hind leg still managed to keep him awake, and the two bandages were starting to itch. A humble attempt to remove them with his teeth had been unsuccessful, so he tried to ignore them.

He was on the verge of sleep when he heard a loud clatter, and he lifted his head from the soft straw that covered the stable floor. The door had been forced open, and was letting the cold air in. When he noticed Ramsey stagger inside with his feet crusted in snow, Theron smiled, and tried to get up. Ramsey promptly told him not to move.

"Happy new year, Ramsey," he beamed, dry straw sticking to his fur. Ramsey replied brusquely, with a tentative sideways glance at the dark horse; then, much to Theron's surprise, the goblin

425

marched up to him and flung his thin arms around Theron's neck. He was crying again. "Ramsey, what's wrong? Are you Okay? Are you hurt?" Ramsey shook his head and kept weeping. "Please, Ramsey, tell me what's the matter."

"I'm sorry, I'm so, so sorry for anything I ever did to hurt you…"

"No, Ramsey, it's not a problem. What's the matter?"

Ramsey dug his fingers into the coarse layer of purple hair at the troll's neck. His voice was suddenly faint, filled with regret and sincerity so raw that Theron could not move for fear of shattering him. "I can't tell you how sorry I am for everything. I'd be dead now if it wasn't for you…"

Theron smiled softly, and tried to speak just as calmly. "I haven't done anything, Ramsey."

"Yes you have. You've been there. Nobody else has ever been there."

As though he did not really want to, Ramsey gradually loosened his grip and pulled away, brushing his sweaty hair from his eyes. Theron beheld him then as somebody quite different, not the Ramsey he had met so long ago, back in his home forest in Merlockiara. This new goblin was insecure and vulnerable; he was not an uncaring, selfish thief who was mindlessly bitter about the world. He just looked like an underfed goblin who had for too long been deprived of basic comforts and safety.

"I just…I just wanted to tell you that."

"Tell me what?"

He huffed and sagged somewhat – that was more the Ramsey that Theron knew. "You're trying to make me say it again on purpose, aren't you? Well then, once again, I just wanted to say that I'm *sorry*. And that I'm glad that you're with me." He looked at the floor, kicking some straw away from his feet, and earning a grumpy snort from Terak's restrained horse. "I really am. I'd be pretty damn bored without your company."

"And I would be mad at myself if I let you risk your life without me there to look after you." Ramsey shrugged with a grin, an I-would-still-manage-perfectly-well-by-myself-thank-you

426

expression rooted in his features. "Is it much further to go, Ramsey?"

"No, it's not. We're almost at the most dangerous point of this journey. So let's enjoy these last few days while we can, eh?"

***

The still night air was static and chilly against Ramsey's bare skin. His old shirt removed, he leaned sombrely out over the windowsill of his snowy white room, gazing upon the darkened streets below. The final guests from Andel's party had long departed, and had disappeared into their warm houses under the sharp eyes of the town watchmen, who even now were scouring the roads on horseback, their lanterns swinging like sunspots in the dark.

The number seventeen. Ramsey had seen it in the mirror, etched into his skin as though by a scalding chisel. Terak's story had been true. His heart sank with the very weight of that wretched number. Then the story of his father had been true, also…

He reached to the nearby table and retrieved his small slip of paper from under a pencil that he had borrowed from the reception desk. On it, he had written the single word, '*Dad*'. He could not hold it very long, for it unleashed upon him a sadness that eroded his heart. Instead, he held it out in one hand, high into the darkness of the star-decked midnight sky. A breeze caught it and plucked it away from his fingers, and it shrank to a flitter of white before disappearing over the rooftops.

# Chapter Sixteen

# Dying Dreams

It was early morning, and Ramsey had woken up with a lingering headache. As he lifted his eyes to the window, he realised that it was barely light – the wan glow of the emerging dawn stretched faintly towards Morfran Town through the dark sky, though the moon had already faded. He had left the window open all night long, and the bedroom was cold. He pulled himself free of the blankets. The soft cloth fluttered against the wound in the middle of his back, causing him to wince in pain. His fingers found the dreaded mark, raised and heated as though something fearsome had awoken beneath his skin.

The floorboards creaked under his feet as he crept from his room and began his cautious descent of the staircase, leaving his room unlocked behind him. Every stair squeaked and moaned with his frail weight, no matter how slowly and delicately he took each step. The whole tavern was cold, and the monochrome painted walls and beams made him feel very visible in the emerging light of morning. He slunk downwards, his breath in his throat, and listened cautiously for any noise. Apart from the tiniest hint of muffled snoring, nothing stirred.

Finally at the bottom of the staircase, he glanced briefly around the reception hall and returned the borrowed pen to a ceramic pot on top of Andel's desk. He shivered. Morfran Town was under several inches of snow, yet he had been thoughtless enough to leave his bedroom window open and sleep with his shirt off. He had a feeling that he would be trembling all day.

Somehow, after learning the truth about his late father, discovering that he had Utipona Madness and realising that his lifelong shoulder pains had been caused by a huge brand mark in the middle of his back, he had been too exhausted to remember such trivialities.

"Ah, Master Ramsey."

Ramsey jarred and swung around to face the staircase, withdrawing his right hand from the door handle. Terak was standing several steps from the bottom, a floor-length, black dressing gown wrapped around him, though his alert expression betrayed no traces of sleep. Ramsey couldn't just run. He stepped forward, and bowed his head towards the vampire. "Lord Terak."

This term of address made Terak smile. He stood at the base of the staircase with intrigue. "Why are you leaving so very early, my boy? It is not yet morning."

"How did you know to follow me down here?"

The vampire conceded to answer, though he had asked a question first. "I had a feeling that you were leaving. My species is not unlike the elves, Ramsey. I could sense your distress, and that you were moving downstairs...given your situation, I guessed that you were going to sneak away. Why would that be, pray tell?"

It was no use. Ramsey couldn't hide anything from the Xavierania lord. More than any other factor, this particular vampire had a certain atmosphere about him that made Ramsey feel the need to comply with whatever was asked. "I wanted to get away before any of you woke up," he admitted, wringing his bony hands. "Truth be told...I don't have any money to pay for my stay here, and I didn't want you all to find out and think less of me."

430

"Somehow I think that running away would be no less cowardly," mused the other. Ramsey blushed and felt his trachea tightening.

"I had money, once. When I first set off from Merlock. Then in BlackField Town, the tavern where I was staying got burned down, and I lost everything apart from what I carried on me. I'm sorry." Terak scrutinised him for an instant, but the vampire's velvet eyes were soft. Ramsey's heart perked.

"Well, in that case, it is just as well that I offered Andel payment for your stay." Ramsey's heart gave another jump, and he breathed. "I offered, but he declined, saying that since he always lets myself and Synor stay for free, and since he took such a shine to you, he decided to give you a courtesy stay. I had an inkling that you didn't have any money."

Ramsey's eyebrows shot up. "You really have a knack for perception, don't you? It's going to get creepy if you can tell me much more."

"I think I told you too many details about yourself last night." Ramsey stayed put, watching as Terak moved around to the back of the reception desk and bent, as though to retrieve something heavy from the floor. Too relieved to move, Ramsey did not pry, and averted his eyes out of politeness. Andel's pet kitten was curled up on one of the chairs, its paws over its face as it snoozed. "Ramsey, if you will come here for a moment."

Ramsey obeyed, and moved around to join Terak at the rear of the desk. Ramsey noticed, among other things, a tattered copy of The Scaless Scriptures, a jar of colourful mints, and some well-chewed cat toys arranged randomly on a shelf next to the padded chair. Terak looked ceremoniously proud as he presented Ramsey with a fairly flat, rather long package bound up with heavy, brown cloth and sharp string. The goblin stumbled under the sudden weight, stared at the bundle in his arms, then looked up at Terak wordlessly.

"Open it," said the vampire, his face alight with a smile. "Just consider it my personal contribution to the welfare of Merlockiara's monarchy."

Ramsey knelt and laid the cloth-wrapped weight upon the stone floor to untie the strings. He did so quite easily (sometimes it was useful to have such thin fingers), pulled the thick material aside, and found a folded stack of brand new clothing, a tough, leather tunic, and primarily, what had comprised the bulk of the package's weight; a gleaming, silver blade, three feet long, sturdy yet slender, its hilt decorated with a crimson motive in the shape of a snake. His mouth fell slack, and he looked up at Terak, who, in a standing position, towered mystically above him.

"This…this is…"

"Consider them late birthday presents, if you will." Ramsey stared at the contents of the unexpected parcel, his eyes swallowing everything at once, the short sword in particular. He had seen far bigger weapons in his lifetime, but for his size and weight, the blade looked perfect. "And be sure to give Morgan my fondest regards when you see him."

Ramsey laughed, reaching out to hold the magnificent weapon. It felt like liquid strength in his nimble grip. "I suppose you have a 'feeling' about that, too?"

"I have feelings about many things. I know that Morgan is alive, Ramsey, and when you find him, that blade and the tunic should give you a fighting chance against the dragon. I also decided that you could make good use of some new clothes. You have heart, dear boy, and I stand by my previous statement. Your father would truly be proud of you."

"I wish I knew." Ramsey flexed his fingers, experimenting with different ways to hold his sword. He tossed it from hand to hand, a new surge of resilience running through him. This was something real, that he could literally hold in his hands, and soon it would be his chance to prove himself, and to test his real strength. It was this strength that kept him going from day to day, striving forward while convincing himself that the poor child was still alive. "I owe you so much…"

"Think nothing of it."

"How can I? Ever since I arrived in this town, something's been happening to me…it's funny, I've never had anyone care so much for me without even knowing me. Theron is different, of course, but Andel, and you as well..." He thought hard for the words to continue, and swung his sword towards a filing cabinet as though trying to stab his voice into action. Terak watched him with quiet confidence. "Everybody here has been so good to me. I really will miss you and Andel...and I'm still thankful to Synor for saving my life."

"It was his instinct to do so. Do not worry, Ramsey. We will see one another again; I am certain of it. May Scaless grant you speed and good fortune for the remainder of your quest."

A moaning creak on the staircase, and a near hysterical voice sliced through the silence of the hall. "*Rammy!*" Andel, also clad in a dressing gown, and looking as though he had a moderate hangover, scurried down the stairs and assaulted the two of them behind the desk. He grabbed onto Ramsey's torso. "I thought I heard someone sneaking around. How could you go without saying goodbye? I haven't even given you your present yet! Wait right there." His attention then switched to one of the many desk drawers in their vicinity, and he rummaged around inside them at random, looking for something.

Ramsey decided that all of this physical contact with vampires was causing his constant headache, and stood still, his sword held firmly in his right hand. He felt so fuelled with confidence and vengeance that his fingernails scraped against the engraved hilt. An abrupt exclamation of triumph from Andel suggested that he had found his quarry, and he spun around to face Ramsey and Terak with a smug smile.

"Rammy, alias Ram, alias Ramsey," he began, his glazed expression hinting that the world was spinning slightly inside his head, "I have here, for you, another traditional custom of our race, an item of sentimental worth that I made myself." He gestured for Ramsey to hold out his free hand, which Ramsey did; Andel slapped a handcrafted bracelet of blue and green beads into the goblin's open palm. "That is a life bracelet, Rammy – the blue and green represent life, you see. What you do is you make a wish relating to your life, then put it on your wrist or ankle, and when it eventually wears off, your wish will come true!"

"Thank you," responded Ramsey with gratitude, looking down at the beads on their black chord. Any vampire custom was more appealing than the 'neck kiss' greeting of the night before.

Andel was luminous with pride as Ramsey admired the jewellery. "Just thought it would come in handy when you're heading off to face the dragon."

"Yeah, I'm sure it will." For the time being, he slipped the bracelet into his trouser pocket, then bent to retrieve his new clothing and brown tunic. Then he looked up. "How do *you* know about the dragon?"

"Terak told me," came the brisk reply, as Andel returned his attention to another drawer. He bustled around inside for a moment, then snapped upright, and marched out of the room, through the glass-panelled door, in the direction of the dining room. Ramsey was left staring at Terak with a mixture of curiosity and disapproval. The remaining vampire smirked.

"Well, it isn't as though Andel can do any harm," he reasoned. "He was interested and wanted to know why I was spending so much time talking to you last night."

"And I suppose your apprentice with pink hair knows about all this as well?"

"I try not to trouble him with my business matters. I don't tell him *everything*."

Andel was back in a trice, carrying a black bag over his right shoulder. The bell tinkled merrily as he forced his way through the door. "Here you go, Rammy. I've got you some stuff here that I made myself, just basics, but I figured that you would need some food for your journey." He shoved the pack into Ramsey's already well-laden arms and continued, barely pausing for a breath. "And before you go, Rammy, let me give you some further words of advice."

"Yes?" Ramsey was relieved when Terak took the initiative to help with the heavy load. The taller vampire took hold of

Ramsey's new clothing and his bag of supplies and supported them in the crook of one arm. Andel puffed up with pride.

"Well, take care, Scaless bless you, don't forget us, come back soon, send letters – but most importantly of all," gushed Andel, trying to stand tall like Terak but swaying nonetheless. "most *importantly* of all – I have some wise words for you on behalf of my late uncle, Rammy. Well, my uncle wasn't called 'Rammy', I mean…oh well, you know what I mean!"

"Yes…?" droned Ramsey, though a smile was plastered to his face.

"My uncle used to say to me, as I was sat upon his knee and he was smoking his pipe, he would say to me, 'Andel' he would say, 'Andel – never, never, never, never, never, never, never, never *smoke'*." (Here Andel added a pronounced lisp to the words of his uncle.) "Then I would say, 'But uncle, *you* smoke', and he would reply, 'Don't do as I do, do as I *say*!' And I would say, 'But uncle, that makes no sense!', and he would say '*Life* makes no sense!' – So there you go. A safe trip to you, Rammy. Scaless' speed!"

He slapped Ramsey heartily on the back and embraced him as though he was about to cry. Ramsey had a dumbfounded expression that refused to shift from his face, and Terak laughed, though it was a restrained, tight sort of laugh, as though he could manage nothing more.

"Dawn is gathering, my boy. You should depart soon, if you wish to leave before the whole town wakes."

"Oh, yes, of course." The concept of time had escaped Ramsey for a brief moment, as though he had been standing in a limbo filled with silver swords and senseless health advice. He felt a distant sort of pain that stemmed from somewhere between his shoulders, and he realised that Andel had smacked against the brand mark on his tender skin. He had been up too late to feel energetic so early in the morning, but nonetheless jump-started himself into action. "Thank you both, for all of your help. I've hardly thought about that bloody dragon the entire time I've been here."

435

"It's been a pleasure!" Andel hugged him again, then stepped away with a slight push against Ramsey's chest. "Now go on, be off with you! Don't want to keep Morgan waiting, do you?"

"Of course not. I'll be with him before he knows it." Andel returned Ramsey's confident smile, and Terak watched them, sagely, saying nothing until Ramsey approached him to reclaim his fresh clothes. "I don't know how I'm going to carry all of this."

"There's room in the bag to fit your clothes inside," said Andel. Ramsey blinked, then stared at Terak.

"You two have been conspiring against me, haven't you?" he grumbled.

Terak handed Ramsey the clothes as the goblin stooped to pack his belongings. There was no genuine anger in Ramsey's statement, but all the same, the slight flare in the goblin's aura alerted Terak to the evil disease that had long ago afflicted Ramsey's body. It would not worsen, Terak was certain of it; but still, to see such a young person so badly hindered by a terrible illness flooded him with guilt. He had told Ramsey about his father, about his past, about his relation to King Viktor – but Terak could not rid him of the Utipona Madness. Ramsey would bear it for the rest of his life, like his appendix scar and the ghastly label on his back.

"The Ash Mountains are very near, Ramsey," informed the larger vampire, though it was a needless statement. Morfran Town literally existed in the shadow of the mountains, which were no more than an hour's trek away. "Though it has been a long time since I travelled those paths, I can safely tell you that the best way through the closest mountains is the one that passes under them. The mountains are riddled with caves and tunnels, so you will have no trouble finding your way in."

"I don't know if that sounds worse than walking over the top."

"Believe me, it is far safer. Once you emerge beyond the southernmost range of the mountains, you will be able to continue above ground, as the land is more accessible from there onwards. I don't suppose the dragon will have based itself far from its food source."

"Right..." Ramsey sighed. His bag was neatly packed, all of Andel's food packages cushioned at the bottom, and in his final act of preparation, he clutched his sword in hand and slid it into the left side of his belt. It felt comfortably cool through his trouser leg, like a shard of ice. "I really hope I can do this..."

"Of course you can, Ramsey. I have complete faith in you. We shall meet again, I promise you." Terak was a proud and impressive creature to behold. Ramsey felt awfully measly beneath the vampire's firm gaze, and lost faith for a second or two, but a glimpse of Andel in the corner of his eye, leaning against the reception desk with a fixedly dizzy expression, perked Ramsey up, and sent a burst of determined fire through his body. "That's the spirit, my boy. You can tell me all about your adventures when next we meet."

"Here, here!" exclaimed Andel without provocation, his headache finally getting the better of him. "And me and Synor will get in line to hear about them, too!"

***

There was a pronounced chill in the early morning air, enough so that their lukewarm breath formed as condensation in front of their faces. They stood side by side; their long, silver shadows stretching across the crystalline carpet of snow. Two vampires waiting on the doorstep of a tavern, both wrapped up in similar dressing gowns, brilliantly pale yet dark against the blotchy landscape. The snow no longer fell, and a solitary line of footprints marred the otherwise perfect coating of white upon the ground.

"The rest is up to him, now." Terak stood majestically alongside the slumping form of Andel, who was leaning against the doorframe and mumbling to the cold air. The larger vampire craned his vision beyond the rooftops to where the mountains jutted forth from the green, frosted landscape. His hair, ruffled from sleep, seemed to swirl and dance even in the absence of a breeze. "I just regret that I could do nothing practical to help him."

"Don't take this the wrong way," began Andel, thus preparing Terak for a tactless statement typical of Synor. "I like Rammy and all, but he's pretty messed up, as far as his history goes. You couldn't have done anything."

"But it is imperative that I aid him as far as I can, so that he may complete this journey and return Morgan to Merlockiara."

"Imperative or not, he had a messed up childhood, and you can't expect him to get over all that info in the space of a few hours." Andel insisted, though his dreary tone lacked real assertion. He had the air of someone who resented the very concept of getting out of bed. "You've done all you can, right? So don't worry about it. He'll be fine. At least, he'd better be, because I want him to tell us all about it when he gets back. It's ruddy boring around here."

The deep, crunching sound of heavy paws upon fresh snow alerted both of them at once. Theron, looking far more energetic than before, emerged from around the side of the black and white building, Ramsey positioned atop his hairy back. The troll snorted water vapour into the air, and it rose and disappeared amidst the chill. Ramsey, firmly clasping one strap of his new supply pack with one hand and Theron's brown mane with the other, looked outwardly concerned, somewhat sad, but the spark of determination igniting his bright face set his emotions very much apart from sorrow.

Theron lumbered towards the two figures, tentatively putting weight on his bandaged legs, and Ramsey looked down at the vampires, mixed feelings jabbing at his subconscious until he didn't quite know what he was feeling. Gratitude, for Terak's advice and Andel's hospitality. Sadness, for having to leave so soon. Anger, at the dragon that had taken an innocent boy from his bed as he slept. Theron, as a simple creature, had a simple, tender expression upon his still-wild features.

"Oh, go all ready!" whinged Andel, grinning from ear to ear. "Before we caught up with long goodbyes!"

"Good idea," agreed Terak, waving to Ramsey as the goblin and the troll passed by, leaving broad paw-prints in their wake. "May the Great Lady protect you, my boy. Scaless' speed!"

"And write to me, Rammy! That's; Andel Numair, Andel's Tavern, Morfran Town-"

"Don't worry, I will!" responded Ramsey, as Theron paused one last time to allow him to wave farewell. "Thanks, both of you, and take care."

Terak waved calmly in quiet confidence. Yes, this goblin would definitely be one to make it. "Use the blade well, Ramsey, and do not be afraid of fate. Scaless can be kind, as well as cruel."

Ramsey wasn't sure whether or not this information was supposed to inspire confidence within him. With a final pronounced wave and an unusually cheerful call of goodbye, he whispered to Theron, and the troll took off at a brisk pace and set off along the road. Stirring up the snow behind them, Theron galloped up the white-washed street, Ramsey sitting erect upon his back like a soldier going to war – beyond Morfran Town, to where the mountains met the earth.

*** 

Meanwhile, at the Dragon Temple atop the most sacred mountain in all of Grenamoya, the demon Pain had been roused from meditation, and now occupied himself with one of the Great Dragons' most powerful relics.

*Show me…show me this boy…*

A misty array of colours swirled inside the glass sphere before him. Its stand took the form of a sculpted, stone snake, with its coils and head wrapped around the crystal globe. The eyes were brilliant, white gemstones, and as such were beautiful but lifeless, glinting against the backdrop of stormy sky. Pain concentrated, forcing every last reserve of his mental power into the sphere to command it. The colours swelled into a glowing, marbled pulse; then they bled into black and faded altogether. The temple shook with the force of his rage.

*Damn it! Why will you not obey me? Show me the goblin who seeks to rescue Prince Morgan!*

A flutter of pigment, as faint as a blush, ignited and died in the same moment. He snarled and clasped one heavy paw over the orb.

"Ulyssis!"

Several prolonged seconds passed before the patter of large, flat feet alerted Pain to his servant's arrival. The former human drew near to where the porcupine was hunched near a grand window, and bowed half-heartedly. Ulyssis' irises flashed violet beneath his eyelids.

"You bellowed, sir?"

Pain's face hardened; black lips parted to expose two rows of jagged teeth. Ulyssis did not flinch, his glowing gaze directed at the floor. "You have become disobedient, Ulyssis, and now you dare to disrespect me! How very cowardly, how very pathetic. How very *stupid*. Don't provoke me. Now come here – I am not yet strong enough to control this artefact, but I think that maybe, if we combine our energy, we may have more success."

With a rancid, murderous expression etched in his slimy features, Ulyssis submitted to his master's bidding, and approached. He could feel Pain's eyes slicing through his consciousness, as though trying to visualise a motive for the sudden indignation; but Ulyssis would not let himself be scrutinised, and he blocked Pain's stare. Instead, he too gazed into the empty, glass orb, and breathed a rattling sigh.

"You cannot control this, master, because it was made to be controlled by the Great Dragons. Naturally, your presence repels it."

"I'll make it listen," snarled the larger of the two, once more taking hold of the smooth glass with one paw. "So help me, I'll make it obey! Show me the boy!"

He closed his eyes in concentration, and Ulyssis focused his mind also, though he kept his eyes resolutely open while he did so. Power channelled through both of them, from one to the other, and then converged inside the sphere as they touched it. It flared to life suddenly, and Pain opened his eyes in a flash. He could feel something moving.

440

"Yes...yes, come now...show me that goblin..."

Ulyssis watched in fascination, intrigue hidden behind a rather grim expression. Colours danced and twisted like ribbons within the glass, and then began to form shapes, that were blurred at first, then swam into focus. Two pale figures standing against a background of white, one taller than the other, both shielded against the cold air by black dressing gowns. They laughed, and the sound drew them into sharp focus – two vampires, one of which was hugely familiar to both Pain and Ulyssis.

"Well, now, this crystal has found our dear comrade Terak. What a pleasant coincidence."

Ulyssis spat on the floor in a fury, his claws still touching the orb. "I don't wish to look upon him! This is not what you asked to see."

Though the two faces were somewhat fuzzy through the glass, as the vampires spoke, the two onlookers could hear their every word. The smaller of the two, whom Pain did not quite recognise, kept laughing and slumping sideways against the other. Terak tried to support him.

"*I swear, you giggle much louder and you'll wake your brother!*" scolded the voice of Terak, which had a vaguely metallic sound to it, ringing like stricken iron. "*Don't lean on me so. You'll wake up the whole town, let alone Synor.*"

Pain grimaced, his canine face tight with thought. He had heard that name before.

"*What are you worried about? My brother's quick-tempered enough, but he sleeps like a troll. No worries!*"

"*You'll be the death of me one day...*" groaned Terak. The very sight of his distorted, glinting face in the orb made Ulyssis' blood churn. The privilege of Terak's death would be *his* some day, if he had things his way. The distance did nothing to quell his anger.

"*On my head the water runs, down onto my tummy-tums-*"

"*Right, that's it, no more singing. I've had it with you – get back inside!*"

The pastel shades flashed and swept into a different image at Terak's fading, tinny words. Before them, the face of another vampire came into sharp focus. Asleep and resting in an ample bed, eyes softly closed, the third creature with dramatically bright hair and plum-coloured dark lips said nothing – but the manifestation of his drowsy features brought a crooked grin to Pain's hairy face. Ulyssis saw this grin, one he remembered all too well.

"What is it, master?"

Pain's grin widened into a monstrous, open-mouthed gape; the dulled light flashing off his razor-sharp teeth sent a wave of momentary horror through Ulyssis. Surely he would have fled, or at least turned to the floor, had he not been so accustomed to his master's fiendish expressions of glee.

"I know this vampire. He is not the boy I have searched for, but now I see it…Synor, Heizenthly's son – yes, I see it now! This one has her magic. He would be a most useful ally in my quest to reclaim my island."

With his eyes, Ulyssis traced a line down his shoulder, along his arm to where his gnarled fingers brushed against the glowing orb. Synor's serene face still burned strongly within. "I am afraid he would do us little good, my lord. *Terak*," (He spat again at the mention of this name.) "has been training him to refrain from the use of aura magic. As such, he is not as powerful as his mother was."

Silence ripped through the air for a moment too long. Ulyssis was struck by Pain's eyes upon him once again. Strange, how eyes can have such physical impact upon someone.

"How do you know all this?"

*How do you know all this?*

Pain's spoken words echoed a second time inside Ulyssis' head, and there they struck him almost dumb. His own voice fled from him; he replied telepathically.

*When you called me, I was in Morfran, in Oouealena, and I saw them. I also saw the goblin you seek.*

Black claws scraped against the cold stone. *And you did not tell me? Ulyssis, you cursed fool!*

Pain was readying to strike him down, and Ulyssis fell back to avoid the blow. The orb, now devoid of energy, died once more and lay empty. Ulyssis summoned all the defiance left inside him and shouted; "I thought you knew everything!"

*Don't you ever, ever raise your voice to me, or I'll send you back to the hell you created for yourself! Beyond me and this temple, there is nothing for you, Ulyssis, and if you forget that, you will not live long enough to regret it! I could kill you, but you do not want to die. I cannot let you die. I will not kill you. You suffer enough for your sins in your current state. Get off the floor.*

Ulyssis obeyed, shaken once again. His face was devoid of emotion, saliva running down his lips and chin.

"I am sorry, master."

*You are forgiven. As long as I need you, Ulyssis, you will always be forgiven. Now, tell me what you learned about this boy.*

Nerves twitched beneath the inhuman creature's crimson, scarred flesh, giving him the appearance of a restless, itchy cat that had been skinned to the veins. His taut, slender muscles would have been elegant, were it not for the jagged ribcage, venomous claws and the deformed, ugly skull that dominated his physical body. All the horrors in Pain's soul bore down upon the ex-human, and shaped Ulyssis appearance accordingly.

"The boy is called Ramsey; orange skin, long nose, black hair, about five foot seven inches tall, visible scarring on the left hand. He stayed in a place called 'Andel's Tavern' with Terak in Morfran Town, and he is travelling north to the mountains, with a troll, to rescue Prince Morgan. At this rate, he may reach his goal within the week."

*Then we do not have much time. Ulyssis, you must go, quickly, and inform Kamror about this. He must go to his son's aid and eradicate that little opportunistic goblin before he reaches the mountains. Go at once, Ulyssis. And unless I direct you otherwise, come straight back when you have accomplished your mission. One more diversion, and you will answer for it in blood.*

\*\*\*

Despite the ebb in the snowstorm of previous days, the morning dawned grey and bleak over northern Grenamoya, like a sheet of frosted glass. The mountains, haggard and haphazard, loomed precariously towards the sleepy town of Morfran, as though bent by the storm, threatening to topple at the slightest change in the wind. The steep slopes leading up the base of the southernmost mountains were bare and craggy, with little opportunity for sight-seeing, still crusty with the remnants of ice and slush. Nonetheless, Ramsey decided to take a rest before daring to venture into one of the many damp-looking mountain mines, and found an uncomfortable, bare boulder on which to sit, to change his musty outfit and allow Theron to relax his limbs.

The cold, dry air hung all around them like stone, making it hard for Ramsey to feel motivated. His heart was heavy, though his steps were consistently brisk. While not walking, he displayed his instinctive quickness in his manner of dressing and investigating his various food packages; he darted behind a dry thicket to change his trousers and remove his shirt, returning to Theron with the sturdy, leather tunic firmly in place over his torso. Its fit was remarkably close.

"So, what do you think? Fashionable, aren't I?" he invited, giving a mock twirl and setting his hands on his pelvis. "Does this suit me?"

"If you want my honest opinion," began Theron, smiling broadly, as was his manner. "I'd say that...earthy colours suit you, is what I'd say."

"Great."

Ramsey ran his fingertips down the front of his tight tunic, admiring the firm, tough feel of the brown leather. For an instant, he became distracted, and his thoughts wandered several paces away from where he stood, as though he were looking at himself from a distance, and feeling unsure about what he saw. He was certain that he did not resemble a warrior. Anything heavier than leather would have weighed him down, so steel or chain-mail or dragon scale (to be ironic) would have hindered his slender frame.

444

He felt secure enough with his current tunic, and tried not to dwell on the fact that he was small, skinny and easily bruised.

"Don't do that, Theron – they're for your own good."

Theron glanced up sharply at the sound of Ramsey's voice, like a startled dog caught in the middle of chewing its master's slippers. With a resigned huff, he stopped harassing the bandage on his foreleg and turned his attention to the mottled ground. "I'm sorry to be holding you up, Ramsey. It won't be long before I'll be better. The doctor said that I only need a day or two, and I can take these things off."

"Yeah, well, leave them on for the meantime. I'm not prepared to go marching all the way back to the town to get you fixed up, and there is absolutely *no* way that I'll wait around for you if your legs fall off. I've come too far to go back now."

Theron looked towards the east, where the sun had risen boldly over the horizon. It seemed to spite the morning's gloom with its frail rays of pink light. "If my mum could see me now...I don't know what she'd say, but I know she'd be surprised." Ramsey sat himself back down on his miserly boulder and pulled a black shirt on over his head. "And she would be proud of me for following you and believing in you. And she'd be angry over these stupid injured legs," he grumbled, raising his two bandaged limbs, "and she'd tell me to be more careful of myself. But I don't really mind, not as long as I'm helping you."

He never looked at Ramsey as he spoke, staring instead at the faint clouds taking form in the east like streamlined, rosy fish.

"Isn't it amazing what they can do with medicine? Ever since that doctor had a look at me, I've felt loads better. It's like magic or something."

"'S not magic," mumbled Ramsey from the rumpled collar of his shirt. Theron laid his head down on his huge paws and looked benignly at the goblin; Ramsey straightened his clothes, took a sandwich from one of the many packets inside his bag, and leant his elbows on his knees. "It's cleverness. I've always been hopeless at anything medical, but...well, the vampires are like the elves," he stated, instantly realising that he had picked up on Terak's words from that very morning. "They can heal, they can work miracles without using magic. And they love one another without worrying about what other people might think or what-have-you. They care for one another. Which is more than I can say about my own people…"

"Oh Ramsey, don't feel that way."

"But it's true!" exclaimed Ramsey, sandwich still in hand. "My race is probably the most stuck-up, uncaring, pointless race on this whole island! Nobody cares for one another. I've spent my whole life in exile, living near a town filled with self-obsessed ninnies, who never even spare a thought for their fellow goblin. Nobody took me in. I was orphaned, my mum was long dead and my dad was taken from me, but nobody took me in. Nobody…nobody cared…and it's so, so sad, looking back on it all, when I see guys like Andel and Terak back in town, who treated me so well, not even knowing who I was. It's just…"

His fingers dug narrow trenches in the fresh bread as his grip tightened around the sandwich. He wasn't even sure why he had taken it from the bag, since he wasn't especially hungry. His nerves had been shaken. His fist was literally shaking.

"It's just *sad*. That's all it is. And this prince, this little boy, he has the chance to have what I never had. Just twelve years old, like I was when my father died – he's been separated from his dad, and I'm going out of my way to make sure he goes home, and gets to see his father again. I never had the chance to see my dad again. I won't let Morgan go through what I went through, royalty or no royalty."

He noted the irony in his statement as it left his lips. Morgan really wasn't a prince, he was not related to King Viktor – not even as distantly as Ramsey himself was. He was a child, though, and a child who had been taken from his father. That was what counted.

Theron held an expression like a thoughtful grizzly bear, his brown eyes set and glossy, wild and dark. "Something happened to you in that town," said he at length, distracting Ramsey from his sandwich yet again. "You aren't quite the same. I don't really know

446

why, but you just feel different. I admire you so much, though, and I'd follow you into the dragon's mouth if I had to."

Ramsey chewed plaintively on his sandwich (which on closer inspection turned out to be a chicken sandwich), his elbows still pivoted upon his bony knees. "Yeah. I know you would."

A flock of clouds drifted overhead, barely distinguishable from the murky, grey flood of bare sky. A thin shaft of lemon-tinted light penetrated the dark from the east, casting a sharp, sickly line up the side of the tallest mountain. They didn't know how early it was, but once they entered the mountain tunnel, everything would be dark, and time would not matter until they emerged at the other side.

Theron knew they would make it – of all the strange, new experiences he had endured on his travels with Ramsey, being underground, inside a mountain no less, certainly sounded like the most unfamiliar. Goblin and troll ancestry had its roots somewhere in the bowels of Grenamoya's great mountains, but thousands of years above ground in more favourable environments had stripped them of their instincts.

"It's funny," coughed Ramsey, having finished his sandwich. "I know I'm almost there, and that I'll probably be holding that twelve-year-old kid in my arms before long, but I feel as though I'm going to my death all the same. Does that sound funny to you?"

Theron sighed. He stood to stretch his stiff legs. "I'm scared too, Ramsey, but I couldn't live with myself if I let you go on alone. I'm here, for what I'm worth in this state…"

"You're worth more than all the scales in King Viktor's royal vault," announced the goblin as he, too, stood for a stretch. He rubbed his lower back ruefully, as though something with very large teeth had bitten him there. "No, scratch that – it sounds too sentimental. But all the same, I appreciate your help. A whole lot." He smiled, hoisting his new, black bag onto his shoulders, his sword tucked safely into his belt. "Thanks."

The gaping blackness of the mountain tunnel stretched towards them like fingers, pulling them into the dark. From the outside, the passage looked wide and tall enough to accommodate Ramsey and Theron walking side by side, but still Ramsey struck out in front, his troll companion following in his usual doting manner. There was no rank stench of death, no hint of an ambush – just the usual murky, moist smell so often associated with underground tunnels. The smell, Ramsey hoped, indicated that there was water trapped somewhere inside the mountain, which would certainly be appreciated after wandering for days in the dark. If they made it that far.

Judging the nearest cavern to be as acceptable as any, they marched forth, into the mountain, under the teetering cliffs of black stone – onwards through the damp mine, determination in their hearts. They had only been walking for under two minutes when the vague light of the morning was severed completely, leaving them in the pitch blackness, with only one another's breathing to determine which way they were walking. Ramsey gave up on movement altogether, and was promptly trampled by one of Theron's heavy paws.

"Yeow!"

"Oh! Ramsey, is that you?"

"Who else could it possibly be? Theron, get your damn foot off my body!"

"Sorry, sorry. So…what should we do now?"

He heard Ramsey cough. "How should I know? Give me a minute."

Their voices echoed up and down and round and back again, striking their ears from all directions. Theron moved back, and slumped awkwardly against something cold and hard and vertical, which he assumed to be the wall of the tunnel. He had thought that the passage was wider, mere moments ago.

He heard what sounded like Ramsey pacing, but it was more likely that the goblin was hopping on the spot, as he tended to do when aggravated. Theron couldn't even see the white of the bandage on his foreleg. The acute, desperate depth of pure blackness was astounding. Not a sliver of light broke through the solid, lumpy rock.

"Theron? Is this you?"

"I'm over here."

Their voices sounded from several metres apart, echoing back and forth like panicked bats.

"...How did you get all the way back there?"

"I haven't moved, Ramsey."

There was a scuffling noise, and Theron felt Ramsey's small presence draw nearer. A cold, bony hand touched his rough bandage. A sigh of relief. "Great, there you are. Now..." Ramsey paused again, pursing his lips under the cloak of icy black that covered them. He heard a tiny, wet noise; Theron had blinked. "I can hear you all right. As long as we stay close together, we'll manage. Stay near me, 'Kay?"

"But how can I tell where you're moving?" Theron's deeper voice rumbled along the tunnel and answered them once before rattling away into the unknown. It was impossible to tell where they were. Ramsey took hold of Theron's broad chest, pulling firmly on the damp fur.

"I'll guide you along, so we won't get separated. Now...the vampires would have told me if these passages were dangerous, but all the same, I think we should keep our voices low, unless we lose one another."

"All right."

Theron padded along quietly behind Ramsey, guided by frequent, sharp tugs on his fur, which would have felt painful had his skin not been so thick. Ramsey was very small and slight and fragile to look at, but his brief moments of strength and courage lit a warming fire in Theron's heart, a fire that burned with his own courage, and the instinct to survive.

His sharp eyes, and the sharper eyes of his small friend, could detect no movement in the gloom. Some other instinct drove them onwards, upwards, downwards, sometimes almost backwards, wherever their invisible path led them. They felt the walls, but found no complex network of twists and turns, no tunnel to follow except one – and they forced themselves to be fearless.

The cold, murky ground dug into their bare feet, sometimes smooth and lumpy like cobbles, sometimes littered with shards of broken rock. Every now and again, they would hear movement and feel the cold rush of tiny animals around their ankles. The rocks creaked, and however the travellers turned, left, right, up or down, the faint sound of running water grew nearer, sometimes seeming to be on the other side of the very walls. The trickling sound soon became annoying, though, as most things did to Ramsey. It would have been rather pleasant, but he was stuck in a pitch black tunnel, not knowing where it might emerge, and he could not bear to think about bathrooms.

They paced through the foul pitch, which seemed to draw ever closer until it touched their faces and licked at their shivering bodies. Something sharp and hard crunched against Ramsey's right arm, and he cried out, releasing his hold on Theron to grip his wound. The tunnel was turning again – this time to the north. They had swerved and careened around so many times during hours of mindless wandering that Ramsey wasn't exactly sure which way they were headed. He just prayed that the tunnel wouldn't lead them to a dead end and force them to march all the way back to try another passage.

"I wish I knew what time it is," mused Theron harmlessly, voicing Ramsey's own thoughts so acutely that the goblin fell back against the hard wall. "Oh, I hate not seeing the sunset. I've always loved sunsets."

"The sunrise was pretty good this morning," added Ramsey, feeling his way across the wall, and eventually sitting down near a patch of icy damp. "Sunrises are always good. I can still remember…feels like decades ago now. I can remember looking out of my tree-house every morning to watch the sun rising over the island. I guess sunsets are more romantic and everything, but sunrises have their own charms, as well."

"My mum loved sunrises. She said that sunrises were beautiful because they had all her favourite colours mixed together." Ramsey heard Theron moving in the dark, and felt the heavy movement of air that indicated that the troll had laid himself down nearby. "It must be night time. I'm so tired already."

"You never know. Maybe it's the effect of constant darkness, making us feel prematurely exhausted. We have been walking almost solidly since dawn, remember."

Ramsey stifled a yawn; Theron mumbled lethargically, the sound of his shifting paws scraping through the stillness. Even in the depths of blackness, where Ramsey could see no more clearly whether his eyes were open or closed, he felt himself drifting into uncomfortable sleep. His head was ringing with silence, the constant, damp sound of water keeping him on the brink of consciousness until it died in the dark.

He could feel Theron breathing at his side, the cold, bristly wall of fur rising and falling against his knee. He could not tell if the troll was asleep, as Theron's breathing was naturally slow and deep. Not the vaguest glint of warm eyes penetrated the thick air.

His pack served as a somewhat awkward pillow, and he curled his toes, drawing his feet near to his body. The squelch of his own saliva in his throat was louder than the cobra dragon's cry. In pure darkness, in the depths of silence where no comforts were near; truly this was the perfect place to live out a futile, troubled existence. Months ago, when he had lived all alone, he would have paid handsomely for such solitude. Now, it choked him.

He dreamed vividly that night, the colours searing his already forgetful mind, stabbing his consciousness with orange, red, green, blue – all the colours he remembered, which felt strangely incredible in the emptiness. A male goblin stood tall and proud before him, wearing a finely crafted suit of armour with a red snake upon the mailed chest. He could not tell if the goblin was himself or his father. Either way, the figure soon vanished, and a huge tide of green, filthy light poured from the very place it had stood, and a scream sliced the sickly clouds, distorted and frantic, stemming from all around. He felt himself running, he could see the dream moving past him. The clouds descended like toxic smoke and constricted his lungs, amplifying the scream until it became unbearable.

451

"I don't know what I'm doing..." he heard himself say, though nobody was near. "I don't know where I'm supposed to be going..."

Groping through the unknown, the smog devoured his searching hands and he fell to his knees, covering his ears. He felt something unnatural against his left ear, and wrenched his hand away to see that the flesh was rotting from his fingers.

"No, I don't know what I'm meant to be doing!" he called to the dark, his voice thin and brittle like dead leaves. "I've got to find the prince!"

Hands on his back; thin, skeletal hands, but warm and tender. He was pulled to his feet. His father, nearly identical in appearance to himself, yet stronger in the face, loomed from the darkness. It billowed angrily around him, ready to strike and close in once more.

"I've got to find the prince!" Seven years – seven years of anguish and painful loneliness, desperate for one last chance to speak with his father, and that was all he could say. "I don't know where I'm going."

*We only hurt you because we love you...*

Despair shot through him like shattered glass. His father could not answer him while the other voice continued to speak. Ramsey could think of nothing else but his aimless questions – his voice faded into the background, even as he felt his lips move. Shouting did not help. "I don't know what I'm doing!"

*We must protect you, little boy. You have no mum and dad, do you?*

His voice burst out of him as sharp and stuttering as a sneeze, but he found strength within it to pull himself free. "No! No, I had a dad! My dad was still alive! You took me from him!" He choked, his eyes stinging with the toxins in the air. His father looked at him, *beyond* him – a fraction shorter than Ramsey, with creases at the corners of his eyes and mouth, glowing through the murky shroud like a burning star.

It nagged at him again. "I don't know where I am!"

*Lie down and be silent! We shall beat you again if you don't stay your tongue!*

"No..."

*Orphan boys die every day! Nobody will miss such a worthless life!*

"No! You have no power over me! You're not real!" He spun around, the darkness thickening overhead. "Dad!" His father gazed at Ramsey through bland, emotionless, brown eyes. "Dad, please...! I don't know what I'm looking for!"

"It doesn't take twelve years for a father to love his son. It takes root from the start, and is slow to die once it is there. The love for a precious child is divine indeed."

Ramsey stared. The smoke filled his chest, sickness rising in his stomach. He was too nauseated to stand, but refused to fall. His heartbeat was mad and painful inside him.

"In all this time...you've never said a word to me. Please – no, don't go! I don't know where I'm going!"

But his father receded into the bursting, venom-coloured clouds, his expression never changing, even as he muttered; "You will understand one day."

"No, please don't leave me!" He staggered forward. Something snagged his legs and he fell face-down onto the crumbled, black earth beneath an endless, rancid sky, his face smeared and stinging. "Not again! Please!"

It all burst in a shudder of white and sapphire, then burned strongly black behind closed eyelids, and everything crashed to a throttling halt. He felt cold, still air against his cheeks and gasped. He opened his eyes with a start. As he did so, something flashed pale in front of his face – some sort of small, moist animal, which let out a shriek and scrambled away through the dark. He could see nothing.

"Theron!"

He groped in a blissful blackness devoid of smoke, and his reach fell upon two furry cheeks and a damp nose, close at his side. "It's all right, Ramsey. I'm here." Ramsey clung to him like a toddler to its favourite blanket, feeling the grimy fur between his fingers, and wishing to see that comforting face for just a moment. He felt absurd and ashamed of himself, but even in the dark he could not hide his distress. "You were dreaming, Ramsey. I heard you groaning something rotten."

Still holding tightly to the fur with his right hand, Ramsey touched his own clammy face with the other, to confirm that his skin was intact. "Damn it, I'm sorry…how long was I asleep for?"

"Not an hour," came the close response, deep and cherished. "What were you dreaming about?"

"Just things." Ramsey replied hastily and moved to look away, realising at the last minute that he could see nothing at all in any nameable direction. He slumped back against the bare stone and felt his stomach with one palm. "Things goblins dream about."

"Lady goblins?"

Ramsey snorted, hugging himself and smiling into the black air that flanked them. "Not likely, when I've got all this other stuff to focus on! I'm not one-track minded, Theron. I'm not sure what sort of things your species likes to think about in the pitch darkness, but I've got better things to worry about. I shouldn't have fallen asleep…" he added mournfully, his voice edged with annoyance. "We have no idea what sort of monsters could be lurking around."

"I'll stay awake to protect you," suggested Theron, feeling rather guilty than Ramsey had taken offence to his prior comment. No reply at all came from the goblin, apart from the soft rush of his breathing, which rasped in Theron's ears. The silence was far more disconcerting than it was comforting. He could smell the tiniest scent of mildew in the unmoving, dank air.

At long last, Ramsey said, in a transparent voice; "There was a man in my dream, in fact."

Theron perked curiously. "A man?"

"Not a human, of course – I mean a male goblin." The black bag rustled tiredly as Ramsey shifted his weight against it. "My dad."

Theron could not see, but the expression on Ramsey's obscured face somehow leaked into his words, and the troll became sombre and leaned close to the voice once more. "What happened in your dream, Ramsey?"

Ramsey smirked. It was a painful expression to form, even in pitch darkness. He reached out again, and nudged Theron with his knuckles. "I don't want to fall asleep here tonight, so I can tell you a story if you like. I've never really told anyone a story before, but I've got one here that's very close to home, even while I'm so far away from where I used to call 'home'. Do you want to listen?" Theron nodded, and Ramsey felt it with his wrist. "Well, then, it all began nineteen years ago, and even before then – it all started with an unmarried king and the girl who became my grandmother."

# Chapter Seventeen

# Ramsey, Theron And The Dragons

Through the empty, harmless night, Ramsey recalled to Theron all the details he had learned from Terak; the royal scandal, his father being driven away, the death of his mother and placement of himself in an orphanage that poisoned him with evil. By the time Ramsey had reached the moment of adoption by his biological father, Theron was shaking quietly as he listened, keeping fiercely close to his spindly friend in the dark. He didn't like all the sadness in this story; he didn't like it at all. And yet he couldn't close his ears to Ramsey's tale, as it flowed from the goblin's mouth without a hitch.

Ramsey's tone was sombre yet amazed, which was a peculiar combination. He seemed to discover the story anew with each spoken word. Revelations tickled his mind like remnants of his nightmare, so faint that he could barely focus on them long enough to work out what they were.

But somehow, he felt it – he had known some of the story before Terak had told him. And now he felt satisfied, yet he ached for more. So did Theron, but in the troll's case, he ached for a happy twist in the tale. None came. He grunted softly, looking at Ramsey though he could see nothing of the goblin's figure or features.

"A stranger knew more about me than I did," concluded Ramsey at last, many hours into his story, which had switched back and forth across an uncertain span of time with Ramsey's increasingly frustrated remembrances, and thus had taken very long to tell. "And all the pain I felt in my upper back was a big brand mark, of all things!"

"I think I saw it," ventured Theron, "when you had a bath in the lake, and I saw your back…it was something like a circle with a picture in it."

Ramsey smirked, realising that Theron could not read. "It's the number seventeen in a circle. And it's disturbing to find out that you had such a clear view of my body, too."

"No…! I-I didn't mean to look, and I only saw you from the back, and you were waist-deep in water, so-"

"Never mind." He reached out and patted Theron firmly on the snout. "It's in the past. Like lots of things. My dad, that orphanage, my life back in Merlock…"

"And my mum, and my forest home," added Theron.

Ramsey nodded; despite the darkness, such instinctive gestures were difficult to repress. "Yeah. I'm…well, it's partially my fault that the dragon attacked your forest in the first place, but Merlock got burned to the ground as well, so that leaves both of us without a home to return to. But nonetheless, we're here now, and we're almost at the end of it all. If we find our way out of this mountain I don't think I'll care any more, quite frankly." He stuck out one foot to feel around in the dark. A worn, cold slab of stone served as a convenient footrest. "I don't really want to go back at all."

Theron laid his head back down on his paws, having been alert all throughout Ramsey's story. "I know what you mean. That forest was all I had. And now, out here in the wild, anything less would feel very cramped."

There was a scuffling noise as Ramsey shifted into a more comfortable position. He opened the top of his pack and felt blindly inside, suddenly hungry and cold. His fingers fell upon various packets of food, several sets of clean clothes, and something cold and hard that seemed rectangular in shape. He couldn't see to investigate, and so retrieved the nearest item, which he identified as another sandwich. He pulled a few from the bag and set them on his lap, tucking in straight away with rampant hunger.

"Want some?" he offered through a mouthful of bread. "Sandwiches."

Theron smiled, flattered by the unexpected offer. "No, thank you," came the reply, accompanied by a low rush of breath. "I can go without eating for months, and you can't."

The grinding noise of Ramsey's small, sharp teeth grated through the mute blackness. "Must be handy, not needing to eat a lot. I mean, I can go for a good while without eating, but it doesn't help a goblin's figure to do that. I look worse than half of the zombies did back in Morfran Town."

"You do not," insisted Theron affectionately. He took a sniff at the air. "We trolls do most things slowly. We don't have to eat much, don't move around too much normally, don't think too much, talk slowly, reproduce very slowly – that's why there aren't many forest trolls like me any more. We do everything too slowly."

"I've heard crocodiles can do that. Go for ages without eating, I mean. And they live really long lives. So I guess that's a lesson for the lot of us." Ramsey took an invisible bite from his third sandwich, still gazing emptily straight ahead.

Theron laughed. "I was never this active before I met you. We aren't great travellers; at least we bigger trolls aren't. Other sorts travel, I think, but I wouldn't know."

"That doesn't stop you talking, though."

"No...it doesn't. Huh. That's weird, isn't it?"

"Yep. Certainly is."

Ramsey reached for another sandwich, and realised that the pile on his lap had diminished. Still hungry, he rummaged around inside his supply pack yet again to find anything edible. He wished that he had the tiniest flicker of light by which to see, so that he could investigate the rest of the food packets properly. In their current situation, he couldn't tell what anything was, and almost tried to 'open' one of his new shirts to feel what was inside. It was a miracle that he didn't rip it in two.

"Are you all right, Ramsey?"

"Yeah, just having a look in here. Not literally, given the circumstances," he added, not wanting Theron to take his answer the wrong way and cause more confusion. His fingertips brushed against something remarkably cold and round, like a perfectly polished stone. Intrigued, he grasped the smooth object in his right palm and withdrew it from the bag to have a better feel. Needless to say, he could not discern anything of its appearance. He rolled it idly between his fingers. It was quite heavy, about the size of a golf ball.

Probably another one of those strange vampire customs, he thought. Whatever it was, he hadn't noticed it on the first inspection of his bag.

He pinched it thoughtfully with his thin fingers. Before his very eyes, a tiny, burning light shattered the pitch black air. It stabbed into his retinas and he quickly shielded his face with his spare hand, jolting back against the cavern wall. Theron's head jerked in the direction of the yellow flame, and he stared through slitted eyes.

"Ramsey? What's that?"

"I don't know! I just found it in my bag." For a moment Ramsey was frightened, not knowing what the glinting light was or why it was there, but he opened his eyes, the tiny ball still held at arm's length. "I can hardly see a thing!"

Theron blinked sharply a few times, his vision fuzzy, the shape of the glowing orb imprinted behind his eyelids. The light was tiny, but uncomfortable and faintly alarming after the bliss of pure darkness. He shook himself and blinked again, resolutely. "It's pretty."

As abruptly as it had lighted, the glowing ball grew dim and fizzled away like a candle flame, leaving them in the dark once more. The dark seemed far more imposing and evil in the aftermath of momentary hope. Both troll and goblin breathed a sigh of frustration.

"Whatever it is, it's broken!" snapped Ramsey, casting the marble-like object away into the black with a dull *clang!* that shook the stone. "Damn it! We'll just have to carry on as we were, Theron. We've managed so far."

"It didn't even stay bright long enough for us to talk..." lamented Theron, resting back down upon his paws like a caged tiger. "I hate it down here. Trolls were never meant to be underground."

"I think you'll find that they were." Ramsey curled up into a tight ball, resolving to fall asleep and wake up in more pleasant surroundings. "And so were goblins. We've just come a long way, I guess. We've both got relatives who are probably mining away beneath some wretched mountain right now. So we should try to think about how they would act."

Something small and invisible scuttled along the tunnel, weaving its way between both travellers, and disappeared, seemingly in the way they had come. Neither one of them moved. "You don't want to know my relatives," replied Theron at last. "I never had many, and most of them were mad, or died strangely."

"And *my* only living relative is an ugly, fat guy who spends all day sitting on a shiny chair working out new ways to be useless. So let's never talk about any of them."

The sound of scratching and squeaking penetrated the darkness above their heads, like hundreds of minuscule, fluttering wings. Ramsey scrambled out of his ball formation and leapt to his feet to equip himself, but instead tripped over Theron's nearby foreleg and crumpled to the blackened floor. He shouted, Theron barked and leapt to attention, and together, blinded by the oppressive void, they gaped towards the ceiling, backing up against one another until they touched. Ramsey heard Theron say something, but it was lost amidst the noise, like rodents skittering across the cavern roof. The clang of Ramsey's sword against bare rock was swallowed by the shrieking.

"Stay close, Theron, don't lose me!"

The words had barely left his mouth when the whole cavern burst into glimmering, brilliant light, blinding them more severely than the total darkness. Ramsey cowered against Theron, who blinked up at the ceiling with his mouth agape, his fangs shining behind his hairy lips. Ramsey gasped and gripped his sword.

The burning blanket of tiny lights descended upon them like falling stars, and settled around them, illuminating their startled, weather-beaten faces. Ramsey stared at Theron through narrow eyes, and the troll gazed down from his splendid height, no less confused than his companion. The sparks separated, clustered, and some of them danced right in front of Ramsey's nose. They moved like tufts of dandelion caught in the breeze, and they radiated a comforting warmth that blushed Ramsey's skin. One glimmer even settled on the tip of his nose, and several others ventured to join it.

His vision finally focused upon them as they fluttered and buzzed like bees. They were tiny, glowing insects, so small and numerous that Ramsey could not really make out their physical shape. They might have been luminous bats, for all that he could see – intricate, winged bodies with lighted abdomens and shiny, beetle black eyes. Their combined energy revealed the entire chamber in which Ramsey and Theron had rested, and Theron himself turned to Ramsey, several hundred sparks flittering around his head.

"I don't think they will hurt us, Ramsey," he said, his whole face glowing absurdly with a halo of tiny creatures. The level of noise they made was incredible for their size. Ramsey couldn't help himself, and laughed out loud with pure relief.

"Come on, then!" He hopped to one side, then back again, and the tiny fluttering animals followed him. They stayed close to his skin, and some even settled in his hair. "These little things can light our way!"

462

"Do you think they'll stay with us?"

Ramsey tightened his lips, blinking towards the luminescent swarm that danced above their heads. "We'll take the chance. We haven't really got a choice, have we? Let's go."

With the benefit of sight, Ramsey and Theron found themselves in a peculiar cavern of dull rock, much taller than it was wide. The walls were cracked with patterns as complex as spider webs, and moisture shone through, trickling down the bare stone. Ramsey quickly lifted his bag onto his shoulders and marched ahead, striding past the gloomy walls that blinked yellow with the movement of the glowing insects. They hummed and whirred merrily, drawn to Ramsey like moths to a lantern, and Theron ambled behind, keeping a close eye on the goblin.

The jagged stone flashed at them from all sides, and the tunnel widened further, seeming to twist back on itself yet again. The travellers followed without question, not even venturing to speak as their shining escorts led them forward and danced around Ramsey's cheeks like burning gnats. Theron snorted a few of them away from his nose, and hurried along behind Ramsey until at last they strode side by side. Elusive, pale animals scuttled away from the swelling glow, keeping concealed in the shadows, their massive, globular eyes gleaming out from the dark.

Neither Ramsey nor Theron could hear running water over the sound of the glowing creatures, and yet they sensed it was nearby. The ground became slippery, almost resulting in an accident for Theron with his bandaged limbs, and was distinctly cold to the touch. The still air carried no stench, other than the dank, moist smell of old rock that had followed them since the previous morning.

At times, the air became stiff and thick, so that it was painful to breathe, and they had to take a rest. They passed through many separate chambers of damp stone, all connected along the single, twisting tunnel. Still, no other passages led away from their one route, and the pulsing swarm of creatures danced like miniature fires above them, waiting whenever the travellers rested for a while, and fluttering around the walls of the cavern.

Ramsey heaved a tired sigh. Theron found himself unwilling to rest, and paced around anxiously whenever the goblin decided to sit down. Ramsey quickly surrendered to his friend's urgency, and trudged ahead with wet footsteps, tiny lights leaping around his head.

Stalagmites erupted from the gnarled rock in these chambers, mirrored by stalactites along the ceiling, which jutted downwards like enormous fangs closing in around them. The smell of sulphur tickled Ramsey's nostrils, and he hurriedly covered his nose.

"Eeugh! Oh yuck. Theron, get over here!" The troll did as he was told, and moved alongside Ramsey at a comfortable pace; apparently he did not notice the smell. "Look, if this stink gets much worse, I say we go back, because if we're heading into some kind of…of…*sulphur mine*, I don't exactly want to continue."

"What smell, Ramsey?"

Ramsey's face fell, then became tight as he scrunched up his eyes, nose and mouth against the stench. "Oh, never mind! I forgot that you're probably too smelly to notice anything that smells less than twice as bad as yourself." He shook his head and coughed. "This stink just came out of nowhere. Scaless, I hope nothing bad has happened. It would be just my luck, you know, to come all this way, through fear and doubt and evading many creatures that wanted to eat me, just to be killed in the end by a bad smell!"

Theron hardly had time to laugh, for at that very moment, they emerged on a ridge of stalagmite teeth, and found themselves gazing into the most brilliantly-lit, tall, wide cavern in the whole of their journey. The ceiling had to be a hundred feet high, dripping with stalactites, and almost completely obscured by the dancing brilliance of thousands of glowing insects. Their rampant buzzing echoed around the massive cavern, and as they watched, the small animals that had lit their way departed, and fluttered away and upwards to join the flood of light high above.

Ramsey stared in complete and utter shock and amazement; Theron's gaze had fallen to the ground, where a massive silver pool, decked with tall rocks and a shimmering waterfall, took up the main body of the chamber. He snorted and smiled.

"Ramsey."

"What?" With a sniff, Ramsey turned back to Theron, his eyes wide with marvel.

"Look over there. There's the water we could hear." He pointed with his bandaged forepaw, grinning. The precipice they stood upon was like the enclosing lower jaw of an immense creature, and they shakily made their way down to the flat of the cavern floor, the desperate magnificence of the light blinding them whenever they looked up. The wet rock beneath their toes reflected the dazzling glow and their down-turned faces, and Ramsey laughed.

"We made it through those tunnels alive, Theron!"

"But where are we?"

Ramsey swallowed and rubbed his temples. He could no longer smell sulphur. "I haven't got a clue, so really, this hasn't helped at all. We're not at the other side, and as far as we know, maybe this path will never lead us out to the mountains. So..."

Something moist made a scuttling noise to their left, and they turned in a flash. From behind the ridged contours of a particularly large stalagmite, a pale, frog-like face emerged, with skin the colour of the vampires' and deep black eye pupils. They both stopped in their tracks. The little creature blinked massively at them, then crawled out from behind the rock, loping like a dog. Another similar animal squirmed out from behind the same formation, and suddenly the walls were swelling and dripping with animals, like insect larvae.

They crawled down from high above, some pulled themselves free of the grey lake and shook themselves dry. Their eyes were huge and dark, glimmering green like a cat's eyes under the sharp light. One ventured near to the two travellers. Its spindly toes were webbed, and along its neck, back, and elbows were beautiful, pale fins. Its tail was like that of a mermaid, yet slender like a snake. It was two feet tall, walked on all fours, and teeth protruded from between its scaly lips.

"Don't move," whispered Ramsey to Theron, his voice pulled taut. "We mustn't alarm them."

The animals in themselves were not threatening to look at, but it was the sheer number of them that prompted Ramsey to be wary. The entire cavern was so pale that the creatures gleamed like white marble, shiny and stiff. Ramsey tried his friendliest smile, which under the circumstances was hard to muster. He only succeeded in looking ill.

"Hello," he greeted tentatively, to test their reaction. They just gaped at him, drawing nearer and blinking like owls. "Um...my name is Ramsey, and this is my friend, Theron. We are trying to get to the mountains, so...um...is this the...er...right way?" Theron shook his head, and Ramsey grumbled at him. "I'm trying my best!" he hissed.

"You are going right way," said the creature in a tightly-strung, fairly high-pitched voice. Its skin was moist like a frog's, but on closer inspection, its face was more reptilian. "Why you come here? Get out of morlona's cavern!" A clamour of agreeing, scratchy voices chimed from the walls and the lakeside and all around, and Ramsey took a step back. "You leave, now!"

"But we're not doing any harm," reasoned Theron, despite Ramsey's moan of despair. "Can you please tell us the way out? We don't know where to go."

The small, aggravated animal pointed starkly towards the back of the huge, rocky cavern – a wide, dark tunnel, also fringed with stalagmite teeth, led away from the bright chamber, and into the dark once more. Ramsey tensed. They would be awfully lucky if they could entice their glowing insect escorts back down from the ceiling. "It's that way! You leave, now, and let us be!"

"But we're not doing anything!" growled Theron, looming tall over the frantic, wet animal. Ramsey cringed and mumbled something in the troll's direction, but Theron did not notice. The creature was staring upwards with visible fear. After all, Theron was huge, especially when compared with something that stood barely higher than his ankle. "Can you give us some more help that that? We are going to rescue a prince from a dragon."

"Cobra dragon? Ha!" said the little animal, its twelve toes all scratching against the ground at once. "You have no chance against cobra dragon! Morlona dragon, we much smaller, and we live in mountain first! Then cobra dragon come and take over mountains so morlonas cannot go outside! Forced to live underground!" It scratched and growled, the other small dragons crowding behind it. Under Theron's severe expression, the dragon's dark eyes flashed to the ground and it huffed its bony chest. "You go to get cobra dragon, then morlonas are grateful. Go through tunnel, then straight on until you reach the fork, go left, and-"

Theron sat down on his haunches. "Is it very far?"

"Morlonas go along path many times."

Ramsey shrugged, resigned to leaving the conversation to Theron for a change. With his hands in his pockets, he looked around, and walked idly towards the side of the lake, which glowed white and silver under the light from the ceiling. The other small dragons watched him intently as he moved, but did not flee or attempt to hurt him. He raised an eyebrow as a group of them dove back into the lake with a resolute *splash!*, and stared around curiously, while only half listening to Theron's deep voice. He prayed that everything would go smoothly for once.

"No! No, no, no! No morlona will lead you through mountain, it too dangerous for us! We die, the snakes and snake dragons kill morlonas."

"We would be safer with a guide than without one."

"Yes, but you are big, strong troll! Very big, you much safer. Morlona, we killed by cobra dragon, and we killed by basilisks living in mountains, in dark places! Basilisks very small snakes, no problem for big troll."

Ramsey eyed the lake water questionably. Truth be told, he was very thirsty, but with a thought as to exactly how much of the dragons' daily life was spent in it, he declined from taking a drink. He decided that uncomfortable thirst was preferable to a mouthful of dirty water.

He stared at his own reflection, amusedly watching the silhouettes of the fish-like dragons converging beneath the surface.

No doubt, they were looking up at him to determine how dangerous he was. Much as he would have liked to, he could see no nearby stones small enough for him to throw into the water. Then again, maybe it was better not to provoke these creatures, especially when they were on the verge of offering help. Funnily enough, these 'morlonas' did not faze him. Very little ever fazed him anymore.

It was then that he noticed another pale dragon sitting at the side of the lake, atop a smooth, flat stone the size of generous dinner plate. This dragon was quite separate from the others, and had apparently not reacted to his and Theron's arrival at all. Its face was turned away from Ramsey, and its tail was coiled around its skeletal body. Ramsey could not explain why he felt the urge to take a better look. His hereditary curiosity spurred him on, and he crawled around to the other side.

"But please, for the sake of the prince."

"No! Only crazy morlona would go and risk life out in the mountains! Very risky, big cobra dragon takes all life! Doesn't matter if it dragon or not! Cobra dragon kills everything, and we safe here. You kill dragon, you have our thanks, but we not go out there."

Ramsey found himself gazing down upon a dragon that was more bones than flesh, curled up almost irritably on the small plateau, its bulbous eyes closed. Like its fellow creatures, it had fins on its tail, elbows and back, as thin and fragile as a fish's, and a small crest on the back of its head, which lay flat against its neck in sleep. It had a large head, and protruding, triangular shoulder blades sprouted from its white skin, to either side of its clearly-defined vertebrae. Long claws, three toes on each foot, were curled up beneath it as it dozed.

Unnerved, and worried that it might be dead, Ramsey defied all of his cautious instincts and tapped the animal on the tip of its blunt snout. It leapt to attention and spat aggressively at him.

"*Bakka!*" it snarled, rising from the flat stone and promptly turning to face the other way. Strangely, it seemed to keep its eyes closed. He was certain that small, water-dwelling cave dragons didn't make random exclamations in their sleep. Then again, based

468

on his recent display of dream-related motions, he couldn't be sure. It settled on the rock with a rattling, dry gasp, and some of the nearby dragons leered close for a look, their big eyes blinking like dead moons.

Once more defying his better instincts, Ramsey reached out to nudge the animal in the ribs. He didn't know what 'bakka' meant, but he was sure it didn't mean anything good. "Hello," he greeted with as strong a tone as he could muster. "I just wanted to see if there was anything wrong with-"

The creature whirled around and snapped at him again, its curved teeth inches from his arm, and he backed away at last. He stared down at the little animal as it twitched and grumbled in its vaguely manic way. Then he realised that its eyes were open; it was blinking right in front of him, but its eyes were as blank as the transparent white of its eyelids. Milky, glistening orbs set in its head, gleaming beneath the yellow light. It was shouting in a direction that was slightly to Ramsey's right. The little dragon was blind.

"Ramsey, are you all right?" asked Theron with a sigh, leaning on his bandaged legs with some discomfort. He too looked at the animal then, and his expression merged into something akin to sorrowful comprehension. "I thought we said that we wouldn't aggravate them."

"Yeah, well, I just wanted to see if the little guy was Okay," protested Ramsey, blatantly ignoring the barrage of strange words that poured from the blind creature. "Can't win them all. You had any luck over there?"

"Not really...all I can get is directions, and then the dragon got half-way through those, and forgot where to go next. So I don't know what we can do from here. We can't stay here." All around them, in an ever-closing circle of moist, leathery hide and delicate fins, the dragons were observing them with heightened interest, though not in a dangerous manner. Most of them were regarding Theron with some criticism. "We're making them upset."

"Damn right you making upset!" shrieked the little blind dragon, now leaping up and down on the wet ground at Ramsey's

feet. It was still aiming its empty gaze somewhere to Ramsey's right, in-between him and Theron. "You waking Blanoka up, Blanoka is not appreciating that! Get away from Blanoka, bakka!"

"All right, settle down!" Ramsey edged away, narrowly keeping an inch away from the irate creature, who swiped madly at the air in front of his damp face. Theron shuffled aside, strangely alarmed by the dragon's minuscule advance. The others were not reacting in such a way, and now seemed entirely friendly in comparison. In fact, the other dragons watched the blind Blanoka with deep apprehension. "Look, I didn't mean anything by it."

"Bakka! Get away from Blanoka, go away, get away!" Tripping on a rock, the dragon fell on his face and squawked with pain. The other dragons began to snigger. He rose to his thin legs, trembling like a fawn. "Be shutting up, and get rid of smelly newcomers!" he said, his gaze now firmly on Ramsey. "Smelly, smelly, smelly!"

Ramsey stuck his hands on his hips, not caring that the beast could not see. "I do not smell!" said he, turning to Theron for support. "We've been through more than any of you will ever go through while stuck in this mountain, and all we want is some help! I'm trying to rescue one of my fellow goblins from a dragon, the same dragon that apparently drove you into this mountain in the first place!"

"Find your own way out!" said another dragon, ignoring Blanoka. "Not our concern!"

"But we don't have time to be wandering in the dark for days and days!" Ramsey's fists were clenched against his chest. "We may already be too late!"

A sudden flash of inspiration struck him, and he reached into the large bag that he still carried on his back. As he moved, some of the dragons finally noticed the sharp sword hanging at his belt, and they did not like it at all. Fins bristled like wrinkling paper in the gaping cavern.

The light over their heads grew and pulsed, the wet chamber rocks below gleaming like seashells. Ramsey found a packet of unidentified food in his pack, and held it out towards them.

"I can give you food, and...and anything else that I can spare! Please, we need someone to get us through the mountain, just until we reach the other side, and we won't ask for anything else. Please."

"Food?" inquired one dragon with interest, cocking its amphibian head. "What food? Good food?"

"Shiny things!" said another, drawing close to Ramsey and admiring the bracelet of green and blue stones that hung around the goblin's thin ankle. "Got more shiny things, have you?"

"Um...I don't really think so, but- no, you can't have that bracelet! It would be bad luck if I took it off." Theron tensed, readying himself to defend Ramsey if need be. The dragons swallowed every movement and every word that crossed Ramsey's lips. Theron sat down again, resting his heavy backside with a huff. Blanoka felt him sit down, and scuttled towards him, his pink mouth agape like a snake about to swallow its prey. "I don't really know how I'd survive, but I can't sacrifice a twelve-year-old boy for my own benefit, so if one of you will come with us, I'll give you all the food that's in my pack."

Silence.

"Please, it's urgent!"

"No!" said the small dragon that Theron had spoken to, its wet feet flapping on the stone. "Suicidal mission, we get killed! Basilisks kill and eat many dragons, we no know how many are eaten, or where basilisks live! Cannot risk losing clan to the evil snakes!"

"I'll fight off anything that comes near," contributed Theron in his steady, deep tone. "We will all be safe."

"No! Basilisks tiny, but can kill with a single look in the dark, and morlonas see in the dark – one look, then dead! If I had a million chillens, I'd not give them to you to put in danger!"

"This is completely mad," mourned Ramsey, one hand over his eyes. "Theron, let's give this up. We managed before, we'll manage again. No point in bothering with such selfish cave creatures, anyway! Some thanks we get, for going off to kill your greatest enemy!"

"Food?" piped up the small dragon known as Blanoka, his blue crest twitching like a fish. "You have food?" None of the other dragons paid any attention, but Ramsey and Theron turned with a start. The blind creature was gazing distantly in a direction where nothing was, coiling his body like a cat readying to spring.

"Yes, we have food..." began Ramsey, his voice quiet and curious. Theron watched as the goblin moved closer to the little animal. "And we can offer you all that we have, and then you can come straight back here, and we'll protect you."

"Blanoka is liking the sound of this offer, smelly ones," said the dragon, snorting to illustrate his point. "Other morlonas cruel to Blanoka, laugh at him! Blanoka is brave, Blanoka will go with you when they too afraid!" The other animals murmured collective sounds of displeasure, and Blanoka laughed aloud with a gaping, sharp mouth. "Blanoka gets food, and Blanoka has not eaten for a week! Leave this stupid place! Blanoka will be showing you the way! Blanoka is your best choice!"

"Theron agrees," said Theron. Ramsey smirked.

"Blanoka will say farewell to cruel morlonas! Nasty morlonas never give Blanoka food, for he is blind!"

Ramsey could feel his optimism draining away. Surely this was not their ideal guide for such an important part of their journey, but judging from the blank faces of the surrounding dragons, he and Theron had no choice. This blind creature was certain to test his patience. "So, will you come with us or not?"

"Are you stupid, stupid head?" he responded, his pale eyes gleaming like round eggs. "Blanoka is saying yes, yes, Blanoka will come!"

"If Blanoka knows what's good for him," growled Ramsey right back, his teeth clenched, "he will stop bloody well speaking in the *third* person."

"Do not be making fun of Blanoka's mannerisms!"

Ramsey sagged and slumped his heavy shoulders, weighed down by the bag on his back. "Right-ho, I guess we'll have to work on that one...so, when can we get going?"

"Now!" replied the blind dragon enthusiastically. "Blanoka will go now! Blanoka is not being afraid! Blanoka is far braver than other morlonas, for other morlonas can be killed by bad snakes! Blanoka cannot see, for he is blind! Blanoka is safe from their evil eyes!"

A thin sort of pessimistic recognition sprouted within Ramsey. Of course – if the dragon could not see, then a basilisk's glare in the dark was not a threat. He still didn't like the concept of those most ancient of deadly snakes, but if he had no choice, he would rather take the risk with a guide that would get bitten well in advance of him or Theron. He was no longer the grouch who had left Merlock with money in mind, but still, his own survival counted if he was to rescue Morgan. He moved to extend his hand, but remembered quickly that Blanoka could not see.

"Um, right, then...shall we go?"

Theron stood up. "Maybe he wants to say goodbye to his family," he suggested. Blanoka twitched like a vine.

"No, Blanoka is not having anyone worth saying goodbye to! We get going now, save time, Blanoka gets his food!" The dragon then set off in a random direction, his head held high and his blind eyes wetly blinking. Ramsey and Theron stayed put, watching Blanoka's erratic movements, until, with a brief sniff at the ground and a flutter of his fins, the dragon aimed himself at the gaping tunnel. Ramsey and Theron consented to follow, neither one of them looking back. "It being this way! You see, Blanoka knows his way! But Blanoka cannot see, for he is blind!"

Ramsey leaned close to his hairy companion and whispered; "I think this little guy is going to give me a serious relapse with my bloody incurable madness."

"It won't be so bad." Theron smiled, though deep inside, the goblin's words had sent frost through his belly. It had been distressing enough to hear about Ramsey's traumatic childhood. The news of Ramsey's illness had devastated Theron, who vowed to keep his feelings under wraps, at least until the two of them were safely at home; if either one of them found a home at the end of the day.

If only they could find Prince Morgan alive and well, and take him home.

Theron felt something tighten in his chest. Ramsey was not looking at him. From somewhere up ahead, a crack and an echoing shout of "Bakka! Who is putting pointy rock there? Bakka, *bakka*!" whisked him back to the cold task at hand, as the light retreated, and blackness swallowed them like a monstrous toad.

***

From the morlona cavern onwards, the mountain tunnels took on a twisted nature, in a very literal sense. The passages wound this way and that, closing in on themselves and one another, branching out from their wide, damp tunnel, into narrow openings that were far more wet and smelled like mould. Blanoka the cave dragon scuffled noisily ahead, shining like a splash of water in the faint flicker of light from stray insects that clung to the walls. Accustomed to the gloom once more, Ramsey and Theron followed with uncertainty and curiosity at the same time, constantly listening for the vaguest echo of a basilisk's hiss. The network of mountain tunnels had the atmosphere of a snake, like an emaciated constrictor that was attempting to devour itself.

Ramsey hugged himself hopelessly, grateful for the warmth of his thick tunic and his long-sleeved black shirt. His bare feet were swollen and bloody, so it was just as well that he had lost all feeling in them. Theron's breath gushed through the air around them, though he did his utmost to remain quiet. From up ahead, Blanoka skittered through the dark, his snout to the ground and his ratty tail in the air, his fins swishing like fleshy flags.

"This way!" he would shout every now and again, at the same volume regardless of whether they were near or far. "Not being long now, Blanoka will show you the way! You must be being keeping of your promise to Blanoka!  Blanoka does not being trusting goblins!"

Ramsey puffed angrily from between his chapped lips. "Charming."

"Never be trusting goblins," said Blanoka to no-one in particular, his voice low but frantic nonetheless.  Theron shook his head like a horse, the faint light shining along his back and mane. The air was becoming thinner, and at last, they seemed to be ascending on a near-constant basis.  Their dark path was currently sharp and slippery, and both Ramsey and Theron had a hard time climbing it with nothing to stabilise them.  Blanoka went onward, not sparing a blind glance, up into the cold, harsh air. "Come on, come on!  No use being lagging behind!"

"No use being *nagging*, either!" retorted Ramsey from somewhere further down the sloping tunnel, unaware of whether he was lying on his back or on his stomach.  All he knew was that most of his clothing was wet.  Blanoka snapped at him to hurry up, so he decided to comply with as little fuss as possible, encouraging Theron, who was even further behind.  Perched like a lofty cat upon a dark shelf, Blanoka looked down at them with a superior, unseeing expression on his white face.  Long, webbed toes and scaly feet had ensured him an easy climb.

"Hurry up, hurry up!" insisted Blanoka, producing a loud sniff that echoed down the steep tunnel. "Blanoka will not be waiting here forever!  Being hurried up, now, stupid-heads!"

"*You*," snapped Ramsey as he scrambled his way to the peak of the moist slope, "are the most annoying, loud, ugly little-" It was then that he noticed the cold, wispy air stroking his cheeks, and the sallow, blue glow of the night sky bearing down upon his bright skin.  He swallowed, he turned, and realised that he was out in the open.  The wind ruffled his hair and tore at his clothes; a particularly frigid, mountainous wind.  Blanoka looked blindly up at him with a toothy grimace. "…little…"

"Annoying, loud, ugly little what?" prompted the small dragon in his high-pitched, erratic voice. "What are you being wanting to say to Blanoka, hmm?"

"Theron!" Ramsey scurried part-way back down the dark slope and shouted to his companion. The troll was still struggling to climb with two bandaged legs. "We've made it, Theron, we're outside! We're at the top!"

"Already?" came Theron's disbelieving response.

"Yes! Yes, we're here! Theron, come on, hurry up! The view is amazing!"

Blanoka cleared his throat nasally. "So, is Blanoka doing a good job?"

Practically jumping for joy, Ramsey steadied his steps and fell back against the bare rock face. Theron's loud grunting edged nearer with every breath, resonating up and down and back through the murky cavern. "I thought...I didn't think we were this close," marvelled Ramsey, one hand in his hair, gasping with excitement. "I thought we'd be wandering for days!"

"Three quarters of a day," corrected the dragon with a hiss. "It not taking long time for Blanoka to bring you here. Blanoka is taking the short way around, always."

"Ah, right. Thanks." Ramsey bent to touch Blanoka's snout, but the dragon somehow sensed his movements and shied away with a reproachful, empty gaze. "I guess we haven't come far, but I did promise you my food, so I'll give that to you now."

"That is being good. Hurrying up!"

Ramsey fell to his knees to fish some food out of his too-heavy supply pack. Maybe it was a good thing to give this cave dragon his food – at least his bag would be much lighter. He tried to think of it in that manner, and not as the unnecessary depletion of provisions for the sake of a six-hour wander through a mountain.

With a final huff, Theron pulled himself free of the narrow tunnel and shook his whole body like a wet dog. Ramsey paid this no heed, for he was too well accustomed to Theron's habits; Blanoka, on the other hand, seemed able to interpret the actions of those around him, and was unimpressed by the shaking.

They stood precariously upon a rather narrow precipice of rock that shone midnight blue under the glow of the moon. Lost somewhere amidst a forest of mountains, their cliff towered high above many of these, giving the travellers a generous view of the jagged landscape. It was as though they had stepped forth into a different world, one made of sharp peaks and stone instead of the grassy, rolling plains of Oouealena that they had left behind. All they could see was grey for miles and miles, stretching north, and to the east and west like the spines of a dragon; armour-plated and impenetrable, and unerringly cold and barren.

The night sky was teeming with stars that glittered as brightly as the tiny insects of the mountain. The moon was motionless and watery in the sky, as though somebody had just painted it onto the dark canvas of sky and scattered diamond dust all around. Theron saw Ramsey before him, surrounded by blue and a halo of light, and breathed a rusty sigh. To feel the moving air in one's lungs was a blessing.

Blanoka eagerly tucked into the food items that Ramsey laid out before him; some sandwiches of various sorts, some more rice delicacies and several soft, round things that smelled of sugar. The dragon eagerly took these, and set about enjoying the rest without a further word for Ramsey or Theron. Ramsey contemplatively chewed the corner of a chocolate slab that he had found in the bag, standing once more to stare out over the world. The wind rattled in their ears. Blanoka was lost to them, his mouth full of food.

"Look at that, Theron," breathed the goblin after a few mouthfuls of chocolate. Theron did as he was told, and pronouncedly looked towards the moon. "Brilliant, isn't it? Come on, we can't wait up here until we freeze to death. We need to find some shelter, and I wouldn't go back in that tunnel if someone paid me to." He beckoned, shivered once, and took off down the rugged, crumbly mountain path. Theron moved to follow him, then paused.

"Ramsey, what about…?"

The goblin stopped in mid-step. He had known that Theron would instinctively pause to say a further farewell, but Blanoka needn't feel more important than he was. "Let's just go, Theron. I can't stand this mountain, that tunnel, or anything to do with it. Come on, now. I don't want to go without you, but I certainly don't want to stand out here in the cold longer than we need to."

"But Ramsey, just to be decent…"

He spun around, his limbs rigidly stuck against his sides. "Decent? Look, I haven't got anything else to say to that slippery little skeleton. Come on." Theron stayed put, indecision playing on his furry features. Ramsey snarled. "Come *on!*"

"The poor thing can't see, Ramsey, we can't treat him badly."

"For Scaless' sake, Theron, you don't have to go around feeling sympathy for every damn creature in the universe. Just come on, will you? He's eating, anyway." Blanoka was still slurping and munching on the various treats that Ramsey had laid before him, and didn't pay attention to either one of them. He didn't even notice Theron's defence of him, and continued to eat regardless. "He's insulted you as often as he's insulted me. He doesn't deserve your consideration, he barely even deserves to be near you at all, so let's just leave him to his food. I'm fed up of the sight of him."

The wind was so cold that it was almost disabling. Already wearied from their journey under the mountain, it was a wonder that Ramsey and Theron were able to stand; yet still they did so, resolute and hardy against the dull grey sky, the air streaking their cheeks. Ramsey's face was gradually engulfed by more and more of his own hair. Blanoka's jabbering and crunching was the only noise that penetrated the swirling clamour of wind for an instant. Ramsey and Theron stared directly at one another, then Ramsey turned and set off along the crooked path alone.

"You can come along if you like, but I'm not waiting around."

"Oh Ramsey, you know I can't let you go ahead by yourself!"

Ramsey did not turn, the edges of his figure blurred by the wind. "You'd better hurry up then, 'cause I'm not staying."

Theron shook, his whole body shuddering with the extreme cold, his fur stiff with grime. He felt his chest tighten. The frosty air was forcing its way into his lungs. Ramsey did not stop.

"Don't be that way!" Theron called, his voice lost the moment it sprang from his mouth. "You don't mean that! After all we've been through!"

But Ramsey did not hear. Theron sank backwards in despair, his eyes bleary from the chill. Behind him, Blanoka snorted through his food and barked, scattering his meal.

"Basilisk!" he shouted in a thin, choked cry. "Basilisk! It is here!" Theron turned sharply and went to the distressed creature. Blanoka's blank eyes were bulging hysterically. "It being here! Run for your lives!"

It was enough to get Ramsey darting back towards them through the night fog, and his face was livid.

"Will you get that little moron to shut up?" he bellowed. Theron cowered and Blanoka continued to twitch madly in all directions with his nostrils flared. The little reptile screamed, and Ramsey leapt to restrain him. "You'll have the dragon upon us, you little blighter!"

Something above them creaked and slithered; the sound of hard muscle uncoiling, wet like rain. Ramsey's hands fell short of Blanoka's throat, and he looked up, warmth trickling out of his stomach until his whole body was frozen. Blanoka sobbed. Theron's claws grated against stone.

A blade-shaped, scaly head crept through the darkness of rock above them, fangs as long as Ramsey's forearms, dripping black with blood. It's sinister, gleaming face recoiled then, and from its claws fell the partially-devoured carcass of a cow, which dropped onto the stone path with a squelchy thud between Theron and Ramsey.

They had found the cobra dragon, they had caught it in the middle of a meal. A terrible, glistening hood of green and purple scales burst from its neck and it screeched, and it leapt at Ramsey from twenty feet above.

"Basilisk!"

Blanoka's voice shattered as the dragon fell towards them. They scattered like sheep, Ramsey and Theron to opposite sides. At first the striped body tumbled beyond them, but the creature lurched itself upright, suspended on terrible wings, and dove at Ramsey again. He fell back against the clammy rocks, looked to Theron, and grabbed his sword from his belt. Blanoka trembled like a white mouse between Theron's thick legs, and wailed his own doom at the top of his lungs.

"Get back!" was all Ramsey could think to say to the dark face. "I'm warning you!"

He pointed his sword directly at the dragon, his knuckles bleeding and grazed. The monster fluttered in the night sky before them and beyond them, its gruesome wings spread to cover the stars; Ramsey could feel its anger boiling through his skin. It did not attack.

Ramsey's outstretched arms trembled, and fell like twigs, the sword now dull and damp. Theron did not move. Blanoka began to wail and curse. The crash of the dragon's wings filled the island, thundering over the mountains like the Doom Storm of Lady Scaless herself. Its face was death, and its mouth gaped red as it plunged. Ramsey met it with his sword.

Theron saw a flash of scales against metal in the dark. His heart leapt to his throat, and he saw Ramsey backing away down the craggy path, stick-thin arms and cold steel fending off a massive monster. It looked bigger now than when Theron had fought it. The tear in its wing flapped like seaweed against the sky.

It lunged at Ramsey with claws and fangs and pure muscle, breathing no fire. It was full of meat and too bloated to summon flame. As soon as Theron realised this, he took his chance and sprang to Ramsey's aid, leaving Blanoka alone and cursing on the path.

The ledge was narrow and fragmented. As he leapt, Theron felt his bandages slip free of his limbs like liquid, and his legs were strong again. The cobra face darted and sliced past Ramsey's arm, lodging in the stone for the split-second that it took Theron to charge. The dragon squawked and lashed out when Theron's jaws trapped its neck, and though it easily shook him off it lost its balance and stumbled away, twirling downwards. Ramsey's stomach was bleeding. With a nod, Theron galloped away down the path, his mane flying in the wind, and Ramsey ran after him, one hand holding his abdomen.

The dragon rose once more and its cry deafened them. The rock slipped and skidded under their feet but still they ran. They could not fight. Theron did not stand in challenge. Ramsey knew at that moment that he could never kill the dragon. He could chase it to the ends of the world, armed with the island's finest weaponry, and still the creature would fly free to do battle with him another day. It would never die, and by Scaless, neither would he.

Its roar clattered over them like spiked armour and Ramsey covered one ear with his free hand out of sheer agony. It crashed into the mountainside above them, and rocks fell around their heads. It was slow but still it danced with deadly grace as though all the skies were made for it alone. The path broke up as they fled.

Suddenly, in the middle of his sprint, Ramsey's legs fell numb and he stopped. Gasping, he turned, and saw the grey mountainside and navy sky of night time stretching far, far behind him. Theron did not see him stop, and the dragon pursued the hulking troll, Ramsey slipping from its gaze. Ramsey clutched his sword and ground his teeth.

"Damn me for a fool!" he hissed, and ran back the way he had come. The instant he turned, the dragon whirled with a shriek and shot after him, wings blazing thunder through the sky. Blanoka stumbled and writhed on the path, too disorientated to make his escape. With a frantic swoop, Ramsey snatched the morlona in his arms and veered back in the other direction. The cobra dragon tried to grab them, missed, and soared overhead into the sky in a torrent of sticky venom. "Let go of my face!" shouted Ramsey, trying to pry the screaming Blanoka from his head and running desperately back down the road. Blanoka let go with a gasp of shock and instead wrapped all four limbs around Ramsey's chest.

Ramsey's arms were free and he clutched his sword with both hands as he ran. He could hear the dragon behind him, outrage spilling through its fearsome cry, and he felt the wake of its great wings on his skin, billowing hot air. Even burdened with a full stomach it was still swift, but Ramsey was quick with the thrill of life and he was faster. The thud of its wings on the dense air beat through the mountain and made the rocks shudder. Ramsey could feel it in his ears.

It was high above them now, darting to overtake them, and its sleek, yellow belly glinted in the starlight. Ramsey forced himself not to look up and just ran, cutting his feet on the sharp rock. He heard something scraping up ahead, and caught a glimpse of Theron through the wet mist in the dark; the troll was waiting for them, his muscles taut and ready to fight. Ramsey yelled at him to run, and together they fled down to the shadowed side of the mountain.

The fog split down the middle as the cobra dragon burst its way through. It veered and lunged with insane fury, missing them by inches and retreating again. Ramsey saw it then, its great head gleaming and its eyes burning like a rhôniae's eyes. It had to be thirty feet from its snout to its tail, and its muscles rippled wetly in the faint light.

He couldn't look away, so powerful was his anger and fear as Blanoka clutched around his torso, and Theron shouted but Ramsey did not know what he said. Elegant scales the size of polished pebbles sparkled in the moonlight, the long, whip-like tail lashing through the clouds above them. It saw Ramsey falter and took its chance to dive, but at the last moment they ducked through an arched overhang of grey rock, and the dragon could not halt itself in time.

It slammed into the rock, its head, neck and one wing lodged through the stony archway, the rest of its body wriggling and struggling at the other side. The impact shook the mountain and sent another cascade of stones down onto the path. Ramsey and Theron turned at once to see what had happened, but they did not linger, and sprinted out of sight, Blanoka in tow. The cobra dragon writhed, pulled its neck backwards and its body forwards, tried to tuck its immense wings against its body, but it was too exhausted and shocked to pull free. With a bellow and a feeble puff of flame, it drooped against the harsh road, its sleek body in disarray, twitching once in a while and causing the stone to crumble like snow.

# Chapter Eighteen

# The Climb

Ramsey, Theron and Blanoka stayed hidden in the shadows for a long time after the cobra dragon became stuck, regardless of how safe they should be if they moved. Ramsey could see nowhere to begin his search amongst the ocean of cliffs and stone, and didn't object to a brief rest. He needed to pull himself back together. He felt as though a few shreds of himself had been scattered underground, some dropped in the snow in Morfran Town, and a drip or two lay neglected in his old tree-house. He had long forgotten the smell of the damp wood and the sound of Merlock market in the early morning.

"That being very close indeed!" said Blanoka out of the blue, louder than was needed. "You are being saving Blanoka's life! Blanoka is grateful, Blanoka will follow you to the ends of the island, he will!"

"Oh great," mused Ramsey, distracted by the glint of moonlight off the mountain peaks.

"And Blanoka will be doing anything you want, no matter what it is, or how dangerous it is being! Blanoka will repay you, good sir!"

"You don't have to." Ramsey was being genuine; he didn't terribly want Blanoka to stick around for the remainder of their journey. Theron, on the other hand, stuck by his previous conviction, and was delighted by Blanoka's sudden acceptance of them. Perhaps, thought Ramsey, a dragon so small has only the room for select emotions and opinions in its little skull at any one time, and that was why Blanoka had changed his tune so dramatically. He didn't feel that the morlona's devotion would aid them. Blanoka seemed desperate to prove his worth.

"Oh, but I will!" he said. "See, Blanoka is being honest! Blanoka will be trying to talk properly." Then he added, "I."

"Speaking in the third person does no more than make you sound needlessly eccentric," decided Ramsey aloud. "There's no reason why you can't sound sane, so please do."

There was a crash and a thud of rock from somewhere out of view – the dragon was moving again. The three travellers were perched upon a rather bare rocky outcrop under the light of the moon, sheltered from the dragon's view by a sheer rock face; a few clumps of scraggly weeds clung to the mottled stone, the wind had died down, and the fog cleared as the night dragged on until morning.

Dawn seemed to come early in this part of the island, and unaware of falling asleep, Ramsey suddenly found himself waking with the palest light of morning upon his skin. Blanoka had been talking all night long, perhaps unaware that the goblin had dozed off. Theron lay still, but he was awake, and his fur was dull. Stray strands of his hair were illuminated by the sallow light, and Ramsey watched the glow for a while, breathing tightly and listening for the sounds of breaking rock.

His whole body was heavy and stiff, he felt as though he might never move again. He began to feel physically sick, realised that he was hungry, but found himself too drained to reach for his backpack. Blanoka continued to talk, and Ramsey registered for the first time that the little dragon was sitting on his lap.

"Are you being Okay?" asked Blanoka eagerly in a high tone. "Blanoka is not meaning to go on and on and on, you tell Blanoka when he can be quiet."

"Shush…" said Ramsey with a start, his ears picking up the faint sound of straining rock. "The dragon's moving again." Blanoka was silent for the first time in hours.

There was a scratch, then a thud, then a roar, and then it sounded as though the whole mountain was collapsing on one side. Fire erupted from the hidden side of the mountain, where they could not see what had happened, and suddenly the dragon soared into view, its sleek coils and muscles writhing and stretching in the sky. The morning was dim, and it did not see them, but Ramsey saw it clearly in the barely existent light, and finally beheld once more the jaws that had dealt him the painful bite at the nape of his neck. Thinking about it made the wound sting, and he would have held it, had he not been restraining Blanoka in his lap.

The dragon whirled through the air, delirious with freedom, stretching its huge, green wings and flaring its dark hood. Its limbs were muscular and slender, its belly was long and its tail coiled languidly behind it – a truly stunning and beautiful monster, but a monster nonetheless. It would have been a pity to kill it, if only Ramsey could. He was not frightened now, while its gaze was not upon him. He sat still, full of awe. In the corner of his eye he spied Theron watching the dragon sombrely; then the troll looked at Ramsey and smiled a tired smile.

"It's bigger than I remember," was all he said. Ramsey said nothing, and continued to stare.

Its bat-like wings spread wide, and with one quick swoop, it dove through the air and circled higher, far above their heads, crying with excitement or frustration; Ramsey couldn't tell. Whatever its feelings, it looked consistently unpleasant and scaly, despite its beautiful patterns and sleek head. Ramsey followed its path and craned his neck to watch it as it darted away northwards for an instant, and set itself down to land atop a steep cliff of marbled rock on the same huge mountainside, where it seemed that a slab of rock the size of Merlock's town wall had broken away.

It shook itself as it settled on the cliff-top, made a soft, hissing cry, and disappeared from view into what looked like, from a distance, a wide cave. It was definitely a cave, one big enough for the dragon to slide into. It didn't re-emerge, and made no further sound. Ramsey's heart made a sudden leap into his mouth and threatened to jump out onto his lap with Blanoka.

"Theron!" he practically shouted to the all ready alert troll. "The dragon's cave is up at the top of that slope. It has to be. Did you see it go in? It hasn't come out."

"Yes, I saw it go in."

"Then that's where it lives, and that's where Morgan will be. He's in there, Theron, I've got to get to him!" He forcibly stood and Blanoka tumbled onto the cold stone with a grunt, but Theron leapt to drag Ramsey back.

"No, Ramsey, you can't go up there. If it sees you, it'll kill you, and it *will* see you if you just wander into its home without planning."

Ramsey objected to Theron's teeth digging into his shirt. "Don't you get what I'm saying? Morgan – Morgan has to be up there! If he's alive, I mean." His expression went from frantic to anxious to determined in the span of a single second, and Theron let go of the shirt. "Of course he's alive, Terak told me he was alive. Terak wouldn't have lied to me, I trust him. And if I don't hurry, if Morgan's still alive, what's to stop the dragon from bloody well eating him right now?" Theron urged him to keep his voice down, which made the goblin more worried. "He could be doing it right now, eating the prince and spitting out his bones! A fat lot of good I'll have done if I let that happen!"

"Just think, Ramsey, before you go barging into that cave without a plan. I'll come with you."

"But we can't waste time! What if he's already dead? Argh...oh damn it, Theron, you're making me upset again..." He wiped harshly at his eyes and glared at Theron as though Morgan was his own flesh and blood, and Blanoka felt the surge of raw emotion as he stood at Ramsey's feet. "Please, no, don't make me wait. If the kid's alive, then I have to go to him now."

"It may not be the dragon's cave."

"It's a cave and the cobra dragon just walked right in and didn't come out, so I think that counts as the dragon's cave, Theron!"

Blanoka piped up interestedly. "You are wanting to save this chillen, yes? Then being waiting until the dragon leaves cave. Then you go in, when dragon is not there."

"No," asserted Theron gruffly. "That's risky, Ramsey wouldn't know when the dragon would be coming back."

"I could tell it to give a warning signal, then!" snapped Ramsey, his whole body stiff and twitching. "What if that dragon doesn't come out for days? Weeks? We'll be stuck standing here like idiots, while for all we know it's sitting in its cave roasting Morgan like a pig! It all ready knows that we're here, so it's got all the more reason to eat him now!"

"Or," said Blanoka, not looking at either one of them, but at the ground, "because of it seeing us coming, maybe it stay in cave short while, then come out again to finish killing us. Blanoka is thinking that is being much more likely." He scratched himself, then turned to Ramsey, blind eyes blinking. "But that is just being what I think."

"I hope you're right," huffed Ramsey with no anger directed at the little dragon this time. He sighed and sat himself back down on the hard rock, his cheeks in his palms. "Oh Scaless, please don't let him be dead."

"If he is, there's no point in risking yourself as well," said Theron. Ramsey broke like a feather.

"What in Grenamoya has gotten into you, anyway? You're not contributing very much, are you? For Scaless' sake, Theron, this is the whole reason I came all this way! Show a little support!" He didn't try to muffle his own shouting. "You're meant to be the optimistic one, so stop talking such misery!"

"I don't want to lose you, Ramsey. You mean a lot to me."

"Oh, whatever."

Ramsey reached for his supplies and rummaged angrily in his backpack for something to eat or drink, desperate to focus on something other than Prince Morgan. He had never been overly fond of food, and knew that it would do little to distract him, but he was swelling painfully with the agony of having to stay put. It made his stomach boil and his head was spinning, his cheeks were damp and his eyes were sore.

He didn't know why he was crying. He might cry if he laid his eyes upon Morgan's lifeless body up in that evil cave, but the prospect of waiting should not have made him so upset. He couldn't take on that dragon alone, and Theron would not be able to hold it off for long. It was all futile, desperately hopeless, and he hugged his bag against his face, tears staining the leather. He cried much more nowadays, he had woken up crying on more than one occasion in recent weeks. He just attributed it to apparently being mad.

"I don't want to lose you, Ramsey," said Theron again, his tone lower. Ramsey did not move his backpack away from his face. "If I lost you after all this, I don't care if you think I'm being over the top, but it would just kill me. If I let you go to your death, I couldn't live with myself."

"Oh..." was all the goblin could say through the bag.

Blanoka had now settled himself between Theron's forelegs, and listened to the conversation with his eyes wide and white. Theron hung his head, feeling stupid himself for getting upset. It had never been in his wild nature to cry. "I can't watch you go to die. I'll see you through to the very end, Ramsey, I swear I will."

"If Morgan's dead..." began Ramsey's muffled voice, but he could not continue, and whined into silence. Blanoka sighed and lay down between the two huge paws. Not a single sound reached them over the barren landscape, and it was as though the whole world was dead, apart from the three of them suspended in space and arguing with tears in their eyes.

"...Please, Ramsey, if this is the right place, we must wait, for your sake and for Morgan's."

"Blanoka would be hoping," squeaked Blanoka, just to get his scaly oar in, "that since he is being a dragon, that you would being listening to his advice on dragons! Blanoka knows about the dragons, you wait, save little chillen when time is right. Not long, Blanoka thinks. Dragon will come hunting travellers, yes it will."

Ramsey was quiet for a moment, then said, "If you say so, and I don't know why I'm listening to your advice – I'll wait. A while. Just a little while, but not too long. If that horrible thing is staying put, then I might as well confront it sooner rather than later. I didn't come all this way to sit around. No, I can't wait here. I have to…"

His eyes traced the severe slope of the broken cliff, top to bottom, and his heart sank. He couldn't judge how high it was, and he didn't need to be up close to determine that it would be near impossible to scale. Maybe there was another way around, but another path might take longer, and he simply couldn't risk any sort of delay.

"I'm hungry and I'm thirsty. I'm going to eat something before I do anything else. Is that all right with you, Theron?"

Theron didn't like Ramsey's hard tone, but replied nonetheless, his head rested dolefully upon his big paws. "Sure, Ramsey. Do whatever you want. Just take some time to think before you try anything dangerous. Promise me."

"How can I do anything but think?" he retorted, emptying the contents of his backpack messily onto the ledge. Food packages spilled everywhere. He seized a heavy, rectangular flask from the pile, seeing that it had a note attached to its lid. He read it silently.

*'Dear Rammy – Hi! Terak told me you would like coffee so I thought I'd pack some for you in case of emergencies! Just don't get addicted, Okay? I hear it can give you wrinkles. See you soon and take care always! --Andel'*

Ramsey smiled thinly and popped the lid off the top of the flask. The strong-smelling, black coffee inside was still hot, and he eagerly poured some into the lid that served as a mug. Theron watched him but was making no responses to activities around him, not even as Blanoka turned to him with a story about life under the mountain. Ramsey felt uncomfortable beneath the troll's gaze, and tried to remain focused on his coffee. He read Andel's note a few times in an attempt to distract his thoughts from Prince Morgan, but still his coffee cup trembled and spilled a little.

The individually-wrapped sugar cubes (each with a different smiley face drawn on it) soon caught his attention, and he added a few to his coffee before pouring himself a fresh cup. The wind howled and rang high above them, but not much of a breeze irritated their skin. Theron's brown mane and the ridge of hair behind either one of his cheeks ruffled ever so slightly, and he hid his face in his paws to evade the gentle movement. Still his greyish fur bristled and twitched.

Blanoka leaned out in the direction of the gathering dawn when he heard the call of birds, and Ramsey watched the throbbing flock of white shapes as it darted and fell and rose again over the clouds. What it must feel like to fly, he mused, hot coffee pressed to his lips. Months ago, he would have sold his very being for such an opportunity, to fly away and be free from his lonely existence. Now, he thought, if he had learned to fly, the cobra dragon would probably stalk him there, too.

Sure enough, as Ramsey had guessed, the flood of white birds on the horizon roused the dragon from its lair, and high above their rocky perch, it surged forth from its dark cave and leapt from the cliff, swooping through the sallow sky and soaring up and up, the birds scattering around it in a myriad of angry cries. Blanoka scurried back until he collided with Ramsey's pile of shirts.

"It being there! Dragon comes out from cave! Now, what is Blanoka being saying about cobra dragon coming out of cave, mmm?"

It moved so swiftly that it was already out of sight as Blanoka finished speaking. It climbed through the sky far above Ramsey's line of vision beneath the outcrop, and seemed to trail away to the south with a thin cry. Its wings left an echo in the air.

492

Ramsey was on his feet, tucking his sword back into his belt with a slicing noise. It was now or never. Blanoka sensed his movement and looked at him, and Theron did the same, but his brown eyes were emptier than Blanoka's. Ramsey sighed and spoke slowly.

"I'm going now. I've got to do this, Theron, I made a promise to King Viktor that I would bring his son back to him."

"Why, Ramsey?" asked the troll, lifting his head. "I trusted you from the start. I was proud to be seen with you, proud to travel with you, but you didn't feel the way you do now until we lost each other. Then you meet some vampires, and suddenly you're all for rescuing Morgan, but no, Ramsey, you can't go risking yourself for him. I've known you these past months, I care for you, I have to protect you, I swore that I would. You mustn't go where I can't follow you…"

"You know very well what happened with Terak, I told you everything."

"But nothing is worth losing you, Ramsey, I won't let you go to die…!"

"Why should I, or Morgan, or anyone have to die, Theron? It's the way things are, and we can't change that."

"I won't stay here and wait for you to die…" Theron's eyes were glossy with tears, but he didn't cry, and he still looked more angry than he did upset. Ramsey felt hollow and stupid under that stare.

"You said I was a hero when I never was. So let me try my best now, let me try. If you really care about me, you'll let me go to prove myself a hero!"

"I won't let you go to die!" insisted Theron again. "I do care about you, I'd die fighting to defend you, but I won't wait around uselessly while you throw your life away!"

"You wanted us to rescue Morgan! So let me go, for Scaless' sake, Theron, or this whole journey will have been pointless!" Theron shook his head and whined. "You can't stop me, you know."

"But we did everything together from when we met, and this was our journey, and I promised that I'd defend you."

493

Ramsey shrugged. "Yeah, well, it isn't our quest, it's *mine*, and it's my responsibility, so for once, just wait here. I will come back, but if I don't…well, then…as I said, I'll come back."

Theron whimpered and berated himself, praying for some wise words to strike him so that he could give Ramsey some final advice, but by the time he had thought of something to say, the goblin was already half-way up the broken path, scrambling his way towards the base of the rock face. Theron perked, fear spreading through his stomach and down his legs, and he sniffed so forcefully that Blanoka almost fainted.

"Don't be doing that!" scolded the little dragon in his taut voice. "We being quiet, cobra dragon not hearing us! We wait and watch, in case it comes back!"

Theron did not question Blanoka's choice of the word 'watch', so intense was his feeling of dread. He watched hopelessly as the tiny, orange blur that was Ramsey arrived at the bottom of the cliff, positioned on a lumpy plateau of stone that had not broken. Ramsey was staring up at the cliff, standing as an ant does next to a brick wall, looking feebly upwards to see the peak so very high above. The mess of black hair swirled in an air current, and Ramsey pushed it free of his face. Theron sighed and eyed the cliff with equal scepticism; Blanoka sat at his feet and cocked his little head with curiosity.

Ramsey had no time to waste. He spat on his palms, rubbed them together and clenched his fists as hard as he could, fuelled by sheer willpower in the face of uncertainty. If anything went wrong, he would either fall to his death or be spotted by the cobra dragon, but either way, he would die a hero, trying to rescue a young prince. Absurdly, this no longer sounded like a sacrifice to him. He knew that he couldn't run away, and he didn't look back.

The rock face was near vertical, and scattered, sharp protrusions in the stone looked like precarious footholds that he might just about be able to climb. He was small, though, and more adept at climbing trees than mountains. The peak of the cliff loomed many, many metres above, flanked by clouds and shining grey in the rising light.

He pressed one hand to the rock, felt it shift beneath his fingers, then grabbed onto a shallow ledge six feet from the ground and hoisted himself up. He groped upwards again, and climbed a further three feet, then seven feet, then ten feet; all the while he wheezed for breath and refused to look down. Slowly, ever so slowly, he climbed the rock face, and as soon as he realised that his feet had left the ground, he finally felt the sun brush his skin again. He braced himself against the hazardous cliff, feet and fingernails digging into the tiny indents in the rock, and forced himself up.

How he could have made good use out of a few rock-climbing supplies. All he had was his bare skin and claw-like nails, but the mountain was unyielding and offered him no easy path. Feeling blindly around on the rock surface, afraid to lift his head from the stone, he clutched any and every orifice and protrusion that he could find. He was breathing faster than he had done when facing the mountain trolls, or the rhôniae, or even the cobra dragon, and his face was still wet, smearing against the grey stone.

No, please no, don't let Morgan be dead...

There was no voice in his head other than his own. Discounting the nightmares, he'd come a long way since first setting off from Merlock.

If this is madness, thought Ramsey, if this is how I'm going to be for the rest of my life, it isn't so bad. I'm an adrenaline-pumped, teenage goblin with a sword. I'll manage.

He groaned when the slight sting of rain itched the back of his neck, begged furiously under his breath for it to die down, and was answered by a warm ray of light from the east. He paused, testing the rock for slipperiness, and clambered on.

He felt as though he was suspended in mid-air, miles above ground, hanging like a star in space. He could neither see nor hear Theron and Blanoka below him, and for an instant he wondered if he should have carried his backpack with him, but it was too late for that now. He inched his way higher and higher, slipping once or twice on slimy patches of rock, clinging like an insect.

All that had happened to him on his journey flooded back to his mind. Apart from cold nights, the odd leak in his roof and scrounging for food every day, his life had been stable once. He had been stuck in a routine for one third of his life, and it had become natural to exist so, all alone and bitter. If it wasn't for the dragon, Ramsey would still be sitting in his tree-house on a hard bed with holes in his clothes.

As things were, he was still alone, still cold, still hungry; but the sharp steel nudging his left thigh had never been there before. His sword reminded him of his duty, and of the vampires in Morfran Town. Yes, he had to live to see them again, so he would definitely survive this.

His rigid fingertips found the sharp ledge at the top of the cliff and clung fast. He grabbed the ridge with his other hand, and using all the strength in both of his thin arms, dragged himself up onto the plateau, his feet scrambling for a firm foothold. He lay, panting, on his stomach for a moment or two, and when he stood, his legs took him forward of their own accord. He straightened his spine and gasped painfully as the darkness of the massive cave loomed at him, dank and immense and, now that he stood before it, absolutely foul-smelling. A blast of stench, thick and abrasive like coal tar, hit him in the face. He staggered forward.

He wanted to run, he needed to run, but he knew he would stumble if he allowed his instincts to take over. The dragon would return and eat him alive at any moment, he had to hurry; time grew sticky like syrup around him, his feet were swamped with fear, he could hear frantic humming in his head.

Please, no, don't let the voices come back. I've come too far for this, I won't die!

A barking echo answered him, and he jumped with shock before realising that it was his own voice shouting back at him. He had spoken aloud. He was far more disorientated than he first thought.

Ramsey entered the cave with the sinking feeling of a man going to the guillotine. Its enormous, black mouth groaned, its walls crumbling and dark with ash. It had a sinister atmosphere that assaulted him as he entered, mixed with a funereal undertone – almost as though something had recently died inside. He froze.

"Morgan?" He coughed on the single word, received no answer, and flew forward to search. The cave stretched far back, beyond Ramsey's scope of vision. Parts of the walls and ceiling had split open with the force of the dragon's wings, and he scoured all the crevices, every little nook for the tiniest trace of life. The powerful stench was pushed to the back of his priorities, for he heard no breathing, no movement at all, save his own heartbeat. "Oh no..."

The floor of the cave was littered with broken rock and piles of unrecognisable remains. The bones and shreds of hair were jumbled together like a gruesome life sculpture, a few cattle skulls mixed into the fray. Ramsey hurried over and ripped the largest pile apart, flinging ribs and old hide over his shoulders. There was some clothing, ripped, green and purple. His fingers fell upon something smooth and hard that turned out to be a goblin skull, but it was far too big to be a child's. He breathed a sigh of relief but still his insides were sobbing. The ground was sticky with dried blood that clung to his toes as he moved.

A small noise echoed through the cave, like crumbling stone, and he leapt to attention, realising seconds later that it was only the noise of dry bones. What remained of the gory pile collapsed, and fragments scattered at his feet. The foul smell of rot and dust billowed up from the torn skin, making him cough. His heart was racing and he could hardly breathe, his eyes watering now from the strong stench that filled his nostrils. It was still raining outside, and the sweltering heat of the cave was laced with the icy chill of morning.

"No..." he panted, standing prone and solitary in the rancid shadows. "No, no, no, no...oh no...please..." He coughed and covered his mouth with one hand, slouching dismally amidst the piles of dead creatures and shattered boulders. The shivers that shook his body were not entirely physical, and most definitely not from the cold. Around him, the whole mountain was creaking mournfully. He wished that Theron was with him.

And then suddenly, faintly, so small that he barely heard it at all, there came a muffled cough and the groan of rock. Ramsey didn't move in case it was he who had made the noise, but then he heard it again, another cough, this one unquestionably real and near. But no voice. Ramsey lost control of himself and ran further into the cave.

"Morgan?" he shouted, listening hard for any more sounds but hearing none. *"Morgan?"* he called out again, stopping still. "Is that you?"

More bones, more piles of carcasses, some of them not long dead. He set upon the nearest one and shouted into it, straining to hear a young male voice from somewhere beneath the bodies. The overwhelming smell of bad meat almost crippled him.

"Morgan, please, you've got to be in here! If you can't speak, don't worry, don't get up, I'll find you, so help me...!" He tore the pile down the middle, not knowing how in Grenamoya he was able to shift the weight of a half-eaten bull, but found nothing. He ran to the others in turn, shouting out but getting no reply.

Voices – he had heard voices in his head, so why not hear coughing? It was just another thing to add to his catalogue of insanity.

The cave was tall and wide enough to accommodate a group of double-decker buses, and still it stretched further and further back into the mountain. Ramsey couldn't look forever, and he knew so, but at that moment, he feared no dragon; and if he died, he vowed to die fighting.

Near to the largest pile of bodies, which Ramsey had successfully toppled, was another tall pile – this one of rocks and jagged stones, as though the dragon had been spring-cleaning one day and moved all of the broken pieces into a corner. Bones were scattered nearby, and Ramsey hurriedly picked through them, the sound of creaking rock growing louder.

He spluttered and covered his mouth again, hurling bones in all directions, making noises that clattered up and down along the tunnel. Amongst the shattering sounds, he thought he heard another cough, but he sagged and dismissed it as wishful thinking.

At least, until he heard it again mere feet away from him.

"Morgan? Morgan!" New power burning in his heart, he stumbled onto the rock pile and wrenched away some of the shards, discarding them in a blind panic of fear and hope. Something groaned and moved beneath the pile, and Ramsey caught a flash of grime-encrusted, pale skin. It was Morgan. "Oh Scaless above!" Ramsey couldn't control his voice and dug furiously at the stones, dismantling the pile from the top downwards, flinging rocks the size of his own head in every direction. "You're alive!"

The boy was indeed alive, but filthy, and he looked very confused through the minute gap between the rocks. The scar on his right cheek was like a stab of lightning in the shadows. "Who are you?" he asked. Ramsey could tell instantly from his voice that Morgan was not well.

"Rammy- no, my name's *Ramsey*, and I've come to rescue you! Hang in there, kid, I'll have you free in no time!" He fumbled, rolling a particularly huge rock to one side, but the pile was deep, and he was barely closer to freeing the prince. Morgan coughed again, and Ramsey abandoned the boulders to reach in through the gap and hold Morgan's hand. "Your skin is like ice. Don't worry, I'll get you out!"

He returned to his laborious task, gasping and panting so hard that his throat hurt. His hands were numb from the work, and he only dropped one or two rocks onto his toes. Morgan didn't ask any more questions, and in fact didn't speak at all. Instead, Ramsey saw him curl up beneath the pile and hug his knees with closed eyes, as though he barely had the strength to move. Ramsey was furious at himself, for taking so long and for allowing Morgan to be kidnapped long enough to get sick. As soon as he got him home, Ramsey would make sure that the prince was seen by a doctor. If he was so desperately ill, he could still die.

"I won't let you die on me!" rebuked Ramsey, making Morgan jolt. "You stay awake, Okay, and be ready to run before the dragon comes back!"

"But-"

"Don't worry, if you can't walk, I'll carry you! Just stay awake!" Ramsey kept eye contact with Morgan through the gap, brown staring into brown, still rolling the stones away with every ounce of strength in his body. Morgan had the biggest tawny eyes that Ramsey had ever seen, and a bright, puppyish expression despite his obvious sickness.

So very unlike Viktor…, Ramsey thought with a grin.

He hadn't needed Theron after all. Dislodging one rock, he abruptly caused several more to cave in on top of Morgan, and he leapt apologetically.

"Sorry! Are you all right?" Morgan coughed and nodded, though his blond hair was now full of dust. "Good. We're almost there!"

The rain was falling hard now, spattering all over the cliff top and at the entrance to the cave. A fresh, stormy wind had picked up and was gusting through the tunnel, whirling all the way down into the depths of the mountain that Ramsey did not investigate. He couldn't remember anything that he had learned about dragons, but he thought that they disliked wet weather, which would make sense if they breathed fire. He didn't have much time if that was the case.

The rock pile was hardly smaller than it had first been, and Morgan was still firmly trapped inside, looking worse for wear. Ramsey couldn't think what to do. Maybe Theron would have been useful.

Rippling with water and soaked to the scales, the cobra dragon veered through the windswept sky, back to its sheltered, warm cave. Its huge wings spread like green tents as it lowered itself to land, and its hood lay flat against its supple, striped neck. It had found no prey, and though annoyed, its appearance was grotesquely calm.

Long toes and claws clattered on the wet stone as it strode into its cave, shaking rainwater off its wings and tail. Globular, yellow eyes glinted like glass in the shadowy tunnel. It hissed comfortably to itself, extending its neck to sniff the air, and as it did so, it smelt fresh goblin, and the metallic tang of a familiar sword.

Ramsey knew he couldn't flee, for he had nowhere to run. He saw the cobra long before it saw him, for it had the rain in its eyes, and did not shake itself free of the blindness until it smelled him. It did not pause this time, did not give him time to feel the full pain of his own terror; it went straight for him, screaming, its wings tucked in to its sides as it had no room to fly. Ramsey could feel its wrath thundering through the ground beneath him, and he drew his sword, refusing to leave the prince.

"Get back you ugly, awful creature!"

Looking back on it, Ramsey wished he'd had something more heroic to say, but he was no warrior, and he was deathly frightened. The dragon halted less than five metres from him, then its mouth gaped wide and it spat a deadly accurate torrent of poison at Ramsey's face. At least, it would have been deadly, had Ramsey not somersaulted out of the way a split-second beforehand. The dragon eyed him suspiciously and advanced, leering close to the pile of rocks as it did so, its every step delicately placed. Ramsey backed up, seeing no other way to evade instant death, and he realised that the dragon was steering him away. Once again, it breathed no fire, but its eyes boiled with venom.

The cobra darted at him with unsheathed fangs and Ramsey dodged right. He struck at its head with his sword, nicking the tip of its snout but no more, and it struck back with a vengeance, missing only because Ramsey ducked behind yet another pile of bones.

The cobra dragon growled and scattered these in its wake as it galloped after Ramsey, swift on its feet but not as fast as the goblin. Ramsey could see nothing to use as a shield, fending off the dragon's strikes with the broad side of his blade; which, though not all that broad, was enough to stop its fangs.

Ramsey suddenly realised that he and his opponent now stood at opposite ends of the cave – he with his back to the open, the dragon with the gloom of the tunnel behind it. He swore as loudly as he could and stabbed at the dragon's foul face, but a sweep of its wing caught him off-balance and he fell. Morgan was far away now, and Ramsey could not squeeze his way past with the monster filling the whole cave with its wings.

He called out to Morgan but the dragon cut him short, knocking him twenty feet through the air to smash into the bloodied cave wall. Ramsey felt something crack inside him and he fell to the ground, everything spinning sickeningly until a cold face materialised above him. It was the dragon, sneering down at him with a mouthful of fangs, its black, forked tongue flicking out at him, wet with poison. He couldn't move his body.

Then the cobra screamed – the most eerie, brutal scream that Ramsey had ever heard from any living being, and he felt warm wetness splatter onto his face and hands. He did not realise that he had stabbed the dragon until he opened his eyes and found that his hair and clothes were gummy with blood and his sword was lodged deep in the dragon's jaw. It wheeled away from him, the sword hanging in its flesh for a moment before clattering to the floor in a shower of crimson, and Ramsey turned, trying to stand. He could taste its rancid blood in his mouth, and was thankful that it wasn't his own.

He stood, clutching his side, sword in hand; but the dragon did not notice him, writhing madly and bashing into the walls, tripping on the discarded bones that littered the floor, wild with agony. It bucked like a horse and tumbled to the ground, spitting pitifully, blood bubbling from its jaws, and Ramsey went forward, not knowing how to kill it, but determined to do it somehow. Its leathery wings flailed hopelessly and drooped at its sides like umbrellas broken by the storm. He was not a killer, he had never been a killer, but he had killed to save his own life and that of his friends, and he would do it now for Morgan.

The dragon lifted its head, its eyes following Ramsey like that of any cornered cobra, and it hissed, dripping blood all down its chest. It still had strength enough to fight, strength enough to kill him, and its fangs stretched long from the terrible mouth, gleaming and red. It tried to spit, but only managed a thin dribble of venom that missed Ramsey altogether.

He moved right up to it, sword held high, and it hissed long and low at him, drawing its fangs to strike back; but before either one of them could attack the other, there was a shout of "Don't hurt him!", and Morgan stumbled around the dragon's fallen body and stood in-between them, arms held out to his side and his expression severe and young. And he was glaring at Ramsey.

"No!" he shouted, his voice hoarse and not yet broken. "No, I won't let you touch him again! You're a monster! Get back, get away from him!" Behind him, the dragon coiled its head miserably to the ground in a pool of its own blood and flicked its tongue. There was absolute fury in Morgan's eyes. "How could you? Get away from him!"

Ramsey was dumbfounded. The dragon's blood was trickling down his face and clothes. "What do you mean?" he asked, gasping. "I've come here to save you, Morgan, to take you away from this dragon! I've travelled miles and miles and more bloody miles to come and rescue you, and now you're telling me not to kill it! It'll kill us, Morgan!" He grabbed the neck of his own shirt and pulled it down just enough to reveal his still painful bite wound. "See this? That *thing* did it to me, and it'll kill you too, and I won't let you die! Come on!"

"No!" said Morgan again, barring Ramsey's way with his thin body. He was still wearing the pyjamas he had worn the night he had gone missing, and every part of him was blackened with ash. The smudge on his right cheek did nothing to hide the pale scar. "He has been kind to me! He has looked after me and given me food, he hasn't done me any harm! What right have you to hurt him?" There were tears in Morgan's eyes now, and Ramsey felt weak with guilt and confusion.

"Why would a dragon kidnap a prince just to look after him? If this monster cares about you so much, it would have left you with your father, where you were happy."

"He's not a monster! His name is Merlock, and he's my friend!" Morgan turned then, and went to cradle the dragon's bloodied head. Its sorrowful eyes peered up at the prince, and no yellow glow lingered in them. They were the colour of wax. "Please, don't hurt him. Just...just go!"

"I'm not leaving you here," said Ramsey firmly, still not really knowing what was going on. The blood was hot upon his skin and it stung. "I came all this way to save you, so I don't know why that dragon of yours thought it had a right to kill me and my friends!"

"He's a *he*, and his name is Merlock!" Morgan's cheeks were pink with distress and Ramsey folded before the two bright eyes.

"Okay, Okay – why does *he* have a right to kill me and my friends?"

The dragon looked at Ramsey again through its colourless eyes, blood still gurgling from its mouth and under its jaw. It hissed softly, still poisonous, as though fatigue alone was keeping it from attacking. "You came to kill my father…" it wheezed at last, its head still supported in Morgan's arms. Ramsey's mouth fell open.

# Chapter Nineteen

# Dragon Flight

The dragon's eyes closed again, and it groaned weakly, its head still firmly supported in Morgan's arms. Morgan stroked its face, trying to wipe away the blood to no avail, speaking softly to the creature and glaring daggers at Ramsey. Ramsey was so perplexed that he found himself unable to move at all. 'Merlock'…where had he heard that name before? His home town, yes, but there was something else behind it that he couldn't quite grasp in such a bizarre situation. He could feel the sweat running down his face. One thing sprung to the forefront of his mind.

"He can *talk*?"

"Of course he can talk," said Morgan severely. "Most dragons can talk, and he's a very clever dragon."

"Then how come he never talked before?"

At this, Merlock raised his wounded head and looked at Ramsey with an emotionless gaze. The blood was everywhere now, and Morgan's clothes were soaked with it. "I've never had any reason to talk to you, you murderer!" snapped the dragon, pulling feebly away from Morgan's arms. "You want to kill my father, you shall never hurt him, not while I'm alive!" The dragon was stationary for a moment, hissing softly, and then he tried to stand. "I won't let you leave here!"

"I swear, I haven't got a damn clue who your father is. I came here to rescue Morgan!"

"You're lying!"

Ramsey gripped his sword again. "I'm bloody well not! Why in Grenamoya would I come halfway across the island to kill some random cobra dragon? If anything, I should kill you, not your old man!"

Merlock sneered, on his feet again though his legs were shaking. "You cannot fool me! I will kill you!"

"No, please!" implored Morgan, in a voice heavy with flu. "I don't want either one of you to do any killing! Killing is never the answer!"

The cobra dragon was amazingly quick to listen. He spat some more blood down his scaly, green chest, and consented to sit down in a relatively calm manner. Feeling as though he should, Ramsey dropped his sword and crossed his arms, also looking at the prince. Morgan smiled.

"That's better. Mister Ramsey, you say you came here to rescue me, but you still had no right to hurt Merlock like that." Merlock hissed with satisfaction, still analysing Ramsey as he might a vaguely tasty-looking pig. "And Merlock, you can't hurt him either, because he doesn't know who your dad is. I believe him."

"But," began Merlock with a brief hissing-fit and a fresh dribble of blood, "but, my father said that there was a goblin coming here to…"

"To what?" Ramsey prompted; but the dragon looked lost, gritting his fangs in disbelief. He glared sharply at Ramsey.

"Do you swear that you have never before heard of my father?"

"Of course I haven't! Who is he? Merlock Senior?"

Merlock didn't react. Morgan was still cleaning the dragon up with the sleeve of his pyjamas, tenderly watching his expression.

"No...no, my father wouldn't...he...he lied to me..." At that moment, Ramsey saw the poison fade from the dragon's patterned face, to be replaced by a veil of absolute betrayal and devastation. The eyes glowed green, then yellow once more. Merlock stared fixedly at the ground in front of his face and stood, long claws grating on the stone, trying to rearrange his crumpled wings. When he saw Morgan's utterly devoted little face looking up at him, the dragon seemed to choke. "How could he do this? How could he? He lied to me!"

"Do you mean to tell me that the only reason you've been chasing me down and trying to kill me is because your dad told me that I was out to get him?" asked Ramsey, rigidly. Merlock nodded, and Ramsey almost collapsed. "Then why in Grenamoya did you kidnap Morgan?"

"Because my father told me to," came the hissing answer. "I don't know why he did."

Ramsey flung his arms up over his head and shouted, "Well that's just great! You've been trying to kill me because of something I didn't do, and you kidnapped Morgan because of something your father said, but you don't know why he said it because he didn't say! Oh yeah, just brilliant. Well, I'm not dead, and I need to take that kid home. Now that you're not going to kill me, please hand him over."

Merlock sighed slowly and addressed Morgan, who looked very small and miserable in his blood-stained pyjamas. "Do you wish to go home, child?" As though he didn't quite want to admit it, Morgan nodded and pursed his lips before looking away, at Ramsey. Ramsey could barely move for the relief rushing through him. "As you wish, then...I have been a fool..."

"It's all very well to admit that now," grumbled Ramsey as Morgan went to him. "Just be thankful that neither me nor my friends got killed along the way, or you'd really have something to be sorry for!"

"You may go on one condition:" hissed the snake dragon, "that you let me take the both of you far away from here, so that I know for certain that you are not going to seek out my father and kill him."

"That suits me fine. Just take us back to Merlock, Merlock."

It hit him then that the capital of their home kingdom had been named after the very first cobra dragon who founded it, 'Merlock'. But this dragon before him – surely this could not be the very first cobra dragon who ever soared over the island…

"Hey," The cobra jerked his neck around to face Ramsey. "Merlock, that name…you're not the Merlock that our kingdom was named after, are you?"

"No," said the dragon with a frown, trailing blood as he ambled his way back to the mouth of the cave. Ramsey followed him, escorting Morgan with a firm hand on the narrow shoulders. "Merlock the Baneful was my grandfather, and he died many, many years ago. I never knew him."

The morning light was abruptly cut off as a slithery, black shape fell onto the cliff top from above, blocking out the sun, causing Merlock to leap back with shock and almost land on the two goblins. Ramsey literally had to drag Morgan with him or the boy would have been crushed.

A loud rattling as cold as hailstones shattered the dimness of the cave, and Merlock answered the shape with an equally harsh noise made deep in his throat. Ramsey couldn't see anything for the blinding glow that surrounded the figure, and he braced himself against Morgan, holding tight. He was sore and exhausted but he was not beyond running away.

Stamping footsteps intruded upon Merlock's cave, and the cobra dragon moved backwards, hissing and whipping his tail through the air, intimidating but not advancing. Ramsey was terrified, trying to imagine anything more terrible than the cobra dragon that had been pursuing him for so long. Something deep in his gut told him that Merlock was facing his father sooner than he would have liked. No other creature on the island, save for Emperor Pain himself, could possibly inspire dread in an already horrendous animal.

509

"My dear Merlock…" It was the most dreadful, icy voice that Ramsey had ever heard outside his own head. It was like the sneering tone of an adder. "What's with all the challenging? Are you not pleased to see me?"

"Why are you here?" asked Merlock. The other creature was evidently grinning, and Merlock's tone was unflinching. Both of them kept hissing between sentences and striking the ground with their tails and claws. Ramsey could feel it through the ground.

"Why?" He was clearly taken aback. "Why does a father ever need a reason to visit his son?" The huge father-of-Merlock forced his way into the cave, pushing his son further and further back until the two of them were inches apart, and Ramsey saw the poisonous face of a near-identical dragon looming in front of Merlock's. Ramsey came to learn, much later on, that this dragon was known as Kamror. The yellow fangs were dripping wet. His gaze fell upon the goblins instantly, and Ramsey felt wretched and naked beneath the burning eyes. *"What…"* began Kamror, "is *this*?" It was a tapered gaze, sharp as a scimitar, cold as poison.

Ramsey was too terrified to find his voice and he felt Morgan shrink back against him. Merlock dove forward to confront his parent, and smouldering eyes locked together like fresh fires. "This goblin came to retrieve Morgan, father! He did not come here to murder you, as you said!"

"He lies!" retorted the other dragon, advancing again with fury. "How can you believe the deceitful words of a worthless goblin over your own father? Ungrateful, after all I have done for you!"

"After all the *lies* you told me, father! You betrayed me! I won't back down this time, father, you lied to me!"

Ramsey grabbed Morgan under the armpits and lifted him to his feet with a whisper, but they had barely moved an inch before Kamror turned on them and leapt at Ramsey with fangs drawn. Morgan screamed and tried to pull Ramsey back, but Merlock moved first, catching his father side-on and knocking him to the ground with the force of an oak crashing down.

The dragons wrestled back and forth through the cave, lunging and missing and striking one another with claws, tails and wings, drawing blood and tearing scales from skin. Merlock had lost so much blood that Ramsey was amazed he could fight, and the pure heat of outrage pouring from them burned in the cavern. Ramsey picked Morgan up and rushed into the midst of the fray to retrieve his sword, and the dragons minced past like courting birds, for between the vicious attacks they circled one another and called like cats.

Swollen muscles rippled beneath the scales as they caught one another and rolled on the ground, crashing into the walls and causing rocks to fall loose from the ceiling. A thick tail swung in Ramsey's direction and he pushed Morgan to safety, realising that he had avoided a potentially lethal injury. The one dragon had a yellow, stinger-tipped tail, in the style of a scorpion, and the muscular stinger ripped through the walls and left gaping fissures in the stone. It would have made short work of Ramsey's tunic.

Without a further thought for his own safety, Ramsey slung Morgan over his shoulder and began to carry him back to the cave mouth. Morgan complained and struggled but Ramsey didn't care, moving as fast as he could and trying to evade the dragons' attention. Kamror forced Merlock under him and slammed him into the rock, giving himself enough time to break free of their conflict and strike Ramsey.

"Oh, not again!" Ramsey couldn't wield his sword while carrying Morgan and he couldn't move out of the way in time. Both goblins were scattered by Kamror's solid impact, and Ramsey felt his neck thud against a sharp lump of rock before Kamror seized upon him and dragged him back. He couldn't see Morgan. All he could see was the green and purple striped face of Kamror drawing near to his own, venom trickling down a pair of hideous fangs. The poison dripped onto his skin and it burned like acid. He reached for his sword and struck the dragon across the face. "Let me go!"

Kamror grunted and spat angrily, but did not release his grip. Blood began rushing to Ramsey's head, and he realised that he was upside-down, suspended above ground in the grip of three blade-like talons. Merlock assaulted his father, and the strike of stone against Ramsey's head as he hit the floor was enough to jolt him back to life. He staggered to his feet again, feeling absolutely sick.

"Morgan! Get over here, wherever you are!"

"Here I am," said Morgan, less than three feet from him. Ramsey stared at him long and hard, then shook his head and covered his mouth with his free hand. "You look awful."

Merlock gained the upper hand for a moment or two. He was at an obvious disadvantage because of his injuries, despite being bigger than his father, and the two remained locked in a stalemate, raised on hind legs as their forelegs wrestled and their supple bodies writhed and twirled.

"Merlock's going to die!" sobbed the prince. Ramsey felt utter helplessness like a block of ice in his stomach. There was nothing he could do. Morgan's watery eyes nagged at him as sweetly as a kitten. "Please…! We have to help him…!"

Merlock struck hard and fast, latching onto Kamror's hind leg and swinging him around inside the cave. Ramsey pulled Morgan out of the way as the dragons wheeled past, Merlock shaking his father like a crazed dog and hurling him out into the open, whereupon Kamror stumbled over the cliff edge and fell out of sight with a furious cry. Merlock, gasping, went to check on the two goblins who stood shivering in the corner.

"Are you all right?" asked he, huskily. Morgan nodded and Ramsey still refused to let go, sword in his other hand. "He won't stay down for long, he'll come back to kill you. We must go, now, if we are to have a chance of getting you home."

The whooshing of wings echoed across the mountains. Kamror rose once more through the sky, tattered wings beating the air, his scorpion tail curled menacingly behind him. It was a sight that Ramsey prayed never to see again. Kamror outside the cave and hovering on air, Merlock within; they were readying to attack when a deep, bellowing battle cry and the thundering of paws echoed up from somewhere deep in the mountain.

Ramsey's despair dribbled away, for it was Theron who came rushing through the dark, Blanoka atop his head, and his eyes wild with vengeance. Ramsey was so delighted that he forgot to speak at all. Theron leapt on Merlock, thinking him to be the attacker, and wrestled him out into the open, knocking him over the cliff the way his father had gone moments before. Ramsey bleached.

"Not that one!" He gesticulated wildly at Kamror. "*That* one!"

Theron skidded to a halt and, for the first time, saw the grotesque form of Kamror flapping like a poisonous bat high above him. Blanoka stared around madly, seeing nothing. Kamror gaped down at Theron with confusion, fangs gleaming, his eyes shining like a spider's. Theron met the dragon with bristling fur and a mouthful of sharp teeth. Ramsey and Morgan ran out after him.

Merlock had not fallen far, and soared up to meet Kamror in mid air. High above the cliff, both dragons sought to kill each other, as though venom itself were running through their veins.

"Ramsey!" Theron ran to his friend and hugged him hard with one paw. "You're alive! I thought you had died!" He noticed Morgan then, and something overcame his features that chased all traces of bloodlust from his brown eyes. He staggered a little and bent on his forepaws, bowing to the prince. "Your Highness...we searched so long, and so far, and..."

Morgan looked warily at Theron, wringing his hands. He looked less like a prince than ever at that moment – a boy who was too embarrassed to accept the most simple, kind gesture. "You can get up," he offered as a suggestion. "I'm not really royalty...my father is, you can bow to him, but please don't bow to me. I'm not a king."

Ramsey smirked and tried to disguise it with a cough. Morgan must not have known the irony in such a statement. Of course he didn't. As far as he knew, he was Viktor's real son. And it should stay that way. "How did you find your way up here?" he asked Theron. Blanoka answered with his usual high-pitched, scratchy tone.

"Blanoka is being good at navigating in mountains, so Blanoka is finding a back way in! Blanoka is being useful, mmm? And what was it being that you were saying about Blanoka being useless and annoying, mmm?"

Above them, the dragons' battle raged on, blazing through the sky. Merlock's breath burned the morning light in shocking blasts of red and orange, and Kamror ducked and dodged as carefree as a dolphin, turning once in a while to retaliate. The rain fell miserably around them, gleaming on their scales and hissing away from the heat of Merlock's fire. Morgan was shivering pronouncedly by now, and Ramsey cradled the boy against him, trying as hard as he could to keep him warm.

"Don't you worry, kid. I'm not going to let you die on me. I'm going to get you home."

He didn't know if Morgan heard him or not.

Merlock had exhausted himself to the verge of collapse. Kamror soared above him, swooping noiselessly like an owl locating its quarry. Merlock watched him cautiously, the tendrils of snake-like hair on his back and tail fluttering like flames in the swollen, rain-tinted wind. Ramsey held Morgan tightly, and felt Theron's body near his own, as warm and steadfast as a bear. Merlock looked defeated and moth-eaten.

"You lied to me!" he hissed, dim amidst the rush of raindrops. "Father, why, *why* did you lie to me? I'd do anything for you, father, I'd have killed them all for you once! But you lied! You ruined it all, father!"

Kamror moved like a shark swimming through the murky sky. From the corner of one eye he spotted Ramsey and Morgan standing motionless like dolls, and he took his chance to dive upon them. Ramsey stepped back, the pain in his abdomen surging as he moved. What had he done? Whatever could he have done to deserve this?

Merlock whirled after Kamror but too late. Ramsey never felt the cold impact of the dragon's body. Instead, he heard a frantic cry piercing the air, similar to Merlock's own cry of agony. Blanoka had leapt clear of the ridge and landed upon Kamror's head, the huge dragon fighting to dislodge the smaller one from his face.

Blanoka bit at Kamror's nose and mouth until the dragon's face bled. The little morlona clung hard like a crab, giving Ramsey the chance to drag Morgan away. As Kamror collapsed onto the cliff top, Theron raced to Blanoka's aid and latched his jaws around the cobra dragon's neck. Blinded by the pain in his face, Kamror flailed and struck out uselessly, swiping his tail under himself to hit the troll.

At this, Ramsey could stay himself no longer, and ran back to his friend, sword in hand. Kamror reeled up, trying to jerk away from Theron's jaws, and with a mighty shake of his head, Blanoka flew through the air and landed with a thump in Morgan's arms. Ramsey drew back his hand, his eyes set on the poisonous, shuddering horror that was Kamror, boring into the monster's heart to where a withered soul grew. The stinging tail struck Theron in the leg and Ramsey plunged his sword as hard as he could into Kamror's gleaming, armour-plated chest. He was blown back almost instantly by the beating of frantic, torn wings, and the gruelling shriek of agony made him cry, crouching on the cliff where he had fallen.

Kamror's serpentine face contorted as he fell once more, blood pouring from his face and neck, Ramsey's sword firmly lodged beneath his right foreleg. The leathery wings collapsed like curtains, the wind whipping noisily through them, and as suddenly as he had appeared, he was gone; spiralling downwards into the darkness of the mountains like a dying vulture, and the echo of his cry was all that remained, like a nightmare chased away in the first glowing threads of morning's light. Merlock watched him fall, silent as a bird, and then came in to land with one last swoop of his wings. Theron was stooping at Ramsey's side, his face a picture of worry.

"I'm Okay, Theron, seriously," Ramsey coughed, wiping some blood and dust from his mouth. "Honestly, you can get off me." Theron snorted and backed up, watching over Ramsey like a sheepdog. The goblin supported himself painfully on one elbow, then rose to his feet, still coughing, holding his chest. "What about you? Theron, you got stung!"

"No, I didn't. The sharp part didn't touch me, it just knocked me sideways a bit. I'm fine."

"Blanoka, then. Where's he gone?"

Blanoka called out from the safety of Morgan's arms, and Ramsey felt so relieved to hear his voice that he had to remind himself of how irritating the little dragon had been so far. Nevertheless, he had played his part in the killing of Kamror, also. "Blanoka is being very safe! Nasty dragon dead? Blanoka is being rejoicing! Blanoka is also being hungry."

Morgan hugged Blanoka's spindly body, supporting the long legs with his arms, beaming at Ramsey. "He's adorable! Where did you find him?"

"In a cave, in a mountain, near a pool, on this journey. That about sums it all up. He's Blanoka, and this is Theron," said Ramsey, indicating the bruised troll. Theron bowed at Morgan for a second time, then nudged Ramsey affectionately in the back. "Ow! Oh...heh. I'd poke you back, but I don't want to break anything. You know, like, my bones or something."

Theron looked concerned, noticing Ramsey's awkward posture. "Are you all right, Ramsey? Are you hurt?"

"No, I'll be fine. Really. The main thing now is for me to take Morgan back home. I don't really know how..." He glanced fleetingly at Merlock, who was 'preening' his wings while seated on the cliff edge, smoothing creases out of the torn flaps. Ramsey wondered what the dragon was thinking. "...How we'll get there."

"I will take you," insisted the cobra dragon. Sore and bloody, he was by no means defeated, and strength swelled in his chest. He relaxed his bright hood, coiling his neck down to look at Morgan, who stood near him, still carrying Blanoka. "I promised to take you, and I will. I am sorry, child, for all the misery I caused you." Ramsey saw Morgan shake his blond head and speak softly to Merlock. The edges of the dragon's deadly mouth curled upwards in a small smile. "I do not weep for my father. Cobra dragons cannot cry. Although, perhaps, I may weep on my mother's side. But those can never be tears of sorrow."

Morgan looked so weak and young next to the towering shape of the dragon that Ramsey felt a surge of ferocity in his blood, and he went forward to put one hand on Morgan's back. The boy turned and smiled a slightly uneven smile that was too high on the one side. Blanoka did not struggle in Morgan's arms. "I think I'm ready to go home," said the prince. Ramsey nodded.

"Yeah." He squeezed the blood-soaked sleeve of Morgan's pyjamas and looked up at the dragon, who looked down at each of them with the wild, docile expression of a charmed tiger. "Me too."

Merlock stretched and tested his wings, sending gales of warm air over the mountainside. With a final pat on the head, Morgan released Blanoka, who instinctively found his way to Theron and sat by the troll's feet. Ramsey's heart was heavy as he contemplated the journey home. Ultimately, he had done what he had set out to do, but still, something small nagged at him. He no longer had his sword, but he didn't need it. He felt bruised from his head to his toes, but there were doctors in Merlock town, so he would not suffer for long.

One look at Theron, and he knew why he felt so downhearted. Though not always fun, the journey had been eventful, and he had travelled with Theron almost since the beginning. He couldn't remember a time, save for those awful hours alone in the Troll Teeth Mountains, when Theron had not been at his side. Theron's presence brought back memories of forests and green fields, of rain and hail and snow; they had faced everything together, and Ramsey had kept Theron near him, no matter how many times he told himself that the troll was nothing but a hindrance. Even when facing dragons twice his size, Theron had no qualms about risking his life to save Ramsey. And there he stood now, with blood-stained fur torn out in places, still with a smile in his eyes.

"So..." began Ramsey, clearing his throat more than once. Behind him, Morgan clambered up onto Merlock's lithe back and nestled himself between the muscles of the dragon's wings. "I guess this is goodbye for a while."

Theron nodded, and his chest rose and fell with a weary sigh. "Only for a little while."

"I shouldn't go...I don't want to leave the two of you all alone. I'd feel like a monster if I abandoned you after everything we've been though."

The troll laughed, and Blanoka skittered nimbly up onto his head. "We'll cope, Ramsey. You need to take Morgan home. We don't mind another adventure, do we, Blanoka?"

The little dragon shook his head, his mouth open. "Not being minding at all! No worries, silly goblin – Blanoka will being protecting your troll for you!"

Ramsey grinned, mirroring Blanoka's toothy expression. "Okay, as long as you promise to keep him under control."

"Being promising!"

Theron made a low, wondering noise that caught Ramsey's attention, and he realised that the troll was regarding Merlock and Morgan, who looked ready to depart. Merlock was warming his wings with further stretches, his colourful features betraying no emotion. Ramsey really wished he knew what the cobra dragon was thinking right then. "I'll miss you. Both of you. Take care of one another and when you can, come and find us, won't you? I've travelled so much that it's made me sick, so you can be sure to find me back at home."

"I'll remember that. Scaless protect you." Theron's smile was incomplete as Ramsey shuffled to where Merlock and Morgan waited on the cliff edge. The dragon's sleek tail was coiled on the plateau, tipped with the same scarlet, snake-like hairs that fringed its back. Ramsey stepped over the tail and climbed up to join Morgan, searching for a firm hold on the hard, scaly back. The morning light had grown into a flourish of blue and yellow, casting warm rays of light upon the mountain and the poised figures that waited on the cliff. The rainbow shivered like a live creature stretching across the sky, translucent and brilliant in the same instant. "Ramsey!"

Merlock froze and lowered his wings, giving Ramsey the chance to turn and answer his friend. "Yeah?"

Theron blinked back his hurt, and fullness flowed into his smile as he said; "Well done."

Ramsey could not stay, for he knew that he had too much to say. He had too many things to be thankful for, too many memories to share aloud, and too many goodbyes to express. The pain had already numbed in his chest, and once again he felt the sting of saltwater in the corners of his eyes.

If he was crying, nobody noticed for all the blood smeared over his skin and clothing. He didn't know how many baths he would need to wash himself clean; Morgan was no better, his hair dark with blood and his clothes sticky with it. The prince's sunny, open face shone through the grime, and his eyes were as bright as amber.

With three deafening beats of the great wings, Merlock took off from the mountainside, flapping hard at first to keep himself aloft, then he soared away through the sky, the two goblins clinging to his neck and shoulders. Theron watched them until they were out of sight, loping across the cliff top to follow them, and Ramsey gave a final wave before disappearing above the clouds on Merlock's back. The mist tousled into broken wisps, then stilled, betraying no sign that a cobra dragon and two passengers had ever gone by.

The world whipped past in a watercolour painting of greens and greys and browns, far below. They were so high that they could look down at the clouds. As things were, Ramsey decided that he didn't like heights and refrained from looking away from what was directly in front of him – Morgan's hair, blood-streaked and untidy, blowing back in Ramsey's face. He was crouching over the prince to ensure that neither one of them fell off, and Morgan didn't seem to mind his rescuer holding tightly to the back of his pyjama shirt. His milky skin was cold and clammy to the touch, so Ramsey made sure not to make contact with it. It only made him worry more.

Morgan eagerly looked down over the side of Merlock's neck, admiring the landscape whenever there was a break in the cloud cover. The air was freezing but the dragon didn't seem to mind, hardly flapping his wings at all and executing superb control over his flight. Ramsey had never flown before and had no idea how fast they were moving, but the barren world above the clouds was silent and still, no birds venturing so high. None of them spoke. Ramsey had nothing to say to either the prince or Merlock. He had a hundred things that he wanted to say to Theron, but he didn't know what any of them were. And to Blanoka...well, he could always offer some food.

Time flew by as swiftly as the houses, hills and trees below them. Soon the earth below them was rugged and entirely green, flecked with copses and little streams, and Ramsey recognised the land as Merlockiara. It was not long before the dull blotch of Merlock's town wall appeared on the cloudless horizon; Morgan spied it and perked up, leaning back against Ramsey for a better view. The older goblin grabbed hold of both of Morgan's arms, pinning him to the dragon's back.

Merlock hissed to himself and swerved abruptly through the air, veering towards the town that shared his name, in preparation for a landing. Ramsey clung fast to Morgan in case either one of them slipped down the slope of Merlock's back as he turned. Merlock gurgled throatily and moved in to hover within the perimeters of the town wall.

As soon as they saw the dragon, the goblins in the town square began to scream and scatter in all directions like insects. Ramsey leaned over cautiously, holding Morgan in place, and it finally dawned on him how terribly the town had suffered since he left. The charred remains of houses that he had known since his childhood lay blackened in the streets, and although some were in the process of being rebuilt, Merlock town was a pitiful skeleton of its former self. The fleeing townsfolk ran into the ruins, while some emerged from the rebuilt structures to see what was going on outside. They screamed, the voices of children merged with the cries of women and the shouts of men, all hurrying to evade the dragon.

With long, slow beats of his wings, Merlock lowered himself gradually until he hovered a short distance above the ground, then he dropped into the centre of the town square with a bump, jolting both goblins from his back. Ramsey lost his grip and fell flat on his face on the cobbles, and Morgan, who had a better grip on the dragon, landed on his feet with no more than a slight stumble. He shook his head, looking around at the townsfolk who were staring transfixed at him and Ramsey. Ramsey went to him and held him firmly, looking at the motley gathering of startled goblin faces all around them. Silence fell, during which the dragon tossed his head and folded his wings neatly at his sides. Bare feet scuffled apprehensively on cobbles.

Morgan breathed so deeply that he began to cough, Ramsey still steadying him with cold, long-fingered hands. He glanced around fearfully, not knowing why he felt so terrified. "Have I been gone so long that they cannot recognise me?" he asked Ramsey in a low whisper. Ramsey shook his head.

"They know you. No amount of grime could disguise someone so beloved to his people." He spoke these words in a voice that was not his own, and he never discovered where they had echoed from, but they came out of him nonetheless. These were Morgan's people and they always would be; the same people who for so long had shut Ramsey out. He had returned their prince to them. That was enough.

Goblins had never been very physical creatures, but goblin women huddled close to their husbands, and children clung tightly to their parents' hands, staring at Morgan as nothing they had ever seen before. Babies born since the prince's disappearance gaped wide-eyed at him like frightened forest animals from their mothers' arms. This jagged shell of a town was not the Merlock he had left behind. He was soon to realise that it never would be.

From the thick of the gathering crowd loomed the worry-lined, blue-skinned face of an individual familiar to both of them. Wrapped up as usual in flowing green and purple robes, the castle herald dropped his basket of shopping and burst his way through the swarm, holding his arms out to Morgan. He embraced the boy heartily, swinging him around in mid-air and praising Scaless at the top of his voice.

Ramsey sighed and stepped away, keeping his distance as the bemused crowd started to hone in on Morgan, their shock and fear chased away by the jubilant realisation that their prince had returned to them. The thrill of noise erupted from all directions, and Ramsey shielded himself near the sturdy, startling figure of the cobra dragon, who just yawned and looked around in a motiveless manner.

"My father," coughed Morgan through the throb of the crowd, pushing the herald's robes away from his face. "I have to see my father. Where is he?"

At this, the herald pulled away from Morgan, though he did not loosen his grip on the prince's upper half. The crowd continued to shout and cry with excitement, but the herald suddenly looked drawn and old, his lips tight and crinkling at the corners. He saw Ramsey, then, when nobody else in the crowd regarded him, and Ramsey instinctively came forward, nudging townsfolk out of his way. "Your Majesty...I am afraid that, during the time you have been parted from us, your father unfortunately...passed away."

The crowd could not have heard the discussion, for everyone else still buzzed with the thrill of the prince's return. Morgan, pale and blood-covered in a tiny clearing of space with Ramsey and the royal herald by his side, heard every word, and he couldn't even think to close his mouth. His bright eyes were glossy. Ramsey felt helpless at the sight of Morgan crying, so protective that a fury burned inside him. He didn't push the herald away; instead he hugged Morgan at the same time, wrapping his bony arms around the prince as tightly as he could. Several people in the crowd marvelled at the gesture.

"I am so, so sorry, Your Majesty..." said the herald, tears in his eyes also. Morgan nodded wordlessly and buried his face against the soft robes, his one hand holding Ramsey's. "He was so upset when you went missing...and the doctors tried everything they could, but...I am afraid that they could not save him."

"It's Okay, Morgan, I'm still here, too," consoled Ramsey, squeezing Morgan's small hand with his own. "For what it's worth."

"No, really, it's worth a lot..." snivelled the prince, wiping angrily at his eyes and getting blood all over the herald's robes. "You brought me back, and I'll never be able to thank you for that...and Merlock, too. Don't let them hurt him."

"Don't worry, he's doing fine." Ramsey quickly looked over to where Merlock was sitting nonchalantly amidst the townspeople, receiving hundreds of nervous stares. "You just worry about yourself, Okay?"

"No...I...if my father...passed away, then..." He sniffed again, clearing his eyes with the herald's sleeve. "I...that makes *me* the king..."

"Oh, Your Majesty, we have been in utter turmoil without you!" beamed the herald, his eyes still red from crying. He took hold of Morgan's free hand with both of his, and then knelt on the cobbles with his head bowed in reverence. "We are your people, my lord Morgan, and may you rule over us well."

Ramsey let go while Morgan tried to get the herald to stand, but his attempt was wholly unsuccessful, for all around them, the other inhabitants of Merlock were also bowing and curtsying one by one, holding one another with their faces alight with nervousness and joy. Hundreds of heads were bowed towards him, hair of all the different colours you could imagine, children falteringly copying their parents.

Morgan turned in a circle, his face smudged with blood and tears and ash, looking utterly perplexed and overwhelmed. Ramsey knew that he didn't need to bow, so he didn't. Instead, he crossed his arms and surveyed the civilians with an air, not of defiance, but of individuality.

"You're the king, Morgan..." he marvelled, drumming his fingernails against his arm. "I'm sorry that I couldn't get you back home in time to see your dad."

Morgan's voice was as soft as snowflakes falling to the ground. "No, it isn't your fault. I can't believe...he's gone...though..."

Ramsey bent over next to the herald to attempt to coax him to his feet. As he moved, a fissure of red-hot pain shot through his right side and everything became fuzzy before his eyes. He hit the ground, falling on his face in a heap at the herald's feet, and the old goblin leapt upright with surprise. Morgan gasped and ran over to his rescuer while the herald called for a doctor, ushering the crowd away from the scene to give Ramsey some air. Being shaken and hearing Morgan shout his name was the last thing that Ramsey registered before he blanked out.

*\*\**

When Ramsey next opened his eyes, he could barely move his body, and his extremities felt limp and sore. He tried to blink his vision into focus, for all he could see around him was an uncomfortable, bright white glow. He could smell flowers and fruit, and fresh air touching his face. The lilac scent of Merlockiara's eternally springtime air wafted in from a nearby window.

He tried to lift his head, but his neck cracked awkwardly when he did so. The ceiling above him was white, the bedclothes around him were white, and his skin, as he looked down at his nearby hand, was a slightly paler shade of orange than usual. He stared at his hand for a while with mild interest, as though it had surprised him by appearing at the end of his bony left arm.

Then he sat bolt upright, swallowing air and staring madly at the scene around him. His mouth tasted foul. Springtime rays of sunlight flittered through the open window and made floating dust particles glow like gold. He was still in bed in King Viktor's castle. It had all been a dream; it had to be.

He pulled himself loose of the bedcovers and realised that he was only wearing a pair of red shorts, the rest of his ungainly figure on view for the whole world to see. He gasped and fell back onto the bed, searching for anything in the room that could prove he had been on a quest for months with a troll named Theron, that they had met a dragon called Blanoka, and rescued Prince Morgan from a monster; but everything was just the same. He felt sick again, and he sank down into the thick blankets, covering his face with his hands. He felt more alone and miserable than he had ever done in his life.

As he sat on the bed, whinging bitterly, the royal herald popped his head through the doorway and greeted him in a voice as cheerful as a sparrow. "Good morning, young sir! You have awakened at last, I see. Come now, you should eat something."

"I don't want to eat something," moaned Ramsey through his hands. "I just want to die."

The herald was alarmed. "Young sir! Never say such things! Why, Morgan would not be alive today, were it not for you."

Ramsey replaced his hands in his lap, his eyes deep and hopeful, the colour of Theron's. "He's alive? I brought him back? This hasn't all been a dream?"

"Why, of course not," laughed the herald, giving Ramsey some clean clothes to wear, which Ramsey readily took. "I am afraid you just had a bit of a mishap with an injury, my boy. Oh, we were so worried! Morgan has hardly left your bedside this whole time. Then again, it has only been one day since you brought him home. Bravo, young sir! Our kingdom cannot thank you enough."

Ramsey tugged the clean pair of trousers on, and when he went to pull his shirt on, he noticed that his chest was bound up tightly in bandages. He stared at the wrappings, then looked at the herald and prompted him for an explanation. The herald complied, lovingly arranging some fresh fruit in the bowl by Ramsey's bed.

"Ah, yes. It seems that you had one or two broken ribs, my boy, and when you came up to me, you managed to shift them into a rather uncomfortable position, and you passed out. Our physician said that you were very lucky that your lung wasn't pierced. You just hurt yourself with your own broken ribs, young sir, but no worries. You shall be right as rain. Ah, such is the cost of rescuing princes nowadays, I suppose." He smiled warmly at Ramsey, genuine gratitude and joy shining through his every movement. Even the fruit in the bowl looked happy.

Ramsey arranged his clothes in a hurry and went to the door. "Where's Morgan?"

"He's in his bedroom, my lad, just pottering about. He has been so worried about you. His coronation has already been arranged to take place in four days' time, so I've encouraged him to enjoy his final moments of childhood. It is a great responsibility, after all, being king, and we were all so afraid that we had lost our monarchy forever."

Ramsey was out of the door in a trice, thinking back to that fateful day, months ago, when the royal herald had guided him along these same corridors to Morgan's bedroom, which back then had been a scene of devastation and loss. The castle staff greeted him as he passed, smiling sunshine at him and spouting words of praise and admiration. He couldn't stop to answer them, because they were all faceless and joyful. It would not deprive them of their happiness to see him walk by. There was only one face that he needed to see, and he found it, as he had expected, in Morgan's chamber at the other end of the castle.

Morgan was sitting on the bed, hunched over one of his old drawings, when Ramsey entered the room. He looked up, and when he saw Ramsey, a smile broke out on his face and he put the paper aside. Ramsey marched right up to him and pulled him into a fiercely protective hug, then contented himself with holding the boy at arm's length. Morgan's smile didn't last long once he spoke.

"They're going to make me the king," he said, low and soft. "I don't want to be the king. I don't have a clue how to be king."

"It's Okay. I know I've said this before, but for what I'm worth, I'm here. I came through a lot for you, and I'm never going to let you suffer the way I did. I lost my dad when I was your age."

Morgan sighed and lowered his gaze, sniffling a little. "I miss my father so much…"

"I know you do, Morgan, but you can get through this. I'll make sure that you always have someone there for you, the way I never had. And you can do your father proud, can't you?" Morgan looked up, brown eyes shimmering brightly, and he smiled again, though his lips and cheeks were turning pink. Ramsey grinned and hugged the boy tightly, rubbing Morgan's shoulders with his knuckles. "I just hope I did mine proud, too."

In the town square, the goblins of Merlock were bustling to life again, going about their daily business with a new sense of vigour, calling to one another and exclaiming that the prince was soon to be crowned king. Homeless families gathered near the fountain, discussing their new housing plans, and children played hide and seek in the half-built alleyways. Elderly couples collected in the streets, saying "Well I *never*!" as they looked towards the sky and saw the coiled, beautiful silhouette of a cobra dragon perched atop King Viktor's castle.

# Epilogue

It was fifteen long years before Pain emerged from his meditation to pose an active threat to Grenamoya Island. With his servant Ulyssis at his side, he remained dormant in the Great Dragons' temple, waiting for an opportune moment to seize control over his rightful lands. With flawed powers, his progress was hindered, but this minor setback could not repress him forever.

At the age of twelve-and-three-quarter years, King Morgan became the youngest ruling monarch in the history of Merlockiara. Unable to bear Ramsey's absence, he asked his rescuer to come and live with him in Merlock castle, where Ramsey spent his days keeping the king company and dispensing advice whenever the royal herald was busy.

Ramsey pondered for a while over whether it would be best to tell Morgan that Viktor had not, in fact, been his father at all; but he decided against saying anything. This was a resolution that made life less complicated for Morgan, who, as king of one of Grenamoya's most important kingdoms, had enough on his plate as it was.

After several months, Theron reappeared in the kingdom with Blanoka, and Morgan was so delighted with the little dragon that he invited both of them to stay with him. At last, Ramsey had everything that he could possibly want – a home, great wealth, friends nearby and a young boy to live for. Morgan would go on to face greater danger and more powerful challenges than those in his past, but though Ramsey could not defend him forever, he was proud to serve under the fair-skinned, beloved monarch, who so long ago had been a little boy shivering in bloodied pyjamas.